"Tell m____
with ____

"Or did the danger of it simply whet your appetite for more?" He pressed his thumb against the vein pulsing so rapidly beneath her soft skin and felt the answering leap as her heart pounded faster. She felt like warm satin. Smooth and creamy to the touch, reminding him how long it had been since he'd tasted the sweeter pleasures of life.

A bolt of static electricity snapped between them, and a tremor shook her from head to toe.

"Get your hands off me!" Khamsin demanded. "Let me go!"

The static sparked again, and she gave a helpless moan. The sound burrowed oddly deep inside him, rousing a response like none he'd ever felt before. Possessive, dominant, compelling.

The little maid felt it too, and she began to struggle in earnest. Her eyes changed color, going from their original storm cloud gray to a bright, strangely shifting silver, as unique as her white-streaked hair. Outside, the wind whistled, picking up enough speed to rattle the windowpanes.

Wynter felt his nostrils flare with an instant stab of aggression, and his upper lip curled back to bare his teeth. He even growled, low in his throat, like a snow wolf warning another male away from his female.

Khamsin's body stiffened, back arching, hips grinding against Wynter's as heat leapt between them, electric and searing.

Outside, lightning flashed, and the window at the Winter King's back exploded with a deafening crash.

By C. L. Wilson

THE WINTER KING
CROWN OF CRYSTAL FLAME
QUEEN OF SONG AND SOULS
KING OF SWORD AND SKY
LADY OF LIGHT AND SHADOWS
LORD OF THE FADING LANDS

C. L. WILSON

The WINTER KING

AVON

An Imprint of HarperCollinsPublishers

AVON BOOKS
An Imprint of HarperCollins*Publishers*
195 Broadway
New York, New York 10007

Copyright © 2014 by C.L. Wilson
ISBN 978-0-06-201897-7
www.avonromance.com

First Avon Books mass market printing: August 2014

Avon Trademark Reg. U.S. Pat. Off. and in Other Countries, Marca Registrada, Hecho en U.S.A.

HarperCollins® is a registered trademark of HarperCollins Publishers.

Printed in the U.S.A.

HB 02.06.2024

Acknowledgments

Writing is a solitary process, but being a writer is not a solitary state. I owe an immeasurable debt of gratitude to the friends, family, and fans who have been and continue to be so supportive and encouraging. I especially want to thank the Starfish Club: Christine Feehan, Kathie Firzlaff, and Sheila English. Our brainstorming retreats are the highlights of my year. Special thanks to my very dear friend and power writing/critique buddy, the supremely talented Karen Rose. Thanks also to my daughters, Ileah and Rhiannon Wilson, for beta reading my work in progress and telling me it was good.

Special thanks to my editor, Tessa Woodward; my agent, Michelle Grajkowski; and the folks at Avon Books, for your understanding, encouragement, and unflagging support. You are great!

Finally, thanks again to Judy York, the cover artist who brought Wynter and Khamsin to life. You promised me no heaving bosoms, gasping mouths, or naked thighs, and you came through splendidly! You even made that sparkly tornado look good!

For My Readers

Thank you so much for picking up this book! And a special thanks to everyone who sent me the wonderful letters of encouragement while I had to step away from writing for a while. Your support means the world to me.

Be sure to visit my website, *www.clwilson.com*, to sign up for my private book announcement list, enter my online contests, and scour the site for hidden treasures and magical surprises.

I'd love to hear from you. You can friend me on Facebook at *www.facebook.com/clwilsonbooks*, tweet me at *@clwilsonbooks*, or e-mail me at *cheryl@clwilson.com*.

PROLOGUE

Scarlet on Snow

King's Keep
Vera Sola, Summerlea

"Do you have to go?" Seventeen-year-old Khamsin Coruscate clung to her beloved brother's hand as if by her grip alone she could anchor him fast and keep him from leaving.

"You know I do. Our treaties with the Winter King are very important."

"But you'll be home soon?" Whenever he was gone, the ancient walls of the royal palace of Summerlea, which had been her home and her prison since birth, seemed somehow more confining, more restrictive.

"Not this time, little sister." Falcon shook his head. A strand of black hair that had pulled free of the queue at the back of his neck brushed against the soft, dark skin of his cheek. "It will take weeks to negotiate the treaties."

Khamsin scowled, and the wind began to gust, sending Kham's habitually untamed hair whipping into her mouth and eyes. "Why does he have to send you? Why can't his ambassador negotiate the treaty? He's sending you away because of me, isn't he? Because he doesn't want you spending so much time with me." Her hands clenched into fists. The wind sent her skirts flying, and a dark cloud rolled across the sun.

Their father, King Verdan IV of Summerlea, didn't love

her. She knew that. He kept her isolated in a remote part of the palace, hidden away from his court and his kingdom, on the pretext that her weathergifts were too volatile and dangerous, and she couldn't control them. That was all true. Kham's gifts *were* dangerous, and she couldn't control them any better than she could control her own temper. Until now, however, he'd never stooped to sending his other children away to keep them from visiting her.

"Here now. Be calm." Falcon smoothed her wayward curls back, tucking them behind her ears. Compassion and pity shone softly in his eyes. "I wish I didn't have to leave you. But Father believes I'll have the best chance of getting what we want from Wintercraig, and I agree with him." Summerlea, once a rich, thriving kingdom renowned for its fertile fields and abundant orchards, had been in a slow decline for years. Although the nobles and their king maintained a prosperous façade for political and economic purposes, beneath the gilded domes and bright splendor of Summerlea's palaces and grand estates, the rough tatters of neglect were beginning to show. "Besides, you won't be alone while I'm gone. You have Tildy and the Seasons."

"It isn't the same. They aren't you." He was the handsome Prince of Summerlea, charming, witty, heroic. He'd lived a life of adventure, most of which he shared with her, entertaining her with the tales of his exploits . . . the places he'd seen, the people he'd met. His hunts, his adventures, his triumphs. No matter how much her nursemaid, Tildavera Greenleaf, doted on Khamsin, or how often Autumn, Spring, and Summer, the three princesses known as the Seasons, snuck away from their palace duties to spend time with their ostracized youngest sister, Falcon was the one whose visits she couldn't live without.

"Now there's a pretty compliment. Careful, my lady. You'll turn my head." He smiled, and warmth poured into her. It was no wonder the ladies of their father's court swooned at the slightest attention from him. Falcon had a magical way about him. He could literally charm the birds from the trees with his name-gift—controlling any feathered creature on a whim—and the weathergift inherent in his royal Summerlander blood was stronger than it had been in any crown prince in generations. It was as if the Sun itself had taken up residence in his soul, and its warmth spilled from him each time he smiled.

Kham took a deep breath. Birds weren't the only creatures susceptible to Falcon's charm. In the face of his warm smile, the sharp edge of her temper abated, and in the skies, the gathering storm began to calm. Perhaps King Verdan truly *had* chosen to send his only son as envoy to Wintercraig for political reasons. Long, long ago, as a small child crying herself to sleep, she'd decided Falcon was the reincarnation of Roland Triumphant, the Hero of Summerlea, the brave king who had defeated an overwhelming invasion force with his wit, his weathergifts, and a legendary sword reputed to be a gift from the Sun God himself. If anyone could coax the cold, savage folk of the north into concessions most favorable to Summerlea, Falcon could.

"Will you at least write to me?" she asked.

"I'll send you a bird every week." He tapped her nose and gave her a roguish grin. "Cheer up. Just think of all the sword fights you'll win when you're fighting invisible opponents instead of me."

Kham rolled her eyes. He'd been teaching her swordfighting for years, but she had yet to best him in a match.

"You know," she said, as they walked towards the doorway leading back into the palace, "it might actually be a good thing that you'll be spending months in Wintercraig."

"Oh?"

"Yes. You can use that time to find out what happened to Roland's sword."

Falcon tripped on an uneven flagstone and grabbed the trunk of a nearby tree to steady himself. "I'm sure I'll be much too busy to chase fairy tales, Storm."

She frowned in surprise. "But you've always believed the stories were true." Blazing, the legendary sword of

Roland Soldeus, had disappeared shortly after the heroic king's death. Legend claimed it was the Winter King, the father of Roland's betrothed, who had spirited the sword away but that one day Roland's true Heir would reclaim it. Every royal Summerlea prince for the last two millennia had dreamed of finding the legendary blade and bringing it back home where it belonged. Falcon had spent years chasing lead after lead, determined that *he* would be the one to find Blazing and restore Summerlea to its former glory.

"What about those letters?" she added. "The really old ones you found tucked in that monastery? You said they proved the stories were true."

"That was six years ago. I was seventeen. I *wanted* the stories to be true." He gave her a quick hug and a brotherly kiss on the forehead. "I've got to run. I'm meeting with Father and his advisors to go over our list of demands and concessions one last time before I leave. I'll see you in a few months."

"I'll miss you every day." She trailed after him, feeling bereft and forlorn when Falcon turned the corner and disappeared from view. But this time, she also felt confused. She'd never known Falcon to give up on something he felt passionately about. And he'd been passionate about finding Roland's sword. He'd been certain he was on the right trail—and certain he was Roland's true Heir. He'd shared his discoveries with her because he knew she was just as hungry as he to find the legendary sword.

So why would he deny it now?

Gildenheim, Wintercraig

"She's not good for you."

Wynter Atrialan, King of Wintercraig, cast a sideways glance at his younger brother. "Don't say that, Garrick. I know you've never liked Elka, but in six months' time, she will be my bride and your queen."

Garrick shook his long, snow silver hair. Eyes as bright and blue as the glacier caves in Wintercraig's icebound Skoerr Mountains shone with solemn intensity that made the boy look far older than his fifteen years.

"You love too deeply, Wyn. From the moment you decided to take her to wife, you've blinded yourself to her true nature."

Wynter sighed. "I should not have shared my worries with you when I first met her." Wyn was an intensely private man, but he'd never kept secrets from Garrick. Not one. Wyn had raised his brother since their parents' death ten years ago. And in those years, he'd never tried to sweeten the ugly world of politics, never tried to gloss over his fears or concerns—even when it came to the more personal but still political matter of selecting a queen. If something happened to him, Garrick would be king, and Wyn didn't want his brother thrown into such a position without preparation.

Unfortunately, the years of openness and plain, unfettered talk had paid unanticipated returns. Because of his unflinching honesty with Garrick, no one knew Wynter better than his young brother. Not even Wyn's lifelong friend and second-in-command, Valik. Such deep familiarity could be as troublesome as it was comforting.

"She is cold," Garrick insisted. "She does not love you as she should. She wants to be queen more than she wants to be your wife."

"Elka is a woman of the Craig. She is as reserved with her feelings as I."

"Is she? So that is why she laughs and smiles so warmly when the Summerlander is near?"

Wynter frowned a warning at his brother. "Careful, Garrick. Elka Villani will be my wife and queen. Insult to her is insult to me."

"I offered no insult. I merely asked a question. And based on my observations, it's a perfectly legitimate one."

"You are misreading what you see. Elka knows it's vital the Summer Prince feels welcome here if we are to come to an amicable agreement." The lush, fertile fields of Summerlea provided much-needed sustenance to the folk of Wintercraig during the harsh, cold months of a northern winter. Their grains, fruits, and vegetables, which Wintercraig bought with furs, whale oil, and forest products, could mean the difference between life and death for his people during years when their own harvests were poor. That had, unfortunately, been quite often of late since the summers had grown shorter and food from Summerlea had been growing steadily more dear after Wynter had taken the throne. Falcon Coruscate, son of the weathermage king who ruled Summerlea, had come three months ago at Wynter's invitation to negotiate terms of a new treaty that would ensure longer summers in the north and more affordable trade in foodstuffs for the winters.

"She makes him feel welcome to more than the court," Garrick corrected. "She flirts."

Wyn arched a brow. "And if she does, where's the harm in it? A pretty face and a sweet smile can persuade a man better than cold figures and dry treaties—especially self-indulgent peacocks like the Summer Prince." He smiled when Garrick rolled his eyes. "You don't remember our mother, but she could charm a Frost Giant into the fire. Father used to call her his secret weapon. Elka merely uses her gifts to aid the realm, as any good queen would."

Garrick gave a snort. "How fortunate that she takes to the task so well. All right, all right." He held up his hands in surrender when his brother's glance sharpened. He paused a moment, using hammer and chisel to chip unwanted ice from the frozen sculpture he was working on, then added, "But even if you trust her, you'd best keep an eye on the Summerlander. He's up to something."

"Foreign dignitaries are always up to something. That's called politics."

"He's been asking too many questions about the Book of Riddles."

Wyn's hand stilled momentarily in its work on his own

sculpture. "Has he?" He tried to pull off nonchalance but shouldn't have bothered. Garrick knew him too well.

"That's what he's really here for. To get the Book and find Roland's sword."

Roland's sword was a fabled Summerlea weapon of inconceivable power. It had disappeared three thousand years ago, not long after the Summer King who first wielded it sacrificed his life to save his kingdom from invasion. Many myths and legends swirled around its disappearance. One of those legends suggested that the Winter King of that time, fearing the sword's power would be misused by Roland's successors, had smuggled the sword out of Summerlea and hidden it in a place it would never be found. The Winter King had also left behind a book of obscure clues and riddles that supposedly led to the sword's secret hiding place, in case his own descendants one day had need of the legendary weapon's vast power.

"Well, good luck to him with that," Wynter said. "The sword is a myth. It's long gone by now, if it ever existed at all. And he won't find whatever treasure the Book actually does protect, either, because he will never find the Book. It's kept in a place no man can go."

"But Elka can."

He scowled. "Garrick, stop. She is my betrothed. She will be my queen. She would never betray me."

Garrick heaved a sigh. "Fine. She is your true and worthy love. I'll never suggest otherwise again."

"Good." Wyn pressed his lips together and focused on the small block of ice sitting on the pedestal before him. Patient as time itself, he carved away the excess ice until he revealed the hidden beauty inside. Fragile, shimmering, a bouquet of lilies emerged, petals curved with incredible delicacy, each flower distinct and perfect, rising from slender stems of ice. "What do you think?" he asked when it was done.

"That's beautiful, Wyn. One of your best yet."

Wyn smiled. When it came to ice sculptures, Garrick

hoarded his compliments like a miser. Only perfection earned his highest praise.

"Do you think she will like it, then? Frost lilies are her favorite."

Garrick stepped abruptly away from his own sculpture—a complex scene depicting a family of deer welcoming their newest, spindly-legged member into the herd—and brushed the dusting of ice crystals from his furs. "Any woman who truly loves you would love it, Wyn. It's obvious how much care you put into it."

"Then she will love it. You'll see."

"I'm sure she will," Garrick said, but his eyes held no conviction.

"Coruscate!" Wynter's roar shook the great crystal chandelier that hung in the entry hall of his palace, Gildenheim. He stormed up the winding stairs to the wing where royal guests were housed and burst into the suite that had been occupied for the last several months by the Prince of Summerlea. The rooms were empty, and judging by the state of the open drawers and the clothes flung haphazardly about, the inhabitants had vacated the place in a hurry.

"He's gone, Wyn." Valik, Wynter's oldest friend and second-in-command stepped into the room. "Laci checked the temple. The Book's gone, too."

Wynter swore under his breath. Barely two weeks ago, Garrick had warned him to keep an eye on the Summerlea Prince, and Wyn had dismissed his concerns with such blind, confidence! "When did they leave?"

"Not long after we left for Hileje. Elka and his guard went with him. Bron didn't think anything of it. The Summerlander kept blathering about not letting some fire ten miles away ruin a good day's hunt."

"We'd better start tracking them, then."

"There's more, Wyn." Valik hesitated, then said, "I think Garrick went after them. He and his friends rode out maybe an hour after the Summerlander. Bron heard them talking about something the Summerlander took that Garrick meant to get back."

Wyn's jaw turned to granite. With Valik close on his heels, he ran back down to the courtyard.

Still saddled and ready to ride, Wynter's stallion was waiting in the hands of a stableboy, and beside him, a dozen of Wynter's elite White Guard held Prince Falcon's valet at swordpoint. The valet looked nothing like the sleek, meticulously turned-out peacock Wynter's courtiers had mocked amongst themselves. He'd traded his velvet brocade livery for rough-spun woolens, a furred vest, and a heavy cloak. His knuckles were scraped, and his face sported a bruised jaw and an eye that was swollen shut and rapidly purpling.

"We found him in the village trying to bribe a merchant to smuggle him out in a trade cart, Your Grace."

"Where is he?" Wyn grabbed the valet by his vest, yanking him up so fast the man's feet left the ground. Wynter was tall, even for a man of the Craig, and holding the Summerlander at eye level left almost two feet between the man's dangling toes and the icy stone of the courtyard. "Where is that Coruscate bastard you serve?"

"I don't know!" Clearly terrified, the man started babbling. "I swear to you, Your Majesty! I didn't even know he was leaving until one of the maids delivered his note. And that only advised me to leave Wintercraig as quickly and quietly as possible."

"In other words, the coward abandoned you while saving his own skin." Wyn threw the man aside. "Lock him up. If we don't find his master, he can face the mercy of the mountains in his prince's stead. The rest of you, mount up. Time to hunt."

Minutes later, Wynter, Valik, and two dozen White Guard were galloping down the winding mountain road that led from Gildenheim to the valley below. Wynter howled a call to the wolves as they went, sending a summons to the packs that were spirit-kin to his family's clan. Wolves were faster in the dense woods, and they tracked by scent rather than sight. The Summerlanders' smell was alien to this part of the world, so the wolves should have no trouble picking up their trail.

He wasn't sure if the prince would try heading south, towards Summerlea, or west to the Llaskroner Fjord. The fjord was closer, and the port there was a busy one, full of strangers from distant lands. For thieves looking to get out of country quickly, that was the better destination. When the wolf call came from the west, Wyn knew he'd guessed right. He whispered to the winds, calling to the old Winterman in the north to blow his icy horn, then summoning the Vestras, the freezing maritime winds of the western seas to send their bone-chilling fog.

As he and his men rode west, following the call of the wolves, the temperatures began to drop. If the Summer Prince fought back with his own weathergifts, that would pinpoint his location. If he didn't, the rapidly worsening weather would slow his escape. Either way, Wynter would track him down and make him pay for what he'd done to the people of Hileje.

The prince had hours on him. That was the purpose of the fire in Hileje—a distraction to get Wynter and his men out of the palace so Falcon Coruscate could steal what he came for and make his escape. But the distraction had been much more than a mere fire. The Summerlanders had raped and murdered dozens of villagers, then locked the rest in the meeting hall and burned them alive.

Eighty-six lives wiped out in one senseless act of violence. Eighty-six innocent Winterfolk who had depended on their king to protect them. And he had failed.

The tone of the wolves' howls suddenly changed, the howls becoming longer, mournful, announcing a loss to the pack. Wynter sent out his thoughts, connecting to the pack mind and seeing through the wolves' eyes as he searched for the source of that cry. He caught a glimpse of scarlet splashed across the snow, bodies that were clothed not furred.

"No!" He knew instantly why the wolves howled and for whom. "No! Garrick!" He spurred Hodri faster, galloping at a reckless pace. The wind whistled past his ears. Snow flew from Hodri's hooves.

It didn't take long to reach the clearing where the wolves had gathered. The smell of death filled the air—a dark odor Wynter had smelled before. It was a scent few men ever forgot.

He reined Hodri in hard, leaping from saddle to ground before the horse fully stopped. The first two bodies were boys Wyn recognized. Garrick's friends. Fifteen and sixteen years old, barely more than children. Arrow-pierced through their hearts. They'd been dead within minutes of being struck.

A moaning cough brought Wyn scrambling to his feet. He half-ran, half-stumbled across the snow towards the source of the sound, but when he got there, he felt as if his heart had stopped beating. He fell to his knees.

The coughing boy was Garrick's best friend, Junnar. He'd been gut-shot, and the dark, matter-filled blood oozing from the wound told Wynter the boy was a dead man even though his body still clung weakly to the last threads of his life.

Junnar lay atop the prone, lifeless figure of Wynter's brother. An arrow—its shaft painted with the Prince of Summerlea's personal colors—protruded from Garrick's throat.

"Garrick?" After moving Junnar to one side and packing his wound with snow to numb the pain, Wyn reached for his brother with trembling hands. His fingers brushed the boy's face, and he flinched at the coldness of his brother's flesh. Garrick had been dead for hours. Probably since before Wyn had left Gildenheim in pursuit. How could Wyn have lost the only family he had left in the world and not known it the instant it happened?

Horses approached from Wynter's back. Then Valik was there, laying a sympathetic hand on Wynter's shoulder.

"I'm sorry, my friend. I'm so sorry."

Wyn nodded numbly. The ache was consuming him. The pain so deep, so indescribable, it was beyond feeling. His whole body felt frozen, like the ice statues he and Garrick carved together.

"Help Junnar." How he spoke, he didn't know. His voice came out a choked, gravelly rasp. "Make him as comfortable as you can."

"Of course."

He waited for Valik to lift Junnar and settle him off a short distance before gathering Garrick's body into his arms. He held his brother for a long time, held him until Junnar breathed his last, and the White Guard packed the bodies up for transport back to Gildenheim. Their hunt for Prince Falcon of Summerlea had ended the moment Wynter found his brother's corpse. But there was no doubt in any of their minds that this was far from over.

Wynter carried Garrick in front of him on Hodri's back, cradling his body as he had so many times over the years after their parents had died and it had fallen to him to raise his brother. He carried him all the way to Gildenheim, releasing him only to the weeping servants who would prepare Garrick and the others for the funeral pyre.

Wynter stood vigil by his brother's side throughout the night. He murmured words of sympathy to the parents of the other lost boys but shed no tears of his own though his eyes burned. At dusk the following night, he stood, tall and dry-eyed beside the pyres as the flames were lit, and he remained standing, motionless and without speaking, throughout the night and into the next morning. He stood until the pyre was naught but flickering coals. And when it was done, and there was nothing left of his brother but ash, Wynter mounted Hodri and took the long, winding road to the Temple of Wyrn, which was carved into the side of the next mountain.

Galacia Frey, the imposing and statuesque High Priestess of Wyrn, was waiting for him inside the temple. She had come the night before to bless his brother and the others and to light their pyres, before returning to the temple to await his visit.

"You know why I have come."

Her eyes were steady. "I know. But Wyn, my friend, you know I must ask you to reconsider. You know the price."

"I know and accept it."

"There's no guarantee the goddess will find you worthy," she warned. "Many men have tried and died."

"You think that frightens me? If I die, I will be with my brother. If I survive, I will have the power to avenge him."

She closed her eyes briefly and inclined her head. "Then take the path to the left of the altar, Wynter Atrialan, King of the Craig. Leave your armor, clothes and weapons in the trunk by the door. You must enter the test as you entered the world. And may the goddess have mercy on your soul."

CHAPTER 1

Wynter's Chill

Vera Sola, Summerlea
Three years later

"He's here!"

The news swept through the royal palace of Summerlea on an icy wind. Smiles froze on suddenly frightened faces. Laughter—so ebulliently prevalent even after the past three years of bitter war and hardship—faded into silence like the last notes of a dying song.

High above the palace, amidst the tangled overgrowth of her mother's long-neglected Sky Garden, Khamsin Coruscate battled an invisible foe beneath the flowering branches of a Snowfire tree, unaware of the fear spreading through the city below. The last few months' unseasonable cold had left all the other trees in the garden winter-bare, but the Snowfire bloomed defiantly. Its long, slender branches were bursting with bold, hot pink blossoms that filled the air with a heady perfume as if to ward off the invading cold with the deep, lusty scents of summer.

Despite the Snowfire's brave show, winter would not be swayed. A light snow had begun to fall, and the tip of Khamsin's nose had gone pink. She paid it no mind. She was engaged in a ferocious sword fight with a powerful and conniving enemy, Ranulf the Black, the villainous king whose attempt to invade and conquer Summerlea was immortalized in Khamsin's favorite book, *Roland Triumphant: Hero of Summerlea.*

As she lunged and parried, locking blades with her invisible foe, Khamsin didn't even notice the approach of her maid, Tildy, until the elderly woman stopped directly beside the Snowfire tree and cleared her throat.

"He's here, dearly," Tildy said.

Khamsin lunged, crowing in victory as her blade struck a killing blow. Straightening, she blinked once to clear her mind of visions of ancient, heroic battles, and squinted at her beloved nurse. "Here? Already?"

"Riding past the Stone Knights, arrogant as you please, not fifteen minutes ago. Your father and the court have gathered in the upper bailey to greet him."

Roland and his foes forgotten, Khamsin snatched up her cloak and the well-worn copy of *Roland Triumphant* that had inspired her mock battle. She thrust through the long, whiplike branches of the Snowfire, ignoring the sound of ripping cloth and even the painful tug of black curls as hair and clothes caught and tore on the branches. "Why didn't you come for me sooner? He'll be coming up the Castle Road by now."

"I came as quick as I could, dearly, but he's an hour early, and these old bones don't move as fast as once they did. Och, now, look at the mess you've made of yourself." Tildy tsked and shook her neat cap of tight silver-gray plaits. She hurried forward, and Khamsin stood with familiar patience as her nurse clucked about her and quickly repinned her hair to hide the distinctive white streaks that threaded like bolts of lightning through her otherwise unremarkable Summerlander black hair. "Half a dozen tears already and mud on your hem. Your father won't be pleased if he sees you like this."

That was nothing new. When in all of Khamsin's twenty years had her father ever been pleased with her? Still . . . she couldn't hold back the hopeful question, "Did he . . . ask for me to join the family?"

The old nursemaid's expression faltered for a moment, pity creeping into her gaze. "No, child. He didn't."

Khamsin drew a breath and buried the hurt with a nod. After all this time, it was foolish to still let the rejection hurt. Since age three, she'd lived as little more than a servant, dressed in cast-off gowns, ignored and forgotten, tutored only because Tildy refused to let the mind of a Summerlea princess go ignorant and unprepared. Few outside the palace gates remembered there had ever been a fourth princess of the Summer Throne. Fewer still knew what she looked like, or even that she was still alive. Nonetheless, at every state function, Tildy insisted on dressing her charge like the royal princess of Summerlea she was, and they would wait together, in silence and dying hope, for the summons that never came.

"It's all right, Tildy." She forced a smile. "I'll just go to the tower and watch from there. The stone amplifies the voices in the bailey, so I'll hear everything. And I'll have a much better view, I'm sure."

"Dearly . . ."

Khamsin didn't want to hear the consolations and excuses, the empty promises that one day her father would realize what a treasure she was. She thrust her book into the nursemaid's hands, lifted the mud-stained hem of her red velvet skirts, and ran.

Hard-soled leather boots slapped on cold stone, and her black cape whipped behind her as she darted through the open garden gate and up the steps to the castle tower. Her mother's garden had been built high on the crest of a small man-made mountain around which the ancient stone walls of Summerlea's palace and surrounding city ringed like ribbons round a maypole. Only the tower proper—the now-crumbling Keep of Kings—rose higher than her mother's beloved Sky Garden. The Keep overlooked the palace's upper bailey and the long, curving lanes that ringed down to the city's main gates and the valley below.

With swift familiarity born of years spent running

wild through the palace's many forgotten places, Khamsin darted through the dim corridors. After her mother's death, the upper reaches of the palace had been locked away, left to weather the years untended and uninhabited. Only a curious child, a princess as neglected as this once-lovely palace realm, had ever dared the King's wrath and ventured secretly within. It was the one place—the only place—Khamsin had ever felt at home.

Her cape caught on a protruding nailhead, and the sudden yanking pull all but strangled her. Khamsin ripped at the frogs that clasped the cape around her throat, tearing one free and ripping the delicate lace at her neckline. The cape fell in a puddle of watered silk and black velvet. The simple golden circlet Tildy had so lovingly settled in place in Khamsin's curls earlier that morning cocked awkwardly over one brow, dislodged by her brief struggles with the cape. With an angry sob, she tore the circlet free and threw it on the pile of silk and velvet.

Her hair came unpinned again, falling about her shoulder in untamed ringlets, the white streaks that had always been so offensive to her father once more in plain view. She didn't care. Let him see her and be enraged. At least then he'd be forced to feel something. Even fury was better than years of neglect.

Leaving her crown and cape where they lay, Kham resumed running. A few moments later, she crossed the wide, cobweb- and dust-covered room that had once been the Queen's Bower.

Silent hulks of furniture, shrouded in linen swaths, filled the room. Along the walls, moth-eaten window hangings and tapestries sagged in mournful tatters. After his wife's death, King Verdan had ordered the bower closed off, Queen Rosalind's belongings covered with sheets and left where they lay.

Across the room, a narrow lip of stairs curved up the tower wall to a small landing and an arched doorway. Kham leapt the stairs three at a time and rushed into the small, covered oriel overlooking the courtyard and city below.

She caught her heaving breath and swiped at the useless tears that still sometimes insisted on spilling from her eyes. She didn't need her father's love. She didn't even need the recognition of her birth status. She had Tildy and her sisters, who loved her despite him. She'd had her brother's love, too, until he'd run off with the Winter King's bride. And, of course, she had her mother's treasures to remind her that Queen Rosalind, at least, had loved her last-born child even if her husband would not.

The clatter of hooves in the courtyard below made Khamsin flinch. She glanced down into the bailey and froze. All thoughts of her father and his long neglect swept away in an instant. Stunned awe took their place.

Now, there was a sight no Summerlander had ever seen before.

Shining white, brilliant pale, like an army of snow-cloaked conquering ghosts, the soldiers of Winter rode proud into the upper bailey of Summerlea's royal palace. And at the army's head, just now passing through the gate, rode the White King himself, Wynter Atrialan, King of the Craig.

He sat on a snow-white stallion, as cold and merciless as a headsman's axe just before the chop. Armor of mirror-polished silver plate gleamed from crown to toe. A long, ice blue cape trimmed in white ermine trailed out behind him, covering his mount's rump and draping down past the Winter King's own armored heels. At the crown of his helm, a tall ruff of white horsehair ruffled in the chill breeze, and his stallion's iron-shod hooves rang out on the worn cobble of the courtyard.

The horse came to a halt. The Winter King swung one long leg over his mount and slid effortlessly to the ground. Summer Sun! He was huge—practically a giant. Taller than any Summerlander, with the broadest shoulders she'd ever seen. Over seven feet of powerful muscles and sheer intimidation. She hadn't expected that. Beneath his silver helm, a mask in the shape of a snarling wolf's head hid his face.

His gauntleted hands rose to unlatch the mask and lift the helm from his head. He tucked it beneath one arm, leaving his sword arm free, fingers resting near the hilt of the now-infamous blade, Gunterfys—Giant Killer. A blade that after the last three years would be better named Ertafys—Summer Killer.

Even from her vantage point high above, she could see the Winter King's face. Square jaw, cheekbones high and shapely, skin a surprising golden hue, the color of browned butter. She'd always thought the folk of Wintercraig would be snowy pale, but they weren't. At least, he wasn't. Which only made his wealth of long, gleaming white hair and startling pale eyes seem all the more vivid.

He was handsome. Beyond handsome.

She hadn't expected that either. Khamsin sucked in a breath, then coughed as the cold air dried and chilled her throat.

Silver-blue eyes, clear and cold as glacier ice, cast upward, finding her in one swift, sharp instant, pinning her in place. All thought fled her mind. She couldn't breathe, couldn't think. She could only stare, captured and frozen, as the Winter King's fearsome gaze held and plundered her.

How long she stood there, motionless, she couldn't say. Each moment lasted a lifetime. First ice, then fire scorched her cheeks. Then ice again when, at last, the Winter King turned his gaze away and freed her.

She stumbled back into the shadows and lifted trembling hands to cover her face. Her heart pounded heavy in her chest, each beat a labored thud. The blood in her veins felt slow and sluggish, her mind dazed, and a distinct chill had invaded her flesh.

She was shivering violently by the time she reached the bottom of her stairs.

"Dearly!" Tildy exclaimed in worried tones. The old nursemaid limped across the room to bundle Khamsin up in the warm velvet folds of her abandoned cape. "What were you thinking, child, to stand up there in the wind with naught to cover you but one thin dress? Your skin's gone cold as ice."

"S-sorry, Tildy," Khamsin apologized through numb lips and chattering teeth. With one long glance, the Winter King had all but frozen her to death. The only spot of warmth on all her skin was the small, rose-shaped birthmark on her inner right wrist—proof of her royal Summerlea heritage.

Wynter cast a cold, keen, wary gaze around the courtyard, missing nothing. The sound from up high a few minutes ago had set him on edge. He'd shot an Ice Gaze at the would-be assassin, only to capture instead a dark, unruly-haired servant girl dressed in some noblewoman's cast-off gown and watching the proceedings in the courtyard with wide gray eyes.

He'd known in an instant she was no assassin. There was something . . . innocent . . . about her. Something intriguing about the wild tumble of black curls streaked with white, like glacial waterfalls frozen against black rock. Well, no matter. He wasn't here to entertain himself with servants—even the intriguing, pretty ones. Not that she'd willingly come within a hundred yards of him again. Had he held his Gaze a moment longer, he would have frozen her where she stood.

Wynter directed his attention back to the royal family of Summerlea, who had assembled on the palace steps as he'd commanded. King Verdan, his dark, swarthy face as full of false pride as ever, stood at the forefront, clad in full court dress. Still fit after thirty years of kingship and decades of indulgent living, the Summer King boasted a vivid masculine beauty. He was tall and well-muscled, with dark, snapping eyes, rich coloring, and an intrinsic Summer warmth so different than the colder, paler folk of the north.

His son, the prince called Falcon, had been much the same.

Was that foreign warmth the temptation that had lured Elka from her vows?

Behind Verdan, standing as close together as they could without appearing to huddle, waited his three lovely daughters. They were—justly so, Wynter now realized—as famous for their exotic beauty as for their Summerlea gifts. What their real names were, he neither knew nor cared. They were easy enough to identify by their giftnames: Spring, the eldest, a tall, cool beauty with bright green eyes and inky hair straight as falls of snowmelt pelting down a cliff side; Summer, the middle daughter, whose thick waves of blue-black hair and summer blue eyes promised a warmth long lacking in the Craig; and the youngest, Autumn, a haughty, exquisite creature of breathtaking beauty, blessed with loose, flowing ringlets of a rare, deep auburn that set off her pansy purple eyes to perfection. These were Summerlea's greatest treasures: the three Seasons, beloved daughters of the Summer King.

The corner of Wynter's mouth curled in a faint smile. This victory would not be without its pleasures.

"King Verdan." He turned his gaze upon the former ally whom he'd spent the last three years bringing to heel. "I have come, as I vowed when last we met on the field of battle, to issue the terms of peace and claim what is my due."

Summerlea's ruler nodded stiffly. "I am prepared to receive and meet your demands."

"Are you? Good." Wynter gestured to the white-cloaked army behind him. "First, you will quarter my men. Your Steward of the Keep will escort my Steward of Troops, Lord Arngildr, on a tour of the city and palace defenses. He will deploy my men throughout the city . . . to discourage any courageous acts of rebellion your loyal followers might entertain," he added with a cold, knowing smile.

Verdan flushed but did not look away.

"You will quarter me as well," Wynter continued. "Richly. With a warm bath and a hot meal to refresh me after my journey. And one of your beloved daughters . . ." He perused the three princesses and settled on the haughty beauty with the flashing purple eyes. "Autumn, I think . . . to share my meal." Again he smiled, without a hint of warmth. "To discourage any . . . overspicing."

"Very well," Verdan bit out, not rising to the bait. "We have prepared a suite for you. Luxurious in every appointment. You will not be disappointed."

"Won't I? I understand the rooms you have prepared for me once belonged to your son, Prince Falcon." He enjoyed the shock on Verdan's face and the quick, panicked flicker of his eyes. Let him wonder how the Winter King had learned that bit of news. "Did you really think I would rest in the bedchamber of the thief who stole my bride and murdered my heir?" Just the mention of that terrible day brought the memory of it back in vivid color. White. The color of fresh-fallen snow. Spruce green. The color of Wintercraig's forest and Garrick's hunting leathers. Red. The color of Garrick's blood. So much blood. Blue. The color of the sky, of Garrick's sightless eyes, and of the Summerlea prince's arrow rising up from Garrick's throat.

Wynter's jaw tightened. The now-familiar burn of power sparked at the backs of his eyes. If he unleashed what lived inside him, he could kill every living thing in the city in a matter of minutes.

"I—but—" Verdan clamped his lips closed and gathered his composure. He bowed. "Then, of course, we will make other preparations."

Wynter blanked the signs of temper from his face. "I understand the upper levels of your tower are unoccupied." He nodded at the stone edifice behind the Summer King. The servant girl was gone from the small oriel above. "I will take those."

"The tower has been unoccupied for years. It has fallen into a state of disrepair. Surely—"

"Consider it a test of your willingness to please me. Your servants have six hours to see to it. Clean, well-appointed rooms, a warm bath, and a hot meal," he repeated. "And your daughter, the princess Autumn, with a pleasant smile on her face, to dine with me. While you see it done, I will tour the city with Valik and your steward."

"But . . . the war . . . your terms for peace?"

"When I am rested and refreshed, we will meet to discuss the particulars of Summerlea's surrender and the price of peace between us." When no one moved, he lifted one mocking brow. "Six hours is little enough time to produce the perfection I demand. Believe me, King Verdan, you would be wise to ensure I am pleased with your hospitality. I am a far less forgiving man than once I was. You and your son taught me the folly of dealing gently with Summerlanders."

"He's taking my mother's rooms?" Khamsin stared at Tildy in dismay. "How could Father allow it?"

The nursemaid gathered a pile of fresh, folded bedclothes and bath towels from a linen room fragrant with rosemary. "He could hardly say no, now could he, dearly?" Tildy answered practically. "Conquered kings may keep their heads but rarely their pride or authority. There's a new king in Summerlea now, child, and his name is Wynter of the Craig. Best we all get used to it."

"But . . . my mother's rooms . . . the Sky Garden . . ."

"Is his, to do with as he pleases." Tildy nodded her head at the open door. "Close the door, dearly, to keep in the scent."

"I don't accept that." She shut the door. "I won't accept that. My mother's rooms are off-limits . . . private. It's been that way all my life."

"That was your father's law. This is the White King's will. We do as he commands now."

"Why? Because he beat a shivering army into surrender? Bah! Politics and the rules of war be damned! We should not bow to this usurper's demands like a pack of frightened mice!" The invasion of her mother's rooms was personal. It was a defilement of a silent, sacred memorial to the beauteous Summerlea queen who'd died long before her time.

Tildy stopped in her tracks, her spine going straight as a poker. She turned and cast a dark glance back at Khamsin, a silent reminder of who had raised whom from infancy. "Politics? Is that what you think this is?" the older woman asked in an arch voice. "Mind your temper, and use that brain God gave you! This isn't politics we're talking about. It's survival. Your father's and your own to boot. Displease the Winter King, and we'll none of us see another spring."

"What joy does a slave find in spring?" Khamsin countered bitterly. "Better to die a hero's death like Roland than live ten lifetimes cowering beneath a conqueror's heel!"

"Hush!" Setting the pile of linens on a nearby table, Tildy crossed the room to take Khamsin's shoulders in a firm grip and shake her soundly. "That is childish idiocy speaking. I've taught you better. Roland died a hero, aye, but his line died with him. You are an heir to the Summer Throne. So long as you and your family live—even one of you—there is hope for us all. Would you fling yourself to your death without a care for those who love you? Without a thought for those whose care you ought to put before your own? Have I failed so utterly that I've raised a blind, vain fool instead of a princess fit to wear the crown?"

Feeling sullen—shamed and wounded by the scold—Khamsin dropped her gaze. "No," she muttered. "You haven't failed, Tildy." She shook free of her nursemaid's harsh grip. Her velvet-clad arms crossed over her chest. "Fine." She couldn't summon gracious defeat, but then, she'd never been able to do that—not even when the defeat was as minor as losing a game of chess. "I will not obstruct." Her eyes flashed. "But I won't help either."

The nursemaid sighed and shook her long-ago-silvered hair. "That would be too much to ask, dearly. I'll be happy just to hear you promise not to summon a cyclone in his bath—especially not when he's in it."

Kham kicked a nearby table leg and scuffed the toe of her leather slipper. Tildy knew her too well. "No cyclone. I promise." Her gaze shot up with sudden defiance. "But I *am* going to collect the dearest of my mother's belongings before he claims her rooms." She'd never dared remove them before now, lest her father discover she'd entered the tower against his will.

"As well you should." Tildy had been Queen Rosalind's nursemaid, too. She had followed her charge from the gentle, oceanside kingdom of Seahaven, twenty-eight years ago, and stayed to raise Rosalind's children as she had raised Rosalind herself.

Tildy started to pick up her linens again, then stopped and turned to wrap Khamsin in a tight, loving embrace. "Don't fight so hard against things you can't change, child. You'll batter yourself to death. Learn to change what you can and accept what you can't. Be the palm that bends in the wind to withstand the gale."

Khamsin stood silent as Tildy walked out the door.

She was no flexible palm. She was, instead, like the Snowfire in her mother's garden, bursting into bright, defiant bloom when temperatures plummeted and snow began to fall, daring winter to do its worst.

She scowled and clenched her long, slender fingers into fists. She'd vowed no obstructions to the claiming of her mother's rooms, and she'd vowed not to summon cyclones in the White King's bath. But if the conqueror harmed her family or her home, she'd make him sorry. Her eyes narrowed, and she felt a familiar electric jolt of energy down to her soles.

Outside, the wind picked up speed.

Wynter frowned. The storm had come from nowhere, quick and violent. The sky overhead had gone dark as slate. Gusting wind howled through winding cobbled lanes and between stone buildings, rattling thick glass windows in their panes. All along the King's Path, the cobbled road that corkscrewed up the palace mount, live oaks and citrus trees battered their brittle, winter-slain branches against the ancient stone walls. Without further warning, the dark clouds opened the floodgates. Rain pelted down, first in painful, stinging drops, then torrential sheets. The Summerlea steward escorting him leapt for the shelter of a covered walkway nearby.

Wynter turned his face up and squinted at the storm-darkened sky. Cold rain sluiced down his cheeks, saturating his hair and soaking the padded tunic he wore beneath his armor. Beside him, Valik, his ever-loyal friend and steward, stood still and watchful, equally as impervious to the downpour.

"There is a weathermage at work," Wynter said. "A strong one."

"Aye." Valik put a gauntleted hand on his sword hilt. "Ill intent?" As usual in the company of foreigners, the steward's clipped speech was trimmed down to the fewest possible words.

"Just a warning, I think." The dark clouds overhead were capable of deadly hail and lightning and even cyclones, but Wynter could sense none of that in the roiling sky.

"Coruscate?"

"I doubt it. If King Verdan wielded this kind of power, we'd have seen it long before now on the battlefield. He's never been able to summon more than a short-lived heat wave in my presence."

"Princess?" Weathergifts were the purview of royal houses, and strong weathergifts rarely passed outside the direct royal line.

"Possibly." Wynter almost smiled at the thought. "That would certainly make things interesting, wouldn't it?"

Valik cast him a flat, emotionless look.

He returned a savage grin and gave a grunt of dark laughter that sounded more like a snow wolf's warning growl. The brief, sharp-edged humor faded as quickly as it had come, and Wynter turned his attention back to the storm. Knowing what was coming, Valik and the rest of the Wintercraig men stepped back to give their king room.

"Well, princess," Wynter murmured, "let's see what you're made of."

He opened the source of his magic and drew power into his body. His vision went hazy white and began to whirl, as if a blizzard blew in the depths of his eyes. Power pushed against the edges of his control, seeking release. He squeezed his eyes shut to keep it caged.

The air around him began to spin, slowly at first, then with increasing speed, capturing the falling rain so that not a single drop touched him. Behind his closed lids, he could see the vortex begin to flash and spark. A crackling sound filled his ears—rain freezing in midair, exploding into brittle, porous ice crystals that showered down upon the ground.

He spread his arms, gauntleted palms facing up. The vortex grew wider still, and faster, until it was a howling wind that drowned out the storm's raucous fury. He held the vortex for several seconds, feeding it power, nowhere near enough to approach his full, lethal strength, but enough nonetheless to make his capabilities known. Enough to make the weatherwitch yelp. He threw his arms up over his head, jerked his head back, and opened his eyes.

Concentrated power, surrounded by whirling wind and ice, shot skyward in a column of blazing light and plowed into the heart of the storm overhead. Lightning exploded across the sky, sending frightened onlookers rushing for cover. Rain froze in midair and shattered, sending a blizzard of ice crystals raining down upon the city.

He felt the weathermage's breathless shock, tasted the scent of definite feminine power and outrage on the wind. And, to his pleasure, a hint of fear. Good. The precocious princess had probably never met her match. Until now.

She would learn, as her father had learned, that the Winter King was no spineless, pampered weakling to be threatened without a care. She would learn, as her brother would learn if the coward ever dared return to face the man he'd wronged, that the wild, impetuous tempest of summer was no match for the hard, relentless dominion of winter.

The first lesson had been given—and received. He felt the Summerlander witch withdraw from the sky. The wind fell silent and, aided by Wynter's magic, the raging storm dissipated as quickly as it had formed, towering black storm clouds melting into thick swaths of winter gray. In the ensuing calm, snow fell in large, soft flakes to blanket the ground below.

Wynter turned to the cowering Summerlea steward. The man's black eyes held raw fear now, and his bronzed skin had assumed a sickly grayish green cast. Good. Nothing birthed respect and acquiescence faster than fear.

"You may continue the tour," the Winter King said.

With visible effort, the steward gathered his composure. He straightened the long folds of his burgundy wool and velvet robes and ran trembling hands through his perfumed hair, smoothing the shoulder-length black curls back into some semblance of order.

"Yes, Your Majesty," he said when he was done, his tone filled with a new, much warier respect. "This way, please." Sweeping one voluminously sleeved arm out before him to indicate that Wynter should precede him, the steward resumed the tour of the palace and city defenses.

As they turned the corner, Wynter glanced back up the road behind, to the upper bailey and ancient keep crowning the city mount. Which one, he wondered. Which one of King Verdan's three lovely, headstrong daughters had thrown down the gauntlet?

Khamsin leaned against the wall, clutching her chest and breathing hard. For the second time today, she'd felt the hard edge of the Winter King's power. Icy, fierce, instantly identifiable, it had plowed into her like a fist to the belly, driving the air from her lungs and sending her staggering backward to slam into the stone wall. Her ears were still ringing, and the lump at the back of her head made her hiss when she ran inspecting fingertips over it.

Summer Sun! She'd never known anyone besides herself capable of generating such concentrated fury in the skies.

She pushed off the wall, winced at the stab of pain from the swan's egg on her skull, and headed down the servants' hall toward the tower at an uncharacteristically restrained pace. No more confrontations for her today. Once she snuck into the tower and gathered up the dearest of her mother's possessions, she would flee back to the sanctuary of her own room and stay there.

For once, she was actually glad her father hadn't summoned her to join the family. No doubt the Winter King would be dining with them tonight, and after two run-ins with him, she would happily spend the rest of her life avoiding a third.

CHAPTER 2

The Price of Peace

Garbed in a plain gray servant's frock, with her distinctive hair hidden beneath a linen kerchief, Khamsin climbed the stairs to the tower floor that housed the Queen's Bower. The sight that greeted her actually stopped her in her tracks.

The melancholy but peaceful silence that had pervaded the King's Keep all her life was gone, ripped away by the mad rush of hundreds of servants sweeping, polishing, waxing, and dusting. Half a dozen carpenters snatched from their workshops worked at a frantic pace to replace rotting floorboards, while drapers tore down moth-eaten window hangings and hung new tasseled velvets in their stead. A small army of footmen carted new furniture up from the lower levels of the palace. Maude Newt, the Mistress of Servants, stood at one end of the room, overseeing the cleanup with steely gray eyes and snapping orders left and right.

Someone bumped Khamsin hard from behind, making her stagger forward.

"Out of the way, girl," a man growled in an irritated voice. He and another man, both sweating from exertion, hauled a large, upholstered divan past and set it down along with a host of other furniture cluttered against one wall on a stretch of mended, waxed, and polished floor.

"You there!"

Khamsin turned to find Maude Newt's iron glare pinned on her.

"Quit gawking like a daft looby and get about your business. We've barely two hours remaining to get these rooms restored and spotless."

An angry retort leapt to Kham's tongue but, remembering her disguise, she bit it back. "Yes, ma'am," she said instead, with galling subservience. The birthmark on her wrist blazed with heat, and the urge to send a little lightning bolt up Newt's skirt was almost more than she could bear. She suppressed the urge with effort, bobbed a brittle curtsy, and sped off towards the door leading to her mother's bedchamber.

I'm here for my mother's things, she reminded herself silently. *I'm not here to teach Maude Newt a lesson even if the wizened old lemon deserves it!*

Controlling her temper had never been easy for Khamsin. Since infancy—since the first sentient days of life in her mother's womb—hot, wild, rebellious emotion had always lain just below the surface, simmering, waiting for the smallest spark to set her off. There were times Tildy despaired of ever teaching her control. There were times Kham despaired of ever being more than the hot, destructive wind for which she was named.

As she crossed the bower to the bedchamber, she felt Newt's hard glare boring into her back, gaining reprieve only when she ducked out of sight through the sleeping-chamber door. Well, at least her disguise seemed to be working. If Maude Newt had recognized her, she'd have run straight away to tell King Verdan that Summerlea's disgrace of a fourth princess was dressed like a servant and skulking in an area of the palace she'd been forbidden to enter.

Khamsin entered the sleeping chamber and froze in her tracks once more. This had apparently been the first room tackled by the crew of frantic servants because its transformation was already complete. Kham could only stand in the doorway and gape.

Her mother's bed was gone. A new, larger bed rested in its place, piled with several thick, fresh ticks that two young maids were industriously covering with scented sheets. The wood floor, scattered with plush woven rugs, gleamed like polished copper. Every last cobweb and mote of dust had been banished from sight. Sumptuous velvet hangings and tapestries robbed the chill from the cold stone outer wall, and a fire blazed in the wide hearth that opened through a shared inner stone wall to the bathing room beyond. A pot of fragrant herbs simmered over the flames to fill both the sleeping and bathing chambers with a fresh, warm scent to chase away the musty odor of neglect.

Others might find the room's transformation a pleasant surprise. Khamsin did not. Anger knotted in her belly. She didn't like change. She didn't like these hundreds of servants invading her mother's space—*her* space—and turning the forlorn but comforting familiarity of her childhood sanctuary into a perfect, spotless foreign world where she no longer belonged.

She turned towards the place where her mother's dresser had stood earlier today, and an invisible fist closed around her heart. The dresser was gone.

She spun around, scanning the room in rapid, frantic sweeps. The irreplaceable treasures she'd come to collect had vanished as well. Where were her mother's golden, gem-studded hairbrush, comb and mirror? Where was the small painted miniature of her mother's likeness? Most of all, where were the two slim, bound books—the gardener's journal and the private diary—written in Queen Rosalind's own hand?

"You two!" she snapped at the young girls making the bed. "What happened to my—to the queen's belongings?"

One of the two girls pursed her lips. "And who is it askin'?" she sneered, scanning Khamsin's modest dress with a dismissive gaze.

Kham's fingers curled in a fist. *I am in disguise. I am a servant,* she reminded herself. *Servants do not rudely order other servants around—unless you're Maude Newt.*

"I'm a new girl, just come to the palace to serve Princess Summer," she improvised. "She sent me to collect a few of her mother's things before the White King takes up residence."

That wiped the sneer off the girl's face. The warm, kind-hearted Summer was beloved by the palace servants. Few would begrudge her the slightest request. In a more accommodating voice, the girl said, "Anything fit for the trash heap has already been taken away. Everything else was carted off to the old solar. If there's anything of the queen's worth keeping, it's most likely there."

"Thank you." Khamsin drew a breath and plunged back into the frenetic rush of the Queen's Bower, weaving through the crowd of carpenters, maids, and other workers. The solar was an adjoining antechamber accessible through a connecting door on the southern wall. Kham reached the door and turned the knob.

Locked. She ground her back teeth together in frustration. The door was locked, and Kham knew who was the most likely person to have the solar key in her possession.

She glanced over her shoulder in Maude Newt's direction. The Mistress of Servants was talking to a tall guardsman wearing the king's livery. Khamsin couldn't hear what they were saying, but when Newt jabbed a bony, emphatic finger towards the queen's bedchamber, it was obvious the woman must have seen through her disguise.

Time to go. She'd come back later after getting a spare key from Tildy. Right now, she'd best make a quick escape before the Newt caught her. The steely-eyed Mistress of Servants would love nothing better than to catch Khamsin in some sort of mischief and report her to the king.

Khamsin ducked through the bower door and shoved past the stream of workers crowding the hall and stairway. Behind her, she heard a man's voice call out, "Princess!" but she ignored him and plunged down the stairs.

She raced two flights down and kept running until she reached her room. She'd barely changed out of the plain frock into one of her sister Autumn's cast-off gowns of spruce green worsted wool when a knock sounded on the door. Kham stuffed the servant's gown and linen kerchief under her bed and ran both hands through her disheveled curls to smooth them before opening the door.

A liveried guardsman—different from the man in the tower—stood outside her door. "Your Highness." He bowed shortly, his face a blank slate. "The king requests your presence."

"What in the name of the Sun were you thinking?"

Khamsin stood stiff and silent, eyes focused blindly straight ahead. Her father, King Verdan, still clad in the formal court dress he'd donned to greet Wynter Atrialan, paced the floor of his private office. Heat radiated off him in waves. He was furious. With her. Not because of the tower, but because of the storm before that.

"Did you think I wouldn't know it was you? Are you that great a fool that you would openly attack the Winter King before the terms of peace are even settled? With half his army waiting in our streets, ready to slaughter us all at the slightest provocation?"

Her gaze snapped up, guilt and worry suddenly swamping her. She hadn't meant it that way. She'd only meant it as a warning . . . something to let the White King know not all denizens of Summerlea were cowed by his presence. She hadn't stopped to consider that he might interpret her storm as an act of war.

"Father, I—"

"Silence!" His hand swept out, cracking against her cheek in a fierce, explosive blow.

Her head snapped back. Tears of pain filled her eyes. Inside her mouth, blood welled up where the edge of her teeth had cut the soft inner lining of her cheek.

"Papa," Autumn protested, half rising from the couch where she and her other two sisters sat, having been summoned as always to witness their youngest sister's disgrace. "You know she didn't mean it. You know how Storm gets when she feels threatened." Storm was Khamsin's gift-name, but only her siblings ever called her by it. Her father never called her anything but "girl."

"Sit down, Autumn, and be silent."

"But Papa—"

"I said *sit!*"

Autumn sat. She cast Khamsin an apologetic glance. Kham shook her head slightly. This was not Autumn's fight, nor was it her place to intervene. Khamsin had long ago outgrown the need for her siblings to protect her from their father's wrath even if they still insisted on trying whenever he was particularly furious.

Her father's full, dark green velvet robes swung as he spun back around towards Khamsin. "Since you obviously cannot be trusted to control yourself, you will remain in your room until the Winter King departs."

She nodded, not daring to speak.

"If you make one more misstep," he warned, "if you so much as ruffle a breeze through the White King's hair or even breathe in defiance of my will, I will cast you out. I will banish you from this kingdom on pain of death. Do you hear me, girl?"

"Papa!" This time the protest came from all three sisters.

Khamsin couldn't gather her thoughts enough to warn them off. Her father's threat was stunning, vicious, and wholly unexpected. She'd known for a long, long time that he didn't love her, but she'd never realized how deep and truly bitter his feelings were. How he must despise her to ever make such a threat.

"Stop it, Papa," Spring ordered. Cool and sensible as always—capable of almost as fierce a temper as Khamsin, but far more able to control it—she crossed to Khamsin's side and laid a protective hand on her arm. "Pain of death? She is an heir to the Summer Throne. There's not a person in this kingdom who would curse their family house by spilling her blood, and you know it."

"It's not Storm's fault the Winter King is here,"

Autumn added. She stood, straightened her deep purple gown with a snap of her wrist, and went to join Spring at Khamsin's side. Her copper curls bounced at she cocked her head to one side and thrust out a delicate, imperious chin. "Everyone in this room knows exactly where that blame lies."

When King Verdan bristled, Summer rose and wrapped her arms around her father's waist. Of all his children, she was his favorite. She was everyone's favorite, blessed with a sunny nature and a ready smile.

"Enough, Papa. I'm sure Storm's sorry for what she did, and I'm sure she didn't mean to endanger the peace. Let her stay in her room, as you suggested, and avoid any further confrontations with the Winter King. The rest of us will do our best to show him how gracious and hospitable Summerlanders can be." She smiled, her deep blue eyes full of forced cheer. "Maybe that will help soften his terms of surrender."

The Summer King regarded his three oldest daughters for a long moment. The heat issuing from his body began to dissipate, and the room grew noticeably cooler. But when he turned back to Khamsin, the loathing in his gaze made her flinch.

"Get to your room, girl. Don't dare step one foot outside your door until I send word that you may. Tildavera will bring you your meals. If I find out you've disobeyed me, I won't kill you or banish you, but believe me, I'll make you wish I had."

Khamsin curtsied and turned for the door. She didn't speak. Tears gripped her throat in a chokehold, and if she tried to say a word, they would burst forth in a humiliating gush. She hadn't cried in front of her father in years—not since the day he'd told her she was responsible for her mother's death.

With half his men deployed at strategic points throughout the city, and the other half taking up positions in and around the palace, Wynter returned to seek the room, bath, and refreshment he'd demanded.

King Verdan himself escorted Wynter through the warm, colorful halls of the main palace building and up several flights of stairs into the old, stone keep that crowned the city. Valik and a prune-faced harridan who'd introduced herself as Maude Newt, Mistress of Servants, trailed behind, along with half a dozen Wintercraig guards.

The air grew a little colder as they entered the keep, the surroundings a bit more lonely and somber, but Wynter actually liked that better than the crowded frills and luxuries of the palace. Cold stone and privacy suited his nature. He was a man who lived in a harsh, uncompromising land of solitude, danger, and stark beauty.

The small party climbed two flights of stone steps in the tower before reaching the floor that housed the newly renovated Queen's Bower. A knot of young, gray-clad serving girls stood at attention just inside the wide, arching doorway that led into the bower. They bobbed erratic, nervous curtsies as he passed.

Wynter walked through a set of wide double doors into the long-abandoned room his spies had told him was a rotting ruin. However deteriorated it might have been before, nothing now could be further from the truth. The room sparkled and gleamed from corner to corner, and the air was rich with the scents of flowers, herbs, fresh sawdust, and a strong sprinkling of bleach. The furnishings were exceptional, both in quality and beauty. Wynter's gaze roved over the room, searching for subtle points of complaint. He found none. Verdan, it seemed, had outdone himself.

"This will do." He glanced at the servant girls. "Prepare my bath."

They squeaked and bobbed and nearly tumbled over each other like a litter of clumsy wolf pups in their rush to do his bidding.

"I will expect refreshments and your daughter's company within the hour," he reminded the Summer King with a cool look.

"Of course." Verdan bowed his head slightly. "Newt here will see to any other needs you may have. Just use the bellpull to summon her." He pointed to a long, tasseled pull near the double doors. "I had thought we would discuss terms in the map room downstairs. Will two hours from now give you sufficient time to prepare?"

"Two hours is fine." He didn't want to leave Verdan stewing for too long, lest worry blossom into something unwise.

"I'll send my steward Gravid to guide the way." Verdan spun on his heel and departed.

The Mistress of Servants lingered behind long enough to drop a quick, deep curtsy and reiterate the offer of her services. "If you need anything, Your Majesty, anything at all, just call on Newt. I'll see you get whatever you desire."

"Very good." There was an obsequiousness to her tone and slyness to her darting gaze that he did not care for. "For now, Newt, privacy is what I desire most. And Newt? Wintercraig kings are addressed as 'Your Grace,' not 'Your Majesty.'"

"I understand, Your Grace. Of course, Your Grace. Just send the girls out when they're done." She bowed and backed out of the Queen's Bower. The doors, now guarded by Wynter's own men stationed outside in the hall, closed behind her.

Silence fell over the bower, broken only by the sound of splashing water coming from the bathing chamber. Wynter and Valik stood still and wordless, watching each other and waiting in patience silence. A moment later, the four trembling young maids emerged from the bedchamber like wary does mincing into an open glade.

"Your bath is ready, sir," one of them whispered.

"Good." Wynter jerked his head toward the double doors. "Out."

The maids bolted.

Valik waited until they heard the sound of the maids' shoes clattering down the stone steps before speaking. "Well, he managed it."

Wynter nodded. "Surprisingly well, too." He stripped off his gauntlets and tossed them on a nearby table, then walked to the two large, glassed windows cut into the stone wall and threw up the sash on each of them. Cold brisk air swirled in, carrying with it a light flurry of snow. He breathed deep and left the windows open so the draft could clear away the sweet, heavy aroma hanging in the room. "It seems Verdan is sincere in his efforts to be accommodating. Perhaps he'll acquiesce to my terms after all, and I can take what I've come for through peaceful means rather than violence."

Valik grunted, plucked a round green grape from a bowl of fruit, and popped it into his mouth. He bit down, then grimaced and spit the crushed grape into his hand. "Sour. You didn't allow warmth enough for their crops to ripen this year."

"That was the plan."

"I suppose. Just didn't think I'd have to suffer the results." He sighed. "I hope there's something decent to eat around here."

"Stay and share my meal with me."

Valik gave a grunting laugh. "Don't think so, tempting though it is. That Autumn is a fine piece of Summerland bounty. They all are. Lucky you."

"Lucky me," Wynter agreed with a smile that didn't reach his eyes.

His friend started to say something—no doubt a continuance of the argument they'd been having since leaving the encampment this morning—but he caught himself, and said instead, "Water's hot. Go bathe. She'll warm to you a bit better if you don't stink of horse and travel."

Wynter arched a cool brow. "I've already told you, she could be cold as a block of ice, and it won't change my mind."

Valik sighed and shook his head. "An occasional chill in the bedroom keeps things fresh, Wyn, I'll grant you that. But cozy your bare ass up to a glacier night after night, and eventually your extremities will freeze and fall off. Including the important ones." He raised both brows suggestively.

Wynter snorted. "No Summer witch has it in her to be that cold." He waved a hand at the door. "Go. Get cleaned up, find some decent food, and meet me in the map room in two hours."

"I've said my piece. Won't say it again." Valik saluted by tugging one of the silvery white braids dangling from his temple, then ruined the image of stoic acceptance by adding, "Will say 'told you so' when the time comes, though." He laughed at Wynter's glare and headed for the door. "Map room. Two hours. I'll be there, my king. Enjoy your meal . . . and your princess."

"Frost brain." The velvet pillow Wynter threw at him bounced harmlessly off the closing door and slid across the floor.

Thanks to Valik's irritating prod, Wynter had half a mind to meet the princess not only stinking of horse but fully armored as well. The scented mist wafting in from the bathing chamber changed his mind. He was tired. He'd been in the saddle, waging war, bereft of female companionship and most of life's gentler pleasures for three years. But the war was over now, and the Summerlea princesses were beautiful. He couldn't deny that a part of him longed to bring a little warmth back into his life.

He walked into the bedchamber, threw open the two windows there, and began to strip in the brisk, fresh air. With deft fingers, he loosened the numerous buckles holding his armor in place and shed the heavy silver plates of protective gear, setting each of them against the wall. His boiled leather inner armor joined the plate, as did the padded gambeson beneath that, and finally the innermost garment, quilted silk that covered him from neck to wrist and ankle.

Naked, he padded into the bathing chamber and stepped into the huge copper tub. A slow smile spread over his face as he slipped into the steaming water. *Winter's Frost, that felt good.* Tight muscles began to relax. He leaned his head back against the broad, curved lip of the tub and stared up at the ceiling from half-closed eyes.

In the Craig, after a particularly cold day, he'd often enjoyed a dip in the hot volcanic springs of Mount Freika or a relaxing steam bath in the caverns beside the springs, but leading this war had kept him from home for the better part of three years. In all that time, he'd not allowed himself indulgences beyond those available to his troops. He'd shared the same hard ground, tepid baths, and plain camp fare as his soldiers. The only amenity he hadn't partaken of with them was women. Elka had stripped him of all warmer passions when she left; the colder ones he'd poured entirely into his bitter, consuming three-year battle for vengeance.

And now, at last, victory was at hand. Summerlea had robbed him of both his queen and his heir. He planned to return the favor.

After his bath, Wynter emptied his saddlebags and donned a flowing, buttonless cream silk shirt and matching woolen breeches. The loosely tied closures bared a casual vee of muscled chest and the cream silk complemented the golden hue of his skin. The breeches and a pair of butter-soft golden leather boots hugged his calves, outlining the muscular legs and hindquarters gained from years of combing the rocky highlands of the Craig.

A knock sounded on the bower door. He walked to the bedroom door, toweling his hair, and despite his own men standing guard, he picked up his sword before calling "Enter!" through the doorway.

The sound of an unlatching lock and the rattle of trays told him his dinner had arrived. He cast a glance through the open doors, counting two—three—maids, and two of his own men watching as they laid out his meal.

He returned to the bathing chamber and left the new arrivals to set up the brief repast, but he kept his sword within easy reach—just in case. The habits of war were hard to break. He was, after all, still a conquering king standing in the heart of the enemy territory.

Wynter tossed the towel on the edge of the bath and ran a brush through his long, pale hair. It was still damp and curled slightly at the ends in the moist warm air of the bathing chamber. He fastened it back with a gilded silver tie and hooked a shining silver ear cuff in the shape of a snow wolf—sign of his family clan—around his left ear. Three silver chains dangled from the ear cuff, each attached to a small silver bell bearing one of three Wintercraig runes symbolizing ice, fire, and the Great Hunt. On his right index finger, he wore his ring of office: an intricately carved platinum signet bearing the royal crest of the Snow Wolf clan. On the little finger of his left hand, he wore another platinum band, this one set with an enormous, breathtaking, blue-white diamond called the Wintercraig Star. Last, he pulled on a short, sleeveless vest of sky blue velvet embroidered in silver threads.

A glance in the beveled mirror hung on the wall reflected back an image of cool, understated elegance. That would do.

He slipped out of the bedroom and halted at the sight of not one but three darkly beautiful Summerlea princesses sitting at the glossy mahogany table.

Spring, Summer, and Autumn had come to share his meal.

In retrospect, Wynter realized, it was a boon to have such surfeit of royal companionship for his repast. He'd thought to observe the Autumn, to determine if she would suit, but enjoying the three of them together gave him a greater understanding of each. He'd taunted them a bit, with their own changed status, treating them more like servants than princesses, just to see if they would be as accommodating as their sire.

They did not disappoint. He'd seen the flash of defiance in Spring's eyes just before she lifted her own wine cup to his lips as he'd commanded, the resentment in Summer's when he'd ordered her to sing while he ate, and the way Autumn's fingers had curled around the knife when he'd told her to cut an apple and feed him the pieces from her own hand after she had taken a bite from each. But he'd also seen each princess shiver when he ran a finger across her soft, pampered skin or leaned a little too close for comfort, and he'd watched each stifle her own flare of temper and bend herself to his will.

They were proud and haughty, like their father, but they were also wise enough to fear the Winter King. And that fear made them swallow their urge for defiance.

When the meal ended, he sent them away, pleased. He'd been right. Any of them would do. That would make things simpler.

Still wearing his cream silk trousers and shirt, with Gunterfys strapped to his hip and Valik striding beside him, Wynter entered the palace's large map room. King Verdan, still in his ceremonial best, greeted Wynter with cool reserve.

"Verdan." He nodded to the older man. Four other men stood beside the king, including the general of the last surviving Summerland army and three lords of the king's council. "You four," he commanded with brisk disregard, "get out."

Outrage flashed across all four men's faces, and across Verdan's as well.

"What? How dare you, sir!" the general exclaimed.

"These men are my confidants and advisors, leaders of Summerlea," King Verdan protested, casting a warning look at the leader of his last remaining army. "They have a right to be present at any peace negotiations."

"Negotiations?" Wynter lifted a brow. "I have come to explain the terms of your surrender. They are nonnegotiable. You can accept them, or you and every living creature in Summerlea can die."

"You're bluffing," one of the other three said. "If you wanted us dead, we'd already be so."

"I do not bluff. I came here to end the war, but only on my terms. Since the day I took the throne, you Summerlanders set yourself against me, thinking my youth made me an easy mark, mistaking my restraint and efforts at diplomacy as signs of weakness. In your arrogance, you thought I could be easily dispatched, and Wintercraig would be yours for the taking. You thought wrong." His eyes narrowed, his expression deadly cold, he leaned forward on the table. Frost whitened the polished surface. "You Summerlanders started this war, but I am here to finish it. You can either accept defeat—and the terms that go with it—or you can die. Either way makes no difference to me. I will take what I came for."

The general flushed a ruddy color and cast an outraged glance at his king. "Sire! There's no need to accept this disgrace and humiliation. Say the word, and we will stand and fight. We'll die to a man, like Roland and his army when they triumphed over Ranulf the Black."

"You wish to die?" Wynter narrowed his gaze on the general. Cold fire came to his call, gathering, burning, at the backs of his eyes. "Very well, then. Die."

The general went stiff, his mouth freezing open in a stifled cry.

"Stop." Verdan wasn't stupid enough to step in the path of the Ice Gaze, but he couldn't stop himself from the quick, instinctive lurch towards the general.

"The wound you dealt me to start this war was personal," Wynter said, holding his Gaze. "The price of peace is personal as well. It does not concern your armies or these men, and their presence is neither necessary nor desired." The general's lips had turned blue, and his skin had gone pasty white.

The Summer King capitulated. "Release him, and I'll send them away."

Wynter blinked and shuttered the power of his Gaze. "Better."

He waited for the three openly terrified lords to depart. The general, shaking uncontrollably, had to be helped out the room by a trio of servants. "Give him a hot bath and wrap him in thick blankets," he told the servants. "He won't feel warm again for several days."

When they were gone, he nodded to Valik, who slipped out the other door, leaving Wynter and Verdan alone.

Wynter crossed his arms and regarded his enemy in silence. The Summer King and his lords were pampered fools. Arrogant and treacherous, yes, but ultimately weak. They had never known true hardship until the hand of Wynter had fallen hard upon them. They roamed the hills and vales of Summerlea, preening and prideful, believing themselves lords of the earth, when in reality they—like the people they governed—were only sheep, fatted and dull-witted by decades of self-indulgence, easily herded to the slaughter.

It had not always been so. Once, long ago, the kings of Summerlea had been lions of men, true heroes, like Roland Soldeus, who had sacrificed everything so Summerlea could live free. But somewhere along the way, that shining spirit, that noble, defiant bravery, had died out. Generations of kings who'd held the fire of the Sun in their hearts had given way to weaker, less noble men, willful, nihilistic parasites who gorged themselves on Summerland bounty and cloaked themselves in the shreds of their ancestors' glory.

And their people, those sheep they kept glutted on a never-ending flow of wealth from the country's fertile fields, vineyards, orchards, and herberies, never noticed the difference.

Oh, they'd rallied a few worthy defenses when Wynter had first marched upon their lands, but he'd known their will would not last. He'd continued to press them, relentless and without mercy, stripping their armies of the few brave souls still among them until only the sheep remained. And then, he'd simply spread winter across their lands and waited. Hardship sapped what tiny flickers of defiance still remained, and the last two battles had been easily won.

"Well?" Verdan prompted when the silence dragged on. "What are your terms? What is the price of peace between us?"

Wyn had intended peace to come only when every Summerlander lay frozen and lifeless beneath a blanket of ice and snow. But the helpful informant who'd snuck into his camps several months ago had convinced him there was another, more satisfying victory to be had.

"Your son, Prince Falcon, stole the woman who was to have been my queen and one of the irreplaceable treasures of my house." Wynter pushed off the map table and began to pace. "He ran off with them both while I was fighting the brigands he sent to destroy one of my people's villages. But that was not enough for him. During his escape, your son put an arrow through my brother Garrick's throat. My brother was just a boy, not yet sixteen, but your son left him to die in the snow and fled like the thieving coward he is."

Wynter turned, his face a frozen mask, his eyes burning ice. "Your son robbed me of my queen, one of my kingdom's greatest treasures, and my heir. You will return to me that which I have lost."

Verdan went pale, and his jaw dropped open in a stunned gape. "I? I'm no miracle worker. I can't return your brother from the dead, and I'm sure your spies have already told you no one knows where Falcon is. Not even I. If Falcon did take your queen and your treasure, as you have claimed, only he would know where to find them."

"A queen, a treasure, and an heir. That's what you will provide me. You have proclaimed many times that the greatest treasures of your kingdom are your lovely daughters. So I will take one of your daughters to wife. She will have a year to fill her womb with an heir to claim both the Winter and the Summer Thrones. If she fails, she will be turned out to face the mercy of the mountains, and I'll be back the following spring to claim another daughter. And so it will continue until I have my heir or you are out of daughters. That, Verdan, is the price of peace."

CHAPTER 3

The Treasure of the Tower

Khamsin approached the closed, freshly gleaming double doors leading to the Queen's Bower. Once more garbed in a gray servant's dress with a cap to cover her distinctive hair and a white bandage wrapped around her wrist to hide her Summerlea Rose, she carried a stack of freshly laundered towels as her excuse to get inside the bower and access the solar to retrieve her mother's things.

The Winter King was in the map room with her father, working out the terms of surrender. Khamsin knew enough about diplomatic negotiations to know he would be gone for hours. Plenty of time for her to retrieve her mother's most treasured belongings.

The Wintercraig guards standing outside the bower doors searched her from head to toe and inspected the pile of towels for hidden weapons. She explained the bandage on her wrist as a burn from the pressing iron and bit her lip to hold back her outrage as searching hands took a bit too much liberty near her breasts. If they were looking for an excuse to do more, she didn't give it to them, and they finished their inspection and let her pass.

As soon as the doors closed behind her, she hurried to the solar door on the southern wall. The key she'd nabbed from Tildy's dresser slid easily into the lock and turned with a satisfying click. The solar door swung open.

Inside, the room that should have been bursting with

Queen Rosalind's treasures was all but empty, only a few shrouded lumps of furniture and a haphazard pile of lamps, artwork, and personal effects remained.

She wanted to weep. They had saved so little. She'd loved every worn stick, every moth-eaten inch of tattered velvet that her mother had ever touched, but her father's servants had discarded most of it as worthless trash.

She forced down the anger and useless sense of loss. "Look on the bright side, Khamsin," she muttered to herself, "at least there's less for you to search through."

She stepped into the solar, leaving the door unlatched and propped open just the tiniest crack so she could hear if anyone entered the bower. With a brisk sense of purpose, aware that each second that ticked by was a moment closer to the White King's return, she began to search. She started with the sheet-covered furniture, pulling cloths away until she found her mother's dresser, where she'd kept the most treasured belongings. Unfortunately, the top of the dresser had been cleared off, and its drawers emptied. Khamsin turned to the jumbled pile in the corner of the room and began rummaging through it.

Halfway through the pile, she found her mother's golden brush, comb, and mirror, and that gave her hope. A layer or two deeper, she came up with the miniature oil painting. Finally, near the bottom of the pile, beneath a tangle of long-outdated gowns, she saw the familiar, cracked leather bindings of Queen Rosalind's handwritten gardener's journal and her diary. At last! Khamsin snatched the books to her chest and bent over them, rocking a little as her breath came in relieved sobs.

Sounds—the click of a door latch, then voices—wafted through the cracked solar door.

Her heart leapt into her throat. She jumped to her feet, her mother's treasures clutched to her heart, and tiptoed to the door to peer out the narrow opening.

A pale-haired man in blue walked past her line of vision. The White King's second-in-command. What had she heard the servants call him? Valik? Then another man, one she knew instantly without even a glimpse of his unforget-table face. White-haired, golden-skinned, clad in creamy silk and a pale blue velvet vest: the Winter King.

What was he doing back so soon? She drew back in in-stinctive fear, terrified that he might turn his ice-cold eyes upon the solar door and find her standing there.

The two of them were talking in voices too low for her to hear. Valik murmured something and headed back to-wards the doors. She heard them open and close. Then the Winter King walked past her line of vision again, and she heard the sound of water running in the bath, muffled by the closing bathroom door.

Time to leave. She stuffed her mother's things in the deep inner pockets of her skirts and crept out into the bower, turning to close the solar door behind her but not daring to lock it for fear the White King would somehow hear the click of the bolt. She hadn't taken more then two steps when a mocking voice froze her in her tracks.

"Well, well, what do we have here? A pretty little assas-sin come to slay the Winter King in his bath?"

Wynter watched the girl—a slender young thing in a gray servant's dress—freeze like a doe scenting the hunter. Her head came up, eyes wide and frightened. She stiffened when she caught sight of him standing in the bedroom doorway, the sound of his bath still splashing merrily away in the empty bathing chamber. Her eyes met his. He smiled, and it wasn't a pleasant expression.

She bolted.

With a darting speed many a runner in his land would be hard-pressed to match, she leapt across the room to-wards the doors. He didn't chase her. He didn't even call out though the guards stationed outside the door would easily have put an end to her flight. He just crossed his arms lazily over his chest and waited while Valik emerged from his concealment behind a large breakfront and blocked her escape route.

She skidded to a halt, half-crouched, arms outflung, and sucked in her breath with an audible gasp.

"Stay a while, won't you?" Wynter murmured. He sauntered closer as she straightened and turned warily back to face him. He'd given Verdan the rest of the day and night to decide which daughter would wed Wynter. Was this assassin Verdan's answer?

He let his gaze wander over the girl's smooth, unlined face. She was quite lovely. Her skin a fine, warm, Summerlander brown, her heart-shaped face blessed with high, sculpted cheekbones, full lips, and a pointed little chin that had the look of stubbornness about it. Dominating it all was a pair of flashing, storm gray eyes beneath dark arching brows.

"Such a pretty face for such an ugly profession."

"I'm no assassin!" she protested. "I'm just a maid. I came to freshen your bath before you returned."

"Truly? But that way"—he tilted his head towards the door in the south wall—"does not lie my bath." His brows lifted in mocking inquiry.

She swallowed, and he could see the vein in the hollow of her throat pulsing like a fluttering bird caught in a snare as she tried to figure her way out of the lie. "I . . . er . . . I . . ." Stammering, openly nervous, she began to back away. Her eyes darted to the left and right, seeking a possible path of escape.

Well, that was interesting. Wynter's initial assumption underwent an immediate reversal. Whatever she was, this girl was no assassin. A professional would have planned an entrance, and exit, and a plausible excuse for her presence if she were caught. And Verdan would have chosen someone older and colder, someone who would have killed Wynter, died trying, or slit her own throat if she failed at both, just to keep from revealing who'd hired her.

One other thing was also clear: whatever her reasons for being here, they had nothing to do with tending his bath.

So, if not to kill him and not to serve him, why had she come?

He nodded at Valik. "Search her."

She stood, trembling and white-faced, as Valik quickly patted her down. Valik's shoulders stiffened when he reached the voluminous skirts. The girl lurched back, trying to keep Valik from revealing whatever he'd found.

Gunterfys flashed. A single drop of scarlet blood welled at the girl's throat and trickled down her skin in the shadow of the shining sword tip tucked just below her chin. Wynter didn't believe she was an assassin, but then again, astonishing though the thought might be, he could be wrong.

"Don't move," he advised. "My blade is very sharp, and Valik's life far more important to me than yours. You wouldn't want to make me nervous on his behalf."

She didn't speak. She didn't dare. If she even swallowed, she'd pierce her throat against his blade, and he could see she knew it.

Slowly, watching for any sudden moves, Valik crouched down and reached once more for her skirts. His hand disappeared into what appeared to be a deep pocket hidden in the gray folds.

Wynter wasn't sure what he was expecting. A knife perhaps, or some sort of poison. Odd how disappointed he felt to see the jeweled comb and hairbrush, followed by a matching mirror. Obviously old, obviously of great value.

"Not an assassin, then," he murmured. "Just a common thief." He pulled the razored tip of his sword back slightly.

The storm gray eyes flashed. With his blade no longer pressed directly against her flesh, she'd rediscovered her courage. "I'm no thief! And even if I were, it would be better than being a cold, merciless killer like you!"

Valik reached into her pockets again and retrieved a small, leather-bound book which he handed to Wynter.

With his free hand, Wynter cracked open the book and

leafed through the handwritten pages, frowning over the detailed sketches of plants and the instructions for their care. "I can understand the gold and jewels, but this? You would risk my wrath to steal this? A gardener's journal?"

The girl surprised them both. She leapt back, away from the tip of Wynter's sword, and delivered a swift kick to Valik's jaw that sent the steward sprawling against Wynter's legs, knocking them both down. She started to lunge for the journal, which went skittering across the gleaming floor, but thought the better of it when Wynter freed himself from the tangle of Valik's limbs and tossed aside his sword to advance on her with unmistakable determination. She spun and raced for the doors.

He caught her just as her fingertips skimmed the brass door latch. One hand wrapped hard around her wrist, the other came up to block the close-fisted blow she plowed towards his head. The little fury meant to black his eye if she could!

He laughed with a mix of amusement and surprised appreciation. She couldn't win. She had to know that. Yet still she fought. He hadn't known there was a Summerlander alive still willing to confront him with such spirited defiance. Entire armies had fallen before him, yet this slight wisp of a girl dared to grapple, barehanded and defenseless, with the Winter King, a man who could slay with a glance.

He dodged a fist meant to break his nose and laughed again, enjoying himself for the first time in a very long while. How lucky for him so few of Verdan's soldiers had possessed such raw, reckless courage! A thousand like her in their ranks, and the war might have ended quite differently.

His humor apparently didn't sit well with her. She snarled and aimed another blow at his chin, which he blocked, as well as a vicious kick to his groin. He managed to block that, too—barely—but the hard toe of her boot still came close enough, with enough force, that his balls tingled from the near miss.

He quit laughing. There were some things a man just didn't find funny.

"All right. That's enough!" He shoved her hard up against the wall, one hand curled around her throat, squeezing just hard enough to make his point. He'd let her have her fun, now he would get his answers.

The struggle had dislodged her cap. Long black ringlets of hair, streaked with gleaming white, spilled halfway down her back. His eyes narrowed on the pale hairs threading through the much darker curls, and he recognized her at last.

"The little maid from the bailey." He regarded her with even greater interest than before. She was the last person he'd ever have expected to find here. "Do you know how very rare it is for anyone who has ever felt my Gaze to risk invoking my wrath a second time?"

Panting, she glared at him. The heat of her Summerlander skin soaked into his hands. She was so soft, so warm. So brave and defiant. More intriguing than any woman he'd met in a long, long while, and undeniably pretty.

"Tell me, little maid, was one brush with death not enough for you? Or did the danger of it simply whet your appetite for more?" He pressed his thumb against the vein pulsing so rapidly beneath the soft, oh so vulnerable skin, and felt the answering leap as her heart pounded faster.

She felt like warm satin. Smooth and creamy to the touch, reminding him how long it had been since he'd tasted the sweeter pleasures of life.

"Is that it?" His voice grew husky. "Was the thievery just an excuse to seek a greater thrill? Perhaps you wondered if the Winter King's blood could run as hot as it does cold? It can, I assure you." He moved closer, pinning her lower body, letting her feel the unmistakable—and growing—bulge in his trousers.

Her face paled, then flushed with color. Her eyes grew huge in her fine-boned face. His free hand slid up her waist to cup one firm, full breast, fingers dancing across the fabric until he felt the satisfying jab of her nipple drawing tight and hard. A bolt of static electricity snapped between them, and a tremor shook her from head to toe.

"Get your hands off me!" she demanded. "Let me go!"

Behind him, Valik cleared his throat in disapproval, but Wynter ignored him. He was toying with the girl—in part, just because he could, but also because every cell in his body was stinging with life and heat for the first time in three long years.

Nor could she hide her answering attraction from him, even though she obviously wanted to. One of the gifts of the Snow Wolf clan was a heightened sense of smell, and though it had been three long years since he'd shared the warmth of female companionship, there was no mistaking the scent of sweet, warm musk emanating from her.

If she were even the least bit as willing as her body so obviously was, he would get rid of Valik and coax her into something a little more mutually satisfying than fisticuffs.

His thumb stroked her peaked nipple through the thin wool fabric. The static sparked again, and she gave a helpless moan. The sound burrowed oddly deep inside him, rousing a response like none he'd ever felt before. Possessive, dominant, compelling.

The little maid felt it, too. And it obviously terrified her. She began to struggle in earnest, slapping his hand away and pulling at the other hand still circling her throat. Her eyes had changed color, going from their original stormcloud gray to a bright, strangely shifting silver, as unique as her white-streaked hair. Outside, the wind whistled, picking up enough speed to rattle the windowpanes.

Valik cleared his throat again. "Enough, Wyn," he chided. "Let the girl go."

Wynter felt his nostrils flare with an instant stab of aggression, and his upper lip curled back to bare his teeth. He even growled, low in his throat, like a snow wolf warning another male away from his female.

His response shocked him. Rationally, Wynter knew

Valik was right. He was many things, most of them unpleasant, but one thing he'd never been was rapist. He had
to let the girl go. But another, far more primitive and fierce,
part of him refused. He had to touch her. Just this once at
least. He couldn't explain the compulsion, but he couldn't
deny it either.

He caught her hands and pinned them over her head,
against the wall. He lowered his head towards her soft,
parted lips. His lips claimed hers, his tongue plunging deep
to conquer the sweet cavern of her mouth, while his free
hand swiftly released the top few buttons at the front of her
bodice. Her skin felt hot to the touch, as if fire burned just
below the flesh. He started to slide a hand inside her loosened bodice, but she tore her mouth from his with a cry.

The window at his back exploded with a deafening
crash.

Wynter cursed himself roundly and released her. He
staggered back two steps and shook his head until the
strange, almost hypnotic sexual compulsion faded, and his
normal, cold clarity returned.

Fool! Idiot! She wasn't the assassin. She was the diversion sent to lower his guard!

He spun around, reaching for his power. It leapt at his
command with crackling, lethal force. To his right, Valik's
sword flashed free of its scabbard with a familiar, deadly
hiss.

Khamsin dove for the bower doors. It wouldn't take either
Winterman long to realize there were no attackers, that
there was only a broken tree branch, lying on the floor
amidst a sea of scattered glass shards, flung into the room
by a fierce gust of wind.

Outside, it was storming for the second time that day,
the sky dark with clouds. The wild strength of the tempest
matched her own mad, riotous feelings. Anger, fear, and—
Halla help her—lust roiled in a fierce tumult in her belly.
The skies echoed her emotions as they always did when

temper or other strong feelings made her lose her grip on the powers of her giftname, Storm. Lightning flashed, and the first, deafening booms of thunder rattled the windows in their panes. Wind howled through the shattered window, and gusts of still-snowy air whirled inside.

The bower doors burst open before Kham reached them. The crash of the window had brought the guards running. She ducked to one side as the guards rushed in, then slipped out behind them and ran for the tower steps.

Time to leave, before she landed in even bigger trouble than she already was.

Halfway to the stairs, she stopped dead in her tracks. Too late.

The large imposing figure of Maude Newt, Mistress of Servants, blocked the only path of escape. She stood at the top of the stairs, flanked by two young maids who'd obviously come to tend the very tasks Khamsin had used as her excuse to get past the guards.

Kham instinctively reached up to pull her cap tighter over her telltale hair, only to plunge her fingers into bare curls. Her cap!

Newt's beady eyes narrowed, and her face pruned tight with triumph and naked loathing. "You!" she exclaimed. Her hand shot out to clamp around Khamsin's upper arm, the meaty fingers almost as strong and viselike as the Winter King's earlier grip. "I knew I'd seen you skulking around here earlier. What are you about? You have no business up here."

Her hard gaze swept over Khamsin, missing no detail of her disheveled appearance, not the loose, wild tangle of hair, not the flushed face, and definitely not the bodice unbuttoned low enough to bare the cleft between her breasts. A sneering, speculative look entered her eyes. "Or did you? Aren't you the sly one. Come to do a little negotiating of your own, eh?"

"You know this girl?" The White King approached, straightening the cuffs of his silk shirt. He'd obviously realized there were no assassins lurking outside in the storm, and he'd leashed his terrible power. His steward Valik followed close behind, rubbing his jaw where it had met the hard edge of Kham's shoe.

Newt gave the White King a tight, obsequious smile. "Indeed I do, sir. A wild, mannerless tatter who hasn't yet learned her place." Her fingers squeezed so tight Kham knew she'd wear a collection of bruises come morning.

She didn't need the warning to hold her silence. The last thing she would do was let the White King know who she really was. Even facing her father's wrath was a more welcome prospect than admitting she was an heir to the throne the Winter King had vowed to destroy.

"I hope she didn't . . . upset you . . . Your Grace?"

Newt looked rather hopeful when she posed that last question, but to Kham's surprise, rather than admitting he'd caught her stealing from the solar, Wynter Atrialan merely gave the Mistress of Servants a chilly look, and asked, "Do I strike you as a man who could be upset by some slip of a servant girl?"

The woman blanched and hurried to recover from her gaffe. "No, Sire, of course not." She bobbed a rapid series of bows and curtsies. "Not in any way, Your Greatness. I never meant to imply any such thing. Please accept my apologies." She started to back away, dragging Kham with her as she went. "Forgive me for allowing this girl to intrude on your privacy. It won't happen again."

He looked at Khamsin, and murmured something she could have sworn sounded like, "Pity." But then his ice-pale eyes flicked back to Newt, and he said, "See that it doesn't," in a voice so cold she was sure she must have imagined the other.

"Pansy and Leila will freshen your bathing chamber, sir." Newt jerked her chin in silent command, and the two trembling maids standing behind her bobbed nervous curtsies and fled past into the bower, all but running as if they couldn't wait to finish their work and leave.

Her hand still clenched tight around Kham's arm, Maude dragged her towards the stairs. Khamsin cast one, last glance back through the veil of her hair, and found the Winter King watching her. He had the strangest look on his face, something oddly wistful and bemused. Then the look was gone. He turned to reenter the bower, and the doors closed shut behind him.

"I've caught you now, girl," Newt crowed with swaggering glee. "Caught you red-handed."

Kham waited only until they were out of sight of the bower doors before yanking her arm from Newt's harsh grip. "Get your hands off me." The idiot woman actually tried to grab her again, but Kham evaded her and gave her a fierce glare. "Touch me again, and I'll make you wish you hadn't," she vowed. Little sparks of energy popped and crackled at her fingertips. She was in no mood for further manhandling, especially not by the likes of Maude Newt.

"You won't be acting so high-and-mighty when the king hears what you've been up to!" Newt snarled. But apparently the threat and the little show of power convinced her that Kham meant business, and she kept her hands to herself. "Get on downstairs now," she snapped. "We're going to see your father."

Khamsin briefly contemplated the idea of running for it and leaving Newt empty-handed, but gave up the idea almost immediately. Newt didn't need Kham in tow. She had witnesses. Half a dozen of them. Even if the White King kept silent, Pansy and Leila wouldn't. They'd seen her distinctive hair, and their livelihoods depended on keeping in Newt's good graces.

Her father was going to be in such a rage when he realized she'd openly defied him and entered the tower. Worse, that she'd been caught there by the White King.

Newt herded her down the tower stairs and through several levels of the palace towards the king's private office. As they walked, Khamsin puzzled over the strange, unseemly twist her foray into the bower had taken. What had come over her? He'd touched her, and it was like electric flame—like the lightning she could summon—shooting sparks through her veins. She'd all but melted, boneless, at his feet. He was the Winter King, her enemy, a man feared for his killing coldness, yet when he'd touched her, she had not frozen. She'd burned.

Her face flamed just thinking about it. About him. His eyes, so pale, so foreign, piercing as if he could see into her very soul. His hands, commanding, callused from years spent holding sword and reins, capable of violence, yet also capable of rousing such . . . incredible sensations.

She shivered and felt the clenching in her loins that left her weak at the knees. Best she stay away from him from here on out.

Far, far away.

"What in Frost's name that was all about?" Valik demanded as soon as the two skittish maids finished fumbling their way through their duties and departed.

Wynter stood beside the broken window, staring out at the storm-tossed sky. The maids had cleared away the broken glass, but the carpenters and glassmakers hadn't yet arrived to replace the window. "I don't know what happened, Valik. I can't explain it."

"I've known you since we were both infants, but I've never seen you act that way before."

"I've never felt that way before."

"What way?"

Wynter glanced down at the cap in his hands, surprised to find his fingers gently caressing the fabric as they'd wanted so desperately to caress the maid's soft skin. He clenched his hands, crushing the cap, twisting the fabric in his hands.

"Driven," he admitted. "Possessive. Enchanted, almost. I touched her and it was like . . . like fire in my soul." He looked out into the roiling clouds. He could still see her in his mind, her flashing eyes and fierce temper, her hair like a night sky streaked with lightning. He could still smell the captivating, enthralling scents of her, the soft aroma of her skin, the heady perfume of her undeniable sexual response that even now made his body grow painfully hard just remembering it. He threw the cap on a nearby table and turned away from the window to pace the gleaming hardwood floor.

"I don't like the sound of it, Wyn," Valik declared, frowning as he watched his king pace. "You dined with the Seasons earlier. Think they spiked your food with arras leaf?" Summerlanders were infamous for their hedonistic ways, and arras leaf was one of their most powerful and renowned aphrodisiacs.

"To what purpose? So I'd plow a chambermaid? Or be off my guard for an attack that never came?" Wynter shook his head. "I'm not drugged, Valik. I didn't leap on those little fawns Pansy and Leila." He hadn't felt so much as a passing interest in either of them even though he'd still been rock hard and aching from his all-too-brief interlude with the storm-eyed maid. "No, it was her. Something about her."

He paced the length of the room again and paused beside the jeweled vanity set and the worn leather gardener's journal Valik had removed from her skirts. Nothing about the girl made sense. Who was she? What was it about these trinkets that were so important? And what was that disturbing enchantment she'd cast over him?

"If the storm hadn't crashed that tree branch through the window, I think I might have laid her down whether she willed it or no. Even with you in the room." He cast a troubled glance at his friend as a new thought occurred. "Have I embraced the Ice Heart so long, I've become it?"

Valik's furrowed brow smoothed. "No, Wyn," he declared staunchly. "You might have swallowed the monster when you set out on this path, but it hasn't consumed you yet. There's still warmth in you. I'd know it if there wasn't." He clapped a hand on Wynter's shoulder. "Forget the maid, and whatever witch's trick she's played on you. Claim your

Summerlea bride. Breed your heir. When you hold your child in your arms, the Ice Heart will melt."

Wynter nodded and took a deep breath. It was the longest speech Valik had made in months. And, as usual, he was right. Wynter was here to claim a royal wife and breed an heir—both for his kingdom and the one he'd spent the last three years conquering.

Fiery little maids—even dangerously enchanting ones—did not figure into his plans.

He would put her from his mind. Tomorrow, he would complete his conquest by taking one of the Seasons to wife, then he and half his army would depart. With a bit of luck and a lot of pleasurable effort, his princess would prove as fertile as she was beautiful, and he'd never set foot in Summerlea again.

Gravid, King Verdan's steward, cast yet another disapproving glance at Khamsin's appearance, sniffed. "His Majesty will see you now." He nodded to the liveried footman attending the king's office door. The footman pulled open the heavy, carved oak door and stood at attention as Newt and Khamsin passed.

They'd been forced to cool their heels in the outer chamber, waiting while the king concluded his meeting with General Furze and three lords Khamsin recognized as chief advisors of the king's council. Khamsin had used the time to button up her dress and try to make herself more presentable. She would have liked to repin her hair, so as to avoid upsetting her father any more than necessary, but Gravid had no pins, and Newt had told him not to send a servant to fetch some. "Let her father see her as she is," Newt had ordered.

Now, with her father's dark, hot gaze searing her where she stood, Kham realized it made no difference anyways. Just the sight of her was offense enough to him.

Newt took every advantage to play it up, all but chortling with glee as she told him all about how she'd discovered the wayward princess acting in direct defiance of her father's kingly will, making sure to put the worst possible spin on the entire sordid tale. "She was there, Sire, in the tower, bold as you please. Hair down, gown unbuttoned. It doesn't take a genius to figure out what she was about."

Khamsin glared at the Mistress of Servants. "I wasn't there to seduce him and you know it, you foul-minded old bat! Tell the truth, if you're capable."

"Silence!" her father roared. He shot a hard look at Newt. "Leave us!" he snapped.

The woman's face fell. She'd obviously been hoping to witness Kham's disgrace and punishment. One hot glance from her king seared away any possible objection. She curtsied and backed rapidly out of the room.

Verdan waited for the door to shut behind her, then advanced upon his daughter, his dark eyes flashing. "Is it true? You went there to play whore to the enemy of this house?"

"No, of course not! Newt is a liar, Father. I ran into her while trying to get away from him, and she knows it."

Her father's brows shot up. "So you admit you were there. In the tower. When I had expressly forbidden you to leave your rooms?"

"Yes, I was there, but—" She didn't dare say she'd gone for her mother's things. To admit that was to admit that she'd been in the tower before, in direct violation of his long-standing royal decree.

"But what? What were you after?" His hand shot out and his fingers wrapped around the same part of her upper arm left tender by Newt's unkind grip.

She'd be bruised for a week. It was ironic. In the last hour, she'd been manhandled by the Winter King, Maude Newt, and her father. Yet of the three of them, her family's sworn enemy was the only one whose hands had left no mark on her.

Verdan shook her with fierce, barely restrained fury. "Are you the traitor in my midst? Are you the one who's been feeding him information?"

Khamsin blanched. "No! Of course not!" *There was a traitor in Summerlea?*

"Don't lie to me, girl!" He shook her again, using both hands this time, making her head snap back and forth until she was dizzy. The book and picture in her skirt pocket banged against his thigh and he froze, scowling with sudden suspicion.

"What are you hiding?"

"N-nothing, Father." The lie popped out, more from instinct than conscious thought, and she immediately wished she could call the foolish words back. *Oh, Kham, you dolt! If you're going to lie, try a lie that actually has a chance of being believed!*

"Empty your pockets. Now, girl!" he barked when she hesitated.

Newt she might defy, but not her father, not her king. At least not openly in his presence. She was well and truly caught. Red-handed, just as Newt had crowed earlier. Kham reached into the depths of the pocket hidden in the folds of her skirt to extract the one remaining book and the framed miniature of Queen Rosalind.

Her father snatched the treasures out of her hands and stared at the small but perfectly executed portrait of his dead queen. With trembling hands, he skimmed the pages of the diary where she'd recorded the events of her last years of life in her own hand. The look in his face was horrible to behold. Staggering loss, utter devastation. If Khamsin had ever doubted her father could love as strongly as he hated, those doubts evaporated in an instant.

He doubled over, shoulders heaving with silent, shattering sobs. Heat gathered, concentrated, poured off him in dizzying waves as the Summer King's own, not insubstantial power, came in answer to his anguish. The portrait and diary in his hands began to smoke, then to Khamsin's horror, burst into flames.

"Father!" She rushed towards him, snatching off her

apron so she could use it to beat out the flames that had engulfed his hands.

But when she neared him, he looked up, and the moment his eyes fixed on her, all his grief, all the devastation of lost love, coalesced into a terrible searing rage.

All focused utterly on her.

Khamsin came to an abrupt halt. "Father?" She'd never seen him look that way at her before. Never. For the first time since childhood, she actually felt frightened of him.

Without warning, his arm swept out and he backhanded her across the face with such force that she flew into the leather chair behind her. She landed, breathless and stunned, fiery pain shooting across her face from the place just below her right eye where his signet ring had smashed into her cheekbone. She cupped a hand over her cheek. The power of his gift was so hot, so raging, his ring had actually burned her.

"You dare?" he snarled, his voice incendiary. "You dare defile her things with the abomination of your touch?"

"She was my mother!" Khamsin cried. Was he really so cruel that he would deny her even a glimpse of her mother's image or the chance to read a word written in her own hand?

"She was my *wife*!" He advanced upon her, eyes shining black and vengeful. For a moment Kham thought he would strike her again, this time a killing blow. She gathered her own power, preparing to defend herself, but at the last moment he spun away. "She was the one thing I loved most in this world, and you took her from me. You and your cursed gifts."

The verbal blow struck harder than a fist, as it always had. "I was a child!" she cried.

"You were a mistake!"

Khamsin's gasp sounded more like an anguished sob. The tears she'd sworn never to shed again in his presence burned at the backs of her eyes, fighting for freedom.

"You should never have been conceived," he continued bitterly. "And if I'd known what you would do to her, I would have slain you in the womb." His rage flared hot again, heat pouring off him in waves that made the room seem to shimmer and dance.

"Twenty years," he snarled, his voice shaking with loathing. "For twenty years, I have suffered the affliction of your existence and the bitter fruits of your rebellious nature and destructive gifts. I will suffer no longer."

Cupping her throbbing cheek, Khamsin watched her father with burgeoning dread as he yanked open his office door and shouted for his steward. He would suffer no longer? What did *that* ominous warning mean?

CHAPTER 4

Veil of Tears

As the city tower rang the dawn bells the next day, and two burly guards half carried, half dragged Khamsin's limp, unresisting body back to her room in the farthest, most isolated wing of the palace, she had her answer.

Her father had given her a choice: death or banishment.

Oh, he hadn't actually *given* her that choice, nor even implied she had one. He'd just taken her to a cold, windowless stone room carved deep into the city mount, far from access to the sky so she couldn't summon its energies to defend herself, and informed her that the White King had come to claim a Summerlea princess as his bride. She would be that bride, Verdan declared, and he caned her viciously every time she refused.

Khamsin, foolishly defiant as usual, had refused a lot.

At first, she hadn't believed King Verdan would go as far as he did, and she was more willing to face a caning or two than face the Winter King's wrath when he discovered the thieving maid he'd caught in his room was to be his wife. She'd seen the hard side of Wynter Atrialan's fury, faced his Ice Gaze, and felt him literally drain all warmth from her body. She'd felt the brutal whip of power in the skies when he'd answered her first challenge. She'd also felt the burning heat of his touch and seen the cold fire of possession flaming in his eyes. If she hadn't escaped him when she had, he would have dominated her will and taken what he wanted, and she would have been helpless to stop him.

"No," she'd told her father. "I won't marry him."

After the fifth caning, the Winter King no longer mattered. It had become a contest of wills: hers against the father's. She thought her stubborn defiance and steely resolve could outlast the Summer King's determination.

She'd been wrong.

Sometime after the twelfth beating, when at least three of her ribs were broken and she doubted there were two consecutive inches of flesh on her back or thighs that weren't raw and oozing blood, she'd finally realized the unspoken choice her father was offering her.

She could marry Wynter Atrialan and leave Summerlea, or she could die.

It was that simple.

For all her defiance, for all the many sorrows of her existence, Khamsin was not ready to surrender her life. When her father raised the cane to deliver the first blow of the thirteenth beating, she agreed to be the White King's bride.

The bloody cane had dropped from her father's hand to clatter on the stone floor, and he'd turned without another word and walked out, leaving the two shaken guards outside the room to gather her up and carry her back to her room.

So here she was. Bloody. Beaten. Defeated in a way she'd never been before. Destined to wed the Winter King. Though how she'd manage that when at the moment simply breathing was a sheer act of will, she had no idea.

The guards came to a halt. They had reached her room.

Pride—and pain—forced Khamsin to stand rather than sag against the one guard while the other opened the door, but when it came time to actually walk inside, she couldn't force her trembling muscles to obey. She took two shaky, wavering steps, and collapsed. Only the quick, sturdy arms of one of the guards, catching her before she fell, kept her

from the further humiliation of landing facedown in an ig-
nominious heap.

He helped her to her bed. "I'm sorry, princess, I'm
sorry," he kept whispering as he helped her lie down on
her belly, then peeled back the light cloth they'd wrapped
around her earlier to hide the bare, oozing skin of her back.

"I never dreamed anyone would do such a thing to one
who bears the Rose," the guard said again. "Forgive me. I
should have stopped him."

She waved him off, eyes closed in utter weariness. "Not
your fault," she mumbled. She just wanted him to leave
and let her rest. Sunlight—what pale bit of it could shine
through the winter gray skies—was streaming in through
the window, its gentle warmth soaking into her raw flesh.
Already she could feel the tingle of her magic returning,
the regenerative warmth and healing light working to
repair the awful proof of her father's rage and loathing, but
at the sun's current strength, it would take days, possibly
weeks before she was completely healed.

She heard her bedroom door open and close as the
guards let themselves out. She closed her eyes, exhaled,
and gave herself over to pain and exhaustion.

How long she floated in and out of consciousness, she
didn't know. It could have been minutes; it could have been
hours. At some point, something tugged her back to awareness.

She heard a gasp of horror and dismay: "Dearly!"

The sound of Tildy's familiar, beloved voice made
Kham want to weep as she had not done once throughout the long, torturous hours of the night. The nursemaid
had been more of a mother to her since Queen Rosalind's
death than Verdan had ever been a father. She had showered Khamsin with constant love and guidance, praising
her when praise was due, accepting the bursts of rebellious
temper that were Kham's nature, never shirking from a
firm reprimand when that was due either.

She'd even administered the cane herself once or twice,

when Kham's transgressions had truly gone beyond the pale, but always—*always*—she tempered those punishments with love and restraint. Never, no matter how deeply Kham vexed her, would Tildy have even dreamed of beating her with such unrelenting brutality.

The ultrasensitive skin of her back felt the disturbance in the air as Tildy rushed across the room and dropped to her knees beside the bed.

"Oh, dearly, what has he done to you?"

Khamsin peeled open one eye. Tears trickled down the nursemaid's wrinkled face as she surveyed the damage Verdan had wrought upon his youngest child.

Kham forced a wry smile. "It feels worse than it looks." She started to laugh at her own, poor joke, but her ribs and the torn skin of her back protested the effort.

"Never," Tildy whispered, "never in all my life would I have believed him capable of this. Foolish, arrogant, unthinking man! How could he commit such a crime?" Shaking fingers covered her mouth. "He's called a curse upon his House."

Sadness wiped the faint smile from the edge of Khamsin's mouth. Her eyes closed with sudden weariness. "No, Tildy," she said. "I did that long ago, when I killed my mother."

"Oh, child." The nursemaid stroked her cheek and bent to press a trembling kiss on her brow. "Don't you ever think that. You didn't kill our Rose."

"The magic was mine." She'd only been three at the time, but she remembered. The lightning crashing all around the Sky Garden, called by a little weatherwitch's temper tantrum. The bolt that struck the oak, shattering the tree's dense heart, and shearing off a heavy branch. Queen Rosalind looking up with a gasp. Khamsin had wiped the terrible memory from her mind until the day her father told her she was responsible for her mother's death.

"It was an accident, child, and that wasn't what killed her. She developed a sickness of the lungs, and she was too frail to fight it. She'd never been healthy after your birth."

"My fault again." She'd heard those stories, too. How she had grown in Queen Rosalind's belly like a cancer, sapping her strength, robbing her of health, draining the very life from her.

"No, child. The doctor had already told both Rose and your father that Autumn should be their last child. But your mother wouldn't listen, and your father couldn't keep away." Tildy's hands, gentle and loving, brushed the tangled, sweat-dampened curls from Khamsin's face. "It's not you your father despises, Khamsin. It's himself. Because he couldn't stay away. When he looks at you, he sees the proof of his own weakness and can't stand it."

A tear—such a useless, silly thing—trickled from the corner of Kham's eye. It flowed across the bridge of her nose, clung for a moment until its own weight grew too great for it to bear, then dropped soundless to the cotton sheets where it was instantly absorbed.

"It doesn't matter," Khamsin murmured. "I'm leaving." She met Tildy's sorrowful gaze and forced the corner of her mouth to tilt up in a smile. "I'm getting married, Tildy."

The nursemaid's chin trembled, and fresh tears swam in her eyes. "I know, dearly," she said when finally she'd regained enough of her composure to speak. "He sent me to speed up your healing. He wants you wed the night after next and gone the following morning."

Wynter stalked the tower ramparts, staring out over the miles of the once-fertile valley that was the heart Summerlea. Snow covered the land from the orchards of the northern foothills bordering the Craig to the vineyards of the rolling western hills to the flat southern fields where the husks of wheat, corn, oats and cotton stood withered and lifeless in their white winter coat.

He'd come to conquer, and he had. Nothing lived here except by his will. The far south, beyond his sight, had yielded food enough to feed the people of this kingdom for a few months more, but after that, without respite from the cold, Summerlanders would begin dying by the thousands.

He would ensure it, did Verdan not agree to his terms.

The clank of metal on stone made him turn. His hand dropped instinctively to cover the hilt of Gunterfys, strapped to his armored waist. He'd been outside the palace today, and though he'd shed his helmet and gauntlets downstairs, the rest of him was still clad in full battle armor. The war might be won, but he wasn't fool enough to trust the Summerlanders with an unobstructed shot at his back.

The grip on his sword loosened when he saw the white horsehair plume of Valik's helmet. "Well?"

His longtime friend approached and held out a sealed roll of paper. "This was just delivered downstairs. The runner is waiting for your reply."

Wynter broke the red wax seal bearing the imprint of Verdan's signet and unrolled the stiff paper. He scanned the inked message once, twice. His lips tightened fractionally.

"Well?" Valik prompted when Wynter lifted his gaze.

"He has agreed. With certain conditions." He held out the note so Valik could read it for himself and watched his eyebrows climb when he reached the last lines of the message.

"The arrogant old bastard. He's ordering you to plow her before you leave."

"Wed her, bed her, and get out," Wynter agreed. "Don't forget that last bit."

"Saw it," Valik said grimly. "He as good as came right out and said blood will flow in the streets if you don't leave the day after the wedding." He passed the message back.

Wynter folded the note and tucked it into the cuff of his armor. He didn't need to read the words again. Every looping scrawl of Verdan's hand was already committed to memory. The message was brief, bitter, and as arrogant as the Summer King ever would be:

*We are agreed. Though I would rather see all
Summerlea laid waste than surrender one of my
beloved daughters to be your wife, one of the princesses
has nonetheless agreed to be your bride. The wedding
will take place Freikasday evening, three nights from
now, and as any concerned father would when his
daughter's life hangs in the balance, I require proof
of consummation before you leave Summerlea. My
physician will examine the princess the next morning.*

*She will be prepared to depart immediately thereafter.
I'm sure the folk of Wintercraig are anxious for your
return, and a prolonged departure would be unwise. As
you know, the citizens of Summerlea are extraordinarily
devoted to their beloved Seasons.*

V

"What answer will you give him?"

Wynter shrugged. "I will accept, of course. It's what I
came for."

Valik's mouth gaped open. "You're serious? You're
going to wed her, plow her, and leave town, just like he
wants?"

He almost smiled at his friend's astonishment. "A
demand for immediate consummation isn't unusual when
great Houses forge matrimonial ties. Whether I do the deed
now or later makes no difference to me, but he obviously
fears I will hold myself from her and use her lack of quickening as an excuse to kill her and claim another princess."
What the Summer King hadn't properly calculated was
how badly Wynter wanted an heir. Though he would quite
willingly strip Verdan of every daughter in his effort to get
one, he'd intended from the start to sow his Summerlea
field with vigor.

"And the speedy withdrawal? You plan to grant him
that, too?"

"I am ready for home. I'm sure you and your men are, too. We've been gone long enough."

"Me and my men?" A fresh spurt of outrage drove Valik's voice louder. "I can understand why you would want to take your bride back to the Craig as soon as possible—I don't necessarily agree with it, but I can understand it—but leaving Verdan Coruscate to his own devices is foolhardy. We'll have a rebellion on our hands before you set the first foot on Wintercraig land."

"That's why your Chief Lieutenant Leirik and half the army are going to stay. You and the rest of the men will accompany me and my bride back home."

Valik's rigid spine went even stiffer. "You're going to put *Leirik* in charge?"

Wynter hadn't thought it possible for Valik to look so upset. He was usually a stern guard of his emotions. "He's capable, don't you think?"

"Yes, perfectly capable. That's not the point. If anyone should stay behind to lead the troops here in Summerlea, it should be me."

"No." He said it bluntly, in a tone that brooked no refusal. "You're coming home with me."

"I'm the Steward of Troops," Valik protested. "I'm your second-in-command. In the White King's absence, the White Sword speaks in his name. That's always how it's been. Keeping the peace in Summerlea after you've gone is *my* duty."

"No."

"Wyn—"

"*No!* Don't ask me again." He glared at Valik. "I've already lost one brother to Summerlander treachery. I won't lose another." The two of them weren't brothers in blood, but in every other way that mattered, they were. They'd been friends since birth, confidants in the awkward years of adolescence, and for the last three years, comrades in arms who'd saved one another's lives more times than either of them could count. Losing Valik was not an option.

Surprise blanked Valik's expression, then understanding crept into his eyes. "Wyn . . ."

Wynter turned away. "I've held the Ice Heart too long. If something happened to you, I fear I'd do the unspeakable."

Silence fell between them, broken only by the distant clatter of the city below and the whistle of the cool wind blowing past.

Wynter turned his face into the wind, closed his eyes, and drew the crisp air deep into his lungs. Cold as it was, the air was still warmer than the frigid mass that dwelled deep inside him.

Behind him, in a much calmer, even casual tone, Valik said, "Verdan's note doesn't say which one of the Seasons will be your bride."

Wynter's mouth turned up at the corner. Not the smoothest of segues, but he was grateful for the change of subject all the same. Thank Wyrn, Valik wasn't one to wallow in emotion.

"Any one of the princesses will do," he said. His spy had told him Verdan loved each of the Seasons madly, and that was all that mattered. The Summer King would suffer the loss of his beloved daughter, as Wynter suffered each day without his brother.

"I'll inform Leirik of your plans and prep my men for departure."

"Have Verdan's runner inform him that we are in agreement."

"I will."

"And Valik?" Keeping his eyes on the frozen Summerlea landscape, he asked, "Did you find anything more about the little maid?"

"She's the last thing you should be thinking about right now."

"Did you?"

Valik huffed out a breath. "No. I asked around, like you wanted, but no one seems to have heard of a maid fitting her description."

"That Newt woman knew her."

"She's Verdan's stooge. I thought you wanted me to be more discreet. Papa wouldn't be too happy to know his daughter's groom is hunting a mistress before the vows are even spoken—especially if you're right about why he wants to ensure the marriage is consummated."

Wynter opened his mouth to deny that his interest in the maid was sexual, then closed it. Who was he trying to fool? He hadn't sent his best friend and closest confidant on a fruitless search of the palace to find the maid just so Wynter and she could exchange stain-removal recipes. He wanted to find her so he could assuage the hunger that still curled in his belly and had kept his body in a state of semi-arousal ever since.

It was probably for the best that her fellow servants were hiding her from him. Had Valik found her, Wyn honestly doubted he'd have any interest in attending his bride on their wedding night, and that would have caused a number of problems.

"Carry on."

Steel clanked as Valik thumped a gauntleted hand against his chest and bowed. "My king."

When he was gone, Wynter remained where he stood, his gaze sweeping the winding levels of the city below in slow, moody passes. He should forget her, just as Valik said, but he couldn't. The little maid, with her storm-cloud eyes and storm-tossed hair, simply would not leave his thoughts.

The rest of the afternoon and the following two days passed without event. While the palace below was in a flurry of activity preparing for the royal wedding and subsequent feast Verdan had insisted on hosting, Wynter spent most of his time sequestered in the bower, signing grants of office for the Wintercraig men who would be putting the country back in order after his departure, and poring over maps and the stacks of active treaties he'd ordered brought to him from Verdan's library. Before his invasion, Summerlea had had a thriving trade with numerous kingdoms and several enviable strategic alliances. It was Wynter's hope to reestablish both commercial and diplomatic ties once the transition of power was complete.

As for the current royal family, after Wynter's departure, the deposed king would be exiled to one of his smaller country estates, away from Summerlea's political heart, and kept there under guard to dissuade him from fomenting rebellion. The two Seasons Wynter was not taking to wife would remain in the city under Leirik's watchful eye—hostages in case Verdan did anything foolish. Active rule of the country would pass to Wynter's appointed governor: Leirik at first, then a nonmilitary figure when the country restabilized; and once Wynter had his heir, he would marry off the other Seasons to neighboring princes in return for economic, political, and military favors.

The terms were more than generous. Verdan kept his head, and his daughters retained their titles as princesses of Summerlea. The prince, Falcon, had, of course, lost his lands, title, and inheritance, but so long as he stayed beyond the Wynter's reach, he could keep his life. All things considered, the deposed king had little to complain about, and the signed and sealed parchments outlining the transition of power were now neatly packed in Wynter's own correspondence bags.

By sunset on the third day, he had completed all of the most pressing paperwork, and the only vital document left that required his signature and seal was the marriage certificate that Verdan's steward Gravid had delivered personally. Two copies of the certificate—one for him and one for Summerlea—lay before him. He picked up the top copy and regarded the simple piece of parchment that, once signed, witnessed, and consecrated before a priest, would make a princess of Summerlea his queen.

Her Royal Highness, Angelica Mariposa Rosalind Khamsin Gianna Coruscate.

That was the name of the stranger who had agreed to be his wife.

Which Season she was, Wynter still hadn't a clue. He'd asked Verdan, whose only response had been a curt, "Does it matter?" It didn't, or rather shouldn't. And he'd be damned if he'd ask the pinch-faced prune of a steward waiting to take a signed copy of the certificate back to Verdan. Whichever one she was, the princess and her witness had already signed both copies of the marriage document.

Her signature was shaky, he noted, as if she'd been trembling (or crying?) when she'd signed. His lips thinned. Poor little flower. Such a terrible fate, to be his queen. He dipped his quill in the inkwell and signed first one copy, then the other, with a steady, sweeping flourish, then added his own pale silver-blue wax impressed with Wintercraig's Snow Wolf seal beneath the red wax medallion bearing the Summerlea Rose.

He passed the documents to Valik, who signed as his witness, then sanded both signatures, waited a few seconds for the ink to dry, and handed one copy to Gravid.

"Well," he murmured after Verdan's steward had departed, "that's that."

"It is," Valik agreed.

"There's only the wedding and bedding left."

Valik grunted.

"When is the ceremony?"

His friend glanced at the small brass clock set on a nearby table. "In an hour."

"Guess we'd best both get ready." Neither of them was dressed for a royal wedding.

Valik looked at him askance, and it was no wonder. Wynter had never been one to drag his feet. Why was he dragging them now?

"Full plate mail?" Valik asked.

He considered it, then shook his head. "No," he said. "No, I feel in the mood for a fight, if he's fool enough to give me one, but I won't go looking like I'm expecting one."

He rose to his feet and paced restlessly. Signing the marriage certificate should have left him filled with cold triumph. Instead, he felt hollow.

"Wyn?"

"What?" He turned to regard his lifelong friend.

"Put her from your mind."

"Is it so obvious?"

"It is to me. I've never seen you like this. I don't know what spell the little witch cast on you, but I don't like it. You don't know who she is or where she came from. For all you know, she was a Coruscate spy sent to find your weaknesses. Forget her."

"It's not just her, Valik." *Liar*, his mind immediately whispered. "I can't help thinking there must be more than this. The victory doesn't feel . . . complete."

"Give it time." Valik clapped him on the back. "Tonight you claim your prize. After a few pleasant hours in the soft company of your Season, I've no doubt you'll feel better."

"What do you mean she isn't going to be ready for the wedding?" Verdan glowered at the old woman who'd been his wife's beloved nurse, then caretaker of his wild, unmanageable youngest child. "You've had the better part of three days."

"And I've spent all of that just trying to undo the worst of the injuries you dealt her!" Tildavera snapped. "I've done everything in my power to speed her healing. Ointments, herbal baths, I even ordered the servants to bring up all the growing lamps we've been using to keep some measure of fresh fruit and vegetable on your table. The best I've been able to do is help her breathe without pain and grow a thin layer of new skin over most of the lacerations you inflicted." She put her hands on her hips. "There's no possible way she can stand before the priest or sit for hours at the wedding feast in her current condition."

"Unacceptable. I've already told the Winter King the wedding will take place tonight, and he's already agreed to it. You're supposed to be a master herbalist. I let you go to her only on the condition that you could get her fit for tonight. Now can you do it or not?"

The old woman got an affronted, self-righteous look on her face. "I am indeed a master herbalist, but no amount of herbal remedy or even full summer sun could possibly erase what you did to her—not in the short time you've given me. It will be a week at the earliest before she's fully healed. If you wanted her capable of wedding, you should have restrained yourself rather than beating her within an inch of her life!"

"Watch your tongue, woman." Lifelong retainer she might be, but Tildavera Greenleaf had long ago forgotten her place.

"Or what? You'll beat me, too?"

"Don't tempt me." He paced the office floor, thinking rapidly. Yes, he'd been harsh, but the damnable girl had refused to bend, and he'd been forced to break her. He'd been counting on the nursemaid's skill with herbs and the girl's own cursedly efficient self-healing abilities to mitigate the worst of the wounds he'd inflicted. "If you can't have her ready for the wedding, Tildavera, you can at least have her ready for the wedding night."

"Surely you're joking."

"Do I look like I'm joking? Aren't you the one who said consummation was the only way to ensure the White King wouldn't demand the marriage be annulled once he realizes he's wed to that . . . abomination instead of the Season he's expecting? Have him wed her and bed her and whisk her out of the city before he realizes he's been duped, you said."

"That was before I knew you'd beaten her near to death!"

"She'll survive. She always does. But the reasons for insisting on consummation haven't changed just because the hour grows late, and you've discovered that your skills aren't quite what you've always touted them to be."

He kicked at the small scorch mark on his office carpet left by the burning ash of Rosalind's picture and diary.

Many potentially lethal accidents had befallen the girl in the years following Rosalind's death, most of them natural, a few less so, but she had survived each one unscathed. Contagion never touched her, deadly blows turned away at the last moment, even the few grievous wounds she'd suffered over the years healed swiftly, without infection or scarring. It was as if the gods themselves sat on her shoulder, protecting her from sickness and peril.

Well, now he had an opportunity to rid himself of her once and for all, and he wasn't about to suffer her presence a moment longer than necessary.

"There will be a wedding. By proxy if necessary." He stopped pacing and looked up. "Come to think of it, that's probably the best solution all around." The idea hadn't occurred to him until now, but it had great potential. "One of the Seasons can stand in for her . . . Autumn, I think. He showed interest in her."

His mind churned through all the possible ways the plan could go wrong and all the ways to keep that from happening. "We'll keep Autumn heavily veiled—and make up some excuse for it, of course—and have the girl switch places with her when she goes to disrobe for the wedding night. If he does insist on seeing his bride's face before the vows are spoken, he'll think he's getting exactly what he wanted. You could even put a little something in his drink to disorient him and ensure he consummates the marriage without realizing she's not one of the Seasons."

His biggest fear all day had been that Wynter Atrialan would learn his bride's true identity *before* he bedded her and annul the marriage. But this . . . this could work. After all, for all that he despised her, the girl was a princess of Summerlea . . . she did bear the Rose . . . and Wynter had not demanded a *particular* daughter to be his wife. He'd just said to choose one. Any fault in not knowing what he might get lay entirely with him.

If the Winter King happened to kill the girl in a fury when he realized how he'd been tricked . . . well, he'd just be ridding Verdan of the albatross that had hung around his neck for the last two decades.

Verdan turned and frowned at the old nursemaid, who was still standing near his desk. "Are you still here, Tildavera? What are you waiting for? Go make this happen."

"Haven't you heard what I've been telling you? You wounded her severely. Even if Autumn stands in for her at the wedding, healing Khamsin enough to withstand a consummation tonight is beyond even my skills."

He lifted a speaking brow. "Don't be so modest. I've seen you fix a posset that had a gutted soldier laughing and smiling only hours after his intestines had been stuffed back inside him. The girl's wounds might not have healed enough to let her stand and walk about, but the pain is something you can mask. Especially as all she has to do is lie there and spread her legs."

"Blessed Sun!" she exclaimed. "How can you be such a monster? You're her father! Rosalind was her mother! Hate the part of you that lives in her if you must, but how can you hate the part of her that came from our Rose?"

Heat rushed into his veins. "She murdered my Rose. I don't just hate her, I loathe the very air she breathes!" he spat. He turned away, fighting to rein in his temper before Tildavera earned more than sharp words. "Make her ready, Nurse. And close the door behind you when you leave."

Khamsin dragged herself across the room, using each stick of furniture as a crutch to help her keep her feet as she shuffled back from the tiny bathing room towards the lamplit bed. The thin silk robe she'd draped around her body brushed against the fragile new skin on her back, each light touch sending bolts of pain shooting through her, and despite Tildy's constant ministrations, Kham's muscles had stiffened up so that every step punished her for making the effort. Of course, considering that earlier today she'd barely been able even to sit up without screaming, the ability to move about the room at all was nothing short of a miracle.

How she was going to stand before a priest for a lengthy wedding ceremony was another matter altogether.

The White King, like her father, did not strike her as a man who brooked delays, but just traversing the small distance from bed to bathroom left her breathless, weak, and dizzy. Even if King Verdan had her carried into the church, how could she stand before the altar under her own power to recite her vows?

Curious, testing herself to see how much she could bear, Khamsin straightened her back and released her hold on the furniture.

She stood there, swaying slightly, counting each second as it passed.

The door opened, Tildy's voice cried out, "Dearly!"

Forgetting herself, Kham instinctively turned towards her nurse. Pain shot down her back. Muscles seized, and her knees buckled. She cried out and grabbed hold of the furniture, barely managing to stop herself from collapsing to the ground.

"What are you doing? You're in no condition to be up and walking around." Tildy rushed to Khamsin's side and nudged a supporting shoulder under her arm. "Here. Hold on to me. I'll help you back to bed."

"I can't. I've got to get up," Kham protested, but she didn't have the strength to struggle as Tildy herded back towards the waiting bed. "The wedding's only a few hours away." Now that she understood the full extent of her father's loathing, she was ready to have the marriage over and done with. Whatever Wintercraig held in store, it couldn't be worse than what her father would do to her if she stayed here.

"Autumn will stand as your proxy," her nurse soothed. "The wedding will take place without you. You need to rest and concentrate on healing." She pushed aside the heavy drapes she'd hung to prevent her herb-infused healing steam from dissipating, and ushered Kham towards the waiting, lamplit mattress. "Come lie back down, dearly. I'll fix a posset for the pain and freshen the ointment on your back and the herbs in the kettle. Hedgewick can bring up a few more lamps from the cellar."

Khamsin's hand shot out, closing round the bedpost. "No, Tildy."

"Shh, all right, dearly," the nursemaid soothed. "No more lamps. It's already bright and warm as a summer morning anyways."

"No," Kham said again. "I'm not talking about the lamps. I'm talking about the wedding. I will say my vows, not Autumn."

"Out of the question! You can hardly stand!"

"He hasn't broken me, and I won't give him the satisfaction of thinking he has," she rasped. She didn't have to say who "he" was. "I made this choice. *I* will see it through, not Autumn." Her legs were shaking, the muscles in her legs weak. She clutched the bedpost tighter.

"Khamsin . . ."

"You cannot dissuade me, Tildy. I've had the last three days to think about this." She lifted her chin and called upon every ounce of haughty Coruscate pride to keep her standing. "For the first time since my mother's death, he's going to have to admit—in public and before the court—that I, Khamsin Coruscate, am a princess of Summerlea. How could you possibly imagine I would let one of my sisters stand in my place when that happens?"

Tildy bit her lip, and her brow wrinkled with concern. "Khamsin, listen to me. You don't understand. As far as Wynter Atrialan knows, Summerlea only has three princesses. He only knows their giftnames, and we can't run the risk of having him discover that the Khamsin Coruscate he agreed to wed is not Spring, Summer, or Autumn."

Khamsin's brows drew together. "Why would he care? A princess is a princess."

"Not to your father, and not to him. He knows how much your father loves your sisters. He wants to strike a blow to Verdan's heart by taking one of the Seasons to wife. If he discovers the deception before the marriage is consummated, he can simply annul the ceremony and marry one of your sisters instead. Your father doesn't want that to happen, and neither do I. This is your chance to get out of Summerlea. Sooner or later, your father will find a way to kill you if you stay. I've no doubt of that now. Wintercraig is the safest place for you—at least until your brother returns to us."

"Falcon isn't coming back. If Summerlea hadn't lost the war, he might one day have returned, but now? It would be a death sentence."

"Perhaps not. Your brother didn't just steal the Winter King's bride when he fled Gildenheim. He also took an ancient treasure called the Book of Riddles—a book he believed would lead him to the secret hiding place of Roland's sword. He's been searching for the sword ever since."

Khamsin's jaw dropped. "Blazing? Falcon's searching for Blazing?" She shook her head, remembering that day in the Sky Garden so long ago, when she'd suggested he search for Blazing. Remembering Falcon's stumble, which she'd attributed to an uneven paving stone rather than a guilty conscience. Remembering how he'd scoffed at the idea as a child's fairy tale. And all the while, searching for the sword had been his intent. The pieces clicked into place like the sliding parts of a puzzle box. "That's why Father sent him." Not to train Falcon how to negotiate a treaty, and not to charm the Winterfolk into better concessions, but to charm someone—probably Wynter's bride—into helping him steal the Book of Riddles.

Kham swallowed hard, astonished that she'd never figured it out before. Like everyone else, when told the story of Falcon's falling in love and eloping with the Winter King's bride, she'd accepted it without question.

"Even if that's true, Tildy, how could you possibly know it?"

"Given the right herbs, a man will tell you any and

everything he knows." Tildy raised her brows pointedly. "And from the latest I could glean, your brother is very close to finding the sword. Once he does, your safety is guaranteed. With Blazing in his possession, he'll be strong enough to win back the freedom of Summerlea and claim the throne for himself, as he will surely do once he realizes the crime Verdan has committed against his own House."

"And if Falcon doesn't find the sword?"

"You'll still be Queen of the Craig and safe from your father's machinations. Which is why it's imperative this wedding to take place, and in order for that to happen, the Winter King must believe he's wedding a Season."

"Even if I veil my face and pretend to be one of my sisters, what's to stop the White King from killing me the moment he discovers the truth?" Khamsin pointed out. "I've met him. I've felt his power. He doesn't strike me as the forgiving sort."

"He demanded one of Verdan's daughters to wife. He'll get one. He may be angry when he discovers you're not the Season he was expecting; but once the marriage is consummated, his own honor will keep him to the terms of his agreement. Ultimately, it's an heir he's after, one capable of ascending both the Summer and Winter Thrones."

"How can you know that, Tildy? And don't tell me he talks under the influence of herbs, too. You've never even met the man."

A strange look crossed Tildy's face. A flash of regret, a hint of shame, followed directly by grim determination.

Khamsin's knees gave out, and not even pride could keep her standing. She collapsed to the bed, realization dawning. Shock made the muscles of her face go lax. "But you have met him, haven't you, Tildy." Dismay, accusation, horror: All crept into her voice. "You're the traitor who's been feeding him information."

Tildy's jaw clenched, and her chin thrust out. "I'm no traitor. I'm a loyal servant of Queen Rosalind. I swore on her deathbed that I would do everything in my power to ensure your well-being, and that's exactly what I'm doing."

"By betraying my family to our enemy?"

Tildy held out her hands. "Dearly—"

"Don't call me that!" Khamsin cried, flinching away from those treacherous, once-loved hands. "How long have you been spying for him?"

The nurse heaved a great sigh. "Six months."

Khamsin's shoulders slumped. Six months. Since before the last two fierce battles that had sealed Summerlea's fate. "Did you help him destroy my father's armies?"

"Of course not! Summerlea's defeat was already certain. I simply helped him understand he could achieve the victory he wanted without razing Vera Sola to the ground."

"You're the one who told him about Falcon's room. You encouraged him to demand the bower." The pieces all fell into place. "You wanted me to go up there and retrieve mother's things. You were hoping I would run into him."

"I had to know if you and he would suit. I would never have let you wed him otherwise. The results have been promising. He hasn't stopped asking about you, and his steward has queried half the palace about the maid with the white-streaked hair."

A chill shivered across Khamsin's skin. Fear, partly, but partly something else. Something that left behind heat, not cold.

Immediately on the heels of that shiver came a new realization that made the blood drain from her face.

"*You're* the one who convinced King Verdan that I should be the Winter King's bride. You're the reason he took me into the mountain and beat me until I agreed to this marriage." She pressed the heel of her palm against her chest, trying to stop the painful ache of her heart. "Why?" Her lips trembled. "Am I really such a monster? All these years, I thought you loved me. Has that all been a lie?"

"How can you even suggest that?" Tildy cried. "Everything I've done I've done for love of you and your mother."

"For love, you sent him to beat me into submission?"

"I told you, I had no idea that your father would dare brutalize you the way he did. Until then, I hadn't realized how truly mad he has become. But his behavior only assures me that I did the right thing in encouraging this marriage." Tildy reached for Khamsin's hands, but when Kham flinched away, the nurse drew a breath and bowed her head. "One day, dearly, you'll see this was the only way I could protect you. If you were to remain here, in Summerlea, Verdan would find a way to kill you. I'm certain of it."

Khamsin crossed her arms. "And you think my fate will be any different with the Winter King?" The memory of his touch, his voice, made her shiver.

"Wynter Atrialan wants heirs. Once you wed him, you'll be safe from your father's wrath, and once you provide him with his heirs, your position as his queen will be secure. If your brother returns with Roland's sword, you and your children will be safe. If he doesn't, your children— Rosalind's grandchildren—will inherit both Summerlea and Wintercraig. It's the best future I could have hoped to give you, dearly. All you need to do is let Autumn stand as your proxy, then you consummate the marriage before he discovers the truth."

The idea that Falcon might truly be the long-awaited Heir of Roland who would return the legendary sword, Blazing, to Summerlea seemed such a fantasy, she didn't spare it a thought. But the other . . . how Verdan would howl to see Khamsin's child on the throne of Summerlea. How he would rage and storm about. That thought alone was almost enough to convince her.

Even without that satisfaction, she had to admit that Tildy was right. If Khamsin didn't get out now, her father would find some other way to rid himself of her. The gods and her own good fortune had kept her alive until now, but she couldn't count on such graces forever.

She clutched the silk robe closer about her neck and winced as the fabric pulled the tender wounds on her back.

"Very well," she agreed. "I'll wed the Winter King, but not by proxy. Veil me as heavily as you must to hide my identity, but either I stand to speak my vows, or they will not be spoken."

"You're too weak, and you're in too much pain," Tildy protested. "I can see it on your face. You can't possibly make it through the ceremony and the wedding feast."

Khamsin smiled grimly. "I wasn't asking for your permission, Nurse Greenleaf. I was explaining the conditions of my cooperation. The only thing I require from you is your herbalist skills to mix up a fresh ointment for my back. You will find a way to block the worst of the pain, and I'll find a way to make it through this farce."

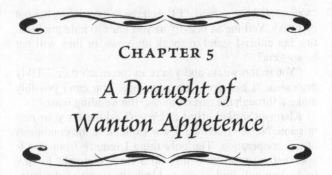

CHAPTER 5

A Draught of
Wanton Appetence

Wynter stood at the chapel altar, his temper increasing by the moment. The wedding should have begun thirty minutes ago, but the bride had yet to make her appearance.

"Think she's got cold feet?" Valik murmured under his breath.

"She's about to get a lot more than that," he muttered back. The temperature in the chapel had begun to drop, proof of his blossoming ire. The Winter King would not kindly suffer humiliation at Summerlea hands.

But just as Wynter prepared to summon his power and send this city plunging into ice, a commotion arose at the far end of the chapel.

Garbed in deep sapphire velvet, the same stunning shade of blue as the waters of Lake Ibree in the heart of the Craig, Wynter's bride had arrived. Verdan stood before her, looking like he'd swallowed something vile, while she stood in the chapel doorway, Spring and Summer at each elbow. Autumn, then, was to be his queen.

If not for the simple process of elimination and his own memorable sense of smell, he would not have known it. She was so heavily veiled that even when she stepped up to take her place beside him, he couldn't make out the shadow of her features behind the layers of concealing silk. But her scent was familiar . . . perhaps even a little overpowering. She'd not applied her perfume quite so liberally the day she and her sisters had joined him for a meal.

Suspicious, he frowned and drew her scent deeper into his lungs, examining. No, she smelled of Autumn, even beneath the perfume, but there was something else mixed in. He couldn't make it out. It was masked by the strong smell of herbs: wintergreen, poppy, a few others he didn't recognize. Was she so unwilling that she'd had to drink a cup of strong courage before entering the chapel?

He reached for her outer veil, and Verdan all but leapt between them.

"Remember your promise, sir!" he hissed. "Do not shame her before the court!"

Ten minutes before the wedding had been scheduled to start, Verdan had come to the groom's dressing room to speak with Wynter. The princess had been weeping over the prospect of leaving her home and family, he said, and she didn't want to shame herself by letting the court see her blotchy and red-eyed from tears. Wynter had agreed to leave her veil intact.

Now, he shriveled his bride's father with an icy glance. When Verdan stepped back, Wynter bent close to her ear, and whispered, "Willingly or not, Autumn, you have consented to be my wife. I will have what I want from you, but this marriage doesn't have to be a battle, unless you make it so. Remember that." He ran a finger down the side of the silken veils, finding her jaw and caressing it gently.

She trembled. The little puffs of her breath made the silken veils flutter, and the tiny beads on her gown winked and shimmered as her body shook with fine tremors. "I understand," she answered in a voice so low it was practically inaudible.

"Good." He turned to face the priest and nodded.

The wedding ceremony began.

Khamsin stood trembling as the seconds crawled by with excruciating slowness.

For a moment there, at the beginning of the ceremony, she'd thought the Winter King would unmask her, but he had not. Thanks, she supposed, to Tildy.

"Wear Autumn's dress and perfume," she had advised. She'd tapped the edge of her nose. "The Snow Wolf clan sees with more than just their eyes."

Khamsin had passed the two first hurdles of the night: fooling the Winter King and keeping her veils intact. Now she turned all her focused energies on making it through the ceremony without collapsing.

Her lower back burned like fire, each bruised and torn muscle protesting even so simple an activity as standing. Perspiration gathered at her neck and along her spine, trickling down her back beneath the hot velvets, stinging the salved and bandaged wounds. Despite doubling the strength of her salve, Tildavera had not been able to block the pain entirely, and in a fit of spite intended to wound Tildy as she was wounded, Khamsin had declared her refusal to drink any draught mixed by a traitor's hand.

She was regretting that prideful urge now. The throbbing ache from her wounds brought tears swimming to her eyes. She dare not lock her knees for fear of losing consciousness, but finally, in desperation, she reached out to grasp the altar railing and leaned heavily against it.

Beside her the White King—only minutes away from being her husband—took a step closer. "You are ill?"

She shook her head and pushed herself back to her feet before he could take hold of her arm. "Dizzy," she muttered. "I haven't eaten."

To her surprise, the Winter King gave the priest an unmistakable gesture to hurry up. She regarded him in confusion, grateful for the protection of her veils that kept him from seeing her expression. Wasn't he the cold, harsh enemy of her family? Wasn't he the anathema of all she loved? And yet, he'd offered her peace between them—even if that offer had carried the distinct feel of a warning—and now he showed this . . . courtesy.

"Who gives this woman and by what grant?" the priest finally asked, bringing the nuptial ceremony towards its close.

Behind her, King Verdan—she would never call him Father again, not even in her own thoughts—rose to his feet. In a clear voice, he said, "I, Verdan Coruscate, King of Summerlea, give this woman, Her Royal Highness Angelica Mariposa Rosalind Khamsin Gianna Coruscate, a royal princess of Summerlea and an heir to the Summer Throne, by grant of patrimony."

Despite the jab of pain that shot down her hips and the backs of her legs, Khamsin's spine straightened. Her chin lifted. She'd been recognized, at last, before the court and her family as both princess and a rightful heir to the Summer Throne.

Well, that was a miracle worth a caning or two all on its own.

"And does the princess," the priest intoned, drawing her back round to face the altar, "vow to accept this man, Wynter Crystalin Boreal Atrialan, King of Wintercraig, as her husband and liege, binding herself to him, keeping only unto him, accepting his counsel and his care, and offering him all the fruits of her life until the gods call him home?"

"The princess," she said, "does so vow."

"And does the King of Wintercraig vow to accept this woman, Angelica Mariposa Rosalind Khamsin Gianna Coruscate, a princess of Summerlea, as his wife and queen, binding himself to her, keeping only unto her, accepting her counsel and her care, and offering her all the fruits of his life until the gods call her home?"

"The king does so vow."

"Your Highness, please extend your right hand and bare the Rose."

She held out her right arm and turned back the full cuff,

baring her wrist with its unmistakable Summerlea Rose birthmark.

"Your Grace, your left hand, sir."

Beside her, Wynter held out his left arm and, with a strange half smile, flipped back his own silk cuff and turned up his inner wrist to reveal a pale white wolf's head shining against the golden hue of his skin.

She had heard the Wintercraig royal family bore a similar mark to the heirs of the Summer Throne, but she'd never seen one before. It was beautiful, in a cold, fierce, wild way. As she looked at it, she had the strangest vision of that wolf's head coming to life, turning its head to look straight at her, and snarling both challenge and warning. A chill swept through her, brisk and cool, followed almost immediately by a flush of heat as the Summerlea Rose on her own wrist began to burn.

"Your Grace, Your Highness, please join hands." The priest held a short length of tasseled silken cord—the symbol of the union about to be forged—beneath Khamsin's wrist.

Holding her gaze as if he could see straight through her veils, Wynter turned his forearm wolf-down and curled his fingers around hers.

"Before these witnesses, and with the blessings of the gods, let these two people be joined, and may the bond never be sundered." Kham stood stiffly by the Winter King's side as the priest wrapped the tasseled ends of the cords around their wrists and pulled gently. Wynter's cool, icy Snow Wolf slid over dark Summerlander skin to cover Khamsin's Rose.

A jolt of energy shot through her body as the two marks met. She cried out and grabbed hold of the altar rail. Beside her, Wynter's spine went stiff, his muscles rigid.

Lightning flashed in the sky, close enough to illuminate the chapel with a blast of blinding whiteness. Thunder cracked with deafening fury. Women screamed. Several of the tall, stained-glass windows flanking the church nave shattered, and a harsh, icy wind howled in, swirling sheets of snow into the room, blowing out every flame in the room and plunging the wedding party into darkness.

No longer able to force compliance from her legs, Khamsin collapsed against the altar rail and sank to the carpeted steps in a billow of velvet skirts. The loosely tied cords tying her wrist to the Winter King's tugged apart, and her hand fell free.

"Valik," the Winter King snapped.

A match flared. A tiny flame flickered to life. Its pale glow illuminated Valik's cupped hand. As he began to moved towards one of the lamps to relight it, Khamsin glanced up at Wynter. His pupils had gone wide, and his reflected an eerie, shiny red glow.

"Are you all right?" he asked. His concern seemed genuine. For all that his eyes were fierce and his face a frozen mask, a thread of sincerity softened his voice.

"I'm fine," she lied. Her back was on fire. Her vision was blurry. She wasn't sure she could stand again even if she had to—which she did, of course. Somehow, she was going to have to get up and walk out of this chapel under her own strength. She still had to make it through the wedding feast . . . and the bedding.

"That was . . . interesting."

Despite the pain flaring up and down her spine, she gave a quick, wry laugh. "Yes, it was," she agreed.

She knew that when the forces of Winter and Summer clashed—either in nature or on the battlefield—sparks had a tendency to fly. But this was a first. She wasn't sure whether the explosive response was a one-time shock caused by the joining of two powerful forces or the ominous portent of a stormy relationship to come.

Already, the wind had died down, and around the chapel, more lights flickered as the servants hurried to relight the candelabras. Khamsin curled her fingers around the railing and tried to pull herself up. A strong hand cupped her elbow and lifted her easily to her feet. She glanced up in surprise at the Winter King. Was he a kind man after all? "Thank you."

He inclined his head fractionally. "It would not do to have the new Queen of Wintercraig collapse at her own wedding."

The little flicker of warmth she'd been feeling snuffed out. Immediately, she castigated herself for her brief moment of moonstruck fancy. What ridiculous foolish sentimental tripe had she been thinking? Marriages between great houses were about wealth and power, not people. He was concerned about appearances, not her.

"I'm fine. I can walk on my own." She tried to tug her arm free, but his fingers remained clamped around her elbow.

"Allow me to escort my bride to our wedding feast." It was not a request.

Did he think she would bolt? Where would she go?

Even so, her first instinct was to resist his effort to impose his will on her. She hated restrictions of any kind, and she always struggled against even the slightest effort to cage her. She tugged her arm harder. His fingers went cold. Goose bumps pebbled her arm beneath the warmth of her velvet sleeves.

"Do not be foolish, Autumn," he whispered. His voice was soft but utterly without warmth. "I will not tolerate open defiance. Especially not here, in public, before your father's court."

Already her brief spurt of resistance was fading. She didn't have the energy to sustain it. Not now, at least.

Surrendering, she let him lead her down the chapel aisle and outside to the open courtyard that had once been a lush, manicured garden filled with carefully carved and tended hedges and flowering trees surrounding a sparkling fountain. The fountain was silent now, the water drained to prevent it from freezing. The flowering trees were skeletal ghosts standing guard at the four corners, and a light blanket of snow covered the fancifully carved hedges, flower beds, and lawn.

Khamsin drew a deep breath as they headed back to the main palace. The air was brisk and chill, a welcome relief to the stifling warmth of her veils and velvets. It cleared her head, and helped her to remember that the man walking beside her was no gentle lord but a conquering warrior, the enemy to whom she had just been sold as the price of her life and the survival of her family and war-torn homeland.

The wedding feast was a long, dull affair for which Wynter had little patience and even less interest. He suffered it only because he knew his bride—the still-veiled princess beside him—was weak from lack of sustenance. She'd practically collapsed twice on the way to the banquet hall—would have fallen except for his hand at her elbow. He'd suggested she retire to her rooms to rest, but she'd refused, saying she simply needed something to eat and drink. She appeared to have been right. The slender hands carrying the wine cup to her lips weren't trembling half so badly now as they had been an hour ago.

"Eat," he'd commanded when they'd first sat down, and the servants had placed plates of steaming meats and vegetables before them. After her first few laborious efforts to eat with the veils still shrouding her face, he'd ordered her to remove them.

She hadn't. Showing a spine he was beginning to realize was much stronger than he'd originally thought, she'd folded back only enough of the layered silks to bare her chin and lower lip. The rest of her face remained hidden from view.

He'd allowed her the small rebellion. She would learn soon enough that no one flouted his will without consequence. At the moment, he had the victory he'd earned, the princess he'd demanded, and a wedding night yet awaiting him. He could afford to be magnanimous.

A spate of boisterous, drunken laughter made him glance towards the far end of the hall. Verdan, face flushed with drink and probably one or more of the intoxicating herbs offered at all the tables, stood beside a table of Summerlea lords, laughing and lifting his cup in a toast. On the dance floor nearby, a dozen or more brightly clad courtiers twirled and pranced as if they hadn't a care in the world.

Wynter's lip curled. Summerlanders. Self-indulgent, hedonistic fools. Look at them—Verdan chief among them—celebrating their own defeat as if it were somehow their victory. And here he'd thought they would all be crying in their wine, not drowning in it.

Beside him, Autumn set her cup down and pushed back the plate of fruit and cheeses he'd insisted she sample after the main meal. Her father and friends might drink and dance, but she, who was paying the price for their lives, had no appetite for blind frolic.

Nor did he.

Wynter pushed back his chair and stood. He held out a hand to his bride. "Come, my queen. Let us retire."

"What? Surely you aren't leaving so soon?" Verdan, loud and laughing, stumbled forward. The wine in his cup sloshed over the rim.

"It is late, and your daughter is tired."

"But you can't leave without the final toast. It's tradition. Spring! Summer!" Verdan wheeled around and called to his other daughters. "Bring the wedding cup!"

The two princesses came forward, one carrying a large, jeweled goblet, the other a golden pitcher set with sapphires, rubies, and emeralds. Summer poured a stream of dark red wine into the cup in Spring's hands, and Spring offered it to her father. He set aside his own wine cup to take the wedding goblet and raise it up so all in the hall could see.

"A wedding toast," he cried, "to a successful and prosperous union between the Houses of Wintercraig and Summerlea. May my daughter and the Winter King find the happiness they deserve, and may we all find victory in peace."

Echoing cries of "happiness!" and "peace and prosperity!" rang out across the banquet hall as the wedding guests raised their own cups in response.

Verdan handed the wedding goblet to his daughter. "Drink, daughter. The wine is the blessing, and it must be consumed between the two of you. Half to you, and half to your groom."

Autumn hesitated, then reached for the cup and took it from her father's hands. Slowly, she raised the cup to her lips.

Wynter put a hand over hers, halting her. He didn't think Verdan would harm his own beloved daughter, but the strange, smug, expectant air about him raised Wynter's suspicions. *Something* was amiss. "A blessing for peace and prosperity should be shared, don't you think?" He held the Summer King's too-bright gaze. "Join us, Verdan." Without taking his eyes from his enemy, Wynter called, "Bring a fresh cup."

After a brief commotion, a servant appeared, clean goblet in hand. He bowed quickly and offered the cup to Verdan.

Wynter took the jeweled goblet from his bride's hands and sniffed it. The overpowering aroma of the heated wine coupled with an overpowering mélange of spices and herbs. The scents were too varied, many of them strong enough to mask the delicate scents of certain poisons. There was only one way to test the safety of the cup's contents.

He poured a portion of the marriage brew into the Summer King's cup. "You first, Verdan."

The Summer King arched a haughty brow. "So suspicious," he sneered. "Do you think I would poison my own child?" He gave a snort, threw back the wine in one gulp, and tossed the empty cup on the table. The remnant liquid spilled out, staining the white tablecloth between the two kings with drops of ruby red, like blood spilled on snow.

Wynter didn't take his eyes from the other man's face. If there was anything in the wine, it certainly wasn't poison. Even if he might let his beloved daughter Autumn drink a cup of death, Verdan would never sacrifice himself that way. He didn't have the spine for it. And other than a faint increase of heat in the man's already-alcohol-soaked veins, Wynter could detect no effects of any possible additives in the wine.

"Satisfied?" The Summer King sneered. Without waiting for a reply, he turned his attention to Autumn, and said, "Drink, daughter, to your future and the future of Summerlea."

This time, when Wynter's bride lifted the cup to her lips, he didn't stop her. She took an experimental sip, paused, then drained half the wine in three continuous gulps before handing the rest to him.

"To the Heir of Wintercraig," Wynter said. He downed the second half of the wine and thumped the goblet down on the table beside Verdan's abandoned cup.

"Spring, Summer, see to your sister," Verdan commanded. His chin lifted, and his dark eyes snapped with haughtiness. "It is tradition for a bride's female family members to ready her for the wedding night. They will escort her to the rooms we have prepared."

The two princesses hurried around the table and took Autumn's arms. "Come with us, sister," they said, casting nervous glances up at Wynter.

"Valik." Wynter jerked his head towards the women. His steward snapped his fingers and gestured. Four armed Wintercraig guards surrounded them. "Make sure these royal ladies arrive at their destination without incident." Before the women could turn away, he reached out to grasp his bride's bare chin in his hands. A tiny jolt of electricity zinged between them, shooting a thread of heat through his veins that sizzled straight to his groin. His eyelids lowered half-mast over his eyes. "Thirty minutes, wife. And then I join you." He ran a thumb over her full lower lip and caught her faint gasp on his fingertips.

Her sisters tugged her away, and she went with them. His hand fell back to his side, still tingling with warmth as if her touch alone could banish the chill of the Ice Heart.

*   *   *

Something other than wine had been in the wedding cup, Kham knew. She felt energized. Her senses were tingling, her muscles replete with new strength. The pain from her wounds and bruises had all but disappeared. Everything seemed bright and crisp, every sense heightened, magnified almost.

Blood rushed through her veins, and her steps quickened. If someone were to challenge her to a footrace, the way she felt right now she'd not only accept the challenge, she'd likely win.

What had they put in that wine?

She didn't dare ask. Not with Wynter's guardsmen surrounding them.

To her surprise, her sisters didn't lead her to one of the guest wings of the palace but rather directly into the heart of the family wing. Curious. They were heading towards the family's bedrooms. Autumn's bedroom to be exact.

Only, when the doors opened, they revealed a bedchamber very different than the one Khamsin had secretly visited numerous times before.

The elegant but functional bedroom of Her Royal Highness, Princess Autumn, had been converted into a sensual, shadowy garden filled with hothouse blooms and lush greenery. Candles flickered around the perimeter of the room, casting a pale golden glow around the edges of the room and leaving the silk-draped bed a dark, mysterious cavern. Incense filled the room with rich, decadent scents. It was a bedroom designed to seduce the senses.

As soon as the doors of the "bridal bower" closed behind them, Khamsin threw back her veils and turned to her sisters in astonishment. "What's going on here?"

"Tildy warned us the Winter King could identify a person by scent," Summer said. "Since he thinks you're Autumn, Tildy said the wedding night should take place here, in Autumn's bedroom, where her scent is already absorbed into everything."

"She added the flowers and incense to help mask your

own scent," Spring added, "and deliberately arranged the candles so he won't be able to get a good look at your face so long as you keep to the bed."

"Where's Autumn?" she asked.

"Here."

Khamsin turned. Her sister emerged from the connecting wardrobe room wrapped in a forest green satin robe. Her long auburn hair spilled around her shoulders in ringlets.

"Scenting up your nightclothes." Autumn grimaced. "I know I'm clean. I bathed this morning, but there's still something wrong about rolling on sheets and rubbing myself on clothes all day. It just seems so . . . so . . . dirty."

Despite everything, Khamsin laughed. For some reason, Autumn's complaint struck her as funny. "You rolled on the sheets?"

"Tildavera suggested it. She told me to make sure I put my scent on anything you were likely to wear or touch."

Tildy again. Friend, mother, traitor. Kham's humor evaporated. Her hand clenched tight.

"Quickly," Spring whispered. "We don't have much time. Autumn, you and Storm need to change clothes before he gets here. He said we only had thirty minutes, and something tells me he's not a man to run late."

A low heat had begun simmering in Kham's veins. She tossed off the silk veils and tugged at her bodice. "It's hot in here." She ran a hand across her brow, not surprised to find beads of perspiration blooming on her skin.

"We'll open a window before we leave, but first let's get you out of those clothes." Summer's fingers went to work untying the laces at the back of Kham's gown. "Autumn, take off that robe and gown."

Autumn shrugged out of the satin robe, and Khamsin's eyes nearly popped out of her head. "I'm supposed to wear *that*?"

Autumn blushed dark red. "Indecent, isn't it?" The sleeveless, formfitting gown covered her from neck to ankle, but the center panels covering her breasts and belly were virtually transparent—and held together only by three simple ribbon ties that would be all too easy to release. Like the rest of the room, the gown was meant to inflame and dizzy the senses.

"Was that Tildy's idea, too?"

"Well, it certainly wasn't Father's." She hurried into the wardrobe and came back wearing a different robe and carrying the scandalous nightgown.

"Autumn, grab that pot of ointment." Spring pointed to small ceramic pot on a table near the wardrobe door. "Tildy said we had to rub it on Storm's skin. She didn't say, but I guess she meant all over."

"No," Kham said. "Just on my back."

Behind her, Summer let out a gasp as she freed the last of the laces and pushed the velvet gown off Khamsin's back. "Storm . . . what happened to you? You're covered in bandages."

"I know." Khamsin wriggled free of the velvet gown, shoved it down around her ankles, and stepped free of the heap of fabric. She was naked except for a pair of loose-fitting silk drawers and the bandages wrapped around her torso. "Do you have scissors to cut them off? They'll show through that gown, which means I can't keep them on."

"Of course." Autumn ran to a dresser and returned with a pair of scissors. "Here." She handed the scissors to Summer, who immediately began slicing through the strips of linen.

Spring and Autumn let out shocked exclamations as their sister gently tugged the cloth free to reveal the ugly results of Verdan's fury.

"Who did this?" Spring hissed. "Who would *dare*?"

"Who do you think?" Khamsin muttered.

"But why?" Summer's hands trembled on the skin of Khamsin's back. She was the gentlest of the sisters.

"The Winter King demanded a princess for a bride, and the Summer King wanted me gone."

"He wouldn't do this," Autumn protested. "He couldn't. Father wouldn't risk cursing his own House this way."

"You underestimate how much he despises me. I made him angry, then I defied him. He wasn't thinking about the family. He was only thinking of breaking me." She tossed her head. "Hurry. Put the ointment on. We're running out of time."

"You can't possibly mean to go through with this," Spring exclaimed. "Not in your condition."

Now Khamsin did turn around. "I've been in a worse condition for three days now, and I *will* go through with this. It's my choice. This isn't the Summer King's will: It's *mine*. Now, put the ointment on my back so I can finish getting ready. My husband will be here soon, and if the marriage isn't consummated before he discovers I'm not Autumn, everything I've done will have been for naught."

Weeping, Summer dipped her fingers in the pot of salve and smoothed the fragrant gel over Khamsin's battered skin. "I'm sorry, Storm. If we'd known, we would have stopped him."

Khamsin frowned and lifted her hair off the back of her neck. The room was stifling. "It's not your fault. I don't blame any of you. This is between the Summer King and me, no one else. Are you done? Good." She took the nightgown from Autumn and pulled it on. The silk settled against her back, sticking to the still-damp residue from the salve. Even without the heavy velvet gown, she was so hot. "Spring, open the window, would you? I'm burning up."

Her sister hurried to unlatch the window and throw it wide.

"Don't worry sisters," Khamsin added as she climbed into the middle of the dark, shrouded bed. "I'll be fine. I'm actually feeling better than I have all day. Whatever you put in the wedding cup seems to have done the trick."

A cool breeze blew through the window, wafting across

the thin fabric of her gown. A frisson of heat shot through her veins. She couldn't stifle a groan as her breasts and belly tightened with sudden, shocking need, almost painful in its intensity.

Her sisters exchanged long, worried glances. Guilty glances.

And then Khamsin knew why she was so warm. She knew why the pain in her back was gone, and where the seemingly boundless supply of simmering sensual energy had come from.

The wedding cup. Tildy.

"Arras leaf," Wynter spat. "The bastard dosed us with arras leaf!"

Winter's Frost! His sex was hard as ice and all but burning through his trousers. Each step was an agony, the material of his pants rubbing against tight, ultrasensitive skin, setting nerves on fire.

"Son of a whoring bitch. I'll freeze his cock so cold it shatters." He glared at Valik, who was striding quickly beside him. "Better yet, you find the bastard and lock him up. He drank from the same bottle. Tie him up so he can't give himself any relief, and leave him that way 'til his balls turn blue."

"Done. Do you want me to find an herbalist? See if there's an antidote?"

"No. If he was this determined I should plow his daughter tonight, I'll see it done. More's the pity for her. I'd hoped to be gentle." The chandelier above their heads froze, and as they passed beneath it, it gave a loud popping sound and shattered in a cloud of crystal flakes. The Summerlea guard leading the way into the private wing of the palace flinched.

They turned a corner, and Wynter saw the double doors flanked by two Wintercraig guards.

"Your queen's bedchamber, Sire," the guide stammered.

He stepped aside to let Wynter pass, then turned and ran in the opposite direction.

The guards flanking the doors opened them as he drew near. Hot, heavy air swirled out, heady with the dizzying scents of incense and woman.

Wynter strode into the room and stopped in surprise. What surrounded him was no bedroom but rather a lush, sensuous garden, dense with foliage. Lights flickered along the edges of the room, and a carpeted pathway led through a virtual forest of plants and flowering trees and shrubs towards the dark, shadow- and silk-draped bed in the center of the room.

The hiss of Valik's sword leaving the scabbard sounded at his back. "Don't like this, Wyn," Valik muttered, his voice clipped as it always was in enemy situations. "Don't trust it."

A flash of bare skin shone dimly in the great bed, a leg, slender and shapely. Moving restlessly, rubbing against the silken coverlet with the same desperate hunger that filled Wynter's own body. This was no ambush. It was just that fool Verdan's determination to see the Winter King fulfill his part of the marriage bargain.

"Get out," Wynter barked at the men behind him. "Now. You, too, Valik."

He waited for the click of the latch, then drew a deep breath of the heady, perfumed air and plunged towards the shadowed heart of the garden. The incense was so thick it left him dizzy. The arras leaf made his flesh burn from the inside out. The heat and the assault on his senses jumbled his thoughts. Logic would soon be gone, leaving only rapacious hunger and need.

"Your father is a fool, princess."

He stumbled towards the bed, crawled into its plush softness. A groan broke past his lips and silks and velvets rubbed against his hands. Hot. He was so hot. Every sensation was a torment. His fingers tore at the silk of his shirt and the too-tight bond of his breeches. Fabric ripped, freeing steaming golden skin. It wasn't enough. Not nearly enough.

He reached for her. His hands closed around a slender ankle, ran up towards the softer skin of her thighs. The gown parted without resistance, fabric falling away to bare soft, sweet-smelling skin. Hot, burning skin.

He heard her breath catch, felt her body shift on a convulsive shudder.

"I'm sorry," she gasped. "I didn't know . . . I should have suspected."

His hands tore at the fragile fabric covering her breasts, yanking satin ribbons free. The soft, round weight of feminine flesh filled his palms.

In a groaning voice that seemed torn from her, she cried, "Please."

He bent his head, drawing the tightly pebbled tip of one breast into the scorching heat of his mouth. His tongue swirled around the beaded flesh. His right hand slipped down between their bodies to the soft curls and even softer flesh between her legs. A strangled cry ripped from her throat and her back arched up against him. Hot cream bathed his fingers. Her body shook in a hard, helpless paroxysm of tremors. The heady, earthy scent of female pleasure filled his nostrils. His balls drew tight in an almost painful clench, and his cock pulsed with sudden, straining urgency.

There was no waiting, no long, drawn-out pleasure. Only driving need and hunger. He lifted his head, eyes gleaming in the dim light.

His mouth closed over her, claiming her lips with the same rapacious hunger as he'd just claimed her breast. His hips surged forward with blind, mindless force. Virgin flesh resisted for a brief instant, then sundered. Tight muscle yielded.

His hands clutched hers, fingers twining tight. Icy

Snow Wolf covered burning Summerlea Rose as her body sheathed his in blazing heat.

Lightning seared the sky. Thunder shook the earth with a tremendous, booming crash. Just as it had at the wedding, a wild, storming rush of air swept through the open windows, snuffing every candle and plunging the room into darkness.

CHAPTER 6

The White King's Bride

In the dark of night, while Wynter slumbered heavily beside her, soft hands woke Khamsin. "Come sister," a quiet whisper urged. "It's past three. Time to go while you still can."

She opened her eyes to the faint glow of a shuttered candle. The familiar shadowy shapes of her three sisters huddled beside the bed. They carefully lifted the weighty anchor of Wynter's arm and helped Khamsin slide free and sit up on the edge of the bed.

Satin, cool and slick, spilled over Kham's shoulders, drawing an involuntary hiss from her throat as the fabric brushed across the torn and sensitive skin of her back. She tugged the robe into place and accepted the hands that helped her stand up. Her knees wobbled, and her legs started to buckle. She would have fallen, but Spring and Autumn quickly slipped their shoulders under her arms and took her weight upon themselves.

"Careful," Summer shushed with soft urgency. "You'll wake him. This way. Hurry." The pale, golden glow of Summer's shuttered candle cast a faint illumination across the far wall, lighting the gaping darkness of the open dressing-room doorway.

They had all agreed last night that it would not do for Wynter to wake and find his bride unveiled in the stark, revealing light of day. He was not a man to take deception lightly, and the longer they could hold off the revelation of Khamsin's identity, they'd decided, the better. And to ensure that he would sleep through her depature, one of the incenses that had burned in the chamber last night included a powerful sedative.

Khamsin cast a glance back over her shoulder. In the faint reflective glow of Summer's lamp, she could see the shadow of the Winter King, large and magnificently naked, sprawled facedown across the bed. A sharp bite of warmth drew her womb tight at the dimly illuminated sight of rounded, curving buttocks, broad, heavily muscled shoulders, and powerful limbs. Summer Sun! If not for the silky spill of winter white hair, she might think Roland himself lay there in her marriage bed.

For all that he was fearsome, for all that he could freeze a body with a single look, she suspected there were worse fates for a woman than to be tied in marriage to such a man.

Despite his reputed coldness, despite even her own painful wounds, when he'd touched her, he'd turned her body to living flame. And no matter how much she might wish otherwise, she knew that wasn't just the arras leaf. It frightened her, that power he seemed to have over her. Frightened her . . . and intoxicated her. Even now, she could feel the hunger growing again, the pull drawing her towards him. She tamped it down and resolutely turned away.

Leaving Wynter to his drugged slumber, her torn back aching fiercely, Khamsin crept from the bridal bower and exited through the servants' corridors to avoid the detection of the guards posted at the bedroom door. Summer hurried before them, holding her lamp. Autumn and Spring kept supporting arms around Khamsin. Together, the four of them climbed the narrow, lamplit servants' stairs and made their way to the remote wing that housed Kham's rooms.

Thankfully, Tildy was not there. The nurse had vacated her post and left behind healing cream, a collection of growing lamps, and a pot of herbs on an unlit burner with instructions to simmer the contents for their healing vapors. Khamsin's sisters helped her to her bed, rubbed the cream gently on her torn back, and started the herb pot simmering. To her surprise, they insisted on staying with her.

"We'll each take turns watching over you," Autumn said.

"There's no need," Khamsin objected. "You should go, before anyone finds you here."

"It's the least we can do, Storm," Summer said. She smiled so sadly, Kham wanted to weep. "Don't fight us on this, sister. In your current condition, you know you can't win."

"I'll take first watch," Spring said. "There's a bed in the next room. You two go get some sleep. I'll wake you in a few hours." When the others were gone, she bent over and brushed a spiral of dark, white-streaked hair from Khamsin's forehead. "Poor little Storm," she murmured. "Don't fight so hard against everything. You'll batter yourself to death."

Khamsin turned her head away. When she heard Spring sigh and move to the corner of the room to take Tildy's chair, Kham let the tears gathered in her eyes spill silently into her pillow.

Wynter woke alone.

He knew it before he opened his eyes. Knew it the moment he smelled the scent of his bride, not warm and womanly soft but cooled by the hours that had passed since her departure. She'd left him. In the middle of the night, while he slept in a drugged and exhausted stupor, she'd fled.

Damn her.

He opened his eyes and jackknifed up into a sitting position on the bed. He would not tolerate arrogance, he would not tolerate defiance, and he would definitely not tolerate rejection from his bride. She would come when he called and stay until he bid her go. That was a lesson he would see to it she learned as soon as he tracked her down.

He rubbed his jaw. The arras leaf had left him with a

foul taste in his mouth. His bride's cowardly flight had left him with a temper to match.

He rose and yanked on his clothes. He winced a little at the sting of the scratches clawed down his back, then smiled in spite of everything. He'd not been the only one maddened by lust last night. Her passion had been just as wild and overwhelming as his. Not a bad way to start a marriage. His smile disappeared. Then again, her enthusiasm probably owed more to the arras leaf they'd both consumed than anything else. Certainly, the moment her head had cleared of the drug's effects, she'd fled.

He glanced back at the bed and frowned at the brownish smears on the white linens, recognizing the sight of dried blood. Much more of it than he would have expected from a virgin's breach. Guilt assailed him as a different explanation for his bride's flight occurred to him. Had he . . . *hurt* her?

Wynter put his hands to his head, closing his eyes and trying to remember, but so much of the night was a blur. He remembered bodies, scorching heat, the slick, clenching feel of hot flesh sheathing him with unbearable tightness. Lips . . . hot and gasping. Breasts . . . Winter's Frost, what breasts—plump little pigeons, fitting perfectly into the broad palms of his hands, driving him mad with their lush softness and stabbing, hard peaks.

He'd not been kind or gentle. He knew that. The tormenting burn of arras had driven him wild. But . . . *hurt her*? Had he done so? Had she cried out against him? Had she begged him to stop and he, too drunk on her father's idiot drug, not listened?

Wynter hung his head in shame and closed his eyes against the silent accusation screaming at him from the bloodstained sheets. Brute. Monster. Rapist.

He was a man of devastating strength, with all the terrible risks and responsibilities that entailed. Even amongst the hard, tough men of the Craig, he stood head and shoulders above most, with bones like Wintercraig granite and rock-hard muscle to match. He had faced a Frost Giant in single combat and emerged victorious. He knew no woman's strength was a match for him. He knew he could kill with a blow. Always—*always!*—he kept himself in check when dealing with those weaker than he. He wasn't above threats—a healthy dose of fear was an excellent antidote to recklessness—but he'd never unleashed his brute force against a woman, and it near slayed him to think the first might have been his wife.

He drew a deep breath and caught his emotions in a firm grip. Too much of his discipline had been torn away, by anger and arras and overwhelming passion. He was a Winterman, King of the Craig. Wintermen were not plump, self-indulgent peacocks like their southern neighbors, who wallowed in emotion and called it sensitivity. Wintermen were disciplined, unflappable, stoic, as any man must be to survive the rugged, unpredictable, and oft-inhospitable challenges of life in the Craig.

Instead of wasting his time worrying, he would track down his bride, discover if he had indeed harmed her, and make restitution if he had. But none of that changed the fact that he had made her irrevocably his. He had wedded her and bedded her, and there was no turning back.

So today, whether she liked it or not—and no matter what sort of brute she thought him—his Summerlea princess would be leaving with him, heading back to the cold, fierce beauty of the Craig. Where, he thought grimly, she would learn to face him with her grievances rather than flee like a thief in the night.

It took Wynter the better part of an hour to track Autumn down. He found her just as she was leaving a chamber tucked away in a remote part of the palace.

She looked shocked and horrified to see him. Those pansy purple eyes had great rings beneath them, as if she had slept nary a wink since sneaking from their bed, but it was the fear that struck him like a blow. The door behind her closed with a snick, and she stood before it as if frozen in place. Her voice shook as she said, "Your Grace—you startled me."

He raked her from head to toe with a cool, brisk gaze. Her wrists were bare, the dark, creamy skin smooth and unmarred by any sign of last night's passion. He was sure as often as he'd rubbed his face against her, tasting her skin and breathing in her intoxicating scent, there would be some small abrasion from the edge of his teeth or the rasp of his stubble. Some proof of his claim. Yet her skin remained smooth as rose petals.

"You look no worse for the wear," he murmured. "I did not hurt you, then." The relief he felt was immense, even if some primitive part of him found its fur ruffled by how untouched by him she appeared to be.

"I . . . no, you didn't hurt me."

"There was blood on the sheets . . . more than I had expected. Did I . . . wound you?"

She blushed and looked everywhere but at him. "No, of course not," she assured him in a faint voice. "There is a wound on my back . . . it must have opened while . . . er . . . during . . ."

Wynter closed his eyes in a brief moment of thanks. "I am glad to know the cause was not any harm I did you," he said, "but why then did you leave me? Without even a word?"

She swallowed, and he watched her throat move convulsively. She licked her lips and seemed to be having trouble thinking what to say to him.

"I had hoped to wake beside you," he told her. "I thought perhaps we might enjoy with clear heads what your father's drug clouded last night." He let his eyes warm, watched the flutter of her pulse in the delicate skin of her throat. She was shockingly beautiful. No doubt about it. But where was the hot rush in his veins? Where was the electrifying connection between them? Surely that had not all been the arras leaf?

His hands rose to cradle her neck, fingers curled just

past her spine, thumbs resting lightly just below her chin. He forced as much gentleness as he could muster into his smile. "Surely, I gave you some pleasure?"

Her cheeks flushed a dusky rose, and she gave a muffled groan of embarrassment. "Please, Your Grace, this is unseemly."

His brows shot up. She'd been no shrinking flower last night. She'd been pure enchantress, untutored but just as driven as he. Just as ravenous for him as he for her. "Unseemly? My queen, the women of my land would say 'tis far more unseemly had I taken my pleasure from you and given you none in return." She tried to flee, but he caught her and held her fast. He thought—unkindly, it seemed, to make such a comparison—of the little maid who would have spat defiance in his eye rather than whimper as Autumn was now doing. *Be still, Wyn,* he chided himself. *Forget that maid. She is none of your affair.*

"Come now," he told his reluctant wife. "You fled in the night, without cause that I can see, and now you say a man's wish to pleasure his wife is unseemly? I know you Summerfolk are not so timid with your desires. Or is it the touch of a Winterman you cannot abide in the light of day?"

"No . . . it's not that . . . it's . . ."

"Then you will grant me a kiss, wife," he interrupted in a tone that brooked no refusal, "and greet me as you should have done more properly at daybreak. In my bed. Where I left you last, and from whence you admit I gave you no cause to flee."

His thumb traced her lip. He bent his head to hers. With a protesting squeak, she yanked free of his hand and turned her head so that his lips landed not on her mouth but on the high, flushed curve of her cheek. She pushed ineffectually against his chest, but he caught her hands and twined his fingers with hers.

Her scent wafted up to him, gardenias and herbs. Familiar . . . yet not. He frowned and leaned closer, inhaling, separating the scents, examining the flavor of them. Something was different . . . missing. She smelled plainer, less intoxicating than she had last night, and there was none of his own scent upon her. Had she spent the morning ridding herself of all traces of him?

He glanced at the fingers clasped in his own and the frown became an outright scowl. She'd removed his ring, the Wintercraig Star. What kindness he'd hoped to show her shriveled. Her fingers were bare, as if she thought that would undo the vows they had spoken and consummated. Icy rage flooded his veins.

"Not even one day wed, and already you try to deny me? You flee my bed, scrub my scent from your body, refuse my kiss, and now I see you have even discarded my ring? Is this how Summerlanders honor their word?" He glared, feeling the power surge within him, the cold anger gathering.

"Your Grace!" she exclaimed. "You're freezing my hands!"

He released her with a snarl and thrust her from him. "We leave for Wintercraig within the hour. You will meet me in the bailey by ten o'clock. And when you come, my ring had best be back on your finger. Do you understand me, *wife*?" He was angry enough to be pleased at the way she blanched and nodded. "Do not defy me on this. I promise you will not like the consequences."

The princess—his queen—clutched her throat with shaking, ringless hands and nodded again. Gritting his teeth against the cold rage burning inside him, he spun on his heel and stalked away.

"Oh, Storm, this was all a mistake. We must find a way to have the marriage annulled." Distraught, her hair disheveled by the last several minutes of running wild fingers through it, Autumn looked more unsettled than Khamsin had ever seen her before.

"The wedding cannot be annulled," Khamsin pointed out. "That was the entire point of last night—to ensure the knot was permanently tied."

"But the things he said . . . what he thought to do . . ." Her face flushed bright red. "He tried to kiss me! Right there, in the hall!"

Kiss? "You didn't let him, did you?" There was a fierce snap in Kham's voice that made Autumn look at her in surprise. The very thought of the Winter King and her sister locked in an intimate embrace sent a violent shudder down Khamsin's spine. The brush she was holding in her hands grew hot, and with a hiss of pain, she dropped it into the half-filled water pail beside her bed. The hairbrush—bearing the imprint of her clenched fingers melted into its metal grip—sizzled when it hit the water.

"No!" her eldest sister exclaimed. "Of course, I didn't. I was terrified if I showed the slightest encouragement, he might flip up my skirts and 'pleasure me' as he called it, right there in the hallway! He's a brute! A barbarian!"

"He's my husband," Khamsin corrected. On her left hand, the heavy, beautiful diamond ring winked up at her, its platinum band a cool circle undamaged by the heat that had melted the hairbrush moments ago. "And he thought you were me—or rather that I was you. How did he find you? What did he want?"

"How should I know how he found me? Someone must have seen Summer and Spring leaving earlier and figured it out. As for what he wanted—I'd say it was you! Or me, because he thought I was you, pretending to be me. Oh, you know what I mean!" She threw up her hands. "Your wounds bled on the sheets—quite a bit, apparently—and he came to make sure he hadn't sundered you in his great lust last night. I told him he hadn't." She peered uncertainly at Storm. "He didn't, did he? Because you didn't say, but I hoped the blood was from your back."

"No, he didn't hurt me." Khamsin reached into the water pail to retrieve the now-cooled brush and dried it off before brushing her hair into some semblance of order.

He'd worried that he'd wounded her. He'd set her on fire, showered her with gift after selfless gift of pleasure, shattered and remade her time and time again in a crucible of devastating ecstasy—and he worried that he'd been too rough. She'd deceived him—was deceiving him still—and he, the supposedly heartless ice man from the north, had come to make sure he had neither harmed nor disappointed her on their wedding night.

She lowered her eyes to hide the vulnerability and guilt that one simple gesture of kindness made her feel. *Oh, Khamsin, why must everything you touch get so wrong-headed?*

She rolled the length of her hair into a knot and pinned it to the back of her head, wincing a little as the gesture pulled the still-tender new skin on her back. Several more hours of sunlamps and herbs had provided enough healing that she could at least dress without needing drugs to keep her standing. She'd eaten earlier, her belongings were packed, now all she needed to do was don her veils, and she would be ready to go.

She looked at herself in the mirror. Was she different? She felt different. Her face was wan beneath its rich, Summerlander brown. She pinched her cheeks to add color and touched the raised ridges on her cheekbone where her father's heated signet had burned her, branding her with the Summer Rose. Tildy had wanted to heal that, but Kham hadn't let her. She wore it as a badge—a reminder of her home, and of the Summer King who despised her.

What would Wynter do when he learned the truth of their deception? Would he kill her? Freeze her on the spot with that deadly Gaze of his? Or would the devastating passion they'd shared last night stay his hand?

She tossed the remaining few personal items from her room in a small satchel and pinned the heavy veils in place over her hair. "It's time," she said. This continued deception was a farce, but one she was committed to carrying out. If she could just make it to the carriage without being unmasked, then she would have some hope of making it past the city gate before she was discovered. And if she could make it past the city gate, she had a chance of reaching the first posting stop without being discovered. The farther they got from Summerlea before Wynter realized how he'd been tricked, the less likely he was to kill her on the spot and return for a different princess.

Or so she told herself.

"Storm," Autumn murmured. Tears welled in her eyes. "It should have been me. I should have told father I would be the Winter King's bride. I was the one his eye settled on first."

"Don't torment yourself. This was my choice." Khamsin forced a smile, trying for brightness, hoping that at least she'd avoided terrified. "You know how I've always dreamed of the ancient heroes who saved Summerlea. Well, this my chance to play Roland Triumphant."

"Roland died, Storm."

The bright smile faltered. "Yes . . . well . . . maybe Roland isn't the right example." She drew the veils down over her face, took a deep breath, and opened the door.

Downstairs, the court had gathered. Spring and Summer were waiting at the top of the stairs, and they took up flanking positions at Khamsin's sides as she grew near, threading their arms supportively through hers. Together, they descended the palace steps.

The Summer King was there, too, looking pale and pained. Too much drink, Kham thought, then remembered how Wynter had forced him to share the wedding cup. Ah, that explained it. But judging from the worn, unhappy look about him, he'd not spent his arras hours gorging on shattering pleasure as she had.

There was no remorse in his eyes, only fierce loathing, which he tried to hide with a false paternal smile for the benefit of his court. "Daughter," he murmured, and stepped forward to embrace her. "Enjoy your life," he taunted on a hiss meant for her ears only. "What's left of it."

She stood stiff and suffered the peck to her veiled cheek.

She wanted to taunt him back, to sneer and inform him she had survived the worst he could dish out and would survive Wynter as well. But that had yet to be seen.

Metal clanked against stone. A cold, harsh wind swept into the palace, sending Summerlander skirts and doublets swirling. Several ladies cried out and clutched at fashionable curls tossed into disarray.

Outfitted once more in full plate mail with Gunterfys strapped to his side, Wynter strode into the marbled greeting hall. Temper snapped around him like crackling frost. He caught sight of Khamsin, and his mouth flattened to a grim, bloodless line.

"Veils again, my queen?" he sneered. He approached her with such scarcely contained force, she was surprised his boots did not strike sparks against the ground. His gaze flickered down to her hands. The sight of the large blue-white diamond glittering on her left hand made the line of his mouth soften slightly. "So, you *can* follow directions. That's something, at least." He caught her hand in his, and the now-familiar flash of energy leapt between them at the point of contact. His pale brows drew together, the golden brown skin furrowing, winter blue eyes narrowing.

Oh no.

Her fingers curled, and she gave her hand a tug, trying to free it from his grip. He would not allow it. He lifted her hand, examining the ring of faint bruises and the even fainter abrasions from where he'd pinned her hands to the headboard in one of their more passionate moments last night. His thumb brushed across the Summerlea Rose burning on her inner wrist. He splayed her hand against his, threading his fingers through hers as if measuring how her hand fit in his.

Slowly, inexorably, he brought her hand to his lips, and on the pretext of pressing a kiss to her hand, he breathed her in, drawing her scent deep into his lungs. A faint shudder rippled through him, followed by absolute stillness.

His eyes flashed up, bright and piercing, burning

through the thick layers of her veils. Khamsin froze. Her heart slammed against her ribs. He knew. He'd touched her hand, breathed in her scent, and without the potency of arras to muddle his senses, he'd deciphered the truth in mere seconds.

His hand shot out. Fingers curled around the corners of her veil and gave a swift yank. The pins holding the veils in place pulled loose. The unanchored layers of cloth slid free and fluttered to the ground. Cool air swirled around Khamsin's bare head, tugging at the white-streaked curls dislodged by the sudden removal of her veils.

"The little maid," he muttered, sounding dazed. The moment of shock didn't last long. His other hand shot out. He grabbed her by the throat and dragged her close. His eyes flared with ice-bright magic, and frost crackled on every surface of the room, leaving Khamsin and all the Summer King's court shivering with the icy force of Wynter's fury.

"Who are you?" he demanded. "And no more lies." His voice was so cold and throbbing, the chandelier shivered overhead, and several of its frozen crystal drops shattered.

Khamsin forced herself to lift her chin, forced her eyes to meet his with as much calm as she could muster. "I am the princess Khamsin Coruscate. Your wife."

Wynter paced the gleaming, intricately inlaid parquet floor of the luxuriously appointed private parlor Verdan had led them to after Khamsin's unveiling. All three of the Seasons—Autumn included—stood pale and silent, ringed protectively around the little storm-eyed maid who bore the Rose and claimed she was Wynter's bride. Verdan stood off to one side, smug and arrogant despite the pallor that testified to the torment he'd suffered last night. Valik guarded the door, silent and watchful. He knew how close his king's temper was to breaking, and he knew what that would mean.

Wynter stopped pacing. The sudden cessation of motion

left the restless, wild energy of his magic with no outlet. He held himself still, letting the power gather and his anger grow so cold it burned.

"I offered you peace, Verdan," he said softly. "You answered with deception." In a sudden explosion of motion, he spun around and lunged towards the Summer King. Gunterfys whipped from its sheath in single, flashing moment, and the business end of the razor-sharp blade kissed the vulnerable skin right beneath the Summer King's jaw. "Give me one reason why I should not separate your head from your shoulders right now."

"I did not deceive," Verdan retorted. The edge of his arrogance wilted a little, but he still met Wynter's cold eyes head-on, without flinching. "You asked for a princess to wife—one of my daughters. I gave you one."

"Liar! It's well-known you only have three daughters."

"It's well-known I have only three? Or only three are well-known?" Verdan countered.

Wynter's eyes narrowed. The girl bore the Rose. He couldn't deny that. He considered trickery—that Verdan had somehow managed to fake the royal mark—but there was no way to fake the surge of energy that sparked whenever Wynter's Wolf covered the girl's Rose.

"A by-blow?" he asked. That would explain why he'd not heard of a fourth princess.

"I wish she had been. Then, at least, my wife would still be alive."

"Father!" Summer and Spring exclaimed in unison. Autumn just curled her arm more tightly around the girl as if to ward off the king's cruel claim.

The girl—Wynter's wife—winced and extracted herself gently from her sisters' protective clutches. Her chin lifted. "King Verdan has four daughters," she said. "All of us are legitimate heirs to the Summer Throne, though until our wedding last night, he'd only officially recognized my three older sisters. He blames me, you see, for my mother's death."

Though she spoke softly, defiance sparked in her eyes. Wynter noted the pride, too, made obvious by the way she held her small chin so high. The pain, however, was so carefully shuttered he almost missed it.

"He couldn't banish me outright," she continued, "so instead he kept me confined to a remote part of the palace, away from the court, and away from him. Then you came."

Images spun in Wynter's mind like leaves on the wind. His first sight of the girl, standing in the oriel near the Queen's Bower, garbed in cast-off gowns, as neglected as the tower around her. The way she'd snuck into his room—not a thief, just a girl retrieving her dead mother's treasures. The gloating and open malice of Verdan's toady, that Newt woman. The servants who claimed they knew nothing about her.

The corner of Verdan's lip pulled up in a sneer. "You wanted a bride, Winter King. Well, now you have one. And may she deliver upon your House the same plague of misfortune and heartache she's brought to mine."

Wynter stepped back and sheathed Gunterfys before the urge to slay Verdan overcame reason. Though his bride was not the Season he'd come for, the terms of the peace had still been met. He would not be the first to break them, no matter how strong the temptation.

His enemy had outwitted him, he acknowledged grimly. He'd come to claim a beloved daughter, to make Verdan suffer as painful a loss as Wynter had when Garrick was slain. Instead, Verdan used the terms of peace as an opportunity to rid himself of a daughter he despised. The wedding was no punishment for Verdan. It was a boon.

Wynter turned to the girl. The lethal threat of the Ice Gaze burned at the back of his eyes, and he knew he looked frightening. "Come here," he commanded.

The Seasons clung to her as if to hold her back and keep her safe from him. Verdan's dark eyes gleamed with triumph. He was all but gloating. No doubt he and his daughters thought Wynter would kill the girl now. That was the reputation Wyn had spent the last three years earning. Those who deceived him died. Usually by ice, sometimes in a messier fashion.

But Wynter remembered other things about last night. He remembered the slow, careful way his bride had walked to the altar. The curious smell of poppies and herbs that had made him wonder if she'd sought courage from a potion. The flinch when he'd put a hand at the small of her back and the way she'd refused to surrender her gown in bed—even when the only thing it covered was her back. Most of all, he remembered the blood—too much blood—on the sheets of their bridal bed.

Khamsin stilled her sisters' objections and pulled away from their fearful grips to approach him. He learned something else about his wife that moment. She was brave. He could see the paleness beneath her dark Summerlander skin, could smell the fear on her, but still she came to him, step after courageous step.

"Take off that cape," he ordered, when she drew near.

For a moment, he thought she might defy him, but apparently she thought the better of it. She fumbled with the golden frogs at her throat until the fasteners slipped free. Fur-lined wool puddled at her feet.

"Turn around."

She obeyed, then flinched at the snick of metal against scabbard as he unsheathed his dagger. He lifted the blade to the back of her neck and plunged it downward in a single, carefully guided thrust of restrained violence, slitting the ties of her gown and her underlying corset and chemise in one pass. Material parted, and she flinched again as the room temperature plummeted several dangerous degrees.

With effort, Wynter sheathed his blade, stilled his hands from shaking and pushed aside the fabric to bare her back. He examined the extent of the damage without a word, fingers hovering so close to her skin little bursts of energy arced towards his hands as they passed. From one shoulder to the other, down the length of her spine to the inviting dip just above her buttocks, where her skin disappeared into her skirts, her back was a horror of yellowing bruises, angry red scars, and half-healed wounds.

His hands withdrew. Without a word—he did not trust himself to speak—he bent to retrieve her cloak from the ground and handed it to her. She tugged it back into place to cover her naked back, refusing to look at him. She'd been beaten like a cur, and he could see it shamed her deeply to have him know it.

He would not allow her even visual retreat. Cupping her face in one broad hand, he forced her with gentle implacability to face him. His anger was a burning flame, one that did not emit heat but rather consumed it. It grew even icier when he saw the mark, high on her left cheek. A shape very familiar to him, having only just seen it on scores of documents.

The Rose of Summerlea. The king's royal seal. Not the large, ostentatiously engraved seal of the office of the king, but the smaller simpler version made by Verdan's signet ring. Burned into her cheek like a brand.

"I will not ask who beat you," he said. His thumb brushed across her cheek, over the ridges of the Rose branded into her skin. "As he signed his work, there is no need." Then his voice dropped to a low whisper for her ears only. "Was marriage to me such a terrible fate that this was the better option?"

Her eyes shot up to lock with his. Her full lips trembled. "I—"

His lips thinned, and he stepped back. "Go with your sisters. Put on a different gown. Something loose-fitting that will not damage you further."

He waited for his wife and her sisters to leave the chamber, then advanced on Verdan with slow deliberation.

"You sought to deceive me. You beat your own child within an inch of her life so she would go along with your deception. Which hand did you beat her with, Verdan? Which hand did you raise against the woman you gave to me as wife? This one, I think." His hand shot out, snatching Verdan's right wrist—his sword arm—and holding it in a grip of stone.

"You made a mistake, Summerlander," Wynter continued. "She is my wife now. By the laws of the Craig, it is my duty to seek justice for any crimes done against her—even those crimes committed against her before we wed. The blows you struck against her are now blows struck against me.

For the first time all morning, genuine fear crept into Verdan's eyes.

"This hand, which beat my wife until she could scarcely stand, you will never lift again against another. She lives, and so you live. But the hand you raised against her dies." Power came to his call, burning his veins with ice, traveling down his arm to the hand that gripped Verdan's right wrist.

Verdan hissed as the first, painful tingles of cold shot through his skin. As the blood and flesh began to freeze, his eyes widened, and he began to struggle, but Wynter grabbed him by the throat and squeezed, sending the Summer King to his knees.

The frost spread, creeping up the Summer King's arm to his shoulder and down to the tips of his fingers. His choked cries turned to outright shrieks as the skin of his frozen hand and arm began to harden. Relentless, icy, unmoved by the other man's pleas for mercy, Wynter held his grip until the arm was a dead, useless hulk of flesh.

Through it all, Wynter felt nothing. No remorse, no pity. Not even a particular rage. His heart was an unmoved block of ice in his chest. When he released his enemy, the once-haughty Summer King hunched over his dead arm, weeping and moaning, his body racked by shivers.

"If ever again you consider deceiving me or harming anyone under my care, remember today," Wynter advised in a voice of pure ice. "And consider this also: I will now do everything in my power to ensure that Khamsin's child—

the child of the daughter you loathe—will be the next ruler to sit on the Summer Throne."

Leaving Verdan huddled on the floor, Wynter strode out of the room.

Khamsin was waiting for him outside, standing near the golden Summerlea coach he'd commandeered for the long journey back to Wintercraig. Her sisters were ringed around her, weeping, while she stood stoic and brave despite all she'd suffered. Feeling returned to Wynter in a painful rush, and he wanted to turn back around and freeze what he'd left of Verdan.

Instead, he drew a breath and started forward. "Time to go, wife. Say your farewells."

Storm gray eyes met his. "My fa— King Verdan?"

"He lives, but he will never raise that hand to another. Say your farewells and get in the coach. I weary of Summerlea."

She hesitated, almost as if she considered defying him, then thought the better of it. Turning to her sisters, she gave each a final hug.

"We each put a gift inside the coach for you," Spring told her. "A little bit of Summerlea to take with you to your new home. Remember what I told you last night."

"Write to us," Summer entreated, "as often you can. Let us know you are well."

"I put the growing lamps in the coach as well, and more of Tildy's herbs," Autumn said. "Be sure to use them each night until you're fully healed."

He gave her a few minutes more, until impatience outweighed generosity. Did her sisters not see she was already tiring? "Enough. Get in the coach." He reached for her, and his approach was enough to drive her sisters back, as he'd expected it would. He took her slender hand and helped her into the carriage. At the touch, he felt again that little jolt of electric warmth, and the frigid ice surrounding his heart began to thaw.

The maid Verdan had insisted Wynter take to care for

his bride was already inside, huddled in the far corner of the roomy coach, next to a collection of potted plants—most ridiculously ill suited to the world Khamsin was about to enter. Rosebushes, citrus trees . . . and was that a birdcage? Chirping song warbled from the cloth-covered cage, confirming his suspicions. Winter's Frost! Songbirds. Probably the delicate, summer-fond kind that would keel over on their little pampered birdie feet and die at the first hard frost.

Which idiot sister had given her those things? He was the *Winter King*, emphasis on *Winter*. What part of that did they not understand? He pressed a hand to the bridge of his nose, squeezing as the first throb of a headache began to blossom. She already thought him such a monster that she'd let herself be beat near to death before agreeing to wed him. How much more would she hate him if he let her little tropical remembrance garden die? Or had that been the whole point of such a wedding-gift?

His arrogant claims to Valik and his own original plans to the contrary, Wynter had discovered he didn't want a cold, political marriage. Last night, albeit beneath the influence of a potent drug, he'd shared one of the most intensely passionate nights of his life. With her. Khamsin Coruscate. His wife. Not the studied perfection of Elka's lovemaking but something wild and elemental and very, very stirring. Just one taste had already addicted him. The hunger to experience such powerful, unleashed passion again was already an ache so deep it hurt.

"Are you . . . not riding with me?" she asked when he made no move to enter the carriage.

"No. Get what rest you can. Have your maid see to your back." He slammed the carriage door shut and stepped back. It wouldn't do to let her know the power she held over him. Unwilling though she might have been, she'd had a hand in deceiving him. She was a Summerlander witch, just like the rest of them. He could not forget that.

He whistled, and his white stallion, Hodri, trotted to his

side, tossing his head and sending the long, silvery strands of his mane flying. Wyn thrust a plated boot into the stirrup and swung into the saddle in a smooth, practiced motion. Beneath him, Hodri pranced a little as he adjusted to the weight, then settled.

"Come, my loyal friend," he whispered, stroking Hodri's strong neck. "Time to leave this Summerland behind." He lifted a gauntleted hand, and cried out, "Men of the Craig! The hot springs of Mount Freika are waiting, as are the lonely arms of your wives. Let's go home."

The gathered Wintermen gave a great cheer. Wynter clucked a command, and Hodri began his elegant, high-stepping walk down the long, curving lanes that led out to the valley below and north to the mountains beyond. The carriage holding Khamsin gave a lurch, and the iron-shod wheels began their rumbling forward motion. Within moments, thousands of hooves were ringing against cobblestone, filling the city with the sound of their departure.

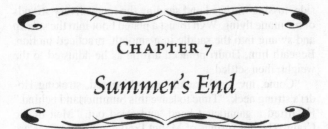

CHAPTER 7

Summer's End

Shards of pain shot up Khamsin's back as the coach jolted northward along the frozen rutted roads of Summerlea. The journey was made longer by the presence of a young maid, Belladonna Rosh, who'd been chattering since the moment they left Vera Sola. At first, Kham had enjoyed the conversation. She'd spent so much time alone, it was nice to have a companion. But after the second hour and the third . . . well, silence was a gift she'd never truly appreciated.

Each hour, Bella changed the dressings on Kham's back and rubbed a fresh layer of cream on her skin, but the dutiful attention made little difference. The meager sunlight that filtered through the gray clouds was not nearly enough to catalyze Kham's natural healing ability, and the constant jostling of the carriage tore open more fragile, healing seams of flesh than Bella's ministrations could keep up with. To make matters worse, Khamsin discovered she wasn't a good traveler. The constant rock and sway of the coach left her feeling decidedly queasy. Her insistence on sitting upright didn't help matters, but she'd had enough of feeling helpless and weak. Eventually, each time the carriage hit a hard bump, Bella would leap across the carriage to Khamsin's side and start wailing over her like she was on death's door.

"For Halla's sake!" Kham finally exclaimed. "If I need your help, I'll ask for it. Until then, go sit there on that side of the coach and find some way to occupy yourself that doesn't include hovering over me."

Bella bit her lip and sank back into the cushioned seat on the opposite side of the coach. She managed to remain still and silent for all of three seconds. Then, clearly unable to help herself, she rummaged around in the small bag by her side, produced yarn and needles, and began industriously knitting away. And resumed talking.

"They say it will take almost a fortnight for us to reach Gildenheim."

Gods help me. "So I understand." Two weeks, stuck in this tiny space, with Bella. Kham would go mad.

Belladonna had only joined Spring's staff a few days earlier. She'd landed the less-than-desirable post as Khamsin's lady's maid and companion by virtue—or, rather, misfortune—of having the least seniority. She was tidy enough in appearance, with big, doe brown eyes, soft skin a few shades darker than Kham's own, and blue-black hair scraped tightly back and confined in a knot at the nape of her neck, but it was obvious Bella had never been a lady's maid in her life. She chattered like a magpie and was altogether too free with her opinions—about everything.

She was none too fond of Wintermen, in particular, and not shy of saying so. "If it took a year to get there, that would be too soon for me. They are savages. Brutes. My cousin's husband's second cousin lives near the border. You should hear the tales she has to tell." The pair of knitting needles in Bella's fingers clacked a staccato beat. "Half-naked men dancing around campfires, smearing themselves with the blood of whatever poor creature they killed on a hunt. Howling at the moon like a pack of wolves. More beast than man, they are, full of dark, unnatural ways. You mark my words. This is going to end badly for the both of us."

"They look like a well-ordered, modern army to me," Kham replied, rubbing a hand at her temple. She'd already had several earfuls about the terrible fate awaiting them both in the savage land of the north. "And I've seen no sign of 'dark, unnatural ways.'"

She closed her eyes and leaned her head back against the cushioned seat. Each jolt and lurch of the carriage sent pain shooting up her back and throbbing against her skull.

"Wait until we cross the border, and they're back in their own lands. We'll have to keep a sharp eye out then. Do you know what they do to anyone who breaks their laws? They strip them down to their bare skin, stake them out naked on a glacier, and leave them to die. 'Mercy of the mountains' they call it. Ha! Mercy indeed!" The girl's furiously clacking knitting needles suddenly fell silent.

After a few moments, Kham peeled open one eye to find Bella biting her lip and regarding her with a look she could only describe as consternation.

"What is it?"

"I . . . nothing. Nothing." The girl bent her dark head back down to her yarn and needles. But rather than resuming her knitting, she just sat there, worrying the thread in silence.

"Bella . . ."

"It's not my place to say."

For hours, the girl wouldn't shut up, and now Kham couldn't get her to talk. Another hard jolt of the carriage sent pain shooting across Kham's back. Her stomach lurched. Unwell, and irritated by Bella's uncharacteristic reticence, she snapped, "Oh, for the love of Helos, spit it out already!"

Bella's head shot up in surprise. She looked like a kicked puppy.

Kham groaned. Wonderful. Bella was her sole companion. Inexperienced, talkative, and far too opinionated she might be, but she was also the only face from home Khamsin was likely to see in Wintercraig. Alienating her was pointless.

"I'm sorry," Khamsin apologized. The words came hard. After a lifetime of her sire finding fault with everything about her, she hated to admit when she was in the wrong. Much better to stick out her jaw and take whatever punishment came her way than make herself vulnerable by admitting fault. "I shouldn't snap at you. But if something is troubling you—as, clearly, it is—you need to tell me."

The maid bit her lower lip. "It's just that . . . well, I overheard something I wasn't supposed to . . . something concerning the Winter King's plans for . . . for . . ."

Kham fought the urge to scream. Honestly, did she have to drag the truth out of the girl word by word? In a voice that struggled to remain calm and even, she pressed, "The Winter King's plans for what, Bella?"

"For *you*, ma'am."

Kham sat up a little straighter, wincing as the motion pulled at her wounded back. "What do you mean? What sort of plans?"

Bella's smooth brow crinkled in distress, and she started picking at the yarn hanging from her needles again. "I—"

"Bella. What sort of plans?"

The girl swallowed. "He intends to kill you, ma'am. At the end of the year, if you don't bear him an heir, he intends to kill you and take one of the Seasons to wife."

Kham moistened her suddenly dry lips. "You heard him say this?"

"Not him." She bit her lip. "Mistress Newt sent me to the king's office to be approved as your new maid, and I overheard the king talking to Master Ogam, my lady. I wasn't eavesdropping," she hurried to explain. "The door was open. I couldn't help but hear."

"Calm yourself." Kham brushed the worried excuses aside. "Are you sure you heard correctly? The Winter King plans to *kill* me if I don't bear him an heir in a year's time?"

"He'll send you to face the mercy of the mountains—and even your father knew what that meant."

Khamsin slumped back against the seat cushion, this time hardly noticing the pull and sting of her wounds. She didn't doubt young Bella for a moment. *Enjoy your life.*

What's left of it. Those were her father's gloating final words to her. No wonder Verdan had been so determined that she would wed Summerlea's conqueror and so smugly satisfied to see her off. He believed he was sending her to her death. He relished the idea. Much as he would have liked to do the deed himself, if she died at the Winter King's hands, Verdan's hands would be clean. There would be no threat of a blood curse befalling the royal House of Summerlea.

"Forgive me. I knew I shouldn't have said anything. My tongue runs faster than my brain, I'm afraid. I'm so sorry, my lady. Really."

"It's all right, Bella." Kham held up a hand to halt the rush of apologies and self-recrimination. "It was right that you told me. I needed to know. You should never be afraid to tell me anything you think is important."

"Thank you, my lady. You're too kind. I'll remember that in future. But, truly, you look pale, and I can't help feeling responsible. I know the news was a shock."

The last thing Kham needed was more hovering. "I'm just feeling a little tired. I think I'll lie down for a bit."

"Of course, my lady. Is there anything I can get you? Do for you?"

"No, Bella. I'm fine." She forced a wan smile. "Please, go back to your knitting."

Kham lay down face-first on the coach seat, using her arms to pillow her head. As Bella's knitting needles resumed their rhythmic clacking, she closed her eyes. She hadn't lied to Bella. She was weary. Her back was hurting, she hadn't slept much the previous night, and the long hours of jostling in the coach had sapped her strength. But the truth was, she needed time to digest Bella's news and decide what to do about it.

The man she'd married had declared war on Summerlea and conquered it, true, but the Prince of Summerlea had stolen Wynter Atrialan's future queen and murdered his brother—his only heir. Many kings had and would go to war over the first offense. All of them would go to war for the second.

Although Wynter was a stranger for all intents and purposes, she could have sworn there was kindness beneath his cold exterior. The way he'd worried that he hadn't pleasured her in their marriage bed . . . the way he'd come to her defense this morning with her father . . . She and her sisters had paused outside the door to eavesdrop this morning after Khamsin's unmasking. A part of her had secretly thrilled at the way Wynter declared himself bound to seek justice for any wound done to her. But could he really share such shattering passion with her, avenge the brutal treatment she'd received at her father's hands, while all the while planning to murder her if she didn't bear him an heir in a year's time?

It didn't make sense. Even Tildy had been sure he was, at heart, an honorable man. Or had all that been a lie, too?

Stop, Kham! Stop! She squeezed her eyes shut and pressed her forehead into the cradle of her arms. Bah. She would drive herself mad, seeing treachery at every corner. Yes, Tildy had conspired with Wynter Atrialan to end the war with a marriage between the two Houses. Yes, she had conspired for Khamsin and Wynter to meet. But she had also spent her life caring for Khamsin, looking out for her, protecting, teaching, and nurturing her. No matter how angry Khamsin was, in her heart she knew Tildy would never knowingly have encouraged this marriage if she'd suspected there was a death sentence hanging over it.

Tildy was no naïve innocent. She'd spent her life in and around courts and all their intrigues. Servants knew the evil that their masters did. She had met the Winter King face-to-face, spent six months sizing him up. She'd seen something in him that warranted trusting him with the royal charge she'd spent her life protecting. She would never have suggested the marriage if she didn't truly believe Khamsin was safer in Wynter Atrialan's keeping than she was in Verdan Coruscate's.

So either Bella had misheard, or Tildy had misjudged Wynter Atrialan.

Because what sort of honorable man would wed a woman with the intent to kill her?

Khamsin must somehow have fallen asleep because, the next she knew, the coach had stopped. The sounds of men and horses moving around filtered through the open windows.

She pushed up into a sitting position and groaned. She felt battered and queasy and notably weaker than she had this morning.

Bella flew to her side. "Your Highness! You're awake. Oh, you don't look well at all."

Kham ignored the hovering and peered out the coach window. "We've stopped?"

"Yes, to rest and water the horses. Your Highness! What are you doing?"

Kham, who had pushed open the coach door, paused to scowl over her shoulder. "I'm getting out of the coach. What does it look like?"

"But—"

"I'm fine. I just need to stretch my legs." Unlike her sisters, who'd been trained from birth to sit through long, boring ceremonies without fidgeting, Khamsin had never known confinement. The forced inactivity was stifling.

The moment her feet touched the frozen ground, however, she half wished she'd stayed in the carriage. All around her, as far as her eyes could see, mile after mile of what had once been verdant farmland lay barren and fallow beneath thick layers of snow and ice. The husks of unharvested crops stood like tattered skeletons in the abandoned fields, a grim reminder of Wynter's devastating march of conquest. Khamsin drew a deep breath of the chill, brisk air and forced back the feelings of sadness that threatened to swamp her. The war was over. Summerlea would bloom once more. Her marriage had ensured that.

Even if that marriage cost her her life.

Bella nodded to a nearby cornfield. "If you want a little privacy, ma'am, that cornfield there looks like the best we're likely to get here."

"Privac—?" Kham broke off. Down the line, a number of soldiers were heading off into the fields. "Oh." She felt her cheeks grow hot. "Er . . . no, Bella, I'm fine. I'll wait until we reach a posting inn."

"That will be a long wait," a male voice declared from behind.

Khamsin spun around, half-expecting to find Wynter there. Her shoulders sagged with something that felt alarmingly like disappointment when she realized the speaker was the White King's Steward of Troops instead.

"Armies don't stop at posting inns," he explained. He watched her carefully, his blue eyes darker than Wynter's, but just as piercing.

Heat flushed her cheeks. Of course armies didn't stop at posting inns. What had she been thinking? Armies were, by necessity, self-sufficient when it came to travel. With thousands of men and horses in the column, it would take every posting inn in a very large city to serve them.

Wonderful, Khamsin. Now, he thinks you're an empty-headed fool. Not that he'd held her in much esteem to begin with, she was sure. She doubted he'd forgotten who gave him that bluish bruise darkening his jaw. She only hoped he didn't hold grudges as bitterly as his king.

So, there would be no convenient posting inn. She cast a considering glance over her shoulder at the cornfield. Though pride insisted she forge bravely through whatever obstacles came her way, just the sight of the snow-covered stalks made her shudder. No, it was out of the question. Maybe later, when she was desperate, but not now. And definitely not with the White King's steward looking on.

"I'm fine," she insisted. "I'll just stretch my legs a bit before we get going again."

The steward's expression didn't change one whit. "As

you wish." He bowed, a brief, curt folding of his body. "My name is Valik. If you need anything, just ask for me."

"Thank you . . ." She hesitated. What had the palace servants called him? Sir? Lord? "Lord Valik," she finished, just to be safe. Better to honor him with a title greater than was his due than insult him with a lesser one. From what she'd observed over the years, nobles would duel over the slightest perceived insult to their vaunted lineages.

Valik turned his head slightly and snapped out a brief command. Six armored men jumped to attention. "These men will guard you while you walk," he said.

"A guard isn't necessary," Khamsin said. "We won't be going far."

"They will guard you all the same. The war may be over, but the peace has barely begun," he explained before she could protest again. "Wynter would kill us all if we took chances with your safety."

Because he wanted the pleasure of killing her himself at year's end?

Kham caught the caustic retort before it left her tongue. It wouldn't do to tip her hand. When the time came, she intended to ask Wynter Atrialan to his face. She'd have a better chance of getting a genuine reaction from him if the question came as a surprise.

"Very well," she answered instead. "I thank you for the consideration." She turned away and curled a hand around Bella's arm. "Come, Bella, let's walk."

Much to her own irritation, Khamsin tired quickly. Within ten minutes, her knees started going wobbly, and she gave in to Bella's badgering and headed back for the coach. There, the young maid insisted on bringing Khamsin a bowl of stew, a hunk of cheese, and a little fresh fruit, but the sight of the food only threatened to further unsettle her travel-tossed stomach. She barely managed a few bites of stew and cheese and one segment of orange before pushing the plate away.

"You need to eat, Your Highness," Bella murmured. "You need to keep up your strength."

"Perhaps later." Kham pressed a hand over her face. "I think I'll just lie down and try to sleep a little more before we get started again. Please, just help me undo my laces—and leave the curtains up. The sun isn't very strong, but it's still better than nothing."

Khamsin stretched out facedown on the cushioned carriage seat while Bella unlaced the back of Kham's gown and pushed the fabric aside to bare her battered skin.

"Shall I put a little more of Mistress Greenleaf's cream on your wounds, ma'am?"

"No, it's been less than an hour since the last time. Leave it for now." She pulled a fringed and tasseled velvet pillow under her cheek and gave a small sigh. Without the constant jolting, the carriage seat seemed a much softer and more welcoming sleeping couch. Weariness washed over her in a sudden wave, and her eyes closed. Despite the light of the winter gray sky shining through her closed eyelids, sleep descended with unexpected speed.

When she woke, the carriage was once more on the move, and Bella was dozing in the corner on the opposite side of the coach. Kham pushed herself up and stifled a groan. The skin of her back felt tight and tender, and her stomach gave a threatening lurch.

A warble called out from the birdcage. Bella had removed the cover earlier in the day. Within the cage, the mating pair of songbirds clung to their swaying perches. A gift from Spring, the birds were Khamsin's favorite: scarlet tanagers. During spring and summer breeding, the male's plumage turned a brilliant shade of scarlet, striking against the glossy black of his wings and tail, but even though it wasn't yet September, both birds still wore the greenish yellow of their winter, nonbreeding plumage.

"Poor little things," she murmured. "You both look as green as I feel."

Remembering the orange she had discarded earlier,

Kham opened the hamper on the coach floor, found the remaining pieces of fruit wrapped in cheesecloth, and slipped one of the plump segments into the bottom of the birdcage. The male was the first to hop off his perch and inspect the fruit. His head dipped, beak nipping experimentally at the bit of orange. A few moments later, his mate joined him, chirping brightly and fluttering her greenish gray wings.

Leaving the birds to their meal, Kham leaned her head back against the cushion and closed her eyes. She couldn't get comfortable. Every lurch and jolt of the carriage pulled at her tender back, and though the cushions were upholstered in velvet, the constant rubbing quickly became a painful friction and forced her to lie back down just to stop aggravating her wounds.

Bella woke and applied more of Tildy's cream, for what good it did. She tried to keep Kham entertained by reading from the collection of Summerlea histories, but the familiar tales didn't hold half their usual fascination. The little bit of food Kham had eaten churned about in her stomach for the next two hours, and when they stopped again to rest the horses, Khamsin voluntarily went racing for the privacy of a snow-blanketed cornfield.

The guards Valik had assigned to her attempted to follow, but she whirled on them. "I will have privacy," she snapped. "I promise if you follow me, it will be the last living thing you ever do." Her hair crackled about her. It wasn't a bluff. Sick as she felt, there was enough sunlight to feed her power, and her limited supply of docile, obedient Khamsin had run out hours ago. Agreeing to eat that godforsaken stew was the last concession she was capable of today.

Luckily for them, their years of serving the Winter King had taught the men when a weatherwitch meant business. They backed off and simply stood guard near the edge of the frozen field.

She plunged deep into the cornfield with no fear of getting lost in the six-foot stalks. The sun, the source of her power, was in the sky. Even hidden behind a blanket of winter gray clouds, she knew exactly where it was and she knew her exact position relative to it. When the sun was in the sky, no Heir of the Rose would ever be lost.

When she reached a spot far enough away from the road to be truly private, she stopped. What remained of the food in her stomach didn't take much coaxing to leave her, and she immediately felt worlds better. She even took the time to step a little farther off and tend to her other needs—an experience she found thoroughly primitive and revolting. She'd never been a pampered princess, but now she realized there were some things she considered basic necessities of life. Like a working toilet. And something besides snow and dried corn husks to go with it.

When she returned to the field, Valik was waiting, blue eyes flashing and a scold on his lips for the way she'd gone off without her guards.

She brushed aside his objections. "There are some matters I refuse to tend to with an audience, Lord Valik. Since you won't give me the luxury of a posting inn, the least you can afford me is privacy." When he opened his mouth to object again, she held up a hand. "That is *not* negotiable."

Valik went off muttering.

Khamsin smiled for the first time all day. The victory was small, but it was hers. Gathering her skirts, she stepped up on the mounting block positioned by the carriage door. A silvery glint at the corner of her eye made her pause and turn. Her smile faded.

Half a mile up the line, the unmistakable figure of Wynter, shining in polished steel armor, was seated on his impressive white charger. The distance was too great to see his face, but somehow she knew his gaze was fixed upon her. For several seconds, she stood there, frozen by some unnameable force. Then a soldier approached Wynter, and his head turned, and the spell was broken.

Khamsin dove for the protection of the coach. Her heart pounded like a hammer in her chest, and her skin felt flushed and chilled all at the same time. She pressed her hands to her cheeks. What was it about the Winter King that drove through her defenses as if they were paper and shattered her senses with a single glance?

"Ma'am?" Bella's dark eyes watched her with open concern. "Are you still feeling ill? Should I call for Lord Valik?"

"No," Kham said quickly. "No, Bella, thank you. I'm fine. I'm feeling much better."

Strangely enough, it was true. Even from a distance, that one brief, electric exchange with Wynter felt like a shot of pure, unrefracted sunlight. The powerful energy of it still tingled throughout her body, shocking and revitalizing.

Unfortunately, that energy didn't last long . . . and neither did the respite from the travel sickness that had plagued Khamsin all day. Shortly after resuming their journey, she was back to feeling green and wishing she were anywhere but in a carriage. The interior of the sumptuous, velvet-lined coach began to feel like a torture chamber.

The light shining through the carriage windows grew dimmer as the blanket of soft gray clouds overhead began to darken.

The first, fat, cold drop of rain splashed against Wynter's sculpted white snow-wolf visor and hit him squarely in the eye, blinding him for a brief moment. A second drop quickly followed the first, then half a dozen more. Within minutes, a steady rain was falling. Thunder rumbled in the distance.

Valik rode up alongside him. "That came up fast," he said.

Wynter nodded, squinting at the horizon, barely visible through the falling rain. They hadn't made as much progress as he would have liked. Irritability made him want to blame his bride for the delay, but he'd been the one to slow his army's usual lightning pace in consideration of the wounded princess following behind him in the carriage. Just as he'd been the one to hold up the column for almost two hours while she'd slept. They'd only made fifteen miles today, considerably less than the forty he expected from an army of Wintermen. Vera Sola was still plainly visible on the southern horizon—or would have been except for the rain—and if he didn't pick up the pace, it would be a month before they reached Wintercraig.

He glanced over his shoulder, towards the carriage following a half mile down the long line of mounted knights and infantry. *She* had not complained about the journey. Even sick as she was—and he knew she was not traveling well—she'd not complained. She'd protested about the guards he'd assigned to watch over her and threatened to fry them if they followed her into the fields when she went to tend to her personal matters, but she'd not voiced so much as a whimper about her illness or their pace, nor placed demands on his men—which was a surprise. Even amongst his own folk, noblewomen were notorious gluttons for attention and indulgence.

"Send word down the line," he said. "We'll camp here for the night."

Valik nodded and started to turn his horse around.

"And Valik? There are lamps in the carriage that are apparently supposed to help her back heal faster. Have them set them up in my tents. I'll see to the men while you get her settled." At Valik's raised brows, Wynter added, "Your face is prettier than mine, or so I'm told. She may find it easier to do what you ask than what I command."

"You're forgetting she kicked me in my pretty face last time I asked her to do something she didn't want to do."

Wyn gave a grunt of laughter. "Better than kicking you in the balls." Then he sobered. "And see to it she actually eats and drinks something." She'd taken little nourishment all day, and though he'd allowed it, knowing anything she ate was likely to come back up once they started moving again, they were stopping for the night now, and she needed to eat. Her body needed sustenance to heal. "If she balks, tell her I'll force it down her throat myself if I must."

Valik shook his head. "I'll let you tell her that." He rubbed his jaw. "I want to be able to chew my dinner."

At first, Khamsin thought the latest stop was just another pause to rest and water the horses. With Bella's help, she straightened her clothing, donned her hooded cloak, and descended from the carriage, hoping to take at least a brief walk to stretch her own cramped legs. Rain was pelting down in gray sheets. Two soldiers stood beside the carriage door, holding up a canvas tarp to protect her from the rain. She waved them off, opening her own oilskin parasol instead. To her surprise, the long column of men in front of and behind the carriage were fanning out along the roadsides and beginning to pitch their tents.

"We're stopping for the night?"

The White King's steward stood waiting for her, still fully armored, but his eagle's head visor had been pushed back to reveal his face. Of the Winter King, there was no sign.

"He's gone to check on the men," the steward said, guessing the reason for Khamsin's searching gaze. He stood, unflinching, as the pouring rain sluiced down his golden brown cheeks. His eyes were a pale blue, but nowhere near as icy as the Winter King's. "He does not rest until all the men and their horses have been seen to."

Khamsin tried not to show her surprise. The image of a caring king, one who put his men's needs before his own, didn't mesh with the harsh, heartless monster most Summerlanders considered Wynter Atrialan to be.

"As his Steward of Troops, should you not be the one checking on the men?" she asked.

Valik smiled without warmth. "My king thought you might find mine a less frightening face. You should stay in the carriage until the tents are up. There's no need to stand in the wet."

"I like the rain. It's cleansing. And why would whether I'm frightened or not make any difference?" she countered. "Fear changes nothing. My fate is the same either way."

"It matters to the king." He gave a short bow. There was a snap to his voice that hadn't been there just a moment ago. "If you want to stand in the rain, suit yourself. Just stay out of the way of the men while they set up the encampment. Loke and Baroc here will guard your safety." He nodded curtly at the two soldiers beside her.

Khamsin wanted to kick herself. Less than a full day into their journey, and she was already turning Wynter's steward against her—not that he'd viewed her kindly to begin with. His jaw probably still hurt from meeting the hard edge of her boot.

"Sir," she said. "Lord Valik." She laid a hand on his arm and snatched it back when his spine went stiff as a pike. She bit her lip, shoved down her innate pride and her own desire to take offense at his flinch. "I'm sorry. I didn't mean to offend you. I only meant that I don't need pampering. I prefer to face my fate head-on—even when it frightens me."

A little of the starch wilted out of him—but only a little. "You are the wife of our king, Your Grace, and by the laws of the Craig, your welfare is his responsibility. He will allow nothing and no one to harm you."

That sounded nothing at all like the Winter King who mercilessly conquered Summerlea, but then again, thus far her every interaction with him had been one surprise after another. "My name is Khamsin," she said. "My sisters call me Storm."

"Storm?"

"My giftname."

"Ah." Valik glanced up at the clouds overhead. "That explains much."

*   *   *

Valik didn't stay to talk. He busied himself instead with overseeing the raising and furnishing of Wynter's tent, though Khamsin noted he actually gave more assistance than supervision.

The Wintermen were swift, efficient folk. In less than fifteen minutes, the towering fourteen-foot center pole and its surrounding eight-foot perimeter poles were in place, supporting the broad circular form of the tent. Once the tent pegs were hammered into place, Wintermen carted rugs, pillows, braziers, and other furnishings inside. To her surprise, they unloaded her possessions from the carriage and carried them inside too: her trunk, Tildy's growing lamps, even the plants her sisters had given her.

She watched her belongings disappear into the interior of the Winter King's tent, and all her brave talk about facing her fears head-on evaporated.

Last night, bolstered by painkillers and arras and shielded by the veils of darkness and deception, she'd unflinchingly—in the end, even eagerly—shared a bed with the Winter King. All fear, all modesty, all reason, had flown out the window after his first, explosive touch. She had lost herself to sensation and the freedom of anonymity.

Tonight was different. Tonight, she would have no arras, no darkness, no veils to hide behind. There would be only her and the man she had deceived into wedlock.

A sudden gust of cold wind made the tent walls shudder and flap. Her oilskin parasol caught the gust and nearly ripped out of her hands. Rain, chill and bracing, splashed her face. She clutched the parasol more tightly and swiped the rain out of her eyes. When she opened them again, Valik was standing there before her.

"The tent is ready, Your Grace." He swept his arm back towards the open tent flap, indicating that she should proceed inside.

She forced her feet to move. The first step was the hardest, the ones after that came easier as pride stiffened her spine. Bella hurried behind her, dodging slushy puddles of snow and mud.

The interior of the canvas tent had been transformed into a plush, surprisingly spacious stateroom. A large brazier circled the center pole, its iron troughs already filled with slow-burning, fragrant wood. Blue-gray smoke from the newly started fire curled up in wispy tendrils, guided by a vent pipe that curled round the center pole like a dragon's tail towards the arch of the tent roof. The pipe exited through a vent flap cut into the highest point of the canvas, and the wind blowing past overhead caused a slight vacuum effect, drawing the smoke outside.

A scattered collection of thick rugs covered the tent floor and softened the hard surface of the frozen ground below. Several folding chairs and a small table had been set up on one side, not far from the fire, and in the back corner of the tent, behind screens of concealing cloth stretched over iron frames what appeared to be plump, down-filled coverlets and pillows had been piled together and covered with blankets and furs. Tildy's growing lamps were positioned around the mound.

"We do not travel in as extravagant a fashion as Summerlanders," Valik said, misunderstanding her silent perusal of the tent.

"It's fine," she assured him. "Much more luxurious than I'd expected." From the whispers she'd heard among her father's courtiers, she'd halfway been expecting cold stone stools and beds hewn from blocks of ice, but this was not at all hard or austere.

"Make yourself comfortable. The cook tents are up, but it will be a while before the evening meal is prepared."

Khamsin's belly lurched at the thought of food. She pressed a hand against her stomach and swallowed back the surge of nausea. "Don't bother on my account, Lord Valik. I'm really not very hungry."

His eyes narrowed, but all he said was, "I'll have the men bring you a little something all the same. Loke and

Baroc will be just outside in case you need them." He bowed again and backed out of the tent.

She waited until Valik was gone before she kicked off her muddy shoes and took her first tentative step onto the exquisite carpets. Stockinged toes sank deep into the soft wool pile. The carpet felt like a cushion of springy moss beneath her feet, surprisingly soft and inviting, like the rest of the furnishings. She approached the brazier, holding her hands out to the welcoming warmth. Already, the inside of the tent was several degrees warmer than the outside, and without the wind and the sting of cold rain cutting through her clothes, it was almost cozy.

The interior of the tent had been decorated, the canvas walls covered in colorful, intricate hunting scenes depicting silvery white snow wolves and white-haired Wintermen on horseback hunting deer, bear, and wild pigs through forests of aspen, spruce, and pine that transformed seamlessly from one season to the next.

The scenes weren't bloody or brutal. They were beautiful—a celebration of nature and survival, with the entire cycle of life depicted in a never-ending circle of seasons. Tucked away within the painting were scenes of nature renewing itself: a tiny fawn curled in the underbrush, a rocky den filled with wolf pups, bear cubs climbing a tree while their mother ate berries from a bush nearby. Eagles and falcons soared overhead, hovering above nests filled with eggs and fledglings. The painting was so vivid, she could almost hear the rustle of the gold-painted aspen leaves shivering in the autumn winds, feel the chill blowing across the snow-frosted tops of the trees in the winter scene, and smell the flowers of the cool mountain summer.

Fascinated, she approached one tent wall to examine it, wondering what sort of paint they'd used that would remain adhered so well to a canvas that was constantly rolled and unrolled and submitted to the harsh conditions of military campaigns. Each line was made up of thousands of tiny little dots of shimmering, multicolored dyes. The canvas had essentially been tattooed, and the artistry and pains-taking attention to detail was astonishing.

Had the Winter King commissioned the illustration? Surely a man who surrounded himself with such exquisite beauty couldn't be a heartless monster?

Behind her, Bella finished cleaning their muddy shoes, lined them up neatly beside the tent flap, then wandered around the interior, inspecting the place with a jaundiced eye and dismissing the exquisite mural with a careless shrug. "Well, it certainly isn't the palace, is it?" she sniffed when she'd finished her inspection.

"That depends on what part of the palace you're used to," Khamsin snapped, irritated by the girl's contempt for the fascinating, foreign beauty around them. The young maid gave her a wounded look, and Kham instantly felt guilty. No doubt Bella had been raised to believe Summerlea was the pinnacle of beauty against which all the world was judged and found inferior. "Remember, Bella," she said in a calmer, more congenial tone, "this is an army encampment. I doubt Roland himself traveled half so well."

"Roland was warrior first and courtier second," a brisk masculine voice said from the tent entrance. "A man after my own heart, even if he was a Summerlander."

Both Khamsin and Bella gasped and whirled around to see Wynter straighten to his full height just inside the tent. His armor was coated in glassy ice where the falling rain had touched the metal plates and frozen on contact. His wolf's head visor was pushed up, out of his face, revealing golden skin and cold, cold eyes.

Those narrowed eyes pinned Khamsin in place. "Valik tells me you've refused the offer of the evening meal."

Kham's throat felt suddenly dry, and her belly took a nervous lurch. "I—"

"You will eat. You can do so willingly, or I can hold you

down and force the food down your throat myself. One way or the other, it makes no difference to me."

What softening she might have been feeling for him froze in a snap. She'd never been one to take orders well. As soon as someone said "you must," her instinctive response was "I won't!" Even when she would otherwise have been happy saying "I will."

Her hands curled into fists. "As I told Lord Valik, I am not hungry." Sparks flashed in her eyes. Outside, lightning cracked, and thunder boomed with enough force to shake the tent walls.

Wynter didn't so much as flinch. "You. Girl. Get out," he ordered Bella. His narrowed eyes remained fixed on Khamsin, unblinking, not flickering for even an instant.

The maid didn't hesitate. Gathering up her skirts, she fled. She didn't even stop to cover her head against the rain that was now pelting down in sheets.

As soon as she was gone, Wynter moved. One moment he was standing by the tent flap, the next he was upon Khamsin, his large hand gripping her by the back of the neck, holding her in place with effortless strength.

"The scent of your magic on the wind is familiar to me . . . Storm. You were the one who challenged me in the sky that first day."

She considered giving him a little taste of lightning, but the way he looked right now, if she attacked, he'd likely just snap her neck. Her jaw tightened as she gritted her teeth and held back her temper.

Wynter smiled, but there was nothing friendly about it. "Don't think for one instant you could actually defeat me. You would only hurt yourself trying. I hold the Ice Heart, and the power of that is something you can scarce imagine." The fingers at the back of Khamsin's neck began to stroke her skin. "Now, my men are going to deliver your evening meal, and you are going to eat it. Every last bite. Do you understand?"

"I told you, I'm not hu—" She broke off in a fit of coughing. His grip had tightened slightly, and his fingers had gone cold. The chill spread rapidly through her skin, making her throat feel so dry she could not continue to speak.

In a voice of toneless calm, he told her, "You are wed to me. Your survival and welfare are my responsibility now, and I will tolerate no defiance in that regard. Best you learn that now, and accept it. Your life in the coming months will be much easier for it." His fingers relaxed their grip just slightly, and the biting cold faded as quickly as it had come. "Now, one more time, you need to eat. You are wounded, and your body needs nourishment, so it can heal."

Her lips compressed in a tight line. Whatever food passed her lips would most likely come right back up, but the mighty Winter King had spoken. "Fine," she snapped. "You want me to eat? I'll eat. Now let go of me." She wrenched herself out of his grip and glared at him.

He regarded her with imperturbable calm. "I'll be back when your meal is ready." He turned and ducked through the tent flaps.

Left with no one on whom to vent her spleen, Kham gave a long, furious hiss of displeasure and kicked a small, glazed pot sitting on the floor near the brazier. Unfortunately, the pot turned out to be cast iron and heavy as a boulder. Instead of rolling across the tent floor with a satisfying rattle, it stayed where it was, and she yelped at the stinging jolt of pain that shot halfway up her leg from her now-throbbing big toe.

Scowling and muttering dire threats against her new husband, she hobbled over to one of the canvas camp chairs. With her back still raw and painful, she couldn't even enjoy throwing herself down on the chair in an angry sulk. Instead, she sat with gingerly care and indulged herself with a black scowl that soon devolved to a self-pitying pout. Outside, threatening crashes of lightning subsided to distant, rumbling thunder and a surfeit of miserable, brooding rain.

*   *   *

True to his word, Wynter returned less than an hour later. Two men followed him through the tent flap, carrying covered trays. The Wintermen set the trays on a long folding table and lifted the lids to reveal hot beverages and an unfamiliar dish of some sort of stewed meat and vegetable. Aromatic wisps of steam wafted up from the plates, but what would normally have been appetizing aromas made Khamsin's unsettled belly lurch. The men set two canvas camp chairs at the table, bowed to Wynter, and left.

Wynter waited in silence, his powerful arms crossed over his broad chest with deceptive indolence. His eyes gave lie to his calm façade. They were the cold, merciless eyes of a predator, unflinching and entirely focused on her. She could almost swear she saw magic gathering in their depths, and she knew his languid pose hid muscles poised to spring at the first sign of defiance.

Pride stiffened her spine. She swallowed her surge of nausea and forced herself to sit at the table. She'd told Wynter she would eat. She would not make a liar of herself.

After the briefest hesitation—was he so surprised she would honor her word?—his arms unfolded, and he took his own seat in a single, fluid motion.

She picked up her spoon, dipped it into the stew and raised it hesitantly to her lips. Her stomach lurched again, but she forced herself to open her mouth and eat. The first, tentative bite went down and, to her surprise, stayed down.

"Not too spicy for you, is it?" the Winter King asked, his pale eyes fixed on her.

"No . . . no, it's fine." It was true. The stew was flavorful without being overwhelming. It actually seemed to quiet the growling churn of her stomach. She waited a few minutes, then tried another bite. When that, too, stayed down, she ate another bite, then another, until half the bowl was gone. She stopped then even though she probably could have finished the bowl if she'd tried. The last few days had shrunk her belly, and she wasn't foolish enough to gorge.

Pushing the bowl away, she sat back in her chair and cast a challenging look at Wynter, silently daring him to insist she continue. He eyed her dish, then tucked into his own without a word, leaving her defiance to fizzle.

Left with nothing to do but sit, she occupied herself by examining the stranger who less than twenty-four hours ago had become her husband. He'd changed out of his plate mail into brown woolen pants, a leather vest, and a full-sleeved, cream-colored shirt made from a thick, soft-looking material that shifted and flowed over his skin every time he moved. His long white hair streamed down his back like a snowfall. The hair at his temple had been gathered back in a silver cuff an inch or two above his ears and braided in three long, thin, silver-beaded braids that brushed across his cheeks as he bent his head to eat.

He was surprisingly graceful in his every move. Kingly. So much more than just brute force wrapped in a danger-ously handsome package. Even his hands, so broad and so capable of destruction, moved with disarming grace and unexpected delicacy as they tore small chunks of bread from a still-warm loaf and handled slender silverware with deft ease.

She couldn't help but recall the way those hands had moved over her, claiming without hesitation, drawing sen-sation after sensation from her untutored, arras-enflamed flesh, until she screamed for him to grant her release. Even now, just watching him spread melting butter on bread sent an unnerving flood of heat sweeping through her.

His nostrils flared, and he stilled for a betraying instant. His lashes lifted, ice blue eyes potent with awareness and a look that made her heart stutter in her chest.

"Hungry for something else, wife?" His voice dropped to a low, rumbling, throaty growl that made the hairs all over her body stand on end.

She drew a shaky breath and closed her eyes to free herself from the arcane magic of his gaze. "No, I couldn't eat another bite," she replied with deliberate obtuseness. "I'm very tired. All I need at the moment is sleep—uninterrupted sleep," she added quickly. The last thing she wanted was for him to think she was issuing an invitation. "On a bed that isn't moving."

He popped the morsel of bread in his mouth and drained his mug of mulled wine before rising and dusting off his hands. "Baroc!"

The tent flaps parted. The young soldier who'd been standing guard over Khamsin earlier stepped inside. "Your Grace?"

"Fetch the queen's maid."

"Aye, Your Grace." The young Winterman bowed and backed out of the tent. Moments later, he returned, with Bella in tow.

Wide-eyed and openly terrified, the young maid looked ready to keel over if Wynter so much as frowned in her direction.

"What's your name, girl?"

"B-Bella, Your M-Majesty."

"It's Your Grace, Bella, not Your Majesty, and your mistress is tired. Help ready her for bed. I understand those lamps will help her back heal, so light them all. We still have a long road ahead of us, and the sooner she is healed, the sooner we can increase our pace." He glanced at Khamsin. "Will you be wanting a bath, my queen?"

The offer surprised her. It was a consideration she'd not expected from him. "No," she murmured. "Thank you, I'm fine."

"Very well." He gestured curtly to dismiss Baroc, then crossed the tent to take a seat at the lacquered camp desk set up in one corner.

Khamsin started to object, then gave it up. There was no point in objecting to his presence. This was his tent, and she was his wife. And except for the fact that darkness and arras had hidden the sight of her from him last night, he already knew her body more intimately than any other person in the world.

Gathering her skirts, she walked to the small sleeping area separated from the main tent by the folding, four-foot-tall screens. With the growing lamps ringed around the sleeping pallet still unlit and the small, makeshift chamber wreathed in shadow, the screened wall offered a small sense of privacy. Her trunk had been set beside the mound of furs and pillows, near the outer tent wall.

"There should be a length of white sheeting in my trunk," she told Bella softly. "Fetch it, please." The young maid lifted the trunk lid and rummaged around inside for a few moments before locating the folded white cloth and handing it to Kham. "Thank you. No, don't light the lamps just yet. Help me out of this gown first."

While the maid unlaced the loose ties at the back of her gown, Kham glanced over the tops of the screens towards Wynter. He was sitting at the camp desk, reviewing a small sheaf of papers, periodically pausing to dip a quill in ink and scratch notations on the papers.

The cooler air of the tent swirled across Kham's shoulders and back as Bella freed the last of the laces, and the gown fell open.

As if he were there on that small breath of air, tasting the warmth of her bare skin, instantly and intimately aware of her, Wynter looked up, directly into her eyes. Kham's breath caught in her throat. She clutched the loose gown to her chest, fighting the shocking desire to let it fall from her body beneath Wynter's burning gaze.

Bella moved between them and spread out the sheet in her hand, blocking Wynter's view. "This is as much privacy as I can give you, my lady," she murmured. "Powerful as he is, I don't think he can see through people."

Kham dragged in a shaky breath and fought the hysterical urge to laugh, wishing she were half as modest as Bella thought she was. She forced her fingers to loosen their grip on her gown. It tumbled down around her ankles in a puddle of fabric. Bella moved with swift industry, wrapping Kham's nakedness in swaths of cool, silky linen. Khamsin clutched the edges of the fabric between her breasts, letting the bulk of the sheeting drape low, just skimming the top of her buttocks and leaving her back bare for healing.

Not daring to glance in Wynter's direction, she knelt on the thick, padded pallet while Bella lit the growing lamps one by one. A muffled sound came from the main tent area, followed by a brief swirl of cold wind. Even without turning to look, Kham knew that Wynter had left.

"I thought he'd never leave," Bella muttered, confirming it. "I don't know what to make of him. He acts so concerned for your health, you'd almost think he actually cared. It's hard to believe he intends to abandon you on some frozen glacier and leave you there to die if you don't give him a child before year's end. Seems cold and unnatural, if you ask me. Now, let me turn these growing lamps up a bit, then you just lie still while I clean your wounds." Bella gently stroked a damp cloth over Khamsin's back. With Wynter gone and the growing lamps turned on full, the temperature in the small sleeping area rose quickly to a warm, toasty bake. "There now, that feels better doesn't it? Summer warm, like home the way it used to be."

It did feel better. The warm light soaked into Kham's skin like rain into thirsty soil. She closed her eyes and murmured a wordless agreement. She heard Bella kneel on the floor beside her, heard the quiet snick of a jar opening, then felt Bella's hands gently began rubbing Tildy's cream into her skin. Her touch was kinder than it had been in the jolting coach, and if Khamsin closed her eyes, she could almost believe it was Tildy, not Bella, tending her with a mother's love.

Tears burned at the backs of her eyes, but she would not let them fall. Her path had been laid out, and Tildy would not ever again walk it with her. Khamsin, who had never truly been alone in the world, would have to learn to be so.

The child who had always found refuge in her nursemaid's maternal love would have to become a woman, strong and self-sufficient.

Because no matter what it took, Khamsin had no intention of letting any man—husband, king, or the Sun God himself—stake her out on a glacier and leave her to die.

CHAPTER 8
A Flame in Snow

Four days later, Wynter paced outside Khamsin's carriage, his body humming with pent-up energy. Valik stood rock still a few feet behind him, no less agitated than Wynter but better able to hide it. Inside the carriage, the Wintercraig army's most experienced surgeon, Jorgun Magnusson, was examining Khamsin, whose health had taken an alarming turn for the worse.

She hadn't complained. Not even once. The stubborn little weatherwitch just suffered her misery in silence and soldiered on. That near-heroic stoicism was not what Wynter had come to expect from Summerlanders, and it would have won his grudging admiration if not for the way she and her maid had conspired to hide her worsening condition from him.

Wynter had slowed his army's pace to a crawl, hoping that would lessen Khamsin's travel sickness. He'd stopped frequently so she could rest, hoping that would bolster her strength, but she'd grown so thin and wan she was near transparent. He'd even drawn back the snow clouds that had blanketed Summerlea skies for so long, hoping direct sunlight would provide her a measure of healing that the growing lamps had not.

This morning, though, she'd been so quiet and withdrawn that he'd paid a surprise visit to check on her himself during their midmorning stop. And he'd caught the maid trying to dispose of the breakfast Khamsin had supposedly eaten three hours earlier! After threatening to freeze the maid with a cold so deep she would never thaw, the truth came tumbling out.

Two days! For two days now, Khamsin had not been able to keep more than a cup of broth in her stomach. And she'd hidden that from him!

His fury at her deception was stronger than any emotion he'd felt since the day he'd learned of his brother's death. He wanted to roar and gnash his teeth. He wanted to stomp so hard the earth would shake and rip trees up out of the ground in a violent rage that would do a wounded giant proud.

Behind him, the carriage door opened, and Wynter spun around to watch Jorgun alight from the conveyance.

"Well?" His jaw clenched as he waited for the surgeon's answer, but he knew, even before Jorgun slowly shook his head, what that answer would be.

"She's much worse, Your Grace. Fever's set in, and her wounds are going septic. If we don't stop long enough to cure the infection and let her fully heal, I doubt she'll reach the borders of Wintercraig alive."

The prognosis left Wynter stunned. Like Valik, Jorgun was no exaggerator. His grave concern meant she was all but knocking on death's door.

"We'll stop here then," Wynter decided abruptly. "And you will do everything in your power to heal her." He turned to his second-in-command. "Valik, ask for volunteers—fifty men, no more—to stay with me and the queen until Jorgun says she's well enough to travel. You and the rest of the men continue on to the Craig. You've been gone from home long enough. There's no need for you to delay your return."

Valik's spine went stiff and a stubborn, all-too-familiar light entered his eyes. "I won't leave my king in the middle of enemy territory with a sick woman. Especially not when that woman is the daughter of your enemy. Not with five hundred men to guard you."

Wynter arched a brow. "You think I can't protect myself without you?"

"I think you'll be distracted. Whether you like it or not, she's gotten under your skin. She's been there since that first day in the tower, and you know it. And I don't trust it. I'll handpick those men—a hundred, not fifty—and *we* will stay with you. The others can go on ahead."

Wynter's eyes narrowed. "You're an impudent get, Valik Stone-skull."

"Take after my friend, the king of rock-headedness." Valik saluted briskly, then turned his mount around to charge down the line.

They set up camp by the road's edge, in the remains of what had been a wheat field. The rest of the army marched north at a brisk pace, carrying Khamsin's young maid with them. She'd protested the dismissal at first until Wynter near froze her with a look. She'd known her mistress's condition was worsening and not only had she not alerted Valik or Wynter to the truth, but she'd helped Khamsin mask the true depth of her illness until it was almost too late.

Valik set up a perimeter around the encampment and appointed shifts of men to stand sentry. A dozen soldiers rode out to hunt for game, while a dozen more headed east along a narrow road to see what they might scavenge from local farmhouses and villages.

Wynter carried Khamsin from the fetid stuffiness of the coach to his tent. Shame and fear battled inside him. She'd lost so much weight, she seemed little more than bones wrapped in a thin casing of flesh.

"Light a fire in the stove, and set out those lamps around the pallet." His men had prepared the surgeon's cot in the center of the tent, closest to the iron stove and farthest from the snowy chill that seeped through the edges of the canvas. Gently, he laid his bride facedown upon the prepared bedding. He turned her head to one side so she could breathe without restriction and smoothed the soft ringlets of white-streaked hair back from her face. Her skin was burning to the touch.

"Stubborn, damned-fool woman," he muttered. "Were you trying to kill yourself?"

He hadn't thought her that sort. She'd struck him as the kind more likely to fry him with lightning than suffer in silence.

Not that she'd been in any shape to summon lightning lately. He'd almost begun wishing for a thundercloud on the horizon and the misery of torrential rain.

He unlaced the back of her gown and parted the loose-fitting fabric. His jaw clenched at the sight of her back. The skin was red and inflamed around the wounds, and infection—quite a bit of it—had most definitely set in. Red streaks radiated out from several of the deeper lacerations, and underlying the scent of blood and pus was the first hint of a smell that made Wynter's blood run cold.

Jorgun, standing near Wynter's elbow, handed him a small, capped pot.

"What's this?" Wynter growled, removing the lid and sniffing the gooey contents within.

"The herbalist's salve. For her wounds."

Wynter recapped the pot and tossed it aside. "What good has it done her? I'll be damned if we waste another second on failed remedies. Don't you have a better solution?"

"I'm a surgeon, not an herbalist."

"But you've treated enough battle wounds to know a few basic healing aids for festering wounds. Tell me what you need. I'll send men to find it."

The surgeon didn't waste time arguing. "I need pine needles boiled in snowmelt for a wound wash to clear out the worst of the infection. Send some men to see if they can find fresh chickweed. If they can't find fresh, then boil some of our dried supply along with chamomile and comfrey for a poultice. I'll need honey to dress the wounds when I'm done, and willowbark tea to bring down the fever. And my king?"

Wynter paused at the outer doorway and glanced back.

Jorgun met his eyes with grim urgency. "If you want her to live, tell the men to hurry."

Wynter gave a curt nod and ducked through the tent flaps.

Within minutes, a cookfire had been built just outside the tent, and several kettles were boiling away, one containing pine needles gathered from a nearby stand of trees, another filled with willowbark for fever. A dozen men were scouring the snow-covered countryside for fresh chickweed, but Wynter wasn't waiting on them. A third kettle filled with dried chickweed, comfrey, and chamomile was boiling alongside the others.

When the pine-needle concoction was ready, Wynter grabbed an old wineskin, packed a funnel with snow, and ladled the steaming wound wash into the funnel. The snow melted and cooled the mixture slightly. He repeated the process, testing the wash against his own skin as Jorgun had instructed, until the wineskin was full of hot, but not scorching, liquid.

Grabbing up a stack of cloths used to bind soldiers' wounds, he carried the pine-needle infusion into the tent and handed it to Jorgun. Jorgun's assistant, Frig, was tucking bolsters of cloth around Khamsin.

"I'll need you both to hold her down," the surgeon said. "She isn't going to like this very much." Jorgun waited for Wynter to grasp his wife's shoulders and Frig to pin her ankles, then he uncorked the wineskin.

The instant the hot, pungent liquid poured over her infected back, Khamsin reared up, writhing and screaming. She would have thrown herself off the cot had Wynter and Frig not held her fast. Runnels of steaming liquid washed over Khamsin's skin and ran in streamers down her sides into the absorbent towels Frig had arranged around her.

The wineskin emptied quickly, but a second was already waiting. As Jorgun aimed the spout of hot liquid directly into the worst of her lacerations to irrigate the inflamed flesh, a stream of filthy invectives poured out of her mouth.

In the distance, thunder began to rumble.

Wynter grinned, teeth clenched. "That's it, little flower. Get angry." But her supply of energy depleted quickly, and before the surgeon emptied the second wineskin, her slender body went limp. Wynter's savage grin faded, and he shared a brief, grim look with Jorgun.

The surgeon continued working in silence, probing Khamsin's wounds, lancing several areas where the infection had gone deep, irrigating everything with fresh pine wash. When he was finally satisfied the wounds were clean, he stepped back and gestured to Wynter.

"Hold her, Your Grace. And get as much of this willow-bark tea down her throat as you can."

Wyn nodded and cradled her against his chest, pouring dribbles of tea into her mouth while Frig and Jorgun replaced the pine-wash-soaked blankets with fresh, dry bedding. When they were done, he laid her back down on the fresh, clean blankets.

One of the men carried in the kettle that smelled of comfrey, chamomile, and chickweed. It was already swimming with soaked linen squares. Wynter fished them out with a stick, wrung them gently—hissing a little at the burn of hot liquid on his palms—and handed them to Jorgun, who placed the steaming, herb-soaked cloths over Khamsin's back.

When the poultices cooled, Jorgun removed them and smeared a generous layer of honey over the open lacerations to help prevent additional infection from entering the wounds.

An hour later, the process started over again. Throughout the afternoon and deep into the night, Jorgun, Wynter, and Frig worked to defeat the feverish infection that held Khamsin in its grip. The battle continued through the next day, and the next, but despite their efforts, the infection would not give up its hold. The poison had settled deep, and no matter what sort of progress they made, a few hours later the battle would rage again.

Close to midnight on the third day, her temperature spiked, and she began rambling in delirium and thrashing about. Electricity crackled along her fingertips as wild energy sought an outlet. A tempest gathered in the sky. The tent walls shuddered in howling gusts of wind. Rain sluiced down in sheets, falling so fast and furious, it was as if a river were pouring from the sky. Lightning shattered the darkness in merciless barrages, illuminating the tent walls like shades over a candle and turning cloud-blackened night as bright as day. Concussive thunderclaps shook the earth and left Wynter's ears ringing.

"Winter's Frost!" The tent flaps flung open, and Valik, who had been standing guard with the men, leapt inside. "That lightning struck so close, it damned near singed my eyebrows!" He scowled at Khamsin's thrashing body. "It's her, isn't it? She's feeding this storm. You've got to knock her out before she kills us all."

Wynter scowled at his friend. "I will not hit a woman, and especially not my wife."

"Wyn, those clouds will spawn a cyclone if she keeps feeding them energy."

"No! She suffers now because of what her father did to her. I will not hurt her more."

"Well, you'd best do something! A few more minutes of this storm, and we'll all die, including your precious Summerlander bride."

As if to prove his point, the whole tent suddenly went bright as day, and a thunderous boom nearly knocked them all off their feet.

Wynter swore beneath his breath. Valik was right. The storm outside was deadly. It had to be stopped. He laid a hand on his wife's burning forehead. Khamsin's fever was driving her delirium, and her delirium was driving the storm. If he could bring down her fever, the storm should calm. Since none of the surgeon's remedies had worked, there was only one other way Wyn knew to lower Khamsin's temperature.

He closed his eyes and drew on the coldness within him, summoning the power of the Ice Heart. Not much. He wanted to cool her fever, not freeze her to death. Even so, just that tiny summoning ate away at the small reserve of warmth inside him.

That was the insidious price of the Ice Heart. Each use of its power, no matter how minute, robbed him of some irretrievable portion of his humanity. After three years of war and death, so little of his former self remained, he felt even the tiniest additional loss like a hammer to the heart. He could literally feel himself growing more distant, more unfeeling, more like the dread, soulless monster of legend.

When the backs of his eyes began to burn, he opened them and stared down at Khamsin, releasing the cold in a long, sweeping Gaze that traveled up and down the length of her body. The temperature around them dropped, becoming brisk. Her breath puffed out in small clouds of steam. His did not. What lived inside him was so much colder than even the frozen wastelands of the north that each exhaled breath grew warmer rather than colder when it hit the air.

He smoothed his hands across her flesh, rubbing the skin so his Gaze chilled but did not freeze and bending close to breathe cool air upon her in its wake. The burning heat in her skin began to cool. Her thrashing stilled.

Outside, lightning still crashed and boomed as strong as ever.

"Well, that didn't work," Valik shouted over the din.

Wynter swore under his breath. "The storm has already gathered enough energy to sustain itself." It was a fearsome storm, far, far worse than the little thundershower she'd summoned last week in Vera Sola. "I'll need to bleed some of it off before things will settle down." Wyn cast a glance back at his friend, and his eyes widened. Valik's hair had begun to lift in a pale halo around his face. The air around him had begun to glow an eerie shade of violet. "Valik!" he cried, "Move!"

Only swift reflexes honed by years of battle saved him. Valik leapt a scant instant before lightning struck the spot he'd been standing. The tent flashed with blinding light, and thunder cracked with earsplitting fury. The canvas caught fire, but pelting rain extinguished it almost as soon as the first flame flickered. Electricity jumped and sparked along the metal binding of the tent pole, then leapt in frenetic arcs towards Khamsin's body.

Her eyes flew open, shifting silver, glowing as the wild energy surged through her. Her back arched; her hands splayed out, fingertips sparking with flashes of light. The curling, white-streaked strands in her midnight hair began to move, rising as Valik's had done on invisible bands of energy while a violet glow surrounded her. She wasn't controlling or feeding the storm any longer, but she was still a lodestone for its energy.

Wynter lunged towards her, but the lightning reached her first. The explosion of it flung him backward with such force that it drove the breath from his lungs. He lay on the tent floor, stunned and gasping as the lightning speared her, filling her slight body with shining light. Another bolt struck, its white-hot charge seeking her out with unerring accuracy.

He lurched to his feet and stumbled out of the tent, summoning his power as he went. He could not control lightning or storms, but by the Frozen Gates of Hel, he could certainly summon enough cold, dry winter to rob this tempest of its fuel. He reached deep into the bottomless well of power that was the Ice Heart, shouting with a mix of pain and defiance as the devastating fury of it ripped through him. His head flung back, his eyes flew open. Power erupted in a shining column, shooting high into the atmosphere. Rain froze and shattered. Water vapor flashfroze to tiny flakes of snow and ice.

He dug deeper into the icy depths of his power, plunging

into the abyss, gathering the bitter cold and driving it into the sky like a sword thrust to the storm's heart. Magic and nature exploded in a collision of power. But a storm—even a great storm—could not sustain itself when robbed of its warmth and moisture. The clouds shrank, bleeding their strength out in showers of brittle snowflakes.

Wynter held the Ice Heart's dread power with unflinching determination, until the wild, roiling storm transformed to clear, cloudless sky, filled with stars so bright they dazzled the eye and a cold so bitter it sent every man and beast in the encampment running for shelter and the warmth of campfires and huddled bodies. Only then did he release his hold on the magic.

His body felt stiff and hollow. As if there were a terrible, empty void within. Some elusive memory niggled at his mind, some faint alarm whose meaning he could not remember. He turned and stepped back into his tent.

Valik had beat out what flames the rain had not extinguished. Now, shivering violently, he was crouched over Khamsin's still form. His hands were shaking with cold as he dragged furs and blankets over her to protect her from the dangerous drop in temperature.

"Does she live?" Wynter asked in a voice bereft of emotion. Some part of his brain remembered that Valik was his beloved friend and that the woman lying on the heap of furs was his wife, whom he was pledged to protect. But the memory felt coldly detached, as if the concept of emotion was little more than alien words on a page. He felt . . . dead inside . . . frozen.

Valik turned to look at him, concern etched across his face. "Wyn? Are you all right?"

"I'm fine." His vision had changed. Everything seemed paler. Whiter. A red glow emanated from Valik's chest and radiated outward through his body, down his arms and legs, growing fainter as it extended. Heat bloom. Wynter was seeing the heat of life in Valik's body.

He glanced down at his own hands and saw white with

the barest hint of pink. The girl . . . Khamsin . . . his wife
. . . looked white, too, but there was something different
about her that he couldn't define. "Is she dead?"

"What? No. Far from it. I don't know how she did it, but
damned if your Summerlea bride didn't just use that lightning storm to heal every wound on her body. Here, see for
yourself." Valik moved aside so Wynter could come closer,
then hissed in sudden surprise as Wyn drew near. "Thorgyll's freezing spears! You're cold as ice!" His body went
stiff. His hand fell to the hilt of the sword still strapped to
his waist. "Wyn?" he asked again in a cautious, clipped
voice. "You all right?"

Wynter ignored him. He crouched down beside the
pallet and reached out his hands towards the unconscious
woman. Now he understood the difference in her whiteness. It wasn't the chill of death. It was heat. A concentrated, simmering well of it. So much stronger than what
lived in Valik that it glowed bright as day. Not the white of
ice, but the white of a blazing summer sun. He could feel it
tingling across his palms, thawing his frozen skin. Nerve
ends prickled with returning sensation.

He leaned closer and drew a deep breath. His eyes closed
as her warmth infused his lungs and drove back the frozen
hollowness inside him. "Yes," he murmured, suddenly
weary. "I'm fine, Valik." He rose to his feet and turned to
clap a hand on Valik's shoulder. "I know what you fear, but
for now, at least, there's no need. Go," he urged, "get some
rest. I'll stay here with her."

Valik reached up to cover Wynter's hand with his own,
and enough human warmth must have returned to Wyn's
fingers to reassure him because he nodded, and the rigid,
battle-ready tension of his muscles relaxed slightly. "I'll
send someone to repair the tent."

Wynter glanced up at the scorched holes in the canvas
roof where the lightning bolts had shot through. Stars twinkled in the crystalline night sky. The air was still now, with
no hint of a breeze. He hadn't been able to feel the cold in

three years, and with the heat radiating from Khamsin's body, he doubted she would be able to feel it either.

"Leave it 'til morning. We'll be fine."

"They can clear up the mess, at least," Valik insisted. He poked his head outside the tent flap and shouted a series of quick commands. Moments later, half a dozen shivering men gathered up the twisted, melted remains of the growing lamps and everything else that had been damaged in Khamsin's delirium-induced storm and carted the wreckage out. When they left, much of the tent had been stripped bare.

Wyn waited until they were gone, then arched a brow. "Satisfied?"

"No. But it'll do for now." After a last, brief hesitation, Valik bowed and left.

When he was gone, Wynter moved back to the pallet and lay down on the furs beside Khamsin, moving close to the waves of heat emanating from her. The pleasure of that warmth sinking into his flesh was sublime, and so sensual it was nearly erotic. He curled and arm around her waist, threw a leg over hers, and snuggled closer.

Once she was healed, he decided, he would find out exactly how much of the shattering pleasure they'd shared on their wedding night had been real rather than arras-induced.

Khamsin woke to the nip of frost in the air and the heavy, warm weight of furs draped over her. She opened her eyes and glanced around to gain her bearings. She was in a tent. Wynter's tent, she realized. Only most of the furnishings were gone, and there was a fine layer of frost lying over everything that remained. The tiny ice crystals sparkled in shafts of bright sunlight like the sugar coating of Tildy's favorite pastry.

Frost? Sunlight?

She sniffed the air and caught the acrid remnants of char. Something had burned, and the scorched smell was familiar. She looked up with burgeoning dread and found bright morning sunlight streaming through dozens of holes in the canvas roof overhead. There were three large, gaping rents, and at least two dozen smaller, coin-sized punctures, all surrounded by a sprinkling of tiny pinpricks. The edges of all the holes were blackened, scorched.

It was as if someone had upended a pail of embers on the roof of the tent. Only she knew no one had. In the way that Wynter could detect the faintest of scents, she could feel the electric echo of lightning. Her lightning.

She'd called a lightning storm down upon this tent. Upon the encampment.

How many men had she killed?

She sat up with a sudden, graceless jolt. The furs covering her body fell away, and she gasped at the slap of freezing air against her naked skin. Naked? She stared down at her bare breasts, the nipples hardened to small, dark points by the cold. Her mind scrambled for the fragments of memories. She'd not felt well. Her back had begun to fester. The last thing she remembered, she'd been riding in the coach, praying for death to end her torment.

Kham reached a hand behind her towards her spine. Fingers fluttered over smooth skin, feeling the small raised ridges of scars but no torn flesh or scabs. She stretched her arms and twisted her back experimentally. There was no pain, not even the twinge of bruised flesh. Her wounds had healed. Completely.

But at what price?

Without warning, the tent flaps parted. Cold air swirled in. Khamsin gasped and slapped her hands over her breasts just as Wynter ducked into the tent, a steaming kettle in one hand and a cloth-covered pot of something that smelled delicious in the other.

All worry over what she might have done evaporated in an instant. Her mind went blank. Her mouth went dry. She couldn't have moved if her life depended on it.

He was nearly naked. Bare-armed, bare-chested, with

shoulders so broad and arms so powerful, he looked like he could bear the weight of the world. Over seven feet of impressive golden muscle, clad in nothing but a grayish white, animal-pelt loincloth and a pair of furred boots strapped to rock-hard calves. Silvery white hair spilled down his back and over his shoulders like a snowfall. The air outside was frigid, but he seemed not to notice it at all. His vivid eyes, pale and piercing, fixed on her with breathtaking intensity.

"You're awake." The look in those eyes made Khamsin shiver and squirm. She'd always thought herself immune to the intense sensual passions that afflicted most Summerlanders. Until now. Just the sight of him made her body melt as if she'd eaten arras straight from the tree.

The flare of his nostrils and the faint, satisfied curve that lifted one corner of his mouth told her he knew it.

Damn him for finding it so amusing. And damn her for not being able to look away.

"Where are we?" she asked, forcing a coolness she was far from feeling.

"About two hundred miles south of the Rill. We set up camp here when you fell ill."

The Rill was the border river that separated Wintercraig from Summerlea. If they were still two hundred miles away, they'd barely traveled ninety miles north of Vera Sola. "How long have we been here?"

"This is the fifth day. The night before last, your fever came to a head. You've been sleeping ever since."

He walked towards her. She stared, fascinated, at the ripple of muscle in his legs and the hard, carved definition of his chest and flat abdomen. The front of his loincloth bore a very distinctive, very large bulge. She licked her suddenly dry lips. The bulge twitched and grew visibly more pronounced. Oh. My.

"Have a care, woman." His voice was a low, throbbing growl. It vibrated across her skin and raised the fine hairs on the back of her neck. "If you didn't need food more than

I need a good fucking, I'd flip you over right now and fill you 'til you scream and beg for mercy."

She should have been shocked by his raw coarseness. Spring and Summer would have gasped in outrage. Autumn would have slapped his face. But she, wild, mannerless heathen that she was, only shuddered with helpless lust. Images from her wedding night flashed across her mind on a hazy rush. Silken skin, unexpectedly soft and fragrant, sliding against hers. Broad hands skimming across her, touching her in ways that made her gasp and quake. A burning mouth, raining fire upon her flesh.

She wrenched her thoughts to the present and her eyes away from all that dangerous, seductive skin and that impressive jut of flesh straining against his loincloth. She forced her gaze back up to his face.

Then wished she hadn't. The look in his eyes was stark and stunning, as powerful and elemental as any storm she'd ever conjured from the skies.

His gaze dropped lower, and she could have sworn blue flames leaped to life in the center of his eyes. She glanced down and realized her hands had slipped from their protective clasps over her breasts. The burnished bronze of one nipple was peeking out between her fingers.

She gasped and snatched a fur, bringing it up to cover herself.

"Don't."

The simple command made her freeze. Then scowl. She cast him a defiant glance and pulled the fur higher.

"We both know I'm only going to take it from you before you leave this tent."

She'd never backed down from a challenge in her life. Not even when retreat served her best interests. Her fingers tightened around the pelt, and she arched one dark brow in return. "You can try, Winterman."

"I'll do more than that, Summerlass." He drew closer and sank to his knees beside her in a single, fluid motion, setting pot and kettle on the ground before him. The long, thick muscles in his thighs bunched and flexed as they absorbed his weight. He smelled of wind and snow, fresh and clean and brisk. Power, a mix of magic and male, swirled around him with dark mystery, deepening his scent with an underlying core of danger. Even without his magic, he would be a formidable man. One to be wary of.

"Here." The rounded top of the kettle was a removable bowl. He plucked it free and poured a stream of steaming liquid into it, then offered it to her. "Drink. You've been too long without food. And be careful. It's hot."

The liquid was a rich brown broth of some kind, and the scent of it made Khamsin's stomach growl. Suddenly, she realized how famished she truly was. Securing the pelt beneath her armpits, she reached for the bowl and brought it to her lips. The first sip nearly scalded her, but pride wouldn't let her gasp and fan her mouth to cool the sting.

He removed a cloth from the pot to reveal a deliciously scented, stewed meat of some kind. "This is *borgan*," he said. "A mix of venison, wild boar, and fowl, flavored with basil, wild onion, and sweetberry and stewed until the flesh falls apart." A small spoon hung from the edge of the pot. He freed it and handed it to her. "It's flavorful, but easy to digest. Try a bite."

She was too hungry to refuse. She dipped the spoon into the *borgan* and brought it to her mouth. The meat was meltingly tender and slightly sweet. "It's delicious," she said, dipping her spoon a second time.

Wynter sat back and watched her eat. He missed nothing. Not the graceful play of her slender fingers. Not the way her pretty lips closed around the spoon or her fluttering pleasure as the sweet flavors of the *borgan* burst on her tongue.

The sight of her made his cock twitch. Ah, gods, he lusted. The need so fierce it was a living thing inside him, a hunger like nothing he'd ever felt before. Not for just any woman. His hunger had a name: Khamsin Coruscate Atrialan, his wife.

Her hair spilled in unkempt ringlets down her back, threaded with those shots of white that fascinated him so. The warm brown skin of her bare shoulders and neck was creamy smooth, the delicate bones more pronounced after her days of illness, lending her a frail air.

She was fragile. He knew she didn't think so. Many fools might agree with her, because her spirit was so fierce she seemed more formidable than she was. But he could crush her bones to dust with one glancing blow.

He remembered the cold fury that had filled him the morning after their wedding, when he'd seen the state of her back and realized the crime her father had done against her. He could still feel the icy rage that made him want to flay the skin from Verdan's bones in retribution and freeze his bloodied corpse in a block of ice so thick he would never thaw, so he would remain an eternal warning to corrupt cowards who would turn their gods-given strength against the women and children they were born to protect.

"How many men died?"

The sound of Khamsin's voice ripped him out of his dark thoughts. He realized he was still kneeling there beside her, his hands gripped in bloodless fists against his thighs, his muscles bunched tight with suppressed fury. A distinct chill was emanating from him. "What did you say?" he asked.

"When I summoned the storm that caused that"— she jerked her chin up, towards the tattered canvas roof overhead—"how many of your men did I kill?"

He glanced up, then back at her. Perhaps if he had never swallowed the Ice Heart, he would not have recognized the look in her eyes. But he had, and he'd lost count of the times he'd come back from battle with that same bitter dread in his eyes, wondering how many friends his power had slain, how many innocent lives were extinguished because of him.

"None, Khamsin. All live."

Her eyes widened. "None? But how is that possible? I

know what my storms can do, and judging by the state of this tent, the storm I summoned was a bad one."

"It was a bad one," he agreed, "but I stopped it."

"You—" Her voice broke off, then she whispered in astonishment, "How?"

"I starved it into submission." Her brow furrowed, her gray eyes filled with disbelief and suspicion. "I use the Ice Heart to steal its heat and moisture," he explained, "so it had nothing to feed on. It died away before it could harm anyone."

"You . . ." She closed her mouth. He saw her absorb what was obviously an astonishing possibility, saw wary disbelief battle the fragile bloom of hope in her eyes. "No one's dead? No one's even harmed? You're sure?"

"I'm sure."

"I—" She dropped her head, lashes shuttering down to veil her gaze. Her jaw worked. When she finally spoke, her voice was a low, strained whisper. "Thank you." She looked up suddenly, her eyes fierce. "Thank you," she said again. This time her voice was firm and fervent. "You don't know how much that means to me."

He smiled sadly because he'd only just realized what similar creatures they truly were. "Yes, *min ros,* I think I do." Like him, she despised the destruction she wreaked. The difference was, he'd chosen to wield his deadly magic. She'd possessed hers since birth.

He rose to his feet. He wanted to comfort her but knew enough about wild things not to be so foolish. "No doubt you'd like a bath." He didn't give her a chance to refuse. He simply stepped outside and motioned to his men. She'd been asleep for one full day, out of her mind with fever for three days before that. He'd never met a noblewoman yet who could stand to go so long without the feel of warm water and soap against her skin.

Khamsin, still sitting on the pallet of furs and clutching several of the pelts to her chest, scuttled back when four soldiers entered carrying in a large, beaten-copper tub. They set it near the fire burning in the iron stove and left. Another four men entered, carrying pails of steaming water. They formed a line leading out through the tent flap. Outside a longer line wound all the way to the large cookfires burning in the center of the camp. Pail after pail of water passed down the line until the tub was well filled. The last of them handed Wynter a stack of linens and a small wooden pail filled with soap, a bottle of fragrant oil, and a washcloth.

Wynter found himself fighting back flares of aggression as he waited for them to finish. The wolf in him was getting snarly about having so many men near his female.

When he was finally alone once more with his wife, the tension of Wynter's protective, territorial instincts faded, but a new tension, sultry and simmering, rose to take its place. He reached for the bottle of oil, unstoppered it, and poured a thin stream into the bath. The scent of mountain jasmine rose up on wisps of curling steam.

"Come, wife." He stretched out a hand towards her. "To your bath."

She didn't move. She continued to clutch the pelt to her chest as if she truly thought he would let her leave this tent before he reacquainted himself with every inch of her skin, every intimate detail of her body, and every breathless nuance of her pleasure. He had an heir to sire, both to ensure the continuation of his line and to free him from the Ice Heart, but even without that, from the moment he'd realized his wife was the intriguing little firebrand he'd not been able to erase from his mind, he'd known he would spend every day of the next year learning her pleasure and teaching her his.

It began now.

"Come," he said again. "I've already acquainted myself with everything you're trying to hide. I've spent the last several days nursing you back from the brink of death, tending every need of your body. There is no part of you I have not seen."

"That is different," she snapped. "I wasn't aware of what you were doing."

"And what of our wedding night? You were aware then. I drank the same arras you did, but I still remember everything. I remembered learning the taste of your skin on my tongue, the weight of your breasts in my hands, the feel of your sex gripping mine. I know you remember it, too. There is no place between us for false modesty."

She still didn't move. "I am not bathing with you here, and that is final."

"You will," he corrected. "If I have to strip those pelts from you and drop you kicking and screaming into the tub, you will."

Her eyes narrowed, beginning to swirl with silver. "You. Wouldn't. Dare."

"Oh, *min ros,* I would." He crossed his arms over his chest. "Wrestling a beautiful, naked woman out of her furs and into her bath? What Winterman worth his stones would pass up a chance like that?"

"I'll fry you before you lay a finger on me."

It was all he could do not to laugh at her outraged expression. She was so fierce for such a tiny woman. Rebellious, headstrong, and so sure of her own power. She probably thought she could take on Frost Giants single-handedly. She definitely thought she could best *him.*

She couldn't. Her power, no matter how impressive, was no match for the Ice Heart. Trouble was, he didn't want to force her. Her father had already brutalized her enough for two lifetimes. Besides, he wanted her bathed, yes, but afterwards he wanted a warm, sweet-smelling, *willing* woman in his arms, not an angry firebrand determined to shoot a lightning bolt up his tender bits.

"I hadn't thought you such a faithless coward. You are a princess of the Summer Throne, wedded Queen of the Craig, and my wife. You swore an oath, before a priest and your father's court, to accept my counsel and my care. You swore to offer me all the fruits of your life. And now, you would deny me that which you swore to offer? Do you have so little honor?"

The accusation stole the silver from her eyes, leaving them pure, plain gray filled with shock and dismay. "I . . . No! Of course not! I'm no oathbreaker."

"Then come to your bath. Accept my care, as you swore you would. Offer me the fruits of your life, that I may dine once more on peace instead of war."

CHAPTER 9

A Fragile Truce

She'd been outmaneuvered.

She knew it, and the brief flash of triumph that lit his pale eyes when she rose to her feet confirmed it.

But what was a woman of honor to do? He'd used the one weapon against which she had no defense. She'd sworn an oath. He demanded she fulfill it. Even Roland would have laid down his weapons and accepted defeat under such circumstances.

Her chin came up. Very well, then. She'd known this time would come. She'd known from the moment he had not slain her for her deception, that he would demand she fulfill the obligations of their marriage. And by agreeing to wed him, she had accepted his right to claim and use her body for his pleasure and the conception of his heirs.

He'd not been an unkind lover that first night. Driven, yes, but except for that first, wild coupling, he hadn't just leapt on her, shoved her legs apart, and stabbed. Even burning with arras, he'd taken the time to ensure her pleasure her first.

Of course, he'd still believed she was Autumn then.

She walked towards the copper tub with its swirling cloud of jasmine-scented steam, towards the man she had accepted as her husband and king. The pelt still clutched in her hand covered her from breast to knee, shielding her from his view but leaving her back bare. Chill air whispered across naked skin, underscoring her vulnerability.

He watched her approach, his unblinking stare cold as ice yet, paradoxically, where it touched her body, her skin felt hot and tingling.

At the tub, she stopped and gathered her courage. His gaze never wavered. He was waiting to see if she was a woman of her word, all but challenging her to prove her cowardice. Her chin lifted and she met his fixed stare with a haughty, defiant one of her own.

She had come. She would obey. But she was neither cowed nor coward.

Khamsin forced her fingers to open and her hands to fall to her sides. The fur slid down her body. It whispered with tormenting friction across the tips of her breasts, then spilled down in a puddle at her feet. Cool air swirled around bare flesh. Already-tight nipples drew even tighter. Her muscles began to shiver, tiny uncontrollable tremors that had less to do with the cold of the air than the sudden flare of heat in Wynter's eyes.

His gaze swept over her with near-tangible intensity, and she was glad she'd waited until she'd reached the tub before releasing the pelt. He had a clear view of her breasts, but little else. Still, that was enough in its own right. The touch of those bright, piercing eyes felt like physical hands skimming across her flesh.

"Your bath, my queen." His voice had gone low, and a raspy edge had further deepened it so that his words came out on a rumbling growl.

Her shivers intensified. Summer Sun, what was it about him that drove all reason from her?

Bath, Khamsin, some tiny, still lucid part of her mind urged her. *Get in the bath.*

With some effort, she tore her gaze from Wynter and glanced down, then frowned in consternation. The copper tub had been made to fit Wynter's near-giant height. The edge of the rim reached higher than her waist, and there were no chairs or stools for her to use as stepping blocks.

"Come here," he commanded in that soft, low growl of a voice, "and I will help you in."

"Come nearer, and I will help you," said the wolf to the foolish little lamb. The words from one of the old fairy fables Tildy used to read to her when she was a child popped into Khamsin's head, the story of a headstrong little lamb who had so wanted to be free of her belled collar that she'd trusted a wolf's offer of assistance rather than heeding her instincts and fleeing to the safety of the flock.

Feeling very like the little lamb, Kham silenced the inner alarms clanging their desperate warning and walked with slow deliberation around the perimeter of the tub. As she rounded the curved corner, she lost the last veil of protection hiding her body from Wynter's gaze.

He examined her with slow deliberation. Pride kept her arms at her side when what she really wanted to do was cover herself and run for shelter. She was slight and had always been. After the last week of illness, she was even thinner now than she'd ever been, but if he found her wanting, he did not show it.

His broad hands slid round her middle, spanning her waist with inches to spare. He lifted her with the barest flex of the heavy muscles bunched beneath his skin, and she rose. When her feet lost contact with the ground, she instinctively clutched his wrists for balance.

Gunterfys. Giant killer. So, he'd named his sword. Feeling the rock-hard bone and unyielding muscle beneath his golden skin, she had no trouble imagining him battling toe to toe, fist to fist, with those ferocious monsters of the high mountains.

He lifted her higher, up over his head. Her breasts brushed against his chin. Wickedly, he held her there for a moment, letting her breasts dangle the merest breath from his lips, watching her with eyes of ice blue flame.

"Lift your feet, little flower," he growled. His breath was

not hot but cold, yet it swirled around her nipples like a breath of fire, making them leap to aching attention.

She bent her knees and lifted her feet clear of the tub's edge. A moment later, she was immersed, tingling from neck to toe where the heat of the water penetrated the chill of her skin. Jasmine steam filled her nostrils with heady scent.

He reached for the bar of soap and a scrap of linen, ducking both into the water and rubbing them together. Her eyes widened when he set the soap aside and began to run the foamy cloth over her arm.

"There's no need for you to bathe me. I can do it myself, or Bella can."

He gripped her wrist, refusing to let her pull away, and continued to scrub. Hand, fingers, up her forearm. "Bella is gone."

Kham's breath stalled. "Gone?" She hardly knew Bella, they'd only been together those few awful first days of travel, but the little maid was all Kham had of Summerlea. A face from home.

"I sent her on ahead to the Craig." His lips thinned. "I should have sent her packing back to Vera Sola. She was worse than useless. Hiding your illness."

"On my command."

His eyes shot up, pinning her with sudden, burning cold. "You think I don't know that?" He finished with her arm and quickly soaped the other. "If she'd acted on her own to deceive me, she wouldn't be headed for the Craig. Or still drawing breath."

He rubbed more soap into the cloth and reached for her breasts. Her hands shot out, one closing around his wrist, the other reaching for the washcloth. "I can do it."

He pushed past her resistance with effortless strength. "Be silent and be still." The cloth touched her breast and began scrubbing in small, brisk circles. "I've already done more than touch every inch of your body and will do so again. This false modesty has no place between us." The cloth scrubbing her breasts slowed. His fingers toyed in the slick, foaming suds, sliding over her skin, cupping her breasts. The pads of his thumbs brushed across her nipples, then lingered to tease the small beads that formed in response. "You have beautiful breasts."

Her brows drew together. "If there's no room for false modesty, there's no room for false compliments either," she snapped. "I know I'm not beautiful."

His gaze lifted. "No," he agreed. "Beauty is too tame a word to describe you." He held her gaze for a long moment, and it wasn't until he turned his attention back to her breasts that she realized she'd forgotten to breathe. "But these," he murmured, filling his palms with the weight of her breasts, "are indeed beautiful. Perfect. You don't know how much I've thought about them. About the way they fit in my hands." Her nipples tightened to tiny pebbles. He smiled a little before coolness shuttered his expression once more. "Stand."

Forcing her hands to remain at her side, she obeyed. Her chin lifted and she refused to look at him as he soaped her abdomen, her hips, her legs. *Think of him as a servant, Kham. A woman servant.* His hands slid up the backs of her legs and stroked her inner thighs. *An old, wrinkled woman servant*, she added frantically.

But the broad hand that slipped between her legs was so large and strong and masculine, she couldn't hold the other images no matter how hard she tried.

Summer Sun! The cloth stroked back and forth between her legs, and there was nothing impersonal or servile about it. Each pass was a languid caress, slow, teasing. Testing. The cloth shifted, and then it was his fingers that stroked her, skin to skin, slick with soap and the warm, feminine cream that betrayed her will.

She sat down with a splash and glared at him.

His lips curved. "As I said, I've touched you before and will again. And you aren't half so indifferent to me as you'd like to pretend, *eldi-kona*." He shifted from a kneel to a half crouch. The muscles in his thighs and belly rippled with fluid, powerful grace as he moved behind her.

His brief humor faded, replaced by a sudden, icy chill. The bathwater dropped several noticeable degrees.

"Stop," she complained. "You're freezing my bath."

"You should have told me what he'd done to you." She heard the scowl in his voice. "On our wedding night, you should have told me." His hands touched her back. She felt the slight tremble in his fingers as he traced the path of her father's cane. "You made a brute of me, when I would not have been one if I'd known."

She turned her head and glanced over her shoulder at him. "You would not have consummated the marriage."

"No."

"That's why I didn't tell you." She turned back around. "You would have found out I wasn't Autumn, and you would have annulled the marriage. You wanted a Season for a wife, not me."

He didn't say anything. He merely began scrubbing her back in silence.

What had she expected? For him to claim that, no, he was happy with the wife he'd gotten? Her jaw firmed. Her chin lifted. "Besides," she declared, "why would you care if you hurt me or not? From what I heard, you've vowed to turn me out into the mountains unless I bear you an heir in a year's time. That's not exactly the claim of a caring man."

"Did your father tell you that?"

"What does it matter who told me? Is it true?"

He tossed the soapy cloth aside, snatched up the small wooden pail, and filled it with warm bathwater. "Close your eyes," he warned the barest instant before he upended the pail over her head. He doused her again two more times.

"Is it true?" she asked again.

He reached for the flagon of gelled hair soap, poured a thick stream of the fragrant, viscous liquid into his palm and worked it into her curls. "I need an heir. I cannot afford unnecessary delay in getting one. Too much is at stake."

She knew ensuring a clear succession to the throne was no small matter. The stability of entire countries depended on it. History books were filled with tales of kingdoms torn apart by civil wars sparked by kings who died without leaving an undisputed heir.

She twisted around to see his face. "And if I don't provide one within the year, you will turn me out into the mountains to die?" she prodded.

He didn't say yes straight out. All he said was, "If you don't provide me an heir, I must take another wife," but she knew what he meant.

She turned away so swiftly, the bathwater sloshed over the rim of the copper tub. She stared, unseeing, at the miniature tempest of waves crashing against her kneecaps.

It was true then. She dragged in a shallow breath and let it out. She had wedded and bedded an enemy king. And if for some reason she did not or could not bear him a child within the next twelve months, he would slay her.

"Well," she said. Thoughts spun in a dizzying whirl, all of them moving too quickly to grasp except for one: *If you don't provide me an heir, I must take another wife.* Her mind supplied the unspoken meaning: *If you don't provide me an heir, you must die so I can take another wife.*

She slid down beneath the surface of the water, submerging herself completely. The lather in her hair streamed out in frothy currents. She ran her fingers through the tangle of floating curls to rinse out the hair soap, then grabbed hold of the tub rim and stood. Water sluiced down in sheets, splashing into the tub in a dozen noisy streams. She scarcely noticed it.

"Well," she said again, turning to him and tipping back her head to meet his gaze. "As the begetting of an heir holds such dire import, I suggest we get to it."

His eyes narrowed, surprise warring with suspicion.

She lifted her arms and made her meaning more clear. "Help me from the bath." The motion lifted her breasts as well, and that caught his eye. His nostrils flared, quivering

slightly as he drew in her scent, then his gaze rose back
to her.

"Grown bold?"

"Bold, I've ever been," she corrected. "It's practical I
sometimes lack."

His hands reached out to clasp her waist, and he lifted
her high as he'd done before, over his head. Beads of water
dripped from her hair and breasts onto his face like a light
rain.

"Put me down. I'm getting you wet."

He grinned with unexpected humor. "Aye, you are, and
you'll get me wetter still before we're done, Summerlass."
The grin turned slow and lazy and full of simmering heat
that made her heart skip. He opened his mouth to catch a
falling drop of water, then he tilted his chin up and licked
the moisture directly from her breasts.

The sensation was indescribable. The chill of the air,
the hot rasp of his tongue, followed by a deeper, more
erotic chill as he blew cold across her mouth-warmed flesh,
making her nipples pucker tight. Then heat again as he
closed his mouth over her skin and drew the tight bud deep
into his mouth. Tongue and teeth and heat and cold worked
sensual magic on her skin until her entire body drew as
tight and aching as the breast he held claim in his mouth.

"Wrap your legs 'round my waist," he growled against
her damp skin, as his tongue drew a burning line from one
breast to the other.

Mindlessly, instinctively, she obeyed. Her legs hitched
up and locked around his waist, heels pressing through
the soft fur of his loincloth to the hard, rounded buttocks
beneath. Free of her weight, one of his hands splayed
against her back, the broad fingers spread wide, holding
her pressed against him. The other wandered lower, curving down the deep valley of her bottom to the petals of her
hottest flesh opened to him by the position of her legs. His
fingers curved up, skimming the slick moisture, stroking.

She gasped and arched her back, the motion thrusting

her breasts closer to his mouth. Her legs clenched tight around his waist. Enemy king or no, in this at least, she bowed to his conquest, and at the moment, it felt nothing like defeat.

She rode his hand, instinct making her thighs and buttocks clench and unclench, lifting and lowering her in an undulating rhythm that was as natural as the roll of clouds across the sky. Her heart beat faster. Her breath came in panting gasps. Heat rolled off her in waves. The tightness in her wound tighter and tighter until she thought the fire inside would burst from her skin like flames from wind-fed embers.

There was no arras in her veins, no Summerlea herb to heighten her sensations. This was pure, natural magic. Almost as powerful a force as weather magic. His north wind meeting her southern heat, the storm building in intensity. Against her closed eyelids, she could see the first white flashes, lightning gathering in black clouds.

His thumb was stroking the small, hard bead of flesh nestled in the folds of her sex. Her body wept from the pleasure of it.

"Wynter." His name was a gasp of air. "Husband!" An acknowledgment of his claim. A cry of both surrender and triumph. Her eyes flew open as the storm consumed her, battering her with shivering streaks of cold and heat. She shuddered and flew apart in his arms.

He held her firm, a rock in the tempest, steady and unwavering. His heavy muscles bunched tight beneath her clenched hands and shaking legs. He wasn't done. He'd fed the storm, let first the cloudburst pour out its strength against him, but even before she could catch her breath, he'd begun to feed the storm again.

She wasn't even aware of how or when he'd stripped his loincloth away. She only knew the moment that he pierced her core. He filled her, stretched her body wide, set her flesh afire from the inside out. His legendary strength held her fast, arms as broad and strong as the branches of the mighty oak, his legs the unyielding granite of the mountain crags. His mouth tracked lines of icy fire across her skin.

"Put your arms 'round my neck, *eldi-kona*." The growl skated across her sensitive flesh like a hand, leaving dancing sparks of lightning in its wake. "Hold tight."

She obeyed without conscious thought. Her arms wound up, around the powerful column of his neck, fingers clasping behind it.

His hands fell to her hips and held her fast, his grip firm yet surprisingly delicate. He could have easily bruised her, and she would hardly have noticed, but when this storm broke, and passion faded back into stillness, her body would bear nary a mark.

Then his hands gripped her tighter, lifted her up, and plunged her back down on his shaft, filling her utterly. Her eyes rolled back in near-fainting pleasure, and every last rational thought flew from her mind. There was no later, there was no before. There was only now. There was only this: the heat, the ice, the consuming, desperate need for more . . . more . . . his mouth, his hands, his tongue. His strength wrapped around her, holding her fast. His sex plunged so deep, she thought she might die. His teeth closed around one nipple, tugging with unbearable torment as he raised and lowered her on the thick column of his flesh again and again.

All the while her fingers dug deep into his shoulders. Her nails raked him. Her passion had far less care than his, more savagery. She was a child of the elements, a mage of storms. Rarely gentle. And never well behaved.

He endured it without flinching, and only growled deep in his throat when her nails broke the surface of his skin. The sound vibrated against her breast and drove her over the edge. Consciousness shattered. Electric threads of lightning shot from her fingertips and raced across his skin, into his veins. Her inner muscles clenched around his sex in wave after wave of powerful, shuddering ripples.

Wynter's back arched. His teeth tugged free of her breast as his head flung back on a shout of triumph and ecstasy.

Her musky, feminine scent swirled around him in heady waves, infusing his senses, driving him wild. His hips pumped with urgent, near-violent thrusts. Once. Twice. Inside her clenching heat, his flesh expanded. On the third driving thrust, he exploded. "Winter's Frost!" he cried, and his seed erupted into her dark heat with such force it was as if his own life were pouring from his body into hers.

Shaking, he dropped to his knees and bore her down to the furs. Her eyes, pure silver only now beginning to shift back to gray, stared up at him in dazed silence. He took her mouth in a brief, conquering kiss, then rolled away onto his back, his lungs heaving like bellows.

Khamsin lay on the furs beside him, shaken and trembling. Not even a whiff of arras had touched her senses, yet this coupling had been even more devastating and passionate than their fierce, herb-enhanced matings.

She drew air into her lungs, forcing herself to breathe deep and even, to gather her shattered wits and calm her racing heart. With effort, she lifted her hands, her arms. Her fingers dragged across the flat surface of her stomach and over her breasts. Still-tingling sparks of sensual energy followed in their wake. The muscles of her thighs and sex continued to tremble, but the earlier, more violent spasms had subsided.

She threw an arm over her eyes. The Rose burned at her wrist, as hot as an ember in her flesh, throbbing in time with her pounding heart. The smell of sex and Wynter washed over her, bringing with it a flood of completeness and a strange, exhausted satisfaction. Her eyes fluttered shut. Just for a moment, she told herself. No more than a minute or two.

How long she slept, she didn't know, but she woke to shadows and lamplight and the feeling of Wynter's hands playing across her body. Blue flame flickering in the depths of his eyes and the silvery whiteness of his hair slid across her skin like falls of snow.

If he possessed even a hint of modesty, he did not show it. He knelt before her naked and unashamed, and held her fast when she would have shied away from the lips that sought out the damp flesh between her legs. What he did with his mouth left her fainting, but even as her body folded, he drew her down upon him and set her afire once more. She'd heard her father's courtiers speculating that the Winter King would be a cold, dispassionate lover at best, but he proved them all wrong. As he had on their wedding night, he demonstrated with breathtaking, mind-shattering mastery that even ice could burn.

Four times more he came to her. Four times more, he drove her beyond reason, beyond thought. Four more times he rode her, his touch like lightning on the wind.

The fifth time, she came to him.

When she did, kneeling naked beside him and reaching out to run a curious finger down the resting length of flesh that now lay limp against his thigh, he gave a wry, weary grunt of laughter. "The mind is willing, *min ros*, but the body, I think, is done."

She glanced up at him, but his eyes were closed, and the small smile that played at the corners of his mouth made her butterflies take flight in her stomach. *Careful, Khamsin. He is the Winter King, not some summer lover. And not Roland either.* She had to guard herself. It would be all too easy with him to forget why she was here, forget that the pleasure he'd just poured out upon her like water from a fountain was but a means to an end.

Bear an heir within the year or face the deadly judgment of the mountains.

Even knowing that, and even knowing he would have shared this same shattering pleasure with whichever Summerlea princess he had wed, she couldn't keep away. For now, at least, he was hers. Besides, if this really was to be her last year of life, she might as well live it large. What had she to lose?

For the first time, she was free of the cage of her father's making, free of his rules and his demands for obedience. She would not willingly step into another. If the Winter King thought to control her, he would find caging the wind an easier task.

Her fingers curved around him, curious, testing. What had earlier been a long, rock-hard column of flesh, was slightly smaller now and soft to the touch. Beneath the flesh ran several long, thick blue veins. He was still damp and sticky from their last coupling, and that stickiness smelled pungent and musky, a mingling of her scent and his. The hair at his groin was thick and short, as silvery white as the hair on his head. Not wiry, and not curly as her own was, but straight and rather soft. Like a wolf's pelt, but not quite so densely furred. Beneath his penis, the large, twin globes of his testicles hung heavy in a sac of flesh.

She cupped them in her hand, scraped fingernail lightly on the underside. A muscle in his thigh leapt. His sex twitched, growing straighter and fuller, starting to rise.

"Does it hurt when it does that?" She'd heard her father's courtiers sometimes cursing the ache in their loins.

She knew the instant his eyes opened, felt the tingling energy of his gaze like sunlight on her skin. She glanced up and, sure enough, found him watching her from beneath the thick lashes of his half-shuttered eyes. "Only if you don't finish what you've started." His voice was a low growl again, and the deep, raspy sound of it sent shivers racing across her body.

"Ah. I'll be sure to finish, then." She turned her attention back to the intriguing mysteries of his sex. She stroked him, traced one long blue vein running the length of his shaft with the rounded edge of a nail, and smiled to herself when, despite his claims of exhaustion, his flesh strained upwards, as if rising to meet her hand. His body was a marvel. So different from her own, yet fascinating and beautiful in its own right.

She curled her fingers around him. The flesh that had only moments ago been soft and malleable was now a thick, rapidly hardening shaft. Her fingers spanned little more than halfway around the base.

She jumped a little when his hand stroked her bare bottom and slid between her heels to caress her inner thighs. One broad finger curved up, found her damp heat, and thrust up while a second finger slid up between her folds and began stroking the tiny nub of flesh that sent flares of electric heat shooting throughout her body. Her inner muscles clenched tight around him.

"Does it hurt when it does that?" he asked with a slow smile.

Her eyes fluttered down, and she swallowed thickly. "Only if you don't finish what you've started." His finger moved up and down inside her, a pale mimicry of what was to come but dizzying in its own right.

He shook his head slightly. "Nay, Summerlass," he denied. "This time *you* finish it."

"How?" She was willing. The ache was there and building. She wanted more than his finger inside her. Her hand clenched tighter around his shaft, moving up and down in a rhythm that instinctively matched his own strokes.

"Mount me. As you would a horse."

"I don't know how. I've never ridden a horse." Oh. She caught her lower lip between her teeth and shuddered on a delicious wave of pleasure. She felt her inner muscles ripple and clench around his finger. It was only the beginning. He'd already taught her to expect much more.

"Then today is a good day to start."

She gasped and nodded. Her eyes fluttered closed. "How?"

She bit back a cry of protest as his hands ceased their erotic magic and slid towards her waist. Damp fingers stroked her thigh. "Put this leg across me and kneel over my body."

She shifted her weight and rose on her knees. He helped her, lifting her by the waist as she flung a leg across his hips and straddled him. Cool air mixed with warm swirled across the hot, damp skin between her legs. The dark, earthy scent of sex wafted around her like a dizzying cloud of incense. She saw Wynter's nostrils flare as the wolf tasted the scent on the breeze. The hands at her waist slid down to her hips and squeezed briefly before sliding between their bodies.

"Now, fill yourself with me and ride." He guided his shaft to the entrance of her body and held it there while she impaled herself slowly on him. Inch by devastating inch, she took him, feeling the burning pull as her body stretched to accommodate him. He watched her with eyes of blue flame and his hands slid up her waist to cup the weight of her breasts in his palms and roll her nipples between his thumb and index finger.

Her body clenched. Her hips bucked.

"Gently, *eldi-kona*. Find your rhythm." His hips rose and fell, showing her the tempo.

She rode. Slowly at first, rocking against him, feeling the tug and burn where her flesh had stretched to accommodate him, then slowly increasing as she grew in confidence, and the heat coiled within her. He rose on his elbows to capture the tips of her bobbing breasts with his mouth. Teeth closed gently around one nipple and held fast, so that every time she rocked, she felt the tug at her breast like a spear of lightning shooting from chest to womb.

"Wynter." She speared her fingers into his hair and gripped his head. He would not let her end the torment. His tongue flicked out in teasing touches, flickering across the tight bead of her nipple in concert with each thrust of her hips.

Her hips rose and fell. The hard, wide shaft worked in and out of her body, in a slow, incinerating slide. "Wynter!" Heat coiled inside her, winding tight.

He grabbed her hips, broad fingers sank into soft flesh and gripped her tight. He lifted her hips and brought her down hard, forcing his body deeper inside her. Up. Down. Up. Down. Up. Slow, burning strokes, each one robbing her lungs of breath, each pulse making her heart race. Down. His own hips bucked up to greet her.

"*Wynter!*" Sensation exploded inside her, radiating out from her womb in jolting electric spikes. Sparks burst in a million dizzying flashes behind her closed eyes. Dimly, she felt the last, pounding thrusts of his hips. Her body exploded again, and she rode the waves of shattering senses into darkness.

When she woke again, sunlight was shining through the holes in the tent roof, and Wynter, fully dressed, was slipping on the last of his armor plate. The wolf's head helm gleamed white and silver in the hands of a young soldier whose battle-aged eyes didn't fit a face that couldn't have seen its first shave more than a year past.

She sat up in surprise and barely caught the covering pelt before it fell away. She was naked beneath the furs, her skin still tingling from the long hours of their coupling.

"This is Stoli." Wynter jerked a chin at the boy. "He'll ride beside you. If you need aught, let him know. Get dressed now. Your clothes are there." A woolen dress, fur-lined cloak, and warm boots had been draped across one of the camp chairs. "You have twenty minutes before my men take down this tent."

He spared a last look at her naked shoulders rising from the furs, long enough for her skin to heat beneath this gaze. Then his eyes shuttered, and she felt the deliberate, distant chill fall between them. What tenderness they'd shared was gone. He took his helm from the boy, ducked out of the tent, and was gone.

Stoli followed seconds later. He didn't look at her, but his bitterness was plain in the stiff, prideful line of his back. He didn't like playing nursemaid to a woman any more than she liked having some downy-faced boy-soldier assigned as her jailer.

Khamsin threw off the pelts and rose. Dizziness made her sway, and she stood still, eyes closed, hands to her head, until it passed. She would dress, and she would eat. She would be in enemy territory soon and would need all her strength and all her wits about her.

Someone had removed the copper bathing tub, but they'd replaced it with a bucket of still-warm, jasmine-scented water, a bar of sweet soap, and a fresh cloth. It had to have been Wynter who'd ordered it, but such thoughtfulness in light of his coolness just now left her puzzled, unsure what to make of him. Was he the enemy king she'd wed or the caring husband seeing to his wife's comfort?

Both, she decided. *Use the care to your advantage, Khamsin, but never lose sight of the enemy.*

She dipped the cloth and soap in the water and hastily bathed as best she could. He'd told her she had twenty minutes, and didn't doubt his men would start pulling up the tent stakes the second that time was up.

Laid across the camp chair beneath the woolen gown was a full white chemise of soft cotton. She tugged it on over her head, and let the billows of fabric drape her still-damp body from neck to toe and shoulder to wrist. Soft, blue lamb's wool skirts followed, then a separate, form-fitting bodice that fastened up the front with two rows of gleaming gold buttons, each bearing the raised stamp of a rose in bloom. The outfit had been Summer's. Khamsin had never owned a gown so fine except for what came from her sisters' wardrobes when the Summer King wasn't looking. The boots were soft kid, with a small, stacked heel, the cloak velvet-lined gray wool, trimmed with the plush, soft fur of a snow lynx around the generous hood. A matching fur muff dangled on a string from one of the cloak's buttons.

She fastened up her boots, ran a brush through her wild curls. She had just picked up the cloak when a youthful voice called coolly, "It's time, my lady."

That brief call was the only warning she received before the tent flaps parted, and Stoli poked his head through.

"Good," he said. "You are ready. The king says you must

eat before we leave. Bjork, the king's cook, has prepared a plate for you. Follow me." He ducked back out before she could answer.

Scowling a little over the boy's high-handedness, she flung her cape over her shoulders and followed him outside. With the exception of Wynter's tent, which a dozen men were already swiftly disassembling, the trampled snow of what had been the army's encampment was barren, smoky tendrils of mist rising up from snow-doused cook fires. Less than a tenth of the original force had remained behind, and they were already packed and waiting on the road, ready to march. The cook wagon was packed also, save a single plate of bread, cheese, and *borgan* and a cup of steaming broth which a large, scarred Winterman who introduced himself as Bjork handed to her.

She thanked him and ate quickly, aware of all the eyes upon her. By the time she was finished, Wynter's tent had been disassembled and loaded for travel, and Stoli returned to escort her to the waiting carriage.

Just the sight of the four-wheeled torture chamber stopped her in her tracks. The meal she'd just consumed churned in her belly.

"Hurry, please, my lady," Stoli urged impatiently. "The day's already half-gone."

Kham swallowed the sick queasy knot in her throat. If she knew how to ride a horse, she would have asked for one. Nodding, she gathered her skirts. *You can bear it, Khamsin. You can bear anything if you put your mind to it. Just open the windows.*

The air of stale perfume and sickness still clung to the velvet-lined interior. She opened the window, turned her face towards the fresh outside air, and breathed through her mouth, praying the gods would be merciful and spare her the travel sickness this time. But with the first lurching jolt of the carriage, she knew no mercy was in the offing.

Khamsin threw open the door on the far side and leapt

to the ground. Her boots sank knee deep in snow, and the dark blue of her skirts and yards of cloak billowed out around her. She stumbled, slapped a hand on an icy tree trunk to steady herself, and took off running for the privacy of the forest.

Shouts rose up behind her, followed by the clatter of horse hooves pounding frozen ground, but she ignored them and plunged into the snow-covered shadows of the trees. She ran until she could no longer see the road or the Wintermen, and then fell to her knees and emptied her stomach into the snow.

When the nausea passed, she staggered back and fell against the trunk of an aged oak tree, sliding down the rough, broad trunk until she was sitting on the ground. She scrubbed her face with fistfuls of clean, cold snow and dragged breaths of cold air into her lungs.

That was how Wynter found her. Her wild, white-streaked curls tangled about her shoulders, snowflakes glittering in the dark of her lashes and skin, her breathing shallow and skin wan. She glanced up at the sound of Hodri's belled bridle, then closed her eyes wearily and let her head loll back against the trunk of the tree.

The acrid scent of sickness curled on the winter wind, and the tension that had gripped Wynter's chest in icy claws began to fade. She'd not been fleeing him. She'd only been seeking privacy to hide her weakness, as all wild things did.

He drew a breath, released it slowly. His fury went with it on a long, chill exhale.

He'd seen her leap from the carriage and race for the cover of the trees, and all he'd been able to think was that she was trying to escape, that she'd sworn to honor her vows and betrayed them at first chance. His fury at the prospect was surprisingly strong and violent. He didn't know why. He'd been expecting deceit from the moment he'd ridden into Vera Sola, and she'd already been party to one lie.

He swung his leg over Hodri's hindquarters and dismounted. The snow came halfway up his calves as he walked to her side.

"I can't go back in that carriage," she said, her eyes still closed. "I just can't."

"No," he agreed. "I can see that."

"If I could ride, I'd ask for a horse."

"If you could ride, I'd give you one." He reached down to take her hand and pulled her to her feet. "Come. Hodri's strong enough to bear the both of us. You'll ride with me."

She gave him such a startled, hopeful look he almost smiled.

"It's no favor," he assured her. "We'll ride hard, and we won't stop often. And you won't find the front of my saddle the kindest seat."

"I won't complain." She wouldn't. Even if the saddle bruised her so badly she could barely walk, she wouldn't make a peep.

He led her back to Hodri, mounted first, then leaned over to grasp her hand and lift her into the saddle before him. Together, they rode back to the rest of the men, and after a brief hour's rest, they were back in the saddle and once more heading north at a punishing pace. Wynter, with Khamsin seated before him, rode in the lead.

It wasn't comfortable. He'd spoken the truth about that. The saddle was crowded, his armor plate against her back was hard as granite, but she didn't care. Anything was better than the closed, miasmic imprisonment of that carriage.

She leaned her head against Wynter's armored chest, tilted her chin into the wind, and smiled for the first time in days.

They rode for eight days. The pace was grueling, the saddle unforgiving, but Khamsin kept her vow not to complain. Despite his outward coldness, Wynter did everything he could to make her comfortable.

The first day of riding sideways across the saddle left her thighs and buttocks black-and-blue from bouncing, and when they stopped for the night, Khamsin remained standing during dinner and barely managed to hobble the short distance to Wynter's tent. He made her lift her skirts to show him the damage. He let out what sounded like a stream of muttered curses in his language, rubbed a healing liniment into her abused posterior, and slept curled tight around her throughout the night. She woke the next morning to find that someone had slit the skirt and the bottom half of her chemise and sewn them back together into wide, loose-fitting trousers. Wynter wouldn't tell her who had done it; he just told her gruffly to put them on and be silent. She rode astride after that.

He drew back the clouds to help her body's sun-fed healing powers regenerate more quickly, and despite the snow on the ground, the warming air and her own hot Summerlea blood soon had her throwing off her cloak. The crisp, cool wind on her face was refreshing, and she loved the free, unfettered feel of it. Even if her hair did keep getting blown into the joints of Wynter's plate mail and ripping out by the roots.

The third morning, ignoring the fierce objections of his men and Valik, in particular, Wynter left off his armor. He claimed it was easier on Hodri—that the armor weighed more than Khamsin, and without it, Hodri would not feel the added burden of a second rider. That made a certain sense, and Khamsin would have believed him without question had she not overheard Valik hissing at Wynter after breakfast that his soft-hearted foolishness was going to get him bloody killed.

"We may have crossed the Rill, but we're nowhere near out of danger. One arrow in your unprotected back is all it takes, Wyn! Put your damned armor back on, and don't give me that blather about weights and double riders! I saw you plucking her hair from your mail last night and scowling like you'd torn it from her scalp with your own two hands. Your mail could rub her skin bloody, and I'd still tell you to wear it."

But he didn't, and from that day on, Khamsin rode snuggled close against Wynter's body, without the wall of cold steel between them. When they made camp, he came to their tent after dinner, rubbed healing liniment on her thighs and buttocks, then curled his body around hers with exquisite care. She slept each night spooned against his large, muscled form, and woke each morn to the dizzying sensation of hard, erect flesh sliding into her body while his hands stroked her breasts and teased the bud of flesh between her legs until she cried out and shattered with pleasure.

On the eighth day, Khamsin caught sight of silvery white shapes darting amongst the trees on either side. Wolves.

"They give escort," Wynter murmured against her ear. "It's not much farther now. We'll reach the Craig by tomorrow midday."

"The Craig? But . . . aren't we already there? We crossed the river days ago." And much to her surprise, the snow that had blanketed Summerlea for the past three years was conspicuously absent on the Wintercraig side of the river. Instead, the land was in full, brilliant autumn bloom, and the only snow she'd seen yet was gathered on the very tops of the mountains.

She felt his smile. "The kingdom of Wintercraig starts at the Rill, it's true; but ask any Winterman, and he'll tell you, these are the Hills. That"—he pointed—"is the Craig."

Khamsin's breath caught in her throat. They'd crested the summit of a small mountain pass, and the trees broke enough to offer up a dazzling view of a wide, forested valley, filled with vibrant autumn color and towering evergreens. In the distance, great, jagged, snow-covered peaks rose up from the ground like ancient walls of stone and ice, filling the horizon as far as her eyes could see.

CHAPTER 10

Wintercraig

Once more clad in full armor that shone dazzling silver and white, with ice blue banners streaming in the mountain breeze, Wynter and his men rode slowly up the winding stone road toward the towering castle perched high atop a steep granite cliff.

Riding sideways before him, draped in another of Autumn's warmest gowns, Khamsin stared up the breathtaking heights and the magical, ice-silvered spires, parapets, and buttresses of the castle that seemed to grow from the very rock itself.

Gildenheim, crown of the world.

Wynter's palace. Her new home.

She turned her head to look at Wynter, wanting to see his face as they drew near the summit. The wolf's head visor was open, but even so, his face was a mask that yielded no secrets. He kept his eyes forward, his face expressionless.

As they rounded the last switchback curve and rode the final stretch of stone road that passed beneath Gildenheim's massive iron gates, Wynter straightened in the saddle, putting a small but notable distance between them. The arm that curved around her waist pulled back and went stiff as an iron pike.

The courtyard was wide and filled with people, with more lining three deep along every stone stairway, parapet and crenellated walk. Soldiers in armor of leather and steel.

Peasants bulky in furs and wool. And on the wide, sprawling palace steps, a host of cool-eyed nobles stood waiting, their regal Winterfolk height draped in fur-trimmed velvets, fine wools, and silk brocades in all the frosted shades of winter: ice blue, cream, white, cloud gray, snow-frosted evergreen, palest taupe.

The peasants and soldiers cheered as Wynter and his army rode past, but the nobles remained aloofly silent. Khamsin regarded them in silence. Tension twisted in her belly. There was not one dark head among them, nor one welcoming smile. Cold and haughty, as icy as she'd first thought Wynter to be, they watched her in silence, spearing her with their unblinking gazes. Never had she felt more alien or more unwelcome.

An older man standing near the bottom step broke away from the crowd of nobles and walked towards Wynter's approaching horse. His white hair was cropped to his chin and swinging with thin braids hung with small silver bells. His eyes were sky blue in a deeply lined golden face, his robes a paler blue, trimmed generously with white fur.

"Welcome home, Your Grace," he said in a voice rough with age. Gnarled hands reached out hooked around the straps of Hodri's belled bridle. "Welcome home, at last."

"Thank you, Barsul. It's good to be back." Wynter looked around the courtyard, his gaze sliding over each and every face crowded around. "This sight is one I've dreamed of now for three long years." He raised his voice so that it traveled easily from one end of the courtyard to the other. "Well met, my friends, my people. At last the war is over." Cheers rose up from all around the walls. He waited for them to die down before he continued. "I bring you victory." More cheers. "I bring you peace." At that, the women shouted with such enthusiasm they all but drowned out the cheers of their men. "I bring you Khamsin Coruscate, princess of Summerlea." He grasped the hood of Khamsin's cloak and drew it back to bare her bronzed face and dark flowing curls, then grasped her wrist and lifted it high, brandishing the Rose. "Now Khamsin Atrialan, Queen of the Craig, and soon, Freika willing, mother of my heirs."

The cheers that followed that outdid all the others, but the eyes of those cheering watched Khamsin without warmth. She knew they did not cheer in welcome of her but rather to celebrate that their king had returned to them, this time vowing his desire for life instead of death. The courtyard erupted in a shower of white and green, as the Winterfolk tossed snowflowers, garlands of twined ivy and holly leaves, sprigs of fragrant fir, and clusters of mistletoe and partridge berry. Symbols of peace and unity and fertility and life. Well wishes for their king and his future heirs.

Wynter dismounted and reached up to help Khamsin down from the saddle before introducing her to the man who had greeted them.

"Khamsin, this is Barsul Firkin, Lord Chancellor of Wintercraig, who served as White Sword during my father's reign."

The old man bowed, his eyes cool and assessing. "Welcome to Wintercraig, Your Grace."

"Lord Chancellor Firkin." Khamsin worked to keep a calm expression as she frantically raked her memory for the protocol to follow when being introduced to high-ranking dignitaries of foreign lands. Was she supposed to extend her hand? Lord Firkin looked surprised when she did, but after a brief hesitation, he lifted it to his lips and brushed a cool, dry kiss across the backs of her fingers.

Wynter removed his gauntlets and splayed one hand across the small of Khamsin's back. Subtle pressure nudged her forward, past Lord Firkin to another, slightly younger man. "And this is Lord Deervyn Fjall, Steward of the Keep."

"Welcome to Gildenheim, the jewel of Wintercraig, Your Grace," Lord Fjall murmured.

"Lord Fjall oversees everything that pertains to the provisioning, protection, and operations of the castle," Wynter said. "If you need anything, his office will handle your request."

Khamsin nodded but didn't offer her hand again.

They moved past Lord Fjall to a towering, ice-eyed woman, whose pale gold hair looked like yards of stiff, curling ribbons piled atop her head. Unlike the wools and velvets of so many others, her gown was a severely cut sheath of pristine white brocade, her cloak an impressive fall of pure white snowbear pelt that draped from shoulder to floor, with yards of the thick fur left to puddle at her feet. Her eyes were so pale a blue, they seemed almost colorless, and Khamsin stifled a shiver.

"Lady Galacia Frey, High Priestess of Wyrn."

Wyrn. Quickly, Khamsin riffled through her small store of knowledge about the northern gods. Wyrn was Keeper of the Ice, the goddess who'd given Thorgyll his freezing spears. Khamsin had never been much of a reader of god lore—except as it pertained to the heroes and warrior-kings of Summerlea—but she knew enough to know that Wyrn was an important and powerful goddess who was supposedly responsible for bringing winter to the world.

Well, if Wyrn were anything like her priestess, Khamsin already didn't like her much. She definitely didn't like the critical way Lady Galacia's eyes swept over her, then turned to Wynter, dismissing Khamsin out of hand.

"We are glad for your return, my king," the priestess said. "Wyrn requests your presence at her altar."

The hand at Khamsin's back twitched ever so slightly. "I will come today, before nightfall," Wynter agreed.

Lady Galacia's tower of frozen curls inclined in a cool nod. "We will await you." She turned once more to Khamsin. "You and I will visit later, at a time of Wyrn's choosing. When that time comes, Lord Fjall will tell you the way."

Khamsin's spine stiffened. *Oh, really?* But before she had a chance to open her mouth, Wynter's hand was firmly nudging her forward.

The next woman in line was a blond-haired beauty with piles of soft ringlets and limpid blue eyes. She clutched Wynter's hands with a fervor that made Kham's eyes narrow. Wynter introduced her as Reika Villani, Valik's cousin. Kham disliked her on sight. There was something about her that reminded Kham of the women who scrabbled to be King Verdan's next mistress in the Summer court.

They continued on down the line. Wynter introduced dozens of people, far too many for Khamsin to keep them straight. The gathered nobles became a blur of golden skin and hair that came in all shades of pale, from golden blond to silver to snowy white. Finally, the introductions ended, and she and Wynter walked up the wide, stone stairs into the palace halls.

If she'd expected Wynter's palace to be cold and austere, nothing could have been further from the truth. The walls were pure granite, but what should have seemed heavy and overpowering had instead been carved with astonishing delicacy. Graceful, curving archways and fluted columns soared high towards a vaulted ceiling. A massive crystal chandelier hung high overhead. All around, adorned with shimmering falls of cut crystal and gleaming patterned streams of silver and gold metals in varying shades, the walls seemed to glow with prismatic hues. Scattered clusters of furniture, upholstered in sumptuous velvets and brocades, added a rich, approachable welcome, and twin silver-gilt stairways, curving like slides of ice, spiraled up to numerous balconied levels overhead.

Khamsin caught herself gaping and had to consciously press her lips together to keep her jaw from falling slack again.

Servants in pale taupe and frosted forest green stood waiting at the base of the curved stairways. An older woman with a white apron pinned to the front of her forest green gown and her white hair caught up in a plait that wound around the top of her head like a crown stood at the head of the assemblage.

"This is Vinca, Gildenheim's Mistress of Servants," Wynter said. "She'll show you to your rooms."

"Welcome to Wintercraig, Your Grace," Vinca murmured as she offered a brief, respectful curtsy. "This way, please." She turned, indicating the curving staircase to her left.

Khamsin glanced uncertainly at Wynter, but he was already striding away towards a waiting cluster of noblemen. She wanted to call out, to ask him where he was going and when she would see him again.

She opened her mouth to call to him, then realized almost Wynter's entire court was watching her, their eyes cool and sly. No doubt they were waiting with bated amusement to see what the little Summerlander witch would do now that her husband had brought her to his palace and abandoned her practically on the doorstep. The hand that had started to reach out for Wynter dropped back to her side and clutched the folds of her gown in a tight grip. Without a word, she turned and followed Mistress Vinca up the stairs.

Being ignored and shuttled off out of view is nothing new to you, Khamsin, she reminded herself sternly. *You've had a lifetime of it. Why is this any different?*

It wasn't. And yet . . . it was.

Since waking in the tent after that horrific storm, she'd hardly left Wynter's side—and he, hers. They'd slept together, ridden together, taken their meals together, woken up in each other's arms.

Oh, Kham, no. You haven't gone and gotten feelings *for him? He's the enemy!*

No, no, not that. Not . . . *feelings.* She knew what he was, and what he would do to her if she didn't bear him the heir he sought. She hadn't forgotten. It was just that . . . well . . . they'd established a sort of rapport between them. They'd become almost friends, in a way.

Friends?

All right. Not friends, exactly.

Not friends of any kind. He is the enemy king who just crushed your country beneath his heel, and you are his war prize. Your only value to him is your womb. You can't afford to forget that. Fail to bear him an heir, and he'll slay you as thoughtlessly as he slew all those thousands of your countrymen.

She knew that. She hadn't forgotten it. How could she?

You're living on borrowed time, and if you let yourself get stupid and sentimental, you'll never survive this. So stop thinking like a girl and start thinking like a man. No, start thinking like a warrior-king. You're all alone in the heart of enemy territory. There's no way to get back home. What should you do? What would Roland do?

Good question. What *would* Roland do if he were trapped alone in enemy territory with no way back home and a lethal deadline hanging over his head? Khamsin's spine straightened. Her chin rose a notch higher. Roland would settle in, establish a home base, familiarize himself with the terrain and its inhabitants. He would befriend every enemy and absorb every bit of knowledge that would help him—if not to conquer, at least to survive.

They'd reached the top of the long staircase and turned left down the balustraded walk that overlooked the entry hall. The people downstairs had started to drift away, but a number of the Winterfolk still remained, and Khamsin was conscious of their watchful eyes upon her.

Let them look. She was Khamsin Coruscate Atrialan, Summerlea princess, and the Winter King's wife. But she was also Khamsin, Bringer of Storms. She was not some helpless victim. She was a daughter of the Rose, Heir to the Summer Throne. Just as Roland had met the enemy and triumphed, so too would she.

Her first order of business would be learning her way around the palace. At Vera Sola, she'd known every nook and cranny of the palace, every hidden and forbidden inch. And that had given her a certain sense of power, of freedom, even sequestered as she was from the rest of the world. The floundering sense of alienness assailing her now couldn't be borne. She would learn the passageways of Gildenheim until she could walk them with her eyes closed. She would discover the palace's secrets and make them her own.

She made careful note of each turn Vinca made as they walked through the palace halls. At the end of the walkway, they turned right through an archway and followed that short, wide hall to a round, open gathering area that linked five corridors. The first corridor on the left led to a long wing that doubled back towards the front of the palace and split into two angled hallways, each terminated by a spacious, skylit vestibule surrounded by several pairs of gilded doors. Vinca took the right fork and approached the large center doors, which were painted silver-blue and chased with platinum bands. Two footmen stood guard outside those doors, and as Khamsin and Vinca drew near, the footmen reached for the crystal doorknobs and swung the doors inward in a smooth silence.

"Here we are, Your Grace," Vinca announced. "These are your chambers."

Khamsin stepped inside and despite her stern admonitions to think like a man and a warrior-king, she couldn't help catching her breath in a dazzled, purely feminine reaction to the spacious elegance spread out before her. Thick furs and brightly woven carpets were scattered liberally across gleaming wooden floors. Furniture of delicate, gilded metalwork and stone sat harmoniously alongside bureaus of rich, inlaid woods and groupings of armchairs and divans. Silk brocade drapes framed a wall of windows that opened to a wide balcony.

A blur of dark, rich color in the sea of glittering winter shades caught her stunned gaze, and she turned towards it and saw Bella.

"Bella!" she exclaimed eagerly. Though the girl was little more than a stranger assigned to serve her, she was from Summerlea, a face from home. They were foreigners together in this cold, icy land, and that forged a unique bond between them. Khamsin almost flung her arms around the little maid before she caught herself. She stifled the urge to give Bella an exuberant hug and settled for a more appropriate, but fervent, clasp of hands. "I'm glad to see you."

"Not half so glad as I am to see you, Your Highness," Bella said. "They made me leave and wouldn't let me go back. I didn't even know if you'd lived or died until yesterday, when the scouts rode in to say the Winter King was coming."

"It's all right, Bella." She patted the maid's hand. "As you can see, I'm perfectly fit."

"Ahem." The slight clearing of Vinca's throat made Khamsin turn. "Your bedroom, Your Grace, is through those doors on the left, as is a private parlor, bath, and dressing room." The Mistress of Servants strode towards the wall of windows and threw open the leaded-glass doors to let in a swirl of crisp air. "From here, you have an excellent view of the mountains, Gildenheim's western gardens, and the river valley. The king has ordered Mistress Narsk to provide your new wardrobe more suited to our climate."

"I don't need new clothes. The ones I have are perfectly fine." The perfumes of her sisters still clung to their gowns. Kham didn't want to lose that attachment to home.

"You'll need something more suited to our weather, ma'am. Winter will soon be upon us, and you'll need much warmer clothes. King's orders."

"I see. Well, then it seems I will be expanding my wardrobe." Kham gave a tight smile. She had no intention of giving up her sisters' things any more than she'd been willing to abandon her mother's things without a fight. This Mistress Narsk could make all the clothes she liked, but that didn't mean Kham had to wear them. Except for outer garments and perhaps a few underclothes more suited to this icy clime, Kham was not going to change who she was or how she dressed.

"Very good, ma'am. Mistress Narsk and her seamstresses will be here at twelve to take your measurements. I'll have a small lunch brought up. Meanwhile, if you need anything, just give this cord a tug. It will ring down to the servants' quarters, and someone will answer your summons."

"Thank you, Vinca."

The woman curtsied. "I'll leave you to get settled."

"Vinca?"

The Mistress of Servants paused. "Ma'am?"

"Who will be giving me a tour of the palace, and when can I expect them?"

Surprise flashed briefly across Vinca's face before being suppressed behind a calm mask. "The arrangements have not yet been made."

"Make them, please," Khamsin said. "For tomorrow, if at all possible. I don't want to feel like a stranger in my new home." Her voice was firm, her gaze steady.

Vinca bobbed another curtsy. "Of course, Your Grace. I'll see to it immediately."

When she left, Bella made a beeline for the open balcony doors and started to pull them closed. "Winterfolk!" she grumbled. "Opening windows every chance they get, even when the air's cold enough to freeze the blood in a body's veins."

"No, Bella, leave it for now. I've gotten used to the fresh air."

Bella stopped, looked a little outraged, then tugged her cloak more snugly about her throat and moved away from the open doors.

Only then did Khamsin realize the girl was wrapped in so many layers she resembled a stuffed Harvest goose. Kham had been so glad to see a familiar face, she hadn't noticed anything else. "I'm sorry. Are you cold? Close the doors then, and fuel the fire."

She watched Bella add logs to the already-burning fire in the hearth, then hold her hands to the heat emanating from the flames and huddle close.

"Does it feel very cold to you?" Khamsin asked. "Outside, I mean."

"As a frost witch's teat," Bella muttered.

Now that was surpassingly strange. Khamsin suddenly realized she hadn't felt the cold in days. Not really. Not since waking in Wynter's tent after her illness. She'd put it down to her Summerlea blood, but Bella was a Summerlander, too, and she was obviously suffering. Was it her magic, then? The heat of her weathergifts?

Curious, she cracked open the leaded-glass door and stepped out onto the balcony. A cold wind caught her full in the face and tore the pins from her hair, sending curls spiraling madly about. She knew it was cold. She could feel the chill on her skin, see it in the frosty mist of her exhale before the wind whipped it away, but it wasn't unbearable. Bracing, yes, but no more than that. Nothing like the cold that had penetrated her bones that day when Wynter had caught her with his Ice Gaze. What did that mean? Assuming it meant anything at all.

Before the war, when the relations between Summerlea and Wintercraig were still congenial, her brother, Falcon, and his friends had often roamed the hills and valleys of Wintercraig—hunting snowbear in the mountains. Khamsin couldn't recall if he'd ever complained about the cold. He'd talked about the snow, the piles of white drifts, high as a man. He'd talked about icicles hanging like crystals from the trees and waterfalls frozen in midplummet. He'd talked about the stark, serene, snow-spangled beauty and the way snow splashed like seafoam around his horse's legs as he rode. She'd drunk the glorious stories of his adventures as eagerly as she'd absorbed the words on the pages of the books she so loved, and if he'd mentioned any unpleasantness, she'd long since forgotten it.

Falcon. Just thinking of him brought a storm of fond memories and bittersweet emotions. Beloved brother. Handsome warrior-prince. Daring adventurer. Charming rogue. How she'd loved him. How she'd missed him.

She'd never understood what madness had led him to throw away his life and toss two kingdoms into turmoil. Tildy's revelation about the Book of Riddles and Falcon's quest to find the sword of Roland had cleared up a good deal of the confusion, but that didn't explain why he'd compounded his crime by running off with another man's bride—a king's bride, no less.

Now, after experiencing the consuming pleasure of Wynter's passion, she had a better understanding of what might have driven her brother on that front.

Where was Falcon? she wondered, staring out over the land where he'd decided to doom them all. Had he found Roland's sword, after all, or had the Book of Riddles merely led him on a fruitless chase after an imaginary treasure? Did he and his Winterlady even know what a terrible price others had paid for their reckless passion and thievery? Did either of them even care?

"He's in Calberna." Lord Chancellor Firkin's gnarled finger tapped a spot on the map laid out before Wynter and drew back quickly at the first telling flash of white in his king's eyes.

Wynter stared hard at the blue-shaded outline of a sprawling chain of islands in the western sea. The familiar, cold bite of vengeance sent streamers of ice racing through his veins, radiating out from his chest. Had the map been a man, it would have frozen dead on the spot. As it was, a fine layer of frost crystallized on the inked parchment, blurring the cartographer's meticulously drawn boundaries and notations. "With her?"

"Yes."

"Do you think they found what they were looking for?"

"It's possible. The prince has been haunting the courts of the West, trying to raise an army he could lead back to Summerlea."

"Has he found one in Calberna?"

"We suspect so. Our Calbernan eyes have gone blind. Four of our informants went missing, the rest have grown too fearful to talk, and three of our couriers were slain, their dispatches stolen."

"Post lookouts along the coast." Wynter ran a finger down the line of Summerlea's western coast. A trail of frost sprouted up in its wake. "Send word to Leirik in Vera Sola. I want Verdan's guard doubled. And send more men to Calberna, to replace those we lost. If Coruscate has found an ally, I want to know it before an army sets sail."

"I'll take word to Vera Sola myself," Valik declared. "If the Calbernans are sending an army, I should be the one to command the battalions in Summerlea."

"No!" Wynter shot a fierce glare at his friend. "You're not going to Vera Sola. I've already told you that."

"But Leirik—"

"You've trained Leirik well. It's his command. Yours is the defense of Wintercraig." He shot a hard, commanding look at Chancellor Firkin. "You've heard my orders. Carry them out."

"It shall be done, Your Grace." Firkin bowed and whispered instructions to two of the noblemen who served him. They each snapped a bow and hurried away. Firkin waved impatient hands at the rest of the council in a silent command to clear the room. When they were gone, he closed the door and approached the hearth.

"Wynter, lad," he said with the affectionate familiarity of an old family friend, "it's good to have you back. You've been away too long." He clapped a hand on Wynter's armored shoulder. "You should get out of this armor. Relax and shed the weight of war. Visit the hot springs of Mount Freika. Run with the wolves. Take your new bride for a ride." He wagged his brows. "Or, better yet, just ride her instead. Start working on that heir you've promised us."

Valik's expression turned sour. "No worries there, Barsul. Believe me, if she doesn't pup in nine months, it won't be for any lack of effort on Wyn's part. He's so besotted, I'm starting to think she's cast some sort of love spell on him." His voice was flat, devoid of any teasing note. Ever since Khamsin had summoned that deadly storm—nearly driving Wynter into the Ice King's grip and miraculously healing herself in the process—Valik had been growing increasingly concerned over what he called Wynter's "obsession" with his new bride. He was convinced there was some sort of subversive Summerlander magic at work.

"Enough, Valik," Wynter growled. To Lord Firkin, he said, "If Calberna has offered Coruscate an army, there's much work to be done to ready Wintercraig defenses. But I see your point," he added when Firkin started to object. "I'll make time for gentler things."

He stayed there with Valik and Firkin for more than an hour, talking not about war but about the Craig, the changes that had happened since he'd left three years ago, the small, personal things Barsul hadn't put to ink during their years of correspondence, and more. Three men had been sent last month to face the mercy of the mountains: two rapists and a child-killer. All had perished in the ice and snow. It was unusual to have so many such crimes in a single month.

Wynter had known one of the men. He'd been a rough sort of Winterman, but Wyn had never considered him brutal enough to ram a fist into his own son's head with enough force to slay him.

"Things are starting to change, Wynter," Lord Firkin said, "and not for the better."

"Is it the Ice Heart, do you think?" he asked. "Has the power grown so strong in me that it can now feed on others?"

"That's a question for Lady Frey."

"Then I suppose I should go get cleaned up and pay her a visit." Wynter took leave of Valik and Firkin and headed up to his rooms. His valet helped him shed his armor and ran a hot bath so he could wash off the stink of travel. Lady Frey objected to the presence of unwashed men in the goddess's temple.

As he pulled on clean clothes, his hand absently rubbed his chest, and he thought about the men who'd met their fate on the mountain. Was he to blame for the madness that had gripped them? He couldn't shake the possibility. His chest still felt cold and tight after freezing that map in the council room.

Valik was right to suspect Kham's Summerlander magic was affecting Wyn, but not in the way he thought. Ever since the night of Khamsin's terrible storm, Wyn had spent most of his time in her company, and he'd realized he felt more human and more at peace than he had in years. He'd hoped that meant the Ice Heart was melting, but today, within minutes of leaving her on the steps of the palace, he'd felt himself growing colder, more impatient, angrier. That brief flash of icy fury that froze the map wasn't dissipating as quickly as it had in the past. And that did not bode well. Not for him, and not for any Winterman.

In fact, the only time he wasn't aware of the cold in his chest was when he wrapped himself in Khamsin's heat.

The front of Wynter's breeches went tight, and he swore softly under his breath. This part of Wynter's obsession, Valik had gotten right. All Wyn had to do was think about the little weatherwitch, and he grew hard as stone. That didn't bode well for him either. She was a Summerlander, sister to Wynter's bitterest enemy, that bride-stealing, child-killer, Falcon. They'd wed not out of affection but political expediency. He knew where her loyalties lay, and it wasn't with him. If he was foolish enough to let himself care for her, she would use his affection, as Elka had, to betray him.

No, so long as that Rose burned on her wrist, she was someone he could never trust enough to love. She was a womb to bear his child. Attachment to her, need—even if only sexual—was dangerous.

And yet, even knowing how vital it was to keep an emotional distance between them, he found himself opening the door that joined his rooms to hers and walking through it.

She wasn't there. He knew it as soon as he entered. Her scent was slightly faded rather than fresh, and there was a certain dull emptiness to the air that would have been charged with energy had she been present.

Her clothes now hung in the dressing room. All her plants and potted trees had been arranged around the upholstered sofa in the reading alcove. Delicate crystal flacons of perfume were displayed neatly on the stone top of her vanity. Wynter made a mental note to return the book and jeweled toiletry set he'd taken from her back in Vera Sola, and to have several of the growing lamps delivered to her rooms to keep her blasted remembrance garden alive.

He wandered from her bedroom into her large receiving parlor. Here, her scent was strongest. She'd stood there, by that couch. He crossed to it and breathed deep. Yes, here. Other women had been with her, half a dozen of them, but hers was a scent easily separated from the rest. So different from her sister Autumn's. How had he ever been fooled before? Hers was a scent so distinct, he would recognize it anywhere now, no matter how diluted.

The cape she'd worn this morning lay draped across the chaise. He bent to pick it up and pressed it against his face. It smelled of her. The jasmine she'd used to wash her hair, and the bold, electric freshness that reminded him of the mountains after a powerful spring storm.

He wanted to close his eyes and rub his face in the gathered cloth, marking himself with her scent, marking her cloak with his. Instead, he forced his fingers open and let the fabric spill to the floor.

"Your Majesty? May I help you?"

Wynter turned swiftly. *Foolish, Wyn! Very foolish!* No one had been able to sneak up on him in years, but he'd been so preoccupied, he hadn't sensed the little Summerlander maid's approach.

"Where is your mistress?"

"In the west gardens, my lord. She said she needed fresh air after Mistress Narsk and the seamstresses left."

Wynter walked to the balcony windows and looked out. Sure enough, several stories down to the west, he found his wife traversing the walks of the terraced western gardens. She'd donned one of her fur-lined Summerlander cloaks, but her head was bare, her distinctive dark hair easy to spot even at a distance.

The moment he clapped eyes on her, he felt the tug in his chest. The yearning to go to her, walk with her, bask in her fiery warmth.

Before he could act on that yearning, logic prevailed. Distance. He must at all costs keep a wise distance. Besides, she needed time to settle in, and he had more pressing matters to attend to.

Resolute, he turned and headed back to his own rooms.

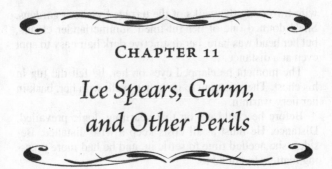

CHAPTER 11

Ice Spears, Garm, and Other Perils

The Temple of Wyrn was built in a cave on the southern face of Mount Vetr. A long, narrow stone road led from Gildenheim's eastern gate, across a bridge to the neighboring peak, and up to the mouth of the cave. Within, the cave's walls and ceiling were coated with ice, and a long promenade led to the wide, rounded main chamber of the temple. There, an altar carved from a block of ice dominated the room, and in the center of the altar sat a chalice of diamond- and sapphire-encrusted platinum, in which burned a cold blue flame that emitted no heat. Crossed ice spears hung on the wall behind the altar, beneath the carved ice mask of the goddess Wyrn.

The last time Wynter had entered this temple, he'd stripped down to his skin and taken the narrow passage to the left of the altar, traveling through a deadly, magical gauntlet littered with the frozen bodies of men who had tried—and failed—the same gauntlet before him. He had survived the tests and made his way to the secret chamber buried deep in the glacier on the opposite side of the mountain, and to the dark pool of liquid ice known as the Ice Heart. That liquid was said to be the immortal essence drained from the heart of Wyrn's once-mortal husband, Rorjak, who'd traded her love for power, using the gifts she'd bestowed upon him to father the Frost Giants and become the first Ice King. It was to slay her husband that Wyrn had fashioned the ice spears and given them to her brother Thorgyll.

Wynter knew the legends were true. Three years ago, he'd put his lips to that liquid ice and swallowed a mouthful of it. The chill had sped straight to his heart and frozen him from the inside out.

"Remembering?" Galacia Frey's voice whispered across the ice, echoing softly.

He turned and saw her standing in the shadows of the entrance that led to the priestesses' private chambers. "Yes."

"You are colder now by far than you were when you left."

Wynter held her gaze. "Yes."

"Is there still hope, do you think?"

"I thought you summoned me to find that out."

Her lips curved in a cold smile. "I did." The smile vanished. She stalked towards the altar, her long snowbear-fur robe trailing behind her. "Approach the altar," she commanded.

There was something about the tone of her voice that put him on edge. Since the day she'd become a priestess of Wyrn, she'd treated him with distant reserve, but this was different. Warrior's instinct made him move slowly, his fingers inches from Gunterfys's grip. He sniffed the air, wondering if the other two priestesses were lying in wait, but he detected only Galacia's faint scent. The temple ice muted smells, and no breeze stirred the air, but if the others were near he would have known. Not an ambush, then.

She stood behind the altar, between the cup of blue flame and the wall of spears, looking regal and reserved. When he continued to hesitate, she arched one haughty, mocking brow. "Afraid, Wyn?" she gibed softly.

The familiar, taunting amusement made him grit his teeth. They'd known each other since childhood. She'd never given much respect to a man's pride—except as a weapon to tweak him with. Obviously, that was still one of her favorite weapons. Regrettably, it still worked.

Damnable woman. He'd show her who should be afraid of whom. Wynter dropped his hand from his sword hilt and leapt up on the altar dais in one swift step. He realized his mistake in an instant.

The world went white.

Air and snow and ice whirled around him in a blinding tempest. He yanked Gunterfys from its sheath. "Galacia!" he roared. The power of the Ice Heart swept over him in a burning rush and gathered at the backs of his eyes. He spun, sweeping Gunterfys and the Ice Gaze blindly in the white wind.

Then froze when the point of a spear pressed against his back.

The tempest slowed to a flurry of snow, then disappeared. He was standing before the altar, facing the wall of spears. One of them was missing. A thick layer of frost from his Gaze lay over everything, except the steadily burning blue of the flame in the cup.

"Drop the sword and shutter your Gaze. Now, Wyn," she snapped when he didn't instantly obey. "Pass the test, and you're free to go. Refuse, and you die now on the point of my spear."

"Damn you for a coldhearted witch!" he hissed, but he knew he'd been bested. Galacia had positioned her spear in the perfect spot. A single thrust would drive it between his ribs and straight through his heart. He opened his fist and let Gunterfys clatter to the floor. The cold rage of the Ice Gaze drained away.

"Good. Now put your hand in the flame."

"Are you mad?" He started to turn around. The spear's needled point dug deeper, freezing his shirt and numbing the flesh beneath.

"Do it," she ordered.

"Woman, you will regret this."

"The regret started long ago. Now, put your hand in the flame." She jabbed the spear in his back again for emphasis.

He shoved his hand into the center of the blue flame

burning in the chalice. The fire flared high in a sudden explosion of red-orange light. He cried out in pain and yanked his hand back. The flesh of his hand was sizzling, and blisters had formed across his palm.

The spear at his back fell away.

He whirled, but she was already gone. He snatched up Gunterfys as she darted around the corner of the altar table. She held the spear pointed towards him and crouched in a defensive stance, ready for battle.

"You'd be dead before you ever drew back that spear to strike," he snapped.

"Perhaps," she agreed. "But kill a priestess of Wyrn in her own temple, and you won't live to cross the threshold."

He snarled at her. While others might doubt the gods still actively manifested their power in the world of men, Wynter knew better. For now, at least, Galacia had won. "You always were an annoying wretch of a girl." He gave her a last, black scowl, heaved out an irritated gust of air, and shoved Gunterfys back in its sheath. "Well, did I pass your test?"

"What do you think?"

He gave her a sullen look. "I think if I hadn't, I'd already be dead."

A ghost of a smile warmed her eyes. She straightened and slowly raised the spear until its sharp tip pointed towards the roof of the ice cave. "The flame only burns flesh that still retains the heat of life. If the Ice Heart had consumed you, the fire would have remained blue and cold." She turned her back to him and set the spear back in place with its twin on the wall.

"You've shown your hand, priestess. If I do become the Ice King, I won't be fool enough to return here and let you prove it."

"I know," she agreed, "but the refusal will be proof enough on its own."

"I am so warned." His pride was still smarting at the way she'd outmaneuvered him. He'd never liked losing to her. He still didn't. "Do what you must, Galacia. You always have." He turned and headed for the entrance to the cave.

"There was a reason I needed to test you today," she called after him.

He ignored her. He'd had enough of her mysteries and torments.

"The *garm* have come."

He stopped. Turned slowly back. The *garm* were deadly, giant wolflike monsters from the ice fields of the Craig, pets and servants of the Frost Giants, Rorjak's deadly minions. His brows drew together in a scowl. "Barsul said nothing of it."

"He doesn't know. I haven't told him. I haven't told anyone until you, just now."

"You've seen them?"

"No. Not seen." Already her haughty air of superiority was returning. She circled the altar, running a long, blue-nailed finger along the edge. "Smelled them on the wind."

"I have not."

"Your nose is full of weatherwitch." She arched a brow. "Did you think I would not scent her on you?"

"I know better than that." Her mother was Snow Wolf clan, like him. Galacia and he had run together with the wolves as children, until Wyrn had called her to service on her tenth birthday. He knew she had enough blood of the wolf in her to grant her a portion of its power. "I wed her to sire an heir, and the begetting of one has proven much more enjoyable than I'd dared hope. Summerfolk are exceedingly passionate."

"So I've heard."

"Jealous, Laci?" he jabbed, unable to resist a taunt of his own. Deliberately, he used the name he'd used when they'd run together as children. Until she'd been called by Wyrn, her parents and his had intended her to be his bride. But as a priestess of Wyrn, her bed was as cold as the goddess she served.

She didn't rise to the bait. "It's good that part of this marriage agrees with you. An enjoyable duty is a pleasure, not a chore, and thus more likely to be completed well and swiftly."

The cool response irritated him, so he dug his next barb a little deeper. "Well, if that's your measure, a dozen of my children should already be growing in her womb."

She gave him a brittle smile. "Only a dozen? You disappoint me, Wyn."

That brittleness shamed him. He'd struck her, all right, and hard, and there was no excuse for it. She'd not chosen her path; it had been chosen for her. Wyrn had called her at age ten, before she'd even known boys were good for more than beating in footraces and games of war. She'd never known a man's love or passion, and never would. She'd never hold a child of her own. "Laci . . ."

She cut him off. Already, the brief moment of vulnerability had passed. She was once more the icy Lady Frey, Wyrn's priestess, coldly distant and impervious to the frailties of human emotion. "In truth, even if you didn't reek of your Summer witch, I'd be surprised if you could detect the *garm*. Their scent is very faint, and I myself can only catch it when the wind is just right. And if not for the dreams Wyrn sends me, I would not have noticed even that. They are still keeping to the mountains, but I doubt it will be long before they grow bolder."

"I will organize a Hunt."

"A Hunt? Where? Through the entire breadth and depth of the Craig?" She laughed shortly. "You won't have any idea where to start until they strike, and you find a trail fresh enough to follow. And the moment you mention the *garm,* your own life will be in danger. There are those who would stab you in the back rather than risk the coming of the Ice King."

"Including you, as I just discovered."

"Including me." Her gaze was every bit as steady as his. "I am Wyrn's, after all."

He gave a rueful laugh. She was an honest woman. Often brutally so, but that was one of the qualities he'd always liked about her. He'd rather have an honest spear aimed at his back than a faceful of lies and political machinations.

"Barsul told me about the men sent to face the mercy of the mountains. Is that because of the growing power of the Ice Heart, too?"

"I don't know," she admitted. "It's possible."

"Then why not kill me now and have done with it? You had your chance. Why didn't you take it?"

"All hope is not yet lost. Besides, I know Barsul told you of Calberna and the Summer Prince. If you are slain, invasion is a certainty, and from more than just Calberna. The only thing that's kept the foreign kings at bay these last years has been the fear that you would turn the power of the Ice Heart on their own kingdoms and lay them waste."

"I suppose I should thank Falcon, then. If not for his efforts to raise a Calbernan army, I would have been greeted with spears instead of wreaths."

The blue-tinted nails idly scraped the ice altar, and the tower of frozen curls tilted slightly to one side. Galacia's pale eyes remained cool and steady.

Wyn scowled at her, recognizing that look. She'd already said all she would. "So the *garm* have come, but I should stay here and do nothing? That is your advice?"

"You should stay here and impregnate your little weatherwitch. *That* is my advice. Your idea in wedding her was a good one. Hold your child in your arms while there's still warmth enough in you to feel the love you need to melt the Ice Heart. The surest way to drive back the *garm* is to rob their masters of hope for victory."

Wynter snorted. "Between you, Barsul, and my queen's own father, I've never had so many friends urging me to bed a woman." Not that the idea of spending the next year in bed plowing Khamsin every chance he got was unappealing.

"It's never been so important. Too much is at stake, and time is a luxury you don't have."

"How long do I have?"

"Not long. Probably less than a year if you continue to use the power. A weaker man would have succumbed long before now."

Wynter absorbed the information without flinching. He'd known how high the price of the Ice Heart could be, but after holding Garrick's body in his arms, no amount of wise counsel could have swayed him from charting his course of vengeance.

"If the *garm* have come," he said, "I will not leave my people unprotected. They must be warned, no matter the cost to me."

"Then send outriders to the remote farms and villages," Galacia replied—quickly enough that Wyn realized she'd already decided what he should do before he'd stepped foot inside the temple. "Claim rumors of marauding dark-wolves. Have the villagers form town watches to patrol the woods and report anything suspicious. Warn them to keep their livestock penned close and avoid traveling through the woods in parties smaller than three. If the *garm* do venture down from the mountains, I doubt they will be bold enough at first to do more than prey on the alone and unwary."

"The moment the villagers find the first tracks, they'll know the truth."

"Yes, but by then, your bride could be pregnant. That may provide hope enough to hold potential assassins at bay. Regicide is not a crime Winterfolk easily embrace."

"Only priestesses of Wyrn, eh, Laci?"

She bowed her head slightly in acknowledgment, her face a cool, expressionless mask.

He shrugged his shoulders to release the gathered tension in them. "Was there anything else, or are we done?"

"We're done," she said. "I'll show you out."

After one last, brief glance at the ice spears and the carved, frozen face of Wyrn behind the altar, Wynter fell into step beside the severe, stately woman who'd once been his friend and intended bride. At the temple entrance, the wind of the high reaches rushed over them, blowing Wynter's hair all around his face. Galacia's stood impervious to it. Like the goddess she served, she was a tower of ice, untouched by the elements.

He spat out a mouthful of hair and bowed to her as temple protocol demanded. "Thank you for the warnings, Lady Frey, and the advice." And because they had once been friends, and there would always be a part of him that wished they still were, he added, "If it comes to it, Laci, there's none I'd rather have hold the spear than you."

As he walked away, Galacia remained standing in the temple entrance, watching him make his way down the rocky path back towards Gildenheim and his Summerlea bride.

"You are wrong, Wyn," she murmured, knowing the wind would whisk her words far away from his ears. If he'd turned at this moment, he would have been surprised by the regret in her pale eyes. "I would not slay you easily. I'd do it, but never easily."

Khamsin scowled as Bella and two Wintercraig maids fussed and muttered around her as they tried to ready her for her first dinner with the Wintercraig court. Summer Sun! Why had she ever thought she *wanted* to take part in the pomp and ceremony of court life? Just preparing for dinner was a production that sapped her patience to a bare thread.

Although there'd been no time in Summerlea to prepare a wardrobe suitable for her role as the new Winter Queen (assuming her father would even go to such expense on her behalf), her sisters had each donated several gowns from their own court wardrobes. Gildenheim's seamstresses had spent several hours "winterizing" one of Spring's gowns with a new, padded silk underdress and a fitted, ermine-trimmed overdress.

"There now, my lady," Bella murmured. She tied off the last stitch to repair some damaged beadwork and snipped the thread, then stood back and ran a critical eye over everything. "All done, and presentable enough for a dinner in any court, I'd say."

Kham's head jerked on a sudden, wincing pain, and she scowled at the Wintercraig maid dressing her hair. "Good, then perhaps you can finish my hair. While I still have some of it left."

"Of course, my lady." Bella dismissed the remaining Winterfolk and set to work finishing Khamsin's hair.

When they were gone, some of the tension drained from Kham's shoulders. She closed her eyes and let the silence wash over her. It was quiet here. Elsewhere in the palace, stone walls and marble floors let sound echo, but here the hardwood floors and the profusion of rugs and hangings helped muffle unwanted noise. And for once, Bella wasn't chattering like a magpie.

Khamsin frowned. Chatter. Magpie.

Birds.

Her eyes opened. She sat up straight. "Bella, where are my birds? The tanagers Spring gave me." In the mirror, Kham saw a strange stillness come over her maid's face. "Bella?"

"I'm sorry, Your Majesty," the girl said. "They didn't survive the journey."

"What? But when did they die? How?"

"I think the cold killed them. It happened the day you were so ill, and the Winter King sent me away. I buried them by the side of the road, back in Summerlea."

Khamsin's shoulders slumped. Poor little things. She'd tried to keep them warm, but apparently it hadn't been enough. The thought of the tiny songbirds with their greenish yellow winter coats lying dead in the snow, their cheerful song forever silenced, made her want to cry.

"I'm sorry, ma'am," Bella murmured.

"No, it's not your fault. Some things just weren't meant

for this place." Kham closed her eyes and fought back the burning press of tears. It was so foolish to cry, but they'd been such sweet, darling little things. And they'd sung so cheerfully together as the coach had carried Khamsin farther and farther from the only home she'd ever known.

By the time Bella finished fixing the last curl in place, Khamsin had her emotions in check. Her eyes were dry, her face composed. Tildy would have been proud.

Kham stood and regarded her reflection with a critical eye. Her gown was silvery white satin, with a heavily beaded bodice, long, unadorned skirts gracefully behind her. Ice blue satin slippers, embroidered with silver thread and crystal beads, peeped out beneath the gown's hem. The ice blue velvet overdress nipped in at the waist and fastened with a row of three diamond and aquamarine buttons. The collar of thick, soft ermine covered her shoulders and framed her bronze face and dark, upswept hair. Wynter's ring, the Wintercraig Star, was her only jewelry.

A knock sounded on the doors in the outer chamber. Bella hurried to answer it. As Khamsin picked up her skirts to follow, a flash of white in the mirror made her spin around in alarm.

Wynter stood inside her bedroom, near her dressing room door. He was clad in white from head to toe. His inscrutable gaze swept over her.

She pressed a hand to her rapidly beating heart. "How did you get in here?"

He waved a careless hand behind him. "There is a connecting door from your dressing room to mine." One would think white would make him seem softer, kinder, less threatening even, but it only made him look taller, broader, and more dangerous. A wolf in lamb's clothing. The hair at his temples had been drawn back again and braided in three thin, silver-ringed plaits that framed his face.

"Wintercraig colors suit you," he said. Before she could do more than blink in surprise at the compliment, he held out a small box. "Here. I meant to return these to you."

Curious, Kham opened the box and looked inside. "My mother's things!" Kham set the box on her bed and pulled them out—her mother's gardening journal, her jeweled brush, comb, and mirror. Kham ran her fingers over the familiar, beloved objects. Emotion welled up so suddenly, she nearly humiliated herself by bursting into tears.

"Thank you." Kham busied herself setting her mother's thing out on her dresser. "These are very dear to me. They're all I have left of my mother." She turned back to find Wynter regarding her with an inscrutable gaze.

"You must have loved her very much."

She'd revealed too much. Not wanting him to use her vulnerability against her, she said, "I'm told I did. She died when I was three." She lifted her chin and added bluntly, "I summoned the storm that killed her."

She'd meant to shock him. And to warn him not to underestimate her or her magic. But instead of responding with wariness or concern or even surprise, his gaze softened, and his voice, when he spoke, brushed across the broken parts of her soul like warm velvet. "I'm so sorry, *min ros*. I can only image the pain you've carried all these years." He stepped closer and slid a hand through her hair, cupping her head in his palm, stroking her temple with his thumb. "But you were a child, Khamsin. A baby. Even if you summoned the storm, no one in their right mind could ever blame you for what happened."

She ached to lean into him, to let the guilt fall away, but she moved away instead, rejecting his comfort and offer of absolution. "You weren't there. You don't know anything about it."

"No, but I *was* there when you awakened in my tent and realized you'd called a fierce storm in your delirium. I saw how alarmed you were by the mere thought that you might have injured someone with your magic. And those were my men you worried about. Soldiers who'd been your enemies only days before." He shook his head. "You aren't a killer, Khamsin. You aren't a monster or a curse on anyone's House. And you didn't kill your mother."

Her throat grew so tight, she couldn't speak. She could only stand there, blinking and trying desperately not to cry.

He didn't try to hold or comfort her again. He merely waited for her to recover her composure, then held out an arm. "Come, Summerlass. The court is waiting, and they will not thank us if we let their food grow cold."

She took his arm in silence and walked beside him as he led her out of their private wing and down to the banquet hall on the palace's second level. She snuck surreptitious glances at him as they walked.

She did not understand this man she'd married. Every time she thought she'd figured him out, he surprised her. How could he be so cold one minute, yet so passionate the next? How could he offer her such disarming kindness and compassion, while planning to execute her at year's end if she didn't bear him a child? Was one aspect merely a show he put on? And if so, which side of him was the mask and which was the true Wynter Atrialan?

Within minutes of entering the banquet hall, Khamsin felt lost and alone, surrounded by cool-eyed men and women who laughed with tinkling little shivers of sound behind fans of snowy-egret plumes. No one was openly rude. In fact, they were all coolly polite. But she was conscious of their eyes upon her, and conscious of her relative small-ness, her foreign darkness. She found herself wishing that she'd worn rich, bold, Summerlea colors tonight—wine, scarlet, emerald green, imperial purple, anything but the pale white and ice blue that made her look like a stranger trying desperately to fit in.

The feeling of alienation was intensified by the presence of Valik's dinner companion, his cousin Reika Villani. Khamsin remembered the sleek, tall beauty from earlier in the day. She was the woman who had gripped Wynter's hands with such fervor at the reception. As it turned out,

Reika was actually Valik's cousin by marriage, the daughter of his uncle's second wife. Apparently, she had become a close friend of Wynter's years ago, when he and Valik would hunt on the old man's abundant acreage.

Seated between Valik and Wynter at the dinner table, the golden-haired beauty spent the entire meal entertaining everyone with humorous anecdotes and prompting them to share their own adventures. She did it in a way that seemed so innocuous on the surface yet had the effect of drawing a distinct circle of friendship in which Khamsin clearly did not belong. "Oh, Valik, tell the queen about the time you wrestled that boar to its knees," or "My king, tell her about the time you found the ice dragon's nest."

To Khamsin's right, Lord Chancellor Firkin and his wife, Lady Melle, listened to Reika's conversation with indulgent smiles and murmured occasional asides to Khamsin to explain some of the customs and terms that might be unfamiliar to her. Whether they were blind to their countrywoman's actions, approving of them, or merely trying to smooth over a potentially awkward situation, Khamsin didn't know. But she had been raised in the shadows of the Summer court, where Summerlea courtiers regularly spoke of passion and desires through subtle and not-so-subtle body language, and she understood the woman's meaning all too easily. Reika Villani was staking her claim.

Khamsin was no fool and no starry-eyed romantic either. Sex in Summerlea was pleasurable entertainment shared by most courtiers without regard for marital status. Fidelity was rare, and in arranged marriages, virtually nonexistent. Logically, she knew she should not expect Wynter to be faithful to her, but after sharing such deep intimacy and shattering pleasure with him, the idea of another woman in his bed made Khamsin grip her eating utensils with unnecessary force.

Reika was also the sister of Wynter's former betrothed. That came out during the course of the meal, too, in another anecdotal tale that ended with, "Who knew you were going to fall so deeply in love with my sister Elka?" At the mention of Elka's name, dead silence fell across Wynter's end of the banquet table. And in a truly gifted performance of tearful remorse, Reika cast Wynter a fluttering, fragile, sorrow-filled glance—complete with two perfect, crystalline tears shimmering in her limpid blue eyes—and said, "Oh, Wyn, I'm so sorry."

He covered her hand with his, and gave her long, thin fingers a squeeze. "It's all right, Reika. The past is gone."

Khamsin stared at Wynter's hand touching the Villani woman's, and something very dark and very unpleasant swelled inside her. She reached for her silver water goblet and drank, hoping the icy snowmelt would cool her temper.

Wynter removed his hand, and that helped more than the ice water. But then Reika launched into another series of humorous tales about their adventures, and she seemed to take Wynter's brief, conciliatory handclasp as an invitation to touch him freely. She started brushing the back of his hand with her fingertips, squeezing his arm as she laughed, leaning towards him and bumping shoulders in a way only intimates had a right to.

So much for Khamsin's earlier plans of learning the lay of the land and befriending the locals. This woman was the enemy. And the rest of the court, eyeing her with such indulgence and laughing their approval of her behavior, were enemies, too. Khamsin clutched her goblet tightly. Outside, the clouds gathered, and the banquet-hall windows began to rattle.

"Oh dear," Lady Melle murmured. "It sounds like we've got a bit of a storm brewing."

Wynter and Valik glanced out the darkened windows then, in unison, turned to Khamsin. Wynter's brows drew sharply together. She knew her eyes were pure silver now and swirling with magic.

"Khamsin?" Wynter half rose from his chair and leaned towards her.

Crystalline laughter pealed out. "Oh, Wyn," Lady Reika grabbed his arm as if to pull him back, "remember the time when we—"

BOOM!

Lightning split the sky, so close, the banquet hall went blinding white. A deafening crack of thunder made ladies scream in fright, then burst out in peals of nervous laughter.

Khamsin set down her silver water goblet, which now bore the distinct impression of her fingers melted into the metal. All the ice in the goblet was gone, and the water was steaming. She pushed back her chair to stand. "I'm sorry. It's been a long day. Please excuse me."

"Khamsin!" Wynter growled, reaching for her. She skirted his outstretched hand and walked swiftly for the door.

Behind her, the silence exploded in a sudden buzz of conversation, and she heard Lady Reika's voice asking, "Wyn? What just happened? Did *she* do that?"

Bella was sitting at the secretary, scratching an ink-dipped quill rapidly over a scrap of paper, when Khamsin burst in. The little maid leapt to her feet and whirled towards the door, one hand clutching at her throat. The other swept out, knocking over the inkpot and spilling black ink across the paper. "Oh, Your Majesty!" she exclaimed. "You gave me such a start." She started mopping up the inky mess with the ruined remains of her letter and several other sheets of paper. "Is dinner over so quickly?"

"It is for me." Khamsin headed for the bedroom, tearing off her velvet overdress as she went. She reached for the laces at the back of the satin gown, but the ties were hopelessly tight. "Come help me out of this dress."

"Of course, Your Majesty, but I need to clean up this mess and wash the ink from my hands before I dare touch that gown."

"A stain or two wouldn't hurt it," Kham muttered under her breath. But she raised her voice, and called, "That's fine. There's a storm outside. I'm going out on the balcony to enjoy it." She pulled open the leaded-glass doors that led to a private balcony circling the castle turret where her bedroom was located. The wind rushed to greet her, cold and hard and stinging with icy rain, but she only spread her arms and lifted her face up to meet it. This storm was strong but not deadly. She'd left the banquet hall before it had become so.

Her skirts whipped wildly around her legs, the pins pulled loose in her hair, and long, curling strands of white-streaked black blew around her. She breathed deep, drawing the chill, fresh air into her lungs, and turned her face up into the sluicing streams of rain. Storms, for all their rage and potential danger, were cleansing and ultimately calming. She gave her temper up to the winds and wished her body could float up and join it. What joy it would be to skate the skies on swirling black clouds or ride the lightning as it raced miles in mere instants.

She stood there for a long while, letting the wind whip at her, the rain soak her through to her skin, until the last remnants of her hot anger had faded away. When she was finally calm again, she went back inside. Bella was gone. Kham poked her head in the main parlor and called to her, but got no response. The girl must have gone to wash up in the servants' washroom down the hall instead of doing the reasonable thing and using Kham's bathing chamber.

With a muttered curse, Kham returned to her bedchamber and tried once more to untangle the knotted ties at the back of her bodice. Really, how ridiculous was it that ladies wore fashions they could not put on and take off without assistance? Men weren't such fools.

She twisted her arms, fumbling blindly with the ties. The rain had soaked the fabric and swollen the cords, making them even harder to unknot. Her chin dropped down to her chest. The wet, tangled curls of her hair fell forward and dripped a steady stream of water on the floor that joined the greater puddle seeping from her gown.

"Summer Sun!" she exclaimed bitterly, giving the ties a furious yank.

"Let go. You're only making it worse."

Khamsin froze at the low rumble of Wynter's voice and the jolt of electricity that jangled across her nerves when his fingers brushed against hers. She stood still, her heart in her throat, while he tugged at the ties of her gown. After a few moments, the ties loosened, and the fabric at the back of her gown parted. She started to clutch the gown to her when Wynter slid it from her shoulders, but she remembered her oath of matrimony and let the gown fall.

His hands went to the ties of the silk underdress, loosing them with similar ease. "Why did you summon the storm?" he asked, as the ties slipped free. "And why did you leave?"

Holding the last flimsy shred of protection to her chest, she stepped away and turned to face him. "You aren't so blind as that."

He wasn't, and he surrendered the pretense without a fight. "She is just a childhood friend, nothing more."

"She wants to sit on the Winter Throne," Khamsin countered, "or at the very least, lie in the bed of the man who does."

"Reika?" He laughed and shook his head. "She'd sooner bed down with a wild wolf. I'm too big and rough for her. She wants a man with poetry in his heart. She's said so many times."

"Has she said so since the day you chose her sister over her?"

His look of consternation was all the answer she needed.

There were benefits to living in the shadows as Kham had done all her life, being unseen, unnoticed. One of those benefits had been to watch the court ladies work their wiles on the men, to observe not only what they said to men's faces but also what they said behind their backs. Khamsin had no doubt Reika's youthful protestations had been flirtation, intended to call attention to her delicate femininity and instruct Wynter how to woo her.

Unfortunately for her, Reika hadn't realized Wynter would interpret her protests so literally. And Kham had no intention of letting her amend her past mistakes.

"I swore an oath to offer you the fruits of my life," she told him. "You swore the same to me, and you promised to keep only to me. As I honor my oaths, I expect you to honor yours."

Surprise flashed across his face for the briefest instant before he marshaled his features into an inscrutable mask. "You ask me for fidelity?"

She hadn't meant to. It had just sort of popped out. But now that she had, she wasn't going to back down. She lifted her chin. "I demand it. Considering my life lies in the balance, it's only just that you restrict your . . . breeding efforts . . . solely to me."

He took a single, purposeful step towards her, a predator stalking prey. His eyes burned like blue flame. "Is that the real reason? Because you fear death?"

Every instinct for self-preservation screamed at her to back away. Pride would not let her. She had issued her challenge, and she would stand her ground. "What other reason could there possibly be?"

He took another step towards her. A growl vibrated deep in his throat.

Her body went weak, legs nearly collapsing beneath her. Heat burst across her skin in dizzying waves. That was so supremely unfair. One intent look, one low, thrilling growl, and she went up in flames.

His nostrils flared, and the muscles in his jaw clenched hard as stone. With a swiftness that left her blinking, he reached out one hand and snatched the underdress from her hands, leaving her standing naked before him. He didn't even bother to remove his own clothes. He simply freed his jutting sex from his trousers, lifted her up with both hands, and lowered her onto his shaft, growling, "Put your legs around my waist" as his hips surged forward, and his body drove deep into hers with devastating effect.

Then again, she thought dazedly as the first orgasm exploded across her body, perhaps instant, undeniable lust wasn't so unfair after all.

He bent her backward, one hand holding her spine, the other clutching her buttocks, lifting and lowering her with effortless strength as he bent over her body. His mouth moved across her neck and breasts, nipping, licking, leaving trails of heat and ice burning together in lines of indescribable pleasure. His voice whispered over her skin. "Tell me, Khamsin, why you demand my fidelity. Tell me why." Whether he was using magic or not, she could not tell, but the words acted upon her like a persuasion spell, dragging the truth closer and closer to the surface with each whisper and each thrust of his hips. "Why Khamsin?" His body drove into hers, then withdrew with aching slowness. "Why?" Another thrust, deeper, making her gasp and shudder. "Tell me."

She grabbed the soft folds of his shirt, wanting skin beneath her hands, not cloth. "Because," she bit out, "I will not share with her or any other woman." Power crackled at her fingertips. The shirt singed in her hands and shredded from his body like paper, baring the silken skin and hard muscle of his arms and chest and back.

"I will not share this." She dug her fingers into heavy muscles of his chest, then dragged her arms around, running her hands up his back to clutch his shoulders. Her body pressed against his. Her thighs clamped tight around his hips. Her inner muscles clenched his shaft, clinging tight as she lifted her body up and held his gaze with the burning fire of her own.

"I will not share you." Still holding his gaze, she drove her body down onto his. Tiny threads of lightning danced over his skin in a shocking web of blue-white light. He gave a choked cry. His spine arched. His buttocks clenched tight. The tendons in his neck stood out like cords of steel. His hips surged again, powerfully, rising up to meet her downward slide. She felt the shock of it to her bones.

"I will not share," she cried out fiercely, one final time as both of them shattered.

When the firestorm passed, Wynter lay on the bearskin rug beside his wife. He stared up at the frescoed ceiling overhead and tried to regulate his breathing and gain some measure of strength back in his muscles.

Winter's Frost! What she did to him.

Although the cold, logical part of Wynter's mind whispered, *Leave her now. Keep a wise distance,* he did not. He stayed with her throughout the night, waking her countless times to claim and reclaim her in the darkness. She was like a drug in his system. Every time he touched her, every time he sank his body into hers, she drove him to heights he'd never known, and he would think, *This is it. This will sate me.* But scant hours later, he would wake again, even more hungry for her than he had been before.

If it was an enchantment, as Valik feared, it was a very powerful one. The only saving grace was that she seemed as incapable of denying him as he was of denying her.

He woke her one last time just as dawn was breaking in the eastern sky. He let his hands skim across her soft skin, relearning the already-familiar curves of her flesh, and watched the passion bloom in her eyes, turning the gray to shifting silver. He smiled in triumph when her hands reached for him, and smiled again when he lowered his head, growled softly in her ear, and felt her body quake. His Wolf called to her as strongly as her scent called to him, and she opened to him like a summer bloom to the sun.

She was so fierce, so passionate, so willing in this, at least, to give him everything without caution or restraint. And so boldly, so fiercely insistent that he be faithful. Elka had never been so possessive. No woman ever had. Not of him. No woman until Khamsin.

One thing was certain: Keeping her at a wise distance was going to be exceedingly difficult.

Her hands clutched at him. Her power sparked across his

skin, driving all rational thought from his mind. There was only wave upon wave of hot pleasure, driving need, sensation and instinct and the feel of his body pumping rhythmically into hers, pushing them both higher and higher. Her volatile heat gripped him tight, burning, scorching. Her hands urged him on. She sobbed his name on a keening cry that broke into a scream as the climax swept over them both.

Later, when he could breathe without gasping and see more than flickering stars in a field of blackness, he bent over her limp body as she drifted back to sleep, and whispered in her ear, "I am no oathbreaker either, wife. I will honor my vows."

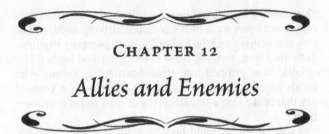

CHAPTER 12

Allies and Enemies

When Khamsin woke again, full daylight was streaming through her bedchamber windows, and Wynter was gone.

She laid her hand on the empty sheets. They were cool to the touch. Her body was aching and sore in more places than she'd ever known existed, but already the need for him was rising again. Her fingers smoothed over the indentation in the pillow beside hers and plucked a long, silvery white strand of Wynter's hair from the linen. She brushed the strand across her lips, remembering the feel of his silken hair sliding over her as his body surged against hers. She wished he'd stayed. She wished she'd woken, as she had so many times in the night, to find him there beside her, his eyes intent, his magnificent body stretched out on the sheets, naked and inviting.

A knock sounded at the bedroom door, and the door swung open. Bella entered, carrying a thick robe draped over one arm.

Khamsin tucked the strand of Wynter's hair beneath her pillow and sat up, dragging the linen top sheet free to wrap around her body. She sniffed the air. A warm, delicate aroma had wafted into the room. "Is that jasmine tea?"

The maid gave a smile. "Mistress Greenleaf said it was your favorite. There's a pot steeping on the hearth. Will you rise, or shall I bring you a cup here?"

"I'll get up." Khamsin smothered a yawn and stretched. "What time is it?"

"Half ten, ma'am."

"What? Half past ten?" Kham leapt from the bed. "Why didn't you wake me? What about Vinca and the tour of the palace?"

"The king left word that you were not to be disturbed. Mistress Vinca has rescheduled your tour of the palace for this afternoon. Lady Firkin has arranged a luncheon for you with the ladies of the court before that. Mistress Narsk delivered a new gown for the luncheon a few moments ago." Bella held the robe open for Khamsin, who swung her legs over the side of the bed and stood. As Khamsin thrust her arms into the robe's sleeves, Bella added, "And Lady Villani is waiting in the parlor. She said she needed to speak with you. Shall I tell her to come back later?"

Khamsin froze. "Lady Villani?" What could Reika Villani possibly want? Khamsin put a hand to her tangled hair. She looked a mess: bed-rumpled, her lips still swollen from Wynter's passionate kisses, faint marks on her neck where he'd nipped at her skin. Reika Villani would take one look at her and know how Khamsin had spent her night. Kham's eyes narrowed. "No," she said slowly. "Thank you, Bella, but I'll see her now." She tightened the robe's sash. "I would like a hot bath though when I return, and a little something to eat. I didn't have much of an appetite last night, but now I'm famished."

She opened the door to the parlor and stepped through. Reika Villani was standing near the hearth, looking out the bank of windows across the valley far below. She turned at the sound of the opening door. Her gown and hair were as pale, elegant, and perfect as they had been last night, her face a confection of graceful features dominated by big, heavily lashed blue eyes that narrowed as she took in Khamsin's rumpled appearance.

"Your Grace." Reika curtsied in a smooth, unhurried motion.

"Lady Villani," Kham murmured in reply. How odd her new title sounded after a lifetime of being just "Storm," "dearly," or "girl." "You caught me just rising from bed. I didn't get much sleep last night." She smoothed a hand across her rumpled hair and gave what she hoped looked like an embarrassed smile. Reika's lips tightened, and Khamsin turned to reach for the teapot in order to hide the flash of triumph she feared might show in her eyes. Those years of watching from the shadows had not gone to waste. She understood the manipulations and maneuverings of court ladies, and even though she'd never participated in their intrigues before, she had claws of her own and was not averse to using them.

Last night, she'd been too weary from travel, too unsettled by the strangeness of her new environment, and taken aback by Wynter's apparent obliviousness to what Kham considered Reika Villani's blatant drawing of battle lines. This morning, she was none of those things. Hours of incendiary passion and the memory of Wynter's voice whispering that he, too, would honor his vows left her feeling far more secure in her new position and determined to put Reika Villani firmly into hers.

"My maid has prepared a pot of jasmine tea," she said, pouring the fragrant liquid into a warmed porcelain cup. "Shall I pour you a cup?"

"Thank you, but no, Your Grace," Reika demurred. "I'm not very fond of tea."

Kham blew on her drink to cool it. The first sip made her reach for the sugar. Bella had steeped it so long it had gone bitter. She sipped again, then added more sugar and turned back to her elegant guest, who was watching her intently.

"To what do I owe the pleasure of your visit this morning, Lady Villani?"

The woman smoothed a hand over her expensively gowned hips and summoned a surprisingly convincing expression of worry and remorse. "I'm afraid we may have somehow gotten off on the wrong foot last night."

"What makes you think that?" Kham asked in a mild tone. She lifted her teacup and regarded Reika over its rim.

"Well . . . I . . ." Clearly, she hadn't expected Khamsin to play ignorant. "The way you left the dinner . . . it was obvious you were upset." She took a half step forward, wringing her hands. Kham thought that was a particularly nice touch. "It's just that Wynter—ah, I mean, the king—and I are such old and dear friends. I fear we might have made you feel a little left out."

"Don't trouble yourself, Lady Villani. I understood perfectly the nature of your relationship with my husband."

"Oh . . . well, that is good . . ."

"Yes, it is, though perhaps not in the way you mean. Roland Soldeus always said understanding the nature of one's enemy is the path to ensuring his defeat."

Great blue eyes blinked in charming confusion. "Enemy? Defeat?" Reika gave a tinkling laugh. "You have me at a loss. Surely you're not suggesting that I—"

Khamsin lifted a hand to cut her off. "Lady Villani, please. Spare me your fluttering lashes and false confusion. I am not susceptible to your charms."

Lady Villani made one last attempt to cling to her illusion of innocence. "I'm sure I don't know what you mean."

"Let us be frank with one another. You want my husband. I will not share him with you. There, the matter is out in the open now, and the battle lines are drawn."

"Indeed." Reika's voice had a new, hard edge that hadn't been there before, and her eyes changed from limpid pools to glittering stone. "Well, like your countrymen before you, *Summerlander,* this is one battle in which you will find yourself far outmatched."

Khamsin took another sip of her tea and curled her fingers around the porcelain cup. Energy from the confrontation was gathering inside her, and she could feel its electric warmth beginning to speed the blood in her veins, making the hot tea seem cooler by comparison. "It must have been very hard for you to want a man so badly only to have your sister snatch him away. And then, after she left him, and he was free once more, to have him go off to war for three long years and return with yet another woman on his arm, a wife no less. You have my sympathy. I know what it is like to want something you cannot have."

"Keep your sympathy. I have no need of it." The corner of Reika's mouth curled in a sneer. "He only wed you to secure the peace and breed an heir acceptable to both kingdoms. You are simply a means to an end, chosen for your bloodline, nothing more. Any Summerlea princess could stand in your stead."

The words struck deep, catching Khamsin unprepared and surprisingly vulnerable. Reika wasn't telling her anything she didn't already know, so why did it hurt to hear it?

Stung, and wanting to sting back, she touched the faint abrasions Wynter had left on her neck and forced a smug, triumphant smile. "Really? Then he truly is an amazing master of deception, to be able to feign such convincing passion again . . . and again . . . and again . . ."

The woman went quite still. For a moment, Kham thought her barb had struck home, but Reika was not so easy a target. Her eyes grew calm and intent. "Yes," she agreed smoothly, "he is a very . . . intense lover and skillful enough to make a woman lose all reason. It's one of the things I've missed most these last three years. And I can see how an inexperienced girl might assume the power of his sexuality implies a bond that doesn't really exist."

Kham's confidence faltered. She would have sworn Reika and Wynter had never been lovers. She lifted her teacup and took a sip to hide her dismay.

Reika stood beside Khamsin, smiling with cool serenity, no doubt silently gloating that her second, well-aimed blow had struck home even more deeply than the first. And that made Khamsin's temper simmer.

Walk away, dearly. Tildy, who understood peace, would say. *Just walk away.*

But Roland, who understood war, would have offered different advice. *Behind your enemy's smile lies treachery. Show him that behind yours lies steel. Fail to do so, and you only make him bolder.*

Khamsin stared down into the fragrant, golden brown depths of her tea. She was no wise, peaceful Tildy, no matter how she might try. She was a daughter of the Sun, capable of warmth, but just as capable of fire and lethal volatility.

Khamsin tightened her grip on the teacup and turned back to face her adversary. "What do you know of the Heirs to the Summer Throne, Lady Villani?"

Blond brows drew together in a delicate frown. "I beg your pardon?"

"The Royal Family of Summerlea—my family, and my ancestors before me—what do you know of us?"

"I . . . don't understand how that has any bearing on this conversation."

"It has great bearing. Have you ever heard of Roland Soldeus—Roland Triumphant, the Hero of Summerlea? No? Perhaps you should do a little reading, broaden your horizons." She flashed a brief, tight smile. "Roland once crushed a well-supplied army of fifty thousand invaders with scarcely three thousand men of his own. They say he blazed bright as the sun, and that his sword shot beams of burning fire, and that his enemies burst into flames before him, and the charred dust of their bodies blew away on the fierce, hot winds—the khamsins—he could summon at will. My family can trace its lineage back to his brother, Donal. The same powerful blood that ran in Roland's veins runs in mine."

She looked up and captured Reika Villani's gaze with her own. "I did not retire from the banquet hall last night because I feared you. I left because I feared what I might do to you if I stayed." Curling clouds of steam rose up before her face. She saw Reika glance down, saw her eyes widen in shock at the sight of Khamsin's tea bubbling madly in its cup. "Do not make yourself my enemy," she concluded softly. "Do not poach what I have claimed as mine."

Dark movement glimpsed from the corner of her eye made Khamsin turn. Bella stood in the doorway. "Your bath is ready, Your Majesty," she said.

"Thank you, Bella." Kham set the teacup down on a small lamp table near Reika's frozen figure. "And thank you for coming, Lady Villani. Our discussion has been very enlightening. I hope I've made my position clear. Bella will show you out."

Fired up by her confrontation with Reika Villani, Kham waved aside the pale cream gown Bella had laid out for this morning's luncheon with the ladies of the court and chose instead to garb herself in bright, vivid, Summerland colors. Thus armored, she marched down to the small banquet hall where the ladies had gathered and met their cool gazes, head-on. She had not come to these people as a supplicant, but as a queen. *Their* queen—even if only for the next twelve months. They would give her the respect and deference due her station.

Something of that determination must have shown on her face because the ladies all curtsied deeply upon her arrival and regarded her with wariness.

"Your Grace, this way, please." Lady Firkin gestured towards the table. "You were so tired from your journey. I thought a more informal luncheon today would be a good way to introduce you to the ladies of the court."

Kham eyed the banquet table, laden with extravagant gold, silver, and crystal place settings, each chair attended by a private footman. *This was informal?* She hesitated to think what a dinner of state might look like. But she murmured something polite to acknowledge Lady Firkin's thoughtfulness.

For the next forty-five minutes, Kham pasted a pleasant expression and did her best to contain her restlessness as Lady Firkin introduced her to the ladies of the court. Tildy had spent countless hours training Khamsin for just such an event. A princess of the Rose was expected to be a gracious hostess of her father's kingdom, and in keeping with those duties, she was expected to remember names, titles, and other pertinent information about the courtiers and guests who frequented her father's court.

Unfortunately, Kham had never been particularly good at those lessons, and though she was careful to repeat each lady's name three times and came up with mnemonics to tie the name and the face together (Crooked nose, Lady Ros. Catty smile, Lady Wyle), it didn't take long for her to become overwhelmed. There were only a handful of ladies she remembered from yesterday's introductions: Lady Firkin, the tall, imposing priestess Galacia Frey, and, of course, Reika Villani, who was there, smiling as if she and Khamsin had not just squared off as enemies less than two hours ago.

Aware that this morning's confrontation with Valik's cousin had only been the first salvo in their personal war, Khamsin watched Reika from the corner of her eye, noting which of the ladies paused to speak with her and which sat closest to her. Kham had no doubt Reika would use every tool in her arsenal to achieve victory, including conscripting her friends into her service. Since Khamsin couldn't very well go around asking everyone if they were Reika's confidantes, she would simply have to be observant and take care to watch her back.

Turning to the Winterlady at her side—what was her name? Oh, yes, crooked nose, Lady Ros— Khamsin said, "Tell me a little about yourself, Lady Ros. Where are you from and how long have you been at court?"

Finally, a quiet gong called the ladies to luncheon. Khamsin took the queen's seat at the head of the table, conscious of the many eyes upon her as the servants offered her all manner of strange, unfamiliar dishes. She tried to steer clear of foodstuffs she couldn't identify or those with an odd smell, especially after the fishy aroma of several different seafood dishes left her feeling rather green about the gills.

"You don't like fish, Your Grace?" Reika Villani asked after Kham waved away a particularly odiferous mackerel dish. "How unfortunate. Seafood is a staple of every Wintercraig meal." Her tone made Khamsin's aversion sound like a calamitous shortcoming.

Kham's jaw clenched. "Quite the contrary, I love fish," she declared, and just to wipe the mocking, superior smile off Reika Villani's face, she forced herself to accept a portion of the next fish dish that came her way. Though the smell and texture made her want to retch, she ate several bites, holding Reika Villani's gaze the whole time.

Two seats down on Khamsin's right, Galacia Frey watched the visual skirmish between Reika and Kham, and when it was over, she gave Kham what looked like an approving nod and tucked into her own meal. Kham would have basked in what felt like a small victory, except that for the rest of the meal, what she'd eaten kept trying to make a reappearance. Outside, pale gray clouds began to gather in the clear, sunny sky.

After the meal, Galacia Frey took her leave, and the rest of the women retired to the gathering room next door to work on needlecrafts and socialize. Khamsin was hopeless with a needle and woefully inadequate as a casual conversationalist. Her questions sounded more like interrogations, and because she was so uncertain as to which ladies were Reika Villani's cronies, her own answers were so guarded they came across as curt and off-putting.

Only with Lady Melle Firkin was Kham able to relax. The wife of Lord Chancellor Barsul Firkin had kind eyes, a warm smile, and a disarming way of putting Khamsin completely at ease. Within the first half hour of the luncheon, Lady Firkin's polite, deferential use of titles gave way to "my dear" this and "my dear" that.

With any other person, Khamsin might have stiffened

up and drawn away from such familiarity, but she couldn't bring herself to rebuke the elderly woman for speaking to her more like a daughter than a queen, especially when the lady confessed, "Lord Firkin and I had a daughter, Astrid. She died of lung fever when she was seventeen. You remind me of her. She had the same fire in her eyes that you do. She never backed down from anything, even things that frightened her." Then she patted Khamsin's hand, smiled, and said, "I have a good feeling about you, my dear. I think you may be just what our king and this court has needed for a long time."

"Thank you, Lady Firkin," Khamsin said with a small, genuine smile.

"Please, call me Lady Melle. I'm not much of one for standing on formalities. I hope you don't mind. The king has been like a son to Lord Barsul and me. We helped raise young Prince Garrick after their parents died."

"How did the king's parents die?"

"Frost Giant attack. Such a tragedy. Wynter barely escaped with his life. And then to take the throne so young. He wasn't even sixteen. Such a burden for a boy to shoulder, especially when some took his youth as a sign of weakness. But weakness is a trait no one who knows him would ever associate with Wynter of the Craig."

"No, I would imagine not," Kham agreed. She started to ask Lady Melle more questions about the man she'd married, but Lady Wyle came up and asked Lady Melle to join a card game. Lady Wyle invited Khamsin to join as well, but the lady's insincere smirk of a smile and too-watchful eyes made Kham decline.

"No, please go on. I don't play cards." Most court card games required four or more to play, so Kham, always alone, had never had the opportunity to learn. And the last thing she wanted to do when her sisters and brothers had snuck up to visit her was while away their precious, purloined time with card games.

It didn't take long for Khamsin to regret letting Lady

Melle leave her side. Sitting alone, without Lady Melle's warm presence to buffer her, she was acutely aware of the Winterladies watching her every move, many of them sly-eyed, sumptuously gowned adversaries waiting for the first sign of weakness.

Tension coiled inside her. Sitting still for any length of time had never been easy for her, and sitting there while her every move was watched and measured was indescribably unpleasant. She was a child of the elements, accustomed to doing as she pleased and running free through the abandoned towers of the King's Keep. She wasn't made to sit for hours on end, confined and coiffed, surrounded by women whose conversation revolved around fashion, running households, and raising children. Kham would much rather be outside with the men, watching them train with their weapons—better yet, swinging a sword of her own. Falcon had often practiced with her, and those were some of the happiest times of life.

Her foot started tapping. Conversation dwindled. Ladies cast sidelong glances her way. She jammed her feet against the ground and kept them there.

Conversation resumed. More baby talk. More discussion of ribbons. One of the ladies had a new maid to dress her hair, and wasn't she doing a splendid job?

Kham's fingers began to drum restlessly against the armrests of her chair.

The lady with the hairdressing maid glanced Kham's way, bit her lip, and fell silent.

Kham clutched the armrests as if her life depended on it.

Outside, the thin clouds that had gathered during the luncheon grew heavy and dark.

"Oh, dear." Lady Ros glanced out at the rapidly darkening sky. "It looks like we're in for a bit of a storm."

"That came up fast," another woman murmured. "There wasn't a cloud in the sky this morning."

Now they were going to talk about the weather? Kham leapt to her feet, unable to bear it any longer.

All the Winterladies rose as well and looked her way. "I have a bit of a headache," Kham lied, working hard to keep the bark out of her voice. "I think I'll go for a walk outside."

Lady Melle cast a glance out the windows, where rain had begun to fall. "A walk, my dear? In the cold and rain?"

"I like the rain," Kham snapped, and the shocked, hurt look on Lady Melle's face made her feel like a brute. She took a breath, forcing down her temper. "I'm sorry. This headache has me on edge. But I do like the rain, and the cold doesn't bother me."

"Of course, Your Grace." Lady Melle's polite use of Khamsin's honorific instead of the warm, maternal "my dear" made Kham feel even worse. The white-haired lady waved to one of the footmen. "Send for our maids, Gunter. We need oiled jackets and rainshades. The queen wishes to go for a walk."

"No, Gunter, wait." Kham held up a staying hand. "Lady Melle, none of you need to come with me. Stay here inside where it's warm." Lady Melle had a surprisingly stubborn look in her eyes, so Kham moved closer and dropped her voice to a low whisper to admit, "This morning has been just a little . . . overwhelming. I need some time to myself."

And then, because it suddenly occurred to her that Lady Melle's determination to accompany her stemmed from reasons other than politeness and court etiquette, she added, "I won't go far. I'll keep to the gardens you can see from these windows."

After a long, considering moment, Lady Melle waved off Gunter the footman, and said, "Of course, my dear. Go have your walk. Only please don't stay out too long. The king would have my head if you caught cold."

Kham beamed her first genuine smile in the last two hours. "I never catch cold." Impulsively, she threw her arms around the older woman and kissed her on the cheek, then just as quickly jumped back and blushed, very conscious of the Winterladies whispering behind their fans. "I'm sorry," she muttered. "I don't suppose I should have done that."

She'd never had cause to put Tildy's comportment lessons into real practice, but she did know queens didn't go about throwing their arms around their ladies and smacking kisses on their cheeks.

Lady Melle, once she got over her surprise, just smiled even more warmly than she had before and patted Kham's hand. "There's nothing to be sorry for, my dear. Gunter, send someone to fetch the queen's wrap, then please escort the queen to the east garden."

Fifteen minutes later, with a warm fur coat over her red velvet dress, Kham turned her face up to the icy drizzle that even now was softening to a fine mist as the dark clouds began to lighten and break up. She took a deep breath of the clean, brisk air, flung her arms out, and whirled in a circle. Summer Sun, that felt good!

The garden was empty and quiet. The bustling sounds from the two large baileys at the front of Gildenheim were muted here. Several fountains burbled peacefully among manicured walks. Instead of beds of bright summer flowers, the gardens here had been planted with evergreen shrubs and sculpted trees and plants that sported bright leaves or berries in shades of purple and red and a ghostly silvery gray.

There was a maze in the center of the garden, grown from holly bushes. Kham glanced back at the arching windows of the banquet hall where she had lunched with the ladies of the court, then turned and dove into the maze, following the twisting paths between the dense hedges. It wasn't a particularly difficult maze, and Kham found the center after only a couple of wrong turns. There, a ring of wooden benches surrounded a lovely, three-tiered fountain.

Scarlet flashed at the corner of her eye, and she turned her head to see a bright red cardinal alight atop one of the benches on the other side of the fountain. She smiled. She'd always loved birds. They reminded her of her brother because wherever Falcon went, birds always congregated.

They flocked to him with the same eager devotion as his many beautiful female companions.

Kham watched the cardinal hop down and peck at the cold ground beneath the bench and wished she'd brought bread crumbs from the luncheon. She'd have to do that tomorrow.

A shadow passed over the center of maze, and the cardinal took wing, disappearing into the dense holly bushes. Kham glanced up to see a large, snowy white falcon soaring across the sky. It circled Gildenheim on outstretched wings, then dove in to land on a window ledge near the top of the castle's tallest spire.

"Where are you, Falcon?" she murmured aloud. Had her brother finally found Roland's sword? And if he had, when he heard about the conditions of her marriage—the threat hanging over her head—would he come to Wintercraig to save her? That was just the sort of grand, heroic gesture Falcon loved most.

So why did the idea of Falcon riding to her rescue fill her with dread?

Her gaze wandered down the gray stone spire and traveled across the rings of fortified battlements that protected Gildenheim as if it were the greatest treasure of the kingdom. She thought about the cheers of the people gathered in the bailey to greet their king and his new bride, and the genuine care and concern he'd shown for the villagers they met along the way.

She was married to Wynter of the Craig. She was his now. His wife, his queen . . . and his key to retaining unequivocal control of Summerlea once she gave him an heir. After the last weeks together, she knew enough about her husband to know he would never surrender anything he considered his. If Falcon came for her, there would be battle, a war that would not end until either Falcon or Wynter lay dead.

And if Falcon had Blazing, the victor would not be Wynter of the Craig.

For no reason Khamsin cared to examine too closely, that thought left her feeling more ill than the awful fish dishes she'd not been able to escape at lunch.

Kham met with Vinca later that afternoon, but the tour of the palace wasn't remotely as helpful or extensive as Khamsin had hoped it would be. They visited only the kitchens, wine cellars, the servants' quarters, and portions of the lower four levels of the main palace.

Kham didn't like the wine cellars. They'd been dug deep into the mountain, through solid rock, and they reminded Kham too much of the place King Verdan had taken her to beat her into compliance with his plans. Especially since her connection to the sun disappeared when she stepped across the cellar threshold.

Rattled by those memories, her curt, "Yes, quite impressive," and the abrupt way she then turned and headed for the door didn't win her any points with Vinca or the wine steward. She was too proud and too protective of her vulnerability to apologize for her behavior. Instead, she announced briskly, "I believe I've seen enough of the kitchens. I would prefer to spend the rest of our tour above stairs."

She didn't draw an easy breath until they reached the first floor, and she stood in a beam of sunlight shining through a large, arched window.

Wynter's palace servants were too well trained to show disapproval, but the tiny hint of warmth that had been in Vinca's voice at the start of the tour disappeared after that visit to the cellars, and it never returned. With cool, dispassionate efficiency, Vinca escorted Khamsin through the lower four levels of the palace proper, which housed banqueting halls, the throne room, rooms of state, and an entire wing of rooms they did not enter, which Vinca said were used by Wynter, his cabinet, and the many folk involved in the governance of the kingdom. In addition, there were all manner of parlors and galleries and a tremendous library that would have made Summer and Spring sigh with pleasure. Everywhere were terraces and balconies overlooking the mountains, the valley below, Konundal, the village at the foot of Gildenheim's mountain, and the many, multi-leveled gardens built into the side of the mountain and integrated into the palace itself as it went up and up.

At the fourth floor, Vinca turned to Khamsin and announced the end of the tour. "What about the rest of the palace?" Kham gestured to the gilded stairways twining up to floors they hadn't visited yet.

"Naught that would be of interest to Your Grace," Vinca said. "Mostly just rooms used by the nobles and visiting dignitaries and their servants when they are at court, and most of those are empty now."

"How many more floors are there?"

"Another ten, not counting the towers, but three of those are servants' quarters."

Kham gasped. "So many?" She'd realized Gildenheim was massive. She just hadn't realized *how* massive.

"There was talk of building an upper palace before the war." Vinca smiled with pride before she caught herself and marshaled her expression back into a cool mask. "Things are much quieter here these last three years."

Kham shook her head. "If Gildenheim got any larger, you would need a horse to ride from one end of the palace to the other."

"Winterfolk are a hardy breed, and walking does the body good," Vinca replied crisply. Then she sighed, and admitted, "But an expansion is unlikely to happen anytime soon. Wars are costly, and not just to the treasury."

A brief, tense silence fell between them at the reminder of the terrible price of war.

Vinca cleared her throat. "If there won't be anything else, Your Grace? Dinner will be served in less than two hours, and I have a number of duties yet to attend to."

"Of course. Thank you very much for the tour, Vinca."

"My pleasure, Your Grace. Shall I escort you back to your chambers?"

Kham wasn't ready to go back to her rooms. She wanted to explore a little more. "No, you go on. I'll find my way there."

Vinca made no move to leave. She gnawed on her bottom lip, then said, "The king would not be pleased if I were to abandon you here alone."

"If I tell you to go, you aren't abandoning me." Kham's mouth twisted in a sardonic smile. "Believe me, if the king doesn't like it, he'll know where the blame lies." When Vinca still remained where she was, Kham arched a brow. A flicker of irritation stirred in her breast. "I'll be fine, Vinca. I need to learn my way around. Now is as good a time as any."

Left with no alternative but to leave or directly disobey the woman who was—however temporarily—her queen, Vinca dipped a curtsy and made her way back downstairs.

Once she was gone, Kham turned and started down the wide corridor that led to another set of stairs. Ten more levels? Plus all those towers and turrets? Her pulse quickened. She was an explorer at heart. Quiet, abandoned places with their musty old secrets had been her home for years, and she'd spent a lifetime ferreting through forgotten treasures, imagining where they'd come from, who had left them there.

True to Vinca's word, however, the fifth floor was nothing more than living quarters for palace guests—many of those rooms unoccupied, and utterly disappointing on the hidden-treasure front. Still, she opened every door that wasn't locked and peered inside.

The rooms were graciously appointed, luxurious without the sometimes garish opulence of the palace at Vera Sola. Kham didn't want to admit it, but the restrained elegance of these rooms appealed to her. And every one of the rooms, occupied or not, was maintained in a perfect state of readiness.

She was inspecting a small study, admiring the cream brocade couches and the beaded embroidery of ice blue velvet drapes, when a young maid approached and bobbed a quick curtsy.

"Begging your pardon, Your Grace. It's half past six, and the king sent me to escort you to your chambers to change for the evening meal."

Had Vinca reported that she'd left Kham unattended in the upper levels of the palace? Or had one of the servants on this floor taken exception to her poking her nose in all the rooms?

Kham considered sending the maid back without her, then discarded the notion. If she defied him, Wynter's next emissary would likely be one of his White Guard, and she had no desire to be marched back downstairs like a wayward prisoner. Her exploring for the day had come to an end.

"What's your name?" she asked the maid, as they made their way to the main staircase.

The girl looked surprised. "Greta, Your Grace."

"Have you worked here long—at the palace, I mean?"

"Since I was eight, Your Grace."

Kham frowned. "Eight seems awfully young to go into service. Is it customary for Wintercraig children to work at so young an age?"

Greta lifted her chin. "My father died in a Great Hunt not long after Prince Wynter became king. My mum had four children and a fifth on the way. The king saw to it that we had a roof over our heads, food in our bellies, and work, because Winterfolk don't take charity. Mum works in the kitchens. I started doing top-floor work until I was old enough to move downstairs."

"Top-floor work?"

"Keeping the upstairs tidy. Seventh floor and higher." She bit her lip. "No one really uses those rooms anymore," she admitted, "but the king wouldn't let Mistress Vinca close them up even during the war. Said it was important to keep the palace ready for whatever the future holds. It's mostly the little ones who tend the unused rooms."

"The little ones?"

"Too old to stay in the nursery but too young to do heavy work. Mostly they just dust and sweep and change the linens. Like I did when I first came here. My sister Fenna still does top-floor work. But she's ten next year, and she'll be training with the seamstress."

"What about your brothers and sisters?"

"My brother Skander—he's sixteen—works in the stables, but he'll be training for the White Guard soon. My brother Tarn is an armorer's apprentice. Linnet—she's thirteen—works with the gardener. Some of the little ones work with the gardener, too, during the summer, but this time of year, it gets too cold, so they can't stay out for long. Top-floor work is better. And there's schooling in the mornings."

"What sort of schooling?"

Greta frowned as if the question made no sense. "The usual. Reading, writing, doing figures." She made a face. "History."

Kham's brows raised in genuine surprise. "Where I come from, Greta, there's nothing usual in that. Only the merchants and the nobility educate their children." It was a long-held belief of many a Summerlander noble that their farmhands and manual laborers had no need for books and mathematics. Education tended to give the menial classes "ideas" that caused all manner of societal problems. "And, history is fascinating."

"I could never like it." Greta shook her head. "All those battles and kings and dates. Deadly boring."

"Oh, no," Kham objected. "All those lives, those heroes, those tales of great adventures and sacrifice. It's the very furthest from boring anything could ever be."

"If you say so, Your Grace." The young maid looked unconvinced.

"I shall prove it to you. When is the next history lesson?"

"History is every Thorgyllsday at ten o'clock."

"Excellent. Next Thorgyllsday, you will escort me to

wherever these lessons are held, and I'll share a bit of history from my country that I promise you is anything but boring. It's the story of Summerlea's greatest king, Roland Soldeus."

Greta didn't look too enthusiastic about the prospect, but Kham attributed that to Greta's self-professed dislike of history. She'd wager not one of these Winterchildren had ever heard the epic tale of Roland Triumphant. She had no doubt they'd love it as much as she did once.

The prospect of sharing Roland's valiant tale kept her smiling all the way to the dining hall, where the sight of Gildenheim's assembled nobles greeted her like a splash of cold water in the face. As the footman rang a bell and announced her arrival, Kham doused her smile and took a deep breath, girding herself for yet another mealtime ordeal.

The next week fell into a stultifying pattern. Although Wynter ate his evening meals with the court and visited her bedchamber nightly, she saw very little of him during the day. Her attempts to get involved in the actual running of the palace were politely but firmly rebuffed, leaving her to fill her time as best she could. She spent her mornings exploring the upper levels of the palace and talking to the children or sitting in on their lessons. Then came the interminably long luncheon and tedious social hour with the ladies of the court, followed by an hour spent walking through the gardens and feeding the birds—which might have been blessedly private and peaceful had not several of the ladies and several White Guard taken to accompanying her. In the afternoons, she wandered about the palace and tried to get to know the servants and Winterfolk who lived and worked in Gildenheim.

Then Thorgyllsday rolled around, bringing with it the much-anticipated history lesson. Khamsin sprang out of bed, eagerly donned a royal blue gown that had belonged to Summer, and raced upstairs, her copy of *Roland Tri-*

umphant clutched to her chest. When she entered the little classroom, however, instead of a roomful of children waiting for their lesson, she found empty chairs and a history teacher who informed her that all the children had been called away to tend other matters.

"How disappointing," Kham said. "Perhaps I could come back next week."

"I'm sorry, Your Grace," the history teacher informed her, "but if you intend to teach them about Roland Soldeus, I expect their mothers will have work for them next week as well."

She swallowed hard. "I see." All week long, she'd noticed that some of the children had been disappearing from the classes, not to return, but she'd assumed that they'd just been reassigned to work in other parts of the palace. It hadn't occurred to her that *she* was the reason they'd been withdrawn from the classes. "What if I were to teach them about one of Wintercraig's heroes instead?" She didn't know any stories about Wintercraig heroes, but there was a big library in the palace. Surely there must be *something* she could use in there to excite these children about history.

"I don't know, Your Grace," the teacher said. "Perhaps it's best if you leave the education of Wintercraig children to Winterfolk."

Kham stumbled back. There was no misunderstanding this message: She was a Summerlander, and she was unwelcome here. "Of course. I'm so sorry. I didn't realize."

Mortified, Kham spun on her heel and walked rapidly down the hall towards the stairs. All the way, she fought a losing battle with tears and had to duck into one of the abandoned bedrooms to hide when the dam burst and the flood of hot, salty wetness spilled down her cheeks. She'd faced rejection before, and plenty of it, but she couldn't remember the last time anything had wounded her like this. This rejection was personal, and it bloodied her in places she'd thought long ago inured against hurt.

She cried until her tears were spent, then wiped her eyes and sat locked in the room until her face was no longer blotchy or swollen, and her eyes lost their puffy red rims. When she finally emerged from the room, half a dozen servants loitering about in the hallway scattered like mice. Kham watched them go with a hardened heart. She'd offered these people friendship, and they'd thrown it back in her face. She wouldn't make that mistake again.

Lifting her chin and squaring her shoulders, she marched downstairs to her scheduled luncheon with the ladies of the court. There, at least, she had never felt at home enough to let down her guard. And because she hadn't let down her guard, the Winterladies of the court couldn't hurt her the way the upstairs children just had.

Or so she thought until she reached the dining hall, and Lady Melle came forward, smiling sweetly, her hands outstretched.

"Come in, my dear, come in. We were beginning to worry you'd gotten lost." As they took their seats at the banquet table, Lady Melle beamed. "Cook has outdone herself today. She's prepared a special treat just for you. I understand it's one of your favorites." She waved over the first of a line of servants carrying covered trays of food. The server whipped off the deep tray with a flourish. A cloud of steam billowed forth as the servant holding the tray held it out for Khamsin's inspection. "Lutefisk and eels," Lady Melle announced with a happy smile.

Kham's eyes widened, and her nostrils flared at the sight—and dreadful aroma—of the pile of gelatinous white fish surrounded by a sea of broth swimming with onions, garlic, and long black eels. Her stomach gave a terrible lurch.

The Winterladies gasped in surprise as Kham leapt to her feet so fast she sent her chair flying.

"My dear!" Lady Melle cried.

"Your Grace!" someone else exclaimed.

Kham clapped a hand over her mouth, grabbed her

skirts in one hand, and bolted for the door. *Please, let me make it out of the room. Don't let me shame myself before them. Please, let me make it out of the room.*

She didn't make it.

"She puked over lutefisk and eels?" Valik asked when Lady Melle finished her report of this afternoon's disastrous luncheon. "Who doesn't like lutefisk and eels? They're delicious!"

"Valik." Wynter gave his second-in-command a pointed look and jerked his head in the direction of the door. Valik grimaced but tromped out. When he was gone, Wyn leaned back in his chair and regarded Lady Melle over steepled fingers.

"It appears to have been a prank," Lady Melle explained. "Cook received a note saying the queen was pining for lutefisk and eels, declaring it one of her favorites. Needless to say, that doesn't appear to be true."

They were seated in his private office in the western tower. To Wyn's left, a wide window of leaded-glass panes looked out over the Minsk River valley far below. Not that you could see that valley now. Dark clouds cloaked Gildenheim in a heavy mist, harbinger of the afternoon storm that had rolled in like clockwork every day around noon for the past week. The storm should have already broken up, since Khamsin's daily luncheon with her ladies had come to its unfortunate end over an hour ago, but his weather-witch queen was working a different misery out in the sky today, and snow was falling with no sign of letting up anytime soon.

It was early for snow, even in Craig, but whether Khamsin's daily storms or the Ice Heart was to blame, Wynter didn't know.

"Apart from today's unfortunate incident, how is my queen settling in?"

"Truthfully?"

Wyn gave a curt nod.

"She's not." Lady Melle threw up her hands in distress. "I'm sorry, my dearest, but the poor thing's miserable. Our food doesn't agree with her. She can't ply a needle to save her life. The ladies tried reading some of their favorite novels to her, but she grew so restless and impatient, I thought we were going to have a tempest right there in the gathering hall. She likes the outdoors, but she hates having us following her, watching her every move. I thought she might like to take a trip with me down to Konundal, but she doesn't ride, and when I suggested having a carriage brought round, well, I swear I nearly saw some of that lightning Lord Valik says she can call."

Wyn grimaced. "Carriages don't agree with her any better than lutefisk and eels."

Lady Melle's brows rose. "That would have been useful information to know before now, Wynter," she said with an uncharacteristic snap in her voice.

Wyn closed his eyes against the sudden whip of icy temper rising inside him. Before drinking the Ice Heart, Lady Melle's scold would have made him blush in shame. Now it made fury bite hard, the Ice King in him fuming at her impertinence. But Wynter would slit his own throat before allowing himself to harm, either by word or deed, the gentle, big-hearted woman who had been a surrogate mother to Garrick . . . and to himself, insomuch as he would let her. "You know it now, Lady Melle," he said when he trusted himself to speak.

She heaved a sigh, oblivious to her own mortal peril. "Honestly, my boy, could you make this any more difficult? You don't want her wandering all over the palace, you don't want her walking alone outside, you don't want her interfering in the running of the palace, the servants are up in arms over her attempt to interfere in their children's education, and Wyrn knows she can't sit still for any length of time. One short hour after our luncheon pushes her to the very limits of her endurance. I've had several ladies express their concern that she might lose her temper and strike us dead with a lightning bolt. Something must be done!"

"What do you suggest, Lady Melle?" One of the many admirable traits of Lady Melle, she never presented a problem without also offering a solution.

"She needs a friend, my dear. She's a young girl in a strange place. She needs someone she can talk to. Someone she can do things with."

Lady Melle's mouth quirked in a deprecating smile. "I'm too old to chase around with her hither and yon, and the ladies, forgive me, fear her magic and frankly haven't warmed up to the poor thing any more than she has to them."

"Do you have someone in mind?"

"I wish I did. I've been racking my brain. I was going to speak to Barsul about it tonight, see if he could suggest anyone."

"I'll think on it. Thank you, Lady Melle." Wynter stood up, signaling an end to the meeting.

Lady Melle rose and headed for the door, then paused when she reached it. "I like her, Wynter. I like her quite a lot, and I didn't expect to. Yes, she has a temper—and a hard time keeping it contained—but there's also a kindness in her, and a great deal of loneliness. I don't think she's the threat Valik believes her to be. You really should spend more time with her."

"Thank you, Lady Melle," Wynter said again, his voice polite, his gaze deliberately noncommittal.

Lady Melle sighed and let herself out.

The freezing rain and snow continued to fall all day. Wynter left his office early to share dinner with the court, but Khamsin's chair remained conspicuously empty.

"I'm so sorry about the queen's ill health at today's luncheon," Reika said, as the servants carried trays of fragrant fish dishes around the table. "Valik told me she didn't travel well, but I would never have thought her fragile stomach extended to mealtimes. We Winterfolk are such a hardy lot." With a smile, she turned to help herself to a serving of broiled mackerel. "I do hope the coming winter won't be too difficult for her constitution."

Though spoken with solicitous concern, Reika's remark somehow managed to make it sound like Khamsin was a weakling who didn't measure up to the rigorous demands of life in Wintercraig. The implication didn't sit well with Wynter.

"She is much stronger than those who don't know her might think," he replied. "But thank you for your concern, Lady Villani. You remind me that I should go check on my wife." Reika gaped at him as he tossed his napkin on the table and stood. "If you will excuse me."

Wynter strode out of the dining hall and took the stairs three at a time. When he reached the wing that housed his and Khamsin's chambers, he didn't bother with his usual habit of accessing Khamsin's bedchamber through the connecting door between their rooms. Instead, he went straight through the main doors to her suite, startling her little maid, whom he dismissed with a curt command and a sharp wave of his hand.

He found Khamsin sitting on her balcony, wet clothes plastered to her body, her skin ice-cold. He didn't need to ask how she was feeling. Her battered emotions were all too obvious as they played out across the stormy night sky. No cracks of lightning or wild winds tonight. Just heavy clouds and wet, falling snow. She didn't even put up a fight when he scooped her up in his arms and carried her back inside.

Because he'd dismissed her maid, Wynter tended to her needs himself, stripping her of her sodden garments, toweling her dry with soft cloths from her bathing chamber, lowering a fine, fragrant linen gown over her head. Through it all, she stood unnaturally still and docile, without a single toss of her head or rebellious flash in her eyes. When he was done, she climbed into bed and looked at him with dull eyes.

"Will you be coming to bed, Your Grace?"

He wanted to howl. She wasn't some spineless, timid lass. She was Khamsin—Storm—full of fire and defiance and strong, reckless, stubborn will. Until this moment, he hadn't realized how much he enjoyed her wildness, her vitality, or how much he looked forward to seeing it every night.

"No," he said. "You've been ill. You should get your rest."

She didn't toss her head and remind him of his need for an heir or her motivation to provide him one. She merely looked at him for one long moment, then lay down on her side, her back to him, and pulled the covers up around her shoulders.

She looked so small and alone in her vast bed.

Valik would warn him to harden his heart, that she was manipulating him. But Wynter knew from the top-floor maids that Kham had spent the entire morning locked in one of the unused bedrooms upstairs, crying. Hiding her vulnerability as she always did.

It alarmed him that she wasn't hiding it now, and he couldn't shake the feeling that leaving her tonight would be a mistake.

Trusting his instincts, Wyn walked to the other side of the bed, shed his clothes, then climbed into the bed beside his wife. He expected her to turn to him, but she didn't.

Instead, her back still to him, she said, "I thought you weren't going to stay."

Her voice sounded different. Thicker.

She was still hiding her vulnerability, after all.

He reached for her, easily conquering her slight resistance as he turned her over to face him. She wouldn't look at him, damp, spiky lashes hiding her eyes.

"I changed my mind," he said. "I don't want to be alone tonight." Gently, as if she were fragile crystal that would shatter at the slightest pressure, he touched his lips to her eyes, nuzzling away her tears, then brushed soft, lingering kisses across her cheeks until her slender arm twined around his neck, and she lifted her mouth to his.

They didn't speak. They simply loved in silence, letting their hands, their lips, their bodies speak for them. Long, lingering caresses. Tender, healing kisses. The slow, steady glide of bodies moving together in wordless communion.

Afterwards, exhaustion overwhelmed her, and she fell asleep in his arms. He lay there for more than an hour, just holding her and watching her sleep, and he realized that Valik might just be right to fear that Wynter's Summerlea bride was working some sort of enchantment on him. The fiery, passionate, willful Khamsin drew him like a moth to flame and brought those frozen parts of him back to life. But this Khamsin, the wounded, needing Khamsin who couldn't hide her pain, she seeped into the cracks in his icy armor, penetrating much deeper than was comfortable or safe.

He wasn't ready for that, so he left her in the middle of the night.

She wasn't the only one who hid her vulnerabilities.

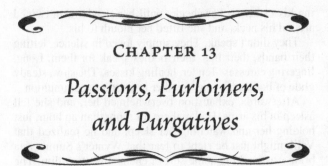

CHAPTER 13

Passions, Purloiners, and Purgatives

Khamsin was both bereft and grateful when she woke up alone the next morning. Bereft because she was becoming used to the feel of Wynter lying beside her, and grateful because his absence excused her from any awkwardness over last night's embarrassing show of weakness.

She took a sip of her morning tea, only to grimace and set it aside. Bitter again. Tildy had always brewed the perfect cup of tea, but Bella clearly needed more instruction. She was either using too many leaves or steeping the tea too long.

The door to her wardrobe room opened, and Bella whisked in.

"Bella, about the tea," Kham began, only to break off with a scowl when she saw Bella carrying a frosted taupe outfit trimmed with white fur. "What's that? I told you to lay out my red dress." After yesterday's humiliating debacle, she was determined to gird herself in her brightest, most defiant Summerlea armor before facing the Wintercraig court.

"Mistress Narsk delivered this this morning along with a note from the king. You're to meet Lord Valik in the upper bailey no later than ten o'clock to receive your first riding lesson."

"Riding lesson?" Every bruised and wilted part of Khamsin's soul suddenly perked up. "I'm to have a riding lesson?"

"Apparently so, ma'am. But you'd best hurry. It's already a quarter 'til nine."

Kham leapt to her feet. Bella had already drawn her bath, but rather than enjoying a leisurely morning soak as she'd intended, Khamsin washed in record time. There wasn't time to dry her hair before the fire, so she toweled it off and secured the damp, unruly curls with a brown bow. Then she threw on her new split riding skirt and fur-lined coat from Mistress Narsk, wolfed down the last half of her now-cold meat pie, washed it down with a few sips of the too-bitter jasmine tea, and bolted for the door.

She reached the courtyard just as Gildenheim's clock tower began to toll ten o'clock.

Valik was already there, and he greeted her with the cold eyes and stony expression she'd come to expect from him.

"This way," he said in a clipped voice. He led her across the courtyard, through the portcullis, and down into the larger, lower bailey that was bustling with industry. Here, a blacksmith's forge, farrier, saddler, and hay barn had all been built along the northern wall to serve the enormous stables carved into the side of the mountain.

A broad-shouldered man with a weathered face and thick queue of ash blond hair met them just inside the building. Valik introduced him as Bron, the stable master.

Bron smelled of horses, hay, and snow, and his eyes were deep, vivid green rather than the typical Wintercraig blue. "I'll bring you Kori to start with," he said. His voice was low and deep and musical—and filled with more warmth than any Winterfolk save Lady Melle had shown her so far. It set Kham instantly at ease. "She's a kind lass, with gentle ways. She'll teach you what you need to know and be patient until you learn it. Later, when you've found your seat, you may want to choose another mount, one with a bit more fire in her soul."

He marched down the corridor, returning a few minutes later with a large, black horse in tow. The mare had a thick, winter coat and a long, striking white mane and tail.

"This is Kori," he said. "Hold out your hand to greet her."

Kham stared at the horse with trepidation. Big as a Summerlea shire horse, with thick powerful muscles and hooves like great, iron-shod rocks, Kori was intimidating. The top of Kham's head barely reached the mare's withers. And that mouthful of very large teeth seemed quite capable of taking off Kham's hand with a single chomp.

Bron smiled slightly and whispered something into the horse's ear. The horse gave a whinnying neigh that sounded like laughter, then tossed her head, sending the long strands of her snowy mane dancing.

"It's a fine compliment that you find Kori impressive enough to fear," Bron said, "but there's no need. She'll not harm you."

"I'm not afraid," Kham lied quickly, then blushed at Bron's steady look. "Well, not much." *At least trying not to be.* Determined not to look like a coward, Kham sucked in a breath and held out her hand, palm up. The animal's nose nudged Kham's hand experimentally, snuffling at her, then the thick, velvety lips nuzzled her palm. It tickled. Kham fought the urge to snatch back her hand.

"She likes you," Bron murmured. "Reach out now, and rub her cheek."

She followed the stable master's instructions, running her hands across the animal's warm, heavy body, learning where and how to touch her and where not to. He showed her how to approach the mare's hindquarters, how to curry her thick hide, how to inspect her legs and hooves and use a hoof pick to scrape the mare's hooves free of collected matter. By the time he was done, Kori was saddled and bridled, and Khamsin had lost a good bit of her fear.

"I'll take Kori's lead myself," Valik said. "The riding ring is a half mile down the mountain."

She started to object to his leading her down the mountain like an infant, but decided not to push the grumpy Winterman. The prospect of her first riding lesson was the greatest treat she'd ever received. If she had to suffer being leashed to Valik as the price of that treat, so be it.

But suffering his brooding, unfriendly silence the whole way was another matter. She was used to people despising her, but she preferred to know the reason why.

"Is it my Summerlander blood you find so offensive, Lord Valik," she asked, as they rode, "or do you dislike me on your cousin's account?"

His expression didn't change. "Why would I dislike you on Elka's account? You had nothing to do with her choices."

"I wasn't talking about the cousin who ran off with my brother. I was talking about Reika, the one who's set her cap for my husband."

That put a crack in his stony expression. Valik's brows shot up. He gave a bark of disbelieving laughter and looked at her like she'd just sprouted a second head. "Reika has no interest in Wynter."

She barely kept her jaw from dropping. "Of course she's interested. I'll wager she's wanted him since the first day she met him."

"You're daft, Summerlander."

"No, but you are blind, Winterman. Good gods." She shook her head. "Who knew men of the north were so easy to deceive?"

Valik's expression went sharp as a razor and hard as stone. The deadly promise of lethal force emanated from every pore, and his eyes were cold enough to freeze the marrow in her bones. "We are not so easily duped, Summerlander. And as your countrymen learned to their woe, we deal severely with those who try."

"Ah, so that's it. You think I'm involved in some plot against the king." She shook her head and rolled her eyes. Anyone who knew her in the slightest—well, any clear-thinking someone, at least—would never contemplate such a ridiculous charge. "In case you haven't noticed, subtleties are not my forte. When I wish someone harm, they storming well know it."

Valik cast a quick glance at the cloudless sky before saying, "So, you're an innocent, are you? As honest as the day is long? It was not you pretending to be your sister Autumn, the Season my king *thought* he was taking to wife?"

She bit her lip. "I never lied. Wynter wanted a Summerlea princess to wife, and he got one. If he neither named the specific princess he wanted—nor lifted my veil to discover which one he was getting—how is that my fault?"

Valik's eyes narrowed. "Lady, you wed and bed my king full-knowing he thought you were another—then say you did nothing wrong—yet you wonder why I consider you as low and untrustworthy as the rest of your kin? What would your father have done, had he found himself so cheated?"

Color stained Kham's cheeks. Verdan would likely have separated his bride's head from her shoulders, then declared war on her kin.

"Exactly," Valik snapped, reading her answer on her face. "Wynter Atrialan possesses more honor in his little finger than your entire family combined, and I will never forget how you used that honor against him. Nor do I intend to let you do so again."

He tossed Kori's lead line to one of the other guards and spurred his mount forward, moving as far up ahead as the lead line would allow. An uncomfortable silence descended. Kham glanced at the others. To a man, they wore blank expressions and kept their gazes fixed straight ahead.

Bron tapped his heels to his mount's side and moved up to the spot Valik had vacated. In a friendly, conversational tone clearly meant to end the awkward silence, he said, "I'm curious that you've never ridden before, my lady. The ladies of your father's court do not ride?"

She forced a smile. "They do, but I was never part of my father's court. He hated me even more than Lord Valik does."

Bron winced. "Forgive me. I do not mean to pry."

"No need to apologize. I've had a lifetime to get used to it." She would never forget or forgive what Verdan had done to her, but from the moment that carriage had carried her past the Stone Knights guarding the gates of Vera Sola, the Summer King had lost the power to hurt her. "My mother's nurse raised me in a remote part of the palace and educated me to the best of her ability, but since I wasn't allowed to leave the palace, I never learned to ride. I confess I'm quite looking forward to it. Other than the journey here, this is the greatest adventure of my life."

"Well, I'll do my best to make the lessons enjoyable."

True to Bron's word, once they reached the riding ring, the lesson was one of the most pleasant experiences of her life, if, perhaps, a little too tame and too short for her liking. Khamsin learned how to mount and dismount, position her feet in the stirrups, and hold the reins. Bron led Kori around the ring on the lead line until he was satisfied Khamsin had gotten the hang of what he taught her. Then he unclipped the chain and let her walk the horse around the ring on her own. The mare, Kori, was a dream: sweet-natured, obedient, and responsive. Khamsin was eager to go on to the second gait, the trot, when Valik declared the lesson was at an end.

"Bron has plenty of work waiting for him at the palace, as do the rest of us."

"Oh, but—"

"There's no need to rush yourself, my lady," Bron intervened when Valik's expression darkened. "We'll have another lesson tomorrow, and I'll teach you the next gait then. For now, why don't you practice what you've learned today and ride Kori back to Gildenheim without the lead line attached?"

"I suppose that's acceptable." She acquiesced with more ill grace than she actually felt, so Valik wouldn't feel compelled to quash the idea just to deprive her. Truth be told, the prospect of putting her newly acquired skills to use was even more appealing than staying in the ring to continue her training.

As they rode back up the hill to Gildenheim, it was all she could do to stop from laughing out loud. She was on a horse, guiding it with her own hands up a curving mountain road, like any other free lady of the court might do. No more prison built of confining walls or her father's harsh governance.

Effervescence bubbled in her veins. Even Valik's glowering presence at her side couldn't dim her happiness. She was wed to a man who might send her to her death in a year, living in a land of haughty strangers who regarded her with all the welcome of a cockroach at a dinner banquet, and currently riding in the company of a man who would rather toss her off the mountain than escort her up it, but for the first time in her life, she felt free.

If Khamsin could have spent every waking hour with Kori and Bron, she would have. She hadn't returned to visit the top-floor children since that awful Thorgyllsday debacle, so except for the all-too-brief daily lessons with Bron, Kham spent most of the next week suffering through more hours of boring teas, luncheons, and social hours that the well-meaning Lady Melle Firkin had arranged.

Of Wynter, Khamsin continued to see little. Except for his attendance at the evening meal and his nightly visits to her chamber—which remained as breathtakingly passionate as ever—he remained sequestered with his councilmen, stewards, and generals in meeting after meeting. Wynter's preoccupation was not lost on Reika Villani or her circle of friends. The whispers and laughter behind their fans grew louder as the days progressed, the sly looks bolder. Khamsin held her head high. She wouldn't give Reika or her friends the satisfaction of knowing how their gloating stung.

Reflecting Kham's mood, the skies over Gildenheim remained a gloomy, overcast gray that drizzled constant snow.

The one bright spot in her days was the time she spent in the riding ring with Bron. The stable master was a kind, patient, and thorough teacher whose gift for calming high-strung horses worked equally as well for calming high-strung foreign queens. Each morning she counted down the hours until it was time for her lesson. When the lesson was over, she counted down the hours till the next day.

By the end of the week, Bron declared that she'd made enough progress to warrant a treat: a ride into the valley to visit the village of Konundal. They never went faster than a comfortable trot, and Valik stayed close by her side, but it was still Kham's first real, independent ride, and she thrilled at her newfound freedom.

When they reached the outskirts of the village, Kham sat up straighter in the saddle and looked around with interest. She hadn't paid much attention when she and Wynter had ridden through on the day of their arrival, but as this was the closest village to the castle, she intended to become very familiar with it.

The buildings were constructed of stone and wood with sharply angled roofs. Scores of stone chimneys rose towards the sky, fragrant wood smoke rising from each one. Cobbled streets had been cleared of snow and covered with grit to keep from turning slippery, and Winterfolk, bundled lightly against what most Summerlanders would consider bitter cold, went about their business as though the frosty air was little more than a spring chill. And perhaps, to them, it was.

For all that it served Gildenheim, the town of Konundal was surprisingly small. What buildings there were could have fit in Vera Sola three times over.

"Our largest cities are the ports Saevar, Loni, and Konumarr," Bron told her when she said as much. "Wynter has smaller palaces in each of them, but the Craig is the true seat of his power."

"I thought the city that served Gildenheim would be larger."

Bron smiled. "Gildenheim is its own city. Konundal is primarily a logging village. Few men of the Craig live in towns. Most have small farms and crofts in the mountains where they raise sheep, horses, cattle, and the next generation of men who will keep Wintercraig strong."

As they rode down the cobbled street, Khamsin was conscious of the stares she received from the villagers, some curious, some openly hostile. In this land of tall, pale-haired, golden-skinned folk, she could never hope to pass unnoticed, even without her escort of a dozen, icy-eyed White Guard.

They left their horses at the village stable and walked down the main street to the tavern for lunch. The proprietor greeted Valik and Bron with warmth and Khamsin with guarded politeness, and led them to a small, private room in the back.

"The last three years don't seem to have been as hard on Wintercraig as they were on Summerlea," Khamsin noted as the servingwoman brought out trays of fresh fruits and vegetables before their meal.

The servingwoman and Kham's guards all gave her sharp looks.

"We have our share of orphans and widows," Valik said coolly.

"Far fewer than Summerlea, I'm sure, but that's not what I meant." She gestured to the obviously fresh produce in the center of the table. "We all but starved this last year. All our crops in the north and many in the south were destroyed by the prolonged cold, but you seem not to have suffered a similar distress."

"It would have been easier on the king to simply cast winter across the entire continent," Bron explained, "but that would have brought suffering to his own people. So instead, he drew entirely on the power of the Ice Heart to create an island of winter across Summerlea while leaving Wintercraig's weather patterns relatively untouched. Our growing seasons have been cooler and much shorter, but we've had them."

"The Ice Heart?" Khamsin repeated.

"The power he embraced when he declared war on Summerlea."

"You mean the power he used to conquer Summerlea was not his own?"

Valik cleared his throat loudly, and Bron fell silent. "The king's powers and where they come from are none of your concern," Valik declared.

"The king is my husband. That makes everything about him my concern. However, since the subject obviously disturbs you, let us choose a different one." She kept her own expression cool and calm. Her initial question had been simple curiosity, but Valik's reaction piqued her interest. The abrupt end of the conversation could only mean there was something about the Ice Heart Valik did not want Summerlanders to know. Her mind seized the thread of the interrupted conversation and followed it down the only logical path. If the Ice Heart was not a power Wynter had been born with, it had come from somewhere.

That last thought led to an even more disturbing contemplation. Could the power be taken from him? Could someone—like herself, for instance—strip Wynter of his devastating power and return the Summer Throne to its rightful heirs?

They passed the remaining time in the inn without incident. The servingwoman delivered their food, Bron and Khamsin were careful to keep their conversations limited to neutral topics, and Valik remained his typical scowling self.

Unfortunately, the meal, though delicious, didn't sit well on Khamsin's stomach. Half an hour after leaving the tavern, her belly churned as discomfortingly as her troubled thoughts. Subterfuge and intrigue did not suit her. Like Roland, she would rather stand in the face of overwhelming odds and shout her defiance than skulk in the shadows and steal victory through ignoble means.

She'd agreed to the terms of peace. She'd wed Wynter of her own free will. She'd pledged her loyalty and the fruits of her life to him. And even if he did plan to turn her out to face the mercy of the mountains if she did not bear him a child in a year, did that nullify her own oaths? Could she continue to take Wynter into her arms and into her body while plotting to betray him? The very idea made her stomach hurt.

Unaware of her increasing distress, Bron escorted her around town and acquainted her with the various shops and shopkeepers. A few greeted her with a frigidness that bordered on hostility, but most seemed more approachable than the nobles in the palace. Kham gave a silent snort. Not that *that* was difficult.

In a field at the far end of town, some sort of gathering was under way. Dozens of tents had been erected, and workmen were unloading dozens more from arriving caravans. Piles of snow cleared from the tent plots formed an odd, impromptu maze of walls and walkways. Khamsin watched three strapping young men wrestle a set of tent poles into place on a freshly cleared plot. The men laughed and joked as they worked, long, fair hair swinging in belled plaits, teeth flashing white and dazzling in golden-skinned faces.

"What is all this?" Khamsin asked, as Bron guided her down a path between two lines of erected tents. Several merchants had already begun to set out their wares: furs and leathers, delicate, multicolored glassware, colorful ribbons, buttons and beads enough to make frippery-loving Summer giddy with happiness.

"The villagers are preparing for a *samdar-hald*," he replied. "A celebration gathering. For at least the next month, Winterfolk from all corners of the kingdom will gather here. There will be hunting and trading and music and dancing, and each week a *gildi,* a great feast, that you and Wynter will attend."

"What are they celebrating? The end of the war?"

"That, too," Bron said, "but this *samdar'*s main purpose is to celebrate your marriage."

Her stomach gave a sudden, unpleasant lurch. She pressed her hand against her belly. "My marriage?" she repeated weakly.

"It's not every day the king takes a wife," a familiar voice drawled from behind.

Khamsin spun around in surprise. "Wynter?" He was standing on the snowy street behind her, clad in a simple huntsman's garb of worn leathers and a white snowbear vest. "What are you doing here?"

"They told me you'd gone riding. Rather than sit in my office envying you, I decided to join you. I trust you have no objections?"

Before she could answer, a shout from a merchant several tents down drew their attention. Wynter snatched her up and thrust her behind him, holding her there with one broad hand, while Valik and the guards spun into action, surrounding them with a wall of steel armor and razor-sharp swords.

"Stop! Thief!"

A small, filthy little figure wrapped in shreds of mangy fur and moth-eaten cloth barreled toward them, only to draw up with in alarm at the sight of the soldiers and their swords. Khamsin had a brief glimpse of wide silvery blue eyes in a grimy face.

A boy. No more than nine or ten. The hand pressing Kham against Wynter's back relaxed.

"Thief! Thief!"

The boy opened his mouth and muttered a curse so foul it singed her ears, then darted towards a snowbanked corridor between the tents.

Wynter caught him in midlunge by the collar of his

moldy clothes and hoisted him into the air. The boy dangled there, limbs swinging wildly, his little teeth bared in a fierce snarl while even fouler curses poured out of his mouth in a defiant flood.

"Silence, boy," Wynter snapped. "You stand in the presence of the queen."

"Sod the farking queen, and sod you, too, you plague-ridden pus bag. Buggering, rat-farking sod! Put me down! Thorgyll freeze off your maggoty balls if you don't!"

"Well, that's charming," Wynter muttered. He grasped the boy by the ankles and dunked him headfirst into a nearby pile of snow. "That's to cool your head, boy," he said when he lifted the boy's snow-covered face back out of the drift. "Now hush."

"Fark you, dung-breath!" The child shook his head, spraying snow and curses in a wide arc.

Wynter clenched his jaw and dunked him again.

"Slime-crapping puke bag!"

Dunk.

"Miserable rat-fark!"

Dunk.

"Dung-eating butt fly!"

Dunk. Dunk.

"Finished?" Wynter asked. The child blinked snow-spangled lashes and glared, but held his silence. "Good." Wynter flipped the boy over, set him back on his feet and settled a firm grip around his thin neck. "Now, what's going on here?"

The merchant, a large, heavyset man bundled in thick but simple woolens and furs, pointed a finger at the child. "He is a thief! That's what's going on. He stole a slingbow from me. Snatched it right off my table, bold as brass!"

"That true, boy?"

The child hawked and spat and remained silent.

Wynter's jaw went hard as stone. "Don't try me, boy. You won't like what it gets you. Empty your pockets. Now," he barked when the child didn't instantly obey.

With a mutinous look, the boy reached into his ragged clothes, pulled out the pilfered slingbow, and flung it on the ground at the merchant's feet. "There! Take your stinking slingbow! Now let me go!"

"What else have you got in those pockets?" the merchant demanded. "What else have you stolen that I didn't see you take?"

"I didn't take nothing else!"

"I told you to empty your pockets, and I meant it," Wynter ordered. He gave the lad a warning shake.

Scowling, the boy began tossing down a veritable hoard of small treasures and trinkets: a handful of copper coins, a ball of twine, several smooth rocks, a collapsible knife, a pair of flint stones, a rabbit's foot, and a silver wristband set with small gemstones.

The merchant pounced on the wristband. "Didn't steal anything else, eh? Then where would the likes of you get this? Or are we supposed to believe it was a gift of the Valkyr?"

The boy lunged forward, almost breaking free from Wynter's grip. "That belonged to my mother, you great boar's ass! Give it back!"

"Your mother?" The merchant laughed. "Right, and I'm the King Under the Mountain. I'll just show this to the other merchants and see if any of them are missing this pretty trinket."

The boy gave a howl of fury and began kicking and flailing wildly. One foot caught Khamsin in the stomach with enough force to knock her down and drive the air from her lungs. She lay on the hard ground, gasping for air and shuddering as clammy waves of nausea washed over her from head to toe.

"Take him," Wynter muttered, shoving the boy—now shocked into fearful submission—towards Valik. He knelt by Khamsin's side and helped her to sit up. "Wife, are you hurt?"

"I'm fine," she muttered. She rose to her feet, then

wished she'd stayed on the ground. Her knees were shaking, and her vision was starting to swim.

"Wife?" The boy was staring at Wyn and Khamsin with wide eyes. "But if she's the queen, that would make you the . . ."

"King," Wynter confirmed.

"Of Wintercraig," Valik added. "Whom you just called a—what was the exact phrase—ah, yes, a plague-ridden pus bag." He gave the child a stern shake.

The boy's golden skin took on a greenish cast. His gaze darted from Wynter to Khamsin and back again. "I-I—"

Khamsin took pity on him. "There's no need to look so frightened. I'm fine." *Liar!* Her stomach, where the child had kicked her, was beginning to cramp. "And I'm sure the king has been called worse." That earned her an arch look from her spouse, which she ignored. "There's no harm done."

"Not that that excuses you from any other crimes you may have committed," Wynter said. "I want the truth of what's going on here. You can start by telling me your name."

For a moment, Khamsin thought the child might remain defiant, but apparently kicking his new queen in the belly and calling his king a pus bag had exhausted the boy's hunger for rebelliousness. At least temporarily. "Kr-Krysti. My name is Krysti."

"Wise decision, Krysti," Wynter praised. "Now, you say this bracelet belonged to your mother. I suggest you take us to her so she can confirm what you say."

"Does she know you're stealing from honest merchants?" the merchant standing nearby piped up.

Krysti cast a sullen glare at the man. "She's dead. She and my father both died three years ago."

"Your mother's dead?" Khamsin repeated. "And that bracelet was hers?"

The child nodded.

"Give it back to him," Khamsin ordered the merchant.

"But Your Grace—" the man protested. He turned to Wynter. "Sire!"

"He said it belonged to his mother," she interrupted. "I believe him. Look at what he pulled from his pockets. Nothing else there seems obviously stolen or unusual for a boy to carry around. And I will not see any child parted from a remembrance of his mother." The cramping in her stomach had become sharp pain. Alternating waves of heat and cold washed over her. She took a breath and swallowed. "If I'm wrong, I will compensate whichever merchant he robbed and see the boy suitably punished. So, give the bracelet back to him. Now."

Glowering, the merchant did as he was told. The boy clutched the bracelet so fiercely, Khamsin knew she'd been right. That small band of silver *was* precious to the boy, and in a way no stolen trinket could have been.

"My thanks." Her skin felt cold and tight. If she didn't find privacy soon, she was going to humiliate herself in front of Wynter, Valik, and half the village, but something about the boy would not just let her walk away. Maybe it was his defiance. Maybe it was the way he clutched his mother's bracelet, as if that small piece of metal held every ounce of happiness in his world. He reminded her of herself. Half-wild, full of fire and fierce rebellion. Desperately clinging to whatever small, precious memories of love he could find.

"Do you have any other family, Krysti?"

The boy's grimy chin thrust up in the air. "No, and I need none. I can take care of myself."

"Clearly not. At least not without stealing." Her lips pressed tight together as her stomach clenched with another sharp pain, and bile rose in her throat.

"Khamsin?" Wynter frowned down at her. "Are you all right?"

She dragged in a shallow breath and waved him off. "You were caught stealing, Krysti. We have returned what you took, and I've offered compensation to any other merchant you may have robbed. You owe me a debt. I claim a year of your service in payment. Starting now. You will be my page. And no more stealing. It isn't honorable." The last several sentences came out in a desperate rush. She spun away. Her belly was rippling with cramps. Sweat beaded her upper lip. "Bron, please have someone escort Krysti back to the palace. I need to—to—"

"Khamsin?" Wynter reached for her arm.

She twisted out of his reach and spun away, walking quickly back towards stables at the center of town where the horses were waiting.

She'd just cleared the last row of tents, when a brutal onslaught of cramps doubled her over. A low cry broke past her lips. Her knees gave out and she sat abruptly in the snow.

"Khamsin!" Wynter raced towards her, dropping to his knees beside her. Valik, Bron, and the guards followed close on his heels, forming a protective line between Khamsin and the crowd of curious Winterfolk. Krysti was still clutched in one of Valik's hands.

"Bron," Wynter snapped, "fetch the horses. Loke, ride back to Gildenheim. Summon Lady Frey to the Queen's chambers. Valik, bind that boy. He's coming with us."

"I didn't mean to hurt her!" Krysti's voice broke the ensuing silence. "I swear, I didn't!"

"Be silent, boy!" Valik barked.

Khamsin laid a hand on Wynter's arm. "Not his fault," she said. "Felt ill since lunch. Ah!" She squeezed her eyes shut and clenched her jaw as another series of violent cramps racked her body. "Merciful sun!" she breathed when the seized muscles finally relaxed.

The clatter of horse hooves on cobblestone announced Bron's return with several horses in tow, Hodri among them.

"You'll ride back with me." Wynter gathered Khamsin into his arms and rose to his feet, lifting her with effortless strength. "No arguments."

"Wyn." Valik's voice was low, quiet, but filled with urgency. "Look." He nodded at the snow-covered ground near Wynter's feet.

Wynter glanced down. His body went still. The arms holding Khamsin clenched a little tighter. "Khamsin . . . you are wounded?"

"No, I—" She frowned and followed his gaze. Bright red glistened in the patch of compressed snow where she'd been sitting. "What in the name of—ah!" Another brutal series of cramps tore through her body.

Her eyes widened in fear as a hot gush of blood soaked her thighs and the dense folds of her skirts.

CHAPTER 14

The Mercy of the Mountains

Rays of sunlight fell over Khamsin's face, bringing warmth and the familiar, energizing tingle of power sparking in her veins. Lost in hazy, pleasant dreams of summer and her brother Falcon sneaking up into the Sky Garden to play Swords and Warriors with her, she tried to resist consciousness, but the dreams faded despite her strongest efforts to cling to them.

She stretched, then hissed as a dozen tiny needles of pain stabbed her abdomen in response. She opened her eyes, blinked at the silvery blue satin canopy overhead, and sat up.

She was in her room in Gildenheim. She sensed the sun's position high in the sky. Her brow creased in a frown. It was midday, and she was still abed?

A whisper of fabric and a cool wind made her turn towards the bedroom door. Lady Galacia Frey entered.

"Ah, you've finally awakened. Good. How do you feel?"

Kham scowled. Feel?

"You lost quite a bit of blood. Between that and the restorative herbs I gave you, you may still feel a little . . . disoriented."

Memories were coming back. Terrible cramping pain. Bright red blood, so much of it the air filled with a sweet, metallic stench. Her own hoarse screams as she writhed in agony, feeling as though her body were ripping apart from the inside out.

"You are a very lucky woman, Summerlander. If Wynter hadn't acted so quickly to get you back to the palace and had the foresight to have me waiting when you arrived—and if your own powers hadn't fought so hard to heal you—you would not be alive."

"What happened?"

Lady Frey gave a small, elegant shrug. "You were poisoned. One of the servingwomen in the tavern in town admitted to putting a Wintercraig emetic called Lady's Blush in your food. She lost her husband, father, and three brothers in the war. Grief turned to madness when she heard you claiming Summerlea suffered more greatly in the war than Wintercraig."

"She tried to kill me."

"Lady's Blush isn't normally lethal. She claims she only meant to make you sick, but she must have been far more heavy-handed with the herb than she admits. One of the side effects is a raised heartbeat and blood that flows much more rapidly through the veins, both of which give the ladies who consume it a blush in their cheeks—hence the name. When the orphan boy kicked you, he must have ruptured a vessel in your womb, and with the Lady's Blush in your system, you began to hemorrhage. If Wynter hadn't used the Ice Gaze to freeze your blood and slow down your heart rate, you would have bled to death before I could determine the cause of your illness and administer an antidote."

"Where is Wynter now?"

Lady Frey turned to a small bedside table on which rested several stoppered flagons. "Attending important matters of state." She uncorked a silvery blue bottle and poured a thin stream of liquid into a crystal glass, then added chartreuse liquid from a small green vial and a powder from a third, capped pot. She stirred the concoction with a long, thin silver wand and turned to offer it to Khamsin. "Here. Drink this. It's a restorative that will help you regain your strength. Drink," she added again when

Khamsin hesitated. A smile flirted on Lady Frey's smooth, pale lips. "I promise, it's not poison."

Kham took the glass and sniffed cautiously at its contents. It smelled of verbena and something she didn't recognize. Deciding that if Lady Frey had wished her ill, Kham would be dead already, she tilted the glass to her lips and drank. The liquid had the slightly thickened consistency of warmed honey and a sharp aftertaste that the lemony verbena couldn't hide. She made a face and handed the glass back to Lady Frey.

"Perhaps not poison, but I think I'll just have broth or *borgan* the next time."

The priestess gave a small laugh. "Wynter is not fond of my potions either. If it can't be killed and stewed or roasted, he wants nothing of it."

"Sounds good to me." She sat up and threw back the covers. A rush of dizziness made her sway, but she fought it off.

"Where do you think you're going?"

Kham glanced at the priestess in surprise. "I'm awake. I'm getting up."

"Absolutely not. I forbid it. You very nearly bled to death. You're still bleeding, in fact, and probably will be for another week or two until your womb heals. Your body hasn't had any substantial nourishment in two days—"

"Two days!" Kham exclaimed.

Lady Frey grimaced impatiently but explained, "It was vital that you stayed as motionless as possible while we tried to stop the hemorrhaging, so I added a sedative to the Lady's Blush antidote. You're only awake now because the worst of the bleeding has passed and because I didn't dare keep you without food any longer. You stay where you are. You're not leaving that bed for at least another day." She turned her head and barked over her shoulder, "Boy!"

A small white-blond head poked through the doorway.

"Has the queen's maid returned from the kitchens?"

"No, ma'am. Not yet."

Kham stared at the child. There was something familiar about him. He cast a shy, hesitant glance in her direction, and his silvery blue eyes met hers. Recognition dawned. The boy. The little pinch-pocket from the Konundal fairgrounds. What was his name?

"Krysti?"

The boy jumped as if a ghost had popped out of the bed, and cried, "Boo!" then lurched into an awkward bow. "Your Grace."

Someone had scrubbed him from head to toe and found him a set of spotless, well-tailored clothes to replace his previous moldy tatters. His face was small and thin, with a pointed chin, arching brows, and a dusting of silvery freckles that looked like snowflakes across the bridge of his nose. The corners of his eyes were tilted up, and the ears peeking through the thick strands of his pale, raggedly cropped hair had a slight point at their tops. If a snow fox had transformed into a boy, Kham fancied he would have looked just like Krysti.

"I am surprised to see you here," she said.

The child shrugged and grimaced. "It's not like I had much choice. Lord Valik brought me here for questioning the day you were—the day you got so sick."

"But clearly he has since let you go. You are not in chains, and someone has obviously provided for you." She gestured to his clean clothes and tidy hair.

"Once they found out about the poisoning, they let me go."

"Yet you are still here. I'm sure you could have run away if you'd wanted to. Why didn't you?"

"You said I owed you a year of service. The king commanded me to stay to serve it." Krysti dropped his head and stared hard at his hands. His fingers were clenched so tight the knuckles were white. "I shouldn't have stolen the slingbow. My parents were honest folk, and they raised me to be the same. I only took it because I was hungry. My traps haven't been catching much, so I thought I'd have better luck with a slingbow." He looked up, his eyes earnest. "Honest."

"I believe you, but since it seems you are to be in my service, I must warn you. I will not tolerate thievery in future. Is that clear? You are a page to the new queen of Wintercraig. Your behavior will reflect upon me."

The child nodded. "Yes, ma'am."

"Excellent. Then for your first task, my young page, please find my maid Bella and tell her I wish to dress."

The boy bowed and darted off. When he was gone, Lady Frey lifted a cool brow. "I've told you how close you came to death, Your Grace. I must insist you stay abed to recuperate. I will summon the king to ensure your compliance if I must."

Khamsin smiled a challenge. "Lady Frey, there are two things about me you should know. First, I am far harder to kill than anyone gives me credit. My sire has been trying for years without success. I am awake and alive, which means I've already survived the grieving widow's attempt. As long as I avoid vigorous activity, sunshine and fresh air should have me completely healed by dinnertime tomorrow.

"Second," Kham leaned forward, and her smile faded, "no one—not my father, not my husband, not the Sun God himself—can make me do something I do not choose of my own will."

Lady Frey's expression did not change. "You are very young to make such a bold statement. Life has a way of throwing such challenges back in our faces."

"What makes you think it hasn't already done so many times over?"

To Kham's surprise, the priestess's cold mask cracked. She smiled. "Ah, now I understand why you have Wynter tied up in such knots. You are a Valkyr in the flesh. He probably can't decide whether to protect you, battle you, or toss you on your back and fark you. Wyrn help him."

Kham tried not to let the shock show on her face. She had Wynter tied up in knots? Was the woman serious?

"What an heir your child will make. Wynter chose well." Still smiling, Lady Frey began to pack her things in a small, fur-lined case.

"He didn't choose me at all." Some perverse need to wipe the smile off Lady Frey's face made her point that out. "He wanted one of my sisters and my fa—the Summer King tricked him into marrying me instead."

"Did he?" Lady Frey chuckled and shook her head.

"You find that amusing? Wynter did not, I can assure you."

"That is not what I find amusing—well, it is, but not in the way you mean."

"Explain."

"You say no one—not even the gods—could force you to accept something not of your own choosing. Wynter is no different, or do you not recognize your own qualities when you see them in another?"

"I—" She frowned. "He signed a treaty. He could not break it once it was signed, and our marriage was consummated."

"My dear girl, Wynter Atrialan turned his back on our laws, the pleadings and threats of his council, centuries of taboo, and his own almost certain destruction to embrace the Ice Heart, Wintercraig's most deadly magic. He used that forbidden magic to wreak three years of deadly vengeance on the whole of Summerlea for your brother's crimes. He was prepared to wipe every Summerlander off the face of the earth. You were all already walking corpses so far as he was concerned. Do you honestly think something as flimsy as a signed piece of paper and a marriage ceremony would have stayed his hand had he not wanted you for his bride?"

The priestess gave a snort of disbelief and shook her head. "Wynter would have parted your head from your shoulders, taken all three of your sisters as concubines, slaughtered everyone else involved in the deception, and frozen the whole of Vera Sola on the spot. After ripping your father's entrails from his still-living body and calling the snow wolves to feast upon them, of course."

Kham's throat felt strangely tight. She swallowed. "He wouldn't have done that. Honor would have compelled him to keep the agreement."

Lady Frey's eyes filled with a mix of pity, irritation, and sympathy. "Honor would play no part in it. He swallowed the Ice Heart. He has used its power to the fullest for three whole years." She stared at Kham's blank face, then her own comprehension dawned. "You don't know what that means, do you? He hasn't told you."

"Told me what?"

Lady Frey closed the lid on her potions case and sat on the edge of Khamsin's bed. "The Ice Heart is a dreadful power. Those who embrace it freeze from the inside out. Once in its grip, compassion and honor are mere things of memory, easily forgotten, just as easily foresworn. Wynter's heart—his humanity—is freezing. He's dying. As I told him, I'm surprised he's lasted as long as he has. A weaker man would have succumbed long ago." Her expression grew thoughtful. "Come to think of it, I suppose Valik deserves much of the credit. Wyn loves him like a brother."

Kham put her hands to her head, framing her eyes and pressing her fingers hard against her temples to block out peripheral distractions and focus on what the priestess was saying. "Wynter is dying, you say. His humanity is freezing. But how has Valik been able to help him?"

"Love, child. That's what it's all about. Wyn is losing the capacity to love—to feel anything. And when all warm emotion is gone, the man we know as Wynter will cease to be. A monster of unimaginable power will inhabit his body—a dark god who was once a man, Rorjak, the Ice King."

"Wyrn's husband? The one Thorgyll slew with his spears?"

"Yes."

Khamsin slumped back against the pillows. She'd read

the legend of Thorgyll and his mighty ice spears. "Why are you telling me this? I'm an heir to the Summer Throne? Aren't you afraid I'll use this knowledge to destroy Wintercraig?"

Lady Frey laughed. It was not a pleasant sound. "Only a madman utterly lost to reason could even contemplate such a thing." She leaned forward, her eyes bleak. "Listen to me, Summerlander, for this is the direst of warnings. If the Ice King is born, there will be no victory for any human ever again. The vengeance Wynter wreaked upon your land is nothing compared to what Rorjak will do. He will cast the entire world into endless winter. Your family's powers, which are derived from the sun, will fade. The Frost Giants and their monstrous wolves, the *garm*, will reign at Rorjak's side, and all humankind will be nothing but meat for their table. It is the day the Frost Giants live for: Carnak, the end of the world."

Even though the poisons had long since been purged from her body, Kham's stomach gave a queasy lurch. "If this magic is dreadful, what on earth are you doing with it? Why would you keep it unguarded for any man to use?"

"Unguarded? The Ice Heart is Wintercraig's most carefully hidden and lethally defended treasure. It is the essence of the god-king Rorjak, the mortal-born man whom Wyrn loved so much, she gave him immortality. Because of her gift, even though his body could be destroyed, his godly essence never could. So after slaying him with Wyrn's spears, Thorgyll gathered that essence and hid it away in a place he thought would be safe. And for thousands of years, it has been. Many have tried to embrace the Ice Heart, but except for a rare few, they died before ever reaching the place of its confinement. Wynter is one of the few. I should have known he would be. He is, after all, a legend in his own right, the man who at the age of sixteen slew a Frost Giant single-handedly."

"If the Ice Heart is consuming him, how do we stop it?"

"Bear him a child. It was love for his brother—grief

over his death—that drove Wynter down this path. Love for his child is the thing he hopes will save him."

"Love can melt the Ice Heart?"

"It's the only thing that can."

"That's why he said if I didn't bear him a child within the year, he'd slay me and take one of my sisters to wife."

The priestess's eyebrows shot up. "He said he'd slay you if you didn't give him a child?"

"Several times. Only he tried to pretty it up with a Wintercraig euphemism, saying he'd send me to face the mercy of the mountains."

Lady Frey scowled and rolled her eyes skyward. "Idiot men. Wyrn save me from them all." She leaned forward, her piercing eyes intent. "Listen to me, Khamsin. Wynter doesn't have a year left. The Ice Heart's grip is very strong, and if he can't break free of it, he will not long survive. As to the mercy of the mountains, I suspect he has deliberately misled you as to what it truly means. No doubt, he thought fear was the best way to force your compliance because he is a great buffoon of a man who does not understand women with the hearts of warriors any more than he understands women with the hearts of snakes." Her lips drew back, baring her teeth in what was a very close imitation of a wolf's snarl.

Despite her initial dislike of Lady Frey, with her chilly aloofness and ice-dagger eyes, Khamsin now realized she could like this woman very much indeed.

The priestess's snarl faded, and she eyed Khamsin in silent consideration. "Perhaps you should get out of bed today after all," she finally said. "I know you'll be doing so anyways as soon as I leave the room, and this way at least I can keep an eye on you for another few hours." She rose to her feet and, without turning her head, called out, "Come in, Summerlander. See that your mistress eats as much as she can, then help her dress. Bundle her warmly. Krysti, go to the stables and tell Bron to prepare a litter." To Khamsin, she added, "And you will promise me to stay in the litter and to tell me the instant you feel the least bit unwell. Agree now, or this will not happen."

"Agreed." The word popped out before she even thought about it. She blinked and gave a wry laugh. "What did I just agree to? Where are you taking me?"

Lady Frey drew herself up to her full height, looking icy, beautiful and remotely regal. "To the slopes of Mount Gerd, to witness the mercy of the mountains."

With both Valik and Wynter gone, there was no one to gainsay Lady Frey. Lord Barsul tried, but he withered quickly beneath the priestess's icy glare. Within the hour, the small party rode out: six armed guards, Lady Frey riding a shining white beauty of a horse, Krysti bundled thickly and riding a shaggy tan mountain pony, and Khamsin borne in a drape-covered litter suspended between two large draft horses.

The litter wasn't quite as stomach-churning a ride as the carriage had been, and Khamsin alleviated her travel sickness by keeping the curtains drawn back. The brisk, cold air on her face and being able to see where they were going staved off the worst of the sickness.

The journey to Mount Gerd was a two-hour, six-mile trek across rough mountain terrain that ended with a nerve-racking traversal of a crumbling stone bridge stretched over a deep gorge between mountains. On the far side of the bridge, perhaps a half mile from the ice-capped summit, a small round lodge had been built into the mountain. Smoke curled from lodge's chimney, and as they approached, two guards in leather armor emerged to greet them.

"Where are they?" Lady Frey asked. "And when?"

"Second elevation, about an hour ago," came the cryptic reply.

"My thanks." The priestess turned her horse left towards a rocky path that curved around the mountain face. The rest of the party followed in single file.

The road turned down, and the air grew slightly warmer as they descended several hundred feet. Stark, snow- and lichen-covered rocks gave way to carpets of ground-hugging juniper. The rocky path split in two. One fork headed down towards the lower elevations, but they did not turn. Instead, they leveled out, traveling laterally across the mountain's face. A few minutes later, the horses slowed, then came to a halt. Khamsin stuck out her head to see what was going on, but all she could see was the back end of her guards' horses. The sound of approaching riders echoed against the stony mountainside. She knew who it was even before she saw Hodri's shining whiteness and Wynter's grim face and blazing eyes. Just the sight of him sent a warm, electric tingle shivering through her blood.

He didn't have the same reaction to her. He took one look at her, and snapped, "Draw the curtains, woman! And pull those furs around you before you catch your death!" He whirled his horse around. "Damn it, Laci! What in Wyrn's name are you thinking? Two days ago, she lay near death, and today you cart her through the mountaintops? Are you mad, or just trying to finish the job that idiot serving-woman started?"

Laci? Kham poked her head back out through the litter curtains and watched Wynter confront Lady Frey. He did not seem the least bit afraid of her as he bellowed insults at her for her "dim-witted bit of insanity" for bringing Khamsin to Mount Gerd.

Lady Frey seemed neither surprised nor impressed by his rage. "I brought her to witness the mercy of the mountains!" she snapped back. "As she was the injured party, it's more than her right, and you know it. Besides, some fool has left her with the impression that the mercy of the mountains is a sentence of certain death—and told her that is her fate if she doesn't bear your child in a year's time!"

For a moment Wynter looked nonplussed—and decidedly guilty—but then his jaw clenched tight, and his teeth bared in a snarl. "She drew her own conclusions. I told no lies."

"Idiot! Lunkhead! Bah! I should leave you to your fate.

If I liked you even slightly less, that's exactly what I'd do." The priestess glared, her usual air of icy remoteness completely shredded.

Kham smiled. Ooh, she could easily like Lady Frey.

"Besides," the priestess continued, "she was awake. If I'd left her on her own, she'd be running around the palace. This way, I've successfully managed to keep her lying down in that litter for several hours."

Kham's smile turned into a frown. Then again, maybe not so easily. She didn't like being manipulated.

Wynter turned his head and caught Kham looking at him. His nostrils flared. "Fine," he snapped. "Show her and be done with it. But then it's straight back to Gildenheim, and she stays in bed the rest of the night and tomorrow with no complaints."

"Agreed," Lady Frey answered before Kham could do more than open her mouth. "Even if I have to drug her again." She cast back a look of such icy promise that Kham scowled and sank back against the litter cushions.

Wynter and his riders turned their mounts around and headed back the way they'd come. The rest of them followed. Several minutes later, the path widened to a small plateau carved into the side of the mountain. Here, the snow had been trampled down.

The horses bearing the litter halted. Wynter pushed aside the curtains and lifted her out, but he did not set her down. "You shouldn't be walking," he growled when she protested. "You shouldn't be here at all, so be silent or I'll stuff you back in that litter and send the horses racing home to Gildenheim."

She scowled her disapproval of his high-handed ways, then tried not to be too obvious when a brisk gust of wind made her snuggle closer to him for protection. Khamsin could see both hoofprints and boot prints all about. On the far side of the plateau, several large iron rings had been bolted into the mountainside. A pile of chain and two empty manacles lay in the snow near the center rings.

The servingwoman was nowhere to be seen.

"There's no one here," Khamsin said.

Wynter grunted. "The mountains have been merciful."

She glared and thumped his steel breastplate. "Enough of this cryptic 'mercy' nonsense. Speak plainly. What happened to the woman from the tavern? Where did she go? Is she dead? Did you even bring her here at all?"

His lips compressed. He strode towards the far side of the plateau. As they neared, Khamsin could see another path leading down the mountain. Fresh footprints had flattened the snow. Wynter pointed down below, where a group of some half dozen bundled people were descending on horseback. "She is there."

Khamsin squinted at the party. "Alive?"

"Against my better judgment." Grim dissatisfaction rumbled in his voice. "I would have cleaved her in two when they first brought her to the palace and told me what she'd done, but Laci, Valik, and Barsul stopped me."

"I don't understand."

"Winterfolk *are* the mercy of the mountains. We live in a harsh world, where our survival often depends on one another. There is no room in the clans for people who cannot be trusted, but we are not brutes or barbarians. The woman admitted to putting a purgative in your food, but, even Laci agreed that if she'd truly meant to kill you, there are dozens of more effective poisons she could have used to ensure your death. Those people down there are the folk from Konundal who were willing to climb the mountain and offer her mercy. She will be taken away from this province. If she ever returns, or commits any other serious crime, she will be taken to the glaciers and left there to die."

Khamsin watched the party below make its way slowly down the mountainside. "And if she had killed me—even accidentally?"

Wynter's jaw hardened. "Then no amount of mercy could have saved her. You are my wife, under my protection. Harm to you is harm to me."

"And if I do not bear the child you require? You would really chain me to this mountain and leave me to face my death?"

"I am the King of Wintercraig and you are my wife. I cannot take another woman to wife so long as you live. The mercy of the mountains is a symbolic death. Just as that woman is now dead to us, so, too, would you be."

She gave a disbelieving laugh. "Symbolically or truly? Do you really think your countrymen would climb the mountain to offer *me*, the daughter of the Summer King, mercy?"

He held her gaze, his own unwavering. "That, Khamsin, depends entirely upon you. Give us reason to believe you are worthy of mercy, and I have no doubt you will find it."

CHAPTER 15

Heroes and Hazards

Khamsin thought about those words all the way back to Gildenheim. Her original plan had been to settle in and befriend the locals with an eye towards using what knowledge she could glean from them to escape the threat of death. Now, she realized, she had even greater reason to put that plan into action. The people she had thought to befriend for information and assistance were the very ones who had the power to set her free should she indeed end up chained to the slopes of Mount Gerd.

When they reached the palace, Wynter plucked her from the litter and carried her in his arms from the courtyard to her bedroom. He set her on the plump, fur-covered mattress with a warning to "Stay there!" then he was gone. Her tingling, vibrant sense of awareness and excitement went with him, but she was too proud to call him back.

She was tempted to rise from her bed, but he'd been wise enough to wring a promise from her that she would not. What pleasure she derived from his trust in her word was completely eclipsed by his willingness to use it against her. But she had given her oath. So, except for occasional trips to the bathroom, for the night and the day that followed, she stayed in bed and soaked up the light from her lamps and the sun and let her body heal.

She would have been bored to distraction except for Krysti. He kept her company the whole second day and turned out to be a delightful companion. He scrounged up a deck of cards, taught her a game called Aces, and they played for two hours. He warned her at the start that he wouldn't let her win, and he didn't. He beat her soundly at every game in the first hour, but she just narrowed her eyes, set her jaw and demanded another game. She won her first hand at the end of the second hour.

"You are a good opponent," she told him with grudging admiration, "but I'm starting to get the hang of it. Don't expect to win as often when we play again tomorrow."

He smiled at the scowl she couldn't quite wipe off her face. "You don't like to lose."

"Never," she agreed. "Not for any reason. I never have. I'm like Roland that way."

"Roland?"

She looked at him aghast. It was plain he didn't know who she was talking about. "Roland Soldeus," she prompted, "the Hero of Summerlea? The ancient king who held back an invasion force of fifty thousand with a mere three thousand men?" Still no recognition. She hesitated for a moment, remembering the humiliating rejection with the top-floor children, but thrust the pain of that remembered wound away. Krysti had sworn her a year of service. He couldn't very well turn his back on her.

"Roland was an ancestor of mine. Well," she corrected, "an ancestor of mine was his brother. I have a book about his most famous battles there on the table. Hand it to me, and I will read to you about the greatest hero who ever lived."

Krysti crawled to the other side of the bed and came back with the worn book with the tarnished silver letters stamped into the spine. Kham opened the book and began to read. In no time, she was as engrossed as ever in the tale of Roland Triumphant. Lying beside her on the bed, his chin propped on his hands, eyes shining like stars, Krysti drank in the tales of the legendary Summerlea warrior with as much eager excitement as she ever had. And when she read the tale of Roland's last and greatest battle, her throat closed up as it always did when she reached the part where his horn sounded a lonely, stirring cry across the valley of dead and dying, gathering Roland's remaining men for one final, desperate charge against the invading hordes.

> " *'They rode, the last one hundred, their banners lifted high.*
> *Their armor gleamed like silver beneath the sun's bright eye.*
> *Before them, clad in golden scales, his brow with sunlight wreathed,*
> *Rode Roland, the Triumphant, the Heir of Rose and Lea.*
>
> *Oh, ever will a man be born more glorious than these,*
> *The greatest sons of Summer led by their shining king?'* "

Krysti's hands clenched into fists, his little face was tense and flushed. "Did they do it? Did they beat them?"

She smiled at him, as Tildy had so often smiled at her. "Be patient, Krysti. Let me finish reading, and you will learn." She bent her head back to the book and continued reading where she left off. " *'The first two lines of Golgoth fell back in dazzled fear, as Roland and the hundred charged forth to meet their spears.'* " The last charge of Roland and the Hundred consumed more than fifteen pages in the book, describing in detail how valiantly those great knights had battled, how each mighty hero had fallen, how the clouds rolled in and cast a gray gloom across the battlefield as if the sky itself mourned their passing. Finally, only Roland and a dozen of his men remained in a field soaked with blood and littered with the enemy's dead. Around them, the last ten thousand of the Golgoth's army drew near, ringing the king and his men. Defeat was certain, but even then Roland would not surrender. He lifted his mighty sword, Blazing, high into the air and called upon the full measure of his Summer gifts.

Overhead, the clouds parted. Those watching from the hills surrounding the battled plain reported seeing a shaft of golden sunlight beam down upon the place where Roland stood, as if the sun itself had answered his call and showered its strength upon him. The last twelve Summerlea knights fell to their knees around him. They bowed their heads and reached out to lay their gauntleted hands upon him. Roland Triumphant gave a final shout, in a voice that boomed across the plain like the thunder of god: *"Avires Coruscate Rosa!"* Long live the Radiant Rose!

And from him exploded a vast, deadly force, like none had ever seen before or since. He flared blinding bright, so bright the watchers on the surrounding hills cried out and shielded their eyes, and rings of blazing golden light rolled out in stunning waves. The light swept across the plains for a radius of two miles, flattening the enemy army, incinerating everything in its path. It was as if the sun had fallen to earth and burst its strength upon the plain. Out and out, the rings of flaming light roared, until the watchers on the mountains cried out in fear, certain they, too, would be consumed by its blazing fury. But just before the deadly brilliance reached them, the fiery light receded like a wave upon sand. The rings raced back towards the center of the field, towards Roland, and met once more with a mighty boom. A tower of light and smoke shot up into the sky, and crackling blades of golden light speared the heavens.

Then it was over. The plain stood barren, emptied of all but a small ring of bodies. Roland's last twelve Summerlea knights were laid out like the petals of a daisy, their armor shining with a high polish, their skin cleansed of blood and the grime of battle, their faces peaceful and untouched as if they had been purified in death. And there, in the center of them all, rising up from a patch of rich, untouched green Summerlea grass, was Roland's mighty sword, Blazing, its hilt pointing towards the sun. The great ruby in its pommel was clear as a star, shining with a radiance unmatched by any diamond or earthly gem. That sword and that unearthly stone were all that remained of Roland, Summerlea's greatest king.

Khamsin closed the book. Krysti had tears in his eye, as moved by the story as she always was. Even now her eyes were damp, and her throat felt closed and aching.

"He was a great hero," the boy whispered.

She nodded. "A hero of heroes. A king of kings. There's never been a man to match him. He led Summerlea to greatness and secured its safety for generations to come. There's a statue of him outside the walls of Vera Sola. He's the first of the Stone Knights guarding the city gates. A statue of his brother Donal, from whom my line descends, stands on the opposite side."

"Where is Roland's sword Blazing now?"

"It disappeared not long after his death, never to be seen again. Many a Summerlea knight has set out to find it, but none ever has."

A brief silence fell. Krysti cleared his throat and said, "Our king, Wynter, is a hero too. A legend in the Craig. Barely two months shy of his sixteenth birthday, he killed a Frost Giant single-handedly."

"I've heard something about that. I understand it's quite a feat."

"It's never been done before. Frost Giants stand fifteen feet tall"—Krysti clambered to his feet and raised his hands far over his head to demonstrate—"and their fists are like boulders. They carry great swords with razor-sharp serrated edges that can shatter swords and cleave fully armored men in two with a single blow." His lips drew back in a snarling grimace, and he hacked and slashed with gusto.

Khamsin hid a smile, charmed by the child's enthusiasm. "And Wynter faced one of these terrible creatures in single combat?"

"He did. He'd only just earned his knighthood. To celebrate, he and his family went ice fishing on Lake Ibree, when the Frost Giant caught them unawares. It struck him a blow that knocked him senseless, then killed his mother and father and was going to slay his brother, the little prince, when Wynter reawakened. Even knowing he was unlikely to survive, Wynter threw himself before his brother, armed only with his sword." He leapt forward and assumed a defensive stance, hands clenched around his imaginary sword. The sword swung, accompanied by hearty slashing and battle noises as Krysti the Giant Killer fought his foe. He stopped in midswing, and added, "Gunterfys was forged in the fires of Mount Freika, did you know? And blessed by the priestess of Wyrn as it was made. They say it is a sword that will never be broken."

"No, I didn't know that." She filed that away, wondering how much of it was true and how much was legend. "I suppose it's only fitting. A mighty hero should have a very special sword. Did Wynter and the Frost Giant fight for hours? Did they battle throughout the day and into the night?"

Krysti gave her a look. "That's only in the legends. Most men couldn't battle a Frost Giant for more than a few minutes and live. As big as they are, they have all the advantage. One blow would shatter a man's bones into dust."

"Ah. Of course. Sorry." Properly chastened, Khamsin nodded. "Go on with your story."

"The battle was fierce—and it did last almost ten minutes. King Wynter—well, he was Prince Wynter then— knew he could not let the Frost Giant's sword or fist strike him. He used his smaller size and speed against the monster, darting in and out, slashing its flesh in a hundred shallow wounds—to weaken him, you know?" The mattress bounced and rolled as he lunged, parried, and hacked at his invisible foe. "But that only made the Frost Giant furious. The creature swung one enormous fist and sent Wynter flying across the clearing. Wynter barely had time to rise on one knee before the monster was upon him, his terrible sword raised high, ready to strike the killing blow."

Even knowing that Wynter had survived the attack, Khamsin felt her body tense. "What happened?"

"There was nothing he could do to stop the blow. All he could do was block it. So he raised Gunterfys with both hands and used it like a shield." On his knees, Krysti demonstrated. "The giant's sword crashed down. Any other man with any other sword would have been cleaved in two right there where he knelt, but Wynter and his sword held fast. The monster's blade shattered. While the Frost Giant stumbled and tried to recover his balance, Wynter jumped to his feet and put all his might into a fearsome blow. The Frost Giant fell, and Prince Wynter leapt upon his chest and drove his sword straight through the monster's heart." With a triumphant cry, Krysti drove his imaginary blade home. His savage expression faded, and he straightened. "Wynter buried his parents there on the mountainside where they died, then he put his little brother on his back and carried him all the way back home. When they reached Gildenheim, Wynter was king, and his sword bore a new name."

"That is a heroic tale, indeed," Kham said. "It should be recorded in a book and passed down through the ages so none will ever forget it."

"I imagine it will be."

Krysti stayed with her past dinnertime until night turned the sky inky black and he could barely keep his eyes open. Bella herded him out and went with him to seek their pallets in the servants' quarters.

As she doused the lights and settled into bed, Khamsin thought of Wynter and the day Gunterfys earned its name. Krysti's retelling of that day had been so vivid. Her heart had gone out to Wynter and to the little prince whose next breath depended solely on his brother's strength and courage.

For the last three years, no Summerlander had said Wynter's name without calling a curse upon it. He was the Winter King, the demon of the north, the enemy.

But now, after hearing Wynter's story, after seeing

the admiration shining from Krysti's eyes, and feeling it echoed in her own heart, she realized that to his own people, Wynter was a hero, as noble and determined in his own way as Roland had been in his.

He wasn't a perfect man. Far from it. He'd made Summerlea pay a terrible price for Falcon's trespass. But, for the first time, she considered how Wynter must have felt when he learned that the woman he loved had run off with Falcon and that his brother, the only member of his family whom he'd been able to save from the Frost Giant's attack, had been slain trying to stop them.

Grief could drive even good people mad. Look at her father's lifelong hatred of her. Look at the woman from Konundal who'd poisoned Kham for an offhand remark.

Wynter's vengeance had been bloody and consuming, but after hearing the story about Wynter's family and the Frost Giant, she was having a much harder time hating him for it. The Sun knew, her own temper was just as volatile and deadly.

If a Winterman had slain her beloved brother, would not she, too, have sought a terrible revenge?

Khamsin was up and about the next day, despite the objections of Lady Frey. "I am healed. The sun has seen to it. See?" She ran circles about the room until she was dizzy. "I was healed yesterday, too, but I stayed in bed as you wanted. Not today."

"No horses," the priestess compromised. "And no running. Keep to the castle."

"Agreed!" She grabbed Krysti's hand, bolted for the door, and that was the last anyone saw of them until they returned, covered with dirt, dust, and cobwebs, to grab a quick lunch. Then they were off again and did not return until supper. The next day, it was the same.

Khamsin reacquainted herself with all the areas of the castle Vinca had shown her, then set about discovering the rest. She and Krysti explored every inch of the Gildenheim, from the damp, pitch-black dungeons to a private tower built near the mountain's peak, accessible only by a long, narrow, winding stairway etched into the mountainside. They discovered it when Krysti—who had no end of interesting talents—picked the lock on a strange wooden door inside one of the guard towers on the battlements.

"I'm not a professional thief," he vowed when he produced the picks, "but you never know when being able to open a door might come in handy—even save your life if the night is cold, and you've nowhere warm to sleep."

"I won't tell," she promised, then grinned, "so long as you teach me how to use those."

He laughed. "Agreed."

A few moments more, and the lock snicked open. Krysti raised the latch and opened the door. Behind it lay nothing but a dark, curving stair, and, well, what sort of adventurers could find a secret stair and not investigate where it led? They slipped through the door, climbed the stair, and found the private tower room perched far above the palace walls. Another quick lock-pick saw them inside.

Inside was a cozy, round, tower room, sparsely but richly furnished. A bed, a desk, a stone hearth with two full buckets of coal beside it, two spacious cushioned chairs facing the hearth, and a large wooden wardrobe. Apart from the one wall that faced the mountain—and into which a small bathroom closet had been built—all the walls were curved and set with high, arched windows that looked out over the castle, the valley, and the vast, seemingly endless range of snowy peaks that was the Craig.

The room was like an aerie perched high above the world. Gildenheim lay sprawled out below her, a shining jewel of snowy, ice-silvered granite. She spied a solitary cloaked figure walking through the uppermost terrace of the western garden. A bird flew down from one of the garden's evergreen trees to alight on the figure's outstretched arm. A few minutes later, the bird took to the air and winged away. A hunting falcon, perhaps? Or maybe a messenger bird, bringing reports from some other part of the kingdom.

She turned one of the chairs from the hearth to face the windows, already planning to claim this isolated spot as her own. Someplace to get away from the eyes of the court and relax.

"I wonder whose room this is?" Krysti said as he knelt to pick the locks on the desk drawers.

She sank into the large, comfortable chair, drew a deep, happy breath . . . and froze. She didn't possess her husband's keen, wolflike ability to discern and identify faint aromas with uncanny accuracy, but she didn't need to. The worn leather chair was steeped in a scent she already knew better than her own.

"Wynter's," she blurted.

Krysti popped up, picklocks dangling from his mouth. "W-w-w . . ." He gulped. "The king's?"

She leapt to her feet. The chair's wooden legs scraped over the stone floor as she shoved it back to its original position. "We should leave."

"Good idea."

They pelted for the door and scrambled down the steep, winding stairs, not speaking again until they were through the tower door and safe once more on the castle battlements. They looked at one another and burst into helpless laughter.

They were still laughing when they ran into Lord Barsul several minutes later.

He eyed the pair of them askance. "Now that's the look of mischief if ever I've seen it. What have you two been up to?"

"Just learning our way around the castle," Kham said. Barsul gave a look of such disbelief she couldn't help but laugh again. "No, truly. That's all."

"Well, from the looks of it, that's trouble enough." He wagged a finger at them. "Don't go poking your noses in places they don't belong."

"What places would those be?" Kham asked, her eyes wide and innocent. "So we know not to go in them."

His eyes narrowed. "Anyplace you have to pass through a locked door to reach, for starters."

Had he seen them on the stairs to Wynter's aerie? She didn't dare glance at Krysti. Lord Barsul would read the guilt on their faces.

"That includes the Atrium on the sixth floor of the main palace, do you hear?" Barsul added sternly.

Khamsin and Krysti exchanged a look. They hadn't finished exploring the sixth floor yet. A secret stair had distracted them.

"Oh, no you don't," Barsul warned, correctly interpreting that look. He wagged a stern finger. "Don't even think about it. Wynter has forbidden *anyone* to enter the Atrium, and unlike some private places"—his eyes flicked up the mountainside—"that's one trespass he won't forgive."

He'd seen them all right.

Krysti, poor boy, was all but shaking in his boots. Kham grabbed his thin hand and squeezed to reassure him. "Thank you, Lord Barsul. We'll keep that in mind. Come on, Krysti, let's go visit the armory. We haven't been there yet." With a quick wave farewell, she dragged the boy with her down the stone battlement steps.

Shaking his head and wearing a smile that wavered halfway between affection and bemusement, Lord Barsul watched them go. When they disappeared around the corner of a building, he turned and made his way along the battlements back to the tower room near the front of the castle where Wynter, Valik, and three of Wintercraig's generals waited.

"Well?" Wynter prompted, as Barsul closed the door behind him.

"They're just exploring."

"Is that what you call spying these days?" Valik grumbled.

Barsul gave him a sharp look. "She's just a girl."

"She's the Summer King's daughter. Do you honestly think she isn't recording everything she sees and hears, and will send it to her father—or worse, her brother—at first chance?"

"Enough," Wynter snapped. "The Summer King may have sired her, but he's no father to her. Do you not remember the state she was in when I wed her?"

"I do remember," Valik said, "but, consider, Wyn, what better way to earn your sympathy?"

Wynter pushed away from the table and straightened to his full height.

"Valik is right, my king," one of Wynter's generals, interrupted. "She may be your wife, but she's still the Summer King's daughter and the sister to murdering bride-stealer Falcon Coruscate. We cannot let down our guard."

"While I appreciate your concern, let me assure you I am neither an idiot nor a lovesick fool. My wife has been under constant surveillance since we left Summerlea, and so will she continue to be. Not because I think she might be working for her father. Any suspicions on that front are misguided. The hatred between them was too real. But I can't forget, it was a Summerlander who suggested I take a princess to wife, and I can't ignore the brother's activities in Calberna."

He stared down at the map stretched out on the table before him and the scattered sheaf of letters beside it. "If our information is accurate, the Calbernan armada will be ready to sail in three months, which means, come spring, we'll have an army on our shores. I'm aware Khamsin might use her 'exploring' to gather information for her brother and his new allies. But she is my queen, not my hostage. She will not be imprisoned. If her wandering gets too far out of hand, I will put an end to it. For now, it suits my purpose to let her roam."

He bent his head, focusing his attention back on the maps spread out before him. The current location and troop strength of all Wintercraig's battalions had been marked.

Calbernans by sea posed a difficulty. Both Wintercraig and Summerlea had too many miles of shoreline to patrol—much less defend. Winter's ice should see them safe until spring, but once the northern passage began its yearly thaw, opening a navigable seaway around the arctic rim, the invaders could land anywhere along Wintercraig's thousands of miles of coastline.

"Reopen all the northern watchtowers and repair the four here that were damaged by last year's storms. I want a pair of scouts at each tower, to be relieved every forty-five days. And send word to Leirik. At a minimum, I want towers built and manned in these locations." He tapped a dozen points on Summerlea's coastlines. "Tell him to move swiftly. Have him muster the locals to aid in the construction." He glanced up. "What are you waiting for?"

Barsul and the generals filed out of the room, but Valik held back.

Wyn shook his head. "Don't," he commanded, hoping to head off his friend's lecture about the danger Khamsin posed to them all.

"All I'm saying, Wyn, is be careful. Get your heir on her as quick as you can, but don't let down your guard. You can't trust what you feel for her. You know you can't. She's a powerful weatherwitch, but who knows what other arcane skills she might possess."

"For the last time, Valik, I'm under no spell."

"Are you not? I've seen the way you are around her, how you can't take your eyes off her. I'm not the only one who's noticed it either. Reika says—"

"Enough!" Wyn pinched the bridge of his nose and battled back the sharp edge of his temper. His friend was venturing into the realm of the ridiculous. "Your concern is noted, Valik. Now, please, you have work to attend to, and so do I." He gestured to the door.

Valik heaved a sigh but bowed and took his leave.

When he was gone, Wynter walked to one of the south-facing tower windows and stared down at the baileys below.

A small figure, easily identifiable by her dark hair and the bright Summerlander skirts peeping out beneath her pale coat, stepped out into the courtyard, a smaller white-blond figure beside her. He watched them cross the bailey and disappear into the slate-roofed armory.

"Is Valik right, wife?" he whispered. "Would you betray me to your brother?" He didn't want to believe it. Everything in him cried out that it couldn't be true. How could she give him such passion in their marriage bed, then plot against him?

But he'd been betrayed by a woman before. He couldn't take the chance he would be betrayed again. There was too much at stake.

Wynter turned away from the window. Laci had banned him from Khamsin's bed to give Khamsin's womb time to heal from the effects of the poison. He would use the time to distance himself from her entirely. Perhaps, with his eye unclouded by desire, he would see her more clearly.

CHAPTER 16

The Gathering Storm

Khamsin saw even less of Wynter over the next several weeks than she had since arriving in Gildenheim. He canceled the *samdar-hald* and *gildis,* spent his days ensconced in meeting after meeting with his councilors, generals, and stewards, and ate his meals in private. The bedchamber adjoining hers stayed silent and dark long past the midnight hour, and the few times she heard him come to bed, she heard him leave again not long after.

Thinking he'd decided to take Reika Villani up on what she so eagerly offered, Khamsin began following him to see where he went at night when the rest of the palace was sleeping. But instead of heading off to meet a mistress, Wynter made his way to the Atrium, the one room in the palace she'd been forbidden to enter. He stayed there for hours—sometimes until morning.

One night, exhausted from spying on her husband, Khamsin dozed off in the adjacent hallway while waiting for him to emerge from the Atrium. She woke sometime later to find herself in his arms, being carried back to her room. She closed her eyes quickly and tried to pretend she was still asleep as he tucked her back into her bed, but he wasn't fooled.

"Have you followed me enough now to satisfy your curiosity, wife? Or must I set guards at your door to keep you in your bed?"

She gave up the pretense and opened her eyes, scowling up at him. "How long have you known?"

"That you were following me? Since the first night." He tapped the side of his nose. "I know your scent, wife. I would know it anywhere."

So much for trying to be stealthy around him. "What are you doing in there?"

"Nothing that concerns you."

She didn't believe him. "Are you meeting someone in there?"

"No."

"So what's in there? Why can't anyone else go in? What are you hiding?"

"What's in there is none of your business. And no one is allowed inside but me because I said so. I am king, and my word is law. That's why." He cupped her face gently. His thumb brushed the rose shaped burn on her cheekbone. "And you will make no attempt to gain access to that room. You will not enter it or send anyone else to enter it in your stead. Is that clear?"

She glared at him in mutinous silence.

Her cheek prickled as the hand cupping her face grew cold. "I will have your word, Khamsin. Now."

"Fine," she snapped. "I won't go into the Atrium or send anyone there on my behalf."

"Good. Now go to sleep. And don't follow me anymore. You're supposed to be resting and healing."

"This is ridiculous. I'm perfectly fine. I heal fast." What she wanted was him back in her bed and at least some small measure of his attention. She was his wife, after all. But pride wouldn't let her ask him to stay. It was too much like begging. Khamsin Coruscate had never begged for a thing in her life. She wasn't about to start now.

But she did catch hold of the hand pressed against her cheek. "I've survived much worse, and you know it."

"Yes, and you and that bastard father of yours drugged me and tricked me into harming you further, then you hid your worsening illness from me until your wounds went septic and you nearly died." He straightened up from the bed, pulling his hand from her grip. "I will not be manipulated into risking your health. Laci said six weeks of rest and healing, and six weeks it will be. Now close your eyes and go to sleep. If I find you wandering around at night again, I will be quite wroth, and you don't want that."

Thwarted, she flopped down on the bed and scowled at him in annoyance. Irritating man. He knew what she wanted. That infernal, supersensitive sniffer of his clearly hadn't stopped working, so he had to know. Because all he had to do was enter the same room, and she could feel herself melting.

"Sleep," he said again, sternly, as if she were a rebellious child protesting against bedtime.

Just for that, she made a show of squeezing her eyes shut. "There. I'm sleeping."

"Good. Stay that way. And for once, wife, do as you're told."

She heard him blow out the candles by her bedside. The light shining through her closed eyelids went dark. She heard the tread of his feet as he exited the room and knew when he was gone by the empty ache that filled the places his presence made warm. With a frustrated groan, she rolled over on her belly and tried to resign herself to another lonely, achingly celibate night without him.

Wynter walked through the connecting rooms to his own chambers and sank down on the edge of his bed. He dropped his face into hands that shook. Wyrn help him. Khamsin had become like a drug to him.

Before her poisoning, the hours he'd spent in her room at night had grown longer and longer. He'd found himself counting down the hours until he could retire to her room, divest her of whatever frothy thing she'd chosen to sleep in, and sink into the seductive heat of her embrace. And even after the sex, when she lay sleeping, he would remain awake beside her for hours, just marveling at the strength of his feelings. Leaving her bed each morning had become an act of sheer will. He could happily have stayed there, his body wrapped around hers, ignoring his duty and the very real threats gathering against Wintercraig. He was tired of war. He wanted peace. He wanted her, Khamsin, his volatile, temperamental, utterly intoxicating wife.

Valik was right. She had too much power over him. If she knew how easily she could drive him to distraction with just a touch, a look, a flutter of those long, silken lashes, he would be undone.

She'd wanted him to stay tonight. If he hadn't pulled his hand free and beat a path back to his own room, he would have joined her in that bed and to Hel with the consequences. And that could have been bad.

She thought she was so tough, so hard to break, so easily and rapidly mended. But he remembered the sight of blood-soaked skirts, the unnatural paleness of her skin as she'd nearly bled her life out before his eyes. He hadn't felt anything close to that stab of terror since the day he'd heard the wolves' mournful howl and known something had happened to Garrick. So no matter how fully healed Khamsin declared herself to be, Wynter wasn't taking any chances.

He lay down on the bed. His body was hard as a rock, and had been from the moment he'd picked her up to carry her back to her room. Finding some other woman to relieve his need was out of the question. Even if he hadn't sworn an oath of fidelity, Khamsin was the only one he wanted. The only one for whom his blood and what remained of his humanity not only warmed, but *burned*.

His hand still tingled from cupping her face, stroking the creamy softness of her dark skin. He lifted his palm to his nose and breathed in the intoxicating jasmine-scented aroma that still clung to him. He reached his other hand down, loosened the laces of his trousers, and curled his fingers around the long, heavy length of his sex. His eyes closed. In the darkness, her face emerged. Luminous silver eyes. Curls of lightning-shot black hair. The fragile, slight-boned beauty of her delicate frame. The full, perfect breasts with their exotic, dark brown nipples.

He remembered how she'd been in the tent after the lightning storm, when he'd claimed her for the first time since their wedding night. Free of wine and arras and whatever else had been in that wedding-cup. She'd been scared, nervous but too proud to show it. But she'd overcome that fear, met his passion head-on, and returned it in full with passion of her own. He remembered, also, their first night here in Gildenheim, when she'd seethed with jealousy over Reika's conspicuous familiarity, and how that anger had led her to stake her claim upon him in no uncertain terms. Her eyes full of storms, her skin hot and electric, facing him without the tiniest hint of fear and demanding his fidelity and attentions. If he hadn't been completely enchanted with her before, that night had done the trick.

He could recall with perfect clarity the feel of her body, so wet and hot, muscles clamping tight around him. The glorious heat, melting the ice that lived inside him, making him *feel*, really feel, like he had not felt for three long years. His hand moved with each remembered thrust, stroking, stroking, until his muscles clenched and his seed spurted across the sheets.

After that night, Wynter made himself even scarcer. He never came back to his room at night. He didn't eat meals with the court anymore. Except for occasional glimpses of him as she and Krysti roamed the palace halls, Kham might have believed Wynter had left Gildenheim altogether.

She almost wished he had. What small gains she'd made with the ladies of the court began to reverse as the nobles interpreted Wynter's absence to mean that the new queen had fallen out of favor. The watchful eyes of the courtiers grew sly and knowing. Polite dinner conversation gave way to subtle innuendo, and titters muffled behind fans, all observed and encouraged by Reika Villani as she held court at the far end of the banquet hall in cold triumph.

Khamsin feared she might fry them all—including her husband—with a lightning bolt if she lost her temper, so she began finding excuses to be away from the palace.

She and Krysti became an inseparable pair. At her insistence, Bron selected a pony for the boy, and the two of them continued Kham's riding lessons together. Once they were both comfortable in the saddle, no place within four hours' ride of Gildenheim was safe from them. Khamsin, Krysti, and their armored guard soon became a common sight in the villages and mountains of the Craig.

And the villagers, despite their wishes to the contrary, soon became the focus of Kham's determined efforts to win them over. With the threat of Mount Gerd looming over her future, she was determined to do everything in her power to ensure that mercy, not death, awaited her.

Befriending Winterfolk, however, turned out to be even harder than winning over the ladies of the court. Winterfolk were wary of strangers, their villages small and closely knit. They were disinclined to be friendly to start with, and Kham's relation to the hated Summer King made them even more standoffish. The first time she rode into Skala-Holt, one of the larger villages nestled at the foot of Mount Fjarmir near the pass that led to Frostvatn on the western coast, many of the villagers actually snatched their children up off the street and hustled them inside as if Khamsin might cast an evil eye upon them, or some such nonsense.

Still, she persevered. Taking unabashed advantage of her rank—hoping the villagers would fear Wynter's wrath too much to snub his queen—she squeezed an introduction out of each person she met. Corbin, the beefy white-haired tanner of Brindlewood; Leise, the curt-bordering-on-hostile pubkeeper in Skala-Holt and her neighbors Derik and Starra Freijel, who raised sheep and spun wool on a stretch of land at the base of Mount Fjarmir: Khamsin committed their faces and many others to memory and made a point of greeting them by name when next they met. Not that it helped. The Winterfolk remained unwelcoming and taciturn.

"This is useless," she complained after yet another day of cold shoulders and unwelcoming villagers. "They'll never see me as anything but a Summerlander."

"Winterfolk warm slowly to outsiders," Krysti said. "If you want them to accept you, you might start by accepting them."

"What do you mean? I'm riding out to meet them. I'm being as nice as I know how. What else can I do?"

"Well, you might try dressing more like us for starters." Krysti nodded at the bright, jewel-toned clothing Khamsin had refused to give up.

"But I *like* my clothes. They remind me of home." The bright colors and rich fabrics made her feel warm, happy. And, yes, defiant. She clung to her Summerland colors as a form of rebellious independence, a symbol of her determination never to be cowed by these harsh, distant people and their cold gray-and-white world.

"I'm just saying, if you dress and act like a foreigner, you shouldn't be surprised when they treat you like one."

Khamsin frowned. She'd watched the Summer court enough to realize the wisdom in Krysti's advice. In fashion, manners, interests, behavior, many of Summerlea's courtiers strove for a sense of personal distinction, but few of them strayed far from acceptable conventions. People were like the flocks of birds she'd watched from her mother's Sky Garden. What one did, the rest followed.

"I'll think about it." That was the most she was willing to concede for the moment. She rebelled against rules and conformity and other people's expectations of her. She always had. If she gave that up—gave up her individuality, her fierce independence—what would be left of Khamsin?

"Even though it may not seem like it, you *are* making progress," Krysti assured her as they rode away from the

Freijels' sheep farm. "That was the first time Mr. Freijel offered to water your horse."

"It was, wasn't it?" She glanced back over her shoulder, at the small, stone cottage built into the side of the mountain. Smoke curled from the chimney. Fat, fluffy sheep wandered the hillside, snuffling at the snow in search of grass. Derik Freijel had already turned away to continue his work, but his wife Starra was still standing on the stoop watching Khamsin and Krysti ride away. Kham raised a hand to wave. Starra did not respond in kind. She merely tucked a flyaway strand of hair behind her ears and ducked inside the family's stone-and-sod home.

"Perhaps we shouldn't read much into that offer to water my horse," Kham said with a grimace. "He was probably just taking pity on the horse."

Krysti glanced back at the small farm and sighed. "Give them time. Even a mountain wears down from the wind."

"But only after a few millennia of effort," she pointed out. "I don't have that much time." She'd been here almost two months already and was no closer to winning over her new people than the day she arrived. Like it or not, her way was not working. She needed to change tactics. "Come on. Let's get back to Gildenheim. I need to speak to Vinca about bringing that seamstress back in."

Wynter noted the change in his queen's attire, as he noticed everything about her. Day by day, bit by bit, she shed her jewel-toned Summerlander clothes for Wintercraig fashions in shades of icy blue, cream, pale taupe, and white.

At first, he approved of the change. Her bright Summerlander colors made it easy to spot her in a crowd, and his eye was instantly drawn to her whenever she entered a room. Since he'd spent the last month trying to avoid being drawn to her, he thought her altered wardrobe would be a good thing.

It didn't quite work out that way. The paler colors set off her dark skin and black hair, amplifying the contrast to an even greater effect, the way diamonds enhanced the beauty of colored gems. Instead of helping her blend in, her new clothes only called attention to how different she was from the rest of his people, how exotically beautiful.

Valik had become so convinced Wynter was befuddled by some sort of Summerlander potion or spell that he'd ordered all of Wynter's food and drink tasted before it touched the king's lips, and he insisted Lady Frey perform dissolution rituals meant to unravel any spell placed upon him. Laci called Valik a fool to his face, but she performed the ritual to keep the peace.

"Idiots and frost brains," she muttered as she stalked out after finishing. "That's what men are. I've no idea why Freika ever bothered creating you. She should have recognized perfection when she created woman and stopped while she was ahead."

Unlike Laci, Wynter wasn't altogether certain Valik was wrong. Everything about his Summerlander queen intoxicated him. He thought about her day and night. He knew the instant she entered any room he was in, and though dozens of courtiers and the entire distance of a vast palace room might separate them, he was acutely and unalterably aware of her every step, every breath, every infinitesimal movement. Not even with Elka had he been so utterly consumed, so helplessly drawn to her. He was the moth, and Khamsin his flame.

And for that reason, though it cost him every ounce of his not-inconsiderable will, he kept his distance.

The six-week anniversary of her poisoning came and went. Laci informed Wynter that he could resume marital relations. But he was wound so tight, he didn't dare. If his wife missed his company, she gave no sign of it. Indeed, she seemed far more intent on traveling the countryside. Scarce an hour went by when he did not hear tell of her latest adventure with that orphan lad of hers. Wynter, consequently, grew surlier and more snappish with each passing day.

"Enough!" Valik exclaimed when Wynter nearly froze him to death during an argument over the kingdom's planned defenses. "This is ridiculous! You're acting like an ice bear with a sore paw. What is wrong with you?"

Wynter scowled. "We're preparing for an invasion we don't have the numbers to repel, our forces are stretched between two kingdoms, and I'm losing my battle with the Ice Heart. What do you think is wrong with me?"

"He hasn't returned to his wife's bed even though I cleared her for relations over two weeks ago," Laci told Valik in a flat voice. "*That* is what's wrong with him. What?" She arched a brow at Wynter's fierce scowl. "Servants talk. I listen."

"That's what this is about?" Valik spun around. "Then *bed* her, for Wyrn's sake. That's what you wed her for, anyways."

Wynter's eyebrows climbed towards his hairline. "Aren't you the one who's been going on for months now about how she's put me under some sort of spell?"

"I'm sure she has! But that doesn't change the fact that you need an heir. Besides, if not pumping the little witch is going to make you this unbearable, then throw her feet in the air and keep them there until your child is born!"

"Or find some other willing woman," Laci murmured, giving Wynter a sideways glance. "I'm sure there's no lack of prospects in your court."

He scowled. "I gave her my word I would not."

"Then do us all a favor and go to your wife," she said.

"You told me to stay away!"

"That was two months ago. I told you stay out of her bed for six weeks." Her mouth drew down in a disgusted grimace. "Truth be told, she was probably healthy enough within a week of the poisoning, but stupid me, I thought you might use the time to get to *know* your wife, not avoid her like the plague."

"You *lied* to me?"

Galacia sniffed. "I gave you the same advice I would

have given any man in that situation. It's not my fault your wife heals exponentially faster than most. But that's immaterial. The point is, you knew you could resume marital activities weeks ago yet you've done nothing about it. And in case it has escaped your notice, the pains you've taken to avoid her have been observed and emulated by your entire court. If you meant to make her life here as miserable as possible, you couldn't have chosen a better method."

Heat stung Wynter's cheeks. "That was not my intent." He wasn't unaware of his court's coolness towards Khamsin, but he'd done nothing to curtail it. And all right . . . perhaps some small, petty part of him *had* wanted to punish her for running about the countryside laughing and enjoying herself while he wanted her so badly, he'd spent the last two months in torment.

"Intent or not, that is the result." Galacia crossed her arms and fixed her cold, glass-sharp gaze upon him. "What are you going to do about it?"

"I'll take care of it." Wynter turned his attention back to the map of Wintercraig spread out on the table before him. The fight he'd had earlier with Valik was over delays with the final preparations at the scouting outposts. Wynter had expected all the outposts to be ready, fully manned, and running drills of the invasion-alert system, but some were weeks behind schedule, and his spies were reporting activity in the Calbernan armada. "Valik, whether they're ready or not, we need to check these defenses." He indicated the scouting outposts and forts along the west coast. "How long will it take you to pack?"

"An hour."

"Good. Then we leave in two."

"Wyn . . ." Disapproval iced Galacia's voice.

"I said I'd take care of it, and I will," Wynter snapped. "But there's a war headed our way, and the defense of the kingdom comes first." He took a breath and turned back to Valik. "Send word to Ofanklettur." He pointed to the southernmost scouting outpost on the western coast. "They are to light the signal fire at noon in two days' time. We ride to Frostvatn by way of the new scout towers." He traced a path from the center of Wintercraig's western coast northward to the isolated fort at the edge of the glacier fields. "I want to see for myself how much they're lacking and how long it takes for the signal to reach from the south to the north."

"Consider it done, my king." Valik marched out of the room.

When he was gone, Wynter closed his eyes and rotated his head to loosen the tension in his neck. He was rewarded with popping sounds, but the tension was still there. And so was Galacia, with her frosty disapproval. Wyn sighed.

"When I return, I'll see to my wife and put the gossip to rest. You have my word."

"I expect you to honor it."

"I always do."

Galacia laid a hand on his shoulder and kept it there even when he flinched. "Wyn, give her a chance. I didn't trust her brother, but she seems an honest sort. You might just have married the best one in the kingdom."

His mouth twisted. "That's not saying much."

"I like her more than most in your court, too."

"That's not saying much either. You've never had much use for nobles of any stripe."

"Don't be difficult. You know what I mean. I know Valik thinks she's a spy, but I've seen no sign of treachery in her. Get to know her. Gods willing, she'll be the mother of your children. You're capable of great love, great kindness. Let her see that."

He took her hand off his shoulder and held it, shaking his head sadly. She didn't understand. She still thought he was the Wynter she'd always known. "I'm not that man anymore, Laci. That man died when the Prince of Summerlea put an arrow in my brother's throat."

"I don't believe that. If it were true, Rorjak would have won long ago."

"He is winning." For the first time, he admitted aloud what he had long suspected. "I can feel him now, there in the back of my mind, waiting. Before this year is out, you'll have to put those spears in the temple to use."

Her brows drew together over troubled eyes. "All the more reason for you to have gone to your wife the instant you could. A child is your best hope of thawing the Ice Heart."

"Perhaps you should have thought about that before telling me to stay away from her." She looked so genuinely contrite, he felt guilty for the jab. "I'm sorry. I know you were doing what you thought was best. Besides, I doubt a few weeks would make a difference. I think it may be too late for me, even if there is a child."

"Don't say that." Her fingers clenched tightly around his. "Don't give up hope. And don't you dare give up without a fight. We need you, Wyn."

He bent his head and kissed her cheek. He didn't have to bend far; she was almost as tall as he was. "You're a good friend, Laci." He pulled back to give her a crooked smile. "Meddlesome, but a good friend all the same. Now, go on. I still have work to do before I leave."

After Galacia left, Wynter regarded the map of Wintercraig's defenses in troubled silence. His people were stretched too thin. The war with Summerlea had cost his kingdom dearly both in lost lives and injuries. With so many of the men at war, most industries in the Craig had struggled by with fewer hands to do the work, and even now were far from prewar production. He'd left half his army back in Vera Sola with Leirik to quell any possible uprisings, and that decision—though necessary—left Wintercraig even more vulnerable. When the armada came, Wynter and his folk would be facing the fight of their lives.

He walked back to the window and stepped out onto the balcony. Drifting snow brushed across his face and caught in the unbound strands of his hair. His gaze scanned the courtyard and battlements, looking for the slight figure he'd seen earlier, before his shouting match with Valik. And there she was, his wife, walking the outer wall, her little shadow, the orphan boy, close on her heels.

She'd already been riding today, but her outing had been cut short because of the storm clouds moving south over the Craig. The snows had come early this year, and the feel of those clouds promised at least another foot of snow before nightfall.

Wynter's chest expanded as he breathed the cold, bracing air deep into his lungs. As if sensing his presence from the other side of the courtyard, Khamsin turned. He knew the instant their eyes met: awareness jolted through him like one of her storm-spawned lightning bolts. His hands clenched the balustrade so tightly he feared he might grind the stone into powder.

That reaction was the real reason he'd stayed away from his wife, despite being cleared to resume marital relations. He remembered the sheets on their wedding bed, stained scarlet with her blood because he'd been too consumed with his drug-amplified lust to notice her wounds or her discomfort. He hadn't trusted himself to go near her until he was certain of his self-control.

But it seemed clear that self-control around Khamsin was a pipe dream. The more he stayed away, the stronger the attraction grew. What he felt for her now so outstripped the arras-driven lust of their wedding night, he could scarce comprehend it. They could not go on this way. *He* could not go on this way.

"When I return, wife, our separation ends. Gods help us both."

The moment Wynter broke eye contact and headed back inside, Khamsin's lungs started working again. She sucked in a deep, shuddering breath, then folded over in a paroxysm of coughing as the cold air chafed her throat and lungs.

"You all right?" Krysti gave her several solid thwacks on the back.

"I'm coughing, not choking." She shoved his hand away and scowled. "Stop hitting me."

"Sorry."

Now he looked hurt. She sighed. That one look she'd exchanged with Wynter across the full distance of the courtyard had left her feeling tightly wound. If she didn't find something to keep her mind occupied, she'd spend the whole day obsessing about why he was continuing to avoid her—and obsessing about him. And that would be a very bad thing. Especially with that snowstorm brewing on the horizon.

Kham turned back to Krysti and forced an overbright smile. "Come show me how to climb like you did earlier when we were out." When riding this morning, they'd stopped by a stream to water the horses, and Krysti had scrambled up a pile of tumbled boulders like a bounding mountain goat. "I want to learn how to do that, too. You think you can teach me?" He'd already taught her how to pick a lock, and she was getting quite proficient at it.

"I don't know. Maybe. But you're not Big Horn clan."

"Does that make a difference?"

"Big Horn clanfolk are born sure-footed. It's one of our clan-gifts. Like the way the king can scent things like a wolf, since he's Snow Wolf clan." Krysti glanced around. "If I'm going to teach you, we need a better place to practice. There's a good climbing wall in one of the upper gardens that wouldn't be too difficult for beginners. We can use that."

"Wonderful. Lead the way." As she followed him, Kham steadfastly refused to glance back at that now-empty balcony outside Wynter's rooms. "So each clan has its own clan-gifts?" she asked, determined to focus her mind on something unrelated to her husband.

"Yes."

"And everyone in that clan shares the same gifts? Not just the clan's ruling family?"

"Weathergifts don't manifest outside the immediate royal family, but clan-gifts are different. All Winter-folk have them. Some clan members have more gifts or a stronger ability in a particular gift than others, but there's always at least one core clan-gift that all members of that clan possess."

Khamsin nodded thoughtfully. All Summerlanders had a way with growing things—that was one of the reasons for the kingdom's exceptional fertility and prosperity—but they didn't have "clan-gifts" like Winterfolk. Occasionally, however, a member of the royal family was born with an affinity for a particular animal, as had happened with her brother Falcon. The royal historians attributed those gifts to the handful of Wintercraig brides wed over the centuries to the Heirs of the Rose, starting with the Wintercraig princess who'd married Roland's brother Donal two thousand years ago.

"How many clans are there?"

Krysti shrugged. "I don't know. Twenty or thirty. Maybe a few more. I was supposed to start learning clanlore three years ago, but my parents died."

In all the time they'd been together, Krysti hadn't opened up about his family. Since she knew what it was like to lose a parent, she hadn't pressed him for more information. Some wounds stayed fresh for a long time. But the fact that he'd brought them up made her think maybe he was ready to talk.

"What were they like? Your parents?"

"Nice. They loved me." He cast her a quick glance, as if daring her to dispute it.

"I'm sure they did." The corner of her mouth kicked up. "You're very lovable."

He flushed a little and gave her a friendly shove. She laughed, glad he'd taken the gentle tease in stride. That told her he wasn't upset with the line of questioning and gave her tacit approval to probe a little further.

"Was your father a soldier?"

"No. He was a tanner and a leatherworker. Mam, too."

"How did they die?"

"Our village burned down, but I don't want to talk about it." Krysti put on a burst of speed, forcing her to jog to keep up with him.

"Krysti!" She chased after him. "I'm sorry. I didn't mean to pry."

"Yes, you did."

She bit her lip. Yes, she had. "I'm sorry."

"Apology accepted. Let's hurry. We're wasting daylight." He jogged up another set of stone stairs, taking them two at a time.

Chastened, Kham followed him in silence. They continued up stair after stair until they reached the uppermost level of the main palace.

"Here we are." The frosted glass roof of the Atrium towered thirty feet above them. Only the palace towers and Wynter's private room built into the mountaintop were higher. Several courtyard gardens had been cut into the mountainside. Krysti led Khamsin to an isolated corner where the outer battlement wall merged with an inner courtyard wall.

"So, let's say you wanted to get to the top of the wall. We'll start with this one." He patted the shorter, inner wall. "Pretend the battlement stairs don't exist. You can still easily scale a small wall like this. Especially if it has handholds like the ones here and here and here." He pointed to a few slightly protruding rocks in the wall. "Watch."

Khamsin stepped to one side as Krysti ran at the corner of the wall. He leapt up, planting his right foot on one wall and left foot on the opposing wall, grabbed the protruding rocks, and scrambled up the corner of the joined walls. When he reached the top, he swung one leg over the inner wall to straddle it and leaned back, turning to grin down at Khamsin.

"There, see? Easy." The whole demonstration had taken less than ten seconds.

"Oh, yes, very easy." Sarcasm dripped from every word. That only made Krysti's grin widen.

He swung his right leg back across the wall and hopped off, landing lightly on the snow-covered grass in front of her. "Probably nothing you should try in a dress, though."

"That's easily fixed." Kham reached down and tucked her skirts into her waistband, leaving her woolen-stocking-clad legs bare. "Show me again, only this time not so fast."

Wynter jogged down the steps of Gildenheim to the main courtyard, where Valik and a contingent of White Guard were waiting with the horses. To his surprise, they weren't alone. Reika Villani stood by her cousin's side, holding the reins to her saddled bay mare.

Wyn frowned and glanced between Valik and Reika. "Lady Villani, you are going somewhere?"

"She's heading home to her family estate," Valik answered. "Reika received word that her father is in poor health. She asked if she could ride with us as far as Skaarsgard. I was certain you wouldn't mind."

Wyn hesitated a brief second, aware of the watchful eyes of his court and the gossip that would ensue. Escorting Reika Villani anywhere could only cause him grief once Khamsin found out, as he knew she would. But what sort of cowardly troll would he be if he refused a lady of his court protective escort to her father's estate for fear of a little gossip?

Shaking off the twinge of concern, he said, "Of course. It will be our pleasure to see you safely to your father's estate."

Reika smiled and curtsied with a murmured, "Thank you, Your Grace."

Wyn glanced up at Khamsin's balcony above. One did not pour fuel on an inferno, then run away and expect others to deal with the resulting conflagration.

"We'll leave in half an hour," he announced. "There's something I must attend to."

Leaving Valik and Reika staring after him in surprise, he jogged back up the steps and into the palace. "Fjall." He called the Steward of the Keep to his side. "Where is Her Grace?"

"She's with young Krysti, Sire. They've been exploring the palace since returning from their ride."

Which meant they could be anywhere. And he had neither the time nor the inclination to rouse the entire castle in search of his wife.

"Thank you." Leaving the steward to his duties, Wynter took the central stairs three at a time and followed the corridors to the private office attached to his rooms. Sitting down at the desk, he drew out a slip of parchment, uncapped the pot of ink, and dipped a quill in.

The inked quill hovered over the parchment for several minutes as he wrestled with what words to write. In the end he decided to stick to the facts.

> *My Queen,*
> *Business of the kingdom has called me away. I return in a fortnight. Keep well, min ros. I will attend you upon my return. Until then, I remain*
> *Your faithful husband,*
> *W*

There. Short, sweet, and to the point. Nothing weak or wistful, but he'd included an endearment and declared his intent to end their estrangement when he got back. And he'd taken the time to write the note in his own hand. That should earn some measure of favor.

He hesitated, debating about whether to address Reika's presence in his traveling party directly, then decided against it. He'd outright declared himself a faithful husband in his note, thus his wife should have no trouble dismissing any groundless gossip that might reach her ears.

Wyn sanded the note, waited for it to dry, then folded, sealed, and addressed it. He carried the sealed missive into Khamsin's chambers and propped it against the mirror of her dressing table, where she could not help but notice it.

Satisfied that he'd done what he could to avert pending disaster, Wynter made his way back to the courtyard and mounted Hodri. The stallion pranced, tossing his long white mane and snorting with impatience.

Wyn patted Hodri's strong neck and took up the reins. "Let us be off."

With a clatter of hooves on gritted cobblestone, Wynter, Valik, Reika, and the White Guard rode out of Gildenheim.

Sore, exhausted, her pent-up frustration now tamped down to bearable levels, Khamsin groaned as she sank into the luxurious, steaming bath Bella had prepared. Her head lolled against the lip of the tub, eyes closed, as she breathed in the patchouli-scented steam.

Her legs and arms felt like jelly, and there wasn't a muscle in her body that didn't ache. She'd practiced under Krysti's instruction until well after sundown. The boy was a surprisingly demanding taskmaster. He hadn't let her quit until she'd reached the top of the wall several times, a feat that had proven more difficult than she'd anticipated given the awkwardness of her voluminous skirts tucked up around her waist and her lack of upper-arm strength.

Tomorrow, first thing, she would start the exercises Krysti had recommended to strengthen her arms for climbing. And the seamstress who'd been remaking her wardrobe would simply have to make her a set of clothes more suited to the sort of active pursuits Krysti and the men engaged in.

She'd seen the women of the Craig working hard alongside their men. She wasn't going to let herself remain some weak, pampered southerner in their eyes. She was going to become a woman of the Craig in every way she could. She was going to learn to climb cliffs, hunt, read the signs of the forest.

Maybe that would earn their approval.

Because being herself certainly hadn't.

This strange dance of avoidance going on between

Wynter and herself had to end, too. Starting tonight. If his seat at dinner was empty again, she was going to track him down and demand that he come to her bed. Considering that her life still lay in the balance if she didn't produce a child, she wouldn't be begging for his attentions. She'd just be demanding he keep up with his part of their marriage contract.

"Bella," she called. She could hear her maid moving around in the bedchamber. Tidying the linens, no doubt, since she'd been bemoaning the Wintercraig maids' inability to fold a crisp corner. A few moments later, the girl popped into the bathing room.

"Yes, ma'am, you called?"

"Lay out the white gown for dinner. The one with the ermine trim." Kham ran a soapy cloth across her outstretched arm. Wynter liked that dress, she knew. The last time she'd worn it, he'd hardly taken his eyes off her.

"Yes, ma'am," Bella said. She started to turn away, then paused. "So you will be going down to dinner tonight, then?"

Khamsin frowned. "Of course. Why would I not?"

"Well, I thought that since the king was gone, you might—"

"The king is gone?"

"Yes, ma'am. This afternoon. He rode out with Lord Valik and Lady Villani."

The bar of soap squirted out of Kham's suddenly clenched hand and landed in the tub with a splash.

"He rode out . . . with Lady Villani?"

"Yes, ma'am." A gust of wind rattled the mullioned windowpanes. Bella flinched and glanced out at the darkening evening sky. "I'm sorry. I thought he told you."

"No. No, he didn't." Khamsin gripped the sides of the tub. The already-warm water was growing hotter by the second. "On second thought, just lay out my nightgown and robe. I'll have dinner in the room tonight and make an early night of it."

"Of course." Bella bobbed a curtsy and left.

Rather than lounging in the tub until the water cooled—which at the present rate was going to be never—Khamsin made short work of her bath and stepped out. She needed no towel to dry herself. The water on her skin evaporated into steam before her feet touched the thick rugs covering the cold stone floor.

Wynter had left Gildenheim without a word to her. And he'd taken Reika Villani with him! He'd sworn to be faithful. To take no other woman to bed. And yet he'd avoided hers for the last two months and was now cavorting about the countryside with that conniving harpy.

She snatched up her robe, shoved her arms through the sleeves, and stalked into her bedroom. Was this some sort of test? To see how far he could push her before she broke? Or had he lied to her from the start? Just told her what she wanted to hear to keep her docile and under control while he went after the woman he truly wanted?

She didn't want to believe she could be so easily duped, but apparently, she could. He'd dazzled her with his great, masculine beauty, seduced her with his oh-so-believable flashes of tenderness and caring. Stupid, naïve idiot that she was . . . she'd fallen for it all.

The bedchamber was warmer than usual, a large fire roaring in the hearth. The flames leapt higher as Bella industriously poked at the logs.

"Those Wintercraig maids opened all the windows this afternoon when they were changing your linens," Bella groused. "Can you believe it? I nearly froze in my shoes when I first came in—such a horrible, icy wind blowing through the place. It's only bearable now because I closed the windows and started a fire. Silly, goose-brained girls. What were they thinking? It's snowing—snowing!"

Kham glanced out the windows. Sure enough, the snow Krysti said had been threatening all day was now falling thick and fast.

"It's all right, Bella," she murmured. "I like the fresh

air, too. It makes the room smell nice, and the cold doesn't bother me. But you go on back to your room and sit by the fire. Take the rest of the night off."

Bella turned in surprise. "But what about your dinner?"

"I'll be fine. I'm really not hungry."

"But—"

"*Please!*" Kham grimaced at the sharp edge in her tone and rubbed her temples. "Please, just go. I'll be fine."

Grumbling about being sent away, Bella left.

Khamsin drew on her nightdress and robes, then paced the room restlessly, hounded by her thoughts and the feelings of anger and betrayal. The roaring fire, rather than comforting her, only made her hot, irritable, and angrier. She'd trusted him. Dear gods, she *had*. The enemy king who'd wed her. He had promised to be faithful, to deal with her fairly, and she'd *believed* him. What a fool she was!

She flung open the balcony doors and stepped out into the storm, hoping the cold and snow would draw the temper from her and calm her down. Instead, the storm grew worse as her agitated weathergift amplified the forces of nature. The wind began to howl. The whole sky was whirling white now, and she couldn't see down to Gildenheim's walls— nor even to the courtyard below. The air around her was hot and steaming—snowflakes evaporating in an instant when they neared her body. Her anger was feeding the storm, all right, but the storm was feeding her anger, just as much.

A frisson of alarm skated up her spine. This was getting bad. Very bad.

"For Wyrn's sake, Khamsin," she muttered, "get away from the sky before you kill someone."

She fled back indoors. In order to break the connection between the storm and her gift, she needed to go someplace deep, surrounded by rock and earth. She waved off the guards standing beside the door to her chambers and made her way downstairs to the kitchens. There, scores of servants bustled about in organized chaos, stirring soups, roasting meats, plating dishes. One look at her swirling silver eyes, however, and they cleared a path without a word.

She ran through their midst and down the stairs to the large, musty wine cellar that had been carved deep, deep into the mountain. Torches burned in sconces along the wall, the only source of light. During her tour with Mistress Vinca, she'd been frightened when her visit to the wine cellar had cut her off from her gift, but if she didn't separate herself from the storm soon, people would die.

When she reached the heavy wooden door leading to the cellar, however, she found it closed and locked. With a scream of frustration, she yanked on the door and pounded the unyielding wooden planks.

"Your Grace? May I be of assistance?"

She whirled around so fast the Steward of Wines, who must have followed her into the cellars, jumped back in fright.

"Forgive me, ma'am. I didn't mean to startle you." His voice shook. He was afraid of her.

He should be.

"Open this door."

"I beg your par—"

"Open it!"

He jumped again. "Of course." He drew the ring of keys from his side. They rattled noisily in his shaking hands. The man skirted gingerly around her and bent to put the key in the lock. Finally, after dropping the keys twice, the steward successfully inserted the right key in the lock and turned. The tumblers clicked. The door opened.

"Give me the keys." She held out an imperious hand.

The steward hesitated. "Madam, if you'll just tell me what you're looking for—"

"Give . . . me . . . the keys. Now."

He handed them over.

"Leave me." Kham didn't wait to see if he obeyed. She snatched the torch off the wall and ran down the long corridor, deep into the cold, shadowy recesses of the wine cellar.

The air was damp, chill, and musty. The flame of her torch was the only light. As she ran, her connection to the storm finally began to wane. She kept running, deeper and deeper into the gloom of the cellar hewn from solid rock, down another set of stairs and back into the deepest, coolest part of the cellar until there was no place left to run. There, before the dark stone wall covered with enormous shelves of dusty wine bottles, she let the torch fall to the stone floor and sank down beside it, pulling her legs up to her chest and wrapping her arms around them.

She could no longer feel the storm outside, only the storm within. The great, wild hurricane of anger and pain that threatened to tear her apart. Her chest was so tight she could hardly draw breath. She gasped for air, and the gasps turned to sobs. The dry, burning pain in her eyes became a flood of tears that could no longer be contained.

Kham buried her face in her arms and cried until her throat was sore and she had no tears left. And when the storm had passed and her tears were spent, she lay on the dusty floor of the wine cellar and stared up at the rocky ceiling overhead.

What was wrong with her that no one wanted her?

She was aware of her shortcomings: her short temper, the violent nature of her weathergift, her need to rebel against authority. But despite those drawbacks, she had always tried to live a good life, be a good person. A person Roland Soldeus would have been proud to call friend. Honorable, loyal, trustworthy, brave.

Maybe she *was* the abomination her father had called her. Maybe everyone else could see the evil in her and *that's* why they reviled her.

Kham gave a harsh laugh and flung an arm over her eyes. Or maybe she was simply stupid and naïve and had spent her whole life trusting the wrong people. Maybe the only person she could trust was herself.

Tired of feeling sorry for herself, scrubbed the dampness from her cheeks and sat up. Time to regroup. She would not let Wynter Atrialan or any other person decide her fate. She was a survivor. She always had been. And she wasn't going to be a pawn in other people's games anymore.

And Wynter Atrialan wouldn't honor his oaths to her, there was no reason she should honor hers to him.

She was done being the docile, agreeable wife. She was going to do what she should have been doing from the very beginning: whatever it took to look out for her own interests. No matter what happened between now and the end of her year as Wintercraig's queen, she was going to find a way to survive and to thrive. And she was going to secure that survival independent of whether she bore Wynter's child or won over the hearts and minds of his people.

With that goal in mind, Khamsin was going to dedicate herself to discovering all the things Wynter didn't want her to know. Starting with whatever he was hiding in the one place in the palace she'd been forbidden to enter. The room he visited in secret when he thought all the rest of the palace was asleep.

Gildenheim's Atrium.

CHAPTER 17

The Frozen Heart of Winter

On silent feet, Khamsin crept across Gildenheim's marble floors. The hour was late. All of Gildenheim was sleeping save the guards who patrolled the outer defenses and the handful who prowled the hallways of the castle in search of mischief-makers and spies. Kham had dodged three of those while making her way from her rooms to the mysterious, forbidden Atrium that only Wynter ever entered.

His predilection for secrecy had actually been a boon to her. If not for those times when she'd followed him from his room to the Atrium, she would not have known the schedule of the guards or the back-stairs path least likely to result in an encounter with some wandering servant or dallying courtier.

The Atrium's twelve-foot-tall doors were fashioned from carved and gilded white wood inset with large panes of frosted glass. Etched snowflakes and curling lines swirled across the glass's translucent surface. The doorknobs were shaped like two great silver wolves rearing up on hind legs, their bushy tails the cunningly disguised lever door handles. Each wolf held a gold ball between its diamond teeth. The ball on the right sported a keyhole.

Kham knelt by the right door, pulled the lockpicks from her skirt pocket, and went to work. Krysti had taught her well. In less than a minute, the lock clicked open. Kham pulled down on the wolves' tails, and the doors opened.

She slipped inside, careful to close the doors behind her, and pulled the shade from her lamp. Light spilled out in a bright circle around her.

"Now, Wynter of the Craig, let's see what you've been hiding." Lifting her lamp high, Khamsin turned to investigate her husband's private sanctum.

She wasn't sure what she expected to find. Private military secrets, perhaps. Treasures vast enough to buy entire kingdoms. Sacred antiquities. Possibly even some dread, terrible evil Wynter hid behind his handsome face and winning smile. (Although despite her best, angriest efforts to paint him a foul, blackhearted villain, she honestly didn't believe that last one.)

But when the light from her lamp spilled out across the Atrium's shadowy secrets, she didn't find dazzling treasure. She didn't find a secret vault of sensitive military or political documents. She didn't find war plans, or holy relics, or a bloody altar to the dark gods.

What she found, instead, was beauty. Breathtaking beauty.

Her mouth open in a soundless gasp of wonder, Khamsin stepped forward into a glorious, ghostly white forest carved entirely from ice. Moonlight, spilling through the leaded-glass dome overhead, sparkled on the delicate, ice-carved leaves and needled boughs, making the entire room shimmer like diamonds in soft silver light.

"Summer Sun." The shocked, reverent whisper echoed in the total silence of the room. She tilted her head back. The life-sized ice trees soared seventy feet high. The Atrium roof soared higher still, and in the space between the tops of the trees and the sheltering glass panes of the glass roof, flocks of carved ice birds were frozen in flight, wings outstretched as they wheeled and dipped through an imaginary sky.

Glittering snow covered the Atrium floor, and as she approached the first few trees of the ice forest, she discovered an astonishingly lifelike baby deer carved from frosted ice standing on spindly legs beneath the watchful eyes of his mother. Just beyond, in a small clearing beside a tiny brook carved of clear ice, a family of Winterfolk were having a picnic.

Snow crunched beneath her slippers as she moved closer and brought her lantern up to illuminate the family. There were four figures: a man, a woman, a young boy, and an infant lying on a blanket between his parents. The sculptures were astonishingly lifelike, right down to the expressions of doting, parental love on the adult faces and the beaming, mischievous exuberance on the face of the boy as he cupped a tiny bird in his hands.

Who had made this place? Why was it here?

She moved deeper into the ice forest. The snow on the ground was packed in places, providing trails that let her walk through the trees without worrying that she might damage them. With each step, she discovered new statues and scenes hidden amongst the ghostly tree trunks. Squirrels, wolves, foxes, bears, birds, flowers, waterfalls, frozen ponds. And everywhere, life-sized ice sculptures of happy families hiked through forest paths, danced among the trees, skated on frozen ponds, climbed frosted rocks and trees.

After the fourth or fifth family tableau, she realized that the people in each exquisitely rendered family scene were all the same. A mother, a father, and two sons—one at least ten years older than the other. The people aged from scene to scene—most notably, the youngest child grew from infant to toddler, and the boy went from youth to young man—but they were the same people, the same family, carved over and over again.

And then she noticed a scene or two that featured only the boys when they were much older. A handsome teenaged boy with hair that tumbled in his eyes. A towering older brother now grown to manhood, with a face she recognized better than her own.

The truth froze Khamsin where she stood. The statues

in this room weren't just beautifully sculpted art. They were carefully rendered scenes from Wynter's life.

These statues were memories. Wynter's memories.

Scenes of his family, his brother, sculpted in ice and hidden here, away from the world. Frozen proof of the love and happiness he'd known before her brother had slain his.

Khamsin tried to stay away from the Atrium. Once she realized the room was a shrine to the family Wynter had loved and lost, going there seemed like an intrusion, a trespass in a sacred space. But the more she tried to stay away, the stronger the place pulled at her.

She told herself not to be driven by her emotions, to keep focused. What was in that room would do nothing to help her survive the coming year. There was no secret, no treasure she could use to bribe her way to safety. No military or political information that might buy her asylum in another kingdom.

And yet, several times a day, she found herself standing before those locked, frosted-glass doors, aching to open them and slip back inside the secret world of happy memories Wynter had created for himself. She'd never known the joy of a close, loving family. Since birth, she'd been reviled, feared, isolated from the warmth her sisters and brother shared, from the love Verdan Coruscate had unstintingly showered upon them. Wynter had grown up with everything that she had been denied: a mother and a father who loved him, laughter, happiness. Belonging.

On the third morning, she gave up her attempts to respect the privacy of his memories. She wanted what she'd never had. Even if she could only vicariously enjoy someone else's frozen memories of what a loving family felt like.

She sent Krysti away on an errand, made her way to the Atrium, and waited until the coast was clear. Picking the lock was easier the second time. She pulled down on the wolves' tails and slipped inside Wynter's frozen wonderland.

In full daylight, the extent of ice forest built inside the Atrium was even more impressive—and more breathtakingly beautiful. With bright sunlight streaming through the glass dome, the frozen forest blazed to pure, radiant, diamondine life. It felt like Halla on earth. Pristine and perfect. And for now, at least, all hers.

She wandered slowly amongst the trees, inspecting and savoring every detail, every leaf, every branch, every delicately etched bird wing, life-sized animal and carved wildflower hidden amongst the trees. Whoever had created these sculptures for Wynter was an incredible artist. What a gift, to be able to form such perfect re-creations of life from blocks of frozen water.

When it came to the scenes of Wynter's family, she slowed even more, committing each face and expression to memory, as if by doing so she could make those memories her own. The soft curve of his mother's lips. The warmth of her smile. The pride in his father's handsome, regal face. The love so plain between them as they watched their children and basked in each other's company.

What was it like to be surrounded by such love and belonging?

She couldn't keep her hands to herself. She found herself stroking frozen flower petals, laying her hand on the cold face of the carved toddler, brushing fingertips across the lips of Wynter, the young man, careful not to let her hand linger, for fear that her Summer-born gifts might melt the ice. Even so, with each brush of her hand, she could almost imagine she was there, enjoying a cool spring day in the forest with a family who loved her.

She closed her eyes and imagined that the ice forest was real, that there was a cool breeze blowing through the frozen treetops, fragrant with pine and spruce and loamy soil damp with snowmelt. And when she opened her eyes again, she could hear the birds singing in the trees, the rustle of squirrels and foxes darting through the shrubs and skittering across the bracken on the forest floor. She could hear the low, manly rumble of Wynter's laughter as he and his brother walked through the woods on a hunt, bows slung across their backs, smiles on their faces as they shared a funny tale. She could hear his mother's voice, calling her children back to her side, telling them to watch their balance by the stream, and his father telling her not to worry so, that their boys would be fine. They were Craigborn, after all.

The game of pretend felt so real she was loath to leave. She managed only because she knew she would be back the next day, and the next.

Krysti grew suspicious of all the errands she was sending him on, so she had to shorten her visits, but each morning she woke up eager to visit again. And each day, she counted down the minutes until she could. She became quite adept at giving would-be spies the slip, traversing up and down the maze of corridors and stairways in Gildenheim only to circle back around to the Atrium once she'd lost her followers.

And when she stepped inside the Atrium's secret world, it was as if every wound and burden she'd ever suffered dropped away.

As strange as it sounded, she'd never been happier. And she never wanted the feeling to end. The days turned into a week. The week turned into a second.

And then, inevitably, Wynter returned.

The familiar, ice-and-snow-capped towers of Gildenheim were a welcome sight.

"Home, at last, Hodri," Wynter murmured. The last two weeks had been long, cold, exhausting, and frustrating. The western defenses were nowhere close to being complete. If Coruscate and his Calbernan friends invaded anytime soon, they would be on Gildenheim's doorstep before Wynter's people managed to rally a defense.

Angry that he'd had to replace three of the garrison commanders and send another two thousand men to defend that dangerously undermanned coast, and weary to his bones because he'd forgone sleep for the last four days in his rush to return to Gildenheim, Wynter wanted nothing more than to enjoy a long soak in a steaming-hot tub and fall into his bed for a full day and night of undisturbed slumber. Maybe then he'd be close to feeling human again.

He touched his heels to his mount's side, and the stallion cantered the remaining distance up the switchback road and through the palace portcullis. Hooves clattered on the courtyard cobbles. The tower lookout had already sent up the cry calling servants to help with the horses and baggage, so as Wynter drew Hodri to a halt, the Steward of the Keep was already standing on the palace steps, waiting to greet him.

"Your Grace." Deervyn Fjall bowed and motioned to a footman to fetch the king's saddlebags.

"Fjall." Wyn tossed Hodri's reins to a stableboy. "Give him an extra ration of oats and a good rubdown. We rode hard the last three days."

"Yes, Sire. We'll take good care of him." The stableboy patted Hodri's strong neck and led him away.

Turning his attention to the Steward, Wyn said, "Tell Vinca I want a hot bath and a hot meal." He started up the stone steps.

"Yes, sir. Of course." Deervyn Fjall jogged up the steps beside him. "Your Grace, you asked me to keep an eye out in your absence." He pitched his voice low so it would not carry.

Wyn paused. "There were more falcons? How many?"

"Three sighted, my lord. We only managed to bring one of them down." Fjall handed Wynter a tiny, curled slip of paper. "We didn't catch the person the birds were intended for. Each time, the falcon flew to a different part of the palace."

Wyn uncurled the message and read the tiny script intended for someone in Gildenheim. His fist closed around the paper, crumpling it, and thrust the wadded slip of paper in his vest pocket. "Thank you, Fjall. Lord Valik and I will take it from here."

"Of course, Your Grace." The Steward of the Keep bowed again.

Courtiers who'd heard the call announcing Wynter's return were lined up along the steps three deep. The lines of them dipped low in a rolling wave of bows and curtsies as he passed. He scanned the crowd, automatically seeking the one face that had been in his mind since the day of his departure. The dark, silver-shot locks in a sea of blonds.

She wasn't there.

Anger and disappointment flared with equal intensity. What now? His queen could not be bothered to welcome him home? There was something more pressing that demanded her attention? Like sending coded messages to her brother, perhaps?

"Where is the queen?"

Fjall blanched white beneath his golden skin. "You said to watch but not to interfere—and not to let her know she was being watching."

"I know what I said," Wyn snapped. "You don't need to remind me of my own orders. Where is she?"

"She's been going there every day since last week. There's no sign that she's done any harm, my lord, but—"

"Where is she?" Ice cracked in his voice.

The Steward swallowed. "The queen is in the Atrium, Your Grace."

"What are you doing here?"

The guttural bark ripped through the still serenity of the Atrium.

Khamsin, who had been sitting in the icy meadow where the sculptures of Wynter and his family were picnicking, jumped to her feet. She turned in a flurry of skirts to find Wynter standing at the edge of the meadow, practically vibrating with fury.

The temperature in the room plunged. The small meal

she'd brought to eat with Wynter's family went white with frost.

"What are you doing in here?" He advanced upon her, each foot falling heavily upon the ground, all but making the earth shake with each stride. "You knew this room was forbidden. You gave me your oath you would not trespass."

Kham found herself retreating two steps for every one long stride Wynter advanced. She hadn't seen him in such a state since the day he'd discovered his bride was not the auburn-haired princess he'd been expecting. No—not even then. She'd never seen him this enraged.

His fingers were clenched in heavy, rock-hard fists. His eyes had gone completely white, and if she hadn't instantly reached for the power of the sun, his Gaze would have frozen her solid where she stood.

She held out her hands in supplication, truly afraid of him for the first time in a long while. There was no hint of the passionate lover or tender husband in the ice-carved lines of his face. He was all ice, cold and harsh and implacable. "Wynter—I—"

"You what? Thought you'd find some valuable military secrets here that you could send to your brother?"

"No!" Her voice cracked. He suspected she was spying for her brother? She ignored the slight twinge of guilt that reminded her she *had* come here looking for secrets she could use to ensure her survival. "Of course not! I haven't spoken to my brother in years! I don't even know where he is."

"Then what are you doing here? Is this how you honor your oaths? Valik was right. I've been too soft, allowed you too much freedom. And you've interpreted my indulgence as a sign of weakness."

"Valik is an idiot!"

"We're not talking about Valik!" His roar blasted out with such force that icy leaves in the tree above Khamsin shivered, cracked and fell from the limbs, showering down in a hail of broken ice. "Valik isn't the one who betrayed my trust, broke my law, and invaded a room he was expressly forbidden to enter! Valik isn't the one who broke his oath! I should have known better than to ever trust a Summerlander. You come from a long line of liars, murderers, thieves, and cheats. Why should I think you would be any different?"

Fire swept through her veins. Anger, fed by the weeks of Wynter's abandonment and her own defensive rage at having been caught intruding, burst to life. Lightning whipped through her veins, heating her blood. Overhead, visible through the Atrium's glass roof, the sky grew dark as clouds gathered.

"You call *my* family murderers? Ha! You have more blood on your hands than Summerlea's last three kings combined! How many of our villages did you raze? How many innocent women and children froze to death or starved in the wake of your conquest? And for what? Because your bride preferred my brother's company to yours! Frankly, after having been wed to you these last months now, I don't blame her!"

His brows shot up, and the temperature dropped commensurately. The sky overhead went white as the gathered clouds began pouring out ice and snow. "You complain of the care I have shown you?"

" 'Care'?" She all but screeched the word. "To what 'care' exactly do you refer? You mean the way you ignore me for weeks on end? That care? Or the way you have made it clear to every member of your court that I am to be ostracized and treated as a source of pathetic amusement?"

"You blame me because you haven't managed to win my people's regard?"

"Of course you're to blame! You've done everything but posted a written edict instructing your people to revile me. You and your precious Valik and that vile cousin of his."

Wind howled through the palace turrets and rattled the Atrium's glass panes. Her anger had started as a defensive response to Wynter's own fury, but as the accusations poured from her lips, Kham began to realize just how much rage and resentment she'd bottled up inside her. And considering that she'd spent a lifetime fighting to keep her temper in check—and usually failing with disastrous results—she could scarcely believe that she'd kept so much emotion contained for so long.

"I made you my queen!" Wynter bellowed. His eyes had gone pure white, and a cloud enveloped the pair of them, shifting back and forth between frost and steam as they both unleashed pent-up anger.

"Queen of what?" she shouted back. "Your indifference? You brought me to this iceberg and abandoned me here!"

"You expected love sonnets and roses? You are here to bear my heir, nothing more."

Lightning ripped across the sky. Thunder boomed, deafeningly close. If she'd ever had any doubt that he considered her anything more than a convenient womb, he'd just cleared that up.

"Winter's Frost! You could drive a saint to murder." Wynter dragged his hands through his hair. "None of this justifies your presence here. This room is off-limits."

"Oh, right! Because this room is just full of secrets that could imperil the kingdom! My gods! Just imagine what horrors would ensue if I told my brother that the Winter King once had a family he loved!"

"This is my place. Mine! I don't want you here! What part of that don't you understand?"

The rejection drove into her like a knife, parting her ribs and ripping into her heart.

Lightning struck the Atrium's roof. The glass shattered.

Wynter dove for Khamsin, catching her around the waist with one big arm and sweeping her off her feet, carrying her clear of the lethal rain of razor-sharp glass. They landed in the snowdrift near one of the statues of Wynter and his family.

But instead of earning Kham's gratitude, Wyn's rescue

only enraged her further. She closed her hands into fists and beat them on his chest. It was like beating a marble statue. He didn't move and her hands throbbed. She shoved against him, writhing and pushing to free herself.

"Get off me! Get off, damn you! Don't pretend concern for my safety. It's just another form of lying, and I'm sick of it! Do you hear me? You're no different than my father!"

Snow fell through the broken Atrium roof in thick sheets, swirling about on fierce gusts of winds, until the entire room looked like a child's blown-glass globe filled with oil and bits of white crystal that, when shaken, would "snow" over some tiny carved scene inside the globe.

"I am nothing like your father." He caught her wrists and pinned her to the snow-covered floor, holding her easily as she struggled and bucked against him.

"No, you're worse. He's at least always been honest about wanting me dead." Her chest heaved. Her whole body was hot and flushed. "There never really was any hope I'd come out of this year alive, was there? You just held out the possibility of mercy to keep me docile and compliant, all the while ensuring none of your people would speak for me when the time came."

He gave a bark of mocking laughter. "You call this docile?"

The laughter made her temper flare like water poured on hot oil. She began to struggle in earnest, writhing and thrashing about in an attempt to break free. During her struggles, her skull whacked into his jaw with a loud crack. Pain exploded across her forehead. She fell back, dizzy and moaning as stars danced before her eyes.

Wynter, barely fazed, flexed his jaw from side to side and glared at her.

"Damn it, Khamsin, stop before you hurt yourself."

"I'm fine." She tugged her arm until he released one wrist, and she laid the free hand against her forehead, massaging the flesh gingerly. "Besides, what do you care?" She gave him a dark look.

"I've told you before. You are my wife and my queen. Your well-being is my responsibility."

"Right up to the time you have me put to death, you mean?" She jerked away from his hand. "I told you I'm fine. And I don't want to be your 'responsibility.'"

His teeth clenched. He gripped her jaw and forced her to look at him. "Just shut up and let me look at that."

She glared up at him. "A little whack on the head isn't going to affect my ability to bear your heir. Of course, how, exactly, I'm supposed to *conceive* that heir when you avoid my bed like the plague is a complete mystery."

The minute the words left her mouth, she knew she'd made a mistake. Wynter went completely still, and his gaze suddenly went sharp as a blade.

"Is that what this is all about? My recent absence from your bed upsets you?" His voice was silky smooth, his eyes searingly intent.

Not for all the world was she going to dignify *that* with an answer. "No, your *lying* to me upset me. If you won't keep your oaths, then I won't keep mine either."

"When have I ever lied to you?"

Her mouth curled. "Don't take me for an idiot. I know you took your harlot with you when you left. Did you think I would just sit here playing the sweet, long-suffering wife while you and Reika Villani fornicated your way across the kingdom?"

His eyes narrowed. "You think Reika and I . . . ?"

"Not just me. The whole court. You weren't the slightest bit discreet. Did you think we all were blind and deaf? Did you think you could just ride off with her for a fortnight, and no one would put two and two together?" When he didn't answer, she slapped at his hands and shoved at him in irritation. "Let me up, Wynter. You're squashing me."

"No," he said slowly. "No, I don't think I will." He caught the wrist he'd freed earlier and pinned her back to the ground. The white Wolf on his wrist brushed against her Summer Rose.

Khamsin gasped. The throbbing pain in her temple evaporated as another, far more powerful and irresistible sensation swept over her. "Stop that."

"Stop what?" His voice had gone low and throaty.

"You know what. You think you can manipulate me with your . . . your wiles."

"You think I have wiles?" He brushed his lips against the soft skin behind her ear, making her shiver violently. "So you are wroth with me for being absent so long from your bed? Is that the real reason you came here? Because you wanted to get my attention?" He blew a soft, icy breeze down her throat. The chill against superheated flesh made her shudder with delicious sensation. Her nipples tightened to hard points, and her mouth went dry.

"I—I—" She couldn't put two coherent words together. She settled for one. "Stop."

His tongue touched her ear lightly in a swift, teasing caress. "I thought you would appreciate my husbandly consideration. Lady Frey said you needed time to heal, so I gave it to you."

"That was weeks ago." His skin smelled so good. Rich and seductive, the scents multilayered: cool crisp winter freshness, underlain with a darker, earthier, masculine scent, and something else she couldn't name that made her body throb every time she smelled it. She told herself she would resist seduction, but she couldn't resist that. She pressed her face to the skin of his neck, breathing him in. Her eyes rolled back in pleasure.

"If you hungered for my touch, you need only have asked." His teeth grazed her skin. Her eyes closed as his mouth found her breast and he bit down lightly, through the crushed velvet of her overdress.

She moaned, her breath starting to come faster. It wasn't fair, the effect he had on her. He pressed his wrist to hers, lowered his voice to that sultry, seductive growl, and every cell in her body started screaming in need.

"How was I supposed to do that when you avoided

me at every turn?" She fixed her eyes on the pulse in his strong throat. A blush rose in her cheeks. She'd admitted her weakness . . . confessed that she'd wanted him . . . that she yearned for him. "And then you left. With Reika Villani." The last popped out of its own volition, the tone hurt, wounded. Ah, gods, she was all but weeping.

He pulled back, his gaze searching her face. "You are jealous?"

"Not jealous. Betrayed." She tried to cling to some measure of dignity. "You swore an oath of fidelity."

"And I kept it. Reika Villani's father is dying. I gave her escort to her father's estate, nothing more. Or did you think I was lying in my note when I vowed to remain your faithful husband?"

"Note? What note?" He was nibbling at her ear now, and her thoughts began to scatter like autumn leaves.

"The one I left on your dressing table."

"There was no note—ah!" His hips moved against hers. Even through the thick layers of her skirts, she could feel the hard ridge of his flesh. Her hips bucked involuntarily, issuing a wordless demand. Big hands slid beneath her skirts, skating up her stocking thighs to the soft heat between her legs. Fingers stroked across hot, slippery flesh, driving her wild.

"Do you hunger for my touch?"

She hadn't even realized he'd undone her laces until her bodice parted, and he used his teeth to lower the front of her chemise, baring her breasts. His tongue swirled around first one nipple, then the other, bathing each in icy fire.

Her hands roved across his back and chest, pulling impatiently at fur and cloth to reach the silky skin beneath. She groaned as the hard, velvety head of his sex pressed teasingly against hers. She reached down to grab his buttocks to pull him closer, wanting him inside her.

His hips didn't budge. And the mouth doing such dizzyingly seductive things to her breasts stopped, too.

She opened her eyes to scowl at him, and found him pushed back on his hands, watching her.

"Do you, wife? Do you want this?" He gave a little buck of his hips. The tip of his sex pushed just inside her, then retreated, leaving the inner muscles of her channel clenching at unsatisfying emptiness. "Do you hunger for it? For me?"

She was done with trying to pretend indifference. He knew it for the lie it was. She wrapped her legs around his waist, her arms around his chest, and surged up against him.

"Yes! Yes, damn you, yes!"

He smiled, and it dazzled her. Then he drove into her, and all coherent thought splintered. She gasped with the sharp ache of pleasure. Her arms tightened around him. Her nails clawed at the layers of fabric still separating her hands from his flesh. Her hips tilted up to meet each of his thrusts, taking him as deep inside her as she could.

Gods, help her. She'd missed this. Missed it more than she had ever let herself admit.

Kham shivered under him—not from the cold ice against her back, but from the heat that boiled inside her with each devastatingly erotic, slow-motion thrust of his body against hers.

"Take this off." She yanked at his vest. "Take it off. Now." He pulled back to shed the furred vest, but she was too impatient to wait for him. She reached for the soft, woven-silk shirt beneath, gripped the sides of the reinforced yoke in her hands, and yanked. The silk ripped with a satisfying noise, baring a broad expanse of silky-smooth golden skin stretched across temptingly well-defined muscle.

Her mouth found his skin. She licked the salty-sweet flavor of his flesh, bit at him, found the hard, tightly gathered coin of his male nipple, and drew it into her mouth. He groaned, and the sound rippled inside her. Her muscles clenched and released and clenched again. She bit down on the pointed tip of his nipple. He gave a guttural roar, and his hips slammed forward, driving her up and back.

Stars exploded, bright, blinding flashes of light, and she screamed as wave after wave of sensation crashed over her. Her hands clutched at his shoulders. Her legs locked around his waist, shaking in helpless abandon.

Wynter held his wife on his chest, his clothes wrapped around her. He'd longed for a long, hot soak in a steaming tub, but this was so much better. The weariness, the irritability, the anger and frustration had all melted away from him the instant he'd buried himself in his little Summerlass.

He ran a hand across her hair, marveling at its soft texture, the way the ringlets curled around his finger, loving the little threads of white shot through all that darkness. Midnight Storm.

"Why did you come here, after promising you wouldn't?"

She glanced up, her gray eyes still touched by passionate silver, looking like shining moons against her dusky skin. "I wanted to know what you were hiding. And I thought you'd broken your own oath, so I saw no reason to keep mine."

"I don't break my oaths. At least until this year is up, the only woman to share my bed will be you and you alone." He could have reassured her again that there was nothing between Reika and him, nor ever likely to be, but he found he liked that hint of jealousy in his hot-tempered wife. No woman had ever felt the need to warn other women away. Elka had known he would never stray and taken his fidelity as her due. He had assumed she was just as faithful, and he'd grown . . . complacent.

"So why did you keep coming when you knew the Atrium contained nothing of value to anyone but me? Oh, yes," he admitted in answer to her look of surprise. "I know you've been here every day for at least the last week."

"You have someone spying on me?" She rolled her eyes. "Of course you have someone spying on me. Probably every person in the palace."

Of course he did. He'd given his foreign bride all the freedom she could desire, or rather, all the rope in the world with which to hang herself. He'd been a blind fool for a woman once before. That was a mistake he would never make again.

"Why did you keep coming back?" he pressed. "What were you expecting to find?" If she was the one sending messages to her brother, she'd had an entire palace to search, places with far more valuable caches of information. According to Fjall, she'd never gone near any of them. She'd come here and kept coming here.

"What was I looking for?" Khamsin's curling black lashes swept down over her eyes, as she surrendered the truth. "The same thing you were looking for when you had this place created, I imagine."

Wyn frowned in bemusement. "What do you mean?"

Her slender fingers trailed across his chest, stroking his skin and stopping over his heart.

He waited, but when no answer was forthcoming, he rolled to one side. She slid off his chest and into his waiting arms. He covered her body with his, bearing his weight on his forearms. The long, unbound strands of his hair fell around his face and hers, secluding them in a veil of silvery white.

"What do you think I look for when I come here?"

She looked up at him. She had only to lift her head a few inches to cover his lips with her own. For a moment, he thought she might try to distract him with a kiss, but instead she only lifted a hand to his face and ran a thumb across his lower lip.

"Love." Her voice was so low, he had to strain to hear it.

He caught her thumb between his teeth and touched his tongue to its tip. "You think I come here looking for love?"

"For the memory of it, yes." She met his gaze directly, and the clear, unwavering honesty in her gray eyes stilled him. "I've been coming here to imagine what it must have been like."

"To love?"

"To be part of a family. To belong."

It had been a very long time since Wynter wanted to gather another person up in his arms and offer them comfort. But the wistful sadness in that hoarsely whispered confession tore at the gentleness he didn't realize still existed in his heart.

As if regretting the vulnerability she'd just revealed, Khamsin pushed against him and tried to wriggle free. He didn't budge.

"You have a family."

"Do I?" Her lips curved in a sad smile. "My mother died when I was three. My father hated me from the day I was born. My sisters and brother harbor some measure of affection for me, but that doesn't mean I've ever been part of a family. Not really. Not like what you've preserved here in this room." Her voice grew husky. She clamped her lips closed and turned her head away, but not before he saw the shimmer of tears spangling her lashes.

The sight of those tiny, glittering drops filled him with both icy rage and terrible, consuming sadness. What miserable excuse for a man would deny his own child, as Verdan Coruscate had denied his fourth daughter?

Wynter brushed his wife's tears from her lashes. She could not be the traitor Valik suspected. No one could be so convincing. He'd been blind to Elka's perfidy because he loved and trusted her. But Khamsin was and had always been the daughter of an enemy king. She'd deliberately deceived him into wedding her when he thought he was marrying her sister. He wasn't blinded by love or trust this time. And when she said she'd come here because she wanted to know what it was to belong to a family—a loving family—he believed her.

He rolled off her and got to his feet, pulling her up with him. He took a few minutes to help her rearrange her clothing and draped his furred vest around her shoulders.

"I made this place for my brother," he admitted. "He

was only five when the Frost Giant killed our parents. I didn't want him to grow up not knowing who they were or how much they loved him. It started as just a single sculpture of our parents, but Garrick liked it so much I made more."

He had succeeded in surprising her. "*You* made this place? You're the sculptor?"

He shrugged. "Ice carving is something of a national pastime in Wintercraig. I started when I was very young and got fairly good at it."

"Fairly? Wynter, there are famed artists in the Summer Court who couldn't match what you've created here."

He flushed a little at her praise, then corrected her misconception that he alone was responsible for the Atrium's sculptures. "They aren't all mine. Garrick did his own carving when he was old enough. It was something the two of us did together."

She gazed around the crystalline world of ice and snow. "Would you . . . tell me about them? Your family?"

A hand squeezed his heart, and Wynter found himself wishing Verdan Coruscate was standing here before him now, so he could choke the life out of him.

He was careful to keep his voice calm as he said, "It would be my pleasure, *min ros.*"

He walked his wife through the numerous trails of the extensive ice forest that he and his brother had created, pausing often to point out a particular piece, or tell her about the memory that had inspired a particular scene. He'd brought Elka here once. She'd admired the beauty of the place, the skill of his and Garrick's sculpting, but she'd never felt the love. She'd never drunk in the memories with eyes that shone like silver moons, or paused so often to laugh over funny little details. Nor had she ever come here on her own to enjoy what he and Garrick had spent so many years sculpting. But Khamsin's enthusiasm and her obvious appreciation for their work was too honest, too compelling, to be false.

What would Garrick have said about Wynter's Summer-lander queen?

Khamsin stopped by a sculpture of his laughing father holding an infant Garrick over his head. Young Wynter and his mother were holding hands nearby, dancing in the grass.

"Tell me about this day," she begged. "What was it like? You all look so happy."

Garrick would have liked her, Wynter decided. He would have liked her very much.

CHAPTER 18

A Surfeit of Snow

The next morning, as Wynter sat in his office reviewing the documents that had stacked up in his absence, it occurred to him that he'd never gotten either the long soak in a steaming tub nor the night of undisturbed sleep he'd been looking forward to. The soak had been shared and short-lived, with most of the steaming water ending up on the floor of his bathing chamber before it had time to cool. And his sleep—what little he'd gotten—had been in Khamsin's bed rather than his own.

He should have been exhausted today. Instead, he felt more invigorated than he had in months. The few hours he had slept, with Khamsin draped over him, had been deep and dreamless and utterly restorative. Despite a second bath they'd shared again this morning, he could still smell her on his skin, and the scent kept distracting him as he attempted to plow his way through the mountain of papers awaiting his review.

The fifth time his mind went wandering while attempting to read the same single paragraph in a report, Wyn gave up. The paperwork would have to wait. He pushed back from his desk and summoned Deervyn Fjall. After explaining what he wanted and sending Fjall to see it done, Wynter went in search of his wife. He found his Summerlass in the grand dining room with Lady Melle Firkin and a dozen ladies of the court.

Wyn paused just outside the doors to observe them. Though the ladies were sitting scant feet away from his wife, there was an invisible but distinct gulf between them. The ladies chatted amongst themselves, never addressing Khamsin except when prodded into conversation by Lady Melle, and even then their voices were cold and clipped. Khamsin's lovely, expressive face was drawn in a blank mask, all her bright vitality and passion tamped down and hidden away, leaving a lifeless, wooden caricature of Wyn's wild summer Rose. The sight made his hands clench, and he had to wrestle his temper and his magic into submission before he stepped into the room.

"Your Grace!" The gathered ladies jumped to their feet and dropped into swift but graceful curtsies.

"Your Grace." Khamsin executed her own, much slower but equally graceful curtsy. "I wasn't expecting the pleasure of your company this morning."

"Were you not?" He bent down and dropped a kiss upon her upturned lips, aware of the ladies watching with avid interest and no small surprise. "I spent the better part of the last two months staying away until you were fully recovered from your illness. I am resolved to make up for lost time. I thought we might go for a ride."

"I—of-of course. I would like that very much."

Clearly, he'd shocked her. Wynter discovered he liked shocking her. He liked the way darker color flooded her cheeks, turning that beautiful brown skin a dusky rose.

"Go change into your riding habit. I'll meet you by the stables. Ladies." He bowed to the women of his court.

The gossip was buzzing before he even left the room. Good. His queen, who had been an outcast in her own home all her life, would not be an outcast in his.

Yesterday, Khamsin had accused him of sabotaging her efforts to fit in with his court and his people. He hadn't deliberately set out to do so, but he couldn't pretend that his determination to avoid her hadn't resulted in precisely that outcome. And Galacia was right, too. He had failed in his duty to look after Khamsin properly. He had contributed to her alienation and misery—he, who was bound by the laws of Wintercraig, to put her well-being before his own.

That disgraceful lack of care ended today.

Over Valik's objections, they rode out alone, without a single guard in attendance. Not the King and Queen of Wintercraig, but Khamsin and Wynter, husband and wife.

Thanks in no small part to the storm, he and Khamsin had generated yesterday, Wintercraig lay buried under three feet of fresh snow. Tree boughs sagged under the weight accumulated on their branches. Travel was possible only because crews of men had been working around the clock since the end of the storm to clear the main roads. Piles of packed snow six feet deep lined the thoroughfares.

Khamsin eyed the wintry scene with open dismay. "Did we do this?"

Wyn hesitated. Even though the ferocity of their storm had faded when anger turned to passion, he hadn't thought to disperse it until hours later. The new accumulation of snow was definitely their fault. He wouldn't lie to her, but neither did he want her fretting all day over something they could not change, so he said, "Winter storms have swept the Craig long before you or I were born. It's the price of living in one of the most beautiful lands in all of Mystral."

"You didn't answer my question."

"Noticed that, did you?" His mouth twisted in a wry smile. "All right, yes, the storm *we* called—you and I together—brought the snow. But it would have come on its own some other time. Blizzards far worse than the one we called are commonplace in the Craig. And we need the snow, Khamsin. We thank Wyrn for sending it. Come spring, the waterfalls will flow from the mountaintops, and our land will turn green and lush and more beautiful than any place in the world."

That mollified her enough to wipe the dreadful guilt from her gaze. She leaned back in the saddle and gazed at the breathtaking scenery around them.

"I can't deny it is beautiful." The mountains of the Craig towered into clear, cloudless blue skies, their jagged black peaks now entirely covered in flows of white. The valley and forested lowland mountains sparkled in the sunlight like the pristine crystalline perfection of the Atrium's ice forest. "You're sure we didn't hurt anyone? No one got caught out in the storm?"

"Winterfolk know how to survive blizzards," he assured her. "No one goes out at this time of year without protective gear and supplies enough to weather a bad storm. And that includes me." He patted the saddlebags and blanket roll tied to the back of his saddle.

"What about the snow on the mountains?" She eyed the towering peaks. "Krysti warned me about the danger of avalanches when we were out riding."

"They are always a danger," he admitted, "but since before my grandfather's time, we have sent teams of men in the mountains to keep the snowpacks under control."

"How do they do that? Are they weathermages?"

He smiled. "No. They're ordinary Wintermen who climb the mountains after every storm to measure the ice packs, and when necessary, start smaller avalanches to clear the snow."

"And that works?" She looked plainly skeptical.

"There are still deadly avalanches, of course, but far fewer than before."

They had reached Skala-Holt, the furthest distance west of Gildenheim Khamsin and Krysti had ever ridden. The villagers Khamsin had been trying so hard to win over stopped in their tracks when she rode in with Wynter at her side.

"I'm hungry," Wynter announced. "How about you? The pub here serves a delicious venison stew."

Khamsin hesitated. Liese, Skala-Holt's pubkeeper

who'd lost her husband in the war, had made it clear Khamsin wasn't welcome in her establishment. Oh, Liese had never outright refused to serve Wintercraig's queen, but her thinly veiled hostility and curt tone had made Kham and Krysti's few visits to the pub very uncomfortable.

"It's already getting late," Kham hedged. "We should be heading back."

But Wynter had already brought Hodri to a halt beside the pub's front door. "We'll eat here," he said. He dismounted and came around to help Khamsin down. He handed the reins of their mounts to a waiting stablelad and, with a cool nod to the gathering villagers, put a hand on the small of Kham's back and escorted her into the pub.

A fire burned merrily in the hearth. Half a dozen villagers were seated at the bar and tables. Liese, the pubkeeper, started to scowl when she saw Khamsin walk through the door, then froze when Wynter ducked in behind her and straightened to his full height. All conversation in the room ceased.

"Your Grace." Liese came around the pub's bartop. Her gaze darted nervously to Khamsin's face. "Your Grace." She dipped an awkward curtsy.

"Good day, Liese," Khamsin murmured.

"I was just singing the praises of your venison stew to my queen," Wynter said. "We'd like two bowls and a loaf of your fresh bread. And two pints of mead."

"Aye, Your Graces, right away." The pubkeeper served them with more deference and alacrity than she'd ever shown Khamsin, and within minutes, they were enjoying a hot, simple meal of truly delicious stew and fresh, fragrant bread slathered with creamy butter.

Wynter chatted with the other patrons as they ate, making a point of including Khamsin in the conversation. Several times, he reached across the table to lift Kham's left hand and press a kiss against her wrist, a gesture not missed by his audience.

When the meal was over. Wynter dropped a handful of

coins on the table, thanked Liese for the excellent food and service, and ushered Khamsin out the door.

"You didn't have to do that," she said as she stepped into his cupped hands for a boost into the saddle.

Wynter played dumb. "I don't mind helping you into the saddle."

She gave him a look, in response to which he arched a single, silvery brow and smiled a challenge. She sighed and shook her head. "I don't need you fighting my battles." She laid the reins across Kori's neck, turning the mare back towards Gildenheim.

"Wrong way, wife," Wyn said as he swung into his saddle. "We're headed west."

She frowned. "Shouldn't we start back? We're already going to be riding most of the way to Gildenheim in the dark." It was mid-November, and the days were short, the sun setting by four o'clock.

"We're not going back to Gildenheim."

"Where are we going?"

He smiled mysteriously. "You'll see."

They rode west another three hours, stopping for the night at an inn in a small village called Riverfall. Khamsin had never met the villagers here, but with Wynter by her side, they were all smiles and warm welcome. They spent a pleasant night spooned together in a soft, warm bed whose rope springs squeaked so loudly Kham could hardly meet the innkeeper's eyes without blushing the next morning.

They set off again at first light, leaving the main road to follow a winding, recently cleared switchback road that zigzagged up the mountain.

The forest was so peaceful. White, covered with pristine snow broken only by the occasional tracks of wildlife. Every once in a while, a flurry of snow would topple from the branches of the trees, disturbed by a winter bird taking flight. The serene quiet was broken only by the steady clop-clop of their mounts' hooves and the chime of the bridle bells.

As they rode up the mountain, they passed a dozen Wintermen coming down, snow shovels strapped to their backs. The men murmured greetings and doffed their hats before continuing down the path Wynter and Khamsin had just traversed.

Thirty minutes later, the cleared pathway ended at a small, frozen mountain lake, which had also been completely cleared of snow, leaving a smooth, silvery surface of thick ice.

Wynter rode Hodri to the edge of the lake and tied his bridle to a tree next to a pile of hay that had been left atop a cleared section of snow.

"Wynter?" What was this place? Obviously, he'd arranged for the road and pond to be cleared so he could bring her here, but she wasn't sure why.

He held up a hand to help Khamsin from the saddle.

"Don't you recognize it?"

"No. Krysti and I never rode this far from Gildenheim."

"My family has a hunting lodge about an hour's ride further up the mountain. We used to come here often when I was a boy. The ice gets thick, and the waterfall freezes every winter." He pointed to an incredible spray of what looked like frosted white stalactites tumbling down the side of the mountain.

The frozen waterfall looked strangely familiar though she was sure she'd never been here before. Then she processed Wynter's comment about his childhood, and the pieces of the puzzle fell into place.

"It's the skating pond from the Atrium!" Now that she'd made the connection, she was shocked at how accurately Wynter had portrayed this spot. "Is there really a cave behind the waterfall?"

"Why don't you go see for yourself?" Wynter turned to the saddlebags strapped to the back of Hodri's saddle and turned back with two pairs of metal blades fitted with leather straps. He patted a large rock. "Sit here, and I'll put on your skates."

She eyed the skating contraptions with trepidation. "I don't know how to skate."

"It's not that hard. I'll teach you." He patted the rock again. When she made no move to do as he said, he arched one silvery brow. "You aren't scared, are you?"

That got her back up. "Of course not."

"Then come and let me help you with your skates."

Khamsin grudgingly went to sit on the rock. Wynter knelt before her and fitted the skating blade to the bottom of her boot. The blade itself was fastened to a hard layer of leather and metal. One set of leather straps tied around the toe of her boot, and another two sets crisscrossed around her heel, ankle, and foot to hold the skate securely in place.

When he finished buckling her skates, Wynter sat beside her to don his own. He stood up and reached for her hands to help her to her feet.

The skate blades immediately tilted sideways, and she fell against Wynter.

"Find your balance. Don't let your ankles fold. Try to stand upright on the blades."

She tried to straighten her ankles, only to have them fold the other direction. "Easier said than done."

"You can do it." He steadied her as she straightened up again. "Good. Now just stand there for a minute. Get used to the feel of balancing on the blades. That's really the hardest part of skating. Everything else is simple."

"All right." She concentrated on keeping her ankles steady. It took a little effort, but all the riding and climbing she'd done with Krysti had strengthened the muscles of her calves and ankles and improved her balance significantly.

"Try to stand without holding on to me."

When she felt steady, she loosened her grip on him, then let go completely. Her ankles wobbled a tiny bit, but she managed to retain her balance.

"Well done. Now, let's get you on the ice."

She nodded and held Wynter's hand as he led her down the snowy bank to the opening in the wall of snow piled around the frozen pond. Wynter stepped onto the ice and glided backward several feet to give her room.

The moment she stepped off the embankment onto the ice, her front foot began to slide out from under her.

"Balance." Wynter caught and steadied her. "Put both feet on the ice. Good," he praised when she did so. "Now, bend your knees and lean forward. That's it. You're doing wonderfully. Now, just hold on to me, and I'll lead you around the ice until you get the feel for the skates."

Khamsin held on to him for dear life, her legs and ankles wobbling terribly as he skated backward and pulled her slowly around the perimeter of the frozen pond.

"You say some people actually enjoy this?" she asked, as they started their second circuit.

He laughed. The low, throaty sound shivered up her spine. "Thoroughly, *min ros*. You'll understand once you get the hang of it. Now, I want you to put your weight on your right foot and start pushing off with your left. Yes, like that. Don't worry. I've got you. I won't let you go."

"I thought you were going to show me the cave behind the waterfall," she reminded him, as they circled the pond a third time.

"That was my excuse to get you out on the ice. It's there, I promise. When you feel ready, you can skate over there and see for yourself."

"I didn't realize you were so sneaky."

"Are you not having fun?"

"I suppose." She was actually. He was smiling. The fresh air, white snow, blue sky, and bright golden sun made her feel happy and light-hearted. It was a perfect, beautiful day. The kind of day he'd sculpted in the Atrium. The kind of day he'd known so many of as a child.

And then she realized what he was doing.

He was giving her a memory of her own to cherish.

The knowledge robbed her of breath and made her throat go suddenly and painfully tight. She blinked back the rush of tears that blurred her vision and threatened to spill over and embarrass her. She coughed to loosen her throat and looked away to hide her unsettled emotions.

"Did you bring Elka here, too?" Good glory! Where in Halla's name had *that* come from? "I'm sorry," she babbled. "Don't answer that. It's none of my business."

"You are my wife. Of course what came before in my life is your business, just as what came before in your life is mine. And, no, I never brought her here. She wasn't much of a skater."

Kham bit her lip. She was curious about Wynter's former betrothed and had been for a long while. Fear of broaching a too-touchy subject and losing what small gains she'd made among the noblewomen had kept her from asking anyone at court about her. But Wynter had just opened that door and invited her in.

"What was she like? Elka, I mean." What about her had so entranced first Wynter, then Falcon that had led two kingdoms to war?

He shrugged. "Tall, cool, beautiful, restrained with her emotions. She had her passions, of course, but she kept them hidden most of the time."

In other words, the exact opposite of Khamsin. "Do you wish I were more like her?"

His head whipped around. "Good goddess, no!" He looked completely shocked. "Have I ever given you cause to think so?"

"No . . . but you like her cousin very much. Don't deny it."

She squawked in surprise when Wynter caught her about the waist and pulled her up against him, leaving her feet dangling above the ice. His head swooped down to claim her lips. He kissed her thoroughly, driving the breath out of her lungs and every last thought of Reika Villani out of her mind. When he set her back on her feet, she nearly went sprawling in an ungainly heap of boneless limbs and jellied muscles.

"You have no cause for concern on that score, *min ros*. Reika Villani is an old family friend and Valik's cousin.

She has never been any more than that to me, nor ever will be. You, on the other hand, are much, much more and have been since the moment I first set eyes on you." He cupped her chin and ran a thumb over her lower lip. His eyes followed the same path with thrilling intensity. "Your father thought he scored a victory over me when he tricked me into marrying you instead of one of your sisters, but he unwittingly gave me the one daughter I wanted most."

"H-he did?"

Wynter smiled, a slow, devastating smile that nearly melted her where she stood. "Oh, yes. Never doubt it."

As abruptly as it had appeared, the smoldering intensity in his eyes winked out, and he pushed her back to arm's length.

"Now, I want you to keep skating, but this time, only hold one of my hands. If you need to stop, for any reason, don't panic. Just bend your knees slightly inward and push out with one or both of your feet. Like this." He released one of her hands and skated a half circle around her, stopping with a sideways motion that scraped a fine layer of powdered ice off the frozen surface of the pond. "See?"

"Uh-huh . . ." Khamsin held Wynter's one hand in a death grip. "All right. Here goes." She pushed off with her left foot, the way he'd shown her. Her ankles wobbled. The skates slid on the ice. She flung her free arm out to the side to steady herself. She started falling backward, and in a panic, lunged for Wynter.

He caught her around her waist to steady her. "I've got you. Don't panic. Just bend your knees. Lean forward over your skates. Keep your balance centered over the skates. There. All right. Try that again."

"I think maybe skating isn't for me."

"I had no idea I'd married such a coward."

"Neither did I, but apparently we were both wrong."

He laughed. "No, we weren't. I wed a fierce and fearless Summerlass with lightning in her hair and a storm in her eyes. Come now, *eldi-kona*. Show me what you're made of."

He thought she was fierce and fearless? Khamsin clenched her jaw and squared her shoulders, determined not to disappoint him. "All right."

She bent her knees slightly, working hard to stop her ankles from wobbling and keep the metal blades of the skates perpendicular to the ice. She leaned forward slightly over her bent knees, as Wynter had instructed, and pushed off with her left foot again.

Whether because she was concentrating more, or because she was simply determined not to fall and embarrass herself in front of him, she managed to maintain her balance. This time, she completed an entire circuit around the pond, holding only one of his hands; and then, feeling slightly braver, she made a second circuit without holding on to him at all.

"Very good, Summerlass. You're getting the hang of it. I knew you could do it." He glided across the ice alongside her, spinning in lazy, graceful circles, his long white hair blowing around his face and shoulders.

"You're showing off."

"No." He smiled. "*This* is showing off." He pushed off with a sudden burst of strength and skated rapidly along the perimeter of the pond, gathering speed as he went. As he circled back around to pass her, he crouched slightly, gathering strength, and leapt into the air in front of her, his body spinning like a top. He landed on one skate several yards away, then twirled, skated back her way, and slid to a stop in a spray of powdered ice.

She gaped at him. "I hope you're not expecting me to try that."

He laughed, white teeth flashing against golden skin. "Maybe one day."

She arched both brows. Maybe never was more like it. "Right . . . um, so where is that cave you were telling me about?"

"This way, little coward." Still chuckling, he put an arm around her waist and skated with her over to the frozen streams of water that had formed layer upon layer of breath-taking falls of icicles. "Crouch down over here, where the ice is thinner. Do you see it?"

She bent over, trying to peer through the slivers of dark space between the frozen streams of water. "I think so."

"Hold on." Wynter slammed a fist into the frozen fall, breaking off several large chunks. "There. Do you see?"

Now she could see the black stone behind the waterfall and the blacker shadow of a small cave bored into the rock at the base of the fall. "I see it. How far does it go back?"

"Twenty feet or so. It gets tight pretty quickly though. I doubt I'd fit more than three feet beyond the opening any-more, but when I was your size, I'd crawl back as far as I could squeeze in. I used to pretend it was a dragon cave, and that if I went deep enough, I'd find the dragon's trea-sure."

It was difficult to imagine him as a child, despite having seen the sculptures in the Atrium. He was so . . . masculine. So intimidating. Seven feet of pure, unequivocal male.

"Did Garrick hunt dragon treasure in this cave, too?"

"Of course. He even found some of the dragon's gold."

Her head reared back. "No, he didn't."

"Oh, he did." Wynter's expression was one of complete sincerity. For an instant, he almost had her believing the dragon's gold was real, until he said, "I know because I put it there myself. Same as my father did when I was a boy."

A laugh broke from her lips. "Did Garrick know?"

"Of course not. Not until much later. That would have ruined the magic."

Something squeezed tight around her heart. She'd never imagined Wynter as a father. Husband, yes. Lover, defi-nitely. King, warrior, hero. But never a father. Not even when she knew he wanted children.

But now, hearing him talk about Garrick, having seen the love he'd carved so clearly into every sculpture in the Atrium, she saw a different side of the man she'd married. And she realized he wasn't the sort of man who would sire children and leave others to raise them. He would be involved in his children's lives, devoted to them. He would be a good father—no, a great one. A father who loved his children. A father who would salt a cave with gold to spark the imagination of his son. The sort of father Verdan Coruscate had never been to her.

And she realized she wanted for her children everything she'd never had for herself: happiness, belonging, security, the knowledge that their parents—both their parents—loved and wanted them.

"Wynter?"

"Yes?"

"Thank you for bringing me here."

He helped her to her feet. "You're welcome, *min ros.*"

"Can we come back again sometime?"

His smile warmed her. "Anytime you like."

They stayed another hour or two at the pond, skating across the silvery ice and talking. They were some of the most enjoyable hours Khamsin had spent in recent memory. She felt like she and Wynter were actually getting to know one another in a way neither time nor circumstance had allowed them to before.

It was odd to realize that Wynter, who knew her more intimately than any man in her life, knew so little about her outside of the bedroom. Or that she knew so little about him. But the more she learned, the more she liked.

He was a good man, this fierce conqueror from the north. The sort of man she'd always admired: steadfast, brave, and true. Not perfect. Thank Halla. A perfect man would have only made her feel miserably inadequate, a hopeless sinner to his shining saint. His temper was every bit as terrible as her own. And he was not one to forgive trespasses. Ever.

But for the first time since their marriage, she could actually envision making a life here. A good life. A happy life. A life with Wynter.

"So what were you and Krysti doing all these past weeks when you went on your rides?" he asked, as they sat on the fallen log to remove their skates.

She shrugged. "Mostly just riding. He took me to several of the nearby villages and introduced me to the villagers." Her nose wrinkled. "They aren't very fond of Summerlanders."

"I doubt there are very many Summerlanders who are very fond of Winterfolk either. War has that effect on folk."

"I suppose. But the war is over. Wasn't that the whole point of our marriage?"

"Old grudges die hard."

She frowned. "What old grudges could your people possibly have? Surely, they aren't all like that woman in Konundal, blaming every death in the war on Summerlea? If you hadn't invaded Summerlea, those Winterfolk would still be alive. And so would thousands of Summerlanders."

She regretted the words as soon as they left her mouth. She and Wynter had been having such a good day. They'd actually been *talking,* communicating, getting to know each other. But the tension that underscored their relationship from the start ratcheted instantly back up as Wynter's expression went from friendly and open to distinctly frosty.

"I did not start the war," he bit out. "Your brother did that when he murdered my brother."

"I realize that," she agreed quickly. "I didn't mean it to sound otherwise." But then her innate loyalty to Summerlea compelled her to add, "But war didn't bring your brother back. All it did was cost more lives."

"So you would have advised me to do nothing?"

"Of course not. But, diplomacy—"

"*Diplomacy?*" Frost crackled across her clothes and the tree trunk. With a curse, Wynter spun around and stalked a short distance away. "From the day I took the throne, your father set out to weaken my kingdom and undermine my rule. He bled us dry for years, raising prices on Summerlea crops, delivering inferior goods, undermining our alliances with other kingdoms. I tried every diplomatic means at my disposal to avoid war. I sent my ambassadors. I welcomed his. The threat of starvation loomed over my kingdom, but still I tried diplomacy. Your father took every concession I offered as proof of my weakness. My restraint only made him bolder, more certain Wintercraig was his for the taking. And then he sent your brother, who again I foolishly welcomed in the name of diplomacy."

"I'm sorry." She reached out to take his hands, hoping to impress upon him the depths of her sincerity. "I'm sorry for all the evils Verdan Coruscate visited upon you. But Falcon—he isn't like that. I know you blame him for your brother's death, but it must have been an accident or self-defense. Falcon wouldn't kill someone in cold blood. He's a good man."

Wynter yanked his hands free. "Tell that to the people of Hileje who saw their loved ones raped and murdered on your brother's command."

Khamsin's jaw dropped. "That's a lie!"

"Is it? I held a nine-year-old girl in my arms as she died from what those Summerlea bastards did to her. And I called the wolves and hunted them down like the animals they were. They told me, as they bled out their lives into the snow. They told me who had sent them. *Your brother.* The worthless bastard you call a good man. He ordered them to attack the village as a diversion, to draw me away from Gildenheim so he and Elka could steal one of the most ancient treasures of my House. My brother Garrick discovered the theft and followed him. And your brother killed him. He put an arrow in Garrick's throat and left him to die in the snow, choking on his own blood." His eyes flared with pale, cold fire, and his jaw flexed. "My brother wasn't even sixteen. He was just a boy."

Khamsin wanted to shout her denial. The words trembled on the tip of her tongue, crying out for release. But they wouldn't—couldn't—fall. The rage—and worse, the raw agony—in Wynter's eyes killed her passionate denial as surely as Falcon's arrow had killed the young prince of Wintercraig.

She swallowed against the hard, painful lump in her throat. "There must be some other explanation." That hoarse, weak denial was the best she could muster. She couldn't hold Wynter's gaze any longer. It hurt too much to see such naked pain in his eyes. If she'd ever doubted him capable of deep, abiding, unassailable love, she doubted no longer. Wynter hadn't just loved his brother—he'd adored him. Every bit as much if not more than she loved her own brother.

But if Falcon had done this . . . if he was indeed responsible for the destruction of an entire village and the rape and murder of innocent people . . .

Wynter cupped a hand under her chin, nudging her face back up and waiting for her to look at him. When she did, he said, "There is no other explanation, Khamsin." The anger and the pain she'd seen a moment ago was gone, replaced by cold, steady resolve. "Falcon Coruscate murdered my brother and ordered the savage death of dozens of innocent villagers in Hileje. I know he is your brother, and I know you love him, but if he ever sets foot on this land again, I will hunt him down, and I *will* end him." He watched her as he spoke, his gaze intent and unwavering. All the while, his thumb stroked her cheek with frightening tenderness. "And the same fate awaits any man, woman, or child in Wintercraig or Summerlea who offers him aid. Don't ever doubt that."

They rode in silence back down the mountainside. The whole way, Khamsin tried to reconcile her memories of the brother she loved and adored with Wynter's account of an evil, cold-blooded killer who sent men to commit atrocities in order to create a diversion. Everything in her rebelled at the mere suggestion that the brother she loved and the architect of the Hileje massacre could be one and the same. The Falcon she knew aspired to the same, brave, noble ideals as their mutual hero, Roland Soldeus. That Falcon wouldn't have—*couldn't* have—condoned the sort of evil Wynter lay at his feet.

No, no, Wynter must be mistaken. There was more to this story. Extenuating circumstances. Something that exonerated her brother or at least made him less culpable for what had happened.

There *had* to be.

As they reached the valley floor and turned east on the main road, they were nearly run over by half a dozen riders galloping at a breakneck pace.

"Ho, there, rider!" Wynter flagged one of the trailing riders down. "What's wrong?"

The rider reined in his horse long enough to say, "Avalanche. A big one on Mount Fjarmir."

Wynter and Khamsin spurred their horses and took off at a gallop down the valley road after the other riders.

When they reached Riverfall, Wynter noted with grim approval the red-striped white flags flying and the flocks of birds already winging away in all directions. Avalanche was one of the deadliest dangers in all the north, and every city, village, and hamlet drilled year-round to know what to do when the red-striped avalanche flag flew. Every village and farmhouse near where the avalanche had occurred would have raised their flags and released birds to all the surrounding towns.

"Skala-Holt?" he barked, as he and Khamsin slowed their mounts before the Riverfall's village hall.

"Aye, Sire!" A man Wyn recognized as Bjork Hrad, the village leader, stepped away from a group of villagers who were packing a sleigh with rescue materials. "Mt. Fjarmir's entire southern snowfield gave way. The patrols headed up after the blizzard blew through, but it looks like they were too late."

"Any word from the village?"

"Only from our scout. Skala-Holt's buried, Your Grace. All two hundred souls."

Wynter spared a quick glance at his wife. She was sitting motionless in the saddle, her face a frozen mask. He could practically feel the waves of guilt washing over her.

"Can you spare an extra avalanche kit?" he asked. Hrad grabbed a pack from the pile being loaded into the sleigh and handed one up to Wynter. "Thanks. Who's keeping the children? I'd like the queen to stay with them until we return."

"No." Khamsin broke her silence. "You're not leaving me here. I'm going with the rest of you to help with the rescue."

"No, you're not." His tone left no room for defiance. "People's lives are at stake. No one will have time to look after you. You'll just be in the way."

"I don't need looking after, and I won't be in the way." She shifted her attention to Bjork Hrad. "Sir . . . Mr. Hrad, isn't it? Please, hand me one of those avalanche kits as well."

"Hrad, don't you dare." Wyn edged Hodri into Khamsin's path, boxing her in. "Khamsin, I'm ordering you to stay here."

She raised her brows. "Haven't you learned yet? I don't take orders well." When he didn't move, she tossed her head, sending dark, white-streaked curls bouncing across the thick ermine lining of her hooded coat. "I'm going. You can try to keep me here, but I'll just find a way to sneak out. I'm very resourceful that way. I'll make my way to Skala-Holt on foot if I have to, but I *will* go, and I *will* help those people. You may be able to kill thousands without remorse, but I can't. I won't stand by and do nothing while they die. I already have enough on my conscience without that, too."

Wynter swore beneath his breath and nodded curtly. "Give her the kit, Hrad. And you"—he jabbed a finger in Khamsin's direction—"you keep to my side at all times. Agreed?"

"Agreed." She grabbed the kit Hrad handed up to her and slung it over her shoulder.

At least, she didn't gloat. That made giving in feel a little less like surrender. "Let's go then." He spurred Hodri forward, picking his way slowly down the road until they were free of the crowded village. "You are a troublesome, hardheaded wench," he muttered to his wife when they were out of earshot of the village.

"Am I? How interesting. I had no idea how closely we resembled each other." She stuck her nose in the air, keeping her gaze fixed firmly forward.

The snippy rebuke left him torn between amusement and annoyance. With anyone else, he would have responded with cold, cutting anger to put her in her place. But the sight of Khamsin's spear-straight spine, the flash of silver in her eyes, that wild, beautiful riot of lightning-streaked black hair, and the soft, full curve of those lips now pursed in indignation melted any chance of anger. In a world where folk lived in fear of his wrath, this slender woman stood toe to toe with him during even his foulest moods, taking the worst he threw at her and firing back as good as she got. She was no meek, domesticated lamb of a woman any more than he was a tame or gentle man.

They'd created that blizzard, the two of them, because he'd raged like a wounded *garm* when she'd discovered the vulnerable remnants of his soul that he'd hidden away from the world. He didn't blame her for the storm. He was the one who'd started the fight. He was the one who'd turned her tempest into a howling fury of ice and snow.

But his Summerlander wife, who believed that her great power was a curse—that *she* was a curse—would never forgive herself if the people of Skala-Holt died because of the storm they'd summoned. And for some reason that had nothing to do with his husbandly duty to protect her from all harm, Wynter couldn't let her bear that burden.

"Yours was not the only magic that helped spawn that blizzard, and you are not responsible for the avalanche. And for the record," he added softly, "I may have killed thousands in the war, but not without remorse. Certainly not when it came to innocents."

The sun was setting, but Skala-Holt was still a hive of activity when they arrived. Winterfolk from every nearby croft and village had come with shovels and strong backs and wagons full of women and youths bearing tents, blankets, food, bandages, and medicine. More rescuers poured in by the minute.

If Khamsin hadn't visited Skala-Holt before, she would not have even known there was a village buried beneath the snow. Except for the few, already-excavated houses, you couldn't see any sign of it. Not a roof, not a chimney. Nothing. Winterfolk were crawling over the snow, using long, thin sticks to probe what lay beneath.

"Halla help them," Khamsin breathed in horror. How could anyone have survived?

As if reading her mind, Wynter said, "Since the fall happened during the day, there's a chance many of them had time to seek shelter."

"A chance?" Despite Wynter's assurances that this wasn't her fault, the mere thought of an entire village dead because of one of her storms made Khamsin's belly churn.

"All the homes have cellars. Hopefully, the villagers had enough warning to reach them before the avalanche hit. That gives us time to dig them out before they freeze or suffocate. Most buried without some form of shelter will die within the first half hour."

She swallowed hard. "What can I do to help?"

He handed her a shovel. "Join a search party and start digging. The men with the probes will set flags everywhere they think they've found survivors."

"What about melting them out? Would that help?"

"You think you can do that?"

"You know I'm not very good at controlling my magic, but I can at least try."

"Then come with me." He held out a hand and led her up onto the spill of deep, packed snow. They clambered over the icy debris until they reached the closest flag—a pennant of red wool fluttering on a long, thin barb that had been thrust into the snow. A dozen Winterfolk were crowded around, digging their way down through the packed snow. They had already cleared a hole about four feet wide and six feet deep, but hadn't reached the top of the villager's house yet.

"The house is another four feet down, at least. See if you can melt down to the rooftop."

Kham bit her lip. Storms, she could summon. Trying to channel heat in such a small area was a different matter.

"What happens if I melt more than just this area?" The mountains were thick with snow. If she didn't concentrate heat in a very narrow radius, she risked flooding the valley with snowmelt. "I don't want to make things worse than they already are."

"You concentrate on raising the temperature. I'll keep the snow on the mountains in check." No hint of fear showed in his expression or his voice. She was struck once more by the reassuring strength that radiated from him. He was a man she would trust to bear the weight of the world. When he wasn't driving her to distraction or irritating her with his domineering ways.

Truthfully, even then, even at his most distracting and domineering, she would trust him to stand between her and danger and rest assured in the knowledge that danger would dash itself senseless against his unyielding will before it ever had a chance to harm her. He was the rock to which an entire kingdom could anchor itself with perfect confidence.

Kham focused her attention on the hole the rescuers had been digging. She wanted to be as strong as Wynter. She wanted to master that calm, imperturbable sense of certainty that surrounded him like a cloak of invincibility. She wanted his people to look at her and see not the daughter of an enemy king but a woman as strong in her own right as the king they adored. Someone who could complement their king's strength, not just shelter in it. A woman worthy of their respect—and of his. A queen.

Wynter's queen.

She focused on the source of her power: the sun's golden white heat. When she summoned a storm, she let anger fuel her power. She knew she could concentrate the sun's heat at least on a personal level, as she did when she melted a metal hairbrush or boiled the tea in her teacup. She knew what that felt like . . . like a storm inside her soul, battering against her skin to gain its freedom.

Summoning that feeling on demand was difficult, so she recalled past wrongs, emotional hurts, wounds that had struck hard and deep and never been forgotten. Her father's face, purple with anger, his eyes flashing a flickering orange like the flames in a hearth. The feel of his signet ring smashing into her cheek, branding her with his fury. Maude Newt and her endless, sneering interference and tattling. Reika Villani trilling with laughter and stroking one slim hand possessively over Wynter's golden skin, turning to regard Khamsin in mocking challenge, daring the pitiful Summerlander to stop Reika from claiming Wynter as her own.

"It's working." Wynter's voice interrupted her increasingly agitated thoughts.

Kham opened her eyes to find herself surrounded by a cloud of steam. Waves of heat radiated from her palms. She was sinking quickly through a large round hole in the snow. Moments later, her feet came to rest on the steep, shingled roof of a house.

"That's good! Stand back, Your Grace. We're coming down." Ropes spilled over the sides of the crater she'd created, and four Wintermen rappelled rapidly down to join her. Three of them immediately pulled hatchets from their belt loops and began hacking a rescue hole in the roof. The fourth held out a hand.

"Please, my queen, if you will allow me? Karl, Joris,

Svert, and I will see to the family. There are many others who could use your help."

Kham blinked. "Of course, I—oh!" She started in surprise as the man wrapped his arms around her. But before she could think to fend him off, he'd looped a harness around her waist and thighs and hooked her to a loop in a second rope. He caught her hands, then dropped them with an exclamation of surprise as the remnant heat scorched him through his gloves.

"Sorry. I'm so sorry." Kham plunged her hands into the packed snow to cool them.

"Hold the rope tight, Your Grace, and don't let go. Understand?"

"I—yes, yes, of course." She wrapped her now-cooler hands around the rope.

"Good." He gave her shoulder an awkward pat. "You did good, my queen." As her jaw went slack in surprise from the unexpected compliment, he cupped his hands around his mouth and leaned back to shout, "Up!"

Kham's rope went taut, and she fought for balance as she was suddenly hoisted up, off the buried rooftop. When she reached the top of the crater, two burly men helped her to her feet while a pair of well-bundled women freed her from the harness straps and rope.

"Come, Your Grace, quickly. Over here."

She caught a brief glimpse of Wynter, who nodded approvingly, before she was hustled off to the closest dig site and asked to summon her magic again.

The sun set, and the rescuers broke out torches to light the area. Kham called upon her gifts again and again, melting her way down to the buried homes so the Winterfolk could locate and rescue survivors. Not every hunt ended in joy. Each time the rescuers unearthed a body rather than a living soul, guilt struck Khamsin hard. That pain fed into her power, keeping her going long past the point of exhaustion, but when the Winterfolk urged her to take a break and rest, she waved them off and stumbled to the next flag in the snow. So long as there were people buried beneath the snow, she was determined to do everything she could to help them.

The last house she uncovered belonged to Derik and Starra Freijel. She stood, swaying, by the lip of the pit she'd melted through the snow and waited for the rescuers to dig through the rubble of the house to find the cellar. At last, the couple and their two children were pulled from their icy prison, and the jubilant shout went up, "Alive! They're alive!"

Thank all the gods. Khamsin took two steps and collapsed facedown in the snow, utterly spent. The frozen flakes sizzled beneath her palms and melted against her overheated face. Her whole body was running such a high temperature, she felt on fire.

Big hands turned her over and gathered her close against a familiar hard chest. She tried to open her eyes, tried to give Wynter some sort of sardonic quip, but the effort was too much. Her head fell limply back against his arm.

Cool lips touched hers, and a refreshingly icy breeze swept over her, cooling her more. "Do that again," she mumbled. "Feels nice." She was rewarded by more cooling kisses against her closed eyelids and hot brow. "I'll be fine in a few minutes. I'm stronger than I look."

"I know, *min ros.* I know." Wynter's husky voice whispered in her ear. "Tomorrow, you'll be ready to fight Frost Giants barehanded, but for now, just rest."

Of the two hundred folk who called Skala-Holt their home, only twenty-one had been lost to the mountain of ice and snow that had come crashing down upon them. It was the most successful avalanche rescue in Wintercraig history, thanks in no small part to Khamsin. That truth did not go unnoticed, and Winterfolk lined up five thick to doff their hats and offer up prayers and thanks as Wynter carried his unconscious queen past. He released her only long enough to mount Hodri, then the gathered villagers handed her back up to him and he carried her before him all the way home, not stopping until they reached Gildenheim.

She did not wake during the long road home, nor when he carried her to her room, nor even when put her in her bed and sat beside her to divest her of her coat and boots and unlace the ties of her bodice so she could breathe without restriction. The only time she stirred, was when he rose from the bed to leave.

Her fingers curled around his wrist. "Stay," she whispered.

She'd never asked him to stay before. Ever. And how shocking that such a tiny little word, such a small, whispered request, could rob the strength from his body and leave him trembling.

"I'm not going anywhere," he vowed. He pulled away only long enough to pull off his boots and clothing, then he crawled into bed and gathered her in his arms, spooning his body against hers. "Sleep, *min ros*." He brushed the hair back from her still-overheated brow and rested his head against hers.

Long after she surrendered to sleep, he remained there, holding her close, breathing in the sweet aromas of her scent and basking in her radiant warmth. He'd been so cold for so long. So numb to any feeling but vengeance and hatred, both of which had burned like icy blue flame in his heart, their bitter, frozen brittleness consuming more and more of him by the day.

Valik and Laci he loved dearly, but only with Khamsin did the ice retreat. Summerlander and daughter of an enemy king she might be, but she was also the only one left in his life who could make him *feel* again. Truly feel, as he had before the day of Garrick's death, before he drank the Ice Heart. There was no doubt in his mind that the fiery, irresistible passion that raged between them was all that was keeping the Ice Heart at bay.

And now, understanding that, he also understood the real reason he'd stayed away from her for so long. It wasn't just because he feared losing control of himself. It wasn't just because he feared he might hurt her. He'd stayed away because of a deeper fear, one he would never admit aloud: that he might surrender himself to Khamsin's beguilement only to find her as false as Elka had been.

Elka's betrayal, he had survived. Khamsin's would destroy him.

Wynter nuzzled the soft, curling mass of dark hair, closing his eyes as he breathed in the scent that had lodged so deep in his olfactory memory that no other woman would ever supplant it. No amount of willpower or self-denial could change that. Wynter now accepted the truth he'd suspected since the day Khamsin had been poisoned and her blood stained the snow scarlet.

His wolf had recognized Khamsin as its mate.

She might betray him to her family, torment him unto madness, bring his kingdom to ruin, but come good or ill, love or hatred, trust or betrayal, Wynter of the Craig would never take another woman to wife.

Because when snow wolves mated, they mated for life.

"Whatever you do, Khamsin, don't betray me," he whispered. "Don't ever betray me."

CHAPTER 19

Shades of Belladonna

For the first time since bringing his Summer-born bride to Gildenheim, Wynter did not return to his own bed before dawn. Instead, he remained in hers, holding her as she slept. He dozed lightly only when his eyelids grew too heavy to stay open, but otherwise remained content with the quiet peace of lying beside her, watching the rhythmic rise and fall of her chest, trying to reconcile the profound desire to protect her with the fear that her loyalty belonged to her brother before him. Verdan Coruscate, he knew, had no hold on her, but her defense of Falcon earlier at the pond had made her feelings for him equally clear.

If she had to choose between the enemy king she'd been forced to wed and the brother she'd idolized all her life, whom would she choose?

The sun was just rising when the bedroom door latch opened with a click and the door swung inward.

The sound fired in his brain like a hammer stroke shattering glass. He had one split second of frozen incomprehension followed by a reaction that was more instinct than thought: *Protect Khamsin.*

With a roar, he sprang up from the bed and landed on the floor between the bed and the door, shielding his wife from view and buffering her from any would-be attacker. Before the door swung more than a few inches inward, his eyes were already blazing with Ice.

"Bella!" Khamsin, who must have been awakened by Wynter's shout, grabbed his shoulder.

That slender hand on his shoulder saved Bella's life. He squeezed his eyes shut to block his Gaze. When he opened them again, the Summerlander maid was standing in the frost-coated doorway, her mouth gaping in shock, staring at him and Khamsin.

"Get out," he growled. His teeth were bared in a snarl, and there was such naked menace in his voice that even without the added lethal force of his Gaze, it was a wonder the maid didn't expire on the spot.

The girl gave a squeak and stumbled backward, closing the door with a slam.

The tension stayed with him for several seconds after she'd gone. He was scarcely aware of the threatening, warning growl that still rumbled in his throat as he waited to see if the interloper would return.

Beneath him, Khamsin made a muffled sound that sounded like a sob. He shook his head to clear the Wolf from his mind and glanced down in concern. Her hands were clapped over her mouth, and her eyes were squeezed shut. But then she drew her hands from her face, and the sound pealed out without restraint, and he realized she was not sobbing.

She was laughing.

Not wickedly, not with sarcasm or arrogance, but with delight. Her eyes were dancing with mischief. "Did you see her face? And yours? I don't know which one of you was more shocked." She laughed again with such helpless abandon he could not take offense. The sound broke over him like a warm summer rain, and just like that, he wanted her.

"You think that was funny?" He rose to his feet and towered over her, naked and without shame or false modesty, watching her dazzled eyes gaze up at him. She wasn't laughing anymore. She was instead looking up at him with undisguised hunger, and he was gladder than he'd ever been for his height, his strength, the broadness of his shoulders, the muscular build of his warrior's body.

He bent and swept her up into his arms with effortless strength and laid her on the bed. "Good morrow, *min ros*," he murmured, bending his head to kiss her lips, then nuzzle the soft skin just behind her ear. "I do believe I could get used to waking up beside you."

Her arms twined around his neck. "Me too." She kissed him, and he felt her grin against his mouth as his body covered hers. "But I think Bella will demand hazard pay."

An hour later, Wynter gave Khamsin one last, lingering kiss, and headed back to his chambers to bathe and dress for the day. She lay there for several, long, lazy minutes afterwards, humming to herself and twirling one long, black curl around her index finger. She rolled over to lay her head on the pillow he'd used, breathing his scent deep into her lungs.

If only all their time together could be as wonderful as this morning. She'd felt so at ease, holding him, touching him, breathing him in, reveling in his closeness. They'd seemed so . . . right. Like two halves of a whole.

It was more than just the sex. Yes, he could just look at her, and she melted. Yes, he made her moan and gasp and explode with a pleasure she'd never thought possible. But this time, they'd seemed . . . closer. Gentler. Instead of their usual rough, wild, passion, they'd shared exquisite tenderness. Afterward, he'd watched her with the strangest expression on his face. As if he was beholding something . . . precious.

Kham ran her hands over her face, letting her fingers linger on her passion-swollen lips. She'd never been precious to anyone. Not that way. Even with Tildy, behind the abundant love had always been a hint of pity, a measure of sadness for the child no one else treasured. With Wynter, there'd been none of that.

Of course, she'd probably misread the look on his face.

Or even if she had read it right, the feeling was probably ephemeral—a fleeting tenderness brought on by the glut of pleasure they'd shared and gratitude for the lives they'd saved at Skala-Holt. Not something to trust. Certainly nothing to think would last.

With a sigh and a pout for the cold splash of brutal practicality that seemed determined to dampen her good mood, Khamsin set aside the Wynter-scented pillow and sat up. Time to steel herself for another cold day in Gildenheim. Throwing off the covers, Kham thrust her feet into the slippers beside her bed and reached for her velvet dressing gown.

"It's all right, Bella," she called to the still-frosty door. "You can come in now."

The door cracked open, and Bella poked her head through, casting a cautious gaze around the room. Once she ascertained that Wynter was indeed gone, she opened the door completely and carried in a tray laden with Khamsin's usual pot of fragrant, steaming jasmine tea and a small repast of smoked salmon, soft, creamy cheese, and thick slices of toasted bread bursting with whole grains and plump nuts. Bella set the tray on the small tea table in the alcove near Kham's bed.

"I am sorry we gave you such a fright earlier," Kham apologized as she took her seat at the table.

"No, no, the fault was all mine, ma'am," Bella demurred. "I didn't realize the king was here, or I would never have intruded."

Kham closed her eyes as Bella ran Queen Rosalind's brush through her hair, enjoying the soothing tug on her scalp. Few things in life were as comforting as having one's hair brushed. Bella pulled Kham's hair back and secured it at the nape of her neck with a ribbon, then reached for the teapot and poured a stream of fragrant, dark golden liquid into the porcelain teacup, adding a cube of sugar before handing it to Khamsin.

Kham took a sip and frowned. "How long are you steeping the tea, Bella?"

The maid stilled. "Five minutes, ma'am, precisely as Mistress Tildy instructed. Is there a problem?"

"It just seems a little bitter. This isn't the first time I've noticed it."

"I'm so sorry. I had no idea." Bella snatched the pot off the table. "I'll go make a fresh pot."

Bella looked so horrified and contrite, Khamsin felt guilty for saying anything. "Please don't bother. It's not that noticeable. Leave the pot. Just try steeping the tea a bit less tomorrow."

"Of course." Bella set the teapot back on the table. "I'm so sorry."

"Sorry about what?"

Kham turned in surprise to see her husband emerge from the connecting rooms that joined their two bedchambers. He hadn't bothered to fully dress. A pair of tawny leather pants rode low on his waist. His feet were bare, and so was his chest. Every broad, magnificently muscled golden inch of it.

"Wynter!" she exclaimed in surprise. Then, remembering Bella, she added a more respectful address, "Your Grace. Has something happened? Is something wrong?" Her first thought was that there'd been another avalanche.

"What?" Silvery brows rose over pale eyes. "No, nothing's wrong. Why would you think so?" He crossed the distance from the dressing room to her breakfast alcove in a few long strides. "Can a man not share breakfast with his wife without causing a stir?" He bent to kiss her up-turned lips, started to straighten, then paused and dipped down for a second, more lingering kiss. When he pulled back, she could only gape at him in wordless wonder. He took a seat—dwarfing the feminine chair with his massive frame—and reached out to place two fingers beneath her chin to gently nudge her mouth shut.

"I—" She was at a loss for words. Aware of Bella's eyes upon them, Kham blushed and blurted, "Bella, fetch the king a plate."

"Of course, Your Grace." The maid bobbed a swift curtsy and hurried out.

"I think I frighten her," Wynter murmured. He looked not the least bit remorseful.

"You know you do. Wasn't that your intention?"

White teeth flashed in a dazzling smile. "Perhaps." He reminded her of Krysti, with that mischief sparkling in his eyes, but there was nothing boyish about the low, husky voice that made her toes curl in her slippers.

Khamsin cleared her throat and reached for her teacup, taking a quick sip of the bitter brew. "If I'd known you wished to join me this morning, I would have had Bella prepare more food. I don't normally eat much breakfast."

He glanced at her plate. "We can share this until she brings more. I'm in no hurry."

"You're not?" Gah, she felt like a ninny, repeating everything he said. But this was the first time he'd been in her bedroom in broad daylight, and for some reason it felt so unsettling. She'd grown used to having him in shadows and firelight. In the bright light of day, he seemed bigger, broader, more real. And so desirable, she could scarcely put two coherent thoughts together.

"No hurry at all. Everyone's been telling me for months to slow down and start enjoying life again." With deft hands, he smeared the creamed cheese across one slice of the toasted wheat-and-nut bread. "I thought we might ride out together again after breakfast. There's still much work to be done in Skala-Holt, and the villagers you saved will want to thank you."

"They don't need to thank me."

"Yes, they do. And they will want to. So just say, 'Yes, husband. I would love to ride with you to Skala-Holt today.'" He layered smoked salmon across the cheese-covered toast, then cut the prepared bread into inch-wide strips.

She honestly couldn't manage a reasonable objection. "Yes, husband. I would love to ride with you to Skala-Holt today."

"Good. That's settled." He lifted the first of the strips to her lips and waited for her to take a bite.

She was intimately aware of his intent, focused gaze as her teeth sank into the moist salmon, cheese, and bread. The combination of flavors burst in her mouth. She chewed slowly and found she couldn't tear her gaze away as he carried the remaining slice to his own lips. She watched his white teeth bite through the food, and all she could think of was those teeth nibbling at her flesh, scraping across her breasts, his lips tracking lines of fire across her body.

He reached for her teacup, and she almost laughed at the incongruous sight of his enormous hand closing around the delicate cup. In Wynter's grip, the cup looked like one of those miniature doll's toys her sisters had played with when they were young. He held the cup to her lips, and she drank without hesitation. The tea could have been as bitter as wormwood, and she still would have drunk it because he had offered it to her.

He turned the cup and, holding her gaze, slowly put his mouth to the spot her lips had touched and drank.

Sweet, smoldering Freika! Kham practically melted.

"If you don't stop trying to seduce me over breakfast, we will never leave this room today," she warned him with a rueful laugh.

Even before she finished her laughing admonition, Wynter's nostrils flared, and his teasing, seductive playfulness gave way to a stiff, distant coldness. His eyes turned snowy, and the tea in the cup turned so abruptly into ice that the delicate porcelain shattered. The frozen brown block of ice that had a split second ago been steaming tea thumped on the tabletop. His fingers fisted around the broken cup handle, and drops of violet-tinged blood stained the tablecloth.

"Sweet Halla!" She jumped up, snatched a napkin from the table, and reached for his hand to staunch the wound. Before she could touch him, his free hand closed around her wrist, and she gasped. It was as if she'd been shackled with an unyielding ring of glacier ice.

"Wynter!" She yanked against him, trying to pull her arm free, but he didn't budge.

He rose to his feet with slow deliberation, straightening inch by massive, aggressive, all male inch, until he towered over her, forcing her to crane her head back to look up at him. His eyes were pure white now, his face hard as graven stone. Gone was the seductive lover, the teasing mischief in his eyes. He was pure, cold, Winter King, full of wrath and ice.

When he spoke, his voice filled her with dread. "You bound your life to mine." Each word tore from his lips with a sound like the very earth ripping apart from unimaginable pressure. The low, dangerous rumble shuddered through her, rattling her bones, making the hairs on her arm stand up. "You promised me the fruits of your womb."

She gaped at him without comprehension. "You said that was what you wanted!" Her throat was dry. The air had gone so cold, each breath scraped through her lungs like sharp knives. What on earth had set him off?

"You smile at me and invite me to your bed. You make me swear to take no other in your place. You act as though you welcome my touch . . . as though you want my child."

"I did. I do! Wynter, for Halla's sake, tell me what's wrong!"

"And all the while . . . all the while as you were smiling so sweetly, welcoming me into your bed and your body, convincing me you were different . . . better than your kin, more honorable and trustworthy . . . *all the while* you were every inch the lying, deceitful, treacherous witch Valik warned me about. A true Coruscate! Corrupt to the bone, just like every other member of your cursed family!"

Frost crackled across every surface of the room and prickled across her skin. Her chest felt tight. Each breath hurt. "What are you talking about?"

"Do you even know what truth is? Or would it burn your tongue like fire to speak it? Do you dare deny your crime?"

"How can I deny anything when I don't know what I'm

accused of?" she cried. As stunned as she was, she was also starting to get angry. How could he have gone from sensual, seductive lover to raging Ice-Hearted bastard in a matter of seconds? What did he think she'd done? "What crime have I committed?"

"This!" He snatched up the frozen block of tea with his bloodied hand and crushed it with one flex of his fingers. "How long have you been drinking this? Since the day you learned that the mercy of the mountains wasn't the death sentence you thought?"

"You're angry because I'm drinking *tea*?" Had the man gone insane?

"Don't play the innocent, Khamsin Coruscate. It doesn't suit you. You know damn well I'm not talking about the tea, but about the poison you brewed with it! Or did you think perfuming your tea with jasmine would hide the odor of that herb from my nose?"

"Poison?" Khamsin gaped at him. "You think I'm trying to kill myself? Are you mad? I just spent the better part of three months trying to win over your people in order to *save* my life."

"Stop!" Wynter shoved her hand away, then snatched up the teapot and flung it at the stone wall. The pot shattered in a million pieces, splattering steaming liquid and shards of broken porcelain in every direction. "Wyrn take you! Quit your lies! What sort of fool do you take me for? We both know you didn't put enough of the herb in that tea to end your own life, only the life of any child in your womb!"

Alternating waves of heat and cold washed over Khamsin, and they had nothing to do with the powerful weather magic brewing in the room. Her stomach flipped, and for a moment she thought the tiny bit of breakfast she'd ingested would make an abrupt reappearance.

"Are you telling me there's an herb in that tea to stop me from having a child?" It was her turn for her voice to go low and dangerous. Her fists clenched at her side. The bitter aftertaste of the tea she'd sipped filled her mouth anew. The frost Wynter had spread across the room began to melt as Khamsin's own anger fueled her power and heat began radiating from her.

For the first time since the rage had come over him, she saw a break in the blizzard in Wynter's eyes. A sliver of doubt crept in. "Are you telling me you didn't know?" He remained stiff, suspicious, but no longer certain.

"That's exactly what I'm telling you." She knew her own eyes had turned to pure, shifting silver. Electricity crackled through her veins. Sparks popped at her fingertips. "What's the name of the herb that's been put in my tea?"

"Black tansy."

"How do you know of it? Does it grow here?"

She could see that he'd begun to believe her. The blizzard in his eyes had slowed to small flurries swirling across the ice blue of his irises.

"Elka used it," he admitted. "Our engagement was long. Neither of us wanted our first child to be born a bastard. And no, it doesn't grow here. She imported it from an herb woman in Summerlea."

It didn't grow in Wintercraig, but it could be easily imported.

Or brought in a coach traveling from Vera Sola.

"Where is my maid, Bella?"

"You killed my child."

Khamsin stood in the cold, drafty stone cell of Wintercraig's dungeon and fought the urge to fry her former maid with a lightning bolt. She'd just come from a meeting with Galacia Frey, and the High Priestess confessed her belief that Khamsin's hemorrhaging womb that first month had, in fact, been the result of a miscarriage. She'd kept her suspicions secret to spare both Krysti and the Konundal woman Wynter's deadly wrath. Not even Lady Frey had suspected the miscarriage was deliberately induced.

Clapped in irons and chained to the floor of the cell,

Belladonna Rosh met Khamsin's accusation with a flat stare and obstinate silence.

After overhearing Wynter and Khamsin's fight and realizing she'd been found out, Bella had tried to flee the castle. She'd nearly succeeded, despite the fact that Wynter had stormed out on the balcony overlooking the courtyard and shouted for the palace to be locked down. In a matter of minutes, the whole of Gildenheim transformed from royal palace into a fortress braced for a siege. The portcullises were slammed into place, the gates behind them closed and bolted with massive slabs of iron-reinforced timber. Wynter's White Guard lined the barbican and tower walls three deep. Every courtier, servant, and civilian not armed for battle disappeared through the closest doorway, clearing the way for Wynter's troops.

With an easy exit blocked, Bella had waited for the initial furor to die down, then attempted to smuggle herself out of Gildenheim in a farmer's cart the following morning. She hadn't counted on the guards searching every pack, wagon, cart, and person coming in or out of the palace. After a brief struggle and a final attempt to flee, she'd been clapped in irons and taken to the dungeon.

"That day in Konundal, when I hemorrhaged so badly I nearly died, it wasn't just the Lady's Blush or the kick to the belly that injured me," Khamsin accused. "You'd dosed me with tansy. You suspected I was with child, and you killed it."

Belladonna turned her head to one side and remained mute.

Wynter, standing behind Khamsin, grabbed Bella's jaw and yanked her back around to face them. "Answer your queen."

Bella looked up then, and her black eyes spat defiance and a depth of hatred Khamsin had never suspected.

"She's your queen, not mine. And you are the soulless bastard that killed my entire family." Bella jerked free of Wynter's grip and glared at Khamsin. "Yes, I suspected you were with child. So I made sure you wouldn't stay that way, and I've made sure you wouldn't conceive ever since. I would do it all again—gladly!—to keep *his* child from ever taking its first breath!"

Khamsin flinched. The confirmation of what had only been a terrible suspicion struck hard. Heat billowed inside her, making her skin feel tight. This woman—this girl she'd trusted—had set out to murder any child that might have taken root in Khamsin's womb.

Wynter gave her shoulder a gentle squeeze. Coolness radiated from his fingertips, drawing the worst of the heat from her rage. She reached up to clasp his hand, curling her fingers around his. More of the anger bled away, as if his touch calmed the perennial storm that lived inside her.

Anyone else would have had to weather her violent emotions until they passed. But Wynter drew the tempest from her heart and banished it with a simple touch.

Kham took a calming breath and blew it out slowly. The murderous rage had passed. The anger was still there, still burning, but it no longer threatened to consume her.

"Verdan, the former king of Summerlea, asked you to do this." She made it a statement. There was no doubt in her mind who had placed Belladonna Rosh in Khamsin's employ.

"He didn't need to ask me," Bella sneered. "I volunteered."

Kham squeezed Wynter's hand again and let that pass. "When we first came here . . . in the carriage when I was so sick . . . you were poisoning me even then, weren't you? You put something in the cream Tildy gave you to treat my back. That's why I didn't get better until you were gone."

The maid's lip curled. "What makes you think she didn't poison it herself?"

"She wouldn't. She would never do anything to hurt me."

"Wouldn't she?" Belladonna laughed. "But then, you thought the same thing about me, didn't you?"

Khamsin took an involuntary step back and bumped up

against Wynter. Tildy couldn't have been involved. *Could she?* She cast a troubled glance up at her husband.

His eyes were cold and hard, and fixed on Belladonna. "How were you communicating with Coruscate?" Wynter asked. "We know falcons were carrying messages into Gildenheim. How were you getting information back out? What information did you provide?"

Black eyes flashed briefly in their direction, then turned resolutely away again.

Khamsin regarded Wynter in surprise. He'd known Verdan was sending messages via bird to someone in Gildenheim? He'd never let on that anything of the sort was happening.

Her brows knit, and she turned to stare blindly at Belladonna and the icy dampness of the dungeon wall.

He'd suspected *she* was the spy, of course, not Bella.

The messages were coming in by falcon. He knew Kham's brother had a gift with birds—similar to his own clan-gift with Wintercraig's wolves—and he knew how much she loved her brother. She'd never made any attempt to hide it. Of course, he would have thought she was spying on behalf of Falcon.

That explained so much. Valik's scarcely veiled dislike that never softened. The guards who accompanied her whenever she stepped so much as a toe beyond the castle walls. Why she kept running into the same servants over and over when she wandered in certain parts of the castle. Even the way Wynter had kept his distance during the day, coming to her only at night and leaving before she woke.

They'd treated her like a traitor in their midst because of Bella. And now Bella's betrayal might destroy the strides Khamsin had made to gain the trust of her husband and his people. The place she'd begun to make for herself here could be utterly ruined. Who would believe she'd been so blind to her maid's misdeeds?

"Is the king right?" she snapped. "Have you been feed-

ing information to Wintercraig's enemies?" A memory rose
. . . the day she and Krysti had picked the lock on Wynter's
aerie. "I saw you in the garden with a falcon. What message
were you sending?"

Bella arched one brow and lifted her upper lip in a sneer.

"Answer me!" Khamsin's hand shot out. Her palm
cracked against Belladonna's cheek. Sparks flashed like
tiny fireflies in the shadowy dungeon. "Tell me what you've
done!"

"Stop, *min ros.*" Wynter pulled her back against his
chest and wrapped an arm around her waist. "She can
cause no more harm, and she will tell us everything before
she faces the mercy of the mountains. But you need not
upset yourself with her betrayals. Come away with me." He
guided her towards the cell door. As they passed through,
he told the waiting guard, "Find out everything. What her
orders were, who they came from. What she sent and to
whom she sent it."

The guard snapped a crisp bow. "Yes, my king."

"Send word when you're done."

"Yes, my king."

Wynter led Khamsin out of the dungeon and into the
sunny courtyard above. The fresh, cold air blew through
her hair, sending her curls flying.

She turned to her husband. Her fingers clutched his soft
leather vest. "I didn't know, Wynter. I know it's hard to
believe I could have been so blind to what was going on
beneath my own nose, but I swear to you I didn't know. Not
about the tea she was feeding me or about the messages
she was sending. I didn't know." It wasn't her life she was
worried about losing. It was his trust. "I would never betray
you that way." She pulled back to look earnestly into his
eyes. "Never."

"*Hossa.* Hush. Do not upset yourself, wife. My men will
get to the bottom of this, then you and I will decide Belladonna Rosh's fate."

"Perhaps I shouldn't be part of that decision." She

crossed her arms over her belly. "At the moment, I don't feel any mercy towards her at all."

"Nor do I, Khamsin, but that won't stop me from passing judgment." Wynter glanced down at Khamsin, and there were snow flurries in his eyes again. "She should have considered that before harming my family."

"Let me get this straight. Your wife, who has been taking tansy daily, said she had nothing to do with any of this, and you *believed* her?" Valik gaped at Wynter with utter incredulity.

"Yes, I believed her," Wynter snapped. "And you can just stop right there. Don't say another word." Valik's response had Wyn bracing for a fight, and he was already so angry that it would be a *very* bad idea. "Khamsin may be many things, but an accomplished liar she is not."

"That remains to be seen," Valik muttered. When the Ice rose in Wynter's gaze, Valik wisely snapped his mouth closed and changed the subject. "And the maid?"

"Graal will find out what she's been up to, and she will be dealt with accordingly." Wynter clenched his fists. "She killed our child, Valik. Khamsin was pregnant that first month, and the maid killed it. That's what really happened that day in Konundal."

"According to whom? Your wife?"

"Laci admitted that she suspected Khamsin had suffered a miscarriage, but she kept silent to spare Krysti and the Konundal woman my wrath."

The outrage and suspicion on Valik's face faded. He straightened to his full height. "Wyn . . . I'm sorry. So sorry."

"The maid was acting on Coruscate's orders." Wyn drew a deep breath, fighting the rage that threatened to turn his blood to solid ice. "He wasn't content with Garrick's death. He means to end my line—and end his daughter with it. He sent the maid to keep Khamsin barren because he thought facing the mercy of the mountains was an automatic death sentence." That realization ate at him. He was the one who'd deliberately misled the Summerlea king about what would happen to his daughter. And Coruscate had latched onto that lie. If Wynter hadn't threatened Coruscate with the death of his daughters, Khamsin would never have been poisoned, and their child would still be alive.

Wynter regarded his friend. There was no other in Gildenheim Wynter loved or trusted more. "Valik?"

"Yes?"

"I haven't asked this before, but I'm going to ask it now. Try to get along with her. She may yet betray me for her brother's sake, but she is still my queen and the only wife I'll ever have."

Valik's jaw worked, but then he nodded. "I'll do my best, Wyn."

"Thank you."

Three days later, Khamsin, Wynter, twelve White Guard, and the four judicars who had heard the testimony of Bella and the witnesses against her all made the long, cold trek up the slopes of Mount Gerd to the place of judgment. They passed the trail leading to the lower levels and instead took the steep, switchbacked path to the icy, windblown peak of the mountain. There, snow swirled in the harsh winds, ice that never melted clung to the black rock in great white sheets. The temperature was so cold, a person could die in minutes.

This was the level of Mount Gerd reserved for rapists, murderers, and traitors. The level from which there was no hope of salvation from kindly villagers in Konundal or the folk of Gildenheim.

The procession came to a halt. Wynter, Khamsin, and the judicars dismounted while several of the White Guard dragged a chained, drooping Belladonna from the prisoner's cart and brought her to stand before the assemblage.

"Belladonna Rosh of Summerlea," the head judicar intoned, "you have been found guilty of treason and of crimes against the person of your queen, and you have been sentenced to face the mercy of the mountains. May the gods have mercy on your soul."

Three days ago, Bella would have answered the judicar's pronouncement with sneering defiance and hatred, but the Belladonna Rosh who sagged in her bonds and shivered in the cold was a far cry from the fiend who'd gleefully crowed her delight over killing Khamsin's child.

Kham stood by Wynter's side as the White Guard dragged Belladonna to the chains hammered into the mountain, stripped away her outer garments, and chained her to a slab of icy rock.

As Khamsin had learned, the worst offenders were not stripped of their clothes but rather warmly bundled, so as to make their death by exposure last as long as possible. And though the grieving mother in Khamsin wanted Bella to suffer for what she'd done, the lonely girl who'd spent the last months viewing Bella as a friend from home couldn't bring herself to inflict more torture upon her former maid. She had asked Wynter to grant Bella the quickest death, and he had agreed.

She pulled her hand free of Wynter's and approached the chained maid. "I wish I could say I forgive you, but I don't. Not for what you did to me. Not for what you tried to do. May the gods grant you no more mercy than you showed my unborn child."

The maid—no, King Verdan's hired assassin and spy—looked up with dull eyes and blunted defiance. "This doesn't end here. I am but one of many."

Kham nodded. "Perhaps. But after today, the many you speak of will count one less among their number."

She returned to Wynter's side. He enfolded her in his arms, pulling her close to his body. He tilted her face up to his and brushed one large thumb across her cheek in a gentle caress.

"Pay her no heed, *min ros*. She's just trying to get under your skin, the same way she did when she tried to make you doubt your old nurse. She knows of no others serving your father here in Wintercraig, and she confessed your nurse had nothing to do with your father's schemes. She said everyone in Vera Sola knew Tildavera Greenleaf's first loyalty was to you."

"You had her questioned about Tildy?" She frowned up at him. "Why?"

"Because I could see that her accusations were troubling you. And I know what it's like to be betrayed by someone you trust. I thought you deserved to know the truth."

He knew her so much better than she realized. She hadn't truly believed Tildy would have harmed her, but the doubt had still been there, poisoning her mind as surely as Bella's herbs had poisoned her body. And he'd seen that and put a stop to it.

"Thank you." She looped her arms around his waist and leaned into him. "Take me home, husband. To Gildenheim."

CHAPTER 20

The Great Hunt

The next month passed in a strange haze of happiness. Or at least Khamsin imagined this feeling was what happiness must be like.

Wynter began to join Khamsin and Krysti on their daily rides. News of her efforts to save Skala-Holt had spread far and wide, and the Winterfolk who had offered her hostility and suspicion now greeted Khamsin with warm smiles and open arms. Valik was actually making an effort to be amiable, and many ladies of the court began including her in their tight-knit circles. Even the mothers of the top-floor children had softened their stance, and allowed her to share the history of Summerlea with their children without protest.

As December deepened and winter solstice arrived, Konundal quadrupled in size. Every room in Gildenheim filled to bursting as folk from all over the kingdom gathered for the grand Festival of Wyrn, which celebrated the official start of winter. Ice sculptors carved enormous scenes and statues from blocks of ice, all lit by a dazzling display of multicolored lamplight each night. Kham's favorite was the breathtaking Ice Palace, a giant, life-sized castle built and entirely furnished with ice. It sported a gathering hall, a dining room set with a complete service carved from frosted ice, tower walls you could actually walk on, and three bedrooms that adventuresome Winterfolk could rent for the night. Wynter tried to talk her into taking one of the rooms, but she refused for fear that she might melt the palace down around their ears.

She felt like smiling all the time. *Her*, Khamsin Coruscate. Even the return of Reika Villani could not dim her happiness.

Each morning, Kham woke in Wynter's arms, his cool body curled against her warmth, his arms wrapped around her, his hair mingling with hers on the pillows. And each morning, she would smile, stretch like a cat, and roll over to look up into those startling glacier blue eyes, and the fire that ever smoldered between them would spark anew.

Lying in her bed as the first fingers of dawn crept over the horizon, Khamsin clutched Wynter's pillow to her face, breathed in his scent, and gave a laughing groan as the scent sizzled through her veins, rousing vivid memories of this morning's vigorous beginning. He was always awake before she was, watching her in silence as she slept, but somehow, that didn't alarm or bother her. Instead, it made her feel . . . protected. Safe. Even . . . loved.

Kham sat up abruptly and flung the pillow aside. Loved? Where had *that* come from?

She pressed her hands to her cheeks. Wynter didn't love her. She wasn't fool enough to ever dream that he would. She was just a means to an end. A womb to carry his heir. She must never forget that. *Never.* To start spinning romantic fantasies involving Wynter was idiocy. Granted, if she did, in fact, provide him the heir he needed, her position as Wintercraig's queen would be secure, but that was politics, not love. Once he had his heir, he might well abandon her bed in favor of another's. The courtiers' sly, tittering glances, which had faded when Wynter began lavishing his attention on her, would once again grow sharp as glass.

A powerful gust of wind rattled the windows in their panes.

Kham caught herself instantly. *No.* She wasn't going to think like that. This last month had been the most wonderful of her life, and she wasn't going to ruin it with wild speculation, foolish dreams, or dark, unhappy thoughts. Wynter didn't love her. She wasn't going to let herself believe he did. But that didn't preclude their building a good life together.

Khamsin shoved the rumpled linens and furs aside and rose from the bed. The instant her feet touched the floor, dizziness assailed her. She swayed and clutched one of the solid wooden posters to steady herself, but the dizziness had already passed. Her stomach growled loudly, and Kham laughed and shook her head. She should have eaten more at last night's dinner meal. If she started fainting from hunger, Wynter would probably insist on hand feeding her himself.

Kham cocked her head to one side, and a slow smile curved across her lips. Come to think of it . . . that had all sorts of interesting possibilities.

With a laugh for her wicked thoughts, she reached for the bellpull and rang for her new maid, a cheery Winterlass named Drifa. Kham had promised Krysti they would make an early start of it this morning. He wanted to take her to a place he claimed had one of the best views in the whole valley.

Wynter looked up as the door to his office opened. Valik entered, but Wyn's automatic smile of greeting died a swift death at the sight of Valik's expression.

"What is it?"

"There's trouble in Jarein Tor. A shepherd came down from the mountains, claiming his flock was slaughtered." Valik's gaze flickered. "He says it was *garm*."

"He saw them?" Skepticism colored Wynter's words. *Garm* rarely left witnesses. If you were close enough to see a *garm*, it was close enough to follow your scent—and fast enough to rip out your throat and belly before you could go for help.

"Not them. He saw the tracks, heard the sheep scream,

and took off running down the mountain. Didn't stop 'til he reached the village."

Wynter nodded. "Send an eagle to Friesing. I want Skyr and his men on their way to Jarein Tor within the hour." If the *garm* had come, he must move swiftly to kill the beast before it grew bold enough to feed on more than sheep. "If the reports are true, we must call the Hunt."

"Done." Valik bowed crisply, pivoted on his heels, and strode out the door.

When he was gone, Wyn forced his clenched fists to relax. Tales of tracks and a sheep's scream from a frightened shepherd weren't proof the *garm* had come. It could be a rogue snow wolf, come down from the glaciers in search of easy prey.

But even as he reassured himself, he knew the words for the lie they were.

The Ice King's minions were gathering to usher in the return of their god. Laci had warned him they would sense the Ice Heart's power growing stronger. And Wynter had already passed the point of no return. With each passing day, the icy void in his chest grew colder and spread farther, freezing what was left of his humanity bit by bit.

The only thing holding it at bay now was Khamsin and her Summer-born gifts. Wynter pushed away from his desk and stood. Speaking of his little Summerwitch . . . he had not laid eyes on her nor had one whispered update about her activities since leaving her bed this morning. That did not bode well. If he'd learned one thing about his wife, he'd learned that Absence of Khamsin held a far greater potential for disaster than Khamsin Constantly Underfoot.

"Hold it steady!" Khamsin shouted.

"I'm trying!" Krysti shouted back. Irritation snapped in his voice. "But I'm just a kid, and you're heavier than you look! I told you I should have gone first."

She looked over her shoulder and down the ladder fashioned from the trunk of a tall, knotted pine and grinned at the boy clinging to the base of the ladder to keep it from rolling. "You're doing fine. I'm almost there."

She reached the top of the tree-trunk ladder and hopped off on the rocky outcropping that jutted out over the tree line to provide what Krysti assured her was one of the best views in all of Wintercraig.

"Coming up!" the boy called from below, and Kham took hold of a broken limb near the top of the tree trunk to hold the ladder steady while Krysti clambered up to join her. He managed in a fraction of the time it had taken her. Of course, he could have climbed the cliff face without a ladder, too.

"What did I tell you?" Krysti dusted his palms on his trousers and gestured to the spectacular vista spread out before them.

"You're right. It's gorgeous. Well worth the trouble of the climb." From the snow-covered spruce on the steep mountainside, to the frosty, evergreen-laden valley below with its wide, rocky river that snaked along the base of the mountains, to the blue, blue sky that seemed to stretch forever, Khamsin was hard-pressed to think of any sight more lovely than the breathtaking grandeur of this rough, rugged land she now called home.

"There is Friesing." Krysti pointed to a distant gathering of shingled roofs and stone chimneys amid the evergreens. "You can barely see Gildenheim from here."

They were a good twenty miles east of the palace as the birds flew. Almost twice that distance by land. Kham bit her lip. She'd grown so comfortable in the saddle, she hadn't even thought about how far or fast they were going. And they'd gone much farther than they ever had before.

She glanced up at the sky. The sun was still high overhead. It was barely past noon, but they would need to start back within the hour. If she and Krysti didn't get home before dusk, Wynter would organize a search party.

"How did you find this place?" She gazed out across the valley and the rolling hills and mountains of Wintercraig's lowlands beyond. Vera Sola had been a man-made mountain in the center of a wide, fertile valley. The view there had been of flat, cultivated farmland. Miles and miles of wheat, corn, barley, and more. Nothing so dramatic and untamed as this.

"I had an uncle who lived in a cabin on Jarein Tor, five miles that way." He pointed to the east. "I used to spend summers here with him, helping him check his traps."

"That must have been fun." Krysti never talked about his family. Of course, neither did she. "I never met my uncle—my mother's brother. He died before I was born."

Krysti started to say something when a high-pitched shriek ripped through the air.

Khamsin nearly jumped out of her skin. "What in the name of Halla was tha—"

Krysti's hand clapped over her mouth—hard. He shook his head. The snowy freckles on his golden skin seemed to disappear as his face lost all color. The hand covering her mouth was shaking like a leaf. Whatever that scream was, it had terrified him.

Krysti leaned slowly towards her until his mouth was pressed against her ear. "Don't . . . move." His voice was a thready whisper. "Don't . . . make . . . a . . . sound."

His fear was contagious. Her heart started to pound. Her throat went dry. She swallowed—or tried to—and nodded.

The scream came again, high-pitched and terrible. Kham scanned the mountainside, trying to follow the sound to its source. She had no idea how far sound could travel. No idea how close the source of that scream might be. She couldn't see anything moving. Just snow and trees and rock and more snow.

"Can you make the wind blow towards us and down into the valley?" Krysti whispered.

Kham hesitated, then admitted, "I would be afraid to try." Wynter could have done it easily, but her ability to control her weathergift was still more chance than certainty.

Krysti took a breath. "That's okay. We're still upwind.

But we need to get away from here as quietly and quickly as possible. Quietly being the most important. Try not to make any noise at all."

"All right."

"You go first. I'll hold the tree."

She eased her way across the rock to the tree they'd used as a ladder.

As she started down the trunk, Krysti said, "Khamsin?"

She paused and looked up. "Yes?"

"If I tell you to run, you get to Kori and ride away as fast as you can."

"What?" She barely remembered to keep her voice to a whisper. "No! I'm not abandoning you here. Don't be ridiculous!"

"We don't have time to argue!" He glowered at her. "You're the queen. It's my job to protect you. I accepted that responsibility the minute I snuck you out without your guards. So this is how it's going to be."

"Krysti . . ."

"If I tell you to run, I'm dead already. So you run! And you don't stop or look back until you reach Gildenheim. Understand?" In that moment, this ten-year-old boy she'd befriended seemed decades older than his years.

She swallowed the dry lump in her throat. "I understand." There was no doubt in her mind they were genuinely in mortal danger because whatever had produced that scream had turned a ten-year-old boy from laughing child to a grim protector willing not only to berate his queen but to sacrifice his life to ensure her safety. Not that she was ever going to let him do that, of course, but she wasn't going to waste any more time arguing about it.

"Good. Now go. And be *quiet*." He cast a quick glance back over his shoulder. "Right now, silence is more important than speed. They can sense both sound and motion, and much of either will give away our position."

They who? She wanted to ask, but she'd already delayed them long enough. Khamsin eased her way down the tree trunk, freezing at each infinitesimal crunch and crack as she blindly tested the limbs to support her weight. *Just get to the bottom, Khamsin. Take your time. Silence is more important than speed.* Climbing down the tree took much longer than her earlier, laughing ascent. She breathed a shuddering sigh of relief when she reached the bottom, then held the trunk to keep it from rolling as Krysti made his way down after her.

He made much shorter work of it, and when he hopped silently to the ground, he held a finger to his lips, and whispered, "Follow me, and try to walk in my footsteps."

The boy's clan-gift and his years of hunting the woods with his uncle served him well. He managed to pick a near-silent path to their horses through the snow, rocks, and bracken that carpeted the forest floor. When they reached the horses, he cut one of the blankets into eight pieces and tied them around the horses' hooves with the roll of twine in his saddlebags. Though the questions were all but burning to get free, Khamsin stayed silent and helped him wrap the horses' hooves. Krysti helped her mount, swung up in his own saddle, and guided them back to the trail that led down the mountainside to the main valley road.

"We need to get back to Gildenheim—fast," Krysti said, as they stopped to remove the cloths from the horses' hooves. "Are you up for a gallop?"

"Of course." Though Krysti was clearly still concerned enough to keep his voice quiet, he wasn't whispering anymore. Kham took that to mean the immediate danger was past. "What was that back there? I didn't see anything."

"Few ever do—at least not those who live to tell the tale." Done unwrapping the horses' hooves, Krysti swung into the saddle and gathered up his reins. "That was a *garm,* the deadliest monster in all of Wintercraig. We've got to tell the king."

The pair of horses thundered down the valley road towards Gildenheim. Long before they reached it, they saw flocks of birds winging through the sky and heard the echoing sound of horns blowing in the villages around them. Three long blasts. Then a pause, then three long blasts again.

"What does that mean?" Kham asked.

"It means the king already knows about the *garm*. He's calling for the Great Hunt."

"I don't understand why I have to stay behind. Galacia Frey and her priestesses are going."

Wynter drew a deep breath and reminded himself to remain patient as his wife crossed her arms and glowered. Ever since Khamsin and Krysti had returned to Gildenheim yesterday, riders had been pouring in through the gates, and the skies were filled with birds sending replies to Gildenheim's summons. Now dawn was near, and enough Winterfolk had gathered to start the Great Hunt. And Khamsin was not happy that she would not be one of them.

"Laci is going because she's the High Priestess of Wyrn. She is the guardian of Thorgyll's Spears, and her presence is required. Her priestesses are going to assist her. They are trained to hunt *garm*. You are not."

"But—"

Wynter held up a hand. "Enough. You are not going, no matter how much you wheedle, shout, or stamp your foot. You're staying here, in Gildenheim, where I know you'll be safe. My mind is made up."

She crossed her arms and glared. She had an impressive glare. Those silver eyes, those brows drawn tight across the bridge of her nose, the way her full lips pursed. Well, maybe not the pursed lips. Those just made him want to kiss her.

He sighed and caught her shoulders. "I need you safe, *min ros*. Don't you understand? When I realized you and Krysti were alone in the mountains where the *garm* had been sighted, I thought I was going to lose you." Just the thought of how close she'd come to death had kept him awake all night long. He didn't want to know that level of fear again anytime soon.

"You think it will be any better for me, waiting around here while you're out hunting these creatures? Krysti told me about them. They're deadly dangerous."

"Which is exactly why we must hunt them down. Once they come down from the mountain, they'll hunt and kill anything that crosses their path—and they'll keep at it until the riders of the Great Hunt stop them."

"All the more reason for me to go with you. This is my home now. I have as much right and duty to defend it as you and Galacia do."

"Khamsin, when we first left Summerlea, Valik wanted to stay behind to govern Vera Sola. As the White Sword, it was his right and his duty. I wouldn't let him stay . . . because I couldn't risk losing him to a rebel blade. It is your right and duty to defend your home—and it gladdens my heart to know you consider Wintercraig that home now— but I need you to stay here, in the palace, where it's safe. I can't risk anything happening to you. If you were hurt . . . if I lost you . . ." He swallowed hard.

Her rebellious, stubborn scowl wavered. "Wyn . . ." The threatening storm in her eyes turned to soft, liquid silver. One slender hand rose towards his face.

He caught her hand and pressed a kiss in her palm. "Please, *min ros*. Promise me you'll stay here, out of trouble. Don't make me command you." He pulled her close and bent to press another kiss on her lips. Not a wild, explosive kiss of passion, but something long and lingering. A kiss that sang a hymn of devotion with each warm breath and brush of lips upon lips. "Please," he whispered when at last he pulled away. "Promise me."

She blinked up at him with hazy eyes and touched her lips in bemusement. "I promise."

The relief that flooded his heart nearly staggered him. "Thank you."

"Now, *you* promise *me* that you'll come back safely."

They both knew any such promise would be a lie, so he said instead, "I'll move Halla and Hel to do so, Summerlass. On that you have my oath."

The hunters had gathered. Scores of Wintermen and a handful of strong, battle-tested women. Instead of shining silver armor, they wore pale leathers bleached to shades of white and cream so they blended in with the snowy forest. All were heavily armed with bows and spears and throwing axes as well as swords. And although each hunter wore an expression as grim as death, the aura of anticipation was unmistakable.

These folk were mountain bred. Hunters, all. And this gathering, despite its serious purpose, filled them with a visceral eagerness.

Wynter swung into the saddle. He had slung a bow and quiver across his back, and Gunterfys was strapped securely to his side. In a Great Hunt, everyone carried both a ranged weapon and a sword. The ranged weapon would be their primary defense, and most prayed they would never need to unsheathe the sword. Against a *garm*, a man's odds of survival dropped sharply in close combat.

Hodri shifted, snorted a puff of vapor into the cold air, and shook his head. For this hunt, he'd been stripped of his usual bells, so the long, wavy strands of his mane, threaded with thin white ribbons, danced in silence against his strong neck.

A clatter of hooves announced the arrival of Galacia Frey and her two priestesses. Clad in white leather and riding snowy white mares, Galacia and one of the other priestesses each held one of the long, crystalline ice spears they had taken from the wall behind Wyrn's altar. All three carried long, curving white bows and quivers full of hollow arrows filled with capsules of concentrated acid.

Wynter glanced up at the balcony high above the courtyard and found Khamsin, dressed in defiant scarlet and gold, standing on the stone walk outside her chamber. The sky was overcast and weeping snow that blew on an occasional fitful gust of wind. She was still not happy to be left behind, but Wynter wouldn't risk her safety in the most dangerous expedition in all of Wintercraig. The Great Hunt never failed to claim lives, and he would face whatever tempest she cared to brew before he let her even chance becoming one of the Hunt's casualties.

Their eyes met. He raised his hand in a faint salute, then led the Great Hunt out of Gildenheim.

Four days later, the riders of the Great Hunt still had not returned.

Khamsin stood beside the mullioned cathedral windows of Gildenheim's large gathering room, staring down in brooding silence at the castle's many terraced gardens. The view was beautiful—the snow-blanketed gardens white and serene, the frozen waterfalls magical, as if time itself had stopped—but even the most exquisite winter beauty couldn't calm her nerves. She didn't want to see frosted evergreens sculpted in perfect shapes. She wanted to see the riders of the Great Hunt coming safely home . . . with Wynter in the lead.

The waiting was driving her mad. Normally, Krysti would have been with her, keeping her entertained and her mind occupied, but since they were confined to the palace, she'd insisted he join the top-floor children for their lessons in the afternoons.

The rustle of skirts behind her made her turn. The other ladies of the court were seated throughout the room, occupying themselves with reading, needlework, or quiet conversation. Lady Melle had set down her needlework and crossed the room to join Khamsin at the window.

"I wouldn't expect them back so soon, Your Grace," she said. "The Great Hunt usually lasts for many more days. I even remember one when I was a girl that lasted three weeks."

"Three weeks?" Khamsin stared at her in horror. Three

weeks of being locked in this castle, waiting, would drive her mad. "How do you bear it?"

"The waiting is hard, I know." Lady Melle's eyes were filled with kindness and sympathy. "And I won't lie and tell you it ever gets any easier. It doesn't. This is the sixth Great Hunt in my lifetime. And every time, I'm a bundle of nerves waiting for the men to return."

"Have you ever ridden with them? I saw other women Hunters besides Lady Frey and her priestesses."

"Single women only. Widowed or never wed. Married women don't ride in the Hunt."

That didn't seem at all fair to Khamsin. "Why not? If they're capable and have the desire, why shouldn't they ride in the Hunt just like the men?"

Lady Melle smiled gently. "*Garm* are the fiercest, most dangerous beasts in the Craig, my dear. Riders die in the Great Hunt—often. You're wed to a Winterman. You've lived among us long enough to know what that means. Our men would die to keep us safe. We remain in Gildenheim, so fewer of them have to."

"Has a king of Wintercraig ever died in a Great Hunt?"

Lady Melle hesitated, then admitted, "Yes."

Kham's mind filled with an image of Wynter, bleeding his life out in the snow. The vision was so horribly vivid that Khamsin spun back towards the window and took short, fast breaths as she battled back an unexpected rush of tears.

Seeing her distress, the elderly lady exclaimed, "Oh, my dear! No, you mustn't think such thoughts." She wrapped an arm around Khamsin's shoulders and pulled her close. "Wynter of the Craig is no ordinary king. It would take far more than a single *garm* to bring him to harm."

Kham leaned into the older woman's embrace. It was the first time since leaving Gildenheim that a woman had offered Khamsin the comfort of a hug, and that nearly broke the dam holding back a flood of tears.

"There now. There." Lady Melle patted Kham's back

and murmured soothing noises until the worst of the emotional storm passed.

Sniffling, wiping at her eyes with the palms of her hands, Kham pulled away and tried to regain a measure of composure. "I'm sorry. I don't know what came over me. I'm not by nature the weepy sort."

"Of course you aren't. These are extraordinary circumstances." The lady positioned herself between Khamsin and the other ladies in the gathering room. "I should have made a point of preparing you for this myself, and I did not. I beg your pardon."

Kham smiled wanly and looked up through tear-spiked lashes. "It's hardly your fault I turned into a waterfall on you." Khamsin gave herself a stern shake and cleared her throat. "I've never been good at waiting. It doesn't look like that's going to change anytime soon."

"None of us are good at it, my queen. That's why the ladies of the court have always banded together in such times. Company makes the waiting easier to bear."

Kham gave a watery laugh. "Yes, well, I don't think needlework will ever make any wait of mine easier."

Now it was Lady Melle's turn to smile. "Perhaps not. We will just have to find other pursuits that suit you better. Reading perhaps? Or a game of cards? I understand you enjoy playing Aces."

"I wouldn't want to bother the others."

"Nonsense. You are our queen, and we are your ladies. We are here to see to your comfort, not the other way around."

Wynter knelt in the crisp snow on the slopes of Mount Trjoll in the Craig. Four days ago, they'd picked up the tracks of the *garm* a scant half mile from the outcropping where Krysti said he'd taken Khamsin. Until that moment, Wynter hadn't realized just how close Khamsin and Krysti had come to meeting the monster face-to-face. *Garm* could cover a half mile in less than a minute. One small change in the direction of the wind, and his Summerlass would never have come home.

Wynter hadn't slept well since.

From Jarein Tor, they'd tracked the *garm* through the mountains to Hammrskjoll, up the mountains and through Glacier Pass in the Craig, then west into the Minsk River valley.

"He's heading towards Skala-Holt," Wyn murmured.

"I'll send an eagle to warn them."

"Let's hope we're not too late." Wyn stood. "Mount up." He swung into the saddle and gathered up the reins.

"Eagle coming in!"

Wyn looked up to see the broad white span of a snow eagle's wings soaring through the blue sky. The bird tucked its wings and stooped towards them, slowing at the last moment to land on Valik's outstretched arm.

Valik removed the message capsule from the bird's leg. He pumped his arm skyward, setting the eagle back in flight, and tossed a small vole into the air. The eagle snatched its treat from the sky and flew off to a rocky outcropping to eat.

"What news?" Wynter asked as Valik scanned the message.

"Word from the men you sent into the Craig to find the *garm*'s den." Valik glanced up, his expression grim. "The *garm* didn't just come down to Jarein Tor. Someone lured it there deliberately.

"Your Grace." A servant Kham didn't recognize furtively handed her a sealed envelope. "I was asked to deliver this," she whispered, then hurried away.

Curious. Khamsin opened the envelope and pulled out the folded parchment inside. Scrawled in a sloppy hand across the parchment, the note read:

The Great Hunt is an ambush. They mean to kill the king to end the threat of Rorjak's return. We

*must warn him. I'll be waiting with the horses at the
old mill at eleven o'clock. Leave the same way as last
Freikasday. Don't let anyone see you. Burn this note.*

The note wasn't signed, but it could only be from Krysti.
Who else knew about last Friekasday's escape through the
hidden door on the western wall?

She thought about Galacia and her priestesses, all
armed with deadly weapons that could kill in an instant.
Much as Kham didn't want to believe any of them would
kill their king, she knew better. The first loyalty of every
priestess was to her goddess, not her king. And no matter
how much Wynter and Khamsin might want to deny it, the
Ice Heart still held Wynter firmly in its grip, and its power
grew stronger with each passing day.

Would Galacia and her acolytes kill Wynter? According to the ladies of the court, the coming of the *garm* was
one of the signs of Rorjak's return. The rumors that Frost
Giants had been involved in the avalanche at Skala-Holt
was another. It was possible the priestesses felt time was
running out.

Khamsin glanced back over her shoulder at the court
ladies playing cards, waiting by the windows, doing anything they could to occupy their time while their men rode
in the Great Hunt. It was a quarter 'til ten. If she retired to
her room, claiming headache or weariness, it might be a
good two to three hours before anyone came looking for
her. Time enough for Krysti and her to be well away before
their absence was discovered.

Kham slipped the note inside her pocket, summoned a
wan look, and went to excuse herself from the court.

Assuming it might be a day or more before they caught up
with the Hunt, Khamsin dressed warmly in knitted undergarments, the wool-lined leather trousers and jacket she'd
had made for her jaunts with Krysti, and a warm, white,

fur-lined, hooded cape that could serve as a bedroll and blanket. Remembering Wynter's comment about how Winterfolk always prepared for the worst, she rolled a change of clothes and a pouch of dried fruit and meat she'd pilfered from the kitchen inside a woolen blanket and slung that across her back. Then she threw Krysti's note in the hearth, watched as it turned to ash, and snuck downstairs to the secret exit she and Krysti had used the day they'd given her guards the slip.

The sun was shining bright in the sky. Khamsin turned her cape fur-side out, pulled the hood over her distinctive dark hair, and waited for the guards to pass before she hurried across the open expanse of snowy rock. Her heart remained in her throat, pounding like mad, until she'd descended the craggy cliff-side trail and reached the cover of the trees growing at its base.

Once safely hidden from view, she ran through the trees toward the old mill. There, two saddled mountain ponies were snuffling through the snow by the creek banks, searching for grass. A cloaked figure was sitting on a rock beside them, skipping stones to pass the time.

A twig snapped beneath Kham's boot as she rushed towards him. The figure leapt off the boulder and whirled around.

Only then did Kham realize that perhaps she should have been more suspicious about the note. Because the identity of the person waiting for her stopped Khamsin dead in her tracks.

"What are you doing here?"

Reika Villani, clad in snug winter white leathers and boots, lowered the furred hood of her thick cape. She'd forgone her usual intricate piles of hair for a pair of braids that made her look more like one of the fresh young girls from Konundal than a veteran of the royal court.

"I'm the one who sent you the note, Your Grace."

Kham glanced uneasily at the surrounding forest, suspecting a trap. Hoping to buy herself time, she said, "What note?"

"Don't play games," Reika snapped. "There isn't time. I know you don't trust me, and I accept the blame for that. But if we don't get to the king soon, he won't come back from the Hunt alive."

"You're right, I don't trust you," Kham agreed baldly. "Why should I?"

"Because my mother used to be a priestess of Wyrn. She was in line to be the next High Priestess when she met my father and fell in love. I know what oaths Galacia and her acolytes took. The minute the *garm* came down from the mountain, Wynter was marked for death."

When Khamsin didn't respond, Reika made an exasperated noise.

"Fine, don't believe me. But I have loved Wynter Atrialan all my life, and I'm not going to sit here and let Wyrn's minions put him in his grave." She stalked over to the grazing horses and took the reins of the brown one.

"I brought you a horse." She swung onto the brown's saddle and indicated the other horse, a black-and-white highland pony even larger than Kori. "You can come with me or not, as you like. I only sent you that note because I thought your magic might come in handy convincing Lady Frey and her followers to back off."

Khamsin hesitated. Every instinct urged her not to trust Reika.

Reika watched Khamsin's indecision and sneered. "Suit yourself. I knew I should have gone myself instead of wasting precious time waiting for you." Wheeling her mount around, Reika went galloping through the snowy forest towards the main valley road.

"Wyrn curse it," Kham swore. If Wynter's life was truly in danger, and she did nothing to warn him, she'd never forgive herself. "I just know I'm going to regret this," she muttered. She grabbed the pony's reins, led the mare over to a fallen tree, so she could reach the stirrups, and swung up into the saddle. A kick of her heels sent the pony leaping forward into a fast canter. "Reika! Reika, wait. I'm coming."

The two of them rode throughout the day and well into the night. They slept in an abandoned hunter's cabin, before heading out again before sunrise the next morning. Reika stopped regularly to call upon her clan animals, the ermine, to help them guide her to the Hunt. They doubled back more than once, going up and down the mountain, then circling back around. If not for the sun in the sky and Khamsin's connection to it, Kham would have been completely turned around. But as it was, she knew they were no more than a day's ride west of Gildenheim.

"This is ridiculous," Kham complained when they stopped yet again, this time to water the horses while Reika consulted her animal guides yet again. "At this rate, we'll never reach Wynter in time to warn him."

Reika cast her a sharp look. "The Hunters are following the *garm,* and *garm* don't exactly run in straight lines for your convenience, Your Grace. If tracking the hunters is too much trouble for you, feel free to go back to Gildenheim."

Kham clamped her mouth shut. After a few more moments, Reika rose from her crouch, dusted the snow off her knees, and remounted her horse.

"They're heading this direction." She pointed up the mountain. "It shouldn't be too much farther now."

"What happens when we find them?" Kham asked. "If Galacia and her priestesses mean to kill the king, surely our presence will force their hands."

"Not if we get to Valik and the White Guard first." Reika dropped back to ride alongside Kham's left flank. "You know, Elka and I used to ride in hills just like these when we were girls. She always dreamed of being a princess. Not me. I always dreamed of being queen."

Kham bit her lip. "Reika . . ."

"Wait." Reika held up a hand. "What's that, over there?" She pointed to a spot off to Khamsin's right.

"What?" Kham peered up the mountain. "I don't see anything."

"You will once the *garm* catch the scent of your blood."

Every nerve in Khamsin's body jangled with alarm. She turned back around in time to see Reika throw back her cloak and raise the weapon concealed at her side.

"Time to die, Summer witch." Reika's beautiful face twisted into ugly lines of hatred. With a scream of rage, she raised her right arm. Sunlight glinted off the weapon clenched in her fist, a long-handled weapon that ended in five splayed, clawlike spikes.

Khamsin jerked around in the saddle and kicked her heels into her mount's sides just as Reika brought her strange blade slashing down. Fiery pain ripped down Kham's back, but it was her mount who caught the worst of the blow as the clawed weapon raked deep furrows across her hindquarters. The mare screamed in pain and reared up on her hind legs, nearly unseating Khamsin. Kham's thighs clenched tight around the mare's ribs, heels digging in as she clung to the animal's back. She grabbed instinctively for the pommel of the saddle with both hands and lost her grip on the reins.

Reika swung her weapon again.

Kham shrieked as pain ripped across her shoulder, arm, and rib cage. The mare's forelegs slammed back to earth, and the horse shot forward in a wild gallop.

Branches whipped across Kham's face, the icy needles slicing at her skin, rough bark scraping hot, painful furrows across cheek and brow. She ducked and leaned low over the mare's neck, burying her face in her mount's mane to protect herself from the worst of the slashing branches. Her back, shoulder, and side burned like fire, and she could feel the blood flowing from the wounds. She didn't dare release the saddle to reach for the reins whipping like ribbons in the wind as the mare ran.

Don't let go, Kham. Whatever you do, don't let go!

The mare bounded over rocks and streams, leapt fallen trees. Jolt after jolt shook Khamsin to her bones, but she clung to the saddle with desperate strength. Her fingers had curved into bloodless talons around the pommel. The muscles in her hands had turned to steel and locked in place.

Then, abruptly, the horse wasn't beneath her anymore. One moment, the mare was galloping wildly through the forest, the next the horse dropped like a stone and propelled Khamsin over her head.

Time stretched as Khamsin soared through the air, spiraling as she went. She caught sight of the overcast sky shining silvery gray overhead and huge drifts of snow gathered at the base of the cliffs directly in front of her. The cliff's ragged black rock rose sharply upwards, its rough surface coated with a thin layer of ice that made the stone gleam with an obsidian sheen.

The next instant, gravity reclaimed her. She landed with a bone-jolting slam atop an unyielding sheet of ice.

Time accelerated in a sudden rush as she spun, spread-eagled, across the surface of a frozen pond. Her feet smacked into the cascade of silvery white icicles that had formed over the waterfall that fed the pond. The ice shattered, and the impact reversed the rotation of her spin and sent her careening, feetfirst into a snowdrift. Great white plumes of snow shot skyward as she came to a jarring halt, then drifted lazily back to earth, dusting her hair and eyelashes with crystalline flakes.

She lay there, stunned and motionless. All the air had been forced from her lungs, and her body seemed to have forgotten how to get more.

Breathe, Khamsin. Breathe.

Her mouth opened. Her throat worked. Seconds later, a long, painful wheeze scraped down the sides of her windpipe.

Deflated lungs refilled. Her eyes rolled back. With that one breath of air, all her other senses leapt back to life with a vengeance. Pain exploded along the hip and shoulder that had taken the brunt of her landing.

She pulled her legs up under her body and pushed up to her hands and knees. Grunts of pain interspersed with bouts of coughing and wheezing as she clambered slowly to her feet.

She wiggled her fingers in her mittens, and flexed ankles, knees, and hips with tender care. Everything was still working. Her nerve endings, especially. Although her hips and shoulder throbbed with each beat of her heart and the furrows down her back and side were dripping copious amounts of blood, she hadn't broken any bones. That was an unexpected bit of good luck.

Kham hadn't counted on surviving the gallop without injury. She'd not been certain she'd survive at all, for that matter. Her horse had been too terrified by Reika's attack.

Kham looked slowly around, trying to get her bearings. She was standing in the center of a frozen pond. A thin layer of snow lay over the slippery surface. And all around the pond, snow was piled high, as if someone had cleared it away.

She frowned and scanned the area again. On the north end of the pond, a black cliff face rose up high above, and a frozen white waterfall spilled down its sides. At the bottom of the fall, a portion of the frozen icicles from the fall had broken away, revealing what looked like the dark entrance to a cave. Her brows lifted as she recognized her surroundings. The skating pond. The one Wynter had immortalized in his Atrium. The one he'd taken her to the day of the Skala-Holt avalanche.

She knew exactly where she was, despite all the circuitous riding she now suspected of being Reika's attempt to disorient her and make her lose all sense of direction. All she had to do was find her horse, and make her way back down the mountain. The folk in Riverfall would offer her aid.

She scanned the white snowdrifts, trying to find the

mare. A splash of dark color at the corner of her eye sent Kham plunging to the left. She slogged her way through higher drifts that had gathered at the base of the trees, trailing drops of blood from her wounded shoulder, and found the mare lying on her side, her neck bent at an odd angle. The horse wasn't breathing.

Kham sank to her knees, brushing snow from the mare's motionless face. Her mittened hands curled into fists, and a familiar, volatile emotion bubbled up inside her.

"Damn you, Reika. You'll pay for this!" The snow clinging to Kham's wool mittens melted and quickly evaporated into a cloud of warm vapor. Overhead, silvery clouds condensed, growing thicker and darker as heat and moisture gathered. She'd worked hard to keep her emotions in check since the day she'd summoned that blizzard that nearly killed an entire village. But the next time she saw Reika Villani, that winter bitch would learn just how fearsome Storm of Summerlea could be.

And then Khamsin heard the growl.

CHAPTER 21

Of Heroes and Harrowing

"The *garm* has doubled back again." Wynter rose from the large, paw prints stamped into the snow along the cliff top and turned a grim eye on Valik and the other riders of the Great Hunt. "It's following the cliffs, heading back down the mountain."

The Wintermen's expressions could have been carved from ice. They all knew what Wyn meant. If the *garm* was heading back down the mountain, it was heading back towards the valley—and the villages. Towards families. Women and children.

Wynter swung into Hodri's saddle. "Let's ride."

He kicked his heels, and Hodri leapt forward. Chunks of ice and packed snow flew up in the wake of Hodri's great hooves as the swift, sure-footed mountain horse raced across the treacherous cliff tops. Valik and the other riders followed close behind.

Wyn kept an eye on the *garm* tracks. The distance between paw prints meant the monster was moving swiftly. The beast knew they were on its trail.

Khamsin's heart sank to the pit of her stomach, and sheer terror turned her blood to ice as she stared at the hideous creature coming towards her.

The description of the *garm* didn't even begin to do justice to the monster's huge, hulking evil. Though big as a horse, the creature's dense white fur blended so perfectly with the snow-covered ground it would have been virtually impossible to detect—except for the eyes.

Bloodred and glowing with a malevolent inner light, those eyes looked like beacons to the gates of Hel.

She'd expected the *garm* to look like an impossibly large, very scary wolf. The paws, the rangy, furred body and shaggy tail did, but that's where the resemblance ended. The same long, thick fur that covered its body also covered its neck and bulbous, earless head in a dense ruff, while a shorter nap grew around the creature's eyes, mouth, and nostril slits. Long, thin, spiky hairs like a cat's whiskers sprouted in abundance from both sides of its short, flattened muzzle and more sparsely on the sides and back of its head. But unlike a cat's whiskers, the *garm*'s long, stiff hairs shivered and undulated with a life of their own. When a small bird took flight from a nearby tree, several of the hairs whipped around to follow its path.

The *garm* had no ears, but it was clear those hairs sensed the vibrations of movement and sound. And with them, the creature literally had eyes in the back of its head.

It also, she realized as the mouth slit opened and the lips pulled back, had longer, sharper teeth and more of them than any creature she'd ever known. Row upon row of curved, razor-sharp fangs unfolded from the monster's upper and lower jaws as its mouth gaped wider. A single bite would slice through flesh and even bone like a knife through warm butter. And with the way the tips of the fangs curved inward, when the *garm* sank its teeth into something, that something wasn't ever getting away.

Kham slowly backed away.

No man can face a garm *alone and live.* Lady Melle's dire words echoed in her mind. *The only chance is to hunt in numbers. Large numbers. That's why we call it the Great Hunt. And even then, men will die.*

And here death was, staring Kham in the face. Drawn by the scent of the blood dripping from the wound Reika had carved down Kham's back.

Blue-white slime dripped from the *garm*'s fangs. One of the droplets landed on the leaf of a holly bush, and the spiky evergreen leaf froze with a crack, white frost spreading instantly across its dark, glossy surface.

The *garm* planted its front paws, swelled its chest and, with an earsplitting shriek, spewed out a billowing cloud of blue-white vapor.

The shriek ripped through Kham's skull. She screamed in pain and dropped to her knees, her muscles seizing. Before she could take another breath, the vapor cloud reached her. Frost crackled across her skin as the mist enveloped her and trapped her body in bands of unyielding ice. Ears ringing, she was dimly aware of the beat of her heart, feeling more than hearing the slow, thudding percussion reverberating in the frozen drum of her chest.

Move, Khamsin! MOVE! Her mind shrieked the command, but her body remained locked in place by the freezing, paralytic effects of the *garm*'s hunting scream and vaporous breath.

Fur rippled along the beast's haunches as the muscles in its hind legs bunched up, gathering power, and six lethal inches of curved, razor-sharp claws dug into the ice as the *garm* prepared to pounce.

If the *garm* touched her, she was dead.

She cast a frantic gaze skyward. Overhead, clouds boiled and wind whipped through the trees in fitful bursts, mirroring the chaotic whirl of terror and desperation rushing through her adrenaline-charged veins. The sun was there, behind those dark clouds. She reached for it, calling on the power and heat harnessed in its bright rays to counter the *garm*'s cold magic.

Please! Please! Help me!

The sun answered with a burst of warmth in her chest

that flowed through her veins to the rest of her body. Her fingers flexed.

The *garm* sprang.

Kham folded her legs and dropped to the ground just as the monster plowed through the spot where she'd been standing. The bitter wind that whipped past in the *garm*'s wake stung the exposed areas of her skin. Kham hissed at the pain and clambered to her feet. Her muscles were still half-frozen and sluggish to respond, but at least she could move.

Snarling, teeth gnashing with furious clicks, the *garm* spun around for a second attack. Long, curving six-inch claws extended from the *garm*'s massive paws and dug deep for traction.

Kham looked around frantically. Behind her lay the cliffs and the frozen lake. She couldn't run that way. Out in the open, she was dead. The creature was too fast, too powerful. She needed cover. Something to hide behind. Something to slow the *garm* down.

Flaming red eyes pinned her with lethal intent. The beast threw back its head, jaws agape. Kham covered her ears against the *garm*'s paralyzing shriek and ran for the trees.

The cold of its ice breath chilled her spine through the thick fur of her coat. She didn't dare slow enough to look back. She could feel the *garm* behind her. A freezing void closing in on her, draining the warmth from everything around it.

Just ahead, a pile of snow-covered boulders lay tumbled in her path. Six feet behind it, the branches of a large spruce stretched out.

Her legs pumped as she raced for the tumble of rocks. For months, she'd chased after Krysti, trying to emulate the effortless way he scrambled up and down sheer cliff faces and treacherous mountain terrain.

Of course, bounding up cliffs and over obstacles with Krysti had been just a lark. A fun way to pass the time.

Now, her life depended on it.

She scanned the boulders as she ran towards them, calculating the distances, the inclines, noting all footholds and determining the path most suited to her own reach and abilities.

There was no time for fear or doubt and no room for error. She could only decide her path, commit to it, and pray she completed a successful run on the first try.

Khamsin put on a burst of speed and leaped towards the first rock. Her foot came down, angled perfectly against the incline. Her right sole made contact. She bent her knee to absorb her momentum and immediately pushed off, springing up and left towards the next rock in the pile. Leaping from foot to foot, rock to rock, she bounded up the pile of boulders and launched herself into the air. Her arms stretched out, gloved hands spread wide.

She caught the spruce branch with her fingertips and kicked up and out to swing her torso over the top of the branch. She pumped her legs again, planted her feet on either side of her hands, and leapt up to grab a higher branch overhead. She scrambled up the branches of the spruce, then paused to see what the *garm* would do next.

Below her, the *garm* leapt for the tree trunk, flexing long, curving claws. Kham's eyes went wide. "Halla help me! The cursed thing can climb, too?"

Sure enough, the *garm* was scaling straight up the spruce's broad trunk, its six-inch claws digging into wood as easily as they sliced through ice and frozen ground. The beast had almost reached Khamsin before she collected herself enough to jump for the next highest branch.

"A giant ice wolf, they called it," Kham muttered as she scrambled up the tree. "Ice wolf, my ass. Show me one wolf—just one!—that can climb a tree!"

The branches grew thinner but more plentiful the higher she went. Hopefully, the thicket would slow down the *garm*—or, if she was lucky, stop it altogether. Khamsin cast a glance over her shoulder and promptly swore the air blue.

"You have *got* to be joking."

Not only did the *garm* run swift as a wolf, breathe freezing mist like a frost dragon, and climb trees as effortlessly as a squirrel . . . but when the spruce branches threatened to keep the garm from its prey, the beast just chewed through them like they were breadsticks.

She scrambled higher, climbing faster, praying as she went.

The crevasse lay in Hodri's path, a long, deep chasm gouged out of the underlying mountain. The crevasse was easily twenty-five feet wide—too far for a horse and rider to jump without considerable risk—but the *garm*'s tracks raced directly to its edge.

The gap might be a risky jump for horse and rider, but apparently not for the *garm*. As he reined Hodri in at the chasm's edge, Wyn could see the disturbed snow on the opposite side where the *garm* had landed after leaping the distance. The tracks continued on from there, still heading directly for the valley, where a thunderstorm was brewing.

He started to turn Hodri left, intending to ride along the chasm's edge until he found a safer place to cross, but a breeze blowing up from the valley brought him up short.

His head reared back, nostrils flaring at the distinctive scent of magic on the wind. Weather magic.

Storm magic.

Khamsin.

Fear struck hard. Wynter's hands clenched around Hodri's reins, knuckles turning white.

She was down there, in the valley. Wyrn only knew what madness had driven his reckless, imprudent wife to ignore his warnings and ride out into the forest during a Great Hunt, but she had. He knew the taste of her magic better than he knew his own.

Kham was down there. And the *garm* was heading straight for her.

For all he knew, it might already be upon her.

He wheeled his mount around and rode back a short distance. There wasn't time to find a safer place to jump. The slightest delay could mean the difference between reaching Khamsin before the *garm* did, or finding her remains scattered across a blood-soaked field.

The latter possibility was unthinkable.

"Come on, boy," he urged. "We can do this. We must. She needs us." He touched his heels to Hodri's side, and the stallion launched instantly into a fast gallop. Great hooves flashed, kicking up clods of packed snow as they raced towards the edge of the cliff.

Wyn heard the approach of Valik and the others as they crested the rise behind him, but he didn't pull up, and Hodri didn't slow.

The gaping chasm loomed before them.

"That's the way, boy," Wynter murmured. He bent low over Hodri's neck and gave the stallion his head.

"Wyn!" Valik gave a shout. "Stop! It's too far!"

Wynter's only response was to urge Hodri to run faster. The drop-off loomed large before them, the twenty-five-foot gap looking more like fifty, but Hodri never faltered. At the very edge of the abyss, when one more step would have sent them plunging to their deaths, the stallion planted his rear hooves, gave an explosive release of power from his massive hindquarters, and leapt off the edge of the cliff.

"Wyn!" Valik cried.

Wyn hardly heard him. Horse and rider soared through the air like one of the mythic Valkyr, the fierce warrior-spirits who rode the winds on ghostly steeds, gathering souls for Eiran, the goddess of death. They came back to earth with a jolt, landing hard on the far side of the crevasse, a scant six inches from the edge.

Roars of victory erupted from the Wintermen gathered on the far side of the chasm.

"You frost brain!" Valik shouted. "You nearly got yourself kill—"

A loud, booming crack split the air. Valik's scold broke off, and the Wintermen fell abruptly silent.

"Wyn!" Valik cried. His voice had gone from angry to alarmed. "Get out of there!"

"Hodri!" Wynter leaned hard over the saddle, digging his heels into Hodri's side and giving the stallion plenty of rein. "Run, boy! Run!"

The ground beneath Hodri's hooves began to shift as the underlying shelf of ice crumbled and fell away.

The stallion scrambled for purchase, barely managing to find solid ground before an enormous lip of ice tumbled down the mountainside.

On the opposite side of the crevasse, Valik and the others brought their mounts up short. What had been a risky twenty-five-foot jump was now an impassable forty-foot-wide chasm.

"We'll have to ride 'round, Wyn. Stay there. We'll cross at the first passable spot."

"I can't. Khamsin's in trouble. Catch up as soon as you can."

"Wyn! Wyn, damn you! Stop!"

But Wyn and Hodri were already galloping away, down towards the valley, towards Khamsin, following the large, platter-sized tracks of the *garm*.

Kham clung to a thin branch near the top of the spruce and screamed down at the still-climbing *garm*. She didn't dare go higher. The branch she was standing on was already bowed beneath her weight—and had started to make alarming snapping sounds.

The storm her unruly weathergift had summoned wasn't helping any. Powerful gusts of wind sent the treetops swaying in all directions, and Khamsin, clinging to the uppermost branches of the spruce, was whipping back and forth through the sky like a ball on a spring. Branches from her own and surrounding trees slapped at her as the spruce swayed, raising welts and scratches on her exposed skin and threatening to knock her from her perch. To make matters worse, freezing rain was rapidly coating the tree branches in layers of slippery ice.

With each passing moment, her perch became more precarious.

A sudden, hard gust of wind bent the top of her spruce tree sideways and smacked her into the branches of a nearby fir. The blow knocked her back. Her feet slipped out from under her, and her mittened hands lost their grip on the slippery, ice-coated spruce branch. She began to slide down the branch, which bent beneath her weight the farther down its length she slipped.

Luckily, she managed to wedge one foot against a knot on the branch below and use that foothold to stop her slide. She clung to her new position and took several deep breaths to calm her racing heart.

As the daze of adrenaline faded, another gust of wind sent the fir and spruce smacking against each other again, their branches tangling together for several seconds, then pulling back apart.

The scowl faded from her face.

An idea blossomed.

A desperate, stupid, reckless idea, granted, but at this point, she was out of options. If she wanted to live, she was going to have to jump. As in let go of the spruce branch she was clinging to for dear life and leap through the air, eighty feet above a boulder-strewn ground, into the branches of one of the nearby trees.

And pray to all the gods that (a) those branches would be strong and supple enough to bear her weight, and (b) that she would actually be able to grab and hold on to them instead of plunging to her death.

Khamsin heaved out a breath. "Well, Kham, you may

die either way, but as Roland always said, 'It's better to die swinging your sword than cowering behind it.' "

She glanced down at the rapidly approaching *garm*, then up at the dark, roiling sky. She fed the storm a little more power, only this time she tried to use that power to direct the storm's gusting winds. Not an easy task. Wind had a mind of its own.

Whether because of her effort or in spite of it, the wind shifted direction again. The fir tree that had knocked her out of the spruce now smacked into her once more.

At the same time, a loud growl sounded below her. Icy cold shivered down her back, and the spruce needles on either side of her suddenly crackled and went white with frost. The branch beneath her feet shuddered.

Her time was up. The *garm* had reached her. If she didn't jump now, she wouldn't get a second chance.

The trees were already springing apart, the distance between them widening rapidly. She released the spruce and pushed off with her feet, diving towards the fir.

The *garm* screamed.

Waves of paralyzing sound enveloped her. Her feet and calves lost sensation as the scream's accompanying vapor made contact. The freezing effect crept rapidly up her body, overtaking her thighs, her waist, her chest. It took all the effort Kham could muster to fight off the brain-scrambling effects of the *garm*'s scream and will the fingers of one hand to close around a thin fir branch. She held on tight as the fir sprang back and yanked her beyond the reach of the *garm*'s freezing cloud.

A furious howl burst from the monster's throat.

Khamsin clung to the fir with all her might, but as the tree straightened, her branch cracked. She fell, crashing through the nest of the thin branches near the top of the fir. Her arms flailed, and she clutched at any and every thing within her reach. A branch caught her behind the backs of her still-frozen knees and flipped her upside down. Another smacked into her shoulder and spun her right side up. Tumbling helplessly, she crashed down through the thicket of branches towards the ground.

A last branch caught her thighs and spun her around. Then there was nothing but air and a thick, white blanket of snow rushing up to meet her. She landed hard on her back. All the air left her lungs on a painful whoosh, and she lay there, dazed and aching and gasping for breath as a hail of ice chips, bark, and fir needles showered down upon her.

Get up, Kham. Get up! Move or you're dead.

Kham rolled to her knees, pushed herself to her feet, then nearly fainted when a stabbing pain radiated up her right leg. Her skirts were ripped near her thigh, the edges of the fabric dark with blood.

She pulled the ripped edges of her skirts apart with trembling hands, afraid of what she would see. A deep, six-inch furrow scored the flesh of her thigh. Blood dripped down her leg.

A loud rustle and the sound of snapping twigs in the trees overhead made her glance up.

She swore again, this time choosing one of Krysti's more colorful and inventive curses. The *garm* had leapt from the spruce to a nearby fir and was quickly making its descent.

Khamsin scanned her surroundings with desperate eyes. She had no weapons. Between her sprained ankle and the wound on her leg, she couldn't run, and standing her ground was out of the question. Even if she stoked the storm overhead, she'd lose control of it before it became powerful enough to be of any use to her. Her only chance was to reach the caves behind the frozen waterfall, scuttle deep into the narrow tunnels, and pray the *garm* couldn't chew through rock the way it did tree branches.

She took off at a fast hobble towards the frozen lake. With each ungainly step, pain shot through the entire right side of her body. Shadows and stars swirled at the edge of her vision.

As she reached the edge of the skating pond, a heavy

thud sounded behind her. She glanced over her shoulder. The *garm* had reached the ground and was racing after her, its enormous legs eating up the distance between them. A trail of brilliant scarlet drops stained the snow behind her.

She gritted her teeth and hobbled faster, slipping and sliding across the ice. The frozen waterfall lay before her. Behind the glittering crystalline icicles, she could see the black stone of the cliffs and the darker shadow of the cave opening.

The thick ice covering the lake groaned and cracked as the *garm* leapt onto its silvery surface and ran towards her.

Desperate, Kham dove for the cave opening, sliding across the last few feet of frozen pond. She grabbed at chunks of ice and stone with her left hand and kicked at the pond's frozen surface with her right foot in an effort to drag herself to safety. Rivulets of icy water dripped down on her from the waterfall, soaking her hair and the skin of her neck as she passed beneath it. She pulled and kicked, dragging and propelling her body farther back into the long cave where Wynter and his brother had played as children.

The *garm* had reached the cave's mouth. Khamsin rolled on her back, plugged her ears, and kept pushing with her good leg to shove herself deeper into the cave as the *garm* shrieked, spewed its freezing vapor, and ripped at ice and rock in an effort to get to her.

Her boots went white with frost, and she lost all feeling in her toes. She screamed and kicked at the *garm*'s nasal slits, its eyes, its jaw, trying desperately to land as many blows as she could while avoiding the rows of deadly, gnashing teeth.

"Get away from me, you Hel-cursed monster!" she screamed. "Get away!" She slammed the heel of her boot into the beast's nasal slits and pushed off. Her good hand closed around a sharp edge of stone. Warm blood filled her palm as the stone sliced her skin, but she tightened her grip and yanked herself a few more inches deeper into the caves.

Suddenly, the *garm* went still. The sensory hairs on the back of its head flattened, pointing in the direction of the cave opening. It tried to turn, but the cave mouth was too small for the *garm* to maneuver, so with one last snarl and a halfhearted attempt to bite her feet, the beast began backing out of the cave.

Kham heard a roar—deep and furious—then the *garm* jerked and screamed like she'd never heard anything scream before. Its eyes rolled. Its head, chest, and forelegs shook and writhed. Then a frothy, blue liquid gushed from its mouth and nasal slits, and it collapsed, tongue lolling across rows of razor-sharp teeth.

A moment later, the *garm*'s body started sliding backward as someone or something dragged it out of the cave. Light flared briefly, then a new shadow blocked out the filtered sunlight shining through the cave's mouth.

"Khamsin? Are you there? Are you hurt?"

Wynter. Khamsin collapsed, shaking, on the damp stone floor.

"I'm h-here," she tried to say, but to her embarrassment, her voice cracked, her throat closed up. A sob broke past her lips. Horrified, she clapped a trembling hand over her mouth to stifle the sound, only to sob again in complete mortification at the feel of warm wetness trickling from the corners of her eyes.

She was crying. *Crying!* Like some weak, spineless coward.

In front of him.

The shame of it burned like a fiery spear to the heart.

His cool hands ran gently up her legs, pausing briefly as they encountered the bloody wound on her thigh. "I have to get you out of here. Tell me if I hurt you."

He gripped her hips and pulled her towards him. Each bump and scrape across the uneven stone floor made her wounds throb with pain, but Khamsin would die before making another sound. As he pulled her towards the mouth of the cave, she hastily scrubbed away her tears and flung an arm over her face to hide her reddened eyes and blotchy skin. The thought of Wynter's seeing her so weak and weepy was more than she could bear.

With such gentleness he nearly made her cry anew, Wynter checked her bones for breaks and inspected the wound on her thigh. She heard rustling followed by the distinct sound of ripping. Curious, she peeked out beneath her arm and saw him using his hunting dagger to slice long strips of leather from the bottom of his vest. He braided the strips into a multistrand leather rope, then sliced a long rectangle of fabric from his linen undershirt. He folded the linen into a pad and placed it over her wound.

"Forgive me, *min ros*. This may hurt, but that cut is deep. I've got to stop the bleeding."

Wynter slipped the braided leather rope under her leg and tied the makeshift bandage securely in place. The pressure on the wound sent pain spearing up Kham's leg, and her body jerked in instinctive recoil. Then the stab of agony passed, and her multitude of wounds began throbbing again.

"Are you hurt anywhere else?"

"M-my b-b-back." As shock set in, her body began to shake.

He pulled her into a sitting position, cradling her against one side of his chest as he inspected the deep furrows scoring her back. "Did the *garm* do this?"

She tried to speak, to tell him what had happened, but the words wouldn't come out. All she could do was shake her head and tremble from head to toe.

Quickly, he made a second bandage and tied it in place over her back. Then his arms closed around her, muscles bunching with effortless strength as he gathered her up and held her close. She felt the cool press of his lips against her hair, breathed his crisp, woodsy scent. His heart was beating so fast and so loud, she could hear it through the thick layers of cloth, fur, and leather he'd donned for the Great Hunt.

The tears she'd fought so hard to battle back welled up again. She gave a choked sob and turned her face into his chest, gripping the fur of his outer vest in one fist and clutching his shoulder in the other as she utterly broke down and began sobbing against him.

His arms tightened further. "*Hössa, min stiarna.* The *garm* is dead. It cannot hurt you anymore." His voice sounded gentler than she'd ever heard it before. Steady, soothing, almost a croon. His kindness only made her cry harder.

"She s-said it was a trap . . . that they meant to kill you . . ."

"Who? Who told you someone was trying to kill me?" When she only sobbed and burrowed deeper against him, Wynter's fingers brushed against her damp cheek. "Look at me, Khamsin."

She shook her head. She didn't want to look at him.

Anger was her defense, the familiar wall of volatility and destruction she'd always used to keep the world at bay, to keep pain and tears at bay. Even as a child, when Tildy had rocked and soothed her over some wound or emotional hurt inflicted by King Verdan, a core of rebellious anger deep inside Khamsin had continued to smolder, giving her strength, shielding the most vulnerable part of her.

But how could she muster a protective shell of rebellion when Wynter gave her nothing to rebel against?

"Khamsin, look at me," he repeated, and his tone was one of such calm, relentless implacability, she couldn't deny him.

Her tear-spiked lashes fluttered. His face came into focus. His eyes so pale and piercing in the masculine, golden-skinned beauty of his face, regarded her with unblinking steadiness. Long, white hair blew about his head and shoulders like ribbons of snow.

"Reika," she admitted. Her gaze dropped and her fingers

plucked at fur of his vest. "I shouldn't have believed her. It was stupid of me. But—but I . . . She said . . ." Kham's voice trailed off.

"She said someone meant to kill me on the Hunt?" he concluded for her.

She caught her lower lip between her teeth and nodded. "To keep Rorjak from returning."

"And you came to warn me?"

She nodded again.

"Why?" His voice had gone husky.

She shivered. The question danced across her skin like the electric purple glow that came when she called the lightning.

Such a dangerous word, "why." Because so often its answer led to places a person didn't want to go. Vulnerable places.

"Wynter, I—" She risked another glance up at him. His features—normally so stern and severe—had softened into an expression that made her chest grow tight. Her gaze skittered away to a point over his shoulder.

The wind from her storm was still blowing. Drifts of snow shifted and moved, looking almost alive.

She frowned. Odd. One of the drifts seemed to be moving *against* the wind, rather than with it. Her mouth went dry as twin beads of glowing scarlet flashed against the stark white of the snow.

She grabbed Wynter's shoulders. "Get down!"

With Khamsin still clutched in his arms, Wynter dropped and spun just as the *garm* sprang towards them. He pressed one of her ears tight to his chest and covered the other with his hand, curling his body protectively around her, as the *garm*'s paralyzing shriek rang out, followed by the blue-white cloud of freezing vapor.

The scream shivered through him like vibrations through glass, and frost prickled across his back. Another man would have been incapacitated, but Wynter had consumed the Ice Heart. Neither the *garm*'s scream nor its freezing breath could harm him.

As soon as the *garm* passed, he flung himself upright. The coating of ice on his back shattered as he stood.

"Khamsin, get back in the cave." He set her down and shoved her behind him, keeping his body between hers and the *garm*'s.

"No, I—"

"Now!" He cut off her protest with a curt, barked command and yanked Gunterfys from its sheath. The *garm* had spun around and was coming back for a second pass. "I can't fight the *garm* and defend you, too, without getting us both killed. Now get into the cave!" He cast one, quick glance over his shoulder. "Please, Summerlass."

He didn't dare watch to be certain she obeyed. The *garm* was already upon him. He spun and sliced as the *garm* leapt, claws outstretched. Burning cold raked his chest, and the beast howled.

The *garm*'s claws ripped through his leather armor like butter and dug deep, burning furrows across his chest. Wyn put a hand to his chest. It came away damp with blood.

Only his blood no longer ran red but violet, and it was cold to the touch. Colder than it had ever been before.

A furious snarl snapped him back to attention. Wyn saw with satisfaction that his was not the only wound struck. The *garm* was limping. Freezing deep blue droplets of the monster's blood dripped down its left foreleg. It was snarling, its lips pulled back, the rows of dagger-sharp teeth gnashing together with audible clicks. Glowing red eyes fixed upon him with unmistakable malevolence as the creature paced around him on the icy lake, waiting for an opening to attack.

Strangely, the sight filled him with hope. He might have drunk the Ice Heart, might already be more than halfway to his doom, but he still remained mortal enough that the *garm* considered him prey.

He gripped Gunterfys more securely and crouched for the beast's next attack.

"Wyn! To your left! Your left!" Khamsin shouted the alarm.

He had heard the scratch of claws on ice and was already spinning to meet the rush of a second *garm*.

Two *garm*? Two? *Garm* were solitary hunters. He'd never heard of a Winterman encountering two at once. Three, if you counted the one he'd already slain.

Wyn rolled to one side, swinging Gunterfys in a wide circle as he went in an effort to gut or at least wound both beasts as they passed overhead. The drops of freezing cold that landed on his skin told him he'd struck a blow.

The sound of crumbling rocks made him look up.

Wyrn save him! Yet another *garm* stood on the lip of the cliff. The fourth *garm* was snarling, fangs bared, claws digging into the ice as it prepared to spring.

He came up sliding on the ice, but there again the dark power of the Ice Heart flowing through his veins stood him in good stead by granting him more traction than he'd thought possible. He leaned forward, putting pressure on his toes, and his backward slide slowed, then stopped altogether.

A flash of dark near the mouth of the cave made him swear and scowl. "Damn it, Khamsin! Get back in the cave!"

She wasn't completely out in the open, just crouched too close to the opening to be truly safe. Not that she, fool woman, seemed concerned about her own safety.

Regrettably, not his either.

He saw her eyes widen just before claws raked down his back. He fell forward onto the ice, and it was only by the grace of Wyrn that he managed to keep hold of Gunterfys as he fell.

The fourth *garm* sprang from the cliff and landed on the

lake directly in his path. The other two leapt towards him from opposing sides.

Wyn twisted to one side, rolled, and popped to his feet as the three *garm* converged. Gunterfys flashed. He spun in a tight circle, not daring to leave his back open to attack. But even in constant motion, even with Gunterfys swinging, thrusting, parrying in constant attack and defense, the *garm*'s sharp claws and sharper teeth ripped through his leather armor and shredded his flesh. Violet blood streamed from his wounds, soaking his garments.

A slash across his thigh dropped Wyn to one knee. He thrust his sword back, over his head to defend against a death bite to the back of his neck, but that bared his chest for a raking blow from the *garm* in front of him.

Muscle shredded as the *garm*'s claws scraped against bone.

He bared his teeth and roared. With every ounce of energy he could muster, he brought Gunterfys arcing over his head and drove the sword hilt deep through the *garm*'s skull.

Its limbs splayed, body twitching spasmodically in death throes.

Teeth clamped hard on his left arm. With his arm locked in its jaws, the *garm* shook its massive head, yanking him off his feet. The other *garm*'s claws raked across his belly. Fire exploded in his abdomen. If he didn't get free of the *garm* holding him by the arm, the pair of them would rip him in two. With his free hand, he punched the monster in its nasal slits and clawed at its eyes. The jaws released, and he went flying.

He heard Khamsin cry his name.

The ice came up fast, and he hit hard. He skidded across the ice, leaving streaks of rapidly freezing violet blood in his wake.

Momentum sent him skidding up the small embankment at the edge of the lake. Gripping his torn belly with one hand, he managed to push himself up on his other hand and his knees and start an awkward, three-legged crawl towards the surrounding forest.

Panting, claws clicking on the ice, the two remaining *garm* loped towards him.

His strength was dwindling rapidly. He was losing too much blood. His thigh, chest, and arm were slashed to the bone, his belly torn open. His sword was out of reach, still quivering in the skull of the one beast he'd managed to slay. He couldn't even summon the strength to stand. Each attempt made agony rip through him while gouts of violet blood gushed from his wounds.

He was done, and he knew it.

It was all he could do to lift his head and face his death head-on.

As Wynter fought the garm, Khamsin cast about the cave, looking for something—anything—to use as a weapon. She found a few rocks, but most were too heavy to throw or too small to be of much use. She snatched up an armful of stones anyways and hurried to the mouth of the cave to throw them, but the rocks fell shy of their targets. She shouted and waved her arms, trying to distract the *garm*. She didn't dare step foot out of the cave because she knew Wynter would sacrifice his own life to keep her safe.

No one had ever risked their life for hers.

No one.

And yet this man, this Winter King, this supposed enemy from the north, had taken on not one but four of the most dangerous monsters in the world to save her.

Khamsin had spent all her life in a fury. Always fighting, rebelling, raging against something. A harsh, hateful parent, her own tempestuous nature, her fears, and her failings.

She'd never known this. The feeling that clamped so hard around her heart it hurt. Whatever it was made her shake, not with fury, but with humility and fear. Fear for someone other than herself.

He—Wynter, her husband—was willing to die so she might live.

Her heart soared when Wynter drove Gunterfys into one of the *garm*'s head, only to sink when one of the remaining beasts sank its teeth into Wynter's arm and tossed him about like a rag doll. Wynter fought back, his free hand curled in a fist that pummeled the beast until it gave one last shake of its gargantuan head, roared, and sent Wynter flying across the lake.

"Wynter!" She screamed his name and lunged forward, gripping the black stone edges of the cave's mouth.

The remaining *garm* loped after him. She could see Wynter struggling to rise, unable to do more than push himself to his hands and knees, his head drooping between his shoulder blades. He was badly wounded. There was no chance he could make an escape, much less fight off the two approaching *garm* bare-handed.

Once the beasts reached him, he would die.

A strange buzzing filled her ears. Khamsin wasn't conscious of moving. She just did. One moment, she was clinging to the mouth of the cave, the next she was staggering across the ice and shouting to get the *garm*'s attention.

Her ploy worked. The *garm* turned her way.

Freezing, blue-white slime dripped from gaping, razor-toothed maws that grinned at her with evil eagerness. The huge bodies began to lope towards her, picking up speed with each step.

Khamsin reached the snowy shore and began to run, leading the monsters away from Wynter.

She raised her arms as she ran, fingertips reaching for the sky, calling upon her gifts with every ounce of power in her, holding nothing back. The storm overhead exploded, clouds boiling out as thick and black as the ash cloud of an erupting volcano. Lightning cracked in a ferocious display. The air around her went violet and half a dozen bolts shot straight towards her.

The lightning speared her, lifting her off her feet in

a blinding flash of searing, brilliant white. Her head fell back, her arms flung out. Tongues of flame raced through her veins. Torn flesh knit together. The air left her lungs, and her mind, her consciousness, went with it, riding the lightning into the sky, joining the storm. Becoming part of its wild, raw, power.

Always she'd been afraid of the storm. Always when the storm truly came alive, its strength had overwhelmed her and escaped her control.

But this time, Wynter's life was in her hands. If she failed, he would die. And this power of hers—this dangerous, destructive, unpredictable power she had cursed and feared all her life—was her only weapon. Her only chance to save him.

She poured everything she had into the winds, into the roiling, crashing clouds. Not trying to control the storm, but trying to set it free. To build its wildness. The air around her went pure violet, glowing, throbbing, dancing across her skin. Energy gathered—both inside her and above, in the black, seething clouds. Her hair lifted in a nimbus of lightning-streaked darkness.

The *garm* screamed, but she could not hear their paralyzing howl above the shriek of the wind. The gaping mouths spewed matching clouds of blue-white vapor.

The sky lit up brighter than a summer day. The air around her flashed blinding white as three massive ropes of lightning snaked down from the sky in the blink of an eye and speared Khamsin.

Her chest expanded on a fiery breath. Pain ripped through her. But she stood firm, absorbing the energy, channeling it through her body, down her arms, out her fingers.

Her hands shot out, fingers splayed. Lightning shot from her fingertips and leapt across the distance to the *garm*. Thunder boomed with such force, the ground shook.

The *garm*, creatures of the remotest, iciest reaches of Wintercraig, didn't even have time to scream. Fire shot deep into massive chests with devastating results. Their fluids flash-boiled into vapor, and their bodies expanded like inflated bladders. Furred skins split and viscous, blue fluid spewed from ruptured vessels.

She held the lightning, pumping the concentrated heat of the sun into the *garm*'s bodies until their fur charred and caught fire. She held it, until the beasts were engulfed in flames and the smell of burnt flesh permeated the air. Held it longer still, until the *garm*'s writhing bodies stopped moving entirely, and their blackened bones turned to ash that disintegrated and blew away on the gusting winds.

Only then did she release the lightning, discharging its remaining power into the earth and draining the volatile storm of energy until the black clouds turned gray and the hailstones mixed with freezing rain became snowflakes tumbling softly from the sky.

Then it was over. The storm dispersed.

Drained of strength, her legs turned to pudding beneath her, and she crumpled to the earth. For a moment, she lay there, dazed and struggling to catch her breath, but the determination that had driven her to call and master the storm now drove her towards Wynter.

She was too weak to stand, so she crawled on her hands and knees. Inch by inch, pushing herself by sheer force of will, she crossed the yards of frozen ground until she reached him.

He lay in a pool of violet-hued ice, still as stone and just as cold. His golden skin looked more like a translucent veil molded over a carved statue than flesh. His brilliant eyes were closed. His chest didn't appear to be moving.

"Wynter?" She laid her fingers against his throat and panicked when she found no pulse. Her only reassurance that he still lived came when she pressed a desperate ear to his chest and was rewarded with the faint, barely audible sound of his heart slowly beating.

"Wynter, I . . ."

Her voice trailed off, and with it went her last ounce of

depleted strength. She collapsed across his chest, and the world went dim.

Her last conscious thought was concern that her storm might threaten them still because she could hear the roll of thunder in the distance. And it was drawing nearer.

CHAPTER 22

Lies, Love, and Loyalties

"She's waking."

Khamsin frowned at the sound of Valik's voice. What was Wynter's second-in-command doing in her bedchamber? Her exceedingly territorial husband would not like that at all.

The thought almost made her smile, until the memories came rushing back.

The Great Hunt. Reika Villani's deceit. The *garm*.

Kham's eyes snapped open, and she sat bolt upright.

"Wynter!"

She cried her husband's name, then fell abruptly silent. She wasn't in her bedchamber. And Valik was not the only Winterman crowded around her.

She was sitting on a narrow bed in a strange room she didn't recognize. Half a dozen White Guard in full plate mail surrounded her, swords drawn, their pale eyes cold, their golden faces frozen in expressions that ranged from impassivity to outright menace.

Her chest went tight, and dread washed over her in an icy wave.

She sought Valik's face in the crowd around her and fixed her gaze on him. "What's happened? Where is Wynter? Does he live?"

All she could think was that Wynter was dead. And a sick, terrible feeling consumed her. He couldn't be dead.

Not him. Not the fierce northern king who fought Frost Giants and won, who battled four *garm* with just his sword and his own fierce will.

Not Wynter.

Not her husband.

Not the man she—she—

"Valik!" she cried. "Tell me what's happened to Wynter!" She lunged forward, rising up on her knees, only to gasp in pain and spin abruptly to one side when one arm was nearly wrenched from its socket. "What in the name of—" Her voice broke off.

A metal cuff circled one wrist. And that cuff was attached to a short length of metal chain that tied her to the wooden frame of the bed.

"Valik!" She yanked at the chain, then turned to him in disbelief. "What is the meaning of this? Why am I chained? Where is Wynter?"

Valik ignored her questions. "What were you doing outside of the palace during the Great Hunt?" His tone was cold enough to freeze water.

"*What?*"

"The king ordered you to remain within the walls of Gildenheim until he returned from the Hunt, yet you defied him. You snuck out of the palace and rode into the forests without guard or escort and without informing anyone of your destination or intent. You will explain yourself!"

She drew herself up, summoning every ounce of royal Coruscate arrogance she could muster. "The Queen of Wintercraig doesn't answer to you, Steward! And as I have already explained my actions to my husband, I am quite certain you are not interrogating me on his command. Now, where is Wynter? I order you to take me to him!"

In a flash, Valik's sword was under her chin, the point pressed against her throat. The other guards raised their swords, too.

"Three days ago, a Calbernan army landed an invasion force in Summerlea, led by your brother, the thief and murderer, Falcon Coruscate. Your father and his generals have escaped their confinement and are presumably on their way to join the Calbernans. And the very day those forces made landfall, you rode out of Gildenheim alone and for reasons unknown."

"What?" Falcon had raised an army? He was waging more war?

"Given what we now know," Valik was saying, "you can understand why the king has ordered your actions thoroughly investigated."

Khamsin stared at Valik in horror. Wynter thought she had betrayed him? Even after he'd risked his life to save her from the *garm*? Even after she'd risked her life to save him, too?

She put a hand over her heart and pressed down in counterforce against the sharp, squeezing pain. *Oh, Khamsin, you fool. He's a Winterman! He protected you for the same reason he always did—because so long as you're his wife, that's his duty. And what have you done? Idiot! Fool! Ridiculous girl! You've gone and fallen in love with him.*

Her shoulders slumped, and her eyes closed in weary despair. "Take your sword from my throat, and I'll tell you whatever you want to know."

Valik must have been convinced because after a silent moment, the sword beneath her chin pulled back. A quick glance showed the others had followed suit.

Kham wrapped her free arm around her waist, holding herself tight, keeping her head bent and eyes down. Her heart was breaking.

Steady, Kham. You've survived worse. Only it didn't feel that way. Even that horrible day in Vera Sola, when her father had taken her into the dark inside the mountain and beaten her to the brink of death, she hadn't felt such despair.

"As I told Wyn—" Her voice came out rough and scratchy. Her throat was tight and dry she could barely speak. She swallowed painfully and forced herself to start again. "As I told my husband, I received a note saying his life was in danger. That people meant to kill him during the Great Hunt. I went to warn him. I thought the note was from Krysti, but instead it came from Reika Villani, and the trap wasn't for Wynter, it was for me."

Several of the men shifted. From the looks on their faces, it was clear they didn't believe her. Valik, however, remained steady and still, his gaze never leaving Khamsin's face.

"What sort of trap?"

"She led me into the forest towards the *garm,* then she attacked me. She had some sort of pronged weapon that cut like sharp claws. Said my blood would draw the *garm.* She intended them to kill me. And if Wynter hadn't come along, her plan would have succeeded."

"Yet here you stand without a scratch on you," Valik pointed out.

"Thanks to the storm. And if you don't believe me, go back to where you found me. You'll find the trail of blood leading back to the place your cousin attacked me."

"And why would she want you dead?"

Khamsin's brows shot up. "Because she wants to be Wynter's queen, of course! That's what she's always wanted."

"You lie!" one of the guards shouted.

"Wulf!" Valik snapped.

"You can't possibly believe her, Valik!" The man named Wulf shot back. "She's a Summerlander. As deceitful and murderous as the rest of her kin. Lady Reika knew better than to enter the forest during a Great Hunt! But this one"—he gestured to Khamsin with his sword—"wouldn't understand the extent of the danger. She probably thought that with the castle emptied, it was the perfect time to send word to her family, or meet with a Calbernan spy. It's more likely the Lady Reika saw her sneaking out and risked her own life to follow her and see what she was up to. And the Summerlander killed her for it."

"Sven! Ungar!" Valik snapped. "Get him out of here."

As the guards marched Wulf towards the door, Kham shook her head and turned to Valik, expecting to see realization and maybe even some hint of apology in his expression. Instead, she found him regarding her with narrow-eyed suspicion. It was the first time in a month he'd regarded her thusly.

"Valik? You can't honestly think that man's accusations are true. Reika told me Wynter's life was in danger in order to lure me out of the palace and into a trap. She's the one who led *me* into the forest. *She* attacked *me*."

When he still said nothing, she threw her hands into the air. "Oh, for Halla's sake! If I was out there meeting with enemy agents or sending secret invasion plans to my brother or whatever ridiculous thing you're accusing me of doing, why would I have stopped those two *garm* from killing Wynter?"

Valik's brows lifted. "You defeated those two *garm*? With Wynter's sword? Forgive me, but I doubt you could lift Gunterfys, much less use it to slay two *garm*."

"I'm not talking about the two *garm* Wynter killed," she retorted. "I'm talking about the other two—the ones that would have ripped him to pieces if I hadn't incinerated them."

"There were no others, you evil bitch!" Wulf shouted from the doorway.

"Sven! Ungar!" Valik roared.

"Sorry, my lord," one of the men escorting Wulf apologized. To his prisoner, he hissed, "Harm to her is harm to him, you idiot. Keep talking, and you'll find yourself chained on the glaciers for treason."

Khamsin turned her attention slowly back to Valik. She could feel the storm building inside her. They didn't know about the *garm* she'd burned to ash with her lightning. They thought there'd only been two of the monsters—both slain by Wynter. But Wynter knew how many he'd faced. If Wynter were the one who had ordered this interrogation, they would know that, too.

She looked up slowly, and she knew by the way Valik went so still that her eyes must have gone pure, shifting silver. Proof of the dangerous, lethal power gaining strength inside her.

"Where is my husband?" she demanded in a low voice. "And cease with your lies. Does he still live?"

A muscle flexed in Valik's jaw. "He lives."

"But he never sent you here. He never told you to interrogate me. He never thought I was my brother's spy."

After a long, bitter hesitation, Valik spat out the truth. "He has not awakened since we found you both."

She closed her eyes and took a deep breath. Wynter had not doubted her. He had not watched her risk her life to save him, then turned around and accused her of betrayal. Her fingers closed around the chain that tied her to the bed. Searing heat bloomed in her palm.

"Then you will take me to him. Now." Her eyes flashed. Metal clanked against the bedpost as the heat-softened links of the chain attached to her wrist pulled apart.

The Wintermen raised their swords in swift response, pointing the business ends her way in naked threat, but just as quickly, her hands shot out, fingers splayed. White-hot electricity crackled at her fingertips.

"Do not," she bit out. "I don't want to hurt anyone, but if you try to keep me from my husband even a moment longer, I'll fry you where you stand."

The guards looked to Valik for guidance, and Khamsin held his gaze, steady and fierce, until he gave a curt nod.

"Very well," he agreed. "I'll take you to him." His eyes turned wintry. "But I warn you, lady, storm gifts or no, harm him in any way, and you won't live long enough to regret it."

With half a dozen swords pointed at her back, Khamsin followed Valik down an unlit hallway and into the spacious gathering room of what appeared to be some sort of hunting lodge. Animal pelts covered the floor and rustic furniture. Antlers and other hunting trophies adorned walls fashioned from tree trunks polished and darkened with age. A fire roared in a huge stone hearth that dominated the majority of one wall.

Galacia Frey stood before the fire. She was still dressed in her white leathers from the Great Hunt. She held Thorgyll's freezing spear in one hand.

The priestess arched a brow. "I take it she convinced you?" she said to Valik.

He grimaced. "In a manner of speaking."

Galacia glanced at the melted chain dangling from Khamsin's handcuff, and the corner of her mouth curled. "So I see."

"Where is Wynter?" Khamsin interrupted. "Valik said he would take me to him." More sparks crackled at her fingertips. If this was another trap . . .

"And so he has," Galacia assured her. She gestured towards the hearth. "The king lies there. In the fire."

"In the—? Are you mad?" Khamsin gasped in horror and spun towards the hearth. The opening was as tall as she was, twice as wide, and easily six feet deep, and inside, stretched out on a raised metal grate and surrounded by orange flames, lay Wynter.

"Blessed Sun! What have you done?" Pushing Valik aside, she ran towards the hearth. She shoved her arms into the flames, intending to grab Wynter and pull him to safety, but before she could secure a grip, Galacia wrapped an arm around her waist and flung her away.

Kham came up fast, magic rising, a familiar violet glow surrounding her.

"Do not." Galacia was crouched for battle. The business end of Thorgyll's glittering crystalline spear was pointed at Khamsin. "The fire does not harm him. He is untouched. Look. See for yourself."

Still holding her magic ready, Kham inched closer to the hearth and risked a swift glance at Wynter. What she saw made her rub her eyes and move closer still. That was indeed Wynter lying on the metal grate in the center of the flames. He was naked, his flesh still torn from his battle with the *garm,* but she could see no hint of injury from the fire licking at his skin.

The flames surrounded him. The heat was searing. Yet his body seemed impervious to its fiery environment.

"What sorcery is this?" She turned to Lady Frey.

"It is the Ice Heart," the priestess replied. "It has him so firmly in its grip, fire cannot harm him now. At most, its warmth retards the final stages of the Ice Heart's conquest. It was the only option I could think of to try to keep Rorjak's essence from consuming the last remnants of Wynter's humanity. The very power that threatens to consume him also keeps him alive." Galacia's mouth turned down. "Gods do not die."

"Is there nothing you can do to revive him?"

"I? No. Not while he remains in this state. To do so would be to destroy us all."

"But you just said the Ice Heart has not fully claimed him yet."

"I said some small part of Wynter remains. And that is true, else his body would have healed itself, and the last battle would already have begun. But he is too far gone, and the power of the Ice Heart is too strong."

"If all hope was lost, you would already have slain him." Khamsin nodded to the crystalline spear clutched in Galacia's hands. "That is one of Thorgyll's freezing spears, is it not?"

Lady Frey lowered the spear and straightened up from her crouch. "You're right, Summerlander. There was one small hope that stayed my hand."

"What hope is that?"

Galacia looked up, pinning Khamsin with a gaze as sharp as the point of her spear.

"You."

"Are you sure about this?" Khamsin stood outside the hunting lodge, staring up at the rapidly darkening sky. Galacia and Valik stood beside the cabin door. "You're assuming a great deal if you think my touch alone can push back the Ice Heart."

"Valik assures me he's seen proof of it more than once," Galacia said.

Kham cast a glance over at Valik. Despite his renewed distrust of her, Wynter's second was convinced that Khamsin's gift-magic was the only fire hot enough to pull Wynter back from the brink of the Ice Heart's grip. Apparently, when Valik and his men had arrived after the *garm* attack, Khamsin was still lying across Wynter's body, where she had collapsed. According to Valik, the moment he separated the two of them, Wynter's body had grown colder, turning icy within a matter of minutes.

He'd kept Kham and Wynter together until Galacia had come up with the idea of putting Wynter's body in the fire.

Now, they all expected Khamsin to summon her storm. Only this time, they expected her to master that storm specifically to superheat her body the way she had when she'd attacked the *garm*. She'd already tried using the crackling electricity she'd managed to generate on her own, but even heat strong enough to soften metal couldn't do much more than thaw the layer of ice that formed around Wynter's body the instant they removed him from the flames.

She needed lightning, and lots of it. She needed the same fury she'd summoned to defeat the *garm*.

The door to the lodge opened, and six Wintermen walked out, carrying the metal grate that held their king. The men laid Wynter's body on the ground before her. In the short time it had taken to carry him from the hearth in the lodge to the fire, ice had already coated his skin.

Khamsin stepped closer. She couldn't get used to the sight of Wynter lying so still, his larger-than-life vitality trapped in a form as rigid and lifeless as those ice sculptures of his dead family that he had enshrined in Gildenheim's Atrium. Even those rare times when she'd awakened to find him sleeping beside her, all it took was the slightest movement, the faintest sound, to bring him snapping back to consciousness, ready for battle.

Ready to protect her from the tiniest threat.

Her. Storm. The forgotten princess hidden away like a shameful secret, the daughter reviled as much for her tempestuous nature as for the dangerous, volatile gifts that came with it.

The first crack of lightning lit the sky, and thunder boomed. Khamsin continued to feed power to the storm, stoking its volatile engine with more heat, more cold, more moisture. Her waterlogged riding skirts whipped around her legs, beginning to steam as her body temperature rapidly increased.

Wynter was the first man who'd ever championed her. The first man who'd ever stood up to her father in her defense. The only man who'd never feared what she was or what she was capable of.

But that wasn't why she loved him. That had merely cleared the path for her heart to follow. She'd started to love him the day she'd entered the Atrium and found herself looking directly into his heart. Or had it been the day in the forests of Summerlea, when he'd shed his armor, exposing himself to an assassin's arrow rather than allow his plate mail to catch on her hair and cause her discomfort? Or the day he arranged for her riding lessons, giving her her first taste of freedom?

Oh, what did it matter? Somewhere along the way, she'd begun to want more of him than mere passion. Somewhere along the way, she'd begun wanting to be not just his wife, but his love. And she'd begun to dream of giving him the child he so desired, not to save herself, but to see warmth and joy replace the icy remoteness in his eyes. Because she wanted to bring back some measure of happiness into his life, to give him the love he'd once known with his family.

To save him, the way he had saved her.

Now, here was her chance.

Kham fixed her gaze on Wynter's still face. With her focus on saving him, her mind didn't have time to worry about the deadly consequences of the storm. And that lack of fear freed her. It was almost like staring at a point in the distance until all the world went out of focus.

Her consciousness separated from her body and spread out once more into the storm, orchestrating the flows of air, encouraging the ionization that unleashed the concentrated power of the sun in the brilliant explosions of light and heat that speared the sky. For the safety of those at the lodge, she tried to keep the lightning in the clouds until the storm had grown so fierce it battered her will, wrestling for freedom.

"You should go inside now." Her voice sounded thick and deep, rumbling like thunder. She didn't know how much control she would have once she unleashed the power currently concentrated in the clouds overhead. Even with the *garm,* she'd only channeled that force—not tried to absorb it into her own body. "I don't want to hurt anyone."

Neither Valik, nor Galacia, nor any of the Wintermen budged. Khamsin didn't take her focus off the storm. She'd warned them. If they chose not to heed her, whatever happened would be on their heads, not hers.

She raised her arms. Warmth became heat. Heat became fire. Fire became a wild, consuming blaze that rushed through every cell of her body. The air around her went violet, glowing with energy. She tilted her head back, closed her eyes, and loosed the bonds holding the lightning in check.

The sky went brilliant white. A lightning bolt, thick as the trunk of a tree, shot from the sky, racing down the tendrils of plasma she'd sent up into the clouds.

Her body shuddered, arching towards the sky as the bolt speared and seared her. For one instant, her entire being seemed to dissolve and scatter to the winds. Mind, flesh, thought, breath, blood, all flew apart in a split second, only to draw back into a cohesive whole the next. She rode the heat, the pain, the wildness as the lightning's energy raced through her body, seeking an outlet. She would not give it that. Heat consumed her, hotter than the sun. She screamed in agony but held fast.

Another bolt ripped from sky to ground, shooting into her body. Then another, and another. Rain turned to sleet, then to hail. Great, plum-sized rocks of ice slammed down from the heavens.

Dimly, she heard someone shouting, "Enough! Khamsin! Enough! You'll kill us all!"

Valik clung to the trunk of a nearby tree. Khamsin watched him through a shimmering, violet-silver haze as he yelled, "Khamsin! Save Wynter!"

She continued to hold up her hands for a few moments longer, summoning more lightning. It shot to the ground, finding her unerringly. Her chest expanded on a breathless, voiceless scream. And then, she pushed out, into the heavens, sending a bolus of energy back up into the clouds, punching a hole in the center of the storm and sending the riotous clouds spinning outward at such speed that the clouds ripped apart and skidded across the sky in harmless bits.

Her skin was incandescent. A near-blinding glow suffused her, illuminating her flesh from the inside out. She could see the faint traceries of her veins, not blue or red, but shining golden white, as if her very blood had turned to liquid sunlight.

She fell to her knees beside Wynter. The ice had formed an inch-thick shell around his body, and his golden skin had taken on a bluish white tint beneath it. She reached out slowly. The power inside her was so hot, she was afraid to touch him for fear she might incinerate him as she had the *garm*. But as her glowing hands hovered over his body, the thick layer of ice enveloping Wynter began to melt, providing the answer she sought. She didn't need to touch him or unleash the concentrated lightning inside her. Her proximity alone was enough.

She passed her hands over his prone form. Icemelt dripped off of him in runnels. She noticed as she did so that her own body was cooling as his warmed. The blue-white tint of his skin faded a little more with each pass. When she was certain her touch would not burn him, she laid her entire body atop his, so that the remaining heat inside her could radiate into his thawing flesh. Closing her eyes, she laid her head upon his chest, threaded her fingers through his, and covered the white wolf on his wrist with her Summerlea Rose.

How long she lay there, she didn't know. Possibly minutes. Possibly hours. Time had no meaning until the moment she heard the first faint throb of sound in her ear. Several long moments later, she heard a second throb follow the first. Now each second of silence seemed to last a century as she waited for the next faint pulse of sound. The next pulse came, a fraction sooner than the last. Then another and another, until a steady rhythm tapped in her ear.

Wynter's heart was beating once more.

The cold, stiff fingers threaded through hers flexed. Barely more than a twitch of movement, but she felt it all the same.

She lifted her head and held her breath as she watched him. His lashes fluttered, lids lifting slowly. She laid her palm against the side of his face, stroking his skin lightly. He was still cold—so, so cold—but his flesh no longer felt like it was carved from an unyielding block of ice.

"Wynter . . . husband." A smile trembled on her lips.

He stared at her for a moment with blank incomprehension, dazed, as if he didn't recognize her. But then, he blinked. His lips moved, forming a soundless word. *Wife.*

Tears sprang to her eyes. "Yes, husband. It's me, Khamsin, your wife." She leaned closer, brushing kisses across his cold skin. "You worried us all."

His lips moved again in another soundless word. *Where?*

"We're at your family's hunting lodge, near the skating pond. You saved us from the *garm*, but were badly hurt in the process. Valik and the Hunters found us. We are safe now, Wynter. You made sure of that." She'd never reassured another person in her life. Never had cause to do so, but the words tumbled out so naturally, the need to put him at ease seemed as necessary as breathing. And she couldn't stop running her hands over his skin, touching him, feeling terrible, icy cold fade as mortal life returned to him.

His body shifted, as if he were trying to rise, but a groan slipped from his lips, and his face creased in pain. Then, to her horror, his eyes rolled back in his head, he gave a ragged sigh, and his body went completely limp.

"Wynter?" She shook him. "Husband?" He didn't respond. Fear rose, swift and hard. She shook him again and shouted for help. "Galacia! Valik!"

The pair were at Wynter's side in an instant.

"He has lost more blood than most could survive, and this wound across his belly is worrisome. The intestine was cut. The risk of deadly infection is very high." Galacia flicked a grim gaze at Khamsin, then turned to Valik. "We need to get him back inside immediately."

"You said if I called the lightning, that would save him."

"From the Ice Heart. And you did—at least temporarily. But these are deadly wounds. Now that his flesh is mortal once more, his wounds have the power to kill him. If I can't heal him, he may still die."

"What?" Outrage boiled up inside Kham. "Why didn't you tend his wounds earlier?"

Galacia gave her a sharp look. "You felt him. His body had turned to ice. How could I tend him in that condition? How could I stitch through skin hard as stone?"

"And now?"

"Now we put my healing abilities to the test."

Kham found herself shunted aside as the men hoisted Wynter up and carried him back into the lodge. Kham stared after them, trying desperately to quell the knot of fear rising in her throat. Wynter could still die.

"Valik." She caught the Steward's arm. "We need

Tildy—Tildavera Greenleaf—my old nurse. There's no better healer in all of Summerlea, possibly all of Mystral. I've seen her bring soldiers back from the brink of death, when every other healer said they could not be saved."

"She's the one who came to our camp, isn't she? The one who sold Wyn on the idea of marrying one of your father's daughters." He gave a derisive snort. "No."

She reached for him again. "Listen to me. I know you don't trust her—or me, for that matter—and I don't care. If Galacia can save Wynter on her own, you won't need to let Tildy anywhere near him. But if she can't . . ." She let her voice trail off.

Valik shook his head. "Even if I said yes, it would take weeks to get word to Vera Sola then get her here. Wynter doesn't have that kind of time."

"No, it won't." Galacia looked up from Wynter's side. "She's already on her way to Gildenheim. Wynter sent for her ten days ago."

"What?" Valik and Khamsin said in unison. They looked at each other, then both turned back to Galacia.

"Wynter sent for Tildy?"

"He never told me that," Valik burst out at the same time.

Laci leveled a stern glance on Valik. "If your king has ceased to confide in you, Valik, perhaps you should look to your own heart for the reason why." Then with a haughty sniff, she added, "He sent for Tildavera Greenleaf because he thought Khamsin would want a familiar face to attend her during her pregnancy."

"My . . . *what*?" Kham's jaw dropped. "Who said I'm pregnant?"

Galacia's brows shot up. "Are you telling me you didn't know?" Her lips tightened, and she glared at Wynter's unconscious face. "I love you dearly, Wynter Atrialan, but you are a great lunkheaded lummox of a man." To Khamsin, she said, "You have been suffering spells of dizziness, yes? Feeling a little queasy at mealtimes?"

"Yes, but—"

"Your scent has changed, too. Wynter pointed it out to me. He said he'd noticed a similar change when you first arrived at Gildenheim, but he didn't realize what it meant until after we discovered what that Rosh woman had done. Your body is changing, thus altering your scent, making you dizzy, and making you queasy, because you are with child."

Khamsin felt dizzy now. She grabbed the back of a chair to steady herself and laid a hand on her still flat belly. "But how can that be?"

Galacia arched an expressive brow. "Considering that you and Wynter have been mating like a pair of mink the last six weeks, I'm assuming that's a rhetorical question?"

Kham grimaced and rolled her eyes. "You know what I mean. Are you sure? There is no mistake?"

"You've had no bleeding since Belladonna Rosh was sent to the mercy of the mountains, have you?"

Kham's face went hot. Mortified to have Valik and all the other men in the room listening to the intimate details of her bodily functions, she shook her head.

"Then there's no mistake. By the end of summer, you'll give birth to the next heir to the Winter Throne. Congratulations, my queen, and please don't tell Wynter I was the one who informed you. He must have been waiting for you to realize the truth and tell him yourself."

"I think I need to sit down." Kham circled around the chair she was clinging to and sank down upon it. She was going to have a child. *A child. Hers and Wynter's.*

"Anyways," Galacia continued briskly, "the point I was trying to make is that Tildavera Greenleaf is at least halfway here by now—probably closer. And if she's as good a healer as Khamsin says, then we should bring her here posthaste."

Kham lifted her head. "Find her, Valik. Bring her here." She took a deep breath and squared her shoulders. "That's not a request. That's a command from your queen."

It was a gamble, forcing him to acknowledge her rank or

strip her of it before the White Guard. If he denied her, she wasn't sure what she'd do. But she was done being the foreigner in their midst. It was past time all of them accepted that she was here to stay.

After several long, tense moments, Valik bowed before her. "Yes, my queen."

Khamsin brushed a cool, damp cloth gently across Wynter's forehead. In the three days since she'd driven back the effects of the Ice Heart, the infection Galacia feared most had set in. A putrescence of the belly, caused by a mix of the slash to Wynter's intestine and the poison carried in the claws and fangs of the *garm*.

Fever raged in the body that had only days before been frozen solid.

Wynter lapsed in and out of consciousness as the infection spread through his veins. Around the wound, his golden skin had turned an angry purplish red, with streaks of inflamed color radiating outward, and his breathing had become shallow and labored. He was clinging to life by a thread, growing weaker by the hour.

If they didn't find a way to draw out the infection soon, he would die.

"Khamsin . . ." Wynter muttered her name as his head tossed on the pillow stuffed with fragrant herbs.

"I'm here, husband." She leaned down to press her lips to his burning forehead. Her fingers squeezed his hand. "I'm right here beside you."

". . . Khamsin . . ." His brows drew together. ". . . the *garm* . . . must save . . ."

"You did save me. I'm right here beside you. You slew the *garm,* husband. We are both safe. They cannot hurt us anymore." She stroked the silvery white hair back from his temples. "Come back to me, Wynter. Please. I . . . need you."

The door to the hunting lodge opened. A burst of cold air swirled through the opening. Valik entered, his boots caked with snow.

"She's here."

Kham turned. "Tildy?"

"Aye. And I pray she's as good as you say she is."

She leapt to her feet and ran outside just as two dozen armed and armored riders came galloping up. Tildy, bundled in so many layers she looked like a stuffed swan, was clinging to the back of one of the riders. Two of Valik's men reached up to help her out of the saddle.

"Tildy!" Khamsin started towards her old nursemaid, then hesitated. For days, she'd been wondering how this reunion would go. She'd been so hard and unforgiving over Tildy's role in her marriage.

But when those old eyes fell upon her, Tildy's arms opened wide. "Dearly!" The face Kham had never thought to see again beamed out from its nest of dark woolens and furs. Then Tildy's arms were around her, and the familiar scent of lemon verbena filled her nose.

"Oh, Tildy, I've missed you." Her own arms came up to pull Tildy close and hold her tight. Kham squeezed her eyes shut against threatening tears as a tumult of emotions welled up. "I'm so glad you're here. Wynter is very ill. Nothing we've tried has worked. The infection grows stronger by the day."

"Of course. Just let me get my things."

"The men will bring your belongings."

Tildy and Khamsin both turned to find Valik close beside them. He was regarding Tildy with the same cold suspicion he'd heretofore reserved for Khamsin.

"Valik, this is Tildavera Greenleaf, my former nurse. Tildy, this is Valik Arngildr, Wynter's Steward of Troops."

"We've met," he said. "Several times, as a matter of fact."

To Tildy's credit, she held his gaze without faltering. "Indeed, sir. I remember the occasions well."

"The question is, who do you spy for now, Nurse Greenleaf?"

"No one, my lord. My days of intrigue are over. I have come only to serve my princess."

"Your queen."

"Pardon?"

"To serve your queen. Khamsin is no longer your princess. She is Queen of the Craig and of Summerlea."

Tildy blinked. "Of course. I but spoke from the habit of years."

Valik inclined his head, his expression inscrutable. "The king lies this way."

Kham gave Valik a questioning look, surprised by his unexpected defense of her position. His response was a curt nod and a stiff bow. One arm extended towards the door in an invitation for her to precede him.

Well, that was interesting. Among themselves, Valik still suspected Khamsin of being her brother's spy, but with outsiders, he circled the spears. Shaking her head in bemusement, Kham led the way into the lodge.

As the men carried in Tildy's bags and boxes of supplies, Khamsin introduced Tildy to Galacia, and Laci brought Tildy up to speed on Wynter's condition and all the remedies they had already attempted.

Tildy listened intently, interrupting only to ask an occasional question. When Galacia finished, Tildy approached Wynter and began her own examination. She inspected the stitched slashes and bite marks that scored his chest, legs, and arms, rolled him to his side to examine the wounds on his back, and gently probed the gaping, infected wound in his belly. Pus and violet-tinged blood seeped out in response to the slightest pressure.

"You say the creature that made these wounds carried poison in its fangs and claws?"

"The *garm*," Galacia confirmed. "Yes. The poison is so lethal, most men would have died within a day of receiving even the least of the king's injuries."

"Is that poison to blame for the strange hue of his blood?"

Galacia hesitated, then said, "No. That is a separate issue."

Tildy looked up sharply. "A separate issue? What sort of issue? What else ails him beside the wounds and poisoning?" She frowned as Khamsin and Galacia exchanged glances. "If you expect me to heal him, you must tell me everything you know about his condition. The smallest detail might be the key to saving his life."

Once, not so long ago, Khamsin would have answered Tildy without a second thought, but these months in Wintercraig had changed her. Her heart—her loyalty—lay here now, tied to the man she had wed. No matter what his feelings for her, no matter what the outcome of their marriage, she would not betray his secrets.

"Galacia is right, Tildy. The color of Wynter's blood has nothing to do with the infection. If anything, the cause of it has probably done more to keep him alive this long than all our potions and poultices. For now, just focus on curing the infection. If he does not soon show signs of improvement, we can talk again."

Kham knew Tildy wasn't happy to be left in the dark, but except for a slight tightening of her lips, the Summerlea nurse was careful not to show it.

"Very well, I'll work with what I can see and what information you feel comfortable in sharing. You were wise to leave this wound open." Tildy gestured to the hole in Wynter's abdomen. "Whoever stitched the torn intestine has a fine hand, but once the intestine is ruptured, controlling the putrefaction is nearly impossible. How often are you irrigating the wound?"

"Every four hours."

"Make it once an hour. I will mix up a special wash to use, as well as poultices to draw out the poison. If he doesn't improve within four hours, I will need to cleanse the entire cavity."

"Tildy." Kham laid a hand on the nurse's shoulder and waited for her to look up. "Can you save him?"

Tildy met Khamsin's gaze with unflinching directness, and admitted, "I don't know. I won't pretend his condition is anything less than dire. But I promise you I will use every bit of knowledge and skill I possess to do so."

The tireless efforts Galacia and Khamsin had been making the last week were nothing compared to the relentless regimen Tildy instituted. In no time, she had Khamsin, Galacia, and every Winterman in the lodge jumping to attention whenever she spoke. They rushed to and fro at her command, fetching whatever items she requested, stoking the fire, assisting whenever she needed another pair of hands.

Valik watched Tildy like a hawk. His suspicious gaze followed each move Tildy made, but the Summerlea healer just bustled about with her usual, focused efficiency, whipping up potions and poultices as if she were safely ensconced in her own apothecary.

She set four great pots boiling on the hearth, each containing a different concoction of herbs, crushed minerals, oils, and various ingredients from the satchels she'd brought with her, as well as other fresh items she sent the men to fetch from the forest and nearest village. She added long strips of linen to one of the boiling pots, handed Galacia a stick, and told her to stir.

"The antiseptic solution must soak the linen fibers completely."

While Galacia stirred, Tildy handed Khamsin a mortar and pestle and ordered her to crush a cup of linseeds, and a dozen cloves of garlic into a paste. Beside Kham, Tildy busied herself grating the bark of a slippery elm into powder.

"I had hoped to find you with child," Tildy murmured as they worked. "You have been here five months, newly wed. As a daughter of the Rose, your fertility is guaranteed. Has your husband failed to attend you?"

The question made Kham's jaw drop. "No, of course not! He has 'attended' me very well—" She broke off, blushing. She glanced over at Valik, who was talking quietly to one of the guards, and lowered her voice. "If you're looking to cast blame for my lack of quickening, look no further than Verdan Coruscate. On his command, the Summerlea maid who accompanied me to Wintercraig was secretly dosing me with tansy. We only recently discovered the truth."

"He wouldn't . . ." Tildy breathed.

"There was a child, Tildy. She killed it."

Horror filled Tildy's eyes. "Oh, dearly, no." She caught Khamsin's arm. "Oh, my dear. I don't know what to say."

Her news about the child she was now carrying was on the tip of her tongue when Valik noticed them whispering and came over.

"Is there a problem?" Valik stopped near the corner of the hearth, one hand resting on the sheathed sword at his hip.

"No," Kham said, as Tildy turned her attention back to the herbs she was preparing. "No problem. Tildy was just asking after my health."

"This is ready," Tildy announced. She took the bowl of garlic and linseed paste from Khamsin and added a measure of castor oil and the slippery elm bark she'd just grated into a fine powder. After mixing the ingredients, she smeared a thick layer of the gooey paste on a square of boiled cheesecloth.

"Fetch your men," she ordered Valik. "You must hold your king down to keep him from struggling. This next part will not feel pleasant."

Valik and five tall, muscular Wintermen ringed Wynter and gripped his limbs. Once they were in place, Tildy poured a steady stream of hot, pungent liquid into the suppurating wound in Wynter's belly. With a roar, he surged up against the hands holding him down. He writhed, muscles bulging, shouting curses and threats while Valik and the others gritted their teeth and fought to keep him down, their own bodies straining with the effort to keep him under control. Wynter's head thrashed, strands of sweat-soaked hair whipping about. The bandage tied over his eyes slipped free and fell to the floor. His eyes opened. The irises had turned a cold, deadly white.

"His Gaze!" Valik cried. "Quickly! Cover his eyes!"

The man closest to Wynter's head reached for the bandage, only to cry out as his fingers went white with frost.

"Wynter!" Abandoning her place by Tildy's side, Khamsin lunged towards the head of the table. She snatched the bandage off the floor and laid it across Wynter's eyes, holding it in place by gripping either side of his head. "*Hossa, min mann*. I'm here. Be calm. Let us help you." She crooned soothing words, but Wynter continued to struggle.

His arm broke free, and he surged up on the table, lifting several men off their feet until two more rushed forward to grab his flailing wrist and pin him back down on the table.

"You!" she barked to one of the men standing near the cookpots. "Come hold this bandage in place."

When the man took her place, she raced around to the side of the table and shoved between the men holding Wynter's arm.

"Let go of his wrist," she commanded. "I've got him." She clasped her husband's hand and pressed the warm red Rose on her wrist against his wolf's head. Energy flared around them in a palpable burst. Wynter's flailing struggles ceased abruptly.

In the still silence, Khamsin clung to him. She folded their joined hands together beneath her as she bent over his body and laid a free hand on his chest. "I am here, my husband. Be calm now. Let us help you. Please, I need you to live. Do you hear me?" She dragged their joined hands to her lips, kissing his strong, blunt fingers, the broad knuckles. There was so much strength—and so much gentleness—in his hands. "I need you to live." Wetness gathered in her eyes, blurring her vision. She blinked, and the tears dropped from her lashes to his skin. "I need you," she whispered into his hand.

"Quickly, Lady Frey," Tildy commanded, snapping everyone back to attention, "pull those linen strips from the pot and set them in a bowl to cool. You there, what is your name?"

"Ungar."

"Ungar, fetch two more buckets of snow. We need to irrigate this wound again."

Tildy worked with swift efficiency, irrigating the wound two more times with the boiling antiseptic wash she cooled by pouring it over snow. When she was satisfied she'd cleared out as much of the infected matter as she could, she packed the wound with the boiled linen strips, laid the linseed, garlic, and castor oil poultice over the top of that to draw any additional infection out, and covered it all with a length of cheesecloth soaked in honey to seal the wound. The whole time she worked, Khamsin remained bent over Wynter, her Rose clasped to his Wolf. That kept him docile though the Wintermen continued to hold him, just in case.

When she was finished, Tildy set out two hourglasses. A large glass that counted down the hour with a steady stream of pink sand, and a smaller glass whose blue sands ran out every twenty minutes. Three times an hour, as the blue sands ran out, she replaced the poultice and honey-soaked cheesecloth with fresh.

Every hour, when the last of the pink sand ran out, Tildy poured an unpleasant-smelling potion made from willow bark, garlic, purple coneflower root, and barberry down Wynter's throat, then summoned them all back to Wynter's side. Valik and five other men would hold him down, and Khamsin would clasp her wrist to his, while Tildy and Galacia removed the poultices and packing, irrigated the wound thoroughly, then repacked the wound with fresh, steaming strips of linen, applied a fresh poultice atop that, and laid a honey-soaked cheesecloth over the entire area.

And so it went the rest of the day, all through the night, and on through a second day. The relentless pace took its toll on all of them, except Tildy, who seemed powered by an inexhaustible supply of energy. Near midnight the second night, when the linen strips they pulled from Wynter's body came away free of infected matter, Tildy pronounced the most immediate crisis passed.

"The next few days will tell," Tildy said, "but so long as the infection does not retake a firm hold, he should pull through."

"Praise the gods." Kham slumped in relief, leaning forward to rest her forehead on Wynter's arm. His skin felt cool again.

A tender hand brushed her cheek. "You should rest, dearly. You're asleep on your feet." Tildy's voice grew crisper as she added, "In fact, all of you should seek your beds. I can manage the next few hours on my own."

"Lady Frey, you and the queen sleep," Valik seconded. "Ungar, Tol, and I will stand watch with Nurse Greenleaf. I insist," he added with cold implacability when Tildy started to object. "Go, Laci, Khamsin. I'll wake you if there's the smallest hint of trouble."

Khamsin was too exhausted to argue, so she just pushed to her feet, stumbled down the hallway to the bedroom she had been using this past week, and fell into bed. She was asleep before her head hit the lavender-stuffed pillow.

Sometime later, while the night was still dark and long before she'd slept long enough to feel rested, Khamsin found herself shaken awake.

"Wha—?" she blinked in groggy confusion.

"Here, drink this."

A wooden cup tapped against Kham's teeth. Warm liquid splashed over her lips and into her mouth. The liquid, whatever it was, had a strong, sharp flavor and a bitter aftertaste. Kham started to spit it out, but more poured into her mouth, accompanied by a command to "Swallow" and a sharp pinch to close her nostrils and ensure she obeyed.

Left with no choice, Kham swallowed, then coughed as some of the liquid went down her windpipe.

"Quickly," the same voice ordered in a hushed whisper, "we don't have much time. I dosed everyone with valerian at the evening meal, but I didn't dare use enough to keep them sleeping for long."

"Tildy?" Kham frowned up at her nurse. "What's going on? Is it Wynter?" Thinking he must have taken a turn for the worst, she leapt out of the bed.

"The Winter King is fine, but it's time for us to make our escape." Tildy shoved a woolen gown and thick, furred coat into Kham's hands. "Here, you'll need to dress warmly. We've a long way to go."

Khamsin stared at the clothes in confusion. "I don't understand. What are we escaping?"

"I'm sorry, dearly. I'm so terribly sorry. I'd heard he was an honorable man, or I should never have proposed he wed you. I never dreamed he would murder his own wife if she didn't bear him a child within the year."

Kham gaped at her nurse as her groggy mind started to make sense of what was going on. "Are you talking about Wynter?" She shook her head. "He isn't going to murder me, Tildy."

"I'm sorry, dearly, but he swore as much to your father, which is of course exactly why Verdan—may he scorch in the fires of Hel!—conspired to prevent you from conceiving a child. I thought by encouraging this marriage, I was sending you away from mortal danger, and instead, I unwittingly sent you into its very jaws. Thank the gods you sent for me before it was too late." She realized that Kham hadn't started getting dressed, and exclaimed, "Hurry, dearly! If we're not well on our way before the valerian wears off, our chance for escape will be lost."

"Tildy, I'm not going anywhere. I know what Wynter told my father, but the 'mercy of the mountains' isn't the certain death it sounds like. I'm in no danger here." Kham laid the dress and coat over the back of a nearby chair.

"You may be willing to bet your life on that, but I am not. And neither is your brother." Tildy snatched the dress up again and sifted through the long folds to find the openings for Khamsin's head and arms.

Kham stared at Tildy in shock. "You've heard from Falcon? But when? How?"

"We've been in contact since shortly after your wedding, when I found out the Winter King intended to kill you if you didn't bear his child within the year. I sent word to him when I found out I was coming here. As soon as we get away from here, I'll send him a signal, and he'll let us know where to meet him." Her face darkened with a scowl. "And you can rest assured, I'll be informing him about your father's latest crime against you. Keeping you barren so your blood would be on the Winter King's hands instead of his own. He has gone mad!" Having located the gown's neck hole, she loosely scrunched up the wool to make a circle of fabric.

"Here. Raise your arms." Tildy held up the gown, ready to drop it into place over Kham's head.

"Tildy." Kham took the dress from her, tossed it on the bed, and caught her nurse's hands. "Tildy, stop. If you sent Falcon a signal telling him we're coming, you'd best send him another one telling him there's been a change of plans. I'm not going anywhere."

"You can't mean that."

"I do. I am Wynter's wife, his queen—"

"Whom he intends to stake out on some mountain glacier and leave to die!"

Kham shook her head. "He isn't going to kill me. If that's what he wanted, I'd already be dead. The only reason he's out there on that table"—she pointed in the direction of the lodge's main room—"fighting for his life, is because of me. I was attacked by *garm*. Just one of them could wipe out an entire village, and Wynter fought off four of them to save me. Does that sound like the actions of a man who wants me dead?"

Tildy looked momentarily nonplussed, but then her shoulders squared, and her jaw firmed. "And if he doesn't survive? I've watched the others closely since I arrived. Lord Valik doesn't strike me as the trusting sort. None of them do. If the Winter King dies, they'll kill you without a second thought."

Khamsin honestly didn't know what Valik and the others would do, but that was the least of her concerns at the moment. "I won't leave him, Tildy. And I'm very sorry to have to do this, but you're not leaving either. At least not until I'm sure he's out of danger."

It took a lot to surprise Tildy, but that did. "You would hold me here against my will?"

"To ensure my husband's survival? In a heartbeat." Kham tried to soften her ruthless declaration with persuasion, reaching for her former nurse's hands and squeezing them gently. "I ordered Valik to bring you here because I knew you were the only person in the world who could save Wynter, and that's what I need you to do."

"And if I nurse him back to fitness, will you come with me then?"

Kham considered lying. Tildy would believe it because it was what she wanted to hear. But she wouldn't do that to her nurse. "No, Tildy. My place is here, with my husband and the people of Wintercraig. This is my home now. This is where I belong."

"But what about your brother? If he doesn't hear from me, he'll assume the worst."

"Are you using preset signals, or can you send him an actual message?"

"Why do you ask?"

That Tildy had answered the question with a question gave Kham all the answer she needed. "You can send messages. Good. Because, I've got one for him."

Khamsin stayed up with Tildy the rest of the night, ostensibly to assist with tending Wynter but really to make sure her nurse didn't sneak off before Valik and the others roused. Her motives left her feeling guilty and a bit vile—Tildy was the closest thing to a mother Kham had, not some enemy— but Kham kept an eye on her all the same.

Her message to Falcon had been short and sweet: Verdan gone mad. I am safe with Wynter. Stay away. We will defend Wintercraig. Storm.

Falcon and his Calbernan allies might have already invaded Summerlea, but hopefully the realization that Wintercraig had not one but two powerful weathermages to defend it would convince them to turn back.

It was something of a relief when Valik woke. He stirred groggily at first, then jerked full awake, bolting upright in his chair and scanning the room with agitated swiftness when he realized he'd dozed off. Finding nothing amiss, his golden cheeks flushed a dusky red. He didn't appear to suspect he'd been drugged, and Kham wasn't about to tell him. Wrong or right, Tildy was family. Unless she directly threatened the safety of Wintercraig, its people, or its king, Kham wouldn't betray her.

Valik cleared his throat, checked on Wynter, then went round the room kicking the other guards awake. "I was just resting my eyes," he declared gruffly when he made his way back to the hearth.

"The last weeks have been wearisome," she agreed without rancor.

Valik rubbed the back of his head, grimaced, and muttered, "Much as I hate to admit it, you were right to send for your Summerlea nurse. She has worked a miracle."

The admission startled a smile from Khamsin. "Miracles are her forte," she said. "And I don't blame you for your suspicions. You love him. You want to protect him from harm." She glanced down at Wynter and caressed his lean, golden cheek with her fingertips, brushing the snowy hair back from his temple. "I can understand that."

Her voice trailed off, and in the ensuing silence, she felt the weight of Valik's gaze. Old instincts kicked in, and she pulled her hand back, burying her softer emotions so they could not be used against her. She took a step away from the cot where Wynter lay. "Of course, he's not out of the woods yet. The slightest infection could destroy all our progress in a heartbeat. But Tildy says she's never seen a man so determined to live."

"He is Wynter of the Craig," Valik said as if that said it all. And perhaps it did.

A huge yawn came upon her without warning. "Sorry. Clearly, I didn't get enough sleep last night."

"Then you should return to your bed." For the first time, Valik spoke almost warmly.

"Maybe later. First, there's something I need to discuss with you and Laci. In private." Falcon had sent birds to follow Tildy. That's how she'd been able to signal him. But that also meant Falcon knew where to find Tildy—and, more importantly, where to find Wynter. Kham had thought about it all night long and realized there was no way she could keep that information a secret.

Before Valik could answer, one of the White Guard entered the cabin. "Eagle approaching."

Valik nodded. "Excuse me for a moment." He took his leave of Khamsin and headed for the door.

While Valik headed out to receive whatever report the eagle was bringing, Tildy called Khamsin to help her with the lengthy process of changing Wynter's poultices.

"He's progressing nicely," she announced when they were done. "He's not quite so rapid a healer as you, dearly, but if I can keep the king still and free of infection for another week, his chances for survival increase tenfold."

"That is indeed unfortunate, Nurse Greenleaf."

Tildy and Khamsin turned in unison to find Valik standing in the lodge doorway. He crossed the threshold and approached the hearth where Wynter lay. His expression was grim, his eyes bleak.

"Like it or not, the king must wake, and we don't have the luxury of another week to wait."

CHAPTER 23

Trust and Treasures

"Guards, protect the king. Do not allow Nurse Greenleaf to administer anything to him until I return." Valik turned to Khamsin. "Walk with me."

Not waiting for an answer, the White Sword strode out of the lodge.

Kham gaped after him. She turned to Tildy in surprise. "What's going on?" Suspicion hit hard. "What have you done?"

Tildy help up her hands. "You have my word, I've done nothing more than you already know. Now, go, quickly. See what your Lord Valik has to say."

Khamsin clamped her mouth shut and hurried after Valik. He and Laci were waiting in the clearing outside the cabin. "Come with us." They turned and walked into the woods.

Valik's and Galacia's long legs covered quite a bit of ground in a single stride, and Kham had to run to catch up to them. They strode through the snow-covered forest and ducked inside a cave a good distance from the cabin. Valik pulled a candle from his pocket and lit it while Laci turned to the mouth of the cave and sketched a design in the air. When she blew on her palm, a layer of ice grew from the rock surface inward until the entire mouth of the cave was sealed by a thick ice wall.

"What in Wyrn's name is going on?"

Galacia spun abruptly around. She clutched Kham's shoulders in a painful grip, her blue nails like talons. "Tell me true, Summerlander, where do your loyalties lie? And I warn you, I will know if your words are false."

Khamsin drew back, offended by both the manner and implication of Galacia's question. "I thought we'd gotten past all this. I'm not a spy."

"That's not what I asked. I asked where your loyalties lie."

"I am Wynter's wife."

"Unwillingly wed," Valik pointed out.

She speared him with a sharp glance. "Perhaps at first," she conceded. "But no longer."

"And if you had to choose between Summerlea and Wintercraig?" Galacia asked. "Between Winterfolk and your family?"

Khamsin wet her lips. Unease curled in her belly. "The eagle that flew in this morning. What news did he bring?"

"Answer the question," Valik snapped.

"I already have," Kham snapped back. The repeated demands to prove her loyalty and devotion to Wynter had grown beyond wearisome. "Time and time again."

"Then once more won't hurt, will it?"

"Oh, for Halla's sake!" Khamsin cried. "This is my home now! More of a home than Summerlea ever was. Is that what you wanted to hear? That my life there was so pathetic, my existence so miserable, that I am happier here—even living under a constant cloud of suspicion and doubt—than I ever was there?"

"And if you must choose, between your family and Wynter," Galacia prodded, "who would you choose?"

"Wynter, damn you! I would choose Wynter!"

"Why?"

Kham's knuckles went white. The words welled up in her throat. They spat from her lips in a fury, each word clear and distinct, no longer bound in silence as they had been in her dreams.

"Because I love him!"

Galacia bowed her head and slowly relaxed her fierce grip on Kham's shoulders. "Thank you. I told Valik as much, but we both needed to hear you say it."

Kham spun around and clasped shaking hands across her chest. She loved him. And she'd revealed that vulnerability out loud. To Galacia and Valik.

She swallowed hard and rasped, "What news did the eagle bring?"

"Our defenses in Summerlea have been defeated. Wintercraig is next."

Kham's breath caught in her throat. She spun back around. "Tell me."

Quickly, Galacia relayed the grim news. Leirik's defenses along the west coast of Summerlea had been overrun by the Calbernans. Aware of Wynter's illness and desperate to delay the invaders to buy time for his king's recovery, Leirik had emptied Vera Sola, leading all but a few hundred of the Wintermen under his command to confront the Calbernan army. But no sooner had Leirik emptied the city of defenders than King Verdan, General Furze, and what remained of the former army of Summerlea had retaken Vera Sola. From there, Verdan's army marched north to join the Calbernans and a force of mercenaries. Leirik and his men put up a strong fight, but cut off from supplies, flanked on two sides and vastly outnumbered, they had been defeated.

"The invaders are even now sailing up the coast," Galacia concluded. "We believe they mean to take Gildenheim."

"What can be done?"

"Very little. Without Wynter and his Ice Gaze, there aren't enough soldiers left to push back a force so large. A contingent of men ride out within the hour to sound the Valkyr's horn in Gildenheim to summon to service every man, woman, and child old enough to hold a spear."

"Women and children? Against the armies of Calberna and Summerlea? Are you mad? They'll be slaughtered!"

"Better an honorable death in battle than life in slavery."

Khamsin gave a choked laugh, recalling the day she had spoken almost the exact same words to Tildy. That day now seemed a lifetime ago. The Khamsin who'd so passionately spat her defiance was practically a stranger to the Khamsin who now stood before Galacia Frey.

"I once believed the same as you do," she admitted. "I would gladly have died fighting rather than surrender Summerlea to your people. But if I had, I never would have known what it was to marry, to love. To be happy. Surely even the smallest measure of hope is better than the certainty of death?"

"You have suffered your father's mercy all your life." Galacia's gaze flicked to the imprint of the Summer King's signet burned into Kham's cheek. "Would you really wish that on anyone else?"

"That's different. He hates me. He blames me for my mother's death. He always has."

"And you're his own kin. What do you think he will do to Wynter? To me? To Valik? To the child you're carrying in your womb? King Verdan has been trying to bleed Wintercraig dry and starve its people into submission since the day Wynter ascended the throne. What do you think he'll do to us once we have no defenses?"

Kham dropped her gaze, unable to argue the point. "If you truly believe sending all of Wintercraig into battle is the right course of action, then why are we standing here? What do you need me for?"

Galacia hesitated, then admitted, "When the men ride to Gildenheim to sound the Valkyr's horn, we want you to go with them."

She glanced between Laci and Valik. "I'm not leaving Wynter."

"You must. He's in no shape to fight the armies assembled against us. Even if he were well, you saw for yourself how close he is to losing his battle with the Ice Heart. We dare not let him use his Gaze again, but without it, we stand no chance of defeating the invaders."

"All the more reason for me to stay here with him." Kham didn't see where this was leading.

"There is one weapon we have left. A weapon the invaders will not expect from us."

"Laci—" Valik gave her a warning frown.

She held up her hands to silence him. "It's the only choice, Valik. Without her, we're doomed, and you know it. This way, we at least have a chance." Turning back to Khamsin, Galacia said, "What do you know about the Book of Riddles?"

Khamsin frowned. What was Galacia up to? "I know that it's reputed to contain clues to the location of Roland's sword. It's what my brother was after when he was here in Wintercraig."

"Among other things," Valik confirmed in a flat voice.

Galacia grimaced at him. "Yes, he took the Book. And it does contain clues leading to the location of Roland's sword. Your brother has spent the last three years deciphering and following those clues."

Kham's mouth went dry. If Falcon had been on the trail of the sword, and now he had amassed an army to attack Wintercraig and reclaim Summerlea . . .

"Falcon has found the sword?" That was the only thing that made sense. He was bringing his army to Wintercraig because he had the sword and was planning to use it to wrest control of Summerlea back from Wynter.

"No, he hasn't. Not yet. The location in the Book of Riddles does exist, but the sword was moved from there nine hundred years ago."

"How do you know that?"

"Because for nine hundred years, the High Priestesses of Wyrn have kept the new location of the sword a secret."

"You're saying you know where the Sword of Roland is?"

"Yes." Galacia took a deep breath, then admitted, "Roland's sword is in the Temple of Wyrn, at the bottom of the Ice Heart."

Khamsin gaped at her. "If that's true, and the priestesses

have been keeping the secret for nine hundred years, then why are you telling me now?"

"Because we need you to get it," Valik said.

Waking was a fight, a slow, clumsy slog through layers of thick, clinging mud. Wynter was exhausted beyond all comprehension, and pain throbbed from every quadrant of his body. He wanted to sink back into the soft, comforting blackness of sleep, but some inexplicable sense of disquiet forced him to rouse.

His eyelids were heavy as lead. Each fluttering attempt to open them sapped his strength, and the darkness called him back with a siren's song. *Rest, Wyn. Sleep. Let it go. Let it all go.*

But beneath that hypnotic, oh-so-tempting whisper, a restless tension gathered in his limbs. It crawled through him like a thousand stinging ants.

With a groan, he forced his eyes open.

Blackness greeted him.

At first, he thought it must be night, moonless and lampless. But he could smell burning wood and feel the warmth of a fire whispering across his skin. Fire meant light. Why could he not see it?

Was he blind? Had they taken his eyes to stop him from using his Gaze?

He shook his head in an involuntary denial. Please, Wyrn, not that. Without his eyes, he had no Ice Gaze, and no ability to see his foes in order to fight them. He'd be defenseless as a babe.

But then he realized that, as he shook his head, the blackness in his field of vision lightened and darkened. He became aware of the rub of cloth, tugging at his hair and skin each time his head shifted.

Something was tied around his head, over his eyes.

He reached for it, fingers fumbling at the folds of cloth to pull them away.

Hands grabbed his. "Calm, Wyn. Be calm. All is well."

The voice sounded familiar. A woman. He quit fighting to reach the bandage covering his eyes and turned his hand to grab hers. Smooth fingers. Cool, long. Slender wrist.

Something missing. Something important. Not her. Wasn't her.

Where was she?

The sense of urgency was a hammer now. Pounding. He struggled to sit up.

"I need some help here!"

Heavy footsteps pounded across a hard surface as men came running. Metal clanked. Chain rattled. Soldiers. Armored soldiers. The smell of dirt, sweat, men. More hands, much larger and stronger, grabbed his shoulders, arms, and legs, holding him down. Pinning him.

He began to fight in earnest. His body arched, his muscles strained.

"Tildy! Get in here!"

More footsteps. These lighter. Leather soles, not boots. Less weight. Shorter stride. A woman.

Was this one her?

The scent of lemon verbena filled his nostrils. Fear and fury swept through him in equal measure.

Not her! Where was she?

What had they done to her?

He roared. Despite the many hands holding him down, his body came up off the table. One arm broke free. He swung. His arm plowed into something hard and sent it flying.

Crash! A raucous clang of metal, breaking glass, many things falling.

More running footsteps. More hands grabbed his free, swinging arm and pinned it back down.

"Why is he waking? You said he wouldn't wake?"

"I don't know. I've never seen anything like it. I dosed him enough to keep ten men down."

"Well, dose him again! Quickly!"

He fought, writhing, roaring. The table beneath him tipped and scooted back and forth.

"Hold him still, damn it! Grab his head!"

Something wet and bitter poured into his mouth. He spat it out and tried to wrench his head free.

"Wyn! Stop it! We're trying to help you. Please, Wyn. Please. You're going to hurt yourself." The familiar voice sounded sad, pleading, worried.

But she was not *her*.

She was one of the ones trying to keep him from her.

He redoubled his efforts to free himself, fighting all the hands holding him down. Pain ripped through him and set his belly on fire.

Where was she? Why wasn't she here?

Had she left him?

A wave of ice swept over the fire, numbing the pain. He went still as stone.

Was that it? She had left him? Abandoned him?

Betrayed him?

"Tildy! Hurry!"

Hands grabbed his face. Pinched shut his nose. Pried open his jaw. More bitter liquid poured in.

He tried to spit that out, too, but now the hands were holding his jaw closed.

He choked, sputtered, started to fight again. The liquid ran down his throat.

Traitors! He would kill them. He would kill them all.

His limbs went heavy as stone. His struggles grew weaker. He couldn't fight. His thoughts grew hazy. But not even the drug that sapped his strength and dragged him back down into the darkness could numb the growing ache in his heart.

Where was she? Why had she left him?

Something was wrong. Very wrong.

When Khamsin and her escort passed through the village of Konundal, they found it deserted. Not a soul to be found and *garm* tracks crisscrossing the snow and slushy streets. Now Gildenheim lay before them. The outer gates were open, there were no men on the wall. Blood and the scattered remains of bodies were strewn across the road.

Ungar held out a hand, waving his men into silence and urging them all to crouch. To a man, the Guardsmen drew their bows and nocked an arrow in place, ready to draw and fire.

"Stay here, Your Grace," Ungar whispered.

"But—"

"Stay! Sven, you, Karl, Leif, and Jan stay with the queen."

Kham glowered but stayed hunkered down, off to one side of the road, while Ungar and the remaining eight of his Guard crept towards the bloody scene outside Gildenheim's gates. Clearly, the *garm* she and Wynter had killed weren't the only ones that had come down from the Craig. She counted at least three *garm* corpses, arrows prickling their hides like porcupine quills, and three times as many dead Winterfolk lying alongside them, some torn to shreds, others burned and bristling with almost as many arrows as the *garm*.

What had happened here?

Ungar and his men passed through the gates and disappeared into the lower bailey. A few minutes later, one of the men came back to wave them in.

Inside the lower bailey, the scene was as grim and bloody as outside the gate, with scores of slain Winterfolk and two more *garm*.

"They came last night, after sunset."

Kham turned to find Lord Barsul, Lady Melle, and a number of others gathered beneath the upper bailey's barbican.

"How many?" Ungar asked.

"Just the five," Lord Barsul said. "But that was enough."

"More than enough," Lady Melle added.

"Where's Krysti?" Kham interrupted, scanning the gathering crowd with worried eyes. "Is he all right?"

"He's fine, my dear," Lady Melle soothed. "Last I saw

him, he was entertaining the little ones in the upper levels of the palace. Telling them stories of Roland Triumphant and Wynter's fight with the Ice Giant—so they knew a few *garm* couldn't defeat you."

Kham smiled with relief and affection.

"Did the *garm* breach the walls?" Ungar asked Lord Barsul.

"They didn't have to. Most of the guards on the outer wall were ice thralls before we could even sound the alarm."

" 'Ice thralls'?" Kham had never heard the term before.

"A corpse possessed by living frost," Lord Barsul explained. "The *garm* killed them with their breath, and they came back as thralls."

Khamsin frowned. "I don't understand. The king and I both survived the *garm*'s breath without becoming one of these . . . ice thralls."

"Aye, but he hadn't returned then," Lady Melle said. "Now, he has."

A sinking feeling in her stomach warned Kham she wasn't going to like what Lady Melle said next, but she asked the question anyways. "He who?"

"Rorjak. The Ice King. He has returned."

CHAPTER 24

Gifts of the Gods

Leaving six guardsmen to help dispose of the dead and sound the Valkyr's horn, Khamsin and the remaining White Guard made their way up the winding mountain road to the Temple of Wyrn. Though she was screaming with mad grief in her mind, Khamsin kept putting one foot in front of the other. If Barsul was right, and the *garm* attack and men turning into ice thralls truly meant Rorjak had returned, then Wynter was lost to her. And if Wynter was lost, then Wintercraig needed her to find the sword of Roland now more than ever.

When they reached the temple, they found it as silent and deserted as Konundal had been. Their footsteps on the carved stone floor echoed in the temple's cavernous main room.

Behind Khamsin, the White Guard pulled their swords.

"I don't like this," Ungar said. "Where are the two priestesses? Lady Frey's with the king, but the other two should have returned here after the Hunt."

"The second spear is still gone." Sven nodded towards the altar at the far end of the room. The wall behind it was bare of the crossed ice spears she'd seen on a previous visit. Only the frozen mask of Wyrn remained, and Khamsin could swear the carved face of the goddess watched her approach with icy eyes. On either side of the altar, soaring archways led to sconce-lit hallways veiled by long strands of shimmering crystal beads. "Maybe they went after the *garm* that attacked Gildenheim."

"On their own?" Ungar shook his head. "I doubt it. Your Grace, wait here with me. Sven, you and the others fan out and search the place."

"But don't go through that doorway to the left of the altar," Kham added quickly.

To the left lies death. Do not cross that threshold.

The men went right through the veil of beaded strings. The beads, which resembled dewdrops frozen on threads of spider silk, tinkled like chimes when they moved, sounding a melodic alarm that echoed through the icy temple. This place might seem open and unprotected, but no intruder could pass beyond the altar room without sounding that alarm.

Several minutes later, Sven and the others returned. "Nothing. The place is deserted. No signs of struggle. Whatever happened to the priestesses, it doesn't appear to be foul play."

The White Guard still insisted on accompanying her through the private residence of Wyrn's priestesses. And truth be told, Kham was grateful for their company. With each step deeper into the heart of the mountain, her connection to the sun waned, leaving her vulnerable and defenseless.

The sooner she got what she'd come for, the sooner she could leave this place.

The last door in the hall was silver gilt and etched with swirling, diamond-studded patterns of windblown snowflakes. Pulling the key ring from her pocket, Khamsin inserted the first of Galacia's keys into the lock and turned it. The beautiful door swung inward, revealing a robing chamber the size of a small chapel.

Kham waited as the men fanned out to search the chamber and connecting rooms.

"It's clear," Sven announced when he and his men returned to the main chamber.

"Good. Now, I must ask all of you to return to the main temple and wait for me there."

Ungar frowned. "We're not leaving your side, Your Grace."

"Oh, yes, you are. What comes next is not for your eyes." There was a door in this room. A door known only to the priestesses of Wyrn. And now to Khamsin, as well.

"At least take my sword." Ungar offered his unsheathed blade to her.

"I can't." Galacia had warned her that no man or mortal weapon could survive the path Kham was about to take. "Now, please, go. You cannot accompany me farther." She waved the guards towards the exit. "If I'm not back by sunrise, then I have failed."

Grumbling, clearly unhappy at being dismissed, the guards nonetheless filed out of the chamber. Once the door was closed and locked behind them, Kham shrugged out of her coat and set to work unlacing her gown. Normally, according to Galacia, the priestesses followed a ritual of cleansing and prayer using the bathing pool, sauna, and steam rooms in the adjoining antechambers, but that was more tradition than necessity, and time was of the essence. Khamsin deposited her shoes and clothes on a bench and slipped into one of the white, hooded robes hanging from a series of wall pegs.

Barefoot and naked except for her hooded robe, she approached the small tabletop altar built into a recessed arch. Two round wall sconces with crystal shades shaped like flames flanked the tiny altar. Kham gripped the crystal sphere at the bottom of the right sconce and turned it to the left, then pulled the flames-shaped shade towards her. With a quiet hiss, the wall behind the altar slid inward and rotated sideways, revealing a secret doorway.

Inside, blue flames flickered in sconces just like the ones flanking the altar. The cool light illuminated the smooth, seamless blue-white walls of a round tunnel carved through solid ice. A puff of cold air flowed out of the tunnel into the warmer air of the private chapel. It riffled through Kham's hair and bathed her face with dry coolness.

Kham took a fortifying breath and stepped into the tunnel.

Without the sun's power to warm her, the icy chill seeped quickly into her body as she walked. Her flesh pebbled, hairs raising on her arms. Her bare feet went numb, then began to burn, but she continued, steadily placing one foot before the other. The tunnel went straight back for about a hundred yards, then curved sharply to the left.

Kham made the turn and nearly fell over the body sprawled across the tunnel floor. She recognized the younger of the two priestesses. Someone must have pierced her with Thorgyll's spear because her body was frozen solid.

So much for the assumption there'd been no foul play.

Khamsin whispered a prayer for the slain priestess, then stepped around her body to approach what looked like a sheet of glass covering the tunnel. As she neared, she realized the glass was a steady, falling sheet of crystal-clear water.

Kham hung her robe beside two others, braced herself, and stepped naked into the wall of water.

The goddess tests all who attempt to enter her domain. Whatever you do, do not scream and do not run. If you panic, you die. Galacia's dire warning made perfect sense now. *Just keep silent and keep moving.*

It was all Kham could do *not* to run. The cold was so intense, she could swear her flesh was being sliced off her bones. Not screaming was easier. She had no breath left in her lungs to make a sound. She forced herself forward, pushing her body through the falling water.

After what seemed like a lifetime, she passed through the icy veil to the open tunnel on the other side. There, the cold air of the tunnel actually felt warm against her skin. Kham continued shuffling forward until she felt a rough, woven mat beneath her numb feet. Finally, it was safe to stop.

To the left, shelves had been carved from the ice, and several pairs of white leather boots with spiked soles had been laid out in a neat row on one of the shelves. Folded, white, fur-lined robes were stacked on another. Khamsin slipped on one of the robes, tying the wraparound sashes at her waist and pulling the fur-lined hood up around her face, then she stepped into the pair of shoes closest to her size and laced them tight. The clothes were much warmer than the thin robe from the purification room, and the spikes on the bottom of the boots gripped the ice when she stepped off the mat, enabling her to walk down the next, descending stretch of icy tunnel.

This part of the tunnel went on forever, long and steep enough to make her knees and thighs ache well before she reached the bottom. It didn't take long to lose sight of the shimmering wall of water and the landing, then there was only endless, descending blue-white ice around her, broken intermittently by the occasional sconce burning its eerie, flickering blue flame. She began counting the sconces to give herself some measure of passing time.

One hundred sixty-five sconces later, the tunnel leveled off and opened to a chamber deep within the glacier on the other side of the mountain.

Khamsin thought she knew what to expect. Galacia had said there was an ice palace, like the one Wynter had taken her to during the Festival of Wyrn. Well, it was a palace, and it was made of ice. But that was where all similarities to the wintry delight she'd visited in the Craig both began and ended. The sheer enormity of what lay hidden in the glacier beneath Wyrn's temple defied description.

The Palace of Wyrn lay situated in a cavern so large it could fit the whole of Gildenheim with room to spare. Massive columns—each wide enough that ten grown Wintermen standing fingertip to fingertip would barely circle them—soared a hundred feet into the air, holding aloft a mighty pediment carved with the bas-relief figures of Wyrn and her once-mortal god-husband Rorjak. Rearing, fifty-foot snowbears stood guard at the base of the broad steps leading into the palace. An ice garden almost as beautiful as the one Wynter had created in his Atrium bordered a wide path that led to the palace . . . all built on a giant's scale.

Khamsin was acutely aware of her own insignificance as she crossed the distance from the tunnel opening to the palace steps. Those steps were as massive as the rest of the palace, each riser easily five feet tall, but in the center, a series of smaller, mortal-sized steps carved into the giant treads allowed her to scale the stairway with relative ease.

At the top, a colonnaded exterior gave way to an enormous, open room dominated by two massive thrones, each holding a gigantic seated figure carved of pure ice. Wyrn, resplendent in flowing robes and wearing a crown of giant sparkling snowflakes. And Rorjak, her mortal love turned god, whose spiky, ring-of-icicles crown struck Khamsin as an eerie premonition of things to come.

A number of passages led from the throne room, but Kham headed straight for the arched, pillared opening at the back. She passed through several more chambers, each more magnificent than the last, but spared the glittering beauty little more than a passing glance. She was on a mission to save the man she loved, and all the greatest wonders of the world could not have tempted her from her path.

At last, she reached the final room at the rear of the palace. The body of the second priestess, frozen like the first, lay sprawled near the threshold. Kham whispered an apology and stepped around the woman to enter the great, domed rotunda.

All around the perimeter of the rotunda, life-sized statues of male and female warriors stood sentry in columned bays. Unlike the other statues in this place or the frozen bodies of the priestesses, each of these sculptures appeared lifelike, as if living people had been posed on their pedestals and encased in a layer of clear ice. Each sported a fabulous jeweled weapon worth a king's ransom. Swords, staves, bows, pikes, shields: treasures to distract would-be thieves from the real treasure in the room, bait for those fool enough to try stealing from a god.

Don't touch anything. The statues are enchanted and will defend what rests here.

At the center of the room, rimmed in a circle of ice blocks, lay what looked like a pool of black oil eight feet in diameter.

This was it. What she'd come for.

Khamsin's nerves jangled as she approached the Ice Heart. The contents of the well were dark and unfathomable, the surface still as glass and glossy enough to see her reflection.

She'd never given much thought to the gods. Oh, she made her devotions to them, of course, but she'd never truly considered the idea that the gods had once walked amongst the people of Mystral, that the tales of their exploits had been true.

Until now.

The gods were real—their tales were true—and the existence of this well of dark power proved it.

And somewhere at the bottom of that black pool—the distilled essence of a corrupt god—lay the legendary sword of Roland Soldeus. She could sense its presence now, as if some part of the sun had broken off and fallen into the well.

Now, she just had to retrieve it.

Despite being buried deep within the heart of a glacier, warmth danced at her fingertips as her power rose in response to Blazing's proximity. Laci's hopes about Kham's ability to withstand the frigid depths of the Ice Heart might actually have merit.

You are a Summerlander, your weathergift one of the strongest in centuries. I'm hoping that gift will allow you to survive the Ice Heart.

A sound, like crackling ice, and a flash of movement in her peripheral vision made Khamsin spin around. Searing pain sliced across her upper arm as the spear aimed at her unprotected back ripped through her furred robe and scored a deep furrow on her arm. Her arm fell limp to her side, paralyzed. Indescribable cold screamed along every nerve ending.

"What the—?" Kham gaped as she got her first look at her attacker. One of the statues had stepped off its pedestal and lunged at her. This one was a woman, tall with long, white hair and blue-white skin. Her eyes were pale and colorless, but just looking at them drained the warmth from Khamsin's skin. She advanced on Khamsin, a long white spear clutched menacingly in her frozen hands. With each measured step, the ice coating her skin cracked and fell away in a thousand tiny flakes, then re-formed almost instantly.

"But I didn't touch anything!" Kham protested. The ice woman clearly didn't care. She jabbed her spear, and only Kham's swift reflexes spared her an impaling. As it was, the spear pierced the sleeve of Kham's robe and froze it solid. Kham's eyes widened. "Wait, is that one of *Thorgyll's* spears?"

The woman lunged, moving far swifter than a block of ice should, aiming a lethal blow at the center of Khamsin's chest.

Kham didn't dare let that spear touch her again. She flung herself backward, bending like one of Vera Sola's famed fire-stick dancers ducking beneath a flaming horizontal pole. The white spear missed Kham's chest but scored a burning line across her jaw as momentum carried her back up. The side of her face went numb, then flamed with pain. She staggered back, stumbling against the blocks of ice surrounding Ice Heart. Tipped off-balance, Khamsin fell backward into the well.

Agony exploded across her nerve endings as the black liquid touched her exposed skin. If passing through the veil in the tunnel had felt like having the flesh flayed from her bones, this was like being submerged in a vat of acid. On her wrist, the red Rose of Summerlea flared with pain and power. Kham fought her way back to the surface and bobbed up, screaming, in time to see the ice creature jab her spear into the Ice Heart. Rippling black liquid froze at the point of contact, crusting over in midripple. The hardening ice spread rapidly out across the surface.

All Kham could do was suck down a gasp of air and dive into the freezing pool before the spreading surface ice closed around her. The error of that instinctive reaction became immediately apparent. The layer of ice now covering the well was thick and solid. She beat against it with bare hands, but it didn't budge. There were a few tiny air pockets—small shallow spaces formed near the apex of the frozen ripples—but those precious breaths would not sustain her for more than a few minutes.

Assuming she survived this murderous cold long enough to drown.

The sword. Khamsin, get the sword.

The Sword of Roland had unfrozen the Ice Heart nine hundred years ago. The sword would be able to break through the surface ice now.

She pressed her lips to the air pockets, sucking in as much air as she could, then she rolled upside down and pushed off the ice, diving down into the Ice Heart.

The world went black and sightless. All that existed was burning cold and pain. The Rose on her wrist burned with a pain so terrible she would willingly cut off her own arm to make it stop. Instead, she kicked and clawed her way deeper into the Ice Heart, dragging herself through the thickening sludge towards the promise of warmth and light that called to her senses. Her lungs burned as fiercely as her flesh, growing tighter and tighter with each passing moment.

She fought the need to breathe until her body rebelled. Her mouth opened against her will, and the freezing black liquid of the Ice Heart poured into her lungs.

Lightning exploded across her cells. A storm like nothing she'd ever conjured roared through her body as her fearsome weathergift battled the bitter invasion of a dead god's icy essence. Flesh and bone savaged one another with brutal claws and razor-sharp teeth, ripping and tearing in a frenzy of ravening hunger.

Kham screamed and screamed and screamed in soundless futility. Her body convulsed, twisting and writhing. The legs scissoring through the thick, oily liquid grew heavy. Each tiny motion became a heroic struggle, then an impossibility as the strength leached from her limbs. Pain faded as her drowning body sank towards the bottom of the well.

Wynter, my love, forgive me. I have failed you.

Was this death?

Khamsin floated in blackness. The pain ravaging her body remained, but it was distant, separated from her consciousness, as if she were a mere observer of another woman's torment. She couldn't see anything, hear anything, and feeling beyond that strangely distant pain seemed an impossibility.

A forgotten memory niggled at her, tugging, pulling, nibbling at the edges of her mind.

The sword, Khamsin. Get the sword.

The sword. Roland's sword. That's what she'd come for, why she was here.

She could feel its presence through the impenetrable darkness. A blossom of beckoning warmth. So near. She reached for it.

The second she did, agony returned full bore—flooding her body, making her writhe and scream in torment. She persevered, fighting to reach the sword with every remaining ounce of strength she possessed.

Please. Please. Please. She didn't pray. She never begged. But for Wynter, she would do that and more. If there was any chance at all to save him, she needed Roland's sword.

There! Numb fingers curled around the sword's hilt. The

moment she touched it, fiery heat roared up her arm, blasting its way through her body in a cleansing burn. With the heat came a flood of images, memories.

Helos the sun god, finding himself so enchanted with the mortal queen of Summerlea that he could not set her from his mind.

Helos pouring his divine essence into the mortal shell of his beloved's husband. And in that husband's skin, with that husband's flesh, the god lay with the beautiful queen. And in the soft, sweet grass beside a still summer lake, with a profusion of red roses perfuming the air, the god gave the Summer queen a child.

Khamsin saw the birth of that child, who became known as Roland Soldeus. The child of Summerlea's king but also the god's divine being, he was the first Summer King to bear the red Rose birthmark on the inside of his right wrist—a mark given him in memory of the time the Queen of Summer had been loved by a god. As her dazed mind processed that, a new flood of memories swept her along like a swift current.

Roland, now a young man, visiting the lakeside where he'd been conceived. And there, rising from the grass, a great and mighty blade, whose hilt was set with an enormous ruby as red as the roses that had blossomed the day of Roland's conception.

Roland reaching for that sword, being swept away at first contact by the same flood of memories that carried her now.

Along with those memories came the realization that the god had placed into Blazing a part of himself, a connection to his divine power and his own memories, so that through the sword, Roland and his heirs could come to know the truth of their beginnings.

Never without his golden sword, Roland had lived up to his divine parentage, leading the armies of Summerlea in battle against its enemies, guiding the kingdom of Summerlea to enviable greatness, peace, and prosperity.

It was that greatness and prosperity that convinced the

equally powerful Winter King to offer his beloved only daughter in marriage to Roland.

Kham stood witness to the day the princess of Wintercraig arrived for her first meeting with her betrothed. It wasn't love at first sight. Far from it, but Roland was dazzled by her pale, exotic beauty and by the fires that burned beneath her cool exterior. With the patience and determination for which he had become renowned, Roland courted his betrothed until, at last, one cool summer night, on the same shores of the lake where the god of the sun had possessed his mortal queen, the Winter princess surrendered to Roland her heart. And there, in the soft grass, like his father before him, Roland claimed his love.

But as Khamsin knew, theirs was not to be a happy tale. Alarmed by the threat of a united Summerlea and Wintercraig, powerful kings from across the sea conspired to destroy Roland and Summerlea. They launched their armada, a naval-borne army the likes of which had never before been assembled.

The sword showed her the very battles she'd spent a lifetime reading about and imagining in her mind. Her imagination didn't come close to the reality.

An ocean thick with ships as far as the eye could see. A coast, overrun by foreign invaders, swarming like ants on an overturned anthill. Roland and his defenders being pushed back and back and back again, until only one final line of hills stood between the invaders and the fertile heartland of Summerlea, where Roland's beloved waited.

Roland, desperate to save his love, calling upon the power of his sword, and through it, the god's own power. And thus came the great, blinding explosion of light, the enormous cloud mushrooming into the sky, the feat that ended Roland's life, defeated the enemy invaders, and forever enshrined his name in legend.

But Roland had not perished without issue as Khamsin and the rest of the world had always believed. His beloved bride from the north discovered after his death that she was with child. To save her child the stigma of bastardy—and to ensure that Roland's only child would inherit his father's kingdom and pass down his great gifts—the Winter princess wed Roland's brother, Donal. And to keep safe her son's true heritage, she spirited Roland's sword away from Summerlea and hid it in her father's kingdom. She intended to retrieve the sword and present it to her son when he reached manhood, but she died in childbirth with her third child. And her father, fearing that King Donal or his heirs would use the power of the sword to subjugate Wintercraig, never returned the blade to its rightful owner. Instead, he hid it securely away and devised an intricate series of clues to lead to its whereabouts, to be safeguarded until such time as an Heir of Roland was born to the Winter Throne. Those clues had been written in a book passed down from one Winter King to another.

But though more than one Wintercraig princess wed into the House of Summer, not one Summerlea princess had ever been crowned Wintercraig's queen. And so the sword remained hidden for many centuries until one enterprising Winter King, having followed the clues to the sword's hiding place, brought the magic weapon back to his kingdom. Although unable to unlock the sword's great power himself—as only an Heir of Roland could do—he thought perhaps the sword's magical, sun-born heat could melt the Ice Heart so he could claim that power, instead. But when he struck Blazing deep into the center of the frozen block of black ice in the Ice Heart well, Roland's sword melted the Ice Heart so completely that the entire frozen mass of it turned liquid, and Roland's sword sank to the bottom of the well, there to remain until a young daughter of Summerlea, a princess of the Rose with the soul of a storm, reached out a hand through the cold darkness to grasp the hilt of Roland's divine sword, Blazing. And at her first touch, the memories stored in the sword poured into her mind, filling her with centuries of history so vivid and real it was as if she'd just lived each event herself.

The flood of memories halted as quickly as they'd begun.

Still clutching the sword, now filled with renewed vigor and sense of purpose, Khamsin planted her feet at the bottom of the well, bent her knees to gather power, and leapt upwards through the long dark of the Ice Heart well, the sword held before her like the tip of a spear.

She burst through the layer of ice sealing the well in a geyser of steam and melted Ice Heart droplets that refroze and fell back to ground as chips of ice. She landed hard, knees bending to absorb the shock.

The sound of crackling ice behind her brought Kham spinning around in time to see the frozen woman heave her spear. The creature's aim was perfect. The spear should have pierced Kham's heart and pinned her body to the rotunda's icy wall. Instead, moving with reflexes and speed she'd never before possessed, Khamsin caught the ice spear in midflight with her left hand and threw Blazing with her right. The sword shot across the distance, and struck the ice woman's chest so hard it sent her flying. She landed twenty yards away and skidded through the rotunda's arched doorway, leaving a trail of blood that changed from blue to purple to red as it went.

By the time Kham reached her side, the icy shell encasing the woman had melted away, leaving a mortal Wintercraig beauty who watched Kham's approach with pain-glazed blue eyes. She lifted trembling hands.

"Please . . ." she begged on a shallow breath. The word came out weak and thick. Blood was already filling her mouth and throat, making it difficult to speak. Kham's had been a death blow, striking lung and heart. "Stop . . . her . . . stop . . ." She broke off, coughing blood.

Kham set the ice spear on the ground, well out of reach, and gripped the woman's shoulders. "Who are you? Who do you want me to stop?"

"Reika . . . she never meant to help me get the sword. . . . she wanted the Ice Heart." The woman's fingers clutched weakly at Khamsin's robe. "She has . . . unleashed him."

"What are you saying? Did Reika drink the Ice Heart? Did she bring Rorjak back to life?"

"P-please . . . tell . . . him . . ." One trembling hand dropped to the woman's chest, fingers closing weakly around the pendant at her throat. "Love . . . him." Then her body went limp, and her head lolled to one side. The hand clutching the pendant fell away, revealing a gold circle carved with the image of a falcon, soaring through beams of sunlight, a rose clutched in one claw.

Khamsin sat back on her heels.

She recognized the pendant. She'd looked forward to seeing it—or rather the man who wore it—every day as a child in Summerlea. It was her brother's personal crest.

The presence of that sigil could only mean that the woman Khamsin had just killed was Elka Villani, Wynter's former betrothed, Reika Villani's sister—and the woman Khamsin's brother had started a war to possess.

"Oh, Falcon." Her brother must have sent Elka to the Temple of Wyrn to retrieve Roland's sword. Apparently, Reika had come along, too, only she'd used Roland's sword as the pretext to gain access to her real goal: the power of the Ice Heart.

Kham's heart slammed against her chest. If Reika was the one who'd summoned the Ice King—if she was the reason for the ice thralls—there was still a chance to save Wynter.

For the second time that day, Kham sent up a prayer. *Please, Helos. Please, Wyrn, let him be safe. Let him still be my husband.*

Hands shaking with pent-up emotion, Kham slipped the pendant from Elka's throat and put it around her own neck for safekeeping. Then she stood, pulled the sword from Elka's chest, and wiped the bloody blade on the still-damp fur of her coat.

She cast one final look at the Ice Heart. Without the heat of Blazing hidden in its depths, what was held in the well was liquid no more. The immortal, indestructible essence of

Rorjak, the Ice King, had returned to the solid, frozen state that Thorgyll's spears had put it in so many millennia ago. She hoped it would stay that way for many centuries to come.

The crack and tinkle of splintering ice behind her chimed a warning. She spun back to find the corpse of Elka Villani once more fully encased in ice and rising to its feet. In an instinctive response born of memories not her own, she stabbed Roland's sword at the rising corpse and cried, "Burn!"

The diamond in Blazing's hilt flared with sudden light. The rose on her wrist went red-hot. A great gout of flame shot from the tip of the sword and engulfed Elka. The Winterlady's arms lifted like a startled babe's, and she burst into flames. Within moments, the body of Elka Villani turned to char, then crumpled to the floor as a formless pile of ash.

"Wyrn and Helos protect me." Kham stared at the sword in her hand. Bright and golden in hue, with a clear, brilliant white diamond the size of a goose egg in its hilt, the Sword of Roland was everything the legends had foretold.

And now, many thousands of years after Roland's death, Khamsin Coruscate Atrialan held the same sword the god Helos had forged for her legendary ancestor and prayed the sword would grant her the power to save her Winter-born love, just as Roland had saved his.

Though, hopefully, with a happier outcome.

He walked through a field of fresh snow. The world was white, crisp, pristine. The sky a blue so deep and rich it dazzled him.

The sun shone high in the sky. A bright, golden white globe.

All around, the trees grew tall and strong, their ever-green branches laden with snow.

He moved silently through the powdery snow. It swirled around his calves, deep enough that he could not see his feet when he walked but so powdery, it was like walking through fog.

Ahead, on the crest of a small hill, stood a large snow wolf. Its fur riffled in the breeze. The wolf howled.

The call caught at a place deep inside him, singing to him in wordless communication, urging him to follow. He walked towards the wolf.

The snow grew thicker. It was up to his knees now. Then up to his thighs. His waist.

The wolf was just ahead now. Its call wrapped around Wynter like a fisherman's net, hauling him closer and closer still.

The snow had reached his chest.

More wolves began to howl. Their howl was a song of warning, sharp and fearful, made up of many voices. He glanced to his left and right, then behind him. Dozens of wolves had gathered on the surrounding peaks. All were barking, howling, baying at him.

He turned back to the wolf he was walking towards.

The snow was shoulder deep now.

The wolf on the hill turned with shocking swiftness.

Only it wasn't a wolf. It was a garm.

Malevolent red eyes gleamed. Rows of sharp, pointed teeth gaped in a ferocious snarl. Past the garm, *down in the valley on the other side of the hill, he caught a glimpse of a mighty army. Frost Giants.* Garm. *Ice thralls. They looked up at him and roared.*

The garm *shrieked, and a cloud of blue vapor billowed forth.*

Wynter shot up out of bed, abruptly and completely awake. The bandage covering his eyes was still tied around his head. He reached up to rip it off.

He was sitting on a wooden table by the hearth in one of the hunting cabins that scattered the mountains of Wintercraig.

At his sudden movement, several guards and Galacia Frey came running. Galacia held one of Thorgyll's spears, ready to strike.

Wynter held up his hands. "It's me. It's still me."

But he wasn't so sure. His chest felt tight and cold. As if everything inside had turned to solid ice.

"Get Valik," Laci instructed one of the guard. The man nodded and sprinted for the door.

"What happened?" Wyn asked. "Where are we?" He glanced down at his body, examining the bandages around his waist, realized that whatever was beneath those wrappings hurt like a Feury.

Quickly, Galacia filled him in. She told him about the Great Hunt. How he'd followed the *garm* track and gotten separated from the rest of the hunters. That the tracks had led him to Khamsin, and between them, they'd killed at least two *garm*. That he'd been hovering on the brink of death or worse ever since.

As Laci spoke, the memories came tumbling back.

"Four," he said. "It was four *garm*. I only managed to kill two of them." He'd fallen after dispatching the second, leaving Khamsin to face the remaining two on her own. Alone and injured.

Khamsin.

"Where's my wife?" He grabbed the edges of the table, bracing himself for the worst. "*Laci, where's Khamsin?*"

"She's safe, Wyn. She's fine. You need to calm down. Now."

Laci hadn't lowered the spear. Her body was taut as a bowstring, her blue gaze watchful and unwavering. The eyes of a hunter, ready to strike. She smelled of fear, but her expression and posture exuded pure, grim resolve.

That's when he realized the wood around his fingers had turned to solid ice.

Wyrn save him. He closed his eyes and tried to push back the glacier running through his veins. He stood on the lip of a precipice. One fraction further—or one crack in the crumbling ground beneath his feet—and he would fall, tumbling into ruin and taking the world with him.

Not today. Not yet. Wintercraig needed him strong enough to defend them. Save Wintercraig first.

He could feel the heat of the fire against his back. He concentrated on that, willing the warmth to infuse his flesh and melt the ice so hungry to claim him.

Where was Khamsin? She could have pushed back the ice with a single touch.

Lacking her presence, he filled the darkness behind his closed eyes with his memories of her face, her smile, her laughter, the silver flash of her eyes when she was angry. The feel of her skin, so warm and soft, smelling of jasmine and wildness, so exotically dark against his own golden flesh. The reassuring warmth of her body nestled against him through the long, dark hours of the Craig's winter nights.

The tightness of his chest had loosened. He drew a breath, then another. The fingers curled so tight around the tabletop relaxed. Moisture gathered as the frozen wood began to melt. He took another, longer breath, and opened his eyes.

Laci was still poised to strike, and Valik had just come in from outside. Wynter looked around the cabin. That woman from Summerlea—the spy, Khamsin's nurse, what was her name? Tildavera Greenleaf—stood beside a table covered with all manner of herbs and pharmacopeia. Half a dozen armored White Guard were also in the room, looking as wary and watchful as Laci. But the face he wanted to see most was still nowhere to be found.

"Where is Khamsin?" he asked.

"I sent her to Gildenheim with some of the White Guard." Laci must have realized that the immediate danger had passed because some of the tension faded from her body. She straightened from her crouch, and the tip of her spear lowered a few inches. "So it's true, what Khamsin said. She really did incinerate two *garm* with her lightning."

Wyn frowned. After he fell to the *garm*, everything got hazy at best. But he remembered the smell of lightning and *garm* vapors. And he remembered sight of his wife running, ropes of lightning shooting down from the storm-tossed heavens, finding her unerringly. Her body, lifting up in the air, lit from within. Two *garm* close on her heels. The devastation of knowing he'd failed her.

"I . . ." He remembered the lightning crashing so close it shook the ground. One deafening crack after another. The smell of scorched flesh. "Yes, she did. She killed them both. With no weapon but her weathergift." He looked up at Laci. "She survived? The *garm* didn't kill her?"

"She survived," Laci said. "She burned them until there was nothing left, which is why some of us didn't believe her at first." Laci cast a disgusted glance at Valik, who had just joined them.

"How are you feeling?" Valik's gaze raked Wynter from head to toe. "You look like Hel."

Wyn gave a choked laugh, then groaned when pain streaked across his belly. "Always full of compliments, you are."

"Thought we'd lost you a time or two. Or four." There was a look in Valik's eyes Wyn had never seen before. And a shimmer of betraying brightness.

"I'm fine." For now. Wyn rubbed his chest. The ice there had softened, but it was far from gone. If he put his hand in Laci's flame right now, the fire would probably remain bright and blue. "How long have I been here?"

"Since the hunt? A week. But we don't have the luxury of staying much longer. Coruscate is making his move." Valik brought Wynter up to speed. "We've only got days—a week at most—before they reach Gildenheim."

"We've got less time and more trouble than that," Wynter said. "The Ice King's army has gathered."

"What?" Valik stared at him in shock. "How is that even possible? Rorjak may be close, but you're still you. We'd know if you weren't."

"I don't know how. But I know that they've gathered. And they know where I am. They're on the way here."

CHAPTER 25

Roland's Heir

"If you move him, he will die. Can't you see that?" Tilda-vera Greenleaf hissed.

Standing in the far corner of the room, and talking in heated whispers, Khamsin's old nurse, Valik, and Laci all thought Wynter was asleep and that they were far enough away that he couldn't overhear them. They were wrong on both counts. Tildavera's latest potion might have kept him unconscious if he'd actually drunk it instead of spitting it in the cloth beneath his pillow, but the little bit he'd actually had to swallow had only left him pleasantly sleepy. And an acute sense of smell wasn't the only advantage of his clan-gift. Sharpened eyesight and improved hearing made it easy to read their lips and pick up the gist of their heated exchange, even while pretending to be asleep.

Tildavera planted her hands on her hips and glared up at Valik and Galacia Frey. "It's only a bit of thread holding his insides inside him. And only my potions keeping him sleeping peacefully instead of writhing about and scream-ing in pain."

"We don't have a choice," Valik said. "You heard him. The Ice King's army is headed our way. We can't stay here. *He* can't stay here."

"If he doesn't stay here, he won't last the journey. You'll kill him!"

"I'm not so easy to kill." Wyn had tired of eavesdropping and pretending to sleep. Let them discuss their options openly. He opened his eyes and propped himself up on one arm. Pain knifed through his abdomen as the movement tugged at his wound, but he ignored it. "I'm like my wife, in that regard, for many have tried and failed. Who knows? Maybe extraordinary survivability is one of the perks of possessing a weathergift."

The aged Summerlea nurse pushed past Valik and Laci and stalked over to his sickbed. "You are supposed to be sleeping." Her face scrunched up in an expression of severe disapproval. She didn't care that he was king. She chided him like she might any misbehaving schoolboy.

He almost smiled. It was clear Tildavera Greenleaf was accustomed to being in charge, and equally accustomed to speaking her mind and having her orders obeyed. But this was one order he had no intention of heeding.

"I've slept long enough. Khamsin told me you were the best healer in all of Mystral, and it's clear she wasn't exaggerating. You did a fine job bringing me back from the brink of death. I'm sure you can keep me clinging to life a while longer."

The old woman's lips pursed. "My patients do not 'cling to life,'" she snapped. "I pride myself on their making a full and miraculous recovery. But carting them all about the countryside with their insides hanging out is not at all conducive to that outcome!"

"Did Khamsin always do as you told her?"

Tildy scowled and switched tactics. "You want to bring Khamsin into this? Fine. So, tell me, Wynter of the Craig, if you sicken and die from that wound, where will that leave her? Alone and undefended against both the Ice King's army and the invaders from Calberna and Summerlea. And if you think that father of hers will lift a finger to ensure her safety—"

"Maybe we don't have to move Wynter just yet," Laci interrupted, as Wynter's expression darkened. "Wyn, you say the Ice King's army knows where you are, and they're coming for you, right?"

Wyn nodded.

"Then staying here buys us time. If you're what they want, they won't go a hundred miles out of their way to attack Gildenheim. Ungar sounded the Valkyr's horn. He's assembling the army. If we stay here, we buy him time and keep the Ice King's army away from Gildenheim—and Khamsin."

Wynter didn't like Laci's logic—mostly because he didn't like the idea of staying here, doing nothing, when enemies were on the move—but he couldn't refute it. The last thing he wanted to do was draw the Ice King's army towards Khamsin. "One more day."

"Three," Tildy countered.

He glowered at her. "That's not an option. Two at the most. Then, whether it kills me or not, we move out."

Once more clad in her own clothes, with the entrance to Wyrn's secret ice palace secured and Blazing safely sheathed in the scabbard she had retrieved from a hidden compartment in Laci's room, Kham picked up Thorgyll's spear and headed for the public altar room to rejoin the White Guard.

The sight of the young boy standing among them brought her up short.

"Krysti! What are you doing here? I thought you were helping out with the little ones."

Her young companion-in-mischief flashed his fearless, *gamin* grin. "You didn't really expect me to stay there when I found out you'd come back. What's that you've got there?" His too-observant gaze latched onto the spear in her hand. "That's one of Thorgyll's spears, isn't it?" He frowned. "I thought only Lady Frey and her priestesses were allowed to touch those."

Before she could answer, his gaze zeroed in on the jeweled scabbard at her side and the sword with the enormous diamond shining brightly in its hilt.

"Winter's Frost!" Krysti swore. "That's it, isn't it? That legendary sword you told me about—Roland's sword, right? The one you said went missing after his death."

"I—yes." The boy was too observant by half. But she trusted him as she trusted few people. "It's Roland's sword. Made for him by the god Helos, himself."

"How did you find it?"

"It's a long story, and I need to get back to the king." She handed the ice spear to Sven. "Here, take this. If we run into trouble, I'll be more help with the sword than that spear."

A look of reverent awe passed over Sven's face as he curled his fist around Thorgyll's famed spear. "I will guard it with my life, my queen."

"And you"—she turned to Krysti—"I need you to go back to Gildenheim and wait for me there."

"What? No! I'm coming with you."

"Not this time. I need you here, where I know you're safe." Whether the Ice King truly had returned or whether she was simply going to confront her brother's army and send them packing, things were about to get very dangerous. Too dangerous for a young boy, no matter how brave he was. "Promise me."

He scowled and kicked at the temple's stone floor. "I promise."

"Thank you." She laid a hand on his shoulder, knowing how hard it was to be left behind. Turning to the others, she said, "Let's go." As they headed towards the mouth of the cave, Kham murmured to Ungar, "Both priestesses are dead, and there was an ice thrall waiting for me when I went to get the sword. It was Elka Villani. That means my brother is probably somewhere near. Tell the men to be alert."

Ungar's square jaw flexed. "Understood, my queen."

"There's more. Before she died, Elka told me Reika

drank the Ice Heart. She said Reika had 'unleashed him.' I think she was talking about Rorjak."

"What?" Initial shock gave way to a string of blistering curses. "What was she thinking?"

As they neared the cave mouth, Khamsin could feel energy throbbing like a heartbeat in the brilliant diamond at Blazing's hilt. The Rose on her wrist warmed and pulsed with the same rhythm. The sky was still dark, but the eastern horizon was beginning to lighten. The sun would soon be rising.

A strong wind blew from the south, chill enough that both guards standing by the cave entrance had pulled down their visors to protect their faces from the bitter cold.

"Karl, Geri, time to go, lads," Ungar said.

Something whistled past Kham's ear. At her side, Sven grunted. Still clutching Thorgyll's spear, he toppled like a felled tree. Khamsin's mind didn't fully process what had happened until Ungar gave a gurgling cry and clutched at the arrow protruding from his throat. Two more White Guard crumpled in rapid succession, leaving only the two by the cave mouth.

"Krysti! Get down!" She spun towards him, her first instinct to protect him, only to stop short. One of the remaining two White Guards was pulling his bloody sword from the back of one of Ungar's fallen men. The other held a sword to Krysti's throat.

"What are you doing? Release Krysti at once!" Kham commanded. She reached for Blazing, half drawing the blade from her belt before a familiar voice called out.

"Storm, don't! They're on our side."

"Falcon?" She pivoted halfway back around as her brother and two white-cloaked Summerlanders emerged from behind a tumble of rocks to her right. "What are you doing here? And what do you mean they're on our side?" She glanced back over her shoulder towards the mouth of the cave. The White Guard holding Krysti lifted his ram's head visor to reveal dark Summerlander skin and cold black eyes.

Movement higher up the hill betrayed the presence of a white-cloaked archer. She only saw the one, but there had to be others. Ungar, Sven, and the other two men had gone down in a matter of seconds. That meant her brother had at least four archers hidden amongst the rocks and snow.

Her fingers tightened on Blazing's grip. Power pulsed against her palm. Playing for time while she evaluated her options, she turned back to her brother. "Falcon, why are you here? Didn't you get my message? I told you not to come."

Her brother, the hero she'd idolized all her life, shook his head, and said, "Of course I came. You're my sister, and I love you. I wasn't about to let Wynter Atrialan stake you out on some glacier to die."

He spoke with such absolute sincerity that Kham's heart stuttered, and for an instant, she truly believed he'd come because he loved her and had to save her. She *wanted* to believe him, just as she'd wanted to believe the best of him all her life.

But she didn't.

"If you came to save me, Falcon, then why are you here instead of at the camp where your bird found Tildy and me?"

"I know what that husband of yours can do, and I know better than to face him in battle without a weapon capable of defeating him. That's it, isn't it? Roland's sword."

She glanced down at the gleaming sword at her waist. Her fingers tightened on the grip. "No," she lied. "It's a replica Wynter had made for me because he knows how much I adore the legends of Roland."

"Oh, Storm, you never were a good liar." Falcon shook his head in reproof. "So, it's really real, and you found it. But how did you know where to look? Was it in the Ice Heart?"

She clamped her lips shut and tried to keep her expression blank, but Falcon had always been able to read her too well.

"So that's true, too, is it? The source of the Winter King's deadliest magic lies inside the Temple of Wyrn?" He arched a brow, and said, "I don't think it's exactly fair that they've been hoarding all this power for so long, do you? Maybe I should pay a little visit to the Ice Heart before I meet your husband in battle."

Her eyes narrowed and she thought of Ungar, Sven, and the people of Hillje, murdered so her brother could claim Roland's sword. "Maybe you should. Just go inside and take the path to the left of the altar."

He laughed without humor. "You've changed, little sister. Three years ago, you would never have considered sending me to my death. Oh, yes," he said when she grimaced, "Elka warned me about the dangers guarding the temple's secrets."

"Three years ago, I thought you were a hero. I thought you were brave and honorable, a Prince of Summerlea worthy of being Roland's Heir. But heroes don't run around murdering innocent people to get what they want, like my men here, and the people of Hillje, and fifteen-year-old boys."

"Enough." All hint of brotherly affection evaporated from Falcon's expression, leaving a cold, hard mask. He extended his hand and flexed his fingers in curt command. "Give me the sword, Storm."

"No." She yanked Blazing free of its sheath and held it before her. The white diamond in the hilt sparkled with light. "You'll get it over my dead body and no other way. I'm taking this sword to Wynter."

Her brother sighed. "You never could do things the easy way." His eyes flicked to a spot behind her, and he gave a sharp nod.

She spun, power crackling up her arm as Roland's sword blazed to life, but the second of the imposter White Guards had crept too near while Falcon and she were talking. He smashed the butt of his sword into her temple. Stars exploded across her vision, then blackness descended.

*   *   *

Khamsin woke with a splitting headache and pain radiating from every part of her body. It was dark, and she was lying on her side beside a fire. Some sort of heavy, hooded cloak was draped around her. She could see the stars overhead, but she couldn't feel her connection to the sun. She groaned and tried to sit up, but her hands were tied behind her back, and her feet were bound. Her brother, Falcon, was sitting a few feet away on a log by the fire, holding Roland's sword.

He turned his head in her direction. "You're awake. That's good. I was beginning to think Verge had killed you."

"He nearly did," she muttered. She struggled unsuccessfully to sit up, then flopped back down with a groan as her head threatened to split in two. "Did he have to hit me so hard?"

The corner of Falcon's mouth curled up in a familiar, wry smile. He came over and pulled her into a sitting position. "To be fair, you were threatening us with a weapon capable of unparalleled destruction. Which is one of the reasons you're tied up and wearing that lead cape."

The flash of affectionate warmth roused by his wry grin winked out. He'd brought a cape lined with lead to cut off her connection to the sun. He'd come to Wintercraig *prepared* to stifle her weathergifts and render her helpless. So much for his claims of wanting to rescue her.

Falcon returned to his seat and resumed his examination of Roland's sword. "It looks just like all the old pictures, doesn't it? I can't believe it's really real."

Once upon a time, she would have shared his awed reverence. No longer. Now he was the enemy, and he'd just stolen a weapon so powerful it could obliterate every living creature in Wintercraig. And he was standing between her and her chance to save Wynter before it was too late.

"Yes, it's real," she said. "What are you planning to do with it?"

Falcon looked up. "Take back what's mine, of course." He caressed the clear white diamond in Blazing's hilt, slid the blade back in its sheath. "I know you think the worst of me, Storm, but I'm not a bad man. I did what I had to do to restore glory to Summerlea."

Khamsin gave a sharp bark of laughter. "Summerlea lies frozen beneath a blanket of snow, its armies slaughtered, its people conquered. Where, exactly, is the glory in that? You think all the children orphaned by the war are singing your praises?"

"Summerlea will rise again. Summerlea will be great once more. The world will tremble at our name, as they did for millennia. This sword ensures that." He patted Blazing's jeweled hilt.

"Do you even hear yourself, Falcon? Is that what you think Roland's sword is for? To make the world tremble in fear?"

"Don't be simple, Storm. To be strong, a king needs to be feared. Nobility is a fine ideal, but real life demands something a bit more . . . practical."

"That's the answer of a weak man, not a strong king."

"So says the woman married to the man who swallowed the essence of a god," he shot back.

Kham looked away. Love and grief had driven Wynter to make a terrible choice, it was true. But at his core, Wynter was kind. His people loved and respected him. Yes, he could be harsh when the situation warranted, but that harshness was tempered with a determination to do what was right rather than what was most expedient or most profitable. He was a fair man and an excellent king, unswerving in his dedication to the safety and security of Wintercraig and its people. Kham had never loved or respected a man more. Not even Falcon.

"Is there any part of the brother I loved that was real?" she asked bitterly. "Have you ever truly cared about anything or anyone more than your own ambition? What about Elka. You haven't even asked what happened to her. Was she just a means to an end like everyone else in your life?"

Falcon's jaw hardened. "Elka betrayed me. She and her

sister went to retrieve Roland's sword, but they never came back."

"Elka didn't betray you. Reika drank the Ice Heart, then she turned Elka into an ice thrall and left her there to kill anyone who came near the Ice Heart or Roland's sword."

"You're lying." But he looked uncertain as he scanned her face.

"No, I'm not. The Elka ice thrall tried to kill me, but I retrieved the sword and killed her instead. She gave me her pendant before she died. If you or your men didn't take it from me, it's still around my neck. Her last words were for you. She wanted me to tell you that she loved you."

He got up and crossed over to where she sat. "Don't try anything stupid," he warned, then untied her cape and pushed it aside to bare her throat. The pendant was still there. He pulled it free and regarded it with an inscrutable look. "When she didn't come to the rendezvous point, I thought she had betrayed me and taken the sword for herself. I was coming to find her when I saw you and your men head into the Temple." He slid the pendant into his pocket and retied Kham's cape. "I'm glad I was wrong about that."

"That's it? How can you be so cold, so devoid of feeling?"

He gave her a look then, a bit wild-eyed, like an animal in pain. "Don't push me, Storm," he warned, and she thought maybe, just maybe, her brother really had loved his Winterlady. That gave her a measure of hope. Maybe she could still reach him, talk sense into him before it was too late.

"Falcon, listen to me. Something bad is happening. Something far worse than another war between Summerlea and Wintercraig. That's why you've got to let me take the sword to Wynter."

"Don't worry, Storm. I fully intend to deliver this sword to your husband myself"—he patted the golden hilt at his side—"point first and straight through the heart."

"I'm serious, Falcon. This isn't some joke! Didn't Elka

ever tell you about Rorjak the Ice King? And Carnak, the end of the world?"

He rolled his eyes. "Those are just fables, Storm. Stories told to frighten children and keep the worshippers of Wyrn paying their tithes to the priestesses."

"No they aren't! Carnak is happening right now. The *garm*—terrible monsters from the remote reaches of the Craig—have been attacking villages. That's one of the first signs of Rorjak's return."

"Is that what all this is about?" He laughed and shook his head. "Oh, Storm, Storm, my gullible little sister. The *garm* didn't attack those villages because the world is going to end. They attacked because my men baited a trail to lead them there."

"*What?*"

He shrugged. "Technically, it was Elka's sister's idea. We needed the temple emptied so Elka could get the sword, and she said the best way to do that was to force your husband to call a Great Hunt."

"Reika suggested luring the *garm* down to attack the villages?" Kham's hands curled into fists. That evil bitch had a lot to answer for.

"We met at her father's estate over a month ago. She was really quite helpful. Doesn't like you much, though, I have to say."

"The feeling is mutual," she muttered. Of course, Reika had helped Falcon. Reika wanted power. When it was clear she was never going to get it through Wynter, she'd found another way. And Falcon was no better. He'd yet again knowingly set innocent men, women, and children up to die as a distraction so he could pursue Roland's sword.

"Have you always been this heartless, and I just blinded myself to it?" she asked bitterly. "Is there anything you wouldn't do—anyone you won't sacrifice—to get your hands on Blazing?"

Her brother's eye flashed a warning. "No, there isn't. And you'd be wise to remember that." He stood up. "I'm going to bed. My men will get you something to eat, and you're not going to give them any trouble. We've still got your little friend with us." He nodded towards a tree about fifteen yards away. Krysti was slumped over and tied to the tree. "If you value his life—which I know you do—you'll behave yourself."

"What did you do to him?"

"Don't worry, he's healthy enough. A regular wild child when he gets a chance. Kicked one of my men in the stones and broke another one's nose on the way here. That's why they tied him up."

Good for Krysti, Khamsin wanted to crow. "He's Craig-bred."

Falcon snorted. "Untamed little monster, more like. Reminds me of you when you were his age."

She glared at him. "Tell me, brother, do our sisters approve of what you're doing? Invading sovereign kingdoms, murdering innocent people, brutalizing little boys?" It would break her heart if her entire family turned out to be as savage and ruthless as her father and brother.

Falcon's dark eyes flashed, and his jaw thrust out. "This is king's business, not theirs."

So no, they didn't know. Kham sighed in relief. Thank Halla for that, at least.

"Get some rest, Storm. We've got a long, hard ride tomorrow, and we won't be slowing down to see to your comfort." He headed towards a tent on the far side of the fire.

"Falcon, please, listen to me," she called after him. "For all our sakes, you've got to let me take Blazing to Wynter. Our lives depend on it. The world depends on it. *Please*."

He just kept walking.

"Falcon!" She jumped up and started after him, only to stop when his men leapt to his defense, swords unsheathed and ready to skewer her.

"You heard the prince," one of the Summerlanders growled. He had several scars across his face and an ugly light in his muddy brown eyes. "Sit down and shut up, or that little Winterbrat over there will pay for your disobedience."

Kham glared at the man and subsided into unhappy silence.

She drank the water they brought to her and, thanks to the sword one of the Summerlander's held at Krysti's throat, she made no attempt to escape when they freed her hands so she could eat the journey cakes and dried meat they offered. Whatever happened, she would need her strength, and refusing food and drink hurt no one but herself. When she was done eating, they rebound her hands and laid her down with a curt command to sleep, but she remained awake for at least an hour, observing her captors.

Falcon was traveling with two dozen men, half Summerlanders, the other half blue-tattooed Calbernans. A small party, much easier to hide in a country as large as Wintercraig. The Summerlanders either ignored her or watched her with cold malice, but she noticed several of the Calbernans frowning in her direction and whispering amongst each other. She recalled from Tildy's endless geography lessons that the island-born Calbernans revered women. They didn't look kindly on anyone who would mistreat them. If she could provoke Falcon or the others into striking her, she just might be able to drive a wedge between the Summerlanders and their Calbernan allies. Kham filed that away for future reference.

Finally, despite the day she'd spent unconscious from the blow to her head, Khamsin fell back to sleep and stayed that way until Falcon came by before sunup to wake her and lead her to a horse.

"I know you've learned to ride, so I'm giving you your own horse so you won't slow us down," he said. "But your hands remain bound, and you wear the lead cape at all times. And Storm? The boy will ride between you and one of my men, chained to both saddles. Unless you fancy the idea of ripping him in two, I suggest you keep close to my men."

Anger curled in Khamsin's belly. Falcon knew her too well. They'd spent too many years together, playing games of war, plotting ways to escape from imaginary captors.

"When did you become such a monster?"

Falcon didn't even flinch. "I am no monster, merely determined and more familiar with your ways than you would like. The child is unharmed, and will remain so as long as you do as you're told. Now get on your horse. We've a long way to ride."

True to Falcon's word, they rode for hours without stopping. When they finally halted to rest and water the horses, the sun had risen, and she did not recognize her surroundings. Kham shook the leaden hood off her head and turned her face up to the sky, trying to pinpoint her location in relation to the sun. They'd traveled west of Gildenheim, towards Konumarr and the Llaskroner Fjord. More than a hundred miles, by her estimate. Well away from the hunting lodge where Wynter was recuperating.

Her only cause for hope was that the deep snow forced Falcon and his men to keep to the roads and established trails through the woods, which improved their chances of being spotted along the way. Wynter had to have scouts. Hopefully, one would cross their path and get word to Wintercraig's forces.

She'd tried to leave a trail behind her by picking threads from her cuffs and dropping them into the snow. Thanks to the Wintercraig colors she wore, those threads would blend so well into the snow they'd be impossible to spot, but she dropped them anyways in the hopes that Wynter's wolves might be able to track her scent.

As she dismounted, Falcon's men lit a small fire and melted snow to water the horses. They didn't bother cooking food. Instead, they passed around strips of dried meat and fruit. Falcon himself removed the bonds around her wrists so she could eat without aid.

Her arms tingled, little knives of pain throbbing up and down, and she flexed her elbows, wrists, and shoulders. Keeping her tied had also robbed her arms of strength. She could barely hold the bits of jerky and fruit offered to her.

She chewed slowly on the tough strips of meat and watched her brother. He was staring into the fire, lost in thought, and it struck her how much older and wearier he appeared. The charming roguishness that had always lurked at the corners of his mouth and twinkled in his eyes was nowhere to be seen. He seemed so different from the heroic brother she remembered that she had to wonder how much of that brother had ever existed and how much was the product of a lonely child's desperate dreams of love and family.

"Is it true you sent your men to rape and murder those villagers in Hileje three years ago?" Falcon didn't look away from the fire. He either hadn't heard her or was ignoring her. "Falcon?" she prodded. "Did you?"

Now he glanced up. "Is that what you think I did, Khamsin?"

"I don't know. That's why I'm asking. I would never have thought you capable of it before, but the last two days have made me realize how little I really know you. Perhaps I never did."

"We were children. Both of us. We're not anymore."

"Did you send them?"

He stared at the piece of jerky in his hand, then threw it in the fire. "Yes, I sent them, but I never ordered them to rape or kill anyone. They were merely supposed to create a distraction that would get Wynter and his men out of Gildenheim."

"Who did you send?"

"Noble Redfern and his friends."

"Oh, for Halla's sake, Falcon."

"What?" He shot to his feet. At least he could still looked shamed. And defensive. "I didn't know what they were going to do."

"You sent a man you knew to be a vile, drunken bastard who found his pleasure raping servant girls in dark hallways. What did you think he and his equally vile cronies were going to do? You knew what sort of atrocities amused them."

"I needed time to get away. Elka and I needed time to get away."

"So, in other words, you loosed the dogs without caring who got hurt or how badly. Just like you did with the *garm*."

His fists clenched. He looked like he wanted to hit something. For a moment, she thought it might be her, but Falcon hadn't become *that* much like their father yet.

"I didn't mean for Hillje to happen, all right? I didn't order it. But I can't change it. I'm sorry, Storm. I'm sorry it happened. Is that what you want to hear?"

"But that didn't stop you from killing Wynter's only brother, did it? Just a boy, barely more than a child, and you shot him in the throat and left him to die in the snow."

"He shot at me first!"

"You were one of the greatest archers in Summerlea!" she fired back. "You could have wounded him. Slowed him down. You had other choices that didn't include killing him. Don't even try to tell me otherwise." He wasn't the only one who'd learned from all the time they'd spent together. Yes, she'd idolized him. Yes, she been blind to the ruthlessness inside him. But she remembered his skills quite vividly.

"And he had talents that went beyond his skill with sword and bow," Falcon retorted. "He was Snow Wolf clan, just like his brother. If I'd left him wounded, he would just have called the wolves to hunt us down. I had the Book of Riddles, Khamsin. *The key to finding Roland's sword.* I wasn't going to give that up. And I damn sure wasn't going to surrender to the king I'd cuckolded and beg for mercy."

"So you plunged two kingdoms into war and ran away. Only to come back three years later to start another war.

Oh, how proud Roland would be to witness the noble glory of his line." Every word dripped with acid, and it pleased her to see how it stung.

Falcon spat in the dirt. "All those tales of Roland were myths, Storm. Legends! A tiny kernel of truth romanticized and prettied up for the ages. But this is real life. Real politics. It's not noble. It's not glorious. It's bitter, brutal, and bloody. That's what thrones are made of. That's what kings are made of."

"No." She'd seen the truth, the story played out in her mind when she'd first gripped the sword. She'd heard the voice of a god, deep and pure, burning through her body like cleansing fire and taking every doubt with it. "Not all thrones. Not all kings. Roland was better than that. My mistake was thinking you were, too."

Falcon's lip curled in a sneer. "And is that husband of yours any better? How many innocents died by his hand? He froze an entire kingdom into submission!"

"Because you drove him to war! Yes, innocents died. But their blood is as much on your hands as his. And if you don't let me take that sword to stop Rorjak from returning, the blood of every last living soul on Mystral will be on your hands as well!"

"Enough!" Falcon leapt to his feet and yanked Blazing from its sheath. The radiant diamond at the hilt's center blazed with light. He jabbed the sword in her direction.

A hot wind sent her hair flying. Khamsin gasped and ducked, covering her head instinctively to protect against the gout of flame she expected to come pouring out of the blade. When the expected inferno did not engulf her, she risked lowering her arms.

Falcon was standing ten feet away, staring at her with an indecipherable expression on his face. The snow around the camp had completely melted, leaving bare, moist ground and the smell of damp wood and bracken.

"I . . ." Her tongue flicked out to moisten dry, trembling

lips. "I thought you were going to—" She broke off. No need to give him ideas.

"What? Shoot fireballs at you?"

Then again, he'd read the same legends of Roland that she had. "Something like that."

"It seems we've both read too many legends, Storm." Anger and bitterness sharpened each word. He shoved Blazing back in its scabbard and slammed the hilt home.

"Pack up," he snapped to his men. "Time to get moving."

"I'm fine! I told you, I'm fine." Wynter glowered at Tildavera Greenleaf, who had been after him the last half hour to leave the military planning to his second long enough to lie down and let her tend his wounds.

The Summerlea nurse sniffed. "You won't be fine if you don't hush and let me do my job. I've let you ignore me long enough. Now lie back, be quiet, and let me look at that wound. It won't take a minute."

"Gah. You are a tyrant, Tildavera Greenleaf. Has anyone ever told you that?" Just to get her out of his hair, Wyn eased into a chaise and leaned back.

"Many a time," Tildy answered without rancor. "Always by patients with more stubbornness than sense." She glanced up to give him a stern look. "And that includes your wife, for as much good as it ever did her." She pulled up his tunic and made swift work of peeling back the bloodied bandage wrapped around his waist.

Wynter scowled at the back of Tildy's gray head as she bent over his belly wound to poke and prod at him and smear some sort of pungent ointment on the wound. She sniffed again and rebandaged the wound.

"Well, you're doing better than you should be, considering all the moving about you've been doing. But"— she wagged a finger under his nose when Wyn started to smirk—"you're still a long way from being healed. One wrong move, and those stitches will pop, and you'll be in one very unpleasant mess."

"Just get me to a point where I can put on my armor and mount a horse. I can't be carried into battle on a sickbed."

"That's out of the question for a week at least. If you go to battle before that, you won't be coming back."

"If I don't go to battle before that, none of us will be coming back," he countered. In a firm tone that brooked no further defiance, he said, "I don't need your approval to do my duty, Nurse Greenleaf. All I require is that you get me in the best possible shape in the time available."

Tildy put her hands on her hips. "Have I not been doing exactly that all this time? Did you think I would stop just because I know you're going to ignore my warnings and do what you want anyways? Which of us raised our Khamsin from the time she was a wee babe? Or do you think *she* was a model patient all those years?"

The laugh slipped past Wyn's lips before he could stop it. "Point taken. She is *much* more hardheaded than I."

Tildy harrumphed. "I don't think I'd go so far as to say *that*. The pair of you seem astonishingly well matched in the stubborn department. There was a time, when she was six . . ."

Telling stories of Khamsin's youthful exploits was a tactic Tildy employed to keep Wynter calm and resting. He'd discerned her ploy from the start, of course, but he played along because he liked hearing the stories of his wife's childhood. Khamsin had run her poor nurse ragged—always getting into some sort of mischief or other, never sitting still for long, thwarting every attempt to mold and confine her. Like the storms that answered her call, she was a force of nature, wild and reckless and free. And Wynter wouldn't have her any other way.

There was a knock on the door, and Valik walked in. Galacia Frey followed close on his heels. Wynter was surprised to see her. She'd taken off without a word last night after receiving a message flown in by a snow eagle.

One look at their grim faces, and Wynter knew their troubles had just increased.

* * *

"So, let me get this straight. All this time, you and every High Priestess before you for the last nine hundred years has known the Sword of Roland was at the bottom of the Ice Heart?" Wynter sat at the hunting lodge's large dining table and tried to keep the freezing power of his Gaze in check. Frost prickled across the wooden tabletop. The pair of them were lucky that the planks of old pine were the only thing frozen at the moment.

"Wyn—"

"And you sent *my pregnant wife* to dive down to the bottom of the Ice Heart—*the most deadly dangerous magic in all of Wintercraig*—to fetch it? Have I got that right?"

"Wyn, you don't understand—"

"*Is that what you did?*" His fist slammed on the desk, and he half rose from the chair.

Laci blew out an exasperated breath. "Yes! Yes, that's what I did. That's exactly what I did, and I would do it again, given the same circumstances." She flung her arms up. "You were unconscious. There was no certainty you would survive, much less be any use to us in battle, and the Calbernans and Summerlanders were invading. We needed a weapon—and that was the most powerful one I knew of."

"And now my wife is gone, Ungar and his men are dead, the sword of Roland is gone, the second of Thorgyll's spears is missing, and the Summerlanders and Calbernans are still invading. Oh, and Rorjak's army is on the march, too. What were you thinking?"

"We were thinking we could save Wintercraig without losing you!" she spat.

"By sending my wife to retrieve Roland's Sword from the bottom of the Ice Heart?" Wynter ran both hands through his hair just to keep from wrapping them around Laci's throat and squeezing tight. He turned a glare on Valik. "And what happened to your suspicious nature? Weren't you the one telling me all along that Khamsin was in her brother's service—that she'd betray me the first chance she got?"

"Maybe I should have listened to myself," Valik muttered. "Maybe that's exactly what happened."

"No!"

All three of them turned in surprise as Tildavera Greenleaf burst through the door leading to the lodge's bedchambers. Clearly, after being dismissed so Valik, Laci, and Wynter could talk in private, Khamsin's nurse had decided a bit of eavesdropping was in order.

"Whatever you believe, you cannot think Khamsin would betray you. She wouldn't. Not to her brother, not to anyone else. I know, because I gave her the chance to do exactly that, and she refused."

Wynter scowled at her. "Explain yourself, Nurse Greenleaf."

"When they brought me to tend you, I was in communication with Falcon Coruscate. I thought you were planning to kill her at year's end, so I arranged to bring her to him." Tildy blurted out all about the birds she'd used to send messages, knocking out everyone with an herb in the evening meal, telling Khamsin to come with her. "But she wouldn't leave you. And she wouldn't let me leave without doing everything in my power to save you, either. If she found the sword, the only place she would have brought it was back to you—to defend you. She loves you, for Halla's sake!"

"Guard!" Wyn called. To the man who answered his summons, he said, "Escort Nurse Greenleaf to the other room and keep her there."

With a look torn between frustration, irritation, and despair, Tildy turned and marched out of the room. The door closed behind her.

"Wyn, if she's right . . ."

"Then Coruscate has the sword, and he has my queen," Wyn summed up grimly.

"He must have solved the Book of Riddles," Galacia murmured. "If he's got that sword . . ."

"Then we are lost." Wynter sank back in his chair. Despair weighted him down. When the only threat was Coruscate and the Calbernans, victory had been questionable. Wynter had resigned himself to giving his life to protect his people. But now with Roland's sword in play and the army of the Ice King on the march, Wintercraig was hopelessly outnumbered and woefully underequipped.

"Maybe not quite yet," Valik suggested. "Roland's sword is supposed to be the deadliest weapon in the history of all Mystral, right?"

"That's what the legends say," Galacia acknowledged. "And considering that without it, the Ice Heart has turned back into an indestructible block of ice, I'm inclined to believe them."

"And you believe it might be effective against the Ice King's army?" Valik prompted.

She hesitated. "I don't know. When I sent Khamsin to get the sword, I was only thinking about using it to repel the invaders since Wynter was so close to turning." She sent an apologetic glance Wynter's way. "But I suppose, considering the effect that it had on the Ice Heart, it might be effective against Rorjak's army."

"Then why not use that to our advantage?" Valik said.

Wynter leaned forward. "What are you thinking?"

"You said Rorjak's army could sense your presence right? That they were coming for you?"

"Yes."

"So, we use that. We use you as bait to lead Rorjak's army straight to Coruscate. Kill two birds with one arrow."

"That could work," Galacia said.

"Or Rorjak could just turn Coruscate's army into ice thralls and double the size of his fighting force in a matter of minutes," Wynter pointed out.

A little of the wind left Valik's sails. "There is that," he agreed. "But do you have a better idea?"

Wynter wished he did. "No."

The three of them regarded each other in grim silence.

Valik was the first to break the silence. "So what do we do, Wyn? What's your call?"

Wynter took a deep breath. "Send word to Gildenheim. I want every eye in the forest looking for Coruscate and his men. We're going to lead Rorjak's army to the invaders. And along the way, we're going to come up with a plan to rescue my wife."

For the next several hours, as she rode in fully hooded darkness, Khamsin replayed the same scene over and over in her mind. Falcon pulling the sword. The diamond in Blazing's hilt flaring to life. The blast of heat that had knocked her back and melted every ounce of snow and ice near Falcon.

Clearly, he'd called on the power of the sword. Just as clearly, he'd released that power at her.

So why was she still alive?

A little flicker of hope flared in her heart as she recalled the angry way he resheathed Roland's sword, and said, "It seems we've both read too many legends, Storm." Maybe Falcon wasn't quite as ruthless as he tried to appear. Maybe *that's* what he'd been angry about—that for all his talk, he didn't have it in him to kill her. Or maybe he'd been mad because remembering their hours of discussion about Roland, all the legends of his heroic tales, had reminded him of the vital aspects of his character he'd sacrificed on the altar of ambition.

Maybe she was getting through to him after all.

Kham hugged that possibility to her heart. He'd loved her once. She was sure of it. Surely some part of the brother she'd idolized still existed inside him. If she could reach *that* Falcon, make him listen, make him understand what was at stake, maybe there was still a chance to save Wynter.

But the next time they stopped, her brother was no longer with them.

"Where is Prince Falcon?" she asked, but the only answer she received was a flask of water shoved in her face and a curt command to "Drink and be quiet, or the hood goes back on."

Anger flared at the man's impertinent rudeness. Prisoner she might be, but she was still Queen of the Craig and a princess of Summerlea. Kham narrowed her eyes and considered setting a fire in the seat of the man's pants. *That* would certainly teach him to mind his manners when dealing with an Heir of the Rose. The thought of it made her smile.

"What's so funny, princess?"

Kham's smile winked out. She cast a withering glare upon the scarred, mean-eyed Summerlander standing to her right. "Your Grace."

"What?"

"The proper form of address when speaking to a queen of Wintercraig is 'Your Grace.'" Each clearly enunciated word ended with a sharp clip.

"How's about I give you the proper form of my fist right across that mouth of yours?"

She smiled, eyes flaring liquid silver. "Oh, by all means, do try."

"Leave off, Blackwood," another Summerlander advised. "Get her mad enough, and that one will fry your balls like eggs on a griddle."

Blackwood shook his fist under her nose. "Saved for now," he muttered, adding with a sneer, "*Your Grace.*"

As the men walked off to tend the horses, Kham measured the location of the sun. They'd traveled another thirty miles since breaking camp this morning. The Llaskroner Fjord couldn't be more than another day or two away. They must be meeting up with the rest of Falcon's army near there.

A careful glance around the camp told her that wherever Falcon had gone, he'd gone alone. For what purpose, she couldn't even begin to speculate, but his absence gave her the chance to draw upon her power without alerting him. Time to make a move.

Krysti was chained to a tree fifteen feet away, but Falcon's men were mostly ignoring him, too. That was a mistake. She saw his fingers working at the hem of his tunic and hid a smile. He kept a set of picks sewn into the hem of each of his tunics because, "A boy never knows when they might come in handy."

She nodded when Krysti glanced her way, then lowered her eyes and reached out to the source of her power, gathering the sun's heat and concentrating it inside her. Her body began to warm beneath its lead blanket. She gripped her chains in both hands, preparing to melt them as she had the chains Valik had tried to hold her with.

Once Krysti got safely away, Khamsin would be free to teach her captors the true meaning of her giftname.

The sound of galloping hooves and the feel of hot, angry weathermagic on the wind made her gasp and release her power.

She turned to see her brother leap off his horse almost before it came to a stop. He crossed the short distance to her side in five long strides and yanked her up to her feet.

"Where is it?" His face was contorted in fury, his eyes wild. "What did you do with it?" He shook her so hard she was surprised her head didn't flop off her neck.

"What did I do with what?" she exclaimed when he stopped shaking her enough that she could speak.

He opened his mouth, then after a hard look at his companions, thought the better of it. Instead, he grabbed her by the arm and frog-marched her into the woods. When they were out of earshot of the camp, he spun her around and yanked Blazing from its sheath.

"No more games, Storm. You tell me what you did with it, or you die right here, and to Hel with any curse on my House."

"Did with what? What are you talking about?"

"The sword! The real sword of Roland! Not this weak-spelled forgery you put in its place!" He shook the sword furiously and flung it aside. It sank into a drift of snow.

Kham's mouth dropped open. She couldn't believe he had just thrown the greatest treasure in the world away like so much rotting garbage. "Are you mad? That *is* Roland's sword."

"Liar!" He slapped her hard, knocking her to her knees. "Where is Blazing? The *real* Blazing?"

She raised manacled hands to her throbbing cheek. "That *is* Blazing. You've felt its power. You called on it early today, during that first stop. You melted everything around us." How could he even think the sword was a forgery? Had Blazing not conveyed to Falcon the same history of its creation as it had the moment she first touched it?

Helos bestows his greatest gifts only on the worthy, Heir of Roland.

The low, multilayered voice boomed in her mind, resonating through every cell in her body. She didn't hear the voice so much as she *felt* it. Each vast and terrible divine tone. It made her tremble in her boots.

Falcon just kept shouting. "Roland's sword was capable of calling phenomenal power! All this does is amplify my weathergift. Any half-witted wizard capable of boiling water could lay an amplification spell on a sword!"

He had not heard the voice.

Falcon had not heard the voice. And if he had not heard the voice, that meant . . .

"You are not the Heir," she breathed.

Falcon stopped in midrant. His body went stiff. His face went hard. "What did you say?"

She stared at Falcon as if she'd never seen him before. And perhaps, until now, she never had. He *had* tried to call on Blazing's power that morning. He hadn't just tried to scare her—he had tried to call upon the sword's magic to kill her the way she had killed the ice-thralled Elka in the Temple of Wyrn.

And the sword had not answered.

She climbed slowly to her feet, never taking her eyes off her brother.

"You are not the Heir," she said again. "Blazing doesn't answer you because you are not the true Heir of Roland."

Her eyes flashed purest silver in an instant. She didn't even need to summon a storm this time. The power she'd gathered earlier came roaring back to life. In an instant, she melted the chain binding her hands and punched through the lead-lined fabric of her cloak like a hot coal through silk. Electricity shot from her palms, striking Falcon on the chest and sending him flying into a nearby tree. His skull cracked against the trunk, and he slid down into a crumpled, motionless heap at the tree's base.

Khamsin ripped off her lead cloak and dove for Roland's sword, snatching it out of the snowbank. Her fingers closed around the hilt. She stared at her reflection in the gleaming blade—the wild, lightning-kissed hair, the quicksilver eyes—and thought, *Fire*. The clear diamond flashed blinding bright, and flame engulfed Blazing's blade.

"Summer Sun," she whispered. "It's me. *I* am Roland's Heir."

"Over my dead body."

She turned to find Verdan Coruscate standing at the edge of the clearing, Krysti held before him, a knife at the boy's throat.

CHAPTER 26

Strange Bedfellows

"How can she be the Heir? It's supposed to be me! It was always supposed to be me!" Falcon paced back and forth across his father's tent. Roland's sword, still sheathed in Falcon's scabbard, lay on a table against the side of the tent. Falcon had thrown it there in disgust earlier. "I'm the one who spent years reading entire libraries of books, tracking down every fragment of a lead. I was the one who followed the trail to Wintercraig and that damned Book of Riddles! I'm the one who spent the last three years traveling from one corner of Mystral to another, risking life and limb to follow the clues in that book! I risked everything to find that sword! It's supposed to be mine! I'm the true Heir of Roland!"

"Yes, you are," King Verdan agreed. "With my sword arm ruined, you are indisputably Roland's rightful Heir." He stalked over to the corner of the tent, where Khamsin was sitting, bound securely to a chair, gagged, and once more draped in a heavy lead-lined cloth. He grabbed her face, squeezing her cheeks and jaw in a hard grip. "What vile magic did you work to make the sword recognize you instead of your brother, girl?"

She glared up at him. The thick wad of cloth tied over her mouth rendered her incapable of response.

Verdan loosened the cloth and let it fall to her chest. "Answer me, girl."

"I did nothing. Clearly, Blazing judged Falcon and

found him lacking." She switched her glare to her brother, and added, "Maybe he should have spent more time trying to emulate Roland's noble qualities—like honor, generosity, and self-sacrifice—instead of murdering, thieving, and whoring his way to the sword's hiding place!"

"You traitorous little bitch!" Frothing with rage, Falcon lunged forward, fist raised.

Kham's chin jutted out, and she braced herself for the blow. "Do it," she dared. "My hands are tied, my magic bound. Hit me and prove once and for all what a fine, brave hero you are."

Falcon swore, and his fist stopped midswing. Perhaps because he still retained the ability to feel shame. Or maybe, just because he remembered what happened the last time he assumed a lead cloak rendered her powerless.

"Do you see now?" Verdan said, waving a hand at Khamsin. "I warned you to send her to Hel with the rest of Atrialan's lackeys. I told you she'd betray her family, her country, and her king at the first opportunity."

"You aren't my king, Verdan Coruscate," she snapped. "And you aren't my family, either. You lost all claim to that the day you dragged me into the depths of Vera Sola and beat me near to death. All the loyalty and devotion I would have given you, if you'd loved me even a little, belongs to Wynter now."

"Love? *You?* I'd sooner love a plague on my own House! I should have drowned you at birth. If I had, my Rose would still be alive."

"So you've said my whole life," she scoffed, "but that's just a cowardly lie." For the first time, his hatred didn't hurt. He had nothing she wanted, nothing she needed, and he had lost all power over her. "Tildy told me the truth. The doctor warned you to stay away from my mother, but you didn't. You couldn't. And do you know what? I don't blame you for that. I know now what it is to love someone so deeply you can't stay away. But do you think for one minute my mother would love the vile, corrupt monster you've become? A man who would plot to kill his own child—*her* child? She would despise you! She would cringe from you in revulsion. She would—"

Verdan's fist shot out. Unlike Falcon, he didn't stop mid-swing. His knuckles struck a hard blow to her jaw.

Her head snapped back from the impact. She and the chair she was tied to fell sideways onto the floor. Kham lay in the dirt, working her jaw, and regarded him with narrowed eyes. "That is the last time you will ever lay a finger on me."

"Or what? You'll call your weathergift, *Storm*?" Verdan laughed. "Go ahead and try. Did you truly think I would be fool enough to repeat Falcon's mistake? This entire tent is lined with lead."

She clamped her lips tight and watched in mute silence as he sauntered over to the table to pick up Roland's sword with his left hand.

"It really is quite beautiful," he murmured. He turned the sword from side to side, watching with almost hypnotic fascination as the light of the tent lamps reflected off the razor-sharp blade. "The weapon of a king."

He closed his eyes and tightened his hand around the grip. When the diamond in the hilt flared with light, Verdan opened his eyes again and smiled.

"I don't know how you could ever have thought this blade was anything but the true sword of Roland, Falcon. Could you not feel the power surging inside it? Trying to connect?" He pulled back the right cuff of his coat, revealing the dark red Rose birthmark on the wrist of his ruined arm. He laid his left forearm across it and gave a small, dazed laugh. "Even though my arm is frozen, my Rose is hot to the touch. The sword knows my blood, and my blood knows the sword."

"Any amplification spell—"

"Would not breathe heat back into the lump of ice that is my arm," Verdan snapped. Then the anger faded from his expression as he once again focused his attention on the blade. "But like you, I cannot access that power. It is blocked from me. Perhaps the sword only recognizes one Heir at a time. Perhaps, if you'd gotten to it first, it would have recognized you instead of her." Verdan regarded Khamsin with cold eyes. "Maybe if she dies, the sword will be free to be claimed again. This time, by its true and rightful Heir."

Falcon looked alarmed. "You aren't seriously suggesting we kill her? You'll call a curse upon our House."

"She *is* the curse. She always has been. Killing her can only set us free."

"Or make it ten times worse!"

Before Verdan could answer, a shrill, ear-piercing shriek rent the air. Another shriek followed the first. Then another.

Then the screams of men began.

Falcon ran to the tent entrance and shoved back a flap, revealing a scene of carnage and chaos. Falcon's small party of men had met up with the rest of their army not long after Verdan's arrival. An invasion force of many thousands of Summerlanders and Calbernans. But their overwhelming numbers seemed somehow smaller now, as half the camp was running and shouting in chaos while enormous, white *garm* darted through their midst, shrieking, spewing blue vapor, and shredding men into mangled bits of flesh and bone.

"Sound the alarm!" Falcon shouted. "To arms! To arms!"

"Free me!" Kham cried. She struggled and kicked against her bonds. "For Halla's sake, untie me and give me the sword. Hurry, or we're all dead!"

"One of us is going to die," Verdan growled. "But it won't be me or Falcon."

Kham gasped as Verdan swung Roland's sword, but instead of biting into her flesh, Blazing sliced through the ropes binding her to the chair. He shoved the sword into his belt to free his hand, then reached down and hauled Khamsin to her feet.

"Father, give me the—" Falcon broke off in surprise. "What are you doing?"

"The sword's useless to us so long as she lives. Time to remedy that problem." Verdan shouldered Falcon aside and shoved Khamsin through the tent flaps, into the path of an oncoming *garm*.

Kham screamed and fell backward, clutching at her father's arm as she tumbled. Her feet slipped on the icy ground, and the sole of her boots caught Verdan in the ankles, knocking his feet out from under him.

With a hoarse shout, Verdan fell on top of her.

She tried to roll free, but he landed on the edge of her leaden cloak and pinned her. The ties at her throat pulled tight against her neck. As Verdan scrambled to his feet, each frantic motion pulled the strings at her neck tighter. Choking, gasping for air, Kham ripped at the ties of her cloak with her bound hands. She managed to free herself and push up to her hands and knees in time to see a glint of malevolent red in a blur of onrushing white. Terror shot through her veins.

Verdan saw the *garm*, too. Shouting, he scrambled to free the sword stuffed in his belt.

The *garm* leapt. Its paralytic scream ripped through the air, and a cloud of blue vapor spewed from its mouth. Khamsin rolled instinctively onto her belly, dragging the leaden cloak atop her as the cloud of freezing cold enveloped them.

Frost crackled in her hair and numbed her legs, and the leaden cloak turned stiff as a plank of wood, trapping her inside a frozen cocoon. She heard her father shout, heard the *garm* scream. Then there was a loud thud, and Verdan collapsed on top of her, his body jerking like a trout on a string. Something hot and wet rained down on the back of her head. She opened her eyes to see blood spurting onto the snow in great, pulsating ruby jets. Roland's sword lay gleaming in the snow several feet away.

Broad, taloned paws pounded the ground as an entire pack of *garm* raced past. More paralyzing shrieks rang out, and the screams of the fleeing Summerlanders and Calbernans cut off in midcry.

Kham pushed against the frozen lead cape and the crushing weight of her father's armored body, barely able to breathe, let alone move. Her struggles caught the attention of a second pack, and two of the *garm* broke from the group to stalk towards her, heads lowered, red eyes glowing with malice.

"Falcon!" Her brother was standing in the tent entrance, watching her struggling to crawl free of their father's corpse. "Help me!" she screamed. "Help me get the sword!"

But instead of rushing to help her, Falcon ducked inside the tent. The flaps fell closed behind him.

"Falcon!"

The scene was far too familiar for her liking, and this time there would be no Wynter riding in to save the day. Panicking, Roland's sword well out of reach, she shoved and pushed against the heavy, immobile weight of her father's body, but it wouldn't budge. Her heart pounded faster than Hodri's galloping hooves. *Think, Khamsin! Calm down, and think! You haven't been helpless a day in your life—for Halla's sake, don't pick now to start!*

The closest of the approaching *garm* growled. Blue slime dripped from its fang-filled mouth.

Kham clawed and kicked at the ground, grunting with effort as she raised herself up on her elbows. Her father's body shifted, sliding down her back and freeing her torso. Now only her hips and legs were pinioned beneath its deadweight.

She reached out a desperate hand towards Roland's sword, hoping the sword's proximity would aid her. A trickle of energy flowed into her veins—a far cry from the heat she could channel from the sun—but it amplified her weather magic, so she wasn't about to complain. The wispy clouds overhead plumped and grew dark with gathering moisture. She fed more energy into them.

The *garm* crouched, hind legs tightening as it prepared to pounce.

Khamsin swore a long string of inventively foul curses she'd learned from Krysti. There wasn't even a hint of the lavender glow around her hands that preceded her ability to summon lightning. And the electrical charge she could generate without tapping into the power of a storm might have tossed a man off his feet but probably wouldn't do much to a *garm*.

Still, it was all she had until the storm brewing in those clouds got going.

Kham focused the energy in her hands until sparks crackled and popped between her fingertips, then let it fly. The electrical charge zinged the short distance to the *garm* and zapped the creature in its nasal slits.

The *garm* yowled in surprise and vigorously shook its massive head. But instead of convincing the *garm* that Kham was more trouble than she was worth, the zap only seemed to anger the beast. Red eyes fixed on her with renewed malice.

She grimaced. Well, that wasn't exactly the result she'd been hoping for.

The *garm* charged. Its gigantic mouth, with all those rows of jagged, dagger-sharp teeth, gaped wide. The long, curved claws dug into ice and gravel. The creature leapt, and Kham braced herself for the killing blow.

To her shock, in the middle of its leap, the *garm* suddenly and inexplicably froze. Literally. The furry body fell out of the air and slid across the frozen ground, crashing into her with a brittle crack. The jolt knocked Verdan Coruscate's body to one side. Kham kicked free and scrambled to her feet.

Only then did she see the ice white spear protruding from the creature's side and the young boy five yards away, bent over, hands on his knees, as he tried to catch his breath after throwing a spear more than twice his size.

The second *garm,* which had been stalking towards her, now fixed its scarlet gaze on Krysti and began to charge.

"Krysti, run!" she cried. He bounded for the closest tree while Kham dove for Roland's sword. Her fingers closed around the sword grip. She rolled to her feet, and cried "Fire!" just as the *garm* shrieked.

Flames engulfed the sword. She swung at the *garm* with all her might. The searing blade of fire halved the *garm's* body and cut off the cloud of freezing vapor in midexhalation. The small, abruptly terminated cloud of blue vapor wisped harmlessly away on a puff of wind.

"Well, that's something you don't see every day." Krysti, who had leapt up a nearby tree with his typical agility, dropped back down to the ground and ran to her side. "I thought you were done for."

"Me, too. If not for you, I would have been." She pulled him close for a quick hug. "How did you get free?"

The boy grinned. "It's a gift."

Despite everything, she laughed. "A darned useful one, too." She ruffled his head. "And the spear?"

"The Summerlander holding it was distracted when the *garm* attacked. I hit him on the head with a rock and took it. I figured we needed it more."

Kham's smile faded. "That we do."

Together, they turned to face the carnage taking place around them. Screams and shrieks rang out from every direction, and blue vapor hung like a mist in the air. A knot of Calbernans were huddled back-to-back, throwing spears at a circling trio of *garm*. A group of Summerlanders were firing arrows on the run. And everywhere, the fallen were rising again, covered in ice.

"We should just leave them to the *garm,*" Krysti said. "They came here to kill us."

"They came here because of Falcon and my father. I can't leave them all to die." Invaders the Summerlander and Calbernans might be, but there was no way she could just walk away and let the *garm* slaughter them. And not just because the fallen were rising again as ice thralls.

"They'd leave us in a heartbeat."

"Perhaps. But that doesn't make it right." She took a deep breath. "Stay here. Find a place to hide." She pulled Thorgyll's spear out of the fallen *garm* and handed it back to Krysti. "Keep this. If the *garm* come back, use it."

"I'm not letting you go off to fight *garm* without me," Krysti protested.

"You're not *letting* me do anything," Kham snapped. Then she winced. She hadn't meant to bark at the boy. "I'm sorry, Krysti. It's too dangerous. I need to know you're safe."

"Safe? Do you see what's out there?" Krysti pointed to a pack of ice thralls attacking two Summerlanders while a *garm* leapt up a tree in pursuit of a third. "I'm a million times safer near you and that sword. And you're safer with me guarding your back."

He looked so small, so young, holding a spear more than twice his size, but so determined and brave as well. She wanted to kiss him. More than anything, she wanted to keep him safe. But he was right. There was no such place in this forest. Not now.

"All right," she conceded. "But don't stick too close. My lightning is dangerous, and I really don't know everything this sword can do."

"Agreed."

"Then let's go." Kham gripped Blazing in one fist and started running towards the knot of Calbernans battling the circling *garm*.

With Blazing in hand, the power that had tingled so tantalizingly out of reach when she was pinned beneath her father's body now came in an effortless rush. It filled Khamsin and the sword in an instant, warm and revitalizing. Heat filled her and radiated out on all sides, melting the snow for six feet on every side. She seized the warm, moist air swirling around her and drove it up into the dry, cold winter skies above. Clouds blossomed and began darkening rapidly, and she laughed at the familiar cool, fresh, electric taste on the wind.

"Stand your ground!" Kham shouted to a half dozen fleeing Summerlander soldiers. "These creatures can be killed! Use ranged weapons! Bows, arrows, spears! Don't let the vapor touch you—and cover your ears against their screams! Fight, sons of Summer! Sons of the Isles! Fight!"

The storm overhead was brewing with power. Lightning crackled and raced across the clouds. The purple glow of plasma gathered around Khamsin. Ahead, one of the *garm* circling the Calbernans froze. The long receptor hairs pointed her way by the dozen.

The *garm* spun and leapt for her, teeth gnashing, blue froth flying from its snarling maw.

"Burn!" she cried, and thrust Blazing towards the beast.

Three bolts of lightning shot down from the sky. In less time than it took to blink, the electric charge passed through her, down her arm, then shot out from the tip of Roland's sword into the *garm* as a single, concentrated flow of power. The lightning slammed into the *garm*, lifting the massive creature off its feet and sending it flying backward through the air. The *garm* burst into flames and landed at the feet of the Calbernans. The flames promptly turned inward, and within less than two seconds, all that remained was a pile of *garm*-shaped ash that collapsed in upon itself and blew away in the next gust of wind.

The second of the dead *garm*'s companions now turned its attention to her, and she dispatched it with similar ease, while the large, blue-tattooed Calbernans threw their viciously barbed tridents at the third, pinning it to the ground. Another island warrior—this one a huge, broad-chested man with long ropes of black-green hair and massive biceps circled by bands of hammered gold—brought an enormous sword arcing down and decapitated the pinned monster with a single, mighty blow. Blue blood spilled out across the snow.

Behind her, Krysti skewered first one, then a second ice thrall with Thorgyll's spear. The thralls froze solid as stone and didn't move again. Just to be sure, Kham stabbed each of them with Blazing's fire and reduced them to ash.

"The *garm* will die," she told the Calbernans, "but you have to burn the ice thralls with fire."

The huge Calbernan who had decapitated the *garm* gave her a savage grin and whirled to slice an ice thrall in half, then dismembered what was left with a few enthusiastic chops of his blade.

"I guess that will work, too," she muttered. A flash of white darting through the trees caught her eye. "Watch out!" she cried to the huge Calbernan. She guided a crackling bolt of lightning that incinerated the *garm* just before it struck the Calbernan's unprotected back. The shower of hot ash washed harmlessly over the islander, turning his blue-tattooed skin a dull, dusty gray. The man's golden eyes blinked, and he lifted a hand in a wordless salute of gratitude.

She pointed to another knot of the embattled Calbernans not too far away. "Your friends over there look like they could use some help. I suggest you grab a few of those bows and quivers over there if you know how to use them. They give a better range than those tridents."

The big, green-haired man barked something in musical Calbernan. The rest of the group plucked their tridents from the dead *garm* and ran to help their comrades, several of them grabbing bows and quivers as they went. The big man sheathed his sword and snatched up four quivers and a long bow.

"Many thanks, *myerina*. Good hunting to you." With a smile, he bowed his head in her direction, gave a graceful, waving salute of thanks, then sprinted after his men.

Kham and Krysti headed off in a different direction to find another target of their own. It didn't take long. All around the camp, the scene was like something from a nightmare. Bodies strewn everywhere. Blood and blue *garm* slime mixing together in noxious purple puddles. Frost prickled across every surface. *Garm* were leaping, shrieking, and spewing blue vapor at everything that moved. Ice thralls were hacking at the living.

The storm overhead boiled with energy. Kham called the lightning and incinerated *garm* and ice thralls left and right. The ease of it stunned her. The storm was so strong now, she should have been fighting desperately to control it, but she wasn't. She could feel and shape the flows of air, summon the lightning or disperse it. The diamond in the hilt of Roland's sword shone like a beacon, and she knew the power of the sword was helping her maintain control over the wild power of her weathergift. With Blazing in hand, she truly was the master of storms.

She and Krysti fought their way across the encampment, dispatching *garm* and thralls with sword and spear and bolts of lightning. Along the way, she caught the scent of another magic on the wind. Bright flashes that had nothing to do with lightning illuminated the bottoms of the dark clouds to her left.

Kham followed the scent of magic and the light flashes to their source, bracing herself to dispatch whatever was there, only to stop in surprise at the sight of her brother engaged in battle.

She'd thought, when he'd left her to face the *garm*, that he would remain hiding in his tent. Instead, he'd retrieved his bow and quiver and was shooting Sunfire arrows at Rorjak's minions. Despite everything, she could not help but feel a measure of pride as each of Falcon's magic-imbued missiles found their targets, exploding *garm* and thralls as his fire clashed with their ice. Grimly handsome, deadly, full of grace and skill, he fought like the Hero of Summerlea she'd always thought him to be.

A tug on her arm pulled her attention away.

"Come on," Krysti said. "Doesn't look like he needs our help. Not that I'd want to give it to him even if he did."

Kham's throat tightened a little. Why couldn't Falcon

have been the admirable man he should be? The noble man she'd thought he was? Was it a weakness in the Coruscate blood that made first Verdan, then his son, lose all sense of right and wrong? Though nothing in her mourned the death of her father—the wounds he'd inflicted were too deep, too many, and far too painful—every part of her wept at the realization that the heroic brother she'd adored and idolized her whole life no longer existed. If, indeed, he ever had.

"Kham?" Krysti's small, white-freckled face looked so earnest. So concerned. "I'm sorry. I shouldn't have said that."

"It's all right." She forced a small, reassuring smile and ran a hand over his spiky white hair. "I love you, Krysti. You are the brother to me Falcon should have been." She bent down to give him a hug and a kiss.

When she pulled back, Krysti's eyes were suspiciously bright, but the boy merely cleared his throat and declared like a true, gruff Winterman, "Well, come on, then. I see more *garm* in need of killing."

Despite everything, she laughed, and a little bit of the heaviness pressing down on her heart lifted. "Lead the way, noble warrior."

Between Falcon's Sunfire arrows, the ferocity of the Calbernans, and the power of Roland's sword, the remaining *garm* and ice thralls were soon dispatched. In the carnage that remained of the invaders' camp, the survivors burned the remains of the dead and tended the injured. There weren't many wounded to speak of. *Garm* were lethally efficient killing machines, and the freezing wounds inflicted by ice thralls sapped their victims' strength and speed, making them easier to kill.

Kham didn't have any idea how many men Falcon and his Calbernan allies had lost, but judging by the grim faces and piles of corpses, the *garm* had winnowed quite a few.

"We should go," Krysti whispered. "Now, before they decide they don't need us anymore."

"Where would we go?" she asked. "Rorjak has returned. And if the number of *garm* that just attacked us is any measure, he's already got a formidable army. There's no way we can face him on our own."

"What are you suggesting?"

"I'm suggesting that we convince Falcon and his allies to join forces with us and confront Rorjak."

Krysti gaped at her. "Are you crazy? They tried to kill us! They came to conquer Wintercraig, not to save us!"

"That was before. Now they've seen for themselves what Rorjak can do. He's not just *our* enemy. He's the enemy of every living soul on Mystral. He's got to be stopped, even if I have to ally with the enemies of Wintercraig to do it." She pulled up the hem of her skirts and cut off a long strip from her white underskirts. She looped the strip around her neck like a scarf. "Come on. And stay close. If they try to use you against me again, this won't end well."

With Krysti at her heels, Kham strode over to a group of Calbernans who were dragging corpses into a pile to be burned. "Take me to your commander. I wish to negotiate with him under the white stole of peace."

The Calbernans paused in their grim work. Several reached for their tridents. They were an intimidating lot, as tall as Wintermen, their bronze skin covered in iridescent blue tattoos. Their muscular physiques were put on impressive display in the blue-green loincloths that hung down to their knees, with gleaming plates of scale-shaped copper armor strapped to their chests, shins, and forearms. Unlike the Summerlanders, who were bundled up against the cold, the Calbernans appeared quite impervious to ice and snow. Somehow, that made them even more intimidating.

Kham stood her ground and kept her expression calm, her gaze steady. Her fingers, however, tightened around Blazing's grip. It was just as well the sword's sheath was still in Falcon's tent. Not having it with her gave her an excuse to keep her weapon drawn and ready for a fight. For all her brave, reassuring words to Krysti, Khamsin's heart was pounding like a hammer. She was taking a huge risk. Just because she helped save these men's lives didn't mean they would feel any debt of gratitude.

Two Calbernans whispered something to one another. The larger of the two, a warrior with a scar running the length of one cheek, and a large quantity of blue blood spattered across his body, stepped forward and waved her over. "Come. I will take you."

Girding herself, Khamsin followed the Calbernan. The rest of the islanders abandoned the burial detail, picked up their tridents, and fell into step around her, effectively boxing her in.

Word traveled quickly as the Calbernans escorted her across the remains of the camp. Curious Calbernans and Summerlanders began to follow them. By the time the Calbernans stopped beside a large bonfire on the other side of camp, Khamsin and Krysti were surrounded by the remaining army of invaders. The man leading them gestured for them to wait while he ducked inside a Calbernan tent. A few moments later, he reemerged. Directly behind him came the enormous Calbernan in the golden armor whose life she had saved at the beginning of the attack. Hope stirred in Khamsin's breast, only to falter when the tent flaps parted again, and her brother Falcon stepped through.

"I told you this was a bad idea," Krysti muttered.

Kham clutched Blazing so tight, her fingers went numb. "You may be right." But it was too late to change her mind now.

"Falcon." Kham acknowledged her brother warily. "I'm glad to see you survived the *garm*."

"You should have escaped when you had the chance, Storm."

"You mean after you left me pinned and defenseless when the *garm* attacked? I wouldn't leave my worst enemy to face that fate—which I proved when I stayed to help the very people who came to destroy my home and kill my people. But even if I could be as self-serving as you, Falcon, there is no escape anymore. Not for me. Not for you. Not for any of us."

"Drop the sword, Kham. If you don't, you won't be leaving this place alive."

Her eyes narrowed. She took a deep breath, then said very clearly, very deliberately, "No."

"Archers!" he rapped out. "Target the boy."

Kham stood her ground. "That won't work this time, Falcon. If you kill Krysti, I will destroy every living thing in this valley." In her hands, Roland's sword went hot, and the diamond in its hilt grew blinding bright. "You know I can do it."

"You're bluffing."

"Not this time." Her steady gaze never wavered. The light in Blazing's hilt grew brighter. "Did you not see what just happened here? The *garm*? The dead arising to fight again? I warned you that Rorjak was coming, and this battle proves it. Carnak is upon us. If any of us hope to survive, we have to stop fighting each other and start working together to defeat the real enemy: Rorjak, the Ice King."

"I came here for that sword, Storm, and I'm not leaving without it."

"It isn't yours, Falcon. It will never be yours. Even if you kill me—even if you kill every living member of our bloodline—Blazing will never answer to you. You are not Roland's Heir."

"Liar! I bear the Rose. I'm as much an Heir of Roland as you—and the rightful King of Summerlea."

"Once, perhaps, but no longer. You threw everything away to go searching for the sword. You betrayed everything Roland ever stood for. Now you are a man without a country, and a prince without a crown. Your weathergift and that Rose on your wrist are the only gifts of Helos you'll ever possess."

"Archers, fire!"

Kham gripped her sword, and cried, "Shield!" A dome

of white-hot flame sprang up around her. Every arrow that flew into the fiery wall disintegrated instantly into ash. She fed more power into the shield, pushing it out along its circumference until the gathered Calbernans and Summerlanders fell back to avoid being incinerated. Within the bright shield, Khamsin turned slowly in a complete circle, targeting each bow aimed her way.

"Burn," she breathed and carefully orchestrated flows of superheated air snaked out from her shield. Summerlander archers screamed as their bows burst into flames.

Kham dropped her shield. A barely caged inferno burned in her eyes as she met her brother's stunned gaze. "I meant to offer you a chance to make amends, to recover some part of the honor you threw away, but if death is your choice, then death it will be. *Fire.*" Flames burst to life along Blazing's shining length. She drew back her arm, keeping the sword pointed at Falcon. "Good-bye, brother."

Before she could loose Blazing's deadly fire, the Calbernan leader standing a few feet from Falcon began to laugh.

"Gods, what a woman!" The Calbernan slapped one massive paw against Falcon's back with enough strength to make him stagger. To Khamsin, the Calbernan said, "I like you, *myerina.* So much more than I like your brother. I will be sad to end your life. Throw down that weapon. Surrender to me now, and I will take you as my *liana* and fill your belly with my offspring."

Khamsin did not take offense. She remembered the lessons Tildy had drummed into her head about the customs of neighboring kingdoms. The Calbernan's threat about killing her was a bluff. Calbernans revered women, having so few females of their own kind. And his offer to take her his *liana*—his wife—was an invitation to live in wealth and comfort beneath the powerful protection and devoted care of a fierce warrior of the isles.

"Regrettably, I must decline your gracious offer, Sealord, and extend instead an offer of my own. Wintercraig has long lived in peace with Calberna. You made yourselves our enemy when you joined forces with my brother and invaded our lands. That foolish act can either end in the slaughter of your army and the destruction of your homeland, or you can renounce your alliance with my brother and join forces with me instead to fight an evil that threatens us all. Do that, and the peace between our kingdoms will continue as if this invasion never happened. You have my word, as Queen of Wintercraig."

The Calbernan cocked his head to one side. The long, dark strands of his hair, wound in dozens of inch-wide ropes slid across his bare, impressively-muscled chest and shoulders. "Death stalks Calberna every day. We do not fear it. But to return home with so many lives lost and nothing to show for our troubles, this would not make my people happy. Besides the prince, your brother, tells me you are queen against your will and for only a year. Forgive me, *myerina*, if I do not consider your word as Wintercraig's queen a reliable star to sail by."

"The Calbernans are circling to our left and right," Krysti whispered.

"I see them," Kham confirmed. In a louder voice, she said, "You have not yet made yourself my enemy, Sealord. I implore you not to do so now. My brother has—unintentionally, I'm sure—misled you about my situation. I am quite happy here, I have a husband I love dearly, and his child already grows inside me."

Falcon regarded her in shock. "You are with child?"

Khamsin ignored her brother and continued addressing the Calbernan. "So you see, Sealord, I will be queen of Wintercraig for much more than a year. Thus, I cannot and will not surrender myself, my husband's child, or my kingdom. Not even to a very handsome and clearly powerful foreign prince, whom I fear has been steered far off course by the counsel of a poor navigator. But I am not an ungenerous woman. Join me to defeat the Ice King, and I will not send you away empty-handed. You shall have wood enough to build twenty ships, and two thousand of Wintercraig's best furs to trade."

"Tsk. Tsk." The Calbernan clucked his tongue against the roof of his mouth. "Falcon, you never told me what a treasure this sister was." He inclined his head towards Khamsin. "Such an offer is indeed tempting, *myerina,* but I did not lead my people to this land seeking merely ships and riches to trade. Your brother promised me wealth, it is true. But he also promised me an unbreakable alliance, bound by blood, and a treasure of treasures to grace the House of Merimydion."

"He promised you a Season of Summerlea, did he?"

The golden eyes gleamed. "Calbernan blood rules the sea. A *liana* with power over weather is worth more to me than two hundred ships and ten thousand furs. I am of age and have earned my right to claim a *liana,* and the Seasons are known to be as gifted as they are beautiful."

The promised bride was for him, which meant he must be the prince of House Merimydion, the royal house of Calberna. What was his name? Kham racked her memory for names of foreign leaders Tildy had drilled into her head. Dilys? "You are Dilys Merimydion?"

The Calbernan inclined his head.

"You are aware, Sealord Merimydion, that the weather-gifts of my family do not pass outside Summerlea's direct royal line. Even with a Season for a wife, it's unlikely your children will inherit the gift—or pass it on, if they do."

"Such is my understanding although your brother made no mention of it." She could see her honesty had earned her a measure of respect. "This does not concern me. Any child of mine will have formidable gifts of his own."

Khamsin's mind raced. As princesses of a still-independent Summerlea, her sisters had never expected a future that did not include being married off to the royal scions of other lands for the benefit of Summerlea. As the daughters of a deposed, enemy king, their future could easily be much less comfortable. They lived at the pleasure of Wynter Atrialan, and they knew it. Still, Khamsin had been given into marriage to a stranger, and she would not force her sisters into the same situation.

"Calbernans hold their wives in great esteem, do they not?"

"The highest of esteem, *myerina*."

"Did Falcon promise wives for your men as well?" Only one of every hundred Calbernan children were female. As a result, the renowned seafarers frequently bought their wives from the slave markets in Lukerne or raided weaker lands across the sea and took women captive to be their brides. She had hoped her first bribe would be tempting enough on its own. So much wealth and so many ships would buy many wives.

"He promised them their pick from the whole of Wintercraig."

Of course, he had.

"That is not going to happen," she told the Calbernan king bluntly. "But, the war between Summerlea and Wintercraig has left many women widowed, their children fatherless. I am sure there are many among them who would look favorably on the offer a union with a man of the Isles if the union offered security for themselves and their children.

"So here, then, is my offer, Dilys Merimydion, Prince of Calberna: If you and your men join me now to fight the Ice King, Wintercraig will provide you wood enough for fifty ships and five thousand of Wintercraig's best furs to trade. You and every Calbernan in this army will also be invited to return, in peace, to the royal palace in Konumarr next summer. There, you, Sealord Merimydion, will have three months to court the Seasons of Summerlea and convince one of them to be your bride. I will also invite any woman of Summerlea or Wintercraig willing to take a Calbernan husband to come to Konumarr as well, and your men will have the same three months to win wives of their own."

The Sealord smiled. "This offer is most generous, *myerina*, to be sure, but why would I or my men sacrifice the certainty of a *liana* now for the possibility of a *liana* later?"

"Trust me, none of you would want an unwilling Summerlea or Wintercraig wife."

"Ah, but any *liana* of a Calbernan would not be unwilling for long." The way he said it sent an unmistakably erotic shiver up Khamsin's body. If she weren't irrevocably in love with her own Winterman, she might actually have considered throwing down her sword and taking Merimydion up on his offer.

Instead, she gave him a sweet smile, and said, "In that case, my lord, three months should be ample time for you and your men to win the consent of your chosen brides. Or," she added when he didn't immediately accept, "I can call upon the deadly power of this sword, and we can all die today in a blaze of Sunfire. And there will be no children and no future for any of us."

The Calbernan Sealord began to laugh again, slowly at first, then with increasing gusto. There was a pleasing, honest sound to his laugh. The kind of sound that said he was a man who lived life to its fullest and enjoyed every unpredictable moment of it. She knew then that she had won. And she knew that her sisters could do worse than to be courted by such a man.

"Well, Sealord, do we have an agreement?"

"That we do, *myerina*. That we do. And if your sisters are half the woman you are, then I am a very lucky son of the sea." Still laughing, his smile dazzling white against the shimmering, tattooed darkness of his skin, the Calbernan called out in the fluid, musical tones of his native tongue. His men lowered their weapons.

"What?" Falcon lunged towards his former ally. "Merimydion, you bastard, we had a deal!"

The Calbernan prince turned swift as a shark, the points of his trident halting inches from Falcon's face. No longer laughing, golden eyes cold and deadly, Dilys Merimydion said softly, "Our deal is done, Falcon Coruscate. Yours are not the only eyes in this forest. I know you struck this brave *myerina*. I know you left her to die. I know she offered you mercy, and still you would kill her if you could. A man who treats a woman—his own sister, no less—with so little care or honor is a man who cannot be trusted. *Myerina*"—the Sealord's cold, predatory gaze never left Falcon's face—"say the word, and this *krillo* will never again pollute your radiance with his presence."

"No. That won't be necessary." To her brother, she said, "You are not the man I once thought you were, but you are still an Heir of the Rose. I will need all the help I can get to defeat Rorjak. Fight with me, Falcon, and I will guarantee you safe passage out of Wintercraig on the condition that you never return and never again conspire against Wintercraig in any fashion."

"Surrender everything . . . for what?"

"For your life, Falcon. That's more than Verdan Coruscate has. More than Elka has. More than the thousands of people who died because of you have. And for a chance to regain at least some of the honor you spent the last three years throwing away. For a chance to be the Prince of Summer you should have been."

Leaving him to mull over that, she turned to the forces gathered around her. "To the Summerlanders among you, I offer amnesty for your rebellion against the King of Wintercraig. I am Angelica Mariposa Rosalind Khamsin Gianna Coruscate Atrialan, princess of Summerlea, Queen of Wintercraig." She rolled her cuff back and thrust her arm into the air, displaying the red Rose on her inner wrist. "I am an Heir of the Rose, Master of Storms, and the wielder of Blazing, the legendary sword of Roland Soldeus. I offer you a chance to return home not to a traitor's death, but to a hero's welcome." She turned in a slow circle, gauging the response. Most of the men looked uncertain. A few remained hostile.

"The monsters that just attacked us? There are more where those came from—as well as an entire army of other creatures whose only desire is to destroy all life and plunge the whole of Mystral into eternal winter. If we don't stop them now, their numbers will only increase. You saw what happened to your comrades when the *garm*'s blue vapor froze them. It will happen again and again, to every man, woman, child, and beast, until the largest army in the world could not hope to defeat them.

"All I ask is that you swear fealty to me and that you follow me now, into battle, as you followed my brother and King Verdan. Do this, and your crimes against Wintercraig's crown will be forgiven. Do it not, and every last one of you will perish in fire and blood. This I swear on the sword of my ancestor, Roland Soldeus."

Wynter lay on his cot, staring up at the roof of his tent. The material was a blank slate of uninteresting tan canvas, unlike the soothing, tattooed beauty of the tent he'd used throughout the three long years of his war with Summerlea. But the very blankness of the canvas was almost hypnotic in its own right.

His eyes unfocused, and his mind wandered through the various scenarios that might unfold in the coming days. He thought about Wintercraig, his childhood, about Garrick. He thought about the day he'd looked up and seen Khamsin watching him from the oriel in the King's Keep, and about their wedding day, the moment when her Rose had first touched his Wolf, and awareness had struck him like a lightning bolt.

Had she gone to her brother willingly? Surrendered to him the greatest weapon the world had ever seen? Or, as Tildy suggested, had she been taken against her will?

He knew what he wanted to believe. His heart ached for Tildy to be right.

Yet some little voice in the back of his mind kept whispering, *Falcon is her brother. The one she loved as much as you loved Garrick. She would never betray him. Not even for you.*

What had he done to ever win her love or loyalty? He'd wed her against her will, all but raped her on their wedding night thanks to that cursed arras leaf, then taken her from everything she'd ever known and everyone she'd ever loved. Yes, he'd made her his queen, but he'd practically abandoned her on his own doorstep, using her body at his convenience, while leaving her alone to face the mockery and derision of his court for weeks on end.

He'd tried to make amends these last months, tried to give her a measure of the care and happiness any wife of his deserved. But how could a few weeks of kindness and attention outweigh a lifetime of love?

Falcon was as much her hero as Roland Soldeus. And with Roland's sword in their possession, the two of them could reclaim Summerlea—or even conquer Wintercraig for that matter. She didn't need Wynter. And considering that she'd incinerated two *garm* even without the added power of Roland's sword, she didn't need to fear Wynter's Gaze either.

Why would she ever choose him over Falcon?

He'd asked the wolves watching her brother's camp, but if any of them had seen her, they'd been slain before they could pass on the knowledge to their pack.

The more he thought about it, the more likely it seemed that Khamsin had gone with Falcon of her own accord. A deep chill rippled through him, sending tremors shuddering through his body. Wynter sat up and swung his legs over the side of his cot.

Just the thought of Khamsin's choosing her Falcon over him made the blood in his veins turn to ice. The cold mass of anger and hate in his chest throbbed like a bass drum made from his living skin stretched over a barrel carved from his bones. *If she betrayed him . . .*

He leapt to his feet. Tension coiled inside him. He clenched his jaw so tight his teeth ached, and his fists so tight the knuckles cracked.

Shake it off, Wyn. Get hold of yourself.

He ducked through the tent flaps. The fire outside was mostly embers now. Except for a handful of White Guard standing watch, the camp was empty, everyone having sought their cots for the night. Overhead, the sky was dark and moonless, the stars shining bright in the clear blackness of the winter night. The forest was silent. Perfectly still. The trees shadowy sentinels standing watch in a star-silvered sea of snow.

Wynter skirted the tent stakes and walked into the dark welcome of the forest.

The night was cold. Even a Winterman might call it bitter. Wyn did not feel it. He just knew that it was so. Cold as snow. Cold as ice.

Cold as death.

His breath did not fog. His feet made no sound as he walked through the powdery snow. No birds in the trees called out as he passed. No creature scurried in the brush.

All around, the moonless dark of the night, the shadows of the forest, the pale silver of the snow enveloped him in still silence. As if he walked alone in a world in which all other life had ceased.

He walked without conscious thought or direction. Putting one foot in front of the other. Breathing in a slow, unhurried fashion.

Gradually, he became aware of something stalking through the trees on either side of him. Furry white shapes, slipping through the silhouetted trees of the forest, their paws as soundless on the snow as his feet. The white wolf on his wrist burned in recognition. The wolves had come to give him escort.

He took comfort from their presence and wished Khamsin had not left. Her absence made him ache, as if some invisible but necessary part of him had stopped working or had gone missing entirely.

When he faced the armies of Calberna and Summerlea, would he find his wife there, on the side of the enemy, taking up arms against him?

His heart wanted to believe she would never betray him after saving his life. His mind, however, kept whispering that he should remember her Summerlea roots, the falseness of her father and brother. Summerlanders weren't to be trusted.

Whether Khamsin had gone to her brother willingly or not, she was still gone. And he was struggling with the idea that he would die without ever seeing her again, without having the chance to tell her—

A twig snapped to his left, yanking Wyn out of his thoughts.

"Who's there?" he called. He scanned the forest, looking for movement, but the night was perfectly still and quiet.

"She has betrayed you," the voice whispered through the trees.

He turned to the right, seeking the source of the voice.

"What you feared has come true."

Wyn spun around. This time the sound seemed to come from his left.

"You gave her kindness, warmth, friendship she did not deserve. You gave her trust. You made her your queen. And in return, she conspires with the enemy."

"Reika." Wyn's lips flattened. "Show yourself, woman. And silence your poisonous words. Do you think I don't know how you hate her? How you plotted to kill her during the Great Hunt? You nearly succeeded in killing us both."

"Is that what she told you? And you believed her?"

Now he could see her, her tall figure shrouded in a hooded cloak, watching from a stand of trees on a rise a hundred yards in front of him.

"You lured her out of the palace. You attacked her and

left her wounded and bleeding. You knew the scent of fresh blood would draw the *garm* to finish off what you started. I'm only alive now because she saved my life. Why would she do that if she meant to play me false?"

"Do you think Valik would have let her take another breath if you had died? Of course she saved you. It was the only way to throw off suspicion until she could attempt another escape." Reika kept her distance. Each step he took towards her, she glided farther back through black-and-white hardwood trunks. "That's the same reason I didn't come to you myself. I knew you would not believe me without proof, so I hid in the forest and waited. I knew she would find a way to escape and go to her brother, and I was right. I followed her to his camp."

Ice stabbed Wyn's chest. "You lie." But even as he protested, a little voice in the back of his mind whispered, *Does she?* Reika was many things, but not stupid. She wouldn't make such claims without some sort of proof.

"Ask the wolves if you don't believe me. She rides now, at the head of her brother's army. She leads the invaders against you."

Wynter didn't want to believe it. Khamsin had risked her life to save him. He remembered the sight of her rushing out, barehanded, to save him from the *garm*. Why would she do that if she meant to betray him? It made no sense.

And yet the little, niggling doubt was there. The chilly, whispering voice in his mind that warned him Summerlanders were not to be trusted, women were not to be trusted. *Khamsin* was not to be trusted.

He pushed back hard against the terrible suspicions of betrayal. Khamsin was headstrong, stubborn, and temperamental, but she wasn't false.

She has lied from the day she first met you, the voice whispered again.

No. She'd never claimed to be anyone other than who she was. She might have passed herself off as a maid—and yes, she'd hidden her identity at their wedding—but she'd never *lied*. At the most, she'd encouraged him to make wrong assumptions. But she'd never actually lied. She was too direct, too honorable, for that. Her idol was Roland Soldeus, for Halla's sake—the most unswervingly honorable king Summerlea had ever known.

Roland is a legend. Falcon is flesh and blood—her brother—and she has idolized him every bit as much as she idolizes Roland—probably more so because he protected her from her father. He gave her love when she had none. Do you honestly think there's anything she wouldn't do to help her brother find Roland's sword and reclaim his kingdom?

"Talk to the wolves," Reika insisted. "Open your eyes to the truth before it's too late."

Wyn didn't want to hear anymore. He didn't want the wolves to confirm Reika's accusations. If they did, Khamsin's betrayal would break him as he'd never been broken before.

He had tried to keep an emotional distance from his wife all these months to protect himself from such a possibility. When he'd been just a man, the heartbreak would be difficult enough. But he was a man who'd drunk the essence of a god—a dark, soulless god who thrived on rage and pain the way an infant thrived on mother's milk.

He knew he shouldn't look. A little more rage, a little more pain and hate, and Rorjak would have all the fuel he needed to overpower Wynter's will, take control of his body, and unleash his evil upon the world.

But when he tried to turn away, he found he couldn't. Perhaps Rorjak had already subsumed Wyn's will to his own. Or perhaps Wyn couldn't deny his own need to know the truth.

He reached out to the wolves.

The invaders broke camp hours before dawn. Falcon rode by Khamsin's side.

"I would never have killed you, Storm," he said as they

rode. "I never would have done that. If I'd wanted you dead, I would have killed you at the temple."

"You let our father throw me to the *garm*, then you left me there to die."

"I didn't leave you there to die. I went to get my bow. By the time I came back, you were already gone."

"Even if that's true, you still tried to burn me with Blazing's fire."

He grimaced and bowed his head. "I was out of my mind. I think I've been out of my mind for a long time. If I'd actually hurt you—really hurt you—I could never have lived with myself." He looked at her with solemn sincerity, his eyes so earnest, pleading for understanding. "All I wanted was the sword, Storm. That's all I've ever wanted."

"I know." Finding it impossible to steel herself against Falcon's eyes, she turned her attention back to the road ahead. "All I ever wanted was to be loved."

"I do love you, Storm. I always have."

"No," she said. "You never loved *me*. Not really. You loved my adoration. You loved the way I idolized you and hung on your every word."

She looked at the man who had been her childhood idol. The handsome, adventurous older brother—she'd thought him so perfect in every way. It hurt so much to realize how wrong she'd been about him. How blind she'd been to the truth.

"But I did love you. I loved you so much I cried myself to sleep every time you went away. You were everything to me. My father, my brother, my friend, my hero. I loved Roland because you did. I wanted to be like Roland, because I thought you were. I tried to be everything you admired because I wanted you to love me and to keep loving me. I even used to tell myself if I was as good and noble and courageous as you, maybe one day our father would love me the way he loved you. I loved you so much I refused to see a single weakness or shortcoming in your character."

"Storm—"

"I didn't even believe Wynter when he told me what you'd done to start the war. I tried to make excuses for you, the way I always made excuses every time you did something selfish or cruel. But no longer. When this is over, you're going to leave Wintercraig and Summerlea. You're going to sail back to Calberna or whatever other land will have you and never come back. If you do that, you can live out the rest of your life in peace, without fear of Wintercraig retaliation for your crimes." She leaned towards him and let her eyes and the diamond in Blazing's hilt spark with deadly power. "But I swear to you, brother, if you ever again threaten my people, my kingdom, or the ones I love, there is no corner of this earth where you will be safe from my wrath. And you know that is no idle threat."

The army of the invaders rode through the predawn forest. Brown-skinned Summerlanders. Iridescent-blue-tattooed islanders in their loincloths, armbands, and protective armor plates, as oblivious to the cold as a pack of Frost Giants. At their head, riding between a massive Calbernan and Falcon Coruscate, unbound and clearly not a prisoner, was Khamsin.

She *had* gone to her brother.

Something squeezed Wynter's lungs tight. He was choking, unable to catch his breath. Terrible pressure gripped his heart as well, tight, burning cold, painful in the extreme. He fell to one knee, clutching his chest. The pain spread out across his chest, down his arms and torso.

He reached out to grab a nearby tree trunk to stop himself from falling over.

Wyrn have mercy. Khamsin's betrayal struck deeper and hurt more than any wound he'd ever known. It twisted and writhed inside him, burned and froze, broke him from the inside out.

A low, keening moan ripped from his throat, the cry of a wounded wolf. Tears, freezing into chips of ice as they fell, tumbled down his cheeks, and he slammed his forehead repeatedly into the tree's rough bark, welcoming the physical pain, hoping it would alleviate the other.

"No. No! Nooooo!" His head flung back, and he loosed the howl into the night sky. A flurry of startled birds took flight.

"She has betrayed you." Each word was like a needle, burrowing under his skin and digging deep into his bones. "There's only one way to stop her. Only one way to make her pay for what she has done."

"No," he whispered.

Reika continued as if he hadn't spoken. "Embrace your power, my king—"

"No."

"Claim what is yours by right—"

"No . . ."

"Punish her for the wound she has dealt you. Punish them all! Make them suffer! Make your enemies cower before you! You are no weakling! You are the Winter King, and you carry inside you the strength of a god! Use it! Unleash your wrath! Wipe your enemies from the face of this earth!"

The words that had started as sharp needles digging into his skin had now become spikes, each one hammering home with brutal accuracy. Anger built inside his heart, pressing outward against the crushing pain of betrayal. He squeezed his eyes shut and flung an arm over his face to stop the wild winter fury raging inside him from breaking free.

"No, damn you! No!"

"She has found the Sword of Roland. She has brought it to her brother, so that they might slay the forces of Wintercraig with its great power!"

If every other claim was a knife driven into his body, that one was the death blow.

Roland's sword. The sword Khamsin coveted as much as her brother. *The sword that was the source of all his pain.*

Khamsin had taken that sword to her brother.

His head lifted. His arm shielding his face dropped to his side.

He had gone completely numb. The hurt over Khamsin's betrayal was gone, as were the tenderer emotions she roused in him. He couldn't feel anything except a freezing, ice-powered fury that spread rapidly to every cell of his body. Everything left of his humanity—his consciousness, his emotions, his memories—seemed to shrink, concentrated into a tiny speck of life buried deep inside a vast, impenetrable ocean of ice.

Like an observer trapped inside a body not his own, he felt the form he occupied push off the tree, felt its spine straighten and stand tall. He opened his eyes. The world had taken on a pale blue tint, as if he saw through colored glass. He glanced down at his hands. A coating of clear ice covered his skin. He flexed his fingers, and the ice cracked and fell away, only to re-form an instant later.

He was frozen, inside and out.

Reika stepped out of the shadows of the trees and pushed back the hood of her cloak. Her lips had gone blue, her eyes the color of Wyrn's sacred, heatless flame, and when she smiled, he heard the faint sound of ice breaking. To her left and right, an army of *garm* emerged from the depths of the snow-covered forest, and behind them, moving with surprising silence in spite of their size, came a company of fearsome, blue-skinned Frost Giants. In unison, Reika, *garm*, and Frost Giant alike bowed down before him.

"Welcome back, my lord Rorjak," Reika Villani greeted. "Long have we awaited your return."

CHAPTER 27

Carnak

"Summer Sun," Khamsin breathed. Dismay and dread poured through her as she looked out across the battlefield. "Krysti, give me that spyglass."

The boy handed it over without a word. She put the glass to her eye.

The Ice King's army covered the entire breadth of the field. Frozen ice thralls—including humans, wolves, and bears—mingled packs of white, all but invisible *garm*, and at least eighty colossal blue monsters that stood close to twenty feet tall.

She'd never seen a Frost Giant and only wished that was still true.

They were fearsome, hideous beasts. Manlike in build, but with bulging hairless blue-white bodies, six-inch claws, and wicked, *garm*like teeth filling their blue maws. In their enormous fists, they clutched great, serrated swords that looked sharp enough to slice a man in two with a single blow. Correction, sharp enough to slice an entire line of men in two.

She scanned the enemy line, then paused as a tall, mounted figure came into view.

Even from the distance, Khamsin recognized her husband—or rather what had once been her husband—and her heart quailed. A terrible change had been wrought over him. All the warm golden hues in his skin had been leeched away, leaving his skin an inhuman silvery blue that made him look as though he'd been carved from a block of pure ice. A crown of jagged icicles ringed his head, and his unbound white hair blew behind him on the wind, snow falling from it in a mist of white. Where he walked, winter fell in his wake. If anything, he looked more beautiful than ever before—like one of his carvings in the Atrium—but also utterly cold, utterly merciless, utterly deadly.

"Oh, Wynter," Kham breathed in horror. Unable to bear the sight of the dread creature that now inhabited her husband's body, Khamsin shifted the spyglass. Her fingers clenched tight as a blue-lipped blonde riding at Rorjak's side came into focus.

"Reika." There was no doubt in Khamsin's mind now of who had killed the priestesses at the temple or why she'd found that ice thrall of Elka beside the Ice Heart. And no matter what else happened, one way or another, before this battle was done, Khamsin was going to dispatch what was left of Reika Villani straight to Hel.

"What is 'reika'?" Dilys Merimydion murmured beside her. The Calbernan had declared that, since she was the one with whom he had negotiated, keeping her alive was the only way to ensure fulfillment of their bargain. He and one hundred of his fiercest warriors had therefore attached themselves to her to ensure her safety.

She spared the Calbernan leader a quick glance before putting the spyglass back to her eye. "A vile creature in need of killing."

"Ah. Yes, many reika there are." He leaned on his elbows, the thick ropes of his green-black hair flopping on the snow, and peered through his own spyglass.

On either side of Reika and Rorjak, the Valik and Galacia ice thralls sat tall and threatening in the saddle. The frozen Galacia no longer held one of Thorgyll's mighty spears. Reika had commandeered it.

Dread filled Khamsin's heart. The ice thralls—man and beast—and Rorjak's army of Frost Giants and *garm* outnumbered her own forces three to one. Even with Blazing, she wasn't sure she and her allies could stand against the power of a god made flesh.

Across the field, the armies of Summerlea and Calberna had assembled. To the left, the forces of Summerlea flew the Coruscate green-and-scarlet banners. To the right, beneath the blue-green banners of the Isles, Calberna's tattooed warriors clutched their gleaming tridents and long, coffin-shaped shields. Fleets of archers were assembled before the infantry, while on the left and right flanks, mounted spearman and crossbowmen waited for the order to charge. Falcon rode at the center of the combined forces, the long curve of his Sunbow in hand. He had replaced his helm with the battle crown of Summerlea.

"That is a large army," Merimydion observed. "Victory will cost many lives. Many times many. When your husband dies today, if you and I still take breath at battle's end, then you will come, too, in the summer to the palace by the sea? With your sisters to be courted for marriage, yes?"

"No." She put her spyglass down. "That will not happen, Sealord, no matter what the outcome of today's battle. The likelihood that I will survive this is very slim. But if do, whether Wynter survives or not, my place will still be here in Wintercraig, defending my people."

"Hhnn." He made a noise somewhere between a grunt, a laugh, and a sigh. "This is a pity, Khamsin of the Storms. You are *myerial-myerinas,* a treasure of treasures. You would mother many great warriors for Calberna."

On the field below, Falcon saved her from further discussion when he pulled an arrow from his quiver, nocked it, and raised his bow high. The archers along both flanks of the main army followed suit. Khamsin was too far away to hear the command, but all at once, arrows went soaring. The arrow from Falcon's bow left a trail of blinding light in its wake.

"There's our signal," Khamsin said, grateful for the reprieve. Merimydion was exotically handsome, surprisingly charming in his own way, and most definitely all male. Had she loved Wynter any less, she might have been tempted to take him up on his offer of courtship. But for her, there would only ever be one man, and his name was Wynter of the Craig.

As the Sunfire arrow flew across the sky, the Ice King raised his sword and slashed it forward.

The Frost Giants roared. Long, loud, terrible, the roars generated gale-force winds—freezing, roiling clouds of snow and ice that raced across the field, swallowing everything in their path. They caught the arrows in midflight, tossing them away like matchsticks.

In the Summerlea ranks, a wave of heat swelled up in response, melting snow and ice as it billowed out to meet the howling blizzard winds. Khamsin felt energy ripple across her skin as the two waves of opposing magic clashed on the field. Storm clouds erupted, boiling up high and fast. Lightning crackled across their surface. Rorjak released his Gaze, and the building storm turned into a white wall of whirling ice and snow.

Ice shot like arrows from massive storm clouds, but Falcon managed to melt the hailstones with his weathergift before they reached the mortal troops.

The tempest called to her gift, power tingling in her skin. She wanted to reach out and shape the flows of winter ice and summer heat. But to do so now would give away their position. She needed to be much closer to Wynter before she revealed herself. The wind blew in her face, making her hair stream out behind her. So long as Falcon kept the storm in the sky, with the wind blasting in her direction and carrying her scent away from the field, she and Merimydion had a chance to flank the Ice King's army.

The Frost Giants roared again. Another wall of ice and snow blasted across the field. This time, on the heels of the howling blizzard winds, hidden from Summerlander view, *garm* and ice-thralled bears, wolves, and snow lions raced towards the mortal lines.

"Let's go," she said. "Even with Sunfire arrows, Falcon's not going to last long against that."

By the time she and her companions circled behind the rear flank of the Ice King's army, the magic of Summer and Winter were clashing as ferociously in the sky as their armies battled on the field below.

Falcon's center line had fallen back, attempting to draw the Ice King's army in so that the cavalry on both flanks could catch them in a pincer and pick off the *garm* with cross fire to give Khamsin time to get as close to Wynter as possible. But as boiling blue clouds of vapor poured over the armies, and the fallen rose again to add their numbers to the Ice King's, it became increasingly obvious that the pincer strategy was going to fail—and fast.

She was going to have to use the storm to slow them down, but the minute she did, Rorjak would feel her magic and track it back to her. She would lose the element of surprise.

"Slight change of plans," she told Merimydion. "Tell your men to brace themselves. It's about to get very ugly for us. And you might want to give me some room."

The Sealord took one look at her face and fell back, shouting to his men in Calbernan.

She tightened her grip on Roland's sword.

"Okay, Blazing," she muttered, "let's see what you've got." If there was any small chance she could still save Wynter, Kham intended to take it. But if he was lost to her, if Rorjak's hold over him was too strong to defeat, then it was her duty to stop him in any way she could. Even if that meant unleashing the same cataclysmic power that had ended the life of Roland Soldeus.

One way or another, the Ice King would never step foot off this field.

"Helos, Sunfather, whatever gifts this sword can give, grant them to me now." She thrust the sword skyward and flung open the doors to her magic, calling to the gods and the sun and the skies with every part of her being.

What answered was far beyond anything she'd ever summoned before.

It was as if a column of fire had descended upon her, igniting her world with heat and flame. Strangely, it didn't burn. Her skin went hot and tight, her hair swirled around her on a sea of heat-spawned winds, but there was no pain. Only a feeling of extreme warmth and the sensation of strength and vitality filling her body near to bursting. The edges of her vision went bright, golden white.

The diamond in the sword's hilt was shining bright as a star, its light near blinding.

In the sky, she could see the flows of air swirling through the storm, like ribbons of blue and red and electric purple. She reached for them and forced them to her will, swirling the flows of warm air round and round in ever-tightening circles as she fed heat and moisture into the storm.

The Ice King roared and wheeled around, unleashing his Gaze. Two dozen Frost Giants followed suit. But even the coldest depths of winter could not extinguish the heat of the sun. The frost of Rorjak's Gaze and the blizzard of the Frost Giants' howls turned to steam, which Khamsin fed back into the storm. Lightning cracked and flashed. One bolt hit a tree near the Ice King's army, exploding it in a burst of burning wood and vaporized ice.

Two dozen *garm* broke from their attack on Falcon's forces, spinning around and galloping directly toward Khamsin and the Calbernans.

"Merimydion!" She shouted to get the Sealord's attention and pointed at the herd of onrushing *garm*.

"I see them! *Calbernari!* To arms!" At his shouted command, his men stuffed wax plugs in their ears to protect them from the paralytic effects of the *garm*'s screams and readied their shields and tridents. Behind them others loosened their arrows.

The *garm* crossed the ground in land-eating strides. They fell upon the Calbernans in a shrieking pack, claws and fangs slashing and tearing. To their credit, the fierce warriors of the Islands held rank. Moving with the inhuman swiftness of ocean predators, they leapt and whirled and twisted to evade the *garm*'s slashing claws and attacked with their own brand of savage ferocity. Ice-coated shields bashed. Tridents stabbed and twisted, shredding flesh with their wicked barbs. Several Calbernans leapt over the backs of their brothers to hack and slash at the wounded *garm* with serrated blades. Red and blue blood ran like rivers across the snow.

One of the *garm* made it through the line of defenders and closed in on Khamsin with lethal speed, only to freeze solid and skid to a halt as Krysti stabbed it with Thorgyll's spear. The boy yanked the spear free and ran to help the Calbernans finish off their lot.

Seeing his *garm* destroyed, the Ice King roared in fury and shouted commands on the howling winds. Twenty Frost Giants sprinted towards the Calbernans. The ground shook with the pounding of their feet as the colossal monsters approached. Massive serrated blades swung like scythes, and despite swift reflexes, more than dozen of Merimydion's countrymen were unable to evade the blades. Sharp, icy steel cleaved them in two.

Khamsin kept her attention and efforts focused on the storm. She fed it more energy and stirred the rotation of the clouds even faster. Several thick, horizontal, spinning ropes formed in the darkening clouds. The sky turned an eerie shade of dark green. Pressure built in her ears, and the sound of wind grew to a roar. The tops of the trees began whipping about. Branches cracked and ripped free, flying through the air like javelins.

The spinning ropes in the volatile heart of the storm dropped down, thick, deadly funnels of wind and vapor that reached for the ground like the fingers of a god.

She sent several of the funnels into the heart of the army

attacking Falcon's troops and directed another at the Frost Giants running towards her position. *Garm,* thralls, even the massive Frost Giants were no match for her whirling winds. The cyclones swept them up and flung them like pebbles through the air. Khamsin drove the vortexes through the Ice King's ranks with ruthless abandon, scattering his troops and breaking his lines while simultaneously calling down the lightning. The dark green sky went blinding white as bolt after bolt after bolt of incinerating fire shot down from the heavens, finding Rorjak's minions with unerring accuracy.

Lightning hit the ground all around Rorjak as Khamsin tried to thin his ranks of defenders. Khamsin aimed a bolt directly at Reika Villani, but the vile woman flung herself out of the way at the last split second, then scrambled to her feet and took off running into the forest.

Across the field, Falcon's forces began closing in on the remaining thralls and *garm*. Lancers pinned the thralls to the ground, leaving infantry to dispatch them. Archers turned the *garm* into pincushions. Red and blue blood painted the snowy field an awful shade of purple.

Rorjak screamed and swept his arms up. Ice-cold wind from the Craig rushed to his call, barreling through high reaches of the sky with incredible speed. The fierce jets of frozen air slammed into the tops of her storm clouds, shearing them away and robbing her storm of its deadliest power. Starved of energy, her cyclones grew thin and ropy, then disappeared altogether.

Having muzzled her storm, the Ice King turned back to Khamsin. He slammed his free hand in her direction, and razor-sharp icicles shot from his fingertips, flying fast as arrows across, straight towards her.

"*Calbernari!*" Merimydion shouted. "*Makatua! Poru myerina.* Shields! Protect the woman!"

Calbernans leapt in front of Khamsin, and Rorjak's ice missiles exploded against their shields, showering them all in a powdery cloud of shattered ice.

Rorjak responded with another fierce, bone-curdling scream and an upward thrust of his hand. The ground beneath the Calbernans rocked and quaked, then split as huge columns of ice shot up from the ground, pulverizing rock in its path and throwing the Calbernans off their feet.

No sooner had the ice columns erupted than they melted down, the water oozing out like clear jelly. It covered the fallen Calbernans, then hardened into an icy shell, cocooning half the men, trapping the others with thick manacles of ice around legs and arms. Rorjak unleashed his Gaze on the lot, freezing them solid.

His path once again cleared, Rorjak turned the full force of his Gaze not on Khamsin but on the sword in her hand. The sword began to shake, and fire and ice battled for dominance. Rorjak began to advance towards her. Clutched in his right hand, Wynter's sword, Gunterfys, was now covered with ice and glowing with blue light. She tried to strike it with lightning, but every bolt diverted before it hit, as if some invisible, impenetrable shield surrounded the Ice King and his sword.

The power of Rorjak's Gaze grew stronger with each approaching step. Kham's hand went numb. The muscles in her arm strained as she fought to keep her grip on her now-violently-shuddering sword.

Several of the ice-trapped Calbernans had managed to hack themselves free. They rose again, but this time as thralls who set upon their countryman in a blizzard of ferocity. A dozen more of Merimydion's remaining warriors leapt into Rorjak's path, putting themselves between Khamsin and the vengeful god. They formed a wall of shields, and held the wall as ice from Rorjak's gaze coated the shields three inches thick. He swept them away with a searing blast of frost and a slash of his sword.

Krysti, who had been icing *garm* with Thorgyll's spear, ran towards Rorjak's unprotected back. The snowy falls of Rorjak's white hair stirred like the sensory hairs of a *garm*. The Ice King turned with the speed of a striking snake. He batted the spear away with his sword and swept Krysti off his feet with a swipe of his left arm.

"Krysti!" Kham cried.

The boy flew through the air and landed limp as a rag doll amidst a sea of dead *garm* and broken Calbernan bodies. He didn't move again.

The ice thrall, Galacia Frey, picked up Krysti's dropped spear and began freezing Calbernans to her left and right as they rushed to surround Rorjak.

Khamsin lunged towards Rorjak, sword upraised, but Gunterfys slammed into Blazing with stunning force. Sparks and ice showered from the two blades. A second, fearsome blow from Gunterfys sent Blazing spinning from Kham's grasp. Rorjak caught her throat in a tight grip and lifted her off her feet.

Stripped of Roland's sword, death mere moments away, Khamsin did the only thing she could think of. She flung open the gates to the source of her power and called the lightning. All of it. Every last ion of energy that crackled through the roiling black storm clouds overhead.

Boom! Boom! Boom! Boom!

One after another, thick, hot, blinding bolts of concentrated electricity arced down from the heavens, following purple threads of plasma to their silver-eyed source. Deafening thunder boomed again and again. The ground shook, knocking combatants off their feet. The wild, hot music of the storm sang through Khamsin's veins, and fire, hotter than the sun, filled her body.

She thrust out her palms, pressing them against the frozen white expanse of Rorjak's chest, and released the power gathered inside her.

Light and heat exploded with a last, deafening boom. Rorjak and Khamsin flew backward in opposite directions and slammed to the ground.

Breath rasping through her bruised throat, ears ringing, Kham pushed to her feet, retrieved her sword, and staggered across the icy ground to the Ice King's fallen form.

There, her legs gave out, and she fell to her knees beside him. A smoldering, charred black hole was burned through his chest plate, but Khamsin wasn't fool enough to think a little lightning could kill a god. She lifted her sword.

"Forgive me, Wynter." Tears filled her eyes. Killing him would be like driving Roland's sword through her own heart, but the Wynter she knew would rather die than let Rorjak live. She wiped her eyes resolutely and prepared to strike the killing blow. "I love you. I love you more than I ever knew I could love anyone."

The bare skin beneath it was blackened as well, but the thick layer of ice that coated him had broken away and not re-formed. A faint hint of golden color had leeched back into his skin. Hope fluttered in her breast. Roland's sword had melted the Ice Heart in Wyrn's Temple. Was it possible her lightning had done the same to Wynter's heart?

She laid a hand over his lightning-struck chest. The thud that answered was so slight, she almost missed it, but it was followed by a second thud, then a third. Weak, sluggish, but a heartbeat nonetheless. A living, beating heart.

"Wynter! Wynter, wake up! Please, beloved. Come back to me." She dropped her sword in order to seize his shoulders and give him a shake. Then she grabbed his face between her hands and chafed his cold skin, all but willing warmth back to his flesh.

"Dear gods, please, please, let him live. *Please.* I'll do anything, give anything, pay any price, only let Wynter live." Muttering frantic prayers over and over again, she pulled him into her lap, cradling his head against her chest, smoothing the cold silk of his hair back away from his face. Hot tears spilled from her eyes and rained gently upon his face. She kissed his cold lips, breathing into his mouth. She clasped his cold hand against her cheek and pressed her lips into the still-icy palm. "Come back to me, Wynter. My husband, my love."

The thick fans of his white lashes stirred, fluttering against his still-pale cheeks.

Her breath caught in her throat as his lashes lifted, and a smile of utter joy broke across her face as she beheld eye of glacier blue rather than the soulless clear ice of Rorjak's wintry stare.

"Khamsin?" He frowned up at her in puzzlement.

She laughed. "Oh, thank the gods for their infinite mercy." She fell upon him, showering him with kisses, weeping with abandon. "I thought I'd lost you forever."

"Lost me? What's going . . . on?" His voice trailed off as he caught sight of the carnage surrounding them. The *garm* and thralled Winterfolk fighting tattooed Calbernan islanders. The maimed bodies of his people littering the snow. "The Calbernans. Falcon." His face lost all expression. He turned back to her and she was horrified to see the blue leaching from his eyes, the golden color leaching from his skin. "You betrayed me. You brought the sword to your brother. You joined them to fight against me."

"No! Wynter, no!" She reached for him with desperate hands as he shoved out of her grasp and climbed to his feet. "I didn't betray you. I would never do that! I *couldn't*! I love you."

"*Liar.*" The voice that emanated from Wynter's lips was no longer his own. It was a dark, raspy, threatening voice, pure evil, filled with corruption and hate and all things vile. Just the sound of it sucked the warmth from her flesh and drained the hope from her heart. The ice that had melted from Wynter's skin re-formed over cold, white, bloodless flesh.

"Wynter, please! Don't do this! Fight him! You can't let Rorjak win. You've got to fight him. Please, beloved. *Please.*" Her chin trembled. Her voice broke, and she began to sob, tears spilling down her face. "I love you. I love you more than I ever thought possible. More than I ever knew I could love anyone. Please, stay with me. *Please.*" Her hands trembled. Her whole body shook, racked with heartbreak.

"You pathetic, mewling *skurm*," a voice sneered at her back. Something white slashed through the air.

Kham gasped and scrambled backward to avoid the killing stab of Thorgyll's icy spear.

Reika Villani had not fled the battle, after all. She had, instead, escaped into the forest in order to circle around and attack her foe from behind. "He is not your love, nor will he ever be. He is Rorjak the Great, God-King of Mystral. And *I* will be the queen who rules beside him through all eternity."

"Like Hel you will." Kham lunged for Blazing. Her fingers closed around the hilt, and she thrust the blade towards the heavens, screaming, "Helos help me!"

Power rushed to her call. The diamond in Blazing's hilt went blinding white. She slashed the blade towards Reika, instinctively channeling the power down her arms and out through the sword the same way she had the lightning. Instead of flames, a concentrated golden white beam of energy shot from its tip.

Reika froze in midlunge, a look of almost comical surprise stamped on her coldly beautiful face. Khamsin scrambled to her feet and spun around, sword drawn back for a second strike. She hesitated in confusion. Reika was still frozen in midlunge. She hadn't moved a fraction of an inch. As Khamsin watched, the skin of Reika's face shifted along an invisible seam, like two blocks of ice moving in different directions. Then her legs folded, and her body separated into two vertical halves that crumpled to the ground. The seared and cauterized flesh of her bisected corpse steamed in the winter air.

Thorgyll's spear dropped to the ground and rolled down the hill, coming to rest at the blood-drenched feet of Dilys Merimydion.

She heard the tinkling sound of breaking ice behind her. A draft of cold air washed over her, prickling her flesh. She didn't need to turn around to know the Ice King had risen again.

Merimydion met her eyes, then glanced at the spear at his feet. She nodded.

"I'm sorry, my love," she whispered. She steeled her heart, clenched her fist firmly around Blazing's hilt, and spun around to stab her blade deep into the Ice King's frozen heart.

A split second before the blade plunged into Rorjak's flesh, she saw the glimmer of blue in his eyes, the shimmer of golden warmth rising beneath the icy white of his flesh. Her arm jerked. The sword that had been aimed directly at Rorjak's heart pierced scant inches above it instead.

"Merimydion, wait!" she cried, but the Calbernan had already scooped up Thorgyll's spear and let it fly. Khamsin had no time to think, even less time to act. Instinct took over.

She leapt between her husband and the icy, irrevocable death rushing towards him.

"Wynter, I—" The breath in her lungs left her in a sudden rush as the spear slammed into her shoulder. The weapon impaled her, piercing flesh and bone, then burying its enchanted point into the thick plate of Wynter's armor. The armor crackled with frost.

Warmth fled inch by rapid inch as the god-killing magic of Wyrn's enchanted spear consumed her.

In helpless, frozen silence, she stared up into the dawning horror in the eyes of the man she loved. And then her world went white.

"Khamsin! *Khamsiiiin!*" Wynter grabbed the cold shaft of Thorgyll's freezing spear and yanked hard. The spearhead was stuck in his armor plate. He yanked again, and again. "Valik! Laci!" Around him, ice was shedding from the members of his army as Rorjak's vile enthrallment melted away. The walking slain collapsed to the ground in a natural death, while the rest emerged from the torpor of their enthrallment in varying states of confusion.

"You, there! Calbernan!" Wyn jabbed an imperious finger at the huge, tattooed brute who'd thrown the spear that impaled Khamsin. A few minutes ago, Wyn had nearly lost himself to Rorjak a second time when his instinctive feelings of betrayal and hate at the sight of the Calbernans fighting alongside his wife had given the Ice King the chance to overpower him again. That one moment of doubt might have doomed Wynter again had not Khamsin slain Reika.

It was Reika in whom the Ice King had fully manifested. Reika, who had lusted for power over everything else, just like Rorjak. To gain that power, she'd surrendered herself to the Ice Heart and to Rorjak. He'd used her as his entrée back into the world, used her to manifest his power. Except, a daughter of Ermine clan wasn't the powerful avatar Rorjak desired for his reincarnation. He'd wanted Wynter, with his royal weathergifts and his Snow Wolf blood.

And that had been his downfall. Because from the moment Wynter saw Khamsin's tear-stained face and heard her sobbing "I love you!" the Wolf in Wynter's blood would not let him hurt his mate. That Wolf had refused to be conquered. He'd held out, fighting Rorjak's attempt to subsume him, until Wynter, listening to his wife's tearful pleas for him to fight, listening to her sobbed professions of love, had realized that even if Khamsin *had* tried to help her brother, even if she had betrayed Wynter in every way, it didn't matter. She was his wife, his queen, his mate. His heart.

And he loved her.

He loved every exasperating, fiery, rebellious, beautiful, challenging, volatile inch of her.

And with that realization, Rorjak lost all chance of claiming any part of Wynter ever again.

"Get over here and help me get this thing out of her!" Wynter snapped at the wary Calbernan. "Move, damn you!"

The islander sprinted over, keeping his barbed trident ready to strike, but when it became obvious Wynter was no longer under the control of Rorjak, the tattooed fellow tossed down his weapon and seized Thorgyll's spear with both big hands. One flex of those enormous biceps later, and the bloodied spear slid free of Khamsin's flesh.

Khamsin's frozen body remained standing, locked in that moment when she'd chosen to sacrifice herself to save him.

"Wyn." Laci stumbled over. Droplets of water and chips of melting ice covered her from head to toe. "Wyrn save us, what happened?"

"That blue bastard tried to kill Rorjak with the spear. Khamsin jumped in front of it to save me. She's still alive, Laci. She's frozen, but I can see the heat in her heart. I can feel it in her blood. And in this." He reached for the hilt of the sword still embedded in his chest, intending to pull it out.

"Wait!" Laci cried. "What if that sword is the only thing keeping Rorjak at bay?"

The Calbernan snatched up his trident again.

"Calm yourselves. The sword didn't drive Rorjak out of my heart. *She* did that. I won't turn again." He yanked the sword, which had only penetrated perhaps an inch of flesh, out of his chest and glared at the Calbernan, who lowered the points of his trident but kept an unblinking eye on Wynter.

"You said this thawed the Ice Heart; maybe it will work on Khamsin, too." Hoping he didn't have to stab her with the blade to get it to work, Wyn pressed the sword against her chest. *Please, gods, let this work.* "Come back to me, *min ros.* Come back to me."

The limbs that had been frozen solid buckled as they began to thaw. Wynter caught his wife's body and cradled her to his chest, careful to keep Roland's sword in place.

"That's it, Summerlass. You can do it." He raised her hand and brushed his lips against the cold, soft skin of her slender fingers. She was so slight to be so brave and fierce. A marvel. *His* marvel. He bent over her, pressing his mouth to her cold, still lips, breathing into her lungs the first warm breath he'd had in years. "I love you." He lifted her closer, trailing a line of kisses from her mouth to her ear and whispered again, "I love you, Khamsin. My own, Summerlass. I don't have words enough to describe how much I love you."

Her throat moved on a swallow. Her lips parted. A small noise breathed out.

"What was that, *min ros*?" He bent his ear to her mouth. "What did you say?"

The fingers in his hand flexed. The lips pressed to his ear moved. And then on a bare whisper of breath, "Try."

He pulled back in shock. Her lashes fluttered. Silver-gray eyes looked up at him expectantly through a fringe of lush, curling lashes. One dark brow arched.

He let out a bark of laughter, hugged her tight, and showered her face with kisses. "I love you more than the sunrise. More than laughter. More than song. I love you more than skating on a frozen pond on a clear winter day or soaking in the hot springs of Mount Freika. I love you more than any man in the history of Mystral ever loved a woman. I love you more than I love making love to you—well, no, wait . . . that's a tie." She punched him weakly in the arm, and he laughed again. Then the laughter faded, leaving a heart so full he thought it might burst inside his chest, and a solemn sincerity that shone straight from his soul. "I love you. Angelica Mariposa Rosalind Khamsin Gianna Coruscate Atrialan. Rorjak will never have a hold on my heart again, because it belongs wholly and completely to you."

EPILOGUE

"Where are we going?" Blindfolded, Khamsin held one hand out in front of her, waving side to side. Although rationally, she trusted Wynter not to walk her into a wall, the instinct to be certain was too strongly ingrained to completely overcome.

"You'll see."

She could practically see the smile in his voice, the mischief sparkling in his pale eyes. He sounded like a boy waking on Wyrn's Day, eager to see what the Old Man of the North had left by the hearth for him.

In the nearly six months since Rorjak's defeat, Wynter and all of Gildenheim had virtually transformed. Gone was the cold reserve, replaced by laughter, warmth, and friendship. With Khamsin celebrated as the savior of Wintercraig, there wasn't a home or hearth in the entire kingdom where she would not find welcome. Even the remaining band of Reika's followers made their peace with her and worked to make amends for their previous transgressions.

Although there had been some rumbling in the court, Wynter had agreed to honor the terms of Khamsin's negotiations with the invaders—even the part where he arranged for Falcon to be escorted to the closest port and put on a ship sailing to the destination of his choosing. Though hardly a day went by that Khamsin didn't think at least one sad thought about her brother, in her heart she was glad he was still alive and out in the world somewhere. And each day, she prayed that Falcon would yet become the man he should have been, a man worthy of the blood that ran in his veins.

"We're coming to another set of stairs," Wynter said.

"Not too many more stairs, I hope." As her belly had swollen with the twin babes she could swear were half-giant, Khamsin had become less and less enamored of Gildenheim's many stairways and labyrinthine corridors. Though it was only June, and she still had months to go before the babies were due, she was already waddling so much she might soon sprout feathers and start to quack.

"Not too many," he vowed.

"Is it much farther?"

"We're almost there, *min ros*." He held her left arm in one hand, and his right hand rested snugly in the small of her back.

She loved the feel of his hands. So big and powerful, yet so breathtakingly gentle and protective. And warm.

Gone was the cool chill that had emanated from his Ice Heart-infused body. Heat now radiated from him like a furnace. Though he could still summon a frosty Gaze when it served him—the divine powers of the immortal essence he'd drunk would always be a part of him—the Ice King's loveless, merciless cold no longer held any part of him in its grip.

Khamsin had studied the histories of Wyn and Rorjak with Galacia Frey, and they both agreed that Wynter was the sort of man Rorjak could have been had the Ice King's heart not hungered for power more than love.

Kham thanked Wyrn and Freika each day that Wynter had made the choice he did.

She heard the sound of someone's whispering, only to be quickly hushed. A slight breeze feathered across her face as a nearby door swung open.

Beneath the mask, Khamsin's nostrils flared. "Something smells lovely." A warm breeze carried the scent of roses and gardenias and rich, loamy soil.

"All right," Wyn said, unfastening the blindfold. "You can look."

Khamsin opened her eyes. Her jaw dropped. The smells of summer had not prepared her for the gift Wynter had created.

They were standing in the Atrium, the place Wynter had kept his frozen shrine to the memories of his family and brother. Only the breathtaking ice forest with all its frozen sculptures was gone. In its place was a lush and fragrant garden, an oasis of Summer, blooming here in the heart of Wintercraig.

"I know you have been missing Summerlea, but since traveling isn't an option until our children are born, I thought I would bring a little of Summerlea to Gildenheim, so you can visit anytime you like."

"It's beautiful. But what about your ice sculptures? The ones of your parents? Of Garrick?"

"I kept a few. I made a cold room behind the Atrium and stored them there. I don't need those memories anymore because I'm going to make plenty of new memories with you. And I wanted this place—the heart of Gildenheim—to be as warm and alive as you've made my heart."

She smiled up at him, blushing a little at the intensity in his gaze. She tugged his hand. "So show me what you've done. I want to see everything."

As they walked, a feeling of familiarity came over her. A brick walk circled the outside of the Atrium, with several walks leading to inner circles. The feeling of familiarity solidified into certainty.

"It's my mother's Sky Garden." She looked up at him in amazed wonder. He'd re-created her mother's private garden: the paths, the flowers, the apple and pear trees growing up the sides of the walls. Oh, it was still young, with years of growing yet to do, but the bones were here. He'd given Kham her favorite piece of Summerlea, here in the heart of the Craig. "But how did you do it? How did you re-create it so perfectly?"

"Valik hired an artist to sketch everything and a gardener to provide all the clippings, seeds, and the like. Your sisters helped me with the planting, using your mother's journals."

"My sisters." It took a moment to process his words. "You mean my sisters are here?"

"Surprise." Spring, Summer, and Autumn stepped out from behind a row of flowering fruit trees.

Khamsin screamed with joy and rushed forward. Happy tears spilled from her eyes as her sisters flung their warm arms around her. "I can't believe it. I can't believe you're here. I wasn't expecting you for another month at least!"

"We wanted to spend more than a few weeks with you before the Calbernans arrive," Summer said.

"Keeping them away from you these last ten days has been more difficult than you can imagine," Wynter said.

"Ten days? You've been here ten days?"

"All this planting took longer than we'd planned," Spring said, "but your husband was adamant to keep us hidden and keep everything a secret until the garden was done."

"If it weren't for Tildy, we might still be working," Autumn added. She nodded to the plainly dressed, gray-haired woman waiting off to one side with Krysti by her side. "She organized us like one of your husband's generals."

Khamsin wiped the tears from her eye and smiled at her nurse. "I wondered what was keeping her so busy this last week." She waved Tildy over and pulled her into a hug. "I know I've never said it before, but I will say it now." She pulled back so she could look directly into Tildy's eyes. "Thank you," she said earnestly. "Thank you for everything. If not for you, none of this would have been possible, and I never would have known such happiness."

The woman who had raised her from birth gave a damp-eyed smile. "I've only ever wanted what was best for you, dearly."

"I know. And I want you to know that I love you, Tildy.

I always have. You're the only mother I've ever known." She hugged her nurse again, wiped away more tears, then laughed and pulled Krysti into a hug, too. "And you! No wonder you've been under my feet all week—you were helping them keep this all a secret—making sure I never got anywhere close to the Atrium or my sisters."

The boy grinned hugely. "I did a good job of it, too, didn't I?"

She laughed. "Clearly."

Spring took her hands. "We want you to know, Storm, that whether any of us choose Merimydion or not, we are all resolved to be here when the babies are born."

"We wouldn't miss the birth of our first nieces or nephews for anything," Autumn agreed. "And if the Calbernan doesn't agree to those terms, then he won't be getting a Season as a wife." She sniffed and tossed her auburn curls.

"Not that that will be a problem," Summer reassured Khamsin with a comforting smile. "From everything I've heard or read, Calbernans cherish their women. I'm sure the Sealord won't mind a small delay to bring his new bride joy." She gave her other two sisters a look of gentle reproof, which was as close to a scold as Summer had ever been able to manage.

"I'm sure he won't," Kham agreed. "He struck me as a good man, or I would never have given him a chance to come within a thousand leagues of any of you." She flung her arms around her sisters. "Oh, I missed you all so much."

With her beloved family around her, filled with more joy than she'd ever known, Khamsin looped an arm around Wynter's waist and strolled through the remaining paths of her own Sky Garden.

"Well?" Wynter murmured, smiling. "What do you think?"

"It's perfect. It's everything I could ever have hoped for." She stood on her tiptoes to wrap her arms around his neck and kiss him. "*You're* everything I could ever have hoped for."

Arm in arm, they walked towards the very heart of the garden, where Wynter had placed a perfect replica of her mother's carved wooden bench. A new, silver-gilt copy of *Roland Triumphant* lay on the wooden slats, waiting for her. Behind the bench, a young, gangly Snowfire tree had been planted in a mound of moss-covered soil. Healthy, strong, already flowering with its beautifully scented white summer blooms, the Snowfire would grow in the coming years and drape its branches like a veil around the bench, waiting for their children to sit beneath its fragrant blooms to read and dream of heroic battles and noble deeds of their ancestors, and imagine the day they, too, would earn the right to protect their kingdom and discover a love to last the ages.